Books by LAURA Z. HOBSON

THE TRESPASSERS
GENTLEMAN'S AGREEMENT
THE OTHER FATHER
THE CELEBRITY
FIRST PAPERS

FIRST PAPERS

LAURA Z. HOBSON

FIRST PAPERS

RANDOM HOUSE NEW YORK

In memory
of
my parents

Adella Kean Zametkin

and

Michael Zametkin

PART

I

ONE

On a barely wooded and sparsely settled hill in the town of Barnett, Long Island, there stood a tall narrow house whose encasing shingles had not yet attained the soft greyness of weatherbeaten wood.

In daylight this house had a faint peach tinge; by night it was the color of wet sand. Built upon a bank of ground sloping sharply back from the sidewalk, it seemed to perch above the pavement, to draw back from the street. In this house lived Stefan Ivarin and his family.

Although half a dozen other small houses had sprung up at about the same time on this same hill, the Ivarin house did not share their neat suburban mood; rather, its structure and character proclaimed a lack of kinship, a wild originality of its own.

Stripped of its embellishing porches, stuck here and there like afterthoughts to break the severity of its outline, the Ivarin house would have emerged as a thin rectangular box, topped by a shingled roof also sloping sharply back, also tall and narrow, its line broken only by a bay window that jutted forward from the roof like a blunt, square nose from a receding brow.

Of porches there was a profusion, two in front, one behind, elongating the house still further, and a stoop at the side entrance. The front porch had slender white posts and no railings; upon its back, in the center, it bore a small square sleeping porch with stout square posts, heavy enough to dwindle the posts below to the semblance of tall white pencils.

The ground on which the house stood was nearly nude of trees, though between sidewalk and curb there were three young maples, still bare though it was early spring. Wires ran from their trunks to pegs in the ground, to support their frail growth against the hill winds that swept across from Flushing Bay, several miles to the north. In the back yard stood a pear tree and a peach tree; the ground there was laid out in the patchwork squares and oblongs of a vegetable garden.

It was at three o'clock on a morning in late March, in 1911, that Stefan Ivarin paused before his house, and drew from it the first sense of peace he had known in all that fearful evening. It was no hour for reflection, yet he stood looking up at it on the rising earth, grateful that he could for a moment forget holocaust and horror. The house had been built two years before, and he himself had been its architect. By profession an editor, lecturer and teacher, he had for decades pursued his hobby of original mathematics, and during the first discussions about building their own house, a year before they were ready to consult an architect, it had seemed easy enough to rough out sketches of rooms and halls and porches, with his wife Alexandra and the children watching him, offering suggestions.

There had been no specific moment when he had decided, We do not need to consult an architect; I will be the architect; this is one way to save money. Those early sketches had revealed how simple, how almost primitive, were the undemanding feet and inches of an architect's plans. All he needed to master were some clinical details about drainage, the heating plan, the electrical system.

And as the plans developed, it had begun to seem natural and just that the first house he had ever owned should be designed by himself, be the creature of his own being, an extension of himself, as were his children or his editorials. Perhaps, like any wife, Alexandra had had misgivings, but with them, the wisdom to silence them, at least at the beginning.

It was only later, when his minutely accurate plans were ready to be translated into builder's blueprints, that she had begun to attack them. Then had come endless discussion, week after week, about matters of looks and convenience; the children had joined in, each offering an objection, a desire, a longing. Even Fira, the baby of the family, had spoken up, vociferous about the stairway.

"I don't *care*," Fee had cried out in defiance, "nobody else has the stairs going up backwards."

He could hear the high excited voice still, and his own burst of rage at all of them, at Fira and Francesca and their mother. Eli had been indifferent, and therefore neutral; but the others were bent on deviling him, wanting only to tear up his months of work and turn to some unimaginative businessman who called himself an architect instead of a sausage maker.

It had been a bad time, a time to forget. Irritability was his fatal weakness, the Greek tragic flaw within him, which the world of his public life knew not at all, and which his private world suffered from too often. If science had evolved some healing drug for the bursting vessels of his equanimity, how gladly he would have become an addict to it, to spare himself the sight of hurt on Alexandra's face, or fear on the children's.

Neither she nor they could fathom the depth of his remorse after one of his outbreaks, nor suspect the self-laceration that followed. About such matters he could not speak; the apology, the abjectness of confession, mended nothing and destroyed something further in his own tissue.

Yet, without passion, he had told himself often, no man rises far above the level of beast or peasant. Placidity was not for the fighters of the world, not for those in the vanguard. To have been a revolutionary at sixteen was no preparation for an equable temper in middle age.

And he was fifty, and beginning for the first time to feel, if only occasionally when he had remained too long at his desk or lectured too heatedly to a large audience—beginning to feel a diminution of his energy and strength, the first sad lessening of himself as he had always been.

I must get more rest, Stefan Ivarin thought an hour later, and mechanically pulled his old silver watch from his pocket. It was past four, no unusual hour for him if he had been waiting for the fever of lecturing to drain away, but later than normal to be writing. An exhausting, shocking night altogether, with the news of the fire stunning the whole world of labor. The editorial he had written at the office for tomorrow's paper was hardly better than reportage; he had ordered a Night Extra with the first terrible list of names, and he had written the editorial in minutes snatched from getting it to press. There was nothing of stature in it, but he had made up for it now.

(5)

For the third time he reread the pages on his desk. After the first paragraph, there was hardly a change or an interlineation.

To put off writing it until the sensible hours of tomorrow had been impossible, just as it had been unthinkable to leave the office until the final toll had come in. The figures kept changing; even at the end thirteen lives were still in doubt, and in God-knew-how-many hospital beds, where the "rescued" clutched with charred and blistered fingers at the last red filament of life, further change was still in the making.

Throughout the afternoon and evening he had felt chained to his desk, a prisoner in a cell of horror and rage. Since the *Slocum* disaster, New York had known no such holocaust, but the *Slocum* was an excursion boat for schoolchildren, so the city could unite in its grief. This time, with labor involved, a thousand attempts would be made to silence the outcry, to stifle the critics.

The attempts will fail, he thought; it's a free country, and labor's voice will be heard. There are those to speak and those to listen and no Siberia to swallow up either speaker or listener.

He folded up his pages, and crossed to the single window in his small room. In the unseasonable cold, the stars shone like ice; the heavens had always moved him, as the purity of mathematics moved him. In his youth when he had found his thoughts studded by sentimentality and superstition, he had often felt that his destiny had been written in those heavens which were shared by his two countries, his native land and his true beloved land. Had he not been born in 1861? Surely, he used to feel, the star of emancipation was high and bright in that year of my birth: in Russia, the Emancipation of the Serfs; in America, the Civil War that was to win the Emancipation of the Slaves.

Emancipation. A beautiful, a noble word, five syllables ringing with every concept of humanity and justice. A lofty music the whole world would one day hear.

He turned away from the window and glanced once more at his desk, as a lover looking back for one last glimpse of his beloved. Two days ago he had found deep gratification in the editorial he had written about the college in Virginia and the history book; the day before that, in his piece about Sir Edward Grey's speech on the armament race in Europe, and a day earlier in the one about the new association for "the advancement of colored people," in which he had challenged its separateness. Poverty was poverty, neither white nor black but poverty-pale, and the drive to end it and advance people should be one drive, undivided, unsplintered.

All three had been strong pieces, work to satisfy a man. But to-

(6)

night's editorial on the fire had a greater immediacy than any of these. It belonged on the front page, not inside; he would order the make-up man to box it next to the news story. The English-language newspapers did that, and there was no reason why the *Jewish News* should not. Another step in Americanization.

Stefan Ivarin stretched and yawned. A strange happiness coursed through him; he had written powerfully in the universal language. Not English, nor Russian, nor French, nor Yiddish, but that international language, the language of protest. In the morning, he would show it to Alexandra.

Too bad she was not awake now. His throat was parched and his tongue burnt; a glass of tea would be agreeable above everything else. Talk would be welcome also; despite his writing, he still felt choked with the need to talk.

Let her rest, he thought, and began to undress. On his desk the ashtray caught his eye: dead stubs crowded it to its rim. The longing for tea, then, was not an excuse to delay going to bed; his throat had indeed been burned dry. He had not been conscious of making so many cigarettes, nor of smoking them. His powers of concentration, at least, were as undiminished and fierce as ever.

I am still concentrating, he thought, still writing phrases in my mind; while this goes on, I would not sleep anyway. In his fingers, he could feel the sting of a scalding glass, in his nostrils the astringent aroma of fresh tea.

Why not? Why this Calvinism that made him fight his longing? He glanced about the room for a moment, peering through his thick glasses, as if looking for some palpable answer to his question. He had already taken off his suit and shoes and shirt, as well as his stiff open-gullet collar and the necktie that lay around its base on the outside. He moved toward his green flannel bathrobe, then veered away from it and went downstairs in his long-legged, tight-sleeved winter underwear and his heavy socks.

He moved softly, thoughtful of the four sleepers upstairs and Alexandra in the small extra room below. As the kitchen light went on, the dog, Shag, began to bark in the back yard, but Stefan recognized the desultory note that meant it would soon cease, and he stood still, waiting for it to end.

He went about the kitchen cautiously, careful of noise as he selected a pan for water and found the wire strainer that fitted inside the rim of the glass tumblers they used for tea. No matter how Americanized he had become about everything else, tea in a cup would always outrage some sensibility deep inside.

(7)

Possessed of the strainer, he turned to the four canisters on the hanging shelf above the sink. He opened the first one; it contained flour. He opened another; it held brown sugar. Then came coffee, then, brown rice.

"Where the devil does she keep the tea?" he asked the quiet kitchen. In his mind, he tried to re-create the path Alexandra traversed as she went about making their tea, and then, nodding to himself, he went out to the pantry.

The crowded shelves dismayed him; he never had been one of those men who were at home with household affairs. Uncertainly he gazed at the salt, cocoa, Mason jars of their own tomatoes, jelly glasses topped with paraffin discs, Eli's huge bottle of malted milk. The familiar square box of tea was not in sight.

Was tea kept on ice? He stared suspiciously at the varnished oak box, still gleaming after two years. The icebox—another *cause célèbre,* like the stairway. From the kitchen he could hear the boiling of the water, and the sense of being driven seized him.

He lifted the lid on top of the icebox; a diminished block of ice was there and nothing else. Forgetting his avoidance of noise, he let the lid drop and flung open the door in the lower half of the icebox. A wild conglomeration faced him but no tea. He seized a lemon, slammed the door and went back to the kitchen. An importance had infused the entire search. To give up the idea of tea now, to go upstairs quietly, to close doors softly, to open his window easily, to get into bed and fall into an unremarkable sleep—none of this was any longer tenable.

Suddenly he spied the square yellow box standing just beyond the breadbox. Relief burst through him, and he tore off the tightly fitted square cover, lowering his face to the good strong smell of the blackish-green spears. Forgiveness pervaded him, toward them, toward Alexandra.

He made his tea and watched the tumbler change color, from white to pale yellow to deep amber. Then he curved his forefinger and thumb toward each other, set the glass within their embrace, with the middle finger as its nether support, and began to pace up and down the room. His left hand could not have borne that scalding heat, but some forty years had wrought the mutation that made it possible for his right. One of his earliest memories, as a small child in Russia, was of his father walking about that dark inhuman kitchen of theirs, with a glass of boiling tea nested in the circle of his fingers.

A continuity, Stefan Ivarin thought, a small immortality. When I

(8)

was arrested, it was a death for both of them, and in '79, when I escaped and left for America, another death—their one son gone forever. Yet there is, somehow, a continuity.

He nodded at his glass, as if in salute. He had not yet tasted his tea; now that it was securely there, compulsion had fled. He enjoyed walking up and down the kitchen; upstairs, in his study, hardly three steps were possible between desk and wall, and when he opened the connecting door to his bedroom, the distance lengthened only another few paces.

Inadequate, it was true. He felt blocked off, barred from freedom, constantly turning back on himself. Perhaps on this one point, he should have given in to Alexandra, and hang the extra cost and the lost work.

The cubicle argument. There had been the stairway argument and the icebox argument and finally the size of the bedrooms. Perhaps if the others had not come first, he would have felt less protective toward his blueprints, less congealed with the ice of resistance at the very mention of the word "change." By that time, he had proved to them all that the stairway could not start up from the front hall at the front door. "If it does," he had said, "the bathroom door upstairs would be like a gate across the top step. Would you prefer that?"

"Can't you put the bathroom somewhere else, Stiva?" Alexandra had demanded. "Did President Taft say it must be just there?"

"President Taft wouldn't mind spending another hundred dollars to lengthen the water pipes!"

In the end, they had abandoned their cry for conformity. He doubted whether it ever crossed their minds, from the moment the house had been completed, that whereas in most houses you saw stairs as you came in at the front door, in this one you found them at the back door, near the kitchen and side porch, and went upstairs to the front bedrooms instead of the ones at the rear.

But, to this day, the size of the bedrooms remained a continuing boil, indurated and tight under their emotional skins. It was probable that he had been overeager to have a wide stairway and open hallway on the upper floor, probable that, buried deep in him, there was some hatred of narrow corridors. Who knew of the thousand concealed longings, wishes, fears, born subterraneously in the seas of fifty years of a man's life?

At any rate, on all his earlier floor plans, the proportions of hallway to bedrooms had been acceptable to the whole family. Only when fluidity had left, only when the builder was pressing him to turn over

(9)

his worksheets for formalization in blueprint, only then had Alexandra begun to demand an overhaul of every dimension and arrangement on the second floor.

As usual, the girls had sided with her. They could not, and she would not, follow him when he explained the additional costs, of juggling beams and uprights about, of shifting pipes and electric outlets. They would listen, and the next day, they would attack him again.

"Each bedroom," Alexandra would tearfully say, "could be ten inches wider, and you would still have your good big hall."

Irascibility was his weakness; the tear ducts hers. The sight of her weeping would snap his control. "A passageway," he would shout. "Like a coldwater flat on Essex Street. Is that the great desideratum of life?"

"But you're making five cubicles for the bedrooms, and a grandstand out of the hall."

"Cubicles! Eleven by thirteen—is that a cubicle?"

"Your bedroom is nine by thirteen."

"But I have my other room too!"

"Another cubicle."

"Is it me you worry about? If it is, let it alone, Alexandra, I beg of you, let it alone."

A bad time, Stefan Ivarin thought now, a time to forget. The bedrooms are a little crowded; I sometimes feel it so myself. But how many human beings on the face of this globe would not consider themselves in palaces, if they had each a bedroom like any one of ours?

Comfort filled him, and pride in his house. He raised his right hand and took his first sip of tea. It had gone tepid, but he did not mind.

Alexandra Ivarin began each day with her own method of physical exercise. A year before, just after her forty-ninth birthday, the doctor had pronounced her flabby as to muscle tone, and had ordered her to take up regular exercising.

Dutifully she had begun calisthenics, following the printed directions he had put into her unwilling hands, and every morning for a week, she spent twelve minutes bending, reaching, stretching and twisting to the accompaniment of a martinet's voice saying, "One, two, three, four, five. And one, two, three four five. And one, two three four five"—a voice she soon detested though it was her own.

After a week, she had quit in rebellion. Then, by some golden accident, the idea had come to her, and she had devised what she called "my dancing."

It had been a revelation of new pleasure, and since logic told her that the same muscles of arms, legs and torso would be in use when she danced, she had never doubted that the curative results were comparable, if not superior, to those the doctor wanted. For more than a year, in winter and in summer, she had kept up her morning ritual; by now she actively looked forward to it each day.

She opened the windows in the living room and wound up the Victrola. It was Sunday morning and still early; there was no chance of the girls coming down, and Eli and Joan slept until ten. Stefan, of course, never appeared before noon, and last night he must have come home later than usual. She peeled off her cotton nightgown, which hampered the freedom of her body, and stood naked, selecting from the small pile of records the Strauss waltz with which she liked to begin.

The music started, and pausing only to get the rhythm set in her mind, she began to hop on her right foot, then on her left. Hop, hop, hop on the right, change; hop, hop, hop on the left. Slide and jump to the right, slide and jump to the left. The hops once more, then a deep bend to the right, to the left.

The delicious melody, a little sugary perhaps but so caressing, so young, was like the clear air blowing in over the fields; her spirits lifted as her breath shortened, and she began to experience that surge of joy which always came to her through these secret minutes of her dancing.

Hop, hop, hop, slide and jump, bend to the right, bend to the left. Vaguely she knew that to others—if anybody could ever see her so— she might seem ludicrous in her dancing. They would see pendulous belly and breasts, grey hair flying; they would see an aging, overweight woman capering and leaping about. It did not matter. In herself, within her muscles and bones and hard-beating heart, was the sense of grace and youth, exhilarating and priceless.

Hop, hop, hop, slide and jump. Never, for the rest of her life, would she forgive Alexis Michelovsky, fine physician, dedicated socialist though he was, for permitting her to get this pendulous stomach, these elongated breasts. Idealism, idealism. All of them in their youth were so fired with scorn for people who thought of looks and money and possessions instead of abiding principles, and Alexis was intimately one of them.

But a thousand times since, she had wished she had gone to a nice American doctor who would have permitted her a maternity girdle for her pregnancies. If Alexis had done so, this disformity might never have begun. When she had asked, a little uncertainly, whether there

were some way of preserving her figure—she had been slender then—
Dr. Michelovsky had looked at her sadly and said, "You too, Alexandra?" as if he were saying *"Et tu, Brute?"*

Then she had been too young, too lacking in courage to tell him it
was no worship of materialism to want her stomach held up. Through
her first pregnancy, her beloved lost child, Stefan, dead at six months
from diphtheria, and then through Elijah's and Francesca's time, she
had helplessly suffered the knowledge of irremediable distention, but
never again had she ventured to ask Alexis to prescribe any escape.
Only when she was having Fira had she turned on him and demanded
an uplifting corset; by then it had been too late.

Hop, hop, hop, slide and jump, bend to the right, bend to the left.
Her blood was racing now, and her breathing a strain. The waltz
ended and she was glad for a moment's rest while she turned the
record, and rewound the machine.

Once, during the summer, Fee, or perhaps it was Fran, had come
downstairs in bare feet while she was still dancing. Luckily, that morning she had on a corset-cover and petticoat, so that she was not undressed. Children were horrified at the sight of nakedness in old bodies, particularly of their own parents. She herself, as a child, had hated
the smell in her parents' room, always thinking of it as an "old smell,"
as if it were a personal failing of her mother and father. Forty years
ago in Russia, even a well-furnished house like theirs, tended by
plenty of servants, must have stagnated with odors from primitive
plumbing and closed windows in a way that was unknown in modern
houses in America.

Alexandra Ivarin glanced affectionately around the room. As she
looked, a darkness stole into her mood; those white naked walls, unpainted plaster still, as on the day they had moved in! When they were
building, Stefan had told her that new plaster had to be given time to
settle, before wallpaper could be put on, and she, in turn, had explained to the girls so that they would not expect decorated rooms to
start with.

Two years had passed, the plaster throughout the house must have
settled as much as it would settle unto eternity, but whenever she
spoke about paper and paint, Stefan grew vexed or angry.

About the house, there never had been any arguing with him, only
fighting or giving in. But by now, these raw dead walls were a torment
to the girls; it was natural for them to want a pretty place to bring
their friends to. Especially Francesca, fifteen next August, and beginning to bring boys home once in a while.

It had been Fran, she suddenly remembered, who had come downstairs barefoot that morning and caught her at her dancing. The child had stopped short and watched, appalled.

"It's my own invention, instead of those awful gymnastics," Alexandra had explained, "it's my dancing."

"Oh, Mama."

Fran had turned away, a tone of helplessness in her voice, as if she had suffered defeat.

"Everything is 'oh, Mama,' " Alexandra had said sharply. "What's wrong with getting my morning exercises any way I like?"

"Nothing's wrong, Mama."

Fran had left the room, sagging in the shoulders. For the rest of the record, she, Alexandra, had stubbornly gone on, but there was no longer any joy in continuing, and for the next few mornings she had been self-conscious even with no one to watch her. Her daughter was ashamed of her, of the way she looked, of the large bulge under her thin slip, of the grotesque figure she made, leaping like Pavlova.

A child, she had thought, Fran is still a child. This lump in my throat is as if I were a child too. She is an American child, what is more; she does not like to be reminded that Stefan and I were once foreigners, coming through Ellis Island like all the others, with that same hunger to get our first papers and start belonging to America.

"Fran," she had called, "I'll be there soon, to get breakfast."

"All right, Mama. I'm setting the table."

She was forgiven, Alexandra had thought. For the moment, forgiven. Remembering it now, however, dampened her spirits, as the sight of the white plaster had done. Stefan could be immovable, cantankerous; to balk at his decision was to bring on a violence that destroyed the whole house.

The second Strauss waltz was ending. She turned off the Victrola and went back to her room, a small one, next to the parlor.

It had started out as the spare room and had become "the sewing room." It was bare except for the sewing machine, the cot, and a chair, but she was sleeping better, since she had turned over her bedroom upstairs to Eli and Joan, and had moved down here. They had protested that they could manage in Eli's room, but she had insisted.

Not only was it too small for two people, but when Eli was having an attack, he needed to sleep alone on that mountain of pillows. If only he would get well, if only he were older, she would be overjoyed about what had happened. A boy like that, though, just past twenty, to have a wife, a baby coming, and his inexplicable asthma—

Perhaps if her first son, the baby Stefan, had lived, she might not have so fierce a joy and pride in Eli, but it was as if he, the living

Elijah, were her first-born. The love that she had for the girls was profound, of course, deep-flowing through every vein. But in her love for Eli was another quality, almost—she had almost thought "worship." That was overstating it, but let it go. One worshiped humanity, one worshiped the ideas which would serve humanity, but also there was, in some love, a breath of worship.

Perhaps what she felt for Eli was a "mathematical" doubling and multiplying for the lost son and the living son. Almost a quarter-century had gone since the baby's death, and yet the same cold fingers of memory reached for her heart whenever she thought of it.

Time flew, life went, the years softened much. But she would never be done completely with that first horror when she watched helplessly as her baby died. She herself had been in her twenties then, a girl still, unused to personal suffering. Twenty-three years ago that had been, twenty-three swift terrible beautiful years.

The thump of the morning newspaper against the porch steps brought Alexandra Ivarin back to the present, and she put on her bathrobe, combed her hair, and went outside for it. Folded and interlocked so that it would not fly apart when it was hurled through space by the newsboy, it sent invitation through her fingers, but she resisted it and went back to the kitchen. She put the percolator and a pot of water on the gas range and then opened the back door, calling to the dog. He came bounding in, a great shaggy beast with energy enough to throw over ten men.

"Down, Shag, down," she cried. Immediately he crouched at her feet, looking up with his brown eyes glistening. She laughed. "You big silly fool," she said, and leaned down to pat his massive head. He was an English sheep dog, unkempt, savage-looking, but gentle and loving. One of her pupils had given him to the children a year ago when he was a tan-and-white puppy; nobody had dreamed then that Shag would grow into this great animal, eating so much, thumping his tail so hard on the floor that the whole house shook. He needed a new kennel; Eli had built this one, allowing what they all thought was plenty of room for Shag's growth. They had been wrong, and Eli kept promising to make a larger one.

"Soon," he would say, "next Saturday at the latest."

But a week of teaching seemed to exhaust him, probably because he was so new at it. Manhood had come to him too fast; six months ago he had begun to earn a living, five months ago he had married, and in two months he would be a father. Too fast, too fast—from the high springboard of boyhood he had dived into maturity. Joan had been nineteen, too, when they met at Jamaica Training School; nei-

(1 4)

ther of them had any experience with love, and they had been over-powered.

Poor children, Alexandra thought, what they must have gone through before they got up the courage to tell us and the Martins.

In Joan, fear was more understandable; her parents, Webster and Madge Martin, were strict, conventional people, good and kind, intelligent, too, since her father was a doctor, but both enslaved by what was proper or not proper, right or not right.

But Eli knew that his own parents set little value on such sanctities as ceremonies; common-law marriage was as legal as any other, if both man and woman were serious in their purpose and not merely having a liaison. Or had the boy been afraid that any parents would abandon convictions and principles when put to the test by their own children? He had been as frightened and miserable as Joan; only after their marriage at City Hall had he regained the appearance of happiness.

From the gas range came the sound of bubbling. Alexandra measured out the Scotch pinhead oatmeal, and stirred it into the boiling water. The sight of the hard little grains pleased her. So much better than denatured foods, she thought. When would people stop killing themselves off with gluey white oats and white flour and white rice and white sugar? Some day she might become a lecturer, too, and tell women about these new discoveries in diet and health. Even Alida Paige, so liberal and modern, lived in the dark ages about such matters; what chance was there for ignorant immigrants on the East Side, filled with their orthodox dietary rules and laws?

She turned away from the range and picked up the squared lump of newspaper, carefully opening its tightly folded bulk so as not to tear it. Every morning, when the boy on his bicycle fired the paper at the porch, it made a woody thump she loved. In the city one never heard these small sounds of village and town, so comforting and neighborly; before she and Stefan had arrived at their great decision to move away from New York, she had always had to go out to buy the morning paper at the corner stand. But here, a mile's walk from Main Street, they had fallen into this Americanism of the thumping paper as if they had all been born to it.

The paper was now open and Alexandra turned it right side up. The front page was splattered with pictures and huge headlines.

154 KILLED IN SKYSCRAPER FACTORY FIRE:
SCORES BURN, OTHERS LEAP TO DEATH

(15)

In the silent kitchen, her gasp was audible. From the black type, words sprang out at her. "700 Workers, mostly girls, trapped" . . . "Bodies of dead heap the streets" . . . "Triangle Waist Factory" . . . "charred skeletons bending over sewing machines" . . . "locked doors" . . . "girls jumping from windows with hair aflame . . ."

"Oh, my goodness," Alexandra Ivarin whispered. She pulled out a kitchen chair and sat down heavily, trying to read the story word for word. But her eyes refused methodical behavior; they leaped from phrase to phrase—the single fire escape, the one stairway, the locked exit, the wooden sewing machines massed so closely that flight between them was impossible.

She turned to the second page and saw that it, too, contained nothing but the fire, and the third page, the fourth, most of the fifth. Lists of the dead stretched on, column after column, and she began to read them. Every second or third name was followed by "age 16" or "age 17." Often the final words to the brief paragraphs were, "Identification by pay envelope."

Children, she thought, half of them were children.

The names were Polish and Russian and Italian—the addresses all on the Lower East Side. Children of the Ghetto, Zangwill had named them, children of poverty and ignorance and injustice.

The fire had begun just before five in the afternoon. In the first hour after the news broke, the *World* said, ten thousand mothers and fathers had flocked to Washington Square, by eight o'clock twenty thousand were there, breaking through police and fire lines under the towering ten-story building, searching for their sons and daughters, begging for the names of the rescued. Her own throat felt their anguished voices, her own breast their pounding hearts. Suppose Eli or Fran or Fee—

"Oh, my goodness," Alexandra Ivarin said again.

"Oh, my goodness what?" It was Fran, coming into the kitchen.

Silently Alexandra handed over the paper. Stefan had known about the fire last night; that was what had kept him in New York so much later than usual. It was two when she had gone to bed, his normal time for getting home, but there had been no sign of him. Now she understood.

"Gee, isn't that awful?" Fran said a moment later.

Alexandra nodded, and said nothing. If she spoke at all, she would find herself explaining why it was not only awful but criminal, that it was not merely an accident but part of a whole system. And Fran would say "Oh, Mama," with that sagging look.

Alexandra turned to the stove and began to serve the oatmeal. Behind her, she soon heard Fran riffle through the rest of the paper. She was looking for the Katzenjammer Kids, Mutt and Jeff, and the rest of the funnies.

As her older sister ran downstairs, Fira Ivarin pulled a white middy blouse over her head and wondered if she would be pretty too when she was fourteen. Three and a quarter years was a horrible time to have to wait to find out. Trudy Loheim, her best friend, was pretty already, prettier even than Fran. Anybody with Trudy's blond hair and blue eyes and wonderful complexion had a big start on being pretty.

Fee slung the folded black silk sailor's tie under the collar of her middy, hooked up her navy serge skirt and went up to the mirror above the bureau, staring at her brown eyes and brown hair. After a moment, she made a face and turned away.

"She'll be a striking woman," Alida Paige had once said to her mother, when they didn't know she could hear them. "Francesca will be a pretty girl, but Fira will be handsome. People will notice her."

Striking, Fee thought, handsome. When all anybody wanted was to be pretty and know how to dance and wear nice dresses from Best or Wanamaker, the way Trudy did. Trudy's father worked in a brewery and was fat and drunk and sleepy, but Trudy looked like a picture in a magazine and had the start of a real shape, even though she hadn't *begun* any more than she, Fira, had. Fran was always talking about everything being different once you began, but she just looked superior if you asked any questions about what it was like.

Her mother had explained everything, because her mother believed in educating children about such things, instead of letting them hear it from their friends, or on the street. But even though Mama went into everything scientifically, she never got to real things like Joan and Eli and their going to have a baby.

Fee glanced toward the next room, now Eli and Joan's. Sometimes she could hear them in there, laughing and talking, and last Sunday morning when Joan felt sick, she had gone in with a cup of hot coffee. Eli was still asleep, next to Joan, and it had made Fee feel queer to see them right out that way, even though she knew perfectly well that married people slept together in one bed. Actually seeing her own brother that way was different from simply knowing, and she had almost spilled the coffee.

There was no sense saying anything to Fran about such things;

(17)

Fran went Miss Ladylike all over and it drove her crazy. And Fran could be mean too. Always teasing her about getting too tall and having wide shoulders, and turning into an Amazon.

"Come on down, Fee," Fran called from the kitchen. "I'm not going to wait around."

Fran was going skating and was letting her go along. Sometimes Fran was wonderful. Fee raced two at a time down the stairs. At the table, Fran motioned to the back porch with her head, and Fee's heart sank. Wearing her horrible old grey bathrobe, Mama was out there, talking to the milkman; he was holding his wire basket, looking down at the floor, nodding his head every other second.

He looked trapped, Fira thought, and shame boiled up for her mother, for the urgent way her mother was talking.

"A hundred and fifty people," Mama said. "It's a crime."

"Terrible," the milkman agreed listlessly.

"Burned alive," Mama said. "Under socialism, it would be the workers who were the most important, not saving expenses on fire escapes. Then such tragedies couldn't happen."

"I guess that's right," he said. "Well, good day, Mrs. Ivarin." He pronounced it Eye-var-*een,* coming down hard on the last syllable. Mama had told him at least ten times to say it as if it were Eee-*var*-in, but the next day he would return to his stupid Eye-var-*een.* Fee couldn't stand him.

"Hello, Mama," she said as her mother came back.

"Good morning, dear."

Fran said, "Mama, do you *have* to talk socialism, every time the milkman comes?"

Fee said, "Fran," in a pleading voice. She hated it when there was a fight.

"You keep still," Fran ordered. "I can say anything I want."

"Girls, girls," their mother said.

"And to the iceman?" Fran went on. "And the grocer and the man who gets the garbage? They don't even listen, and I tell you, it doesn't do any *good.*"

"And I tell *you,*" Alexandra said, "it's the only way the world ever changes." She turned to Fee. "Here's your oatmeal."

"Aren't we having bacon and eggs? Today's Sunday."

"Yes, yes. I forgot what day it was." She set the steaming cereal down and continued addressing Fran. "And the world has to change," she said, pointing to the paper. "Do you want such things to go on happening? If the unions were really strong—"

"The unions, the unions," Fran said under her breath.

Alexandra Ivarin opened her lips to speak, but just then Eli came downstairs, with Joan behind him, and she turned to them. Her eyes lighted at the sight of her son. He was wearing a blue shirt; he looked handsomest in blue. It made his grey eyes change color, like the sky when the clouds broke open. He was average height but well-built and manly; he had always been popular with girls. Joan was sweet and good, not very pretty nor remarkable; if they had not been so hasty, Eli might have had his pick from a dozen more gifted girls later on.

At his greeting, her heart sank. When he drew a breath, she could hear it, rough and hard as if it were made of cord. She glanced inquiringly at Joan, and behind his back, Joan nodded in unhappy confirmation.

"He had a bad night, Mother Ivarin," Joan said, "but he won't stay in bed."

"I'm going for a ride," Eli said.

"A ride," Alexandra said in alarm, "when an attack is starting?"

"It helped last time."

"That motorcycle." His mother put her hand on his shoulder. "If you had a bad coughing spell when you're going so fast, you might be killed."

"Please." He jerked his shoulder to shake her hand off. His wife and sisters looked at him uneasily. But Alexandra thought, He's sick, poor boy, no wonder he's cranky.

T W O

The acrid smoke of Cubeb cigarettes penetrated the thinning screen of sleep, and Stefan Ivarin awoke. It was three days since the fire, and ever since the quarrel with Fehler at the office about the boxed editorial on the first page, he had been sleeping badly; it was remarkable he had not had one of his nightmares.

All his adult life, he had been subject to intermittent nightmares, sometimes once every few months, sometimes once a week. Their coming was unpredictable, with no apparent relation to his waking state of mind, and as apt to occur during periods of tranquillity as during crisis.

Once, when he had been laid up with lumbago, he had mentioned them to Alexis Michelovsky, and again, conversationally, to Dr. Martin, in the process of the two families' early acquaintanceship over Joan and Eli. Both physicians had promptly blamed too much strong tea, too many cigarettes; neither had even paused to wonder why, with the same vast quantities of tea and cigarettes, other nights remained dreamless. Whatever else their predilections, the equations of logic and reason, it would seem, held no appeal to either of them.

Bernard Shaw was right, and not only in being a socialist. Most doctors knew next to nothing, and if they did not prattle about white phagocytes, they usually erupted as learnedly about other nonsense. Alexandra with her newly declared war on "refined" foods probably made more sense than half the accredited physicians.

Not one doctor had found any cause for Elijah's asthma, not one any cure. Though his worst attacks came only once a year or so, these "small attacks" baffled them quite as thoroughly. Rest and medicated cigarettes were their prescriptions, and during the big attack, injections of adrenalin. And a young man of twenty, in the meantime, remained the vessel of a mystery that could destroy his health and his youth.

Frowning, Stefan began to dress. His eyeballs ached with strain, and he felt the first heaviness of a headache. The impregnated air distressed him; he was always sensitive to certain odors, usually the greasy smells from frying, but Eli's rank cigarettes had added a new type.

Fatigue had not vanished with sleep; he was jumpy and on edge. It had been a crushing week, with his usual duties augmented by endless meetings and discussions about strategy over the fire. Relief funds were being organized by religious groups, labor organizations, the Red Cross; churches and synagogues were planning special services for the dead, permits and licenses for parades and meetings were being sought throughout the city.

A funeral procession of three hundred thousand garment workers was being arranged by the Women's Trade Union League; the Cloakmakers were staging a giant mass meeting at Grand Central Palace and there would be another at the Metropolitan Opera House next Sunday.

He had been invited to speak on all three occasions. Gompers and others in the labor movement would be appearing; he was already preparing notes—as if he would ever need them. Every union in the city was calling for tighter enforcement of safety regulations, sufficient exits, fire drills, condemnation of some thirty thousand other deathtraps in which men and women, boys and girls, spent their twelve hours every day. Like every disaster, the fire was the catalyst that had brought a seething new agitation to the ranks of labor. How hideous the price of these catalysts, how tremendous the purchase.

From Eli's room came sounds of coughing; it had been a stubborn attack, passing now, after four days, but leaving the boy depleted and wan. Since it had begun, Alexandra, frightened and weeping, had turned on him each time he left for the office, accusing him of "not caring enough." A wonderful woman, Alexandra, but maddening in her inconsistency.

When Eli was small, she had chided him often about devoting more time to his son, and whenever Eli was ill, "nagging" was the inevitable word that came to the tongue. Later, with the girls, the situation was worse; by then he was on the staff of a morning paper and scarcely ever at home when they were awake.

Like most mothers, Alexandra saw reality, and rejected it. Her mind was host to a vast illogic and nothing would dislodge it for long. She respected, honored, egged on her husband in his chosen work, and at the same time resented the fact that that work prevented him from being "a good father."

"A good father." What was it, this being "a good father"? To love one's sons and daughters was not enough; to carry in one's bone and blood a pride in them, a longing for their growth and development— this was not enough. One had to be a ready companion to games and jokes and outings, to earn from the world this accolade. The devil with it.

He finished dressing and went next door. Eli was propped against four pillows and Joan was reading.

"How do you feel?" Stefan asked.

"Better, thanks."

"He's going to get up after lunch," Joan said.

"Good." Eli was breathing through his nostrils again, distended still, but once more capable of supplying him enough air. That was good. To see him at the worst of a serious attack was a horror: a youngster sucking at space, fingers plucking at his pajamas as if they were made of constricting iron.

"Is your father coming again today, Joan?"

"I think so. To see if Eli can go back to school tomorrow."

"Too soon," Stefen said, with authority. "Don't go for the rest of the week."

"You can talk," Eli said. "It would be my third absence this term."

Stefan said, "Well," and shrugged. Then he turned to Joan, noticing with some surprise how big she was, as if he had forgotten her pregnancy. "And how do you feel, Joanischka?"

"Fine," she said, and laughed. "I never *will* get used to 'Joanischka.'" Like a child, she added, "Don't be sore at me for teasing you, Father Ivarin."

"Sore?" he said gruffly. "Nonsense. It's all in the tone." He hesitated, and then as he left, he spoke past her to his son. "She's all right, Eli, she's a good girl."

Downstairs, the kitchen was empty, but through the windows, he saw his wife working in the garden. At last the weather had turned mild, the earth was thawing, and a haze of young green already touched the fields and trees.

Now for days on end, Alexandra would be out there digging and weeding and planting her lettuces and tomatoes and radishes and beans, even the two rows of corn in the narrow strip left over at the side of the yard. If she suspected that sometimes he was sorry he had calculated costs so closely when they had bought their plot, she would begin at once to press him about the empty lot next them. Better to say nothing.

On what they earned, it was miracle enough that they had finally built their own house on their own ground. Forty by a hundred was the usual plot in this neighborhood; less would have been forbidden by the zoning laws, more would have been aping the rich.

Yet when he watched Alexandra measuring out the inches for her vegetables, he did sometimes speculate on approaching the owner of the neighboring property about renting his vacant ground. It would give her so much pleasure to have a larger garden, and unlike her yearnings when he was planning the house itself, these had some validity.

We'll see, he thought, and stepped to the window and called her. She looked up, raised her forefinger to say she would be in in a minute and went on tamping down the earth around the seeds she had planted. At the side of the garden, Shag was lying stretched out on his belly, his huge front paws parallel before him, a speculative look about him as he eyed Alexandra's activity. Watching him, Stefan thought, There will be problems larger than life when he starts tearing up her plants.

(2 2)

Seating himself at the table, he picked up the paper, and by the time Alexandra came in, he was deeply absorbed. She greeted him and he replied but went on reading. As she set out his breakfast, she kept up a steady questioning about the developing plans for a funeral procession, for the mass meeting; he answered between paragraphs, with a growing annoyance at her persistence.

"We ought to do something ourselves," Alexandra said.

"I gave the relief fund five dollars yesterday."

"I mean, do something here in Barnett," she said. "Out here it's already forgotten, a few days after it happened."

Stefan nodded and went on reading. The final figure was 146 dead. The *World's* coverage was again the largest and the best of any of the papers; even today, the fire was page one, column one, and most of page three was given over to pictures and affidavits. Like the rest, however, the *World* was blaming the disaster on "incompetent government" and overlapping authority between local and state departments. Even the liberal press could not grasp the truth underneath the superficiality.

"Something to make the neighbors remember and think a little," Alexandra went on.

Stefan looked up and said sharply, "Must I leave the room, to read my paper?"

She drew back as if he had thrown something at her, and turned quickly, to hide the ready tears that sprang to her eyes. But he had seen, and, in Russian, he said, "The devil!"

"*Chortu, chortu,*" she repeated after him. "Everything is *chortu,* if I dare open my mouth when you want silence."

He made no answer. Under the table his right foot moved backward under the chair, his leg bent and the knee jutting forward like a runner's at the tape. On the ball of his foot, as if driven by an unseen mechanism, the leg began a rapid up and down pumping. Unlike a tic or tremor, this pumping was something he could instantly control when he knew he was doing it, but it had become so habitual that he usually did not know. It was not always a mark of irritability; at times of delighted concentration over some baffling problem of chess, for instance, it would also begin, continuing until his calf and thigh began to ache.

Now, however, in the sudden silence, he heard his shoe squeak and his rubber heel go tap, tap, tap on the floor. Suddenly eager to soothe his wife's feelings, he brought his right foot forward, in alignment with his left, and set his heel flat on the linoleum.

"You're right," he said, making his tone agreeable again. "Some kind of public protest in Barnett would not be a bad idea."

Instantly smiling, Alexandra wiped her eyes with a kitchen towel. "We'll decide on something. If only there was time to arrange a big meeting in that hall in Jamaica. Alida and Evan would help, and you could speak—"

"Alexandra, I beg you. Not now." Under the table his right foot moved back under the chair once more; his knee rose and fell; this time he did not know it. He bent over his paper, shutting her face out of his line of vision. Without a word, she left him and went back to her garden. Stefan was relieved.

And he was relieved again some twelve hours later, when he returned to the house, to find it already dark. It had been another exhausting day and he needed silence and separateness. He would work out Capablanca's game with Lasker, and go to bed early.

His fatigue was out of proportion to the day; he wondered at it. The trip from New York had taken longer than usual; a lightning storm had damaged power lines, and after the change at Cypress Hills from the elevated, the trolley crawled to Jamaica and Barnett. By the time he had walked the mile up from Main Street to the house, he was conscious of a dragging pain in his back and shoulders.

Only rarely did he regret the decision to move out to Long Island so that the girls, at least, could grow up from babyhood in a thoroughly American environment, but tonight was one of the times. For a man on a morning newspaper—daily except Saturdays—with the first deadline at eleven each night, it was a hard trip, harder than it had been nine years ago when they had taken the step.

When he was a block away from home, Shag heard him and came loping across the empty fields to greet him. Having a dog was charming; there was a great clumsy loving energy about Shag that appealed to him even when he was depressed.

"How are you, boy?"

Shag leaped at him, his weight striking full on his shoulders.

"Down," Stefan shouted. "Lie down." He bent to pat the great animal. "You blockhead you," he said. "Come home and behave yourself."

The lightning storm had wiped the sky clear of cloud, and the rain had freshened the odors of new grass and earth. In the pale light, the house looked beautiful. Stefan Ivarin drew a deep breath and some inner tightness loosened. Walking more easily, he climbed the three concrete steps that rose in the bank of ground, and then the three wooden steps of the porch.

But for once the chess game failed to stimulate him and he left it before the final moves. With vague apprehension he wondered again why he should feel so weary. It was never hard work, long hours, the expenditure of energy which produced this depletion; it was, rather, depression.

Was the situation at the office really growing worse, or did he imagine it? Nonsense, Ivarin thought. I am no skittish youth to be imagining. A clash will come between us. He is heading for a show of power which will kill off one or the other of us.

Well, let it come. If the *Jewish News* is to go in for Joseph Fehler's yellow journalism, I would not remain in any case. Fehler bridles at the phrase, but his schemes are all for sensationalism in the paper. In this too he is an extremist, not in his politics alone. It was a bad day when Fehler was appointed Business Manager, bad for the paper, bad for my peace of mind.

An anarchist for a business manager and efficiency expert—that is a touch of the sardonic for you. Socialism is too moderate for Mr. Fehler, the Socialist Party is too moderate, I am too moderate, Debs is too moderate. Only the Socialist Labor Party—how mischievous political titles could be, concealing disparate principles under similarities, to confuse the innocent or naïve—only Fehler's S.L.P. is any good! Like all extremists everywhere, in Russia, in America, even in the offices of newspapers, Fehler will hurl his little bombs the moment he feels powerful enough to do so. Woe to anybody in his way. Woe to anybody when the extremists win anything anywhere.

Ivarin slowly undressed and went to bed. He had never liked Joseph Fehler, not even at the beginning when he had not yet known he disliked him. On a larger paper, more departmentalized, his path would rarely have crossed that of the Business Manager; for most editors, it was a point of honor to steer clear of "the money side." But the *Jewish News,* though only 30,000 less in circulation than the *Forward,* was informal and loose in its structure and behavior, and when Fehler had come to work some five years before, the staff was still small enough to make this steering-clear impractical. Duties overlapped; to this day sudden disputes could spring up over jurisdiction and boundary lines.

Hiring a business manager at all was a sign of prosperity. Until then, the paper's founder and owner, Isaac Landau, aided by one old bookkeeper, had done all the buying of paper and inks and press equipment, all the billing and contracting and whatever "business managing" had to be done. Ivarin had no taste for such matters, and as insurance against any future invasion, rather made a point of it.

(25)

Fehler was not yet thirty-five when Landau took him on, but he was no neophyte. He had been a job printer, like his father before him, and had gone on from there to magazine and newspaper work in the foreign-language field. He sounded like a native-born American, having lived in the Middle West from the age of one or two until he was grown, but his mother tongue was German and the Yiddish that went with it because his parents were Jews. With three sons, his father had thought ahead to their forced conscription in the German Army and had emigrated after the Franco-Prussian war, settling in Milwaukee because New York had "too many Russian Jews."

The German Jew versus the Russian Jew, Stefan Ivarin thought now, turning over in bed. Maybe that's why I found something objectionable in Fehler from the start. The German Jew buttering his soul with that slippery superiority over the Russian Jew or Polish Jew. An intramural bigotry that outsiders never suspect. But had Fehler been more Russian than all the Romanoffs, we'd have clashed anyway, the moment he proclaimed himself a "philosophical anarchist." What is that indeed, except an anarchist with his tail between his legs? Not precisely the right Damon for my Pythias.

An international metaphor, Ivarin thought, and felt the first vagueness of sleep.

In the darkness Fee woke, shaken by fear and recognition. Her father's voice, full-throated and deep like an animal's, rose and fell in the screaming of his nightmare. For a second she lay still, hoping somebody else would do it this time. Then she sprang up and ran to his room and leaned down over him. "Papa, wake up, Papa."

His screaming rose in volume and she knew he would not wake until she had touched his shoulder. Then he would give one final cry, and it would be over for this time. But the instant of touching him and of hearing that last cry was the worst moment. For another second, she continued to call, "Papa, wake up." Then she forced her hand through the darkness and seized his shoulder.

At her touch his body leaped.

"Wuh-ahhh." It was a sliding groaning howl, followed by abrupt silence. He sat up and, in his ordinary voice, said impatiently, "All right, all right."

"It's me, Papa. Are you up?"

"Yes, yes. I had a bad dream." He stretched his hand out for his glasses, on a chair drawn up to his bed, and as his blanket fell back from his moving arm, a faint sour smell rose to her nostrils. She drew back a step. "Turn the light on, Firuschka."

She crossed the bare floor to the switch, her heart still thudding. He always called her Firuschka when she woke him, and he always said exactly the same words: *All right, all right. I had a bad dream.*

The switch clicked as she turned back to him, reluctantly now that they could see each other. After waking him, she never knew what to say; it was hard even to meet his eyes. But to shake him awake and then just leave without a word seemed terrible.

She stood still, glancing around the room, waiting. Even coming in here at night was strange; everything looked different. His clothes were hung on a knob of his chair; through the open door to his study she could see his papers and equations and books piled on his desk, and the old wooden table next to it, with his chessboard and more books about famous chess players and their tournaments.

In bed, her father was clearing his throat and coughing. "What time is it?" he asked, and she made herself look at him as she answered. "I don't know, Papa," she said. "Late."

He was blinking, and giving his head quick little shakes as if to dislodge the rest of his nightmare. He didn't like pajamas, and in his buttoned, long-sleeved underwear, he seemed smaller and older than he did in the daytime when he was dressed. His neck looked thinner and his head balder. Now he put his glasses on and leaned over the chair to look at his watch. "After three," he said, as if he were angry at the watch. "Go back to sleep, Fira. You'll catch cold."

"All right, Papa. Good night."

Gratefully, she hurried out. It wasn't a very cold night, but she felt shivery just the same. In her own room, the door to the sleeping porch didn't fit tightly at the bottom and wind slithered in like snakes along the floor. But her bed was still warm, and she curled up in it, far down, pulling the blanket up over her hair and around her forehead like a hood.

Of late, she seemed to be the only one who ever heard him. At least she was always the one who had to run in to wake him. Fran insisted she never woke up, but Fira was sure she did wake and then lie there, too afraid to move. Her mother also said she couldn't get upstairs in time to wake him, and Eli and Joan—well, Joan was too new in this house to be the one to do it. Joan never said anything about it, and everybody else was too used to it to ever talk about it.

In the daytime, her father never mentioned his dreams and it was impossible to ask him right out about them. Mama once had said it was always one dream: he was back in prison in Russia and they were flogging him with the knout. When anybody called out to wake him, the voice flowed right into his dream and became the shouts of the prison guards beating him. And when anybody actually touched him, it became the fiercest slash of the knout.

Poor Papa, Fee thought. Even though he never mentioned his dreams, he did sometimes talk about being in prison. He had just turned seventeen when he was arrested, and he belonged to a secret group of students, all of them sixteen and seventeen years old, at the University of Odessa, and all writing and printing pamphlets and articles about the oppression of the Czar and the horrible Russian police. He used to say, "When I was in prison," with a sort of boasting pleasure in his voice, the way Betty Murphy's father would say, "When I was in Paris."

Down the hall, footsteps sounded; it was her father going to the bathroom. He left the door open, and she could hear him. Anger and shame spouted up in her, like jets of hot fluid, drenching and extinguishing her flare of love and pity.

She wished she had a father like Betty's or Trudy's. Their fathers didn't stay up half the night and sleep in the morning when the rest of them had breakfast; Betty and Trudy didn't have to hear that "shush" all the time. "Shush, Papa's sleeping." Or, "Shush, Papa's working." Or, "Shush, Papa's in a mood."

Every once in a while he would get in a mood and fall silent, never looking at anybody, going around for days like a stranger. Late at night, sometimes, she could hear him downstairs talking at the top of his lungs to Mama, as if he were on a platform, lecturing to a thousand people. The sound frightened her and sometimes Fran would listen a while and then look as if she hated him.

Fee didn't hate him; sometimes he was wonderful, and said funny things. If only both of them were more like everybody else's mother and father—without any accent, and not forever talking about a better world for workingmen and ending child labor and sweatshops, and what a great man Eugene V. Debs was, and electing Socialists to Congress, and eating brown bread and brown sugar.

They were both too old to change; fifty was half a century old. She thought of her father dead, lying in bed, his face blue-white and his eyes staring up at the ceiling. She was kneeling beside him, desperately crying, and in a circle around her stood the whole family and their best friends, watching her grief, saying, "Poor child, the youngest, his favorite one."

Fee's throat lumped and she sat up. Leaning across to the other bed she whispered, "Franny, are you awake?" There was no answer, and after a moment, she lay down again and fell asleep.

Suddenly, that afternoon, the sun grew hot and in a day or two the whole hill was green. Outside the Ivarin house, on the three slender maples, twigs and branches swelled and thickened with pale-yellow buds; in the back yard the two fruit trees took on a paler pink. Along the sides of the house and the front porch, lilies of the valley looked out from green sheaths and the Rose of Sharon bushes burst into young leaf.

Walking home from school with Trudy Loheim, Fee swung her books by their leather strap and slung her winter coat over her left shoulder as Trudy had done. It was Friday afternoon and on Fridays they were allowed to make fudge, taking turns at each other's houses.

This was Fee's turn and she was glad. It made her happy to be going home with her best friend in such warm and sunny weather, school over for the week, and somehow the sudden feel of Easter vacation just ahead, and then the whole summer.

A block away from her house, she stopped short, and Trudy stopped too

Even from that distance, she could see something queer about the house. She glanced at Trudy's face, and then at the house once more. Her stomach tightened. The whole front of the house looked black.

It *was* black, she saw a moment later. Both her parents were out on the porch, her father on a stepladder, her mother below him, feeding him lengths of cotton fabric from a bolt she held in her arms. The fabric was black and they were draping the entire front of the house with it.

Any kind of physical work always made her father grumble, and say *Chortu;* the only time he ever spoke Russian was for secrets or when he cursed out loud. Yet here he was nailing the bunting over the doorway, curving it down in a swag, reaching down for the tacks her mother was passing up to him and nailing the swag up at either side. Each porch post had already been twined around with it from top to bottom, and one of the two windows had been framed in it.

She glanced at Trudy and desperately wished today wasn't the day to make fudge. Trudy was staring at the porch, too, not saying anything.

"Oh, Trudy," Fee whispered, "don't tell anybody."

"What are they doing?" Trudy whispered back.

(29)

"I don't know—something crazy and terrible."

They walked onward, slowly. Step by step Fee kept thinking it was terrible to have to go forward, to have to go straight up to the house and hear what they would say, with Trudy right there to hear it too. She was used to the way they talked, but Trudy wasn't. There was no way to stop them, no way to go right past the house as if it had nothing to do with her.

The sound of hammering started again, and Shag's barking with it. By now the girls were only a few feet away, but the hammering and barking covered up the sounds of their approach.

"Hello," Fee called out.

Her mother heard her and spoke to her father. He stopped hammering, but stayed perched up on the stepladder, looking down at them. Shag leaped down the steps and flung himself joyously at Fee, but she ignored him and kept looking up at her parents.

"Hello, girls," her mother said. "Now, Fira, don't look like that until you hear the reason."

"It's a protest," her father offered, in a strange, rather kindly voice. "Hello, Trudy."

"Hello, Mr. Ivarin." Trudy blushed, and turned a little to face Fee's mother. "And Mrs. Ivarin."

"Shag, you *stop!*" Fira cried, grabbing the dog's collar without taking her eyes from her father's face. "A protest?" she asked.

"About the Triangle fire," he said. "Trudy, do you know about it?"

"I think so, Mr. Ivarin," Trudy said uncertainly.

Fee's mother came toward them, unwinding a few lengths from the bolt in her arms, so as not to topple the ladder. She addressed herself to Trudy. "It was in a factory, where the owners saved expenses on fire escapes, and a hundred and fifty workers were burned alive."

Politely, Trudy said, "Oh, yes."

"But, Mama," Fee said, "is anybody *else* putting black all over their porch?"

"I had the idea and we—"

"The whole labor movement," her father interrupted, still sounding patient, like Miss King at school explaining parsing, "is staging public demonstrations. We want to do something too."

"It was my idea," Alexandra began again, but she saw that the child was looking only at Stefan, and she let her voice trail away.

"But, Papa," Fee said, moving closer to the ladder and looking up in entreaty, "everybody will make *fun* of me."

(30)

"It's nothing, Firuschka, let them. When you're older you won't mind."

He turned back to his work and the hammering started again. Shag instantly resumed his barking; together, the hammering and barking were deafening. "Come on," Fee said to Trudy, and ran around to the side entrance. She flung open the door to the back hall, and dropped her coat and books on the floor. Behind her, Trudy said, "Don't you care, Fee. It's not your fault."

"It's horrible," she cried. "I hate it. I just hate it." She sat down on the lower step of the stairway, and put her face on her knees. "Oh, Trudy, I just *can't* make fudge today," she said.

"Let's go up to your room."

"They're so *mean!* They never even *care* what I feel like."

"Come on, Fee, we can go up, can't we?"

Trudy started up the uncarpeted stairs, and in a moment Fee picked up her books and coat and followed her. This crazy stairway! She forgot all about it until something bad happened, but then she could see the blueprints on the table again, and hear their voices, and see her father with his face all red and his foot pumping up and down a million times a minute.

"And I hate this whole house," Fee said to Trudy, flinging herself on her bed. "It's homemade and Dutchy, and I hate it." From below came the hammering, and her parents' voices, and Fee looked at her friend in a passion of misery.

For a moment Trudy said nothing at all. The hammering seemed to grow louder. Then she said, "My father fell down drunk in the kitchen last night, Fee."

Fee raised her head, staring. "He *did?*"

"He just slobbered all over and my mother cried so, and Carl and I had to help her get him up and half pull, half shove him into bed."

"Oh, Trudy."

"So you see."

Fee nodded and felt obscure comfort, and an unexpected gratitude to Trudy, for what, she did not know. Her own father never slobbered or fell down or sprawled on a chair smelling of beer. But Trudy and her brother, Carl, wouldn't trade theirs for hers anyhow.

"When I grow up," Fee said, "I'm going to live in a beautiful big house, with beautiful furniture and wallpaper, and never let anybody but you and Betty and my brother Eli come and see me."

"How about Fran?"

"No."

(3 1)

"And your mother and father?"

"Except for my birthday, maybe."

"Not for Christmas?"

"We don't believe in Christmas," Fee said, "or in Passover, or any‹ thing in a building."

Trudy sat down on the bed, closer to her. "But you believe in God, don't you?"

"I don't know," Fee said. "I know we believe in something but not about listening to your prayers to get A or B on your card, or have it stop raining for Field Day. I asked my father."

"My mother says you believe in a Jew God."

Fee shook her head. Whenever Betty or Trudy talked about church or Sunday school or Jews or Christians, a funny excitement started up inside her, not pleasant or unpleasant, just there.

"And she says," Trudy went on conversationally, "it must have been terrible for your mother when Eli married outside your religion."

Fee sat up, astonished. "But it wasn't," she said positively. "They liked it; it's a principle."

"What *is* that, anyway?"

"Well, it's—" Fee waved her hand vaguely. "Oh, I can't exactly say it right out, but you know, something terribly important."

Trudy nodded. "When I grow up," she said, "I'm going to marry a millionaire and have a governess and a maid and a butler."

The hammering ceased and Fee looked at Trudy in sudden hope. If the black was all on, maybe it wouldn't be so horrible as knowing they were still putting it on.

"I'm going to make lots of money," Fee said after a moment, "and have a tennis court of my own, and a motorcycle. Are you?"

"I'm going to get an auto."

"So am I. A dark red one, like the Paiges'. Mr. Paige took us for a ride last night, me and Franny and Joan and Eli. My mother wouldn't go."

"Franny likes Jack Purney."

"I hate her. She's so stuck-up about how she looks."

Trudy crossed the room to the bureau and looked at herself in the mirror. She picked up a comb and ran it through her hair, shaking her head from this side to that, watching her curls move. "My mother's going to get me a white silk middy," she said. "When I'm twelve."

"Oh, Trudy!" Fee sprang up, her heart squeezing into a hard knob. Trudy had such a lot of clothes, all bought at Wanamaker, and never looking homemade. Trudy called clothes "Dutchy" if they were made by your mother, and said she'd rather die than look Dutchy.

"And maybe a white serge skirt," Trudy added, relishing Fira's anguish. "My father doesn't even know. He's so stingy."

"Mine is too." She took the comb from Trudy, but when she shook her head from side to side, her hair fell like brown rain, straight down. "He wants me to be a teacher when I'm big," she said. "But I'm not going to."

"I'm going to be a secretary, and make a lot of money."

"I guess I will too."

"Let's make the fudge, Fee."

"All right."

They ran downstairs, and while Trudy went into the kitchen, Fee stayed behind and went into the pantry for the milk and butter. That was another thing that was different from everybody else's house, having a kitchen without an icebox right in it. Her father and mother were forever talking about being American and what a wonderful thing it was to live in this wonderful free country where the police never came after you if you believed in things some people didn't like. But they kept right on doing things and saying things nobody else in Barnett ever did. Except the Paiges.

"Here comes Fran, up the hill," Trudy called to her. "Who do you think's with her?"

"Who?"

A vast unwillingness swept through her as she went back to the kitchen. If Fran was bringing that awful Jack Purney home, it would spoil the last chance to get back to the happy feeling she had had walking up the hill before she saw the black house. Jack's forehead was all little tight pimples, like cut velvet, and once when Franny and he were dancing in the parlor and thought nobody could see, he slid his hand all over Fran's chest, and she giggled and said "Don't," but you could tell she liked it.

Fee glanced out of the window. Fran was laughing and looking up at Jack Purney and Fee said, "She flirts, that's what's so icky about her." But the old wonder came, about whether she would be pretty too, and she was almost relieved when Fran's face suddenly went shocked and angry, as she saw the porch.

"Oh, Trudy," Fee whispered, "it's going to be just awful around here tonight. When my brother Eli gets home too, it's going to be just terrible."

(33)

THREE

As a small child, Stefan Ossipovitch Ivarin had heard many times that he was descended from a famous man, the great Lev Isaacovitch Ivarin who, in the sixteenth or seventeenth century, had been Rabbi of All the Southern Russias.

As a man, when he thought of it all, Stefan could still remember the solemnity with which the statement was made; a note of awe would sound in his father's voice, and a sly conspiratorial gleam would brighten his eye.

It was usually his father who reminded him of his heritage, not, as might have been expected, his mother, and it seemed to Stefan that his father's impulse to speak of the great Lev Isaacovitch was always attached to some indignity or failure the driven man had suffered himself. Ossip Petyacovitch Ivarin was a hatmaker, with a clientele of nobles and army officers, earning barely enough to keep his four children and wife, Miriam Solomonovna, supplied with clothing and food.

At the time of Stefan's birth, the family lived in a small town on the outskirts of Odessa. When he was about six, the town had had what the police called "a riot" and what everybody else called a pogrom; the following month a local ukase declared the town "beyond the pale," and with one exception its Jewish families were forced to move. The exception, ordered by the ruling nobleman himself, Count Kyril Cronchev, was made because he was too vain to change hatmakers when at last he had one whose talents suited him to perfection, and too lazy to contemplate the long, annoying carriage trip to the city.

Stefan was never sure whether his memory of the ensuing days was only the memory of what he had heard a hundred times over, or a direct primary memory, so vivid and intact were the sights, sounds, faces, words he carried on through life from that single week. The harrowing images of his mother and father were clearer and more strongly defined than at any other moment of his childhood, particularly on the night when his father announced that they would not remain behind.

"To be like a pet animal," he had suddenly said, "is no good."

(34)

Not for the great-great-great-how-many-times-great-grandson of the Rabbi of All the Southern Russias. If all honest God-fearing Jews could not remain, then the descendant of Lev Isaacovitch most surely would not remain, as a fawning pet of Czar Nicholas himself. If they tried to chain him there, he would still move.

Move they did. In later life, every time a moving van came, Stefan would remember again that collecting of possessions, that packing of crates and boxes, that halting of the clockwork of daily pattern and then the empty stretching-out of time and strangeness before one could feel familiar and at home once more.

To this day, he hated moving. Whenever he and Alexandra had decided to move, at first from one tenement flat to a slightly better one, in New York, then out to one or another of their rented houses in Barnett, and at last to their own house—each time, he had felt an inner trembling of excitement at the sight of the packed boxes and crates, a secret melancholy, deep and hidden.

And always, as if ordered to by some armed sentinel, his thoughts would halt for an instant of time, captives of memory, and he was once more a small boy, the descendant of the great Lev Isaacovitch Ivarin, seeing the sly gleam in his father's eye, hearing the catch in his mother's voice, hearing, somewhere beyond, the sad religious chanting of prayers said for farewell.

Prayers and the grief of farewell had always been linked in his mind, Stefan knew, and had known since he had begun to question his belief in his religion, in any religion.

For all his father's talk about God-fearing Jews, for all the awed reminders of his illustrious ancestor, Stefan knew that his father could not really have been a deeply religious man.

The candles were lit, the Sabbath honored, the orthodoxies followed, but as Stefan came to see later, there was no unwavering passion behind any of it. Otherwise it would not have been possible to persuade his father that his son Stefan Ossipovitch had no true calling for the usual Talmudic or Rabbinical schooling, and would be far better fitted for life if he were permitted to attend the Odessa school of commerce.

And with that much concession granted, the next step had been fairly simple, gently and persistently to nudge his father's mind still further, to accept the astonishing idea of the University itself. It was in the "period of liberalism" when a few Jews were permitted in the gymnasia and universities of Russia, when the leaders among them spoke Russian instead of Yiddish or Hebrew, though they were often accused of being too "Russified" for their own good.

"If it will bring you joy," his father said at last. It had taken longer to win over his mother, but in the end she had agreed, although a nameless apprehension shone in her eyes as she said her last good-bye to him.

And it was at the University that his life exploded into new vigor, new fire and new beauty. For it was there that he had become inflamed with the ideals of every young intellectual of the day, the hot longing to free Russia from Czar and nobles, free her from the degradation of fear as much as the degradation of poverty.

Young Drubhinov had been his first friend in his new life, Pyotr Drubhinov, the first Christian he had ever known enough to love; ex-Christian, rather, since Drubhinov was an atheist. Fair-haired, handsome, son of a noble, Drubhinov spoke out fearlessly against tyranny and oppression, and Stefan found it very moving that it should be such a youth speaking, not as a Jew nor as a serf nor as a dirt-poor worker in the city, but as an idealist, as a young man who, but for the yeasty bubbling of his good heart, might have remained forever within the pleasant circles of acceptance and silence.

It was Drubhinov who had induced Stefan to join the secret group at the University, "The Free Ones of Russia." Sixteen students were members; when Drubhinov introduced him to them, they looked him over with curiosity and some doubt, but also with a certain willingness because Drubhinov was his sponsor. The doubts fled soon enough; a leaflet had to be written and Stefan volunteered to write it that very evening.

Never would he forget the pride that had leaped in his heart when he read it aloud at the next meeting, and his listeners shouted approval. The leaflet was an exhortation to other students to join with them in printing and distributing handbills among the citizens of Odessa, and a day later, Stefan Ivarin, for the first time, had seen words he had written transformed by the majesty of type.

"The Free Ones" did their own printing, on a small handpress they had bought from a junk dealer and installed in the cellar of a private house near the University. In two weeks Stefan had become a slow but reliable operator of the press; in two months he had become adept.

By the beginning of his second year at the University, he, with Drubhinov, headed the policy-making committee of "The Free Ones," and had their first ardent quarrels over ideas. Already Stefan had begun to shape the conviction that extremism, even within a revolutionary movement, was a potential danger, a proposal to exchange an old tyranny for a new. Drubhinov brushed aside his plea for patience, for the education and persuasion of vast numbers of people.

"Will you persuade the Czar and the Cossacks and the landowners, Stiva?"

"Always the Czar and the Cossacks and the landowners! What of our millions and millions of serf-stupid peasants? Must they not be taught to read and reason first? And if not, won't you have to impose a worse terrorism, if you try pure socialism now?"

"You belong in England or France or America, Stiva, with such lofty patience. Not here."

"Perhaps, Petya. Maybe you're right."

It was during a night in May of '78 that Stefan Ivarin met terrorism head on. Working alone in the secret cellar, his eardrums suddenly tore with the sound of smashing wood; his heart caked with fear.

In the next moments, a thousand imagined and whispered-about horrors became real: the booted tread, the shouting voices, the door battered in, the uniformed giants, the questioning from peasant-rude mouths, the glare of hate from zealot eyes.

Name? Address? Occupation? Religion—?

"I have no religion. My father is a Jew."

Sweeping arms gathering up printed pages, eyes glancing, hands flinging them to the floor.

"Who writes this—this pig dung?"

"I do."

"Who else with you?"

"Nobody."

"Who makes it be printed on that—that—" He waved to the handpress, at a loss for a name to fit the machine.

"I do."

"And who helps you?"

"Nobody."

"A wise one! And how many are you protecting with your lies?"

"Nobody. I run it alone."

"And then who takes this pile of lunacy"—here an arm swept the stacked handbills to the floor—"and hands it out to other lunatics?"

"I distribute them myself."

"Come on, move. Get moving."

The first crash of pain, as the two armed Cossacks wrenched his arms half out of their sockets and pushed him ahead of them. Fear made his mouth metallic, fear of what was to come when they had him alone, in the privacy of prison.

(37)

In later life Stefan Ivarin sometimes wondered why his recurrent nightmares included no bit of this first horror he had experienced, why, like dramas gone mad, they always plunged into the second act. It also puzzled him that his waking memories of his arrest never arose at moments of great stress, but at calmer times, when he felt contemplative, when he found himself considering, perhaps, some incident of the day that seemed remote indeed from that long-ago night in Odessa.

Now, sitting at supper, weary from the unusual exertion of climbing the stepladder to tack down the black bunting, Stefan glanced at the four stony young faces of his daughters and son and daughter-in-law, and found himself thinking of his trip to prison.

Somewhere on that trip, he thought, somewhere along the way when I was yellow with fear, it was resolved how my life was to go. Dragging me off between them, they handed me my first papers for what I have become. If they had not dragged me, I might have outgrown my youthful revolutionary zeal as so many do, and become what? A mathematics teacher, a small businessman, an innocuous writer of poetry or novels, with a mild streak of good will running through, to show that I am a lover of humanity.

Ah, these lovers of humanity! Joseph Fehler is a lover of humanity, such an ardent lover he would assassinate any human who disagrees with him about how to love humanity.

And most of the intoners in the churches and the synagogues are lovers of humanity, dribbling saliva-wet platitudes about being meek and accepting pain and privation.

In poor Russia, the Bolsheviki are lovers of humanity, ready to kill Menshevik and Czar alike; woe to Russia if they, not the moderates, gain control when the time comes.

Would-be tyrants, all. But—irony, irony, they sire rebels. Not tyrants, but rebels. That's what they never realize. Those two Cossacks didn't realize it, nor the magistrate after them, nor the guards in the prison flogging with the knout.

All of the small tyrants together sired a larger group of "Free Ones" at the University, sired Drubhinov's determination to manage my rescue, sired the faked entry permit to America, my thirty-four-dollar trip across the ocean in the steerage.

And so, here I sit some thirty years later, safe in a small American town, a free man in a great free country, listening to my children's small misery because the house is draped in black.

(38)

"Everybody will make fun of me!" In varying versions, each of them had said the same thing. After Fira, Francesca; after Francesca, Eli. Joan, the newcomer, had remained silent but what she felt was clear.

Conformists, Stefan thought; they are all strait-jacketed in the norm. In accord with his or her own nature, each of them sings the song of orthodoxy. The youngest cries out in a baby's rebellion, her sister withdraws in remote adolescent silence, and Elijah, the adult, takes refuge in that false intellectualism that fools nobody. "The idiom of one's surroundings," Eli had said, "A protest should be phrased in the idiom of one's surroundings."

Stefan suddenly regretted that it was Friday evening and the office closed. Even upstairs in his room, he would feel the pall in the house; down here the kitchen was choked to the ceiling with it. Alexandra was discoursing on neutral matters—"Twenty-five cents for a pound of butter—two cents for one egg—the poor will starve—" but behind her words fluttered a private agitation, residue of the three separate scenes that had followed the three separate arrivals of the children during the afternoon.

Just as Eli had irritated him the most, so Fran had hurt Alexandra the most, attacking in the most vulnerable spot.

"I'm never going to let another boy come here," Fran cried out the moment Jack Purney left. "You don't want me to know anybody nice." Alexandra's face went tight with outrage, but Fran raced on. "I nearly died, with Jack right here hearing everything you said."

"But you insisted on an explanation then and there. You wouldn't wait."

"You could have not told me. Not right in front of Jack."

Stefan Ivarin directed his glance to his older daughter. Every day she became less the child, more the woman, and with her developing beauty she would soon enough give them a new kind of worry. But in her lowered eyes and straightened lips, there was something disagreeable and guarded.

Next to her was Fira, still stormy and rebellious, but openly so. From babyhood on, there had never been anything enigmatic and closed about her; she loved, hated, laughed, cried—all openly and fully. When her friend Trudy had left, there had been another scene about the black bunting; the house had echoed with Fee's sobs and Alexandra's attempts to persuade and comfort. Supper had brought only a hiatus—what an evening lay ahead!

On the other side of the table, Eli and Joan were putting up a life-

(39)

less pretense of responding to Alexandra's dissertation on high prices. Idiom indeed, Stefan thought now as he glanced at his son. What an argument I could give him! A verbal hiding that his lordly manner asks for. But it would upset Alexandra and ruin my evening.

Again he thought of the office and irritation pinked him. What nonsense, this pious pretense of observing the Sabbath in an office where ninety-five per cent of the staff were agnostic or atheist or at least unorthodox. But even with the office closed, New York might not be such a bad idea. By nine he could be at the café, playing chess or talking over a glass of tea with people who felt no need to instruct him in the niceties of public protest.

"Isn't it so, Stiva?"

It was Alexandra, a new note in her voice. "Isn't what so?" he asked warily, sure she had left the safe topic of high prices.

"That the A.F. of L. has more than doubled in ten years?"

"Tripled," he answered. "In nineteen hundred, it had only half a million members."

Alexandra looked triumphantly at her son. "You see?"

"Just the same," Eli said, "you can't prove they added even one member by doing things like that." He jerked his thumb toward the front of the house.

"And can *you* prove," Stefan answered for Alexandra, "that they did not add even one member by doing them?"

"I bet I could prove that thousands were alienated by such far-fetched—"

"What is this sudden passion for proving?" Stefan interrupted sharply. "Next, you will be 'proving' your point about the 'idiom of one's surroundings.' "

"That's just common sense," Eli said. "Just an understanding of human nature."

"And your mother and I," Stefan replied, leaning forward so that one of his vest buttons clicked against the edge of the table, "have neither common sense nor human understanding. I see."

"Are we going in for heavy sarcasm," Eli asked, "or can we stay in the field of reason?" Beside him, Joan put a restraining hand on his arm, but he shook it off.

"Reason," Stefan said, raising his voice, "is not bandied about so easily. Your 'idiom of one's surroundings' is based on trembling, not on reason."

"Stiva," Alexandra said, "please don't get excited."

Stefan ignored her. "Let me tell you," he said to Eli, "that the pro-

(40)

test which is made 'only in the idiom of one's surroundings' is so polite and colorless that the surroundings do not suspect the protest exists."

"On the other hand—"

"On the other hand, the idiom itself may be so vicious that it cries aloud for protest. Why, right now there's a case in Virginia, a perfect example, I wrote about it. A Roanoke College down there has been using a certain history of the United States—"

"Stefan," Alexandra murmured, "some other time. Your face is getting red."

It was as if she hadn't spoken. Ivarin's gaze stayed fixed on his son's. Vaguely he was aware that the girls both looked fearful; he forced his voice down to a quieter tone. But in the next moment he heard it as loud and sonorous as if Eli were seated in the last row of the top gallery of a large lecture hall.

"This history book, mind you," he went on, "has been in use for years, but suddenly a group of Virginia's citizens discover they don't approve of it. Why? The author, it appears, a man named Somebody Elson, not only writes of the bright side of slavery, the *bright* side, remember, but dares also to include the dark side of slavery. This 'dark side' admits there were sometimes illicit relations between white masters and black slaves. You follow me?"

"What's the connection?" Eli asked impatiently.

"Why, need I spell that out?" Stefan sounded baffled, amazed. "Those citizens of Roanoke, speaking only in the 'idiom of their surroundings,' mind you, now demand, righteously demand—"

Alexandra said again, "Stiva, please."

His glasses had begun to steam over. He seemed to see those far-off citizens of Virginia, see the author, so much one of them that he called the Civil War "a slaveholders' rebellion," and yet a transgressor they had to punish.

"Righteously and idiomatically," he continued, "those Roanoke citizens demand that such an unidiomatic history book be banished by the college. Suppressed. Abolished."

"For God's sake, Pa, nobody means banishing books."

"Conformists always mean banishing books, people, ideas, that do not conform to their own special familiar idiom. And if Roanoke College now gives in, no book in any college will be safe from the next group of citizens with its own pet idiom."

"So one bunch of fools in Virginia," Eli said, "is enough to make every book in every school unsafe. For God's sake."

"You are right; you have a point: this is America, not Russia. And if you thought a little more deeply about what that means, Eli, let me tell you, you would not speak so authoritatively about 'idioms of one's surroundings.' In America, *any* opinion—"

"Oh, Lord," his son said wearily, "here we go again about the greatness of America."

Stefan Ivarin banged his fist on the table so that the dishes jumped. "You will not," he shouted, "not while you live in this house, take that tone of contempt."

"You want me to knuckle down to everything you say!"

"If you'd knuckle *up,* fork up, stand up, with some thinking one can take seriously. Years ago, I warned your mother, she was letting you grow up into a spineless Adonis."

"Stefan," Alexandra cried, springing up from her chair.

"Eli," Joan said softly. "I don't feel very well."

Stefan Ivarin muttered, "I'm sorry, Joan. I get too excited, it's true."

"Oh, poor child," Alexandra said to her. "You look pale. Come, I'll take you upstairs, and you rest a little."

"Eli will take me up, Mother Ivarin." Slowly Joan rose from her chair, smiling as if in regret at leaving a gay party, and they all watched as she and Eli left the room.

The kitchen was silent. Ivarin stared at the oilcloth around his plate, a bright red-and-white-checked pattern, mitered at the corners and tacked on the underside, to keep it taut. His nerves were as stretched as that, nailed down, a crucifix of nerves; he was a fool to argue on these matters with any of them. "America" is not the magic word to them, he thought, that it is to me, liberty is not, freedom not. This, precisely, is where I come closest to Alexandra's weeping, a gulping in my throat, as hard to control as her tears.

"Poor Joan is not used to our ways," Alexandra said to no one in particular.

"She must hate it here," Fran muttered.

"She does not hate it here," Alexandra said sharply. "She loves it, being a member of our family. She and Eli could live with *her* family, couldn't they? The Martins keep inviting them."

"I bet she never heard such fights before," Fran said.

"An argument," Alexandra said sternly, "is not a fight."

"Argument!" Fran let scorn sound in her words. To Fee she said, "Come on, let's get started," and began jamming dishes together, scraping each free of food as she did so. Fee carried glasses and silver to the sink and their mother took out dishpan and soap.

Stefan remained motionless. Joan's device had not deceived him; to her he must have sounded like the czar of the supper table. Not czar; Oliver Wendell Holmes had called it "The Autocrat of the Breakfast-Table." Delightful, full of wisdom and good humor.

Good humor. Ay, there's the rub, he thought. Tonight, good humor had been noticeable by its absence, and Joan had known it as had everybody else. He had an impulse to follow her upstairs and beg her to believe that soft-spoken discussion was impossible for him, and that a raised voice meant intensity as often as it meant anger. He sat on, doing nothing except to wonder why and when this vice had begun. Had his own parents habitually raised their voices? He could not remember.

"You've helped enough," Alexandra said to the girls. "I'll finish."

Fran threw down her towel and left the room. Fee went on working, and Alexandra said, "Go, go. I'll finish." In her voice was the tone that warned Ivarin she wanted to speak to him in private, and he sighed.

"Stefan," she said tentatively when Fira left.

"Yes?"

"If they all feel so terrible about it—"

"You are going to take the bunting down?"

"They all are so miserable."

"Do as you like."

"I'm not 'doing.' But perhaps it's wrong to persist. Can't we talk it through a little, sensibly?"

"Have you no memory, Alexandra? When I was reluctant about your idea, you accused me of indifference. Now you want to back down, and you demand that I approve. I beg you, decide it yourself."

"You won't even talk about it?"

He made a gesture of exhaustion. As she turned abruptly away, he heard the familiar, maddening first sound of her sniffling and then weeping. It is fantastic, he thought, literally a matter of fantasy and dreaming. Even when I give in supinely on something she wishes, we end in anguished tears.

We have always differed in our approach to action; she will never concede that to drill the milkman every day may accomplish nothing but the satisfaction of her need to drill, and that black drapery may be nothing but a desire to wear her socialism on her sleeve. He pushed his chair back. "I'm going to New York."

"At this hour? But why? It's after seven."

"Must I give an accounting of every desire I have to go to New York?"

"But Alida and Evan are coming. I told them you'd be home. You *know* that."

(43)

"Then tell them I'm not home." He opened the door, turned back, and said, "Eli will be only too glad to take the bunting down for you, perhaps even tonight, under cover of darkness, in the perfect idiom of his surroundings."

His angry footsteps sounded through the dining room, through the parlor. The front door slammed. Alexandra's sobs rose in volume, and the girls came running in, Fee burying her face against her mother's waist.

"The big crank," Fran stormed. "The minute I'm a teacher, I'm going to move out of here and never even talk to him again."

"Move *now*," Alexandra said, still crying. "Move tonight. Don't you dare to call him such names while you stay here, that's all."

"*You* call him things, you say he ruined your life, but if anybody else says a word, you stick up for him."

Alexandra stood over Fran, her plump body quivering with anger. "I at least understand him," she said. "He has had a terrible life, from the moment he was born it was hard, and he has become a great man and you are too silly to know it."

"If that's what great men are like!"

"You think a great man is always an angel, day and night? You're a child, you know nothing about life. But go ask anybody in the labor movement—"

"Oh, God, the labor movement."

"Franny," Fee pleaded.

"Ask Eugene V. Debs," Alexandra went on, "Debs himself would tell you your father is—"

"Is it true," Fee interrupted, "that Papa ruined your life?"

"Of course not," Alexandra said. She put her hand on the child's shoulder. "Don't look so frightened, Firuschka," she said. "Nothing's really wrong. This is the way we are, that's all."

"Does Papa *hate* us?"

"No, darling, no. He loves us, he would die for us. But when he's in a bad mood, he can't help it."

Fee stared at her for a moment and then said, "Could I go to the library?"

"Go, both of you. Get some nice interesting books."

As they left, Alexandra thought, I'll tell them about the bunting in the morning. She imagined the relief that would leap to their faces, and her spirits lifted. When the kitchen was at last tidy, she filled the kettle—she and Stefan had made tea-drinkers of the Paiges in the two years of their friendship—and went to change from her housedress. Again she thought of the bunting. She could hear the

(44)

ripping sounds it would make as it was torn down, could see the porch columns emerge white again after their single night of mourning. She sat down suddenly on her bed.

No idea, she thought wretchedly, none, from Christianity to the French Revolution to the first labor union, not one of them would ever have taken root if every parent gave up the moment a child disapproved. Had the children of the abolitionists all applauded when their parents spoke out first against slavery? Had the sons of Socrates and Galileo and Abraham Lincoln approved everything their Papa said or did? And even from a child's point of view—would those young girls of sixteen and seventeen who jumped from skyscraper windows last Saturday, their hair streaming upwards in flames—would they have disapproved of a house draped in black to mourn them?

No, she thought. No. It is impossible. To say nothing to the world? To do not even one small thing? No, it is not possible.

The doorbell rang, and she hurried to answer it.

FOUR

They stood there, surveying the bunting, not only Alida and Evan, but their son Garrett and his wife Letty, who still lived with them. Alexandra touched her finger to the switch and flooded the porch with light; all four looked about them once again, but it was Alida who spoke first.

"Oh, Alexandra," she said in her high little voice. "It's a fine idea. I think we'll do it too."

Gratitude and warmth surged through Alexandra, and as she welcomed them into the house, explaining Stefan's absence as well as she could, saying the girls would be right back, offering them tea, she thought for the hundredth time how fortunate it had been to find such people living a few minutes' walk away.

"A tree introduced us," Evan had once said, and it had become a standing jest between the two families. In fact it had been during the

(45)

final days of building the house that they had met each other, only days after the trees had been planted. One afternoon, when the plasterers were near the end of their task, she and Stefan had walked up the hill from their rented house in the village, and had found two people examining one of the young maples whose trunks were scarcely three inches across inside their swathing of burlap. The man was bending over almost to the ground, his head cocked near the slender trunk, as if he were listening for a heartbeat. On his face was such concern, and in his whole attitude so lively an interest, that Stefan said, "Is anything wrong with it?"

There was a hint of pleasure in Stefan's voice, and Alexandra knew he was pleased to find two nice-looking strangers pausing over his property. She herself had experienced a tingle of satisfaction, almost of importance, as if the three young maples were her children, and talented enough to draw warm attention from passers-by.

At Stefan's question, the man had straightened up, removing his hat, smiling, and saying, "Are you the owners of this house?"

"Yes," Stefan had said, putting out his hand and bowing a little from the waist in the ceremonious way that always came back when he was meeting people for the first time. "Stefan Ivarin, sir, and my wife Alexandra."

"And I'm Evander Paige," Evan had said, grasping Stefan's hand warmly. "This is my wife, Alida."

In the instant of speaking and shaking hands all round, in the ready smile on Evan's and Alida's faces, Alexandra had felt a promise of friendship. Evan was tall and spare, with a narrow gaunt face that reminded her of descriptions of New England farmers, or of Owen Wister's Virginian. His wife was small and thin, still pretty, though she was perhaps the same age as Alexandra. Her blond hair had scarcely any grey in it and Alexandra instantly noted that her navy-blue serge suit swept to her ankles with no bulge anywhere.

"I'm worried about your maple," Evan Paige was saying to Stefan. "We were just passing and I heard the wire singing."

"Off key, I take it?" Stefan said at once, and both the Paiges laughed and looked at him once again.

"Very much so," Evan replied. "It's much looser than the others and if this wind rises, the tree could be wrenched loose by the unequal stress."

"It's very kind of you, sir," Stefan said, "to trouble about a strange tree."

"It won't be a stranger long," Alida had put in. It was a kindly voice and Alexandra's heart opened to it. "We pass here every day.

Our house is just over there, on Channing Street." She gestured toward it and smiled at both of them. "As soon as you move in, we must visit each other."

Then and there, the visiting had begun. When Stefan said he had designed the house himself, Evan seemed impressed and asked to be shown through it; in the empty rooms, their voices rang and echoed, their steps resounded. The Paiges had ended by inviting them to return home with them, and over tea (served in cups) their talk had soon turned to the Inaugural speech William Howard Taft had made the week before. It was Evander Paige's phrase, "Taft's usual tariff promises," spoken with a dry irony, that led Stefan to say, "We seem to feel the same way about many of these matters."

"I voted for Debs," Evan replied. "The third time since Nineteen Hundred."

"My dear sir," Stefan said, "I greet you again. I've been a socialist since I was a boy of seventeen in Odessa." He rose and put out his hand once again to Evan. Evan rose too, and they stood there shaking hands as if each was congratulating the other.

Watching them, Alexandra and Alida Paige smiled at each other like schoolgirls discovering a common joy.

"And if women could vote," Alida added, "I'd have voted for Debs three times too."

They had remained at the Paiges' for an hour, exploring each other as if they were hungry. Evan Paige was a lawyer in New York, and through one of his first cases for a young convict who had broken parole, he had begun to do a good deal of voluntary work with the parole board for the city prisons. He still did, though of late he was increasingly active as attorney in free speech cases, and, with a group of other lawyers and one or two people in government, was trying to form a free speech league, to provide free legal counsel to "offenders" who could not retain lawyers of their own.

They had only one son, Garrett, named after his mother's family, who was to be a chemist when he finished college in June. Another son, Van, had died at fifteen of mastoiditis; he would have been twenty-four now and probably a lawyer like his father.

Alexandra marveled at the way they could speak of their lost son, so calm and measured their tone, so much the victor over the pain that had been theirs and—how well she knew—still was. As she and Stefan were leaving, they met Garry, down from college for spring vacation, a handsome, fair-haired boy nearly twenty-one, spare and tall like his father, and seeming to offer friendliness on trust, expecting it to be accepted and returned, as his parents had done. Garry was

(47)

to be married after Commencement Day to a girl named Letty Brooks. Later on in their acquaintance with the family, they met Letty, but Alexandra had taken a vague dislike to her.

"A snob," she had announced. "Maybe Alida and Evan aren't fashionable enough to suit her. In a house like that, with real Oriental rugs and lace curtains to the floor."

Now, listening to Alida's praise of the bunting, Alexandra saw that Letty alone of all the Paiges looked distant, perhaps even displeased. She was a pretty girl, with wavy black hair and light grey eyes, a startling color effect, and she had a willowy curving figure that any young man must find bewitching. But she, Alexandra, was not a bewitched young man, and she felt the vague dislike.

"But, if Garry was still a child," she said, talking just past Letty's head to Alida, "would *you* do it to your porch?"

"Sure she would," Garry said.

"If I thought of it," Alida said.

"Van and I were always getting some surprise or other," Garry added, "and squawking over it."

"But," Alexandra said to Garry, "you and your brother didn't worry about being called crazy foreigners. That makes a difference."

"We had just as many battles with our children as you have with yours," Alida said comfortably.

"Just as hot ones?" Briefly, feeling it a treachery, Alexandra related the crises of the day. As she spoke, Evan, Alida and Garry occasionally exchanged glances of amusement. "And I really think," she ended, "that it's because Stefan and I still are foreigners in the children's eyes—that's what makes them anxious to be more American than George Washington."

"That may be part of it," Evan said. "But not all."

"Dad," Garrett said, "remember my first bloody nose?"

"Some kid called him a spy," Evan explained. "I was campaigning for Debs; and Van tried to bribe me to quit. They were eleven and thirteen and said I was ruining their lives."

"I wish the girls were back, to hear this," Alexandra said.

"We offered to give up our allowance for a year," Garry said, "if Dad would say he was for Bryan or McKinley and quit talking about the Spanish-American War and pacifism."

"Children always want to run with the herd, Alexandra," his mother put in. "They grow out of it."

"Oh, I hope so."

"By the time I was a senior at Barnett High," Garry ended, "I out-pacifisted even Dad and Mother."

Alexandra's face was alight, and she suddenly said, "Eli and Joan don't know you are here. Excuse me—I'll see if they can come down now. Joan was feeling queasy."

Upstairs, the bedroom door was closed, but Eli's voice came through. They're quarreling, she thought; he sounds just like Stefan. At her knock there was abrupt silence and then, from Joan, "Come in."

"The Paiges are here," Alexandra said. "Oh, Joan, you're already in bed."

"She's so upset," Eli said harshly, "she's sick. I can't have her go through this any more, even once more!"

"Eli," Joan said. "Not now."

"Not now, what?" Alexandra asked. But her heart thickened with the expectation of pain.

"We're getting out, that's what."

"Mother Ivarin," Joan said quickly, "I think it's bad for the baby— I do get so wrought up. If it won't hurt you, we're going to move in with my parents until we can find a place to live."

"Oh," said Alexandra.

"We won't be far away," Joan went on, "and we'll see each other all the time anyway."

"I suppose so." Alexandra looked at her son, her eyes dark with reproach. He turned his head away. "Well, it happens," she said firmly. "I must go down now."

She returned to the parlor, but her delight in the Paiges was covered over as by a thick cloth. The girls returned, and during their greetings, she thought, Soon they'll be the only ones left.

"Garry," she said. "Would you tell about your bloody nose again?"

Listening to his story, Fee sat like a small brown bird, head erect, eyes alert. Fran was attentive too, but in a different way. She seemed suddenly quite grown up, prettier, as if she had matured in the five minutes since she had come in and found them there. Fran sat close to Garry, and as she listened, she gave her head an occasional small toss, almost coquettishly, like a young princess holding her first court.

"But," Fran finally said to Garry, "you could get out there and punch them. Boys can do things, but girls have to sit back and feel dreadful."

Watching her, Alexandra forgot the news of loss she had just received upstairs. Francesca, she thought, my little Franny. Growing up, worshiping at the feet of a handsome young man. It was lovely to see, a token of how it would be in a couple of years when Fran was a young lady at last. It was too bad the Paiges had no unmarried sons.

The thought startled her, but just then Fran turned on the Victrola

(49)

for the ragtime she played incessantly. Alexandra disliked the record Fran chose—it was so suggestive. Everybody's doin' it indeed! The girls, of course, had no idea of it beyond the tinkly little tune. Doing what? The Turkey Trot. As if that purified it.

Garry and Letty began to dance, making their way around the three scatter rugs, woven of strips of colored felt by Canadian Indians, rugs the children hated and which Alexandra loved because Stefan had brought them back from Montreal when he had gone there to lecture last fall. Presents were so rare from Stefan, that the rugs had assumed a symbolic beauty to her. Like the three inkwells he had brought years ago from Wilkes-Barre, the first time he had lectured there to the young union of coal miners. The inkwells were carved out of great chunks of anthracite coal, faceted like diamonds, glistening. The rugs were more important though, more in evidence, seen by everybody, often commented upon by her pupils and by other people who came to the house.

Now, watching Garry and Letty pick their way between them, Fran kicked "the eyesores" aside into a heap. But Alexandra thought only, The child is really interesting in this new role of young lady on the threshold; it is unlike seeing her with that boy Purney and his pimples.

The second time the record was begun, Garry turned to Fran and said, "May I have this dance?"

"Oh, I'd love it." For the first measure Fran stumbled, and her mother gulped for her, but then smoothness came to the two sets of sliding feet, and a lovely rhythmic pulse of pride began to beat. My pretty daughter, she thought, how delicate and slim she is, how graceful, a man's arm around her, glancing up and away so quickly. My Francesca now begins to feel what it is to be a lovely young woman, appealing to a desirable young man.

She glanced covertly at Letty, and a guilt invaded her, but she was flooded with an odd vicarious joy, as if *she* were young and slender and fair in color, as if she were knowing for the first time what it was to dance, not with an ungainly stumbling boy, but with a handsome young man.

As the music ended, Garry turned to little Fira and with a distinct air of courtliness said, "And you, Miss Ivarin, would *you* honor me now?"

Fee giggled and clapped her hands and burrowed down into the armchair, hiding her head against the cushions. Everybody laughed, and another hour slipped by with the easy good nature that seemed to follow Alida and Evan wherever they went. As Fran and Fee finally went upstairs to bed, the little one talking, her sister singing, Alexandra thought with relief, The bunting is already forgotten.

"He'll be a native-born American," Eli was saying to Joan upstairs, "just as we are. Why should the poor kid go through life with a Russian name?"

"But it would hurt your parents so," Joan said. "Just as my parents, and grandparents too, would die if we didn't call him Webster, or Madge if it's a girl."

"Webster Ivarin. My God—Webster Martin Ivarin. What a combination—it's going to drive him crazy, the way Elijah Lovejoy Ivarin did me. Does me."

Joan nodded. She was remembering the night he had told her about his name, the second or third time they'd gone out together.

"Is Eli short for Elihu?" she had asked.

"No. For Elijah."

"The prophet in the Bible?"

"Not exactly," he had said, too lightly. "My parents have made a personal prophet out of this Elijah, the one I'm named for. Elijah Lovejoy of Illinois."

The chill of sarcasm touched his voice, but he went on as if he wanted to get it over. "My private Elijah was an editor, and an advocate of abolition—this was way before the Civil War. Pro-slavery mobs threatened him all the time. But he went right on advocating."

"I never even heard of him."

"The mobs destroyed three of his presses, and told him they'd get him next, but he bought a new press and kept at it. They finally killed him."

"Elijah Lovejoy," she said. "I'm glad you told me about him."

"He had a younger brother, Owen," Eli went on, mollified by her interest. "Owen saw them kill his brother. Then he took over and became an abolitionist leader too."

"Elijah Lovejoy," she repeated. And then suddenly she added, "Your parents must be pretty wonderful, Eli."

"They are," he said. "Really they are. But they do things like that, things that drive you crazy."

He had begun, falteringly, to tell her about his family; it was the first time he had spoken of his parents at all, and she had thought, He admires his father, but he doesn't love him, not the way I love Daddy. And he still hates the name Ivarin, and the name they gave him to go with it.

(5 1)

Now she lay back on the bed, wondering if their own baby would get to hate his name too.

"Webster Ivarin," she said. "Web, they'd call him, Web Ivarin."

Eli looked disgusted. He began to cough, and sat down in a chair near the bed. Even when the spasm came to an end, he did not go on talking; he had learned that it was safer not to start speech too soon.

For how many generations did you have to remain "loyal" to foreign names? For all eternity? It was ridiculous.

Ivarin was hard to shorten. Written down, Ives *looked* close, but the sound of it was unrelated to Ivarin.

Eave—that was better. The first syllable of Ivarin, with an Anglicized spelling. Webster Martin Eave. Eaves would be better yet. Then a little boy would never be teased about being named "Eve."

Webster Martin Eaves, he said, and only when Joan did not stir, did he realize he had not spoken it aloud, but was merely trying it out in his own mind.

How often he had done the same sort of thing with his own name, as a boy and even as a man. Elijah Ivar, Elijah Vareen, Elijah Ives. He hated doing it, he hated the discussion within himself about names, foreign names *versus* American names; he grew agitated when the subject of names entered his mind, unbidden and yet suddenly there, in charge, not to be dismissed. Ivar would sound changed, and Vareen would make people think he had changed from Levine. He always did when he heard names like Le Verne or La Vine or Cone or Cohann.

Since Joan's pregnancy, the unwelcome pro-and-con about Ivarin grew more clamorous and tonight's fight with his father had made a decision seem both easier and more urgent. The arrogant, yelling old fool, red in the face, eyes bulging behind his glasses, that damn foot punching up and down on the floor. What was so wrong about "the idiom of one's surroundings"?

"Maybe we ought to change Ivarin right now," he said. "Even if they raise a row. When you think of the rows we have about everything else. I thought of Eaves—E-a-v-e-s."

Joan sat forward from her pillow; she felt quite well, and she had been enjoying the faint sound of Victrola music floating up through the open windows of the living room downstairs. Being up here with Eli, his rage at his father long since thinned down, was comforting and sweet; alone with her, Eli was so different from what he was in the presence of his parents.

"Eaves," Eli went on. "You say it."

(52)

"Eaves," she said. "Webster Eaves." She cocked her head, smiling a little. "Madge Eaves."

"Mr. and Mrs. Elijah Eaves," he added, leaning closer to her. "If we do decide to, we ought to get it changed now, so it will go on the birth certificate the new way."

She reached her hand out toward his, as if they were making a pact. It meant a lot to him, and it always would mean a lot to him.

"I thought it took a long time," she said, "if you wanted to change your name by law."

"We could at least find out."

"It makes a lot of sense," she said, "doing it in time for the birth certificate."

"We don't have to say anything about it for a while," he said. "We might just get started and then see."

Fran couldn't sleep. Long after she had gone to bed, she kept on reading *The Rosary,* the book she had brought home from the library, a wonderful book, but not wonderful enough to take hold of her whole mind. That time Jack Purney had kissed her was nothing like this, nothing. Garry, she thought.

Her body still felt encircled by his arm; they were still dancing together; she could see the point of his collar like a white triangle before her right eye, and his chin moving when he turned his head. His hand pressed into her back, when he wanted her to turn or change step, with the faintest pressure only, but so firm, so positive, she never once wondered what he meant, the way she did at the gym dances at school. And each time that little signal of pressure came, she closed her eyes and went shivery.

Fran closed *The Rosary* and gave herself up to remembering. Later on, he had asked her to dance again, and it was as if they had learned to dance with each other in the half-hour they weren't dancing at all. Fee was still digging her head into the cushions and being silly, and the Paiges were starting to talk to Mama about politics, and as Fran rose and moved up close to him, she could hear her heart thump.

Garry, she thought again, Garry Paige. Garrett Paige, and he's married and he'll never even think about me again. If he weren't married, he would. He did like me. It went down his arm when his hand pressed my back—

She glanced over to the other bed where her little sister was sound asleep. Fee would stay sound asleep if you shined a flashlight right

(53)

against her eyelids; thank heaven for that. She didn't want to have to talk to her. She didn't even want to get sleepy and go to sleep herself.

All she wanted was to keep feeling this new wonderful way. She wished she had a diary to write in. She could write about the way she felt, just thinking Garry's name. She'd put in about wishing he weren't married, and that she were older, and that they were walking somewhere, all alone in the woods, maybe the wind blowing her hair so he would notice it. He wouldn't say anything about it, but she would know. And then they would come to a clearing or a stone fence and he'd ask her if she were tired, and she'd say, yes, a little, and he'd put his hand around her arm, high up, above the elbow, to help her. Or if it were a fence, he'd probably put his hands on her waist and half lift her up. She could feel him sitting beside her, not looking at her, not saying anything, just sitting there, close enough so she could feel his nearness. He'd probably talk about the way she followed him so easily when they danced, not like some girls who tried to do the leading, and he might tell her she was beautiful.

Twenty-three wasn't too old. Nine or ten years older was just right. Everything about him seemed perfect, even if he was married to that stiff-faced Letty. In a few years, maybe he would get a divorce, or Letty might go insane and be put in an institution. Then after a while Garry would meet her again and say "Francesca" in that deep voice of his, and kiss her and kiss her. Not the way Jack Purney did, all slobbery and quick, but long and slowly.

Oh, God, Fran thought. Oh, God. Somebody like Garry, not anybody at school, and not any of those horrible Yipsel boys. She had warned her mother how it would be at the Young People's Socialist League dance, but Mama wouldn't listen. Each time there was to be a dance, Mama started in again, and finally she made a new dress for her to go in. "You *might* meet a boy there," Mama had said, "and if you do, he won't think you're peculiar because you're a socialist."

"I'm not a socialist. You always say I can decide when I grow up."

"Of course you can. But in the meantime, you might as well meet some boys from nice socialist families."

Finally, she had gone, with Mama, all the way to Brooklyn. Mama had a new dress too, a changeable dark green, but hers was navy-blue *crêpe de chine,* and the skirt came almost to her ankles, as if she were grown-up already. She had her first pumps, too, with French heels, and her black lisle stockings were so sheer they looked like silk. At the last minute, she had been excited about going; maybe there would be some nice boys after all.

But the minute they reached the hall, her heart dropped. They

(54)

were *awful,* shorter than she was, funny-looking, and either Italian or Polish or Jewish or something foreign about every single one of them. There wasn't one boy that looked like the boys in Barnett. The evening had been just terrible, and even Mama had never tried to get her to go back a second time.

Fran shuddered. Even remembering that Yipsel dance was hateful; it filled her with an ache for something she couldn't name. To be eighteen, to go and live in a pretty furnished room in New York, and make new friends that never had to meet her mother and father or see this homemade house of theirs.

Suddenly she got out of bed. She couldn't bear just lying there, wanting things so hard, bursting with *wanting.* Going on fifteen was horrible; everything was a million years off. She went to the bureau and opened the top drawer. Underneath her one sweater was the flat white jar of "Ashes of Roses" rouge she had bought at Gray's Drug Store for fifty cents; she had to hide it because at the first sight of rouge her mother got going on being cheap and the White Slave Traffic and all the rest. Leaning close to the mirror, Fran rouged her cheeks, high on the cheekbones, the way the woman at Gray's showed her. Then she patted her lips with a reddened finger and stood looking at herself.

Jack Purney always says I'm beautiful, and he's never seen me with rouge on. Garry might say she was beautiful too if he saw her this way, instead of the scrubbed-clean look he always saw. He might even realize that she'd be grown-up in two years or so, with her hair up for good, and leaving home for good the minute she became a teacher.

Her longing for that distant time sharpened so much it was pain. Maybe if you had nice parents and a pretty house and no talk about a better world and labor and socialism—maybe then it wasn't so awful being fifteen. Almost fifteen; fifteen in five months. Maybe if you had a tennis court and lots of boys and girls came trooping over, even the stuck-up ones, why, maybe then it would be fun to be in your teens, the way it was supposed to be. Childhood's happy time. Youth's sunny days.

She hid the Ashes of Roses jar under her sweater and got back into bed. This time she turned out the light.

Garry, she thought, Garry.

"Just the same," Letty said, as she was undressing, "I do think it's foolish."

(55)

Garry frowned. Letty, usually so amiable with their friends, always became contentious when they visited or talked about the Ivarins, and tonight she was almost cruel about them and the black bunting. Walking home she had begun to ridicule what they had done as "just plain silly," and she had persisted even after his mother remonstrated about hearing friends attacked the moment their front door closed.

But alone in their own room, Letty came back to the subject again and again, like a child returning to a candy box, insatiable.

"Widow's weeds on a whole porch," she said, "I nearly laughed in their faces."

"Please see that you don't!"

He spoke sharply, and she looked at him with resentment. He was bearing down on her more than he used to; under all his easy ways, he managed to rile her oftener, and it nearly always was about something as out of the way as this. Tonight at supper, before starting for the Ivarins', things had started to go wrong, but he hadn't noticed, no more than his father and mother had. Garry kept talking and talking about a speech by the British Prime Minister or Foreign Minister or whatever he was, warning the world that the competition in armaments all over Europe would lead to the worst war in the whole history of civilization. Garry kept quoting Sir Edward Grey this and Sir Edward Grey that, until finally, as a joke, she accused him of "hero worship."

It didn't come out like a joke; it nearly started a quarrel in front of his parents. That would have been too awful. Garry hated scenes; the slightest emphasis of a word, even when they were alone at home, made him draw in on himself, and if they were at his family's or with friends, he went stone-still inside. You could feel it.

Of course, when he was the one who emphasized words, or ideas, he saw nothing wrong in it. It was a good talk then, a discussion, the breath of life.

She hadn't dreamed of this kind of difference between them when they had fallen in love at the summer hotel in Maine. Garry had told her straight out about his politics and not killing people in wars and all the rest; she was fair enough to admit that. But when a man was in love the way he was that summer, he could *say* that pacifism mattered terribly, but not sound as if anything mattered a button except his longings for his girl, and later, his bride.

"And please don't make fun of the Ivarins any more," he said now, a little less sharply. "I *like* them, and they don't seem silly or foolish or anything else except interesting and nice."

He disappeared into the bathroom. When he returned she was in bed, and he said, "You can keep the light on, if you want to read for a while," and kissed her cheek and said good night. He turned on his side, away from her, and in a moment or two his breathing took on the rhythm of his immediate sleep.

Exasperation stung her; he always fell asleep easily. She wanted to shake his shoulder, make him stay awake a little longer. What was the matter, anyway? Something had begun to go wrong between them—when? How long ago? For what reason? It couldn't be jealousy, but it did make her want to clutch at his actual physical body, as if he were a drowning swimmer, and she desperately trying not to let him sink out of sight.

Imagine, Letty thought, being jealous of pacifism, and politics, and a bunch of crazy Russian Jew socialists. I wish I could tell Gare just once that I do feel they ought to behave better because they weren't born in this country.

But that would start something too serious. Except at the beginning, when being in love and making love and wanting each other was everything there was to life, she knew it was simply sensible to guard every word, every look even, about anybody that was foreign or Jewish, or, of course, pacifist or socialist.

She loved Garry and she wanted him to be happy, so she could never say the ordinary things people said. Not in front of him or his parents. They took their ideas so seriously, all the Paiges, just as they did their religion.

Unitarians could be as ardent as Catholics when it came to believing. Garry's mother quoted the Bible often, and they never missed going to church, but they never criticized people who never went, even downright atheists, and much less agnostic people like the Ivarins, who only said they didn't *know* about God.

"It's a humble enough point of view, this not-knowing," Mr. Paige once said. "Perhaps we who are so certain are the arrogant ones. Believers and atheists are both so positive they're right."

Letty felt the sting of exasperation once more. Garry was always so positive he was right, and about lots more things than his religion. He admitted he was overpositive and said he would have to get over it, but he never had. Once he told her about coming an awful cropper because of it and he seemed rather tickled about it; it was when he was seventeen and had just made the Debating Society in Barnett High. In practice debates he was supposed to take any side assigned to him and put that side across heart and soul.

"But the first time I had to take the affirmative of something I thought all wrong," Garry told her, "I stood there, with my mouth open, just gaping like a fish sucking at air. Not a word would come out, not one. Finally somebody motioned me to get off the stage, and I slunk off, red as a beet."

"Did they put you off the Debating Team?"

"No, they just treated me like a freak. After that they only assigned me to the side I did believe in."

"You weren't a freak," she assured him, "you just had to stick to your guns. It's wonderful, being that way."

But that was just after they had fallen in love. Now, at times, it didn't seem so wonderful. There was so little difference, really, between sticking to your guns and just digging in and being mulish.

FIVE

The moment she walked into the classroom on Monday morning, Fee felt a strangeness there, a waiting. Trudy wouldn't look up from her desk, but stayed behind the raised lid, searching for something, and Betty Murphy said, "Hello," and looked away.

Miss King was wearing a new grey shirtwaist with tiny tucks all over it, and as Fee passed her desk and said "Good morning, Miss King," she couldn't help staring. Miss King always looked so beautiful and her clothes were beautiful, too. Miss King answered, as she always did, "Good morning to you," but she didn't look at Fee either.

The class bell rang and Miss King stood up. "Good morning, class," she said, and they all sat up straight, hands clasped at the edges of their desks, eyes forward. "Good morning, Miss King." But instead of starting right in on fractions, Miss King remained silent. She was looking straight at Fee, and as Fee realized it, her heart skipped a beat.

"Fira," Miss King said, "don't you want to be excused today?"

"Excused?" Out of habit, she stood up, as if she were reciting. "Why, no, ma'am."

"Well, I saw your house all draped in black. If there's been a death in your family—"

"Oh, no, ma'am. Nobody in my family died."

In the row just ahead of Fee, Tommy Gording leaned over to Jack Dryer, whispering. Jack turned around in his seat and stared up at Fee, and Tommy Gording began to laugh. At the side of the room somebody else began whispering and laughing too.

Up forward, behind her desk, Miss King said, "Class!" in her discipline voice and the whispers and giggling stopped abruptly. But the watching did not, nor the waiting. As if a thousand eyes had suddenly been socketed into place all over her head, Fee could see an expectant look on each face in the room, behind her, at either side of her.

"But all that black crepe?" Miss King said. "Did your dog Shag die?"

This time the entire class laughed right out and Fee went rigid. She stood there with her head lowered, and as she shook it from side to side in answer, the rough cloth of her blue middy rubbed first one side of her chin and then the other. She could hear Miss King's ruler, tapping for silence, but she could not look up.

"Then what *is* the mourning for, Fira?"

"Why, it's—"

Her voice caught and stuck. Suddenly she wanted to hit somebody, hit Miss King, hit every boy and girl in the whole room. She wanted to run right home and hit her mother and father.

"It's what, Fira?"

"It's a—well, Miss King—" Her voice surprised her; it sounded like a kindergarten voice, way up high. "It's a protest."

"A *what?*"

"A pro-test," she said in little separate squeaks, "for the Tri-ang-le Fire Vic-tims."

This time the room seemed to rock and shake with laughter, and this time Miss King didn't rap with the ruler. She simply stood still, her eyebrows arched, looking around as if waiting for somebody to explain. Then she said, "Well!" and reached for the lesson book.

Fee sat down, but Miss King still looked puzzled, and when she spoke again, her voice seemed louder and there was an unbelieving sound in it.

"Why then, Fira, your family must be anarchists or socialists or something, isn't that right?"

Fee said nothing.

"Aren't they, Fira?"

"We're socialists, ma'am."

Once more everybody roared and Miss King suddenly said, "Page fifty-seven, class," and there was the sound of books being opened and it was over.

But for Fira Ivarin it was not over. Minute after minute it was not over. Minute after minute she told herself it would never be over, as long as she lived, never never over. Never would she forget that sound of the laughing and whispering; never would she love school again, and be happy at getting A or B-plus. If Trudy or Betty ever asked her to go home, she'd say no; she would just run off alone forever and never even talk to them.

Suddenly a sour nasty taste was in her mouth and her skin went cold and wet all over. She knew what it was, and without raising her hand for permission, she darted to the door. Behind her she heard Miss King say, "Fira—?" but she cupped her left hand over her mouth and ran out. She got into the hall, but before she could even start down the corridor, it started.

She kneeled down on the stone floor. The transom is open, she thought, they can all hear me. On her knees, bending over the sourness there, she began to cry. Her eyes felt as if they were bleeding.

Sounds of music reached out to Fee as she started up the three steps to the porch. She had run nearly all the way home, but she stopped at the front door and couldn't go in. Mama was in there, doing her dancing, and Fee didn't want to see her while she hated her so for what had just happened.

The bright happy music went on, and Fee stood still. She closed her eyes so she wouldn't have to see the terrible bunting, but its blackness was like fingers touching her skin. She heard Shag come bounding around from the back yard and up the steps, and she kneeled down to him and laid her face against his big furry head. "Oh, Shag," she said. Without knowing it, she began to cry again.

Suddenly her mother's voice cried out, "What's the matter, Fee? Are you sick? Why are you home?"

Fee looked up. Her mother was leaning out of the window that opened on the porch and before she could answer, her mother said, "My poor child, what happened?"

The words made Fira's hate dissolve and she ran inside straight into her arms. "Oh, Mama," she said, "Miss King—"

"My poor child," Alexandra said. "You look green, you *are* sick, let me see you." She put her fingers under Fee's chin and raised her head so she could look at her, but in a moment, Fee hid her head against her mother's body, as if the light hurt her eyes.

Her mother was in a cotton slip, and her feet were bare, and they looked so strange and old, so different from her own feet, or Fran's. There were crisscross veins, like blue strings, standing up on them and Fira suddenly had a wild longing to have a young mother who wouldn't die and leave her when she was so unhappy.

"Tell me, Firuschka, tell Mama what happened to you."

She tried to answer, but her words came only in squeezed-out little gasps. "Miss King," she began again. "She saw our house—"

"Yes, darling, yes," her mother said, holding her closely, waiting, not needing to hear more, knowing already. On the Victrola, the forgotten Strauss waltz played on with gayety and sweetness, but Alexandra's heart beat thickly with the oldest pain. To watch your child suffer, she thought, because of you—

Upstairs, Stefan's steps sounded and she knew he had been waked, but Fee was able at last to begin her story, and nothing else mattered.

In the middle of it, Stefan appeared but only Alexandra saw him. He stood motionless just inside the double frame of the dining-room door, listening with her, listening to Fee's mimicry of her own piping syllables in the classroom.

"And then," Fee went on, not seeing him, "Miss King said well, we must be anarchists, mustn't we, or socialists, and I told her we were socialists, and they all laughed all over again and then I knew I had to vomit so I ran out, and then she came out and said to go home—"

"Firuschka," her father said.

Fee looked up, and there he was, as if he'd appeared from the air, silently, in his old bathrobe and long winter underwear, just staring down at her.

"This is bad," he said. "For a little girl to be so unhappy is very bad."

He took her hand and led her toward the dining room; with his other hand he pulled out a chair and sat down. Then he put his arm around her waist and drew her toward him; she could feel the edge of his chair against her legs. She tried to choke back her crying because it always made him nervous to hear crying, but he said, "Cry, cry, Firuschka. I heard what happened. It's very bad, I agree."

Then, without wanting to, or knowing she was going to, Fee started her story over again, from the beginning, as if her father had not just told her he had listened the first time. As she repeated it, her father kept nodding, and once he took off his glasses, and wiped them, and blew his nose. Fee saw that his face was very red and that he kept biting the corner of his lip over and over again.

"You see, Fira," he said at the end, "it's not always easy to be a little girl, when your parents are people like Mama and me. It sometimes is hard. Maybe even too hard."

She pressed herself against him. "Oh, no, Papa, it isn't."

"But," he went on, "to be the little girl of people who believe there could be a better world? In some ways that might be nicer than to be the little girl of people who never think of anything except having fun."

"It *is* nicer."

"When you grow up I think you will feel the way Mama and I feel, but in the meantime, I'm sorry about what happened. Very sorry, Firuschka."

For a moment nobody said anything. Alexandra was looking at Stefan with a private love and gratitude. Then she made her voice practical and said, "Fee, you can read in bed for an hour or two. Would you like that?"

"Later on," her father said, "I could perhaps give you a chess lesson."

Uncertainly, Fee looked from one to the other. A new feeling rippled through her, warm and exciting. Nothing that had ever happened before in her whole life had been like this.

"Read first," her father said, "then later maybe the chess. Have you a good book up there?"

Her mother went up with her, and propped Fran's pillow behind her own, and brought a glass of water and her library book, and opened the window.

Even when her mother went downstairs again, they both kept right on talking about it. Two or three times Fee heard her father say, "Miss King," and as the minutes passed, the new feeling grew. They made her feel important. They were a wonderful wonderful father and mother.

After a while, she heard her father at the telephone asking for a number. Then he said, "Miss Mainley, please." Miss Mainley was the principal of the school, and Fee jumped out of bed and ran halfway down the stairs, calling out, "Please, Papa, don't."

He was already talking. He sounded strange, very polite and formal. "Entirely convenient," he was saying. "And, Miss Mainley, would you be kind enough to invite Miss King to be present as well? Thank you again."

(62)

Fee heard him hang up and then say to her mother, "Of course I will be careful. I will keep so cool it will be like ice."

"Maybe I had better go, Stiva?"

"No. At schools, they do not see so many fathers."

"But if you should get irritated—"

"Under the ice, may I be permitted to be irritated if my daughter is tormented?"

Fee went back to her bed, her new feeling of importance higher than before. Her father wasn't going to his office, he wasn't going to a meeting, or to a lecture; having a tormented daughter came ahead of anything else.

And soon Miss Mainley and Miss King would know it. Even his having a Russian accent wouldn't spoil that. He could be so wonderful when he wanted to be. And it was wonderful that he was going, not Mama. Mama was too fat.

It was early afternoon when Stefan Ivarin, dressed in his best suit, which he wore only on the lecture platform, went through the front door of Barnett's grade school, peering through his thick glasses, as he always did in a strange place. He found a door whose gold-stamped glass pane proclaimed, "Principal's Office," and as he knocked, he sternly reminded himself that he was, if ever in his life, to maintain a glacial tone and manner. As the door opened, a voice said cordially, "You are Fira's father? I'm Geraldine Mainley."

"How do you do, Miss Mainley," Stefan said, taking the hand she offered and bowing a little over it. "Thank you for arranging this visit so quickly."

Geraldine Mainley was about forty, he guessed, with a candid, intelligent face. But her appearance was remarkable; from an extremely slender body there sprang a bosom so ample, so protruding, that he swiftly looked away rather than risk any facial betrayal of the astonishment he felt. Standing near the window was Miss King, whom Miss Mainley introduced. To her he merely nodded, saying, "Miss King." She was young and he could see why Fira always called her beautiful, with her retroussé nose and blue eyes, but he thought, No distinction, quite the opposite.

"Is Fira feeling better, Mr. Ivarin?" Miss Mainley asked as she indicated a chair for him.

"Yes," he answered slowly. "Yes, a good deal. Physically."

Geraldine Mainley looked at him thoughtfully. She had known that

(63)

the Ivarins were in no way the typical immigrant family, and the telephone call had prepared her for cultivated speech, yet now she found herself unable to absorb this man's actual presence. He's like a—a diplomat, she thought, and she glanced at Miss King. Miss King was looking at the floor.

"You must mean," Miss Mainley said, "that she is still upset emotionally."

"Precisely," he said. "And I confess, so am I." He paused, waiting for comment, but there was none. "Not only that she should have been ridiculed in public about the bunting—"

"I merely asked about it out of interest and concern," Miss King put in.

"Children of ten, nearly eleven," Stefan said courteously, "do not vomit over questions that arise from interest and concern."

"I don't know what Fira told you, Mr. Ivarin." She pronounced it Ivverin.

"Nor," he said, "does Fira normally tell lies."

"I'm sure she doesn't. But I simply asked—"

"Permit me, Miss King," Stefan interrupted. "Permit me to explain why I am here. By the way, I asked that you be present because I do not wish to make charges about you in your absence."

Miss King glanced away. Geraldine Mainley said, "It is a grave enough matter, Mr. Ivarin, if a pupil feels ridiculed by a teacher."

"Yet there is a graver matter." Now he turned slightly in his chair, addressing himself only to the older woman. "And this larger matter," he continued, "is that Fira was asked to state whether her parents were anarchists or socialists."

Miss King looked up. "I simply made a remark."

Stefan Ivarin raised a palm of caution, as if to head her off from further folly. "For anybody in authority," he went on quietly, "to interrogate an American about his political belief is shocking. Am I not correct?"

"I would certainly think so," Miss Mainley said. Miss King said nothing.

"It also is illegal," he continued drily. "Not that she was interrogated about her *own* political faith. That I will readily grant. She was asked, it appears, about somebody else's. She was asked, in effect, to turn informer. They do just this in Russia. Precisely this."

"Why, Mr. Ivverin," Miss King said. "That's taking it too seriously."

"My dear Miss King, not too seriously, I assure you. If the day should ever come when an American can be quizzed about his political or religious belief, quizzed against his will, mind you, and by some-one in authority, America will not be the free country it is."

"But I wasn't 'quizzing' her. It was, well, thinking out loud, chat-ting—"

"When one is *required* to answer," Stefan said, "that is not chat-ting."

Miss Mainley said, "No, it could not be."

"I am only too happy to volunteer the shocking information," Stefan went on, with a new crispness in his enunciation, "that I am a socialist. That, however, is volunteering. You follow me?"

He waited until Miss King nodded.

"If anybody in authority," he said, "required me to answer, I'd tell him to go to the devil. And as an American citizen, I would be within my rights."

Geraldine Mainley said, "I'm sure Miss King agrees with you."

"In that case," he said, "she will understand why I now charge her with invading the inalienable rights of an American child."

There was no reply from either of the two. Stefan leaned forward. For the first time, his color rose.

"As to Miss King's rights," he continued. "I assure you, Miss King, I defend your right to ridicule me, publicly, privately, in a lecture hall where I am speaking, or in letters to the newspapers—anywhere, any time, you choose."

"Ridicule?" she said. "I really didn't mean to hurt Fira's feelings. As for my 'right'—"

"Though I defend it," he went on, suddenly sharp, "I also despise the practice of such a right on a child."

Miss King gasped. "Why, Mr. Ivverin."

"Ee-*var*-in," he said, amiable again, "the accent is not recessive. By the way, Fira tells me that though she has been your pupil since last fall, you still stumble over her name, obviously too foreign a name to master. Ivarin." He dismissed the matter with a wave of his hand and rose.

"Thank you, Miss Mainley," he said. "I was ordered by my wife not to lose my temper. I hope I can report a passing mark on that?"

"You can, you certainly can." She rose too, and put out her hand. Her face was miserable, her gaze direct and clear.

He clasped her hand warmly, bowing over it again, and said, "I am grateful you and I understand each other, Miss Mainley; I am glad that I came. Good-bye." He turned briefly to Miss King. "Good day, Miss King," he said.

(65)

"Good-bye, Mr. ur-unn—Mr. Ivarin."

"Quite easy, isn't it?" He smiled and was gone.

SIX

The night the baby was born, Fee was allowed to stay up "as long as you please," and as eleven o'clock went by and then midnight, she realized that having a baby was a far bigger event than the last day of school or the Fourth of July.

It was eighteen days after the day set for his arrival and as those days passed, Eli and Joan and Mama and even Fran grew jumpy about the delay. Eli and Joan had been living with the Martins for about two months, but as the time came closer for Joan to go to the hospital, they came over to the house quite often.

"Mother doesn't even think of how I feel about dragging it out this way," Joan complained once. "She's just so thrilled the baby is co-operating with her fibs to the neighbors."

"A tactful baby," Alexandra remarked.

"*Why* is the baby tactful?" Fee asked, and everybody burst out laughing. It became a family joke, and though her mother did what she called "explain openly," Fee remained puzzled. It was an afternoon in the middle of June when the baby started to get born, and even her father was suddenly excited. He telephoned the paper that he wouldn't be there that evening, and hour after hour, he sat in the kitchen with them, drinking tea and talking. "The second generation of Ivarins to be born in America," he said, sounding happier than Fee had ever heard him sound. "But this time, it's an Ivarin who'll be able to say, 'In America,' when they ask, 'And where was your father born?' "

His voice went thick and funny as he said it, and he began to talk about his first few days in America, about how he kept walking for ten and twelve hours each day, just looking at the houses and the meadows and the Brooklyn Bridge, which wasn't finished.

"The Statue of Liberty wasn't there yet," he said. "Remember that was in 1879, when I was eighteen, but when the ship was entering the harbor, I felt precisely the way they feel now when they look up and see it standing there. Precisely."

"Tell them about the buttons, Stiva."

Fee and Fran knew about Papa's first job in America, sewing buttons on shirts in a factory on the East Side, where he worked for twelve and sometimes fifteen hours a day, earning six or eight dollars a week. But they had heard it only from Mama, never straight from him, and it sounded like a new story now.

He told them of getting a room for three dollars a month on Delancey Street, and board for four dollars, and going to night school for English lessons, because in Russia he spoke "school English" only. Even while he was going to night school for English, he began to give English lessons to other foreigners, whom he called "other greenhorns." During the off-seasons in the needle trades when there was nothing to sew buttons on, when he was laid off without warning for two months at a time, he might have gone hungry without his pupils and their twenty-five cents an hour.

Fee could not imagine her father as a boy of eighteen or nineteen, younger than Eli or Garrett Paige, and she sat listening as if he were reading aloud from a book he had just got from the library. But even in books where people were poor, like *Little Women* or *Rebecca of Sunnybrook Farm,* there was nothing like a man sewing buttons and giving English lessons to foreigners while he was taking English lessons himself.

After another glass of tea and another telephone call to the hospital to ask about Joan, Papa went on and told them about starting to work on a newspaper, a Russian one first, and then a Jewish one, and about going to meetings with other people working in factories, and beginning to lecture to them about unions and sweatshops and child labor. His lectures were also in Russian at first, but later his audiences grew so large he changed to Jewish for that too, although "everybody in the Russian colony," he said, "regarded Russian as their mother tongue and their intellectual cachet."

Fee didn't know what he meant, but she didn't want to ask questions and stop what he was telling them. It was another way he could be wonderful, and it didn't happen often either, any more than his caring about things at school. A long time had passed since that terrible day, two report cards' worth, but she still hated Miss King and Tommy Gording and the others.

Now her father was talking of his own days at school. His voice was very loud even though he wasn't angry, but now the loudness was happy, like the bells on a holiday or kids shouting when a team won.

"Your mother's family were rich," he said. "When she came to America, she had a big trunk loaded down with silver candlesticks and silver dishes and jewelry and furs, but when I was a little boy, my father was a hatmaker and we were always poor. We never had enough to eat, and we lived like cattle in the same room."

"Your mother and father and *all?*" Fran asked.

"My three sisters and I, and my parents. None of us had ambitions for a private tennis court, I can tell you."

"Oh, Papa," Fran said. *"Don't."*

"No, no, I'm teasing you."

Instantly Fran looked wary, and Fee waited to see what would happen. That spring, Fran had begun to talk about how easy it would be to make a tennis court themselves, on the vacant lot next door—"just get the grass off, and level it a little, about four feet would have to be dug off the back end and it would be level. Jack Purney promised to help and we could do it without spending one cent."

"I'll help dig, Franny," Fee had said, half-begging as if she wanted a favor. "I'm awfully strong."

Day after day since then, Fran kept talking about their own court, until at last Mama had openly spoken about it to Papa one evening when he was in a good mood.

"Couldn't we rent the ground next door, Stiva, for a small price, from whoever it is that owns it?"

Stefan had opened his mouth, then closed it. Looking speculative he had then said, "It's amazing, what turns life takes."

"What do you mean?"

"Well, it had occurred to me already that the owner might be only too glad to rent the plot. But I had something else in mind for it."

"What 'something else'?"

"No matter. To tell you now would only provide you with a problem."

"Who owns it?" Alexandra said.

"How should I know that? But banks can tell whose property any lot is, even without searching the title."

"Will you ask them, then?" She sounded vexed, and more urgent.

"Let me pay this month's interest on our mortgage first," he said. "I will hate to explain at the bank that we now need a private tennis court in our family."

"And why not?" Alexandra flared up. "If the child wants it so much she's willing to dig and level and sod it herself?"

(68)

"I can help," Fee said. "Franny said I could."

"Aping the rich," Stefan had said to Mama. "They'll want tiaras next."

Now, when he dragged in the tennis court, both Fee and Fran expected him to launch an attack on it, but the moment passed, and he went back to his childhood. The first big thing he could remember was a night when his mother grabbed him out of bed and rushed him through the snowy streets to a place where twenty of their neighbors were huddled with their own children, all wailing and praying and talking about the pogrom. His own sisters were there, hiding under a table, and at every noise outside, his mother spread her full skirts wide, to cover their heads.

It was the night before Easter; being Russia, though, the land was still locked in ice and the air fluffy with snowflakes. His father was not with them; none of the fathers were with any of the families. There was scarcely any mention of the fathers; once a woman cried out, "He'll be slaughtered like a pig with one stroke of a sword."

There was a suffocating fear in the place, and the crying women were placing benches against the doors, piling one on another until they were like a grandstand at a parade, but a grandstand shoved back on itself so that the rows of benches had become a wall.

"What *is* a pogram, Papa?" Fee asked. She wished he had never begun on this part. She wanted to go back to the English lessons and the buttons and the new bridge to Brooklyn.

"A pogrom," he said. "Po-*grum*—it's a killing of Jews by savages, that's what it is."

"Why?"

"Because they're Jews," he said. "In Russia, Jews were hated so much that drunken Cossacks could kill off a few just for fun, and nobody in the government really minded too much. Christians all, but not Christ-like."

"Oh, Papa." A shudder went through her. This time the word "Jew" and the word "Christian" were producing more than a simple feeling of excitement. "Do they still have pogroms?" she asked.

"Not so many." He caught a warning glance from Alexandra and added, "And never in America, never in this country."

"Never?" Fran asked. "Are you sure?"

"I'm sure. Even in Russia, it's not often, any more, or anywhere in Europe. It's like the Spanish Inquisition or the Massacre of the Christians in the arenas in Rome. History." He looked from one to the other. "Come, come, girls, I did not mean to frighten you, but it's another reason you should be happy you were born in America."

(69)

The telephone rang then and they all jumped. Alexandra got to it first and a moment later she was calling, "A boy, a boy," and then Stefan went to the phone too, and talked for a minute, and then they both kissed each other and Alexandra kissed Franny and Fee. "You're aunts," she said to them, hugging them. "And I'm a grandmother. Webster's grandmother. Imagine!"

Her eyes filled with tears, and she laughed and said, "Oh, my goodness, a grandson." Nobody minded her tears this time, and she didn't try to hide them.

After a moment, Papa said, "Well, one more glass of tea in honor of young Mr. Ivarin."

A few days later school was over and full summer burst upon them with high clear skies and unfaltering heat. On the first of July their second exodus to the beach began. It had always been the "mountains" while they still lived in New York, the mountains meaning any of the small inexpensive towns within sight of the Catskills.

But the summer of 1910 had been a summer of discovery, with Alexandra the Columbus who had found a new world for them, a tent colony on the Atlantic, a few miles east of established resorts like Far Rockaway, Long Beach and Edgemere.

This year's return was scarcely an exodus, for Eli of course would not be going, and Stefan pronounced himself unable to do what he had managed last year, go along for the first day, which was all the time he ever could, or ever did, spend with them "in the country" anyway.

Once the baby was born, Fran and Fee went back to their usual June hatred of school and their usual June longings for vacation. And Alexandra was hardly less eager than they to get back again to her new love, a summer in a tent. That it was a summer without fashion, and with a minimum of convenience or comfort, did not disturb her; that their mode of life for July and August would strike many people as primitive gave her a secret pleasure. "Thoreau," she had remarked once, "would have called our tent a palace."

"Disputing Thoreau," Stefan had replied, "I cannot call it a palace. I'd rather stay right here."

The tent was one of about two hundred, all identical, lined up in seven rows separated by wooden "sidewalks," making a tent city of more than a thousand people on a half-mile expanse of white sand beach directly on the sea.

To Alexandra the tents were compact miracles, livable, quickly cleaned, offering the free charm of life in the jungle or aboard a ship at sea. This year, learning from last year's longings, she was paying ten a month more to be in the front row of tents, with an unobstructed view of the ocean hers "by riparian rights."

"It's worth the whole summer's hundred dollars," she said again and again, "every time I look out the front door. The front flaps."

Each tent, about twelve by fourteen overall, was built upon a wooden flooring, raised on stubby posts a few inches from the sand. A three-foot-high wall of planking extended the full depth of the tent on each side; thus the slope of tan canvas began high enough up so that the floor space was usable over the entire area. One had to stoop only when making up the cots, placed end to end along the walls, two on each side.

A curtained shelf with hooks and nails provided closet space for the few skirts and dresses and coats Alexandra and the girls took with them, and all other apparel was kept in a low old chest, which Alexandra in a burst of gayety had painted a blazing blue.

Fore and aft, the flaps of the tent could be tied back to form large triangles of sky and light; at night, a single electric bulb on the cross-beam gave brilliant raw illumination. The rear of the tent, separated from the main part by inside flaps, contained an icebox and kerosene stove, an oblong table to seat four, open shelves for dishes, a small sink, with a drain and stopper but without faucets or water, and a small washtub, equally deprived. Water, pure but brackish, came from great iron hand-pumps, painted dark green and standing like motionless one-winged birds at crossings of the wooden sidewalks. Clusters of children and adults were always gathered around them, carrying zinc pails into which they pumped up the morning, noon or evening supply.

Even these arrangements did not dismay Alexandra; the one aspect of tent life that she did concede was "primitive" was the lack of private bathrooms.

"But," she said loyally, "they have two modern buildings, with twenty separate places in each. The one thing I don't like is when I'm going there and meet somebody I know, also going there. Such a community of motive!"

This minor flaw was forgotten soon enough and so, for Alexandra Ivarin, the summer of 1911 began beneficently as it had the year before. Life on the beach was delicious, easy, lazy.

"There's nothing to wash and iron, with all of us in bathing suits from morning to night. Nothing to sew. If only Papa liked it here—I feel so selfish!"

She never admitted, even to herself, that it was a relief to be away from Stefan, from the necessity to gauge his moods, from the frequent hurt that blighted her day, that brought her unwanted, shameful tears. The year before, she had ascribed her lift in spirits to the newness of their summer arrangements, which persisted despite her worry about how Stefan would get along. She had hired a Polish immigrant girl to take care of him at home during their absence, a plump young illiterate, who was only too glad to get food, a place to live, and $14 a month. But in a week, Stefan fired the girl.

"She is a chatterbox," he wrote, "whose most fundamental belief is that a newspaper cannot entertain me as much as her conversation does. She also assumes that, like the feudal lords in Poland, I am waiting to order her into my bed. Her willingness begins to get on my nerves."

"Your father will starve," Alexandra had cried to the children, hiding the letter. "A man who can't do a thing for himself, except make tea! I'm going home to see—I'll be back tomorrow."

She had returned, chagrined and relieved. "He boils two eggs till they're like rocks," she reported, "and stands by the stove to eat them. He makes tea, and cuts a slice of bread. Later, he goes to New York and has a real meal at the café. He seems to like it. The house is like a pigsty. You can smell eggshells at the front door."

Only after that episode, was Alexandra able to banish all guilt, and relish every hour of life at the shore. This summer, as she spoke of feeling selfish, she knew that nobody took her seriously. But she was happy.

Early each morning, she would wake with the first outdoor sounds of voices, steps, pails, pumps—wake rested and glad to be done with the non-living of sleep. In her cotton nightgown, she would go to the rear of the tent, reach down for the two bottles of milk set under the extending flap of canvas by the milkman, and transfer them to the icebox.

The iceman had been there even before the milkman, entering the back of the tent on rubber-soled feet, lifting the lid of the icebox and leaving his great lump of ice inside so quietly that the lightest sleeper would never stir.

The morning paper and the mail did not come until noon, but she quickly re-shaped her habit to accommodate this fact. She would then put on the long kimono she had made from the black bunting that had caused such grief, and start for the public bathhouse, carrying her toothbrush and can of toothpowder, a towel, a small covered butter dish in which reposed a piece of soap.

Returning to the tent, she would put on her coffee, and wake the girls. They needed less than ten seconds to dress; she had made them black alpaca bathing suits, with matching bloomers, and these they wore all day long. The color of their skin delighted her, Francesca's a gold-bronze, and Fira's a fierce dark brown.

Alexandra was a good swimmer, and she had long ago taught Eli and the girls how to swim. Now she loved to watch Fran and Fee in the water, though when the breakers were rough after a storm, and she saw their young slender bodies sliding out of sight as they dived under curling tons of water, fear would send a shaft of steel through her heart to tell her that such frailty could never return safely. The cure for this fear was to dive under the same breakers herself, and when she felt her own plump small flesh tightly secure under the ferocity passing above it, she became tranquil about the girls once more.

One morning, however, after perhaps two weeks of this second tent-summer had gone, Alexandra became aware of a faint dissatisfaction, the opposite of tranquillity, somewhere within her, and she realized that she had been harboring it for several days. She could not describe it; it was like a faint sensation of hunger, perhaps ignored to start with, but now grown so energetic one had to pay attention to it.

Did this faint malaise have anything to do with Stefan? With Eli and Joan and the baby? The girls? Could it be that repetition, even of something she loved as much as this glorious blazing-white beach—could repetition cut down the joy? So soon? It was impossible. In relief she began to hum.

Instantly she knew what was wrong. She missed her dancing.

She knew it with complete certainty. And in the certainty was dismay; she did not like to become slavishly attached to anything.

It was obvious that tent life precluded her dancing. Not only was there no Victrola; to dance in front of Franny and Fira was not to be considered; to wait until they had gone swimming and then to lower the tent flaps for privacy, would mean raising the temperature under the morning-hot canvas to suffocating heights, like dancing in a Turkish bath. Impossible.

A hundred Victrolas, a symphony orchestra. Still impossible.

Last summer, her dancing had still been so new that she had bid farewell to it for two months, and struggled punctiliously with the boredom of calisthenics.

And this summer, too, she had summoned up the sturdy realism she liked to think she always showed, and once again said farewell to her dancing until the fall.

How astonishing then, that on this particular morning, without warning, the lack of it should suddenly seem unbearable. It was as if her muscles had at last rebelled at the injustice she was perpetrating on them, at the denial to them of their rightful and habitual pleasure. She was delighted with them; they were entities with a life of their own, capable of making demands, organizing in defiance. They had, in effect, called meetings, taken a vote, gone on strike.

The moment this notion entered her mind, Alexandra Ivarin capitulated.

She gazed down at her body, encased in her own alpaca bathing suit, as if she were greeting each one of her valiant muscles. She kicked off her slippers and moved into the open space in the center of the tent. For a moment she stood still, regarding the open flaps of canvas. The warm air drifting in bore the distant smell of the sea, fresh and heart-lifting. She turned her back on the triangular expanse of yellow light and began again to hum.

The melody of the Strauss waltz was like wine, and a joyous giddiness entered her spirit. Hop, hop, hop on the right foot, change; hop, hop, hop on the left. Slide and jump to the right, slide and jump to the left. The three hops once more, then a deep bend to the right, a deep bend to the left.

It was glorious. Humming became harder as her breathing grew labored, and after a moment, her lips opened of themselves and she gave up humming in favor of singing. Her voice was a high soprano, thin and untrained, but it struck her own ear now as almost beautiful.

On the wooden floor, with nothing but a little space underneath and then sand, her bare feet made more of a thump than they did at home; she raised her voice to compensate for the thumping and slapping and sliding, and the very act of raising it seemed like a new assertion of freedom.

When she reached the end of the melody, she paused, as she did at home when the record had to be turned over. Only then did she become aware of voices behind her, and she looked over her shoulder to the back of the tent. Outside, on the wood sidewalk, watching, were four or five children and several women.

Fleetingly Alexandra thought, Oh, my goodness, it's good the girls aren't here. As the people outside saw her turn toward them, one of the women laughed derisively and left, and another took her child's hand to lead him away.

"No," the child shouted. "I want to see some more."

"Come, Morris," his mother said, speaking in Yiddish. "Or you know what'll happen."

"I want to see the crazy lady do it again."

"You want—" his mother shouted, and slapped him across the face; the child yelled but didn't budge. Once again the raised hand smacked him. His screams rose to the heavens.

By now Alexandra was outside, still panting, but smiling vaguely. To the mother of the screaming child she said politely, "Have you ever tried it?" and at the confused look on the other's face, she repeated her question, this time in Yiddish.

"Tried it?" The woman eyed her cautiously.

"Dancing for exercise," Alexandra said cheerily. "It makes you feel young."

"Young," the woman said. "Maybe a little crazy." She started off, but Alexandra put a hand on her arm.

"Don't go," Alexandra said. "Could you come in for a moment?"

At the astonishment on the other's face, Alexandra said, "You know I'm not crazy, so do come in for a minute. But without little Morris—I really would like to talk something over with you alone."

One of the other women now leaned forward and whispered to the one Alexandra had invited in; the expression on the woman's face underwent a remarkable change. "Why didn't you tell me before?" she demanded of the whisperer, and turning back to Alexandra she said, "Is it true? Your husband is Ivarin?"

"Yes," Alexandra said. Pride in Stefan suffused her. Away from New York, living out on Long Island, it was easy to forget that to people like these, working people from the East Side, Stefan was famous, a public figure, a hero.

"My husband is in cloaks, he's a cutter," the woman said, giving a shove of dismissal to her child, who was still screaming. "He tells me every word Ivarin says from the platform at union meetings. He reads every word he writes in the *Jewish News*. If I had dreamed who you are! But we only arrived here yesterday—"

Alexandra touched her finger to her lips, as if she were hushing a child. " '*Who*' isn't important," she said, leading the way back into the tent, pulling a chair forward for her visitor, and stooping to light a burner on the kerosene stove. "If you would permit me, though, I'd like to talk to you about your little boy."

"My Morris?"

"That's why I wanted you to come in without him. Please tell me your name; I don't know what to call you."

"Godleberg," she said. "I'm so excited I forgot. Anna Godleberg, my husband's name is Dave, the boy is Morris, another boy is Louis, he's four years older, and a baby, Rebecca, we call her Reba."

(75)

"How do you do, Mrs. Godleberg," Alexandra said, as if she were acknowledging an introduction made by a third person.

"About Morris, you said?" Mrs. Godleberg rushed on. "He drives me wild, he's a terror, he never minds me, he—"

"No child," Alexandra put in mildly, "is born a terror. Of course, it's none of my business, but—"

"Please, it *is* your business," the other said. "The wife of Ivarin? Anything you like is your business."

Alexandra dropped her tentative tone. "Then if I may, I think *you* are turning him into a terror."

Her visitor stared at her in amazement. "I'm turning him?" she demanded. "I'd give ten years of my life if I could make him be a good boy."

"Smacking a child across the face," Alexandra said, "yelling at him, shoving him—all of that is old-fashioned now."

There was silence, hostile, unwilling silence on Mrs. Godleberg's part, patient silence on Alexandra's. As she waited, she remembered one of her first pupils, years ago when she also had begun to give private lessons in the evening, to add to Stefan's earnings. At the beginning, whenever she penciled in a correction in the pupil's exercise book, writing in her blue crayon over the misspelled or misused word —whether it was an important error or the merest nothing, the pupil would respond with that same unwilling, hostile silence, as if a teacher were unspeakably rude to teach.

"Old-fashioned?" Mrs. Godleberg asked at last.

"Modern methods of discipline are nothing like the old way *we* were brought up. It's something we can all learn. Have you ever heard of Madame Montessori?"

"Never."

"A woman doctor in Italy, Marie Montessori, the first woman doctor Italy ever had. She became interested in the right way to educate a child, train a child, help him develop—"

For the next half-hour, as she watched her visitor's face grow absorbed in the Montessori Method, as she answered the first uncertain questions, felt the other's springing eagerness to learn, Alexandra Ivarin was elated and happy.

"I only wish, Mrs. Ivarin, I had met you long ago, when I was carrying my first child. How can I know such things? Who is to tell me?"

"Well, I've started," Alexandra said.

"It is too late now. That Morris—nothing I could do, nothing I could learn—"

"Don't be so sure," Alexandra said. "You can at least try. And then, remember, there's your baby, little Reba."

"You remember her name!"

"Even if it *is* late with Morris," Alexandra went on, "you have a fresh start right now, with her."

"Oh, how can I thank you, Mrs. Ivarin? I have a friend here, Sadie Cohen, her two children are worse than my Morris. If she could only hear what you told me—"

"Ask her to come over with you, next time."

"You wouldn't mind? You mean it?"

"I mean it."

And so it was that a few nights later, Anna Godleberg and her friend Sadie Cohen, and Mrs. Cohen's friend Esther Malowitch, and Mrs. Malowitch's friend, Sophie Jabrowsky, all came to the Ivarin tent after supper, and sat on chairs and cots while Alexandra talked to them about the Montessori Method.

Fee and Franny left just before they arrived, to visit new friends at the far end of the tent city. They both told their mother they were glad she was meeting friends of her own, and they had been fascinated by the story of the screaming Morris and his mother (though Alexandra had not deemed it necessary, for the moment, to tell them of the dancing which had brought Morris into her life).

"If you like it, Mama, why shouldn't you have a little lecture club?" Fran said, and Alexandra was relieved that there was none of her usual "Oh, Mama."

"Not a lecture club," Alexandra said. "Only Papa can lecture or write. But teaching is something we both can do, he and I equally."

"You're a teacher by nature," Fee informed her. "Papa said so to the Paiges once; I heard him."

A teacher by nature, Alexandra thought. It's true. It makes me happy when I teach an immigrant how to read English and write it and spell it. But this kind of teaching, about their children who have to grow up here in America? Could any other teaching be as good to do as that?

Off and on, for the rest of the summer, Alexandra gave one or two evenings a week to groups of women like this first group of Anna Godleberg's friends, groups that shifted and changed and grew. At times there were six women to listen to her, at times twenty, using every available chair and cot, sitting on the wood flooring, looking up at her.

Each time she varied her subject matter as the occasion suggested, improvising as she went along, astonished at how she could hold their interest with many of her own favorite topics—the value of whole grains, the danger in denatured foods, the justice of woman suffrage, labor's right to organize and bargain for a ten-hour day and a six-day week, with extra pay for anything over those minimums.

But invariably it was her discussions of their daily problems with their children that awoke the strongest response, the greatest willingness to hear more.

"You must write all this down, in a book, Mrs. Ivarin," Anna Godleberg said on the eve of her departure for the heat of a Rivington Street tenement. "Every Jewish woman in America would read it."

"A book? My husband is the author in our family."

"But men know nothing about children," Sophie Jabrowsky said. "Even your famous husband—is he fine with your children?"

Alexandra passed the question by. But that night, unable to sleep for the excitement racing through her mind, she wondered how one went about writing a textbook for immigrant women. The chief section would be about children; another might give them a basic grounding in diet and health, with perhaps some American recipes, too, and surely a section to teach these poor harried women how to organize their hours, so they would not be forever trapped in the sloppy slavery of housework.

A book! How gigantic a task it would be. A mountain of pages piled up in the eye of her mind; she felt exhausted and dejected at the idea of it. And yet she could not stop thinking about it.

At last her eyes closed and she dozed, waked, slept, but never deeply or surely. At the first sifting of light across her eyelids, she went and sat down at the front of the tent, on the edge of the flooring. To her bare feet the sand was cold, but the pinkish silver tint of it pleased her. The sky was streaked with pearly yellows, and a few stars were still visible, reluctant to yield to the new day. Far off the cries of unseen gulls sounded, and Alexandra's heart seemed to swoop and circle with them, in a reaching thrusting longing for she knew not what.

It was larger than wanting to write a book to help ignorant women with the thousand problems life showered upon them; that was part of it, but it was larger and more formless.

She thought of Stefan, standing at the side of the gas range, eating stone-hard eggs, perfectly contented, doing very well without her, without the Polish servant girl. His life is so full, she thought, that he feels no emptiness, no matter what changes around him.

(78)

So far my life has been as full as his. But Eli is already gone, Francesca has a birthday next month, and even the little one was eleven in June. Life is emptying; it always empties earlier for women than for men.

Jealousy struck her, jealousy of Stefan, of all men. Until they are tottering and senile, she thought, they can go on with *their* kind of usefulness. Stefan will go on lecturing and editing the paper until he is seventy, but in another few years I will be finished.

Fear assailed her, an apprehension she had never known, dark and thick. She stood up, went inside and stood looking down at her two girls, sweet in their young sleep.

For another little while, she thought. A few years more.

SEVEN

Letty heard him coming up the stairs and she went out into the hall to meet him, holding the door almost closed so he could not see past her, into the room. He looked up and said, "You look as excited as a kid."

She said, "I told you I'd finish in time," and lifted his jacket from his arm where he had been carrying it. His shirt was damp through, and he wore the summertime look of all men coming home from work in New York City, but he was cheerful and impatient for her to open the door and let him see.

She waited for an instant and then flung it wide.

He stopped on the threshold. Behind him she said, "They make a difference, don't they?"

"They're beautiful." The three windows that had been tall blank rectangles that morning now were curtained in the dark-red fabric she had been working on for weeks. He looked at the rest of the room, slowly, seeing everything, knowing how much it meant to her that he see and approve. She had done it all; with an occasional workman in for a few hours at a time, to build the bookcases or put up curtain rods, she had created this herself, and she was right to feel proud.

"They *will* like it, won't they?" she asked.

"They'll be flabbergasted."

His mother and father were coming to dinner, "allowed to" at last, two months after he and Letty had moved in, and he tried to see it as they would see it, completed, whole, all at once, not step by step as he had been seeing it since June.

He looked at the long red curtains again, so simple, yet so—what was the right word? He didn't know the proper language for curtains or furniture or ornaments; he was foreign in this world that was so familiar to Letty and so obedient to her skill.

"I'm flabbergasted too," he said and kissed her. "But I've been that ever since I discovered this about you."

She was delighted. "I wish it would hurry and get dark, so we could light the candles for dinner. And it's a pity we can't light a fire too."

"It was ninety-eight in the lab, and in the office one of the stenographers fainted."

It was the first week in August, and the first experience for each of them of a summer in New York. Born in Maine, Letty had never known such relentless heat, worse at night than under the noon sun on a village street at home. But she was so happy that at last they had a place of their own, that she never complained, and never slackened in the thousand things she had set herself to do.

Her own parents would not be able to visit them until Christmas, and the Paiges had understood when she said, "Please not till it's finished. I want everything to be right before you see it."

"Of course not," Alida Paige had said. "Unless I could help with something."

"I don't *need* help, it's such fun. Even though we're still sitting on Garry's books!"

Apart from their clothes and Letty's hope chest half-filled with linen and silver, their possessions were seven crates of Garry's books and five heirlooms of Letty's which could at last be shipped down from Rockland. They had belonged to her English grandmother who had loved eighteenth-century English furniture and had refused to leave it behind when she came to America. There was the "great piece," a Sheraton breakfront in mahogany, a small table, a four-poster bed, with a highboy and lowboy to go with it.

Even before they had found the place they wanted, Letty had begun to plan rooms around these five, to talk of color schemes, to collect samples, to search through newspapers and magazines for pictures of rooms she admired. Her energy astonished Garry, and made him wonder why he had not been more concerned over her previous inertia, now so exposed in retrospect.

Not that he had deliberately chosen to live on so long in Barnett, in his parents' house. When Letty and he had married, his pay at Aldrich and Co. was $25 a week. They had been glad to live at home until they could save; they spent nothing from the money they had received as wedding presents, and they saved steadily. But even when he was raised to $27.50 and then a year later to $30, they had too little for a down-payment on a house or even for renting a house and furnishing it. The weeks dribbled away and when they did speak about searching for a place of their own, it was token talk, easily silenced by irresolution.

Then, late in April, he was made assistant to the head of the laboratory. His pay leaped to $40, with a promise of yet another raise for 1912, if the new division for synthetics turned out well.

At once, Letty and he were infused with the juices of resolve. They became devotees of real-estate advertisements, and overnight Letty was transformed into the most indefatigable of house-hunters, investigating everything offered, from small houses in Manhattan or Brooklyn, to suburban cottages in Westchester or Connecticut, to empty lots in new developments as far out as Manhasset or Great Neck or Hempstead, or as close to Barnett as Jamaica or Hollis or Kew Gardens.

Rents ran from $40 to $50 a month for "a nice one-family house," and the notion of sharing a two-family house was vetoed by Garry as strongly as by Letty. Once, feeling experimental, Letty went to see an apartment, not a house. It was on East Sixty-sixth Street in Manhattan, just off Fifth Avenue. It had seven rooms and a bath and the rent was $50.

"Seven rooms!" Garry said. "What on earth would we furnish seven whole rooms with?"

"Boxes and barrels," she said. "I'd paint them all gold and red, and they'd be beautiful! And don't forget my heirlooms."

They each had grown up in the tradition that "a house of your own" was the universal goal, and they continued their search. But suddenly one evening, Letty said, "If only we could live in New York. Right smack in it. Not here on the Island or up in Scarsdale or out in Brooklyn Heights, but right in the city."

Before he could answer, she went on, "And not in a house. In an apartment." Her eyes bright, her voice animated, she sang the joys of city life, the museums, the lecture halls, the concerts and theaters.

"And no stairs to sweep," she raced on, without transition, "no cellar or attic or porches or back stoop, no ashes to lug out, no furnace, no sidewalks to shovel snow from—"

Garry listened, amazed. Had she wanted to live in Manhattan all along, had she wanted to live in an apartment all along, without being able to say so openly? How complex people were, even the people one was closest to; how hidden, how private.

She had begun to be silent and hidden even about the one disappointment they both shared equally, that they still had no baby. Until recently, she had been open and natural about it, and touching each time she told him, "Oh, Gare, not this month either." At times her eyes would fill, and always she had accepted his comfort and love; when he would say, "We'll have a baby soon, you'll see," she would take it as a promise instead of the voice of his own longing.

But recently she had been silent about what she felt, and now he was discovering that she had been silent, too, about where and how she herself really wanted them to live.

"Darling," he said. "Did you think I'd insist on a house, if you didn't want a house?"

"I never thought about it at all. Oh, Garry, New York would be marvelous."

Now she abandoned every other idea. She saw everything from squalid flats to new apartments on Riverside Drive, she searched Gramercy Park, Fifth Avenue, the side streets, and even a new building a full block in length, fourteen stories high, on Madison Avenue way up in the Eighties, which offered "De Luxe apartments" at rents that started at $200 a month and soared to $325 on the top floor.

She regaled the Paiges with her descriptions of this unbelievable luxury, "with a separate bathroom for every bedroom. Three bedrooms, three bathrooms; five bedrooms, five bathrooms. And I suppose on the top floor with the best apartments, twelve bedrooms, twelve bathrooms."

Never since their honeymoon had she been so good-natured, so amiable about disappointment or weariness, and when he least expected it, Garry would find himself again pondering what had been wrong that now was righted.

He thought, If we had had a baby right away, it wouldn't have gone this way for her. She's out here in Barnett all day with nothing of her own, and she's been bored and I didn't notice, not enough to matter. Desire and sadness rose together in his heart, flowed together and became an unspoken pledge to be more loving to her, to be less absorbed in his work, in books, in politics.

(8 2)

And then at the end of May she found "the absolutely most perfect apartment in all New York."

They had planned to meet at four that afternoon, to see the new library that had opened only the week before. When he arrived at Fifth Avenue and Forty-second, she was already there, and she ran down the white steps toward him, one hand scooping up her skirts, the other holding the brim of her enormous hat.

"I found it," she called out when she was twenty feet away, "a whole floor."

"A whole what?" He was as startled as if she had said, "a whole continent."

"It's three rooms, and a tiny kitchen, in a house that used to be a mansion. They've done it all over, and we have the parlor floor. Wait till you see it—he promised to wait for us. It's at Eleventh, just off Fifth."

He glanced up at the noble white building, considering whether it would be wiser to abandon it or hurry through it first. In some indefinable way, the new library looked as if it had been there, unhurried, untroubled, for centuries of man's learning.

"Let's not race through it," he said. "Let's see your apartment first."

"You're sweet."

Soon they were at the house, going up a flight of wide steps to the floor above the street, being ushered into what the owner called "the drawing room."

Letty said, "There!" and waited.

The room must have been twenty feet long. Garry looked across it, to the three windows that faced West Eleventh Street, and then he looked up at the ceiling which seemed twenty feet above his head. He walked across the newly polished floor to the old fireplace, perhaps once a pure white marble like the great library, now faintly grey.

"There's another fireplace in the bedroom," Letty said.

He stared into the empty fireplace, imagined it hot with burning logs on a winter evening, and he smiled. Then he turned to follow her to the rear of the apartment, past a bathroom (without a window) and a small kitchen (without a window).

"Up there," Letty said, pointing to an expanse of grillwork near the ceiling. "It's a ventilator, the latest thing."

The windowless room wakened an unwillingness in him, but Letty accepted this new condition as if she had spent her life in rooms without windows, where air was sucked in through a lattice of steel.

"This is the small bedroom," she said behind him. "It's sort of

(8 3)

steep and funny, but it would be big enough for a baby's room."

It was a narrow room, no more than seven feet across, though its ceiling was as lofty as in the rest of the rooms. "They made two bedrooms out of the original sitting room back here," Letty told him. "But don't worry about this little one. I'll make the most cunning nursery out of it."

Their bedroom was a third smaller than the drawing room, but it retained proportions that were pure and pleasing. A fireplace made a central focus in one wall, and the two windows looked down upon a square of lawn. At one side of the lawn there was a flower bed; at the other side there was a leafy tree, standing close to the house, leaning into their windows.

"Darling?" Letty finally said, as he stood gazing down at this city garden, pleased beyond reason with it.

He turned and said, "You're right, it's perfect."

"I'll make it wonderful, I'm good at fixing a place up, you'll see. I'm so happy I could die."

Now as he looked at the candles and flowers on the table set for dinner, he knew that in the two months since then, they had both been happier, close again as in their first year. Passion and need, and delight in both, had always been stronger in him than in Letty; now there was a sweet wholeness in her that aroused him constantly, as if they were newly lovers.

This side of her had been hidden, and it was an important side, her talented side, her ability to plan and create. "Taste" was as mysterious as other talent, but now it was clear that Letty had it, though she could never put it into words for him.

When she began to search the big stores for what they needed, her taste was offended and she came home empty-handed day after day. Her handbag was stuffed with lists, made out in her neat handwriting, of things to see; occasionally Garry would read them, wanting to share her problems.

"Five-piece panne plush parlor suite," he read aloud. "Was one hundred and fifty dollars, now seventy-five. What's panne plush?"

"Terrible." She laughed as he went on, male and bewildered.

"Bird's-eye maple dresser, regularly twenty dollars, now twelve-fifty. Buffet, quartered oak, regularly forty dollars, now twenty-five. Brass bed, reduced from fifty to twenty-five."

"Stop it! I saw all of it and it makes you seasick."

"Smyrna rugs, nine by twelve," he read from another list. "Reduced to twenty-two dollars and forty-nine cents. Aubusson rugs, nineteen dollars and seventy-four cents. Ladies' Black Satin Duchesse suit, twenty-six dollars and ninety-five cents, now fourteen dollars and ninety-five cents, instep length."

"I didn't buy a dollar's worth of anything. Yes, I did. One pair of chamois gloves for me, seventy-five cents. And a pigskin belt for you, fifty cents. Your old one's coming apart."

In another few days, she began wandering around the city in search of second-hand dealers. At once, her hopes revived. This was the only way, she said, to do what she wanted without going bankrupt.

As her first purchases arrived, Garry looked at them in disbelief. There were a chest and two small tables crusted with paint, and a set of four chairs which she called "Queen Anne," such wrecks that their springs hung down like torn tendrils of a climbing vine after a storm.

"The wood's there, you wait and see," she said with joy, as a mother might say of a sick child, "His heart is strong."

With these derelicts and with others still to come, she began back-breaking work that made her sing. She would strip them of their layers of paint or varnish, rub them smooth with sheets of emery paper, returning to them day by day until she had restored their natural woods. And then she would wax and polish them, treating each one for a certain time each day until it shone.

But she gave part of each day to a search for old fabrics, and for an upholsterer who would "teach me what I have to know." At last, in the slums of Avenue A near the East River, she found an old Pole willing to show her, right there in his store, for a price of five dollars, how to tie back the broken springs of a chair, how to replace its tattered crisscross of webbing, how to re-cover its seat with the tan fleur-de-lis brocade she had found.

Because the old man liked her, he later taught her, for an extra two dollars, how to make "headed draperies" for the living-room windows.

The days went by, turned into weeks, and still she was not done. They needed a bookcase; shelves could be put up for a song (she found a wonder of a little German carpenter) and they could paint them themselves.

"I'm still within our budget," she would often say. "I'm watching every penny. I've got a head for business, I think."

He looked at her with an exaggerated surprise. "Are you the girl I married?" he asked. "Letty Brooks? Of Rockland, Maine?"

"A Yankee horse-trader," she agreed. "Oh, Gare, it's such fun."

Dinner was a triumph. The Paiges took the apartment to their hearts as if it were a living thing, and Alida kept bringing the talk back to Letty's achievement, her sense of design, her use of color.

"You have a flair for it," Alida said, "a real gift. The way people are gifted at painting, or composing."

"It's just that I love doing it." She sounded diffident, but cannons of pride thundered a private salute within her.

"Flair?" Garry said. "It's downright genius. I might put her to work one of these days, fixing up houses for the Four Hundred, at fat, dishonest fees."

"I'd like it," Letty said. "I've started to worry about what I'll do all day."

"It's too hot to worry," her father-in-law said comfortably, tapping at his forehead with his neatly folded handkerchief. "Did you happen to notice Alexander Graham Bell in the Sunday paper?"

"With his Ice Stove!" Garry said. "I certainly did."

"What 'Ice Stove'?" both women asked.

"It's a contraption that looks like a coal stove," Evan said, "with a step in front of it, and a pipe going up and out the window. The paper said it was down to sixty-one degrees in Bell's study, while the asphalt melted away on the street outside his house in Washington."

"How marvelous," Letty said, and looked questioningly about the room, as if to choose the most appropriate place to set an Ice Stove of their own.

"Maybe some day," Alida Paige said, "we really will have one stove for winter and another for summer. What a wonderful age to be alive in."

"At the office today," Evan said, "a new client told us that an aviator in Brussels just flew three hundred eighty-eight miles without a stop. That broke the world's record by twenty-two miles."

"Did you see the aviation story too?" Garry asked. "Our new Aviation School—the Army's? Wait a minute; I've got the story." He went to the bookcase that balanced the breakfront on the other side of the fireplace. The shelves rose to the ceiling, many of the upper ones still empty; down below, the wonder of a little German carpenter had built four cabinets, with wide doors and brass handles.

Garry opened one of these, and at once found what he wanted, the feature section of *The New York Times*. "I meant to take it with me yesterday," he said. "We have a new man at the lab, Otto Ohrmann, just over from Germany. He's an expert on cellulose and synthetics. I like to talk things over with him."

He spread the paper on the table. "Here we are. Sunday, July thirtieth, 1911."

" 'Aviation School at College Park, Maryland,' " Alida read, " 'To

Train Young Officers in all the Fine Points of Driving an Aeroplane . . . A War Measure . . . Four Government Hangars . . .' "

Letty rose and stood next to Garry, looking at the pictures that ran with the story. Handsome young men in uniform were seated two abreast in the center of aeroplanes that did look murderous with their twin wings stretched thirty feet across.

"Perhaps we're fools to keep on hoping," Evan said, and took the paper. He turned to another page, heavy with headlines and pictures and charts.

PROSPECT OF A EUROPEAN WAR OVER MOROCCO

ENGLAND, GERMANY AND FRANCE MAY BE DRAWN INTO IT; GERMANY'S DESIGNS ON HOLLAND AND BELGIUM

There were graphs showing the relative size of the army in each country, a helmeted giant indicating 600,000 for Germany, a shorter one showing 500,000 for France, and smaller helmeted fellows grading all the way down to a pygmy representing 25,000 for little Holland.

"Boiling up higher every day for a month," Evan said, as if he had not paused, "and still we keep hoping it's only a war-scare, instead of a war."

"Was it a month ago they sent the *Panther* and that other gunboat out?" Garry asked.

"It seems more like a year," his mother said.

They're off, Letty thought, her heart sinking. Now they'll never talk about anything else. She tried to follow what they said, she knew it was important to everybody alive. But she got so bored, trying to read it or to listen to it. The Germans had sent the *Panther* steaming to a place called Agadir in Morocco because they were furious at the French for spreading around down there, threatening German business interests. The French wouldn't budge, and all the papers kept predicting war and denouncing the Kaiser and Germany's "mailed fist."

She did try nearly every day to read about Europe or Washington, but it was like cramming for an exam, forgetting it the minute the exam was over. For the past week, knowing the Paiges were coming, she had crammed even harder, so she would not be left out when they all started on politics. There had been a big speech in London by Mr. Asquith—no, not Asquith, he was the Prime Minister; by Mr. Lloyd-George, the Chancellor of the Exchequer, and the speech made the French happy, and some of the English too, but not pacifists, or parents with sons at school. He had said the Great Powers of the Entente-Cordiale would stand shoulder-to-shoulder in opposition to Germany.

"That would mean war for all Europe," Garry said now, angry and at his most positive. "Every small country would be dragged in, before six weeks were over. Damn it, they're all insane."

"Maybe it'll blow over," Letty began, but nobody heard her.

" 'Thou Shalt Not Kill,' " Garry said. "Except for French and German interests in Morocco!"

He stared at the crystal goblet in his hand, one of a set of original Waterford she had unearthed, but he did not see it. He had forgotten the lovely table, the candles and flowers, the whole room. He had forgotten her, too, and she knew it.

She glanced at his parents' faces; they also had forgotten her. They were lost, gone, far away. And Garry was with them, lost too.

"Is Mrs. Paige coming out alone on the trolley," Fran asked, "or is Mr. Paige going to drive her out in the Reo?"

"The car might not be fixed," Alexandra said. "We'll have to wait and see."

"Not that I care who comes," Fran said. "I just got wondering."

It was a Sunday morning, the twentieth of August, and her own friends from the beach were asked for two o'clock, when her birthday party would begin. Papa, of course, couldn't come, but he sent a dollar bill as a present, and Mrs. Paige and Joan and Eli had all promised to arrive by eleven. Joan and Eli were bringing the baby, his first trip anywhere.

"Won't the baby fall *off* the motorcycle, Mama?" Fee asked as they hurried through breakfast.

Alexandra shuddered. "Don't make me think of it. I begged Eli, literally got down on my knees and begged him not to, but once he decides on something with that motorcycle—"

"You wrote a letter," Fee said. "You can't get down on your knees in a letter."

"Silly-billy," Alexandra said cheerfully. "You're giving *me* English lessons now? Well, why not? But when I think of a two-month-old baby going fifty miles an hour on a motorcycle—"

Fran laughed. "The baby isn't *driving* it, Ma," she said. All week she had been looking forward to Sunday and to being fifteen. Last year she had squirmed at the idea of a birthday party in a tent, but it had turned out a huge success, with colored balloons hanging from the center beam, popping off in all directions with the breeze,

(88)

and with bright tissue-paper streamers floating noisily from the strings that tied back the canvas flaps. Everybody had stayed on and on to play games and sit around singing, until it was dark outside and their little brothers or sisters began arriving to say they had to go home.

This year, she had invited six girls and three boys, and Fee was allowed to ask her best beach friend too. Fran had a new foulard dress in pale blue, that Mama had bought at a sale at Saks for $3.90, and a set of the leather curlers she had always wanted. Her hair was still wound up in them, and Fee kept staring expectantly at the fat knobs all over her head, as if she hoped one would explode and set off the others one by one, like a string of firecrackers.

"Can I blow the balloons up?" Fee asked now, puffing out her cheeks.

"Your lungs are stronger than mine," Alexandra said. "Blow to your heart's content. There, in that white box, on top of the books."

Fee raced across to the cardboard box.

"You do the red ones, Fee," her sister said. "I'll do the yellow ones."

"Mama said I could do *all* of them."

"Well, you can't," Fran said. "I want to do some too."

"But she just said I could!"

"She did not, Miss Selfish."

"She did so, she did so," Fee shouted in sudden fury, stamping her foot so hard that sand flew up in a film from the wood flooring.

"Girls, girls," Alexandra said. "Not today, on Fran's birthday. Here, I'll divide them for you, and no more quarreling."

Fee pushed the box violently away. It fell to the floor, tumbling out blobs of red and yellow, wrinkled and dull. The sight of them touched off new anger in her, hidden and inexplicable, anger at them now, not at Fran. They were supposed to be round and big and shining in the light, but instead they were bunched-up, ugly and lifeless, lying at her feet like dead animals.

She covered her face so she couldn't see them. "Let *her* do them," she cried. "I don't want to do any of them."

"You great big crank," Fran said. "You're getting to be just like Papa."

"I am not!"

"You are so!" Fran said. "I pity your husband, when you get married."

"Make her stop, Mama," Fee stormed, "she always says that."

"Francesca!" Alexandra said. She had to raise her voice above theirs, and suddenly she thought, "We're all fighting, on a day we should be happy." She turned away from her children and started to

(89)

make up her bed, her face dulled with sadness. Behind her, Fee's sobs continued, and without a word Franny took her towel from the third hook, collected her soap-dish and comb, and departed for the bathhouse.

"She's so mean, she gets me sick," Fee said. "I hate her. She thinks she's so beautiful."

"She's not really so mean. Come here and let's talk."

"I don't want to."

"All right, don't." Alexandra went to the icebox, and took out the sliced ham, Swiss cheese, chicken, lettuce, mustard, butter and bread. Then, remembering, she put back the ham, and reached for the quince jam instead. There were fifty sandwiches to make, and a dozen other things to prepare. At times, children were savages, all of them.

Behind her, Fee felt her heart crowd with pain, choke with pain. She had had no idea she was going to refuse to talk to her mother, but the words flew out. It wasn't what she had wanted to say; when she was this angry, something made her say the exact opposite of what she wanted to say, and do just the opposite of what she wanted to do. The words sprang out of her mouth as if they were coming from a stranger's body.

Once they were out, you could never get them back. You could never escape the result of them. No matter how hard you wished you had held them in, you couldn't escape the angry face the words put on the face of the person who heard them. Or the sad face.

This, about the balloons. She had never expected to do all the balloons herself, she had never wanted to, had never imagined blowing up every single one. But the moment Fran said she couldn't, a kind of explosion went off inside, and the words were flying out like sparks, and then everything else was too late.

Just the same, Fran was horrible, to say she was getting to be like Papa. If people were going to pity her husband, she would never never marry as long as she lived.

Desolation washed through her. She looked over to her mother, but she was slicing bread busily, the knife and the loaf all she could think of.

"Mama," Fee said.

"Yes?"

"Nothing."

A moment went by; the knife flashed in the light; slice after slice fell on its side, with Mama pulling the loaf back an inch every two or three slices, to make room.

"Is Franny right, Mama?"

"About what, darling?"

Fee went over to the oblong table. The slices of bread lay like a deck of cards spread out, edge overlapping edge. Beyond them, all the slices of chicken and Swiss cheese looked beautiful, and their smells made her remember that today they were having a birthday party.

"Never mind." She put her finger into one of the holes of the Swiss cheese. "Can I help make the sandwiches?"

"Of course, dear. Wash your hands first. Hurry, we're going to have a lovely day."

It *was* a lovely day. A wonderful, a glorious day, Fran thought again and again as the hours ran away, the most beautiful day of my whole life.

Mrs. Paige had not come alone by streetcar. Mr. Paige had driven her out in their red touring car and—she nearly died when she saw him—Garrett Paige was with them.

Garrett and Letty Paige actually, though she hardly saw Letty until later. But Garry, whom she had not seen once since that time he had danced with her, whom she had thought of every day and every night since.

She felt herself go spinny and faint when he came toward the tent, and she hardly heard Mrs. Paige explain that Letty and Garry had come to visit them just as they were leaving for the beach, and was it all right to ask them along without warning?

"My goodness, of course," Mama said, beaming at all of them.

"Happy Birthday, Francesca," Mrs. Paige said then, kissing her on the cheek and handing her a large box that said *Lord & Taylor, New York*. "I do hope it's the right size, dear, but if it isn't we can change it."

"Oh, thank you, oh, how nice."

"Happy Birthday, Fran," Mr. Paige said.

"Oh, thank you too, Mr. Paige. For my present, I mean."

"Happy Birthday from me too," Garry said. "And me," Letty added.

"Thank you. Oh, it's lovely."

Everybody began to talk then and Fran thought, It happened. Until the last minute, her daydream had kept up, that even though Garry and Letty had moved to New York, somehow when the Paiges came out today, Letty and Garry would come too.

While she was combing her hair and doing her special trick with

(9 1)

her sunburn, the daydream had been so vivid she had turned around once, half expecting to see Garry right there. But it was only Fee, watching what she was doing with her rouge.

"I'm just making it look the way it does at the beginning of summer," Fran explained, adding in a nice big-sister voice, "You can do it in a couple of years. I'll show you how."

It was a trick she had invented herself; instead of using rouge only on her cheekbones and lips, she also dabbed it faintly across the bridge of her nose and on two spots on her forehead, just under her hair at her temples, just like a new sunburn.

It was becoming, especially today against the light blue of her dress, and Eli and Joan, the first to arrive, said she was getting prettier every year.

They hadn't brought the baby after all; a threat of rain had settled that. Their birthday gift to Fran was a pyrography set, because she used to love watching Eli burn out designs in leather and wood with his own set. Fee brought out her present then: a set of jacks, all bright and bronzy, with a red rubber ball. Fran nearly blurted out that fifteen was way too old for jacks, but instead she hugged Fee and with a special look over her head at the others, she said, "They're just what I wanted, honestly. And when I'm not playing with them, you can borrow them and play with them yourself."

Just then the Paiges arrived and the whole day changed.

After the first spinning minutes, all she could do was busy herself with the Lord & Taylor box, and she squealed with joy when she saw what was in it—a real cashmere sweater, the most expensive thing she had ever owned.

"Try it on, Franny," Fee said, and Fran could have hugged her for saying it.

"Later," she said.

"Now, Fran, come on," Fee insisted.

So she did and everybody watched while she slipped it on over her dress. She knew Garry was watching too, although she could not look straight at him, and even before she went to the tiny square of mirror, she could *feel* she looked well in it. In her high little voice, Mrs. Paige said, "I declare, you look a little beauty, Francesca," and Fran nearly ran over and kissed her for saying it in front of Garry.

Fee's friend arrived just then, and a moment later two of her own. The games started, and then there wasn't a minute when she could talk to Garry alone. But not for part of a minute did she forget he was there. And the moment he disappeared, she knew that too, and began to wait for him to come back.

(92)

His father and he had gone off to change into bathing suits, while Letty used the back part of their own tent. Garry came back first; he looked marvelous. He had one of the new suits, without the short sleeves most men wore; it was black with two white stripes around the V neck and the big armholes, and also around the legs, just above his knees.

She felt funny, seeing Garry in a bathing suit for the first time, and she kept trying not to look at him. Then Letty joined him and she looked all right in her navy bloused suit and white cap, like a big puff of rubber over her hair. Her legs looked sort of thick, though, in her long black stockings, and come to think of it, her pleated bathing suit made her look a bit thick all over.

"It looks like rain," her mother suddenly said, "everybody better get your swim in right away. Hurry!"

Fran felt like jumping with pleasure. All the boys and girls ran home to get their suits, and in a moment Garry would be seeing *her* in a bathing suit for the first time too. Her stockings didn't make her look thick, and her bathing suit didn't either.

"Come along, you two," Eli said after supper, "let's take a walk and see if this dump has changed since last summer."

Fran paid no attention to him. By now the birthday party was over. The Paiges and Mama were talking about the big strikes that had started in England and Ireland on Thursday, stopping railroad trains dead. Garry knew more about it than anybody; a friend of his at the lab kept getting letters from relatives in Germany, warning him that the strikes would spread there too, and then to France.

"Come on, Fran," Eli repeated, "let's take a walk."

"Well, the strike's sort of interesting," Fran said. "I'd rather stay and listen."

Alexandra looked at her with new pleasure. "Poor devils, working twelve, fourteen hours a day, seven days a week, for eight or nine dollars a week. A ninety-eight-hour week, for nine dollars."

"It's inhuman," Fran said.

"They'll get their ten-hour day," Garry assured her.

"I *hope* so," Fran said gratefully, as if he had just taken special pains to make her happier.

But Eli insisted. "Don't be a pest on your birthday. Come on."

There was nothing to do but go. Fee had already started, and they went up the beach to where the new dance hall had been built. Inside it, the Victrola was turned up to its loudest, blaring out "Alexander's

Ragtime Band." Above them, though the sky still had a faint orange from sunset, the moon was new and clean, and the wind from the sea was dryer and cooler than it had been all summer. Soon vacation would be over and school starting up once more.

"Let's sit down here," Joan said. They had reached a breakwater sticking out from the ocean, and she felt it with her palm to see whether it was still wet.

Fran sat down beside her, first lifting the skirt of her new dress, and Fee sat on the sand, locking her arms around her knees. From above them, Eli said, "We have a big secret we want to tell you." He sounded serious. "Do you both promise, on your honor?"

Joan said, "We're sure you're both old enough to keep a secret."

"*I* certainly am," Fran said. Loyally she added, "And Fee is too."

"I *have* two big secrets anyway," Fee said, and Fran snickered. One was about Trudy and the other about Betty, and Fee had blatted both of them out the same day she had heard them.

"We know we can trust you," Joan said. "And you won't want to tell your mother and father anyway, because it might hurt them."

"Hurt them?" Fee said.

"Just at the beginning," Joan said.

Fee looked at Fran and then at her brother. She wanted terribly to hear what the secret was, but in a funny way, she suddenly wished there wasn't anything to hear. Fran looked serious, and Fee wondered if Fran was a little afraid too.

"We changed our name," Eli said. "We did it before Web was born, so it could get on his birth certificate."

"Changed it?" they both asked.

"To Eaves. E-a-v-e-s. Eaves. No more Ivarin."

"You didn't," Fran said, impressed. "You never would."

"But I did." He looked at her, then at Fee. "We got the legal part taken care of beforehand, and we know there'll be a peach of a row when we tell Pa and Ma."

"Oh, Eli," Fee said slowly.

"Before Web was born?" Fran asked Joan. "But at the hospital, when we went to see you and the baby, we didn't say 'Eaves.' The nurse called you 'Mrs. Ivarin,' not Mrs. Eaves."

"We wanted it that way, to keep it to ourselves for a while. But Daddy and my doctor are friends, and they took care of the birth certificate."

"Eaves," Fran said. "Eli Eaves. It's grand. But, gee."

They all fell silent, looking at each other, starting to speak, then saying nothing.

(94)

"Will it be awful," Fee asked at last, "when you tell Papa and Mama?"

Eli just whistled, and Fee's wish came back stronger than ever, that there hadn't been a secret to listen to, even one as exciting as this. Through the rest of the evening, when they were back in the tent and couldn't say a word in front of their mother, and even next morning, Fee wasn't over the feeling of being afraid. She wouldn't admit it to Fran. The only thing she did say, the moment they were off by themselves, was that she never knew you could just go to court and change your name to a prettier one.

It was a small matter, Fran said learnedly. You could change your name even without bothering to go to court at all, if you felt like it, like taking a *nom de plume* or a pseudonym or a stage name. The only time the law cared was if you were a criminal, and were changing your name for criminal purposes.

"I could change my name to Francesca Fairbanks," Fran ended, "or Francesca Fiske or anything I wanted. And you could change yours to Fira Foolish or Fira Phooey or—"

"You keep quiet."

"That's what we both have to do, Fee," Fran said, serious and nice again. "We can't even breathe 'Eaves' in front of Mama. She would just die."

EIGHT

"To receive such praise from you," Stefan Ivarin said slowly to the man standing beside his desk in the office, "is, you will admit, an extraordinary experience."

"Now, Stiva," Joseph Fehler said. "It's not so unheard of as all that. If only you could drop the chip on your shoulder." He spoke ruefully, a man regretfully aware of difficulty yet declining to quarrel.

"Last spring, you recall," Stefan said, "I had rather a nasty fight, overruling you, about the box on the front page—"

"But now that *I* want your editorial in a box on the front page,"

Fehler cut in, "the notion becomes anathema to you." He indicated the strip of galley on the desk and added, "For even *one* reader to miss this would be a crime."

Involuntarily, Stefan glanced down, conscious of pleasure, and of annoyance that he should be so helpless in vanity. The moment the galley had come up from the press room, he had sent word to Abe Kesselbaum, the make-up man, that an error had been made; the editorial was for the regular page, in the usual format. Word had come back that by chance Mr. Fehler had happened to read it in proof and had sent word down that it should appear front-page center.

"ASSASSINATE A BOOK?" the headline said, and as Stefan read it again, his satisfaction with it deepened. There was economy there; "ASSASSINATE" brought anarchist idiocy and madness to mind as no other single word in the world could have done.

"You realize," Stefan said, looking up at Fehler, "that if his book ever does get into print, between the efforts of your crowd and any money we raise here, I will still denounce his ideas at every opportunity?"

"Yes, Stiva. I didn't think we had made a convert."

Stefan grunted. He wished he could order Fehler to stop addressing him as "Stiva," but the specific harshness eluded him. The sycophant's tone Fehler had adopted this evening sent a chill of distaste through him, though the office was as clammy hot as if it were August instead of late October. Now, in his final phrase about making a convert, Fehler's disdain for "the softness" of the moderate socialist twanged like a fat 'cello string. Stefan looked down again at the strip of smudged galley.

This paper has fought Anarchism for twenty years. It still does.

Yet it is a shock that in this free country, not one publisher will accept Alexander Berkman's *Prison Memoirs of an Anarchist.* To assassinate a book, we need only to refuse it print.

Readers of the *Jewish News,* so many of whom still recall the tyrannies they escaped from when they came to America, say again and again, " It's a free country," and their hearts hammer with gratitude and love.

But that great banner, "A free country," will wave only while all writing and speaking and thinking remain free, even that which we detest, despise or fear.

Therefore this newspaper now invites its readers to send in money orders for a special fund to publish Berkman's book privately—

As Stefan read on, he was aware of Fehler's eyes upon him, of the triumph in them. He is a fool, Stefan thought; like every extremist, he is so obsessed with his own ideas, he loses the ability to reason as men reason. Now he is certain he is "using" me and the paper. He cannot see that by robbing this book of martyrdom, we not only maintain a principle, but doom the book to the oblivion it undoubtedly deserves.

"I must either overrule you on position, Fehler," he said aloud, "and restore this to the editorial page where it normally would appear, or else, call a special meeting of the policy staff and put this vexing matter to a vote."

Joseph Fehler shook his head. His handsome face, ruddy and still tanned from his late vacation, seemed to elongate and harden. "I will be outvoted," he said. "I am always outvoted here."

Stefan Ivarin picked up a heavy pencil, changed the printing directions on the smudged galley, and shouted "Boy, Boy," until an old man in a sweater appeared and took the galley from him. "Yes," he said to Fehler, "you would be outvoted."

"Your conception of freedom," Fehler said bitterly.

A current of anger shot through Stefan but he controlled it. "This old story," he said wearily. He rose so that he could face Fehler. "If you wish to be in the voting majority, Fehler, you must join the staff of an anarchist paper. Perhaps Johann Most could use your talents as business manager on *Die Freiheit*." Fehler started to reply, but Stefan refused to allow it, his voice growing in volume, ploughing right on. "But here on the *Jewish News,* where you are the single anarchist, among an entire staff of Democrats and Socialists, do you really daydream about majorities?"

"You would celebrate for a week," Fehler said, "if I went to another paper."

"Perhaps not for a whole week."

Stefan felt the heat mounting in his forehead and eyes; in his mind, Alexandra said, "Stiva, please, your face is getting red." He lowered his voice. "Are we to descend to sarcasms now about 'celebrating'? Bickering like young girls with hurt feelings?"

"I did not intend to bicker."

"Neither did I. It does not matter." He seated himself at his desk once more. "What does matter," he said, "is that the owner of the paper approves of your efficiency, whatever he may feel about your political formation. The paper's circulation grows, the income grows, he wants no changes. So it has been for five years, so let it be for another five years."

(97)

"Perhaps," Fehler said, and left the room.

Stefan looked after him. Yes, sooner or later, a show of power, and not over Fehler's anarchism, either. He will choose a more popular arena, where he has more chance to tear me apart.

"It will break his heart," Alexandra said bitterly.

"Mama, please don't cry," Fee begged. "Please don't."

"He'll raise the roof," Eli said. "That I grant, but it won't break his heart. Nothing could."

They were in the kitchen, Alexandra and the girls, Eli and Joan. Alexandra put her hand on Fee's thin shoulder, nodding as if in obedience to the child's entreaty. But tears kept flooding her reddened eyes; nothing under heaven could stop them now.

Joan looked at Eli in reproof for his roughness, and wished he had put it off once again, as he had put it off so many times since they had done it in June. Father Ivarin wasn't there, and maybe that was why Eli had chosen tonight to tell his mother about Eaves. An hour had passed since he had, and all Joan could think of now was how to end it and get Eli home. If he didn't calm down, he wouldn't sleep, and he'd have a frightful day tomorrow. His new school was way out in Brighton Beach and he had to leave at seven-fifteen each morning to get there in time.

"Don't you tell him about it," Joan advised Alexandra. "Eli and I ought to tell him ourselves—we don't want to put it off on you."

"I can't hide a thing like this."

"Can't you make up some excuse? You could say you're worried about the baby, a sudden temperature, something like that. Then tomorrow I'll come back and tell him myself."

"The shock—I'm so distracted—"

Eli exploded. "For God's sake, I can't stand all this," but Joan said to her mother-in-law, "Of course it's a shock."

"I knew what we were in for," Eli added. "If you take it this way, can you imagine *him?*"

"But you decided in May, before the baby was born, and all these months you were living a lie with your own parents."

"Right," he said without any note of regret. "I wasn't going to put Joan through it while she was pregnant. And not right afterward either. I wanted to keep it a secret for as long as we could, a year, maybe more."

At the word, "secret," Fran and Fee exchanged glances. Neither of them had ever had such a secret to keep in all their lives; it had changed their last two weeks at the beach, so they would not blurt it out right in front of Mama. And since getting home, they would talk about it in whispers, if they talked of it at all, and they had each taken a special oath not to tell their best friends. Neither one of them had betrayed the oath.

Until this evening, keeping the secret so well had seemed an achievement, something everybody would praise them for when it was at last revealed. But tonight, after Joan and Eli had told Mama, Joan had let something slip about the walk along the beach on Fran's birthday, and telling the girls about Eaves then.

"You know?" their mother cried, turning on them in disbelief. "You knew this and never told me? For nearly two months, like—like conspirators, you let me live on in a fool's bliss, while you both *knew?*"

"Oh, Mama," Fran said, in her special way.

It infuriated Alexandra. "Oh, Mama, oh, Mama—you take sides against me automatically," she said. "Maybe you also are ashamed of your father's and mother's name."

"That's not fair," Joan put in sharply. "Being ashamed never came into it. Not for one moment."

"No, no," Alexandra apologized quickly. "I shouldn't have said it." With her next breath she added, "Just the same, if our name was Rockefeller or Carnegie, you wouldn't even *dream* of changing it."

Fee looked at her mother with a new interest. Not once, never since the day she was born, had it even once occurred to her that her mother could be wrong, totally, absolutely, positively wrong. But now she was wrong.

"Why, Mama," she began excitedly, "you're saying something that's the exact opposite of—"

There was silence from all of them. Suddenly Fee felt as if she were again standing up alone in the middle of the stage in the auditorium just after Miss Mainley had announced, "The next will be a recitation, 'Sally Ann's Experience,' by Fira Ivarin, sixth grade." Her breath stuck in her throat, and her heart squeezed with knowing she had to begin, that everybody was waiting, and that she couldn't escape until she had recited.

"The opposite of what?" Mama asked, coaxing, as if she knew that whatever was to come, it would be a first step for her youngest child.

"Of what you always say about getting Americanized and being Americans. If our name *was* Carnegie or Rockefeller it would be American *already,* so Eli and Joan wouldn't *have* to change it. They just *did* it for Americanizing, not out of being ashamed."

"Thanks, kid," Eli said, his eyes brightening. "You've got it straighter than Ma has."

His praise made her feel marvelous. But then he said to Joan, "Maybe Fee's just been elected to tell Pop."

"No, I haven't," Fee shouted at him. "Don't you make fun of me, don't do it, don't you dare be so mean and horrible to everybody." And she ran from the room, sobbing, racing up the stairs two at a time.

Down below, they could hear her furious crying, and for a moment nobody spoke. Alexandra thought, Despite Fee's point, I know and Eli knows that being ashamed of a foreign name like Ivarin did enter into it; I'm glad Fee didn't see quite that far.

"I'll come over tomorrow," Joan said, "before Father Ivarin is awake, and I'll tell him myself. Please wait until then."

Alexandra shook her head. "I'll tell him tonight." She looked at Eli. "When he comes home, I will tell him. I couldn't sleep in the same house with him all night, and keep silent about a thing like this."

She dried her eyes on a kitchen towel and went to the sink for a glass of water. Behind her there was silence, and before she turned back to them she said, "It's really time for you to go home. Otherwise Eli will be too exhausted tomorrow, and start another attack."

Upstairs, Fee lay in the dark, waiting for her father to get home. When Franny came up to bed, she pretended to be asleep, her face turned toward the wall, and her arm over her eyes, so her sister couldn't see whether her eyelids moved.

"Fee," Fran whispered as she came in, "are you asleep?"

She didn't answer; she could hear Fran come around to try to see better, but behind her concealing arm, she felt safe.

"I don't believe you," Fran announced after a second or two, but she left Fee's bed and began to undress.

When the light went out, Fee opened her eyes, and lay still, trying to guess what would happen when Papa heard about it. She tried to remember back to the promise on the beach, back to that first instant, that first knowing about Eaves, to see how she and Fran could ever have thought it was all right to keep it a secret from Mama just because Eli and Joan said they should.

Had Eli and Joan made them promise before they told them what the secret was? Or had they first told them about Eaves, and then later on asked them to keep it a secret? It was terrible not to remember.

If you promised to keep a secret before you knew what it was, then you were not responsible for keeping it. At least not as responsible as if you first heard the secret, and then afterwards promised not to tell. Had Eli and Joan told them first, and then made them promise? If it had been in that order, then they really couldn't help keeping Mama in a fool's paradise; there was no way out. She wished she hadn't made Fran think she was asleep; Fran might remember which came first, the secret or the promise.

Maybe she ought to go downstairs now, to explain to Mama that they would rather die than hurt or fool her, but that it had been impossible to do anything except what they did do. It was so mixed up, if being proud of being able to keep a secret could suddenly turn into being so ashamed.

A fool's bliss, Mama had said. She meant "a fool's paradise," and tonight nobody would have joked or teased her about the right way to say it. But at other times they would have, and Mama would have laughed and said, "a fool's paradise, all right. A brochure."

They would have all burst out laughing at "brochure." It was a word that was special for them all, a family word, a family joke that never failed, with Mama laughing as hard as any of them, even though the joke was on her.

It had happened a long time ago, when Fee was only nine, and at first Fee had laughed only because Eli and Fran and Papa had all laughed so hard. Only later did she understand for herself how funny it was and every time the word "brochure" was spoken after that, it just got funnier and more of a special private word.

In a way, it was dirty too, but nobody thought of that any more. The day it happened, Mama had been talking about one of Dr. Wiley's worst enemies, a bad man who owned a big food company and wouldn't stop using preservatives in canned goods, benzoate of soda and coal-tar dyes and things like that, even though Dr. Wiley was part of the Government and Congress had just passed the Pure Food Laws he wanted, laws that everybody had to obey.

This bad man was stubborn and said Dr. Wiley had no right to interfere with a man's private business, and that he was going to fight back.

"So he let out a big brochure—" Mama said.

That was as far as she got. There was a roar of laughter from Papa and Eli and Fran; through the laughter, Mama kept trying to explain that this stubborn angry businessman had written a booklet, had it printed on rich heavy paper, and then had mailed thousands of copies to lots of important people. But it was no use. They wouldn't listen or stop laughing and at last, in a questioning tone, Mama herself repeated, "let out a big brochure." "Oh, I *see*," she said, and began to laugh with them, which started them off once more.

Now in the darkness, Fee remembered how jolly their laughter had sounded, and wished desperately that it were that night again, instead of this awful one of waiting until Papa got home and heard what Eli had done.

Everything was so happy then, with Mama explaining that no matter how brilliant you were about any language you learned when you were grown up, you still could make mistakes in slang or in idioms. Papa had agreed, and told them he had never felt he really knew the English language until the night he had had his first dream in English, instead of in Russian.

This was like a dream too, a nightmare of Mama turning on Fran and her as if they were traitors. It was Eli's fault, for starting it all. Eli was a wonderful brother, but he certainly had a way of doing something and then not worrying about what would happen. Right this minute he probably was sound asleep, not lying awake wondering what his father would do when he walked up the hill tonight and came into the house and listened to what Mama would tell him.

Elijah Eaves. It sounded silly and crazy now, though it hadn't when she first heard about it. About a week after that walk on the beach, Fran had said as a joke, "Maybe I'll do it too, before I start teaching." And Fran had started mimicking her own future pupils in her future classroom. "Yes, Miss Eaves. I'm sorry, Miss Eaves. Good afternoon, Miss Eaves."

Francesca Eaves, Fee thought now. Fira Eaves. She squirmed and wondered if Fran really had been joking. Maybe she should wake her; she would die unless she could hear Fran promise never never to change her name to Eaves, to stay Francesca Ivarin until she got married, and say that Fira would be Fira Ivarin until she married too.

Then when they became Francesca Somebody-Else, and Fira Somebody-Else, it would make Mama and Papa happy, not miserable and angry, the way they were if you changed on purpose.

"Fran," she whispered in the dark. "Franny, are you still awake?"

Fran flopped around, but she didn't answer. Fee tried again a moment later, but there was no doubt about it: she was asleep, and not just paying Fee back. It was comfortable to know that Fran could sleep, and Fee closed her eyes and wondered if maybe she could sleep now too.

.   .   .

It was after two when Shag's huge barking outdoors announced that Stefan was coming home at last. Alexandra went to the front door, but at once changed her mind and returned to the kitchen where she would normally be if she were downstairs at this hour, after giving a late lesson or sewing longer than usual.

She could never do what Joan suggested, and explain her swollen eyes by saying Webby had a sudden high fever. She was never successful with lies, even small social lies to save a friend's feelings about a new hat or a suggested visit, and with something as awful as this, she could not even wait in silence. All evening she had rehearsed what she would say when he did get home. She must not burst out with it; she must help him by seeming calm and strong. To conceal her pain was impossible, but she must somehow manage, must, must, must manage not to let the tears come, nor the break in her voice. If only he could be spared the news itself.

"It won't break his heart," Eli had said angrily, "Nothing could." How cold Eli could be, how indifferent. What was wrong with the boy, that he was capable of such words, so inconsiderate, so—well, let it be said, so cruel? Somewhere along the road from babyhood, Eli had turned a corner and lost his sweetness, his goodness, which was there at the beginning. Was it when Francesca was born?

Eli was nearly six then, and for those six years, he had been undisputed king of the world, his baby world, the only world he knew. Was it rage then, at being toppled from the throne? But all families knew this problem, this jealousy of the firstborn when the second child arrived to dispute his lordly singleness. And surely she had prepared Eli as wisely, as lovingly for the change in his solitary status as any mother could, anywhere on earth.

She would not chide herself too constantly for the faults that showed in Eli or in any of the children. Parents could do much, could love, help, shape, lead, but in the end there surely remained in each being some mysteries of goodness or badness, of strength or weakness, of softness or stoniness.

And Elijah did have this capacity to deal out a blow without the capacity to imagine its stab. "Raise the roof," he could say, but apparently it was beyond him to predict the pain there would be for her or for his father.

If Elijah were not the only son.

If the baby Stefan had lived, there would have been other grandchildren; they would be named Ivarin, and perhaps one at least would be a boy. Then Stefan would not need to feel the way he would now: It will all end with me.

Francesca would marry, and Fira, and their names would be the names of their husbands, and their children's names would be the unknown names too. Ivarin would disappear from the face of America forever.

But that is wrong, Alexandra thought, when we love it so.

When we have worked for it so much, both of us, teaching its new citizens, helping to form its young labor unions which some day will be thought right and good, instead of something crazy and radical. The time will come when it is normal to belong to a union, when every capitalist will bargain and arbitrate instead of beating or slugging or shooting down strikers. The time will come when nobody need starve if they are laid off, when they will save out a few pennies a week during all the years they work, to make some kind of public fund to give them security and dignity when they are at last too old.

All of it will come, and when it does, the name of Ivarin should not have vanished from the face of America, when Stiva worked so deeply, and I too, it must be said, to make greenhorns into Americans, and to make America's workers different from the serfs and slaves and wretches of Europe.

The door opened, and Stefan called, "Alexandra, is that you?"

"Yes, here," she said, "I couldn't sleep."

He came in, his face pale, with the grey look that could mean ill-temper or else ordinary fatigue.

"Why not?" he asked.

"No reason, just not."

He had brought *The World* and *The Call* as well as the *Jewish News* with him, and he put them on the table as he said, "I had a bad time with Fehler. It's getting worse, with him."

"That fool," she said. "What happened?"

He began to pace up and down the small kitchen as he told her of the altercation between them, and though she listened to each word, a part of her mind kept thinking, How can I change the subject to the real subject? How can I prepare him, how lessen the blow to his dignity? Aloud, she made sounds of indignation at Fehler's too-obvious attempt to get Berkman's book on the front page of the paper, and these she alternated with praise and approval of everything Stiva had said and done.

"There will be worse times with him," he ended. "Before too many years have gone by, he will try to seize control of the whole paper, you will see. He will tell me what to write and what not to write. You will see."

"He wouldn't dare," she said. "The readers would rebel, every reader the paper has, if Fehler dared. They would picket the office, they would call mass meetings, they would make it clear enough how they worship Ivarin's work."

He smiled. "You are a wonder, Alexandra," he said. "When it comes to defending one of the children, or defending me, you become a mobilized army, all by yourself."

As he spoke, he passed the chair in which she was sitting, and he paused, as if to take a second look at a stranger. She *was* a wonder in many ways. Of course, she could also drive a man mad, drive him out of the house, make him travel the whole distance to New York to earn a few hours of respite. But that did not alter this other truth: in many ways, there was no one on earth like her. Picket the office, call mass meetings!

"It won't come for a while," he said. "Fehler is clever. He knows he has to wait. In the meantime, I'd rather think of a glass of tea and something to eat."

The water had been boiling for some time; the tea waited in the strainer inside the rim of the tumbler, the lemon was cut, and the sugar bowl set on the table. Alexandra also had set out a package of Uneeda Biscuits and some homemade quince jam.

She waited until he had started on his tea and jam. Then she said, "Stiva, I have something bad to tell you."

"Anybody sick?" he asked. "One of the children?"

"It's nothing like that. It's only something that will make you angry. I wish I could keep it from you."

He put down the square white cracker he was spreading with quince jam, but picked up his glass of tea.

"But you cannot keep it from me," he said. "It is too big; I can tell from the way you look. I did not notice before, I'm sorry."

At the kindness in his voice, the concern in his words, Alexandra felt the familiar, the abominable stinging in her eyes, and she pressed the tip of her right pinkie finger as hard as she could. Fee had once told her that you could hold back a sneeze that way. You had to press the tip so hard it began to burn; perhaps it would work now to hold back something more important.

"It's something Elijah did," she said. The trick must have worked. Her eyes did not sting; the tears had not begun; the break in her voice had not come.

"Something Elijah did that will anger me? Once a day he does something that angers me. He may yet harden into manhood, I do not know, Alexandra, but so far he seems—well, never mind."

The spineless Adonis speech was nothing she could permit just now, she thought. Alas that she could not. How much easier it would be than what was to come in its place.

"This is different, Stiva," she said. "They decided, before the baby was born, they talked it all out, and they both agreed to do this."

Stefan looked at her attentively. This was of major importance, clearly of major importance. But she was unable to tell him. She was afraid to tell him. Afraid of how he would take it.

"They agreed to do what?" he said, with a note of impatience. "Come, Alexandra, you are dragging it out like a French novel. They decided *what?*"

"To change—it's about changing their name. The baby, after all, is born an American, of American parents on both sides, and Webster does not go very well with Ivarin."

"But they picked 'Webster' because of her father." The very act of speaking the words canceled them out. Before she could speak again, he added, "That isn't it. They are not changing 'Webster.' Of course, of course. They are changing 'Ivarin.' "

She said, "Yes, Stiva, yes, that's it." Her voice suddenly roughened, as Eli's always did during an attack. "It is done already. There is not even a chance to argue with them, or persuade them against it."

He said nothing. He did not stir. He simply sat, one hand still circling his half-empty glass of tea, the other lying close and unmoving beside it, like a tired companion.

She watched the hands, unable to look at his face. The silence in the kitchen grew. Outside it began to rain, and from the north a wind blew strong and fresh, the first heavy rain of autumn. Soon the last leaves would drift from the trees, the earth would go brown, and winter be on its way.

"I know how you feel," she said at last. "In my own shock of hearing it, I ran to the telephone but I changed my mind. I could not tell you this—this agony, over a wire strung along a thousand electric poles from here to New York."

He pushed his chair back and began to pace the kitchen once more. He walked up and down, up and down, and then, as if he were throwing off constricting garments, he turned abruptly through the kitchen door, and walked into the dining room, then into the living room, and then into the small front vestibule near the porch. There he turned and traversed the entire route once more.

For a time, Alexandra remained at the table in the kitchen. He was fighting the first rage, the first wound. It was wisdom, and kindness too, to give him time, to wait no matter how long, until he himself felt ready to speak.

Minute followed minute, and still she sat quiet. He had not even asked what they had changed it to. He did not care about the specific; it was the principle of it only, the total of it.

Five minutes went by, then ten. Once she heard him pause, but she guessed he was only making a cigarette, and the sound of his striking a match on his heel a moment later told her she was right. Again he resumed his pacing, still out of sight.

At last she went into the dining room. He had not turned on the light, but against the chalky walls, she could see him clearly. He had wrenched loose the necktie that lay at the base of his stiff wing collar, open at the gullet like an encircling fence with an entranceway cut into it. He seemed less erect than usual, his shoulders were uneven, the right higher than the left, as they always were after he had worked at his desk too long.

He gave no sign that he knew she had come in.

"Do you want to know what name they took?" she finally asked.

"Of course."

"Eaves. They decided finally on Eaves. Webster Eaves, the baby is, and they are Mr. and Mrs. Elijah Eaves."

"Well," he said mildly. "It's euphonious enough."

She was startled. Whatever she had been braced for, it was most certainly not this. Most definitely and clearly nothing whatever like this. Euphonious indeed.

She watched him go through the dining room, the living room, the small vestibule, watched him turn, repeat the whole pattern, turn, repeat. It's like a minuet, she thought. Is he going to say nothing?

"Stiva," she began tentatively. "If you would rather not talk about it now, I would understand."

"Yes," he said, "I would rather not."

"The first shock is terrible for you," she said. "I know exactly what you feel, what the pain is like."

For a moment he made no answer. Then he said, "You agreed we needn't talk about it."

"But to bottle it up inside is worse. I know how it is. I told Eli it would break your heart."

"But it does not break my heart," he said. "I'm afraid you were wrong."

She stared at him in disbelief. His voice was patient, steady, not sharper than usual.

"You mean you do not mind?" she asked.

"Of course I mind. If my only son shelves my name forever, it is inevitable that I mind."

He turned as if to resume his walking, but an exasperated "Stiva!" brought him to a halt.

"Is that all you have to say?" she demanded. "Nothing else?"

"What can I say? He's a married man, a father, it's his life, he's within his rights."

"His rights! Does that give him *carte blanche* to strike a dagger into his parents' hearts?"

He frowned. He always frowned when her language grew "too volatile," as he called it.

"Was there a dagger in my parents' hearts," he asked, "when I was arrested at the University and sent to prison?" Before she could answer, he went on, "And then when I was rescued by Drubhinov, and I left them for America, forever, for the rest of their poor lives— did they feel daggers then?"

"Stiva, what is wrong with you?" she said. "You know this is not the same kind of thing, what Eli is doing."

"True enough. It is not the same. But is also true that he has the right to make his own life."

"He can't make his own life as Eli Ivarin?"

She spoke heatedly and at last, over the words, her voice broke, and her eyes filled. She was furious at Stefan's calmness, his Olympian control. For hours she had been in torment for his sake; now, he was showing her up for a sentimental fool. How perverse he could be, how maddening.

"He has decided," Stefan said, still not raising his voice, but now spacing his syllables, as if he were talking to one of his pupils in Beginner' English, "it will be a better life as Eli Eaves. His ideas about life include, perhaps, matters that do not seem weighty to you or to me."

"Weighty," she said angrily. "What a word to use!"

"But they are weighty enough for him. And he is free to act on anything weighty, you follow me?"

"Free," she cried. "It's inhuman, this logic of yours, I can't stand it."

Abruptly, she started out of the room. At the door, she stopped. "Good night," she said. "It's good you do not suffer about this as I was so sure you would."

His back was toward her, and he did not turn around. She waited an instant, sure he had heard each word anyhow. He continued his pacing, and furious once more, she suddenly screamed at his retreating back, "Because if you did, you could not bear it."

(1 0 8)

NINE

The girls could not believe it. At the risk of being late for school, they made Alexandra tell them every word she could remember about the way Papa had taken it.

"But, Mama," Fran said, "it's a relief, isn't it?"

"I suppose it's a relief."

She said it without conviction. In her old grey bathrobe, which the girls had not seen since spring, she looked greyer and older than usual, her eyes lusterless and her hair still in its short grey braid down her back, despite her rule that nobody could appear at breakfast without a washed face and combed hair.

"But you sound funny," Fran persisted. "I should think you'd be just plain happy that he didn't get mad."

"Yes, darling, you would think so."

Fee, who had been listening in silence, now asked, "Will he be in a bad mood when he gets up?"

"I don't know," Alexandra said. "I can't decide what he feels, no matter what he said last night. It didn't ring true, that's all."

"Then he will be in a mood," Fee said. She sounded resigned, not frightened, but prepared. Now began the uneasy time, the queer time that lasted as long as Papa's moods lasted. Sometimes they were over in a day or two, but sometimes they would go on and on forever.

Out in the vestibule, the telephone began its one-two, one-two that meant it was their half of the party line. "It's Joan," Alexandra said positively, "to find out if I did tell him last night."

Fran and Fee followed her out to the boxlike little hall that held only a clothes tree of varnished oak and a high narrow table for the tall black telephone.

"Yes, I did," Alexandra said at once into it. "He remained—well, judicious. Aloof, that's a better word, Joan." She listened. "No, not angry at all. I was quite surprised."

"Come on, Fee," Fran said. "We'll just make it by the skin of our teeth as it is."

"Go, children," Alexandra said, turning from the telephone to kiss them. "And don't worry."

But as they hurried off, half running to the corner where they had to separate, apprehension spun its faint web across both their faces.

"Franny, will you get home right after last period?" Fee asked.

"I can't. Today's basketball."

"Then I'll hang around Study Hall a while. But don't go for a sundae or anything after basketball, will you?"

Fran promised and Fee went off alone. Off and on during the day her apprehension returned. While Papa was in a mood, he would never look at anybody, never say a word to anybody. Or else he would yell out orders, "Stop that infernal racket," or "Get out of my room—it doesn't *need* any cleaning."

Even the way he walked told you he was in a mood. He would come down the stairs slowly, clearing his throat again and again, making thick phlegmy sounds, not caring whether it made other people feel sick to hear him. If anyone was in the kitchen, he would grump a good morning or a hello at the air in general, and then sit over his paper, drinking coffee but ignoring any cereal or eggs or fruit put before him either by Mama or the Polish servant girl, if this was one of the times they had a new one.

Not once would he look up from his reading; "working," he called it because he was always on the hunt for something to write about. And then the afternoon mail would come and he would start on that. Before the first day of a mood was over, the whole house felt as if somebody were in bed dying. And after the second or third day, the sight of his untouched food could suddenly drive Mama out of the kitchen, out of the house. She would go downtown to Main Street, and stay down there long enough to buy a million dollars' worth of clothes and groceries and jewelry and books. When she finally did come home, he might still be sitting there, and again all he would do would be to grump some words about "going upstairs" or "going to the office."

If she got angry, if she said he was making a mausoleum of the whole house, or worst of all, if she started to cry, he would get up in silence and walk out of the room, go up to his desk and stay there, or march straight to the front door and disappear for New York.

Then Mama really would cry, and who was to blame her? She began to look pale, and half-sick, and after a few days, you would think she had boiled her eyeballs in vinegar.

But he didn't notice. Nothing would move him, nothing speed up whatever mysterious process it was that had set off his mood, that then held him in it, that finally would release its hold, like an illogical policeman suddenly unlocking handcuffs and saying, "That's enough for now, beat it, twenty-three skiddoo."

Mama once said it was more like his having a desperate sickness and then miraculously getting over it. There was no predicting when the disease would strike, and no understanding why it did. Sometimes real troubles would come and he would take them without blinking, serious troubles, like not having enough money for the mortgage, or a quarrel at the office or a lecture that fell flat.

But at some other time, anything might turn the trick and start him off. An editorial of his that nobody mentioned, a strike lost somewhere, some ordinary small thing wrong at home—and one, two, three he was in a mood.

While it lasted, Fran and she spoke in whispers; they tried to avoid him; they never asked him a question, they hated meals and, if Mama had let them, they would have skipped them all, and lived on Hershey Bars and milk.

But Mama would not let them stay away from the table. "It would insult him," she said firmly. "He is your father and he is a good father. He can't help these moods; you don't think he feels happy either, do you? Then grant him a little patience! You know that all of a sudden it will end."

"The 'all-of-a-sudden' is what keeps us living," Fran said bitterly. "If he ever once said he was sorry when it was over."

"Does a man ask his family to forgive him, if he recovers at last from a fearful illness?"

Never again did they bring up the idea of apologies, but now, as Fee started the last period of the day, she kept looking at the big clock over the blackboard and wondering if this would be one of his worst times. At three, Miss Roberts said in a teasing voice, "Well, run along, Fee, have a nice time at your rendezvous," and Fee said, "I'm only going to Study Hall and do homework, Miss Roberts." Miss Roberts was the nicest teacher she had ever had.

But Study Hall was no use; it was empty and spooky. At last she was so jumpy, she left for home ten minutes before Fran's basketball practice would end.

But Fran was already there, out on the porch, waiting. "You're a fine one," Fran said. "Letting me be first home, to do the dirty work!"

"But you said—"

(1 1 1)

"Hiding out like an old scaredy-cat."

"You *told* me—oh, Fran, don't be sarcastic today. You said, on account of basketball practice—"

"Gee, I forgot." Her face softened and Fee felt forgiven and grateful. "Miss Miller got the pip, so practice was off."

Fee bent down to hug Shag, and then straightened up and balanced her strapped books on the porch railing. "Is Papa all right, Fran?"

"He's horrible. I hate him."

Fee said, "Oh, Franny."

"Keep out of his sight, that's all. He's in the kitchen—Mama can't even start supper."

Fee said nothing. A gust of wind snapped at her books, but she caught them in time. After a while, Fran began to whistle "Roamin' in the Gloamin'," and it sounded mournful and lost.

"I'm going in, Fran," she said at last.

"Stay away from the kitchen."

But as if she were pulled on strings, Fee went straight there, and said, "Hello, Papa." He didn't look up; the only sound from him was his heel hitting the floor.

The screen door at the back porch was blowing open and shut, making little rusty squeaks; she thought of hooking it to stop the noise, but she stood motionless, as if ordered to in gym, arms at her side, head up, eyes front. From the sewing room, Mama's foot on the treadle was tapping out another warning like Fran's. Fee wished she had gone in there instead.

Squeak, went the screen door, squeak-squeak. Her father glanced over at it, and Fee moved forward, glad there was something she could do. As she stepped out on the porch, a gust of wind caught the door and flung it back, flattening it with a bang against the shingles of the house. She had to tug and fight it, as if it were a wrestler determined not to be thrown.

Suddenly in the open doorway she saw her father, his hand high and flat on the inside door, the real kitchen door. He slammed it with such violence that the screen door itself jumped in her hands. She thought, It's a wonder he didn't tear it right out of its socket, and the kitchen door too.

There was a strange prickling all over her as if her father had slammed the other door into a thousand splinters, with all their points touching her skin in a thousand places. I hate him too, she thought, he *is* horrible.

She went down into the back yard and then around the house to the small side entrance. Inside the door there, she could look into the kitchen at a slight angle and still see him. He was back at his reading, as if nothing had happened. He turned a page of the paper and folded it with sharp nervous movements of his hands and sharp creasing pressure of his fingers. The page came loose and stuck out from the others. He tried to straighten it, to align its edges with the edges of the other sheets. But the sliding page stuck out further, refusing to fit back into place as he wanted it to do.

He forced it back, shoving it, pulling it, talking in Russian under his breath at it. It still would not obey and at last he jabbed at it with such force that his fist punched through half the paper. He threw the whole thing down; it slipped off the table, scattering all over the floor at his feet.

Watching from the hall, Fee wanted to rush in and shove him and pull him and jab him the way he was shoving and pulling and jabbing the paper, shooting his hand through it, killing it and letting its insides rip and tear and come out and spill all over the floor.

The familiar sliding howling sound woke her, but she lay rigid and unwilling. This time somebody else would have to go in there; this time she could not be the one. Let him have his nightmare, let the prison guards go on shouting and beating him until he died.

Day after day had gone by since he had started having this mood but nothing had changed. One night Mama was so nervous, she telephoned a candy store on Rivington Street, where they would give a message to her new pupil, Mrs. Godleberg, to tell her not to come out tonight for her lesson. In all those days he only once sounded as if he were in a good mood again, but that was over the telephone to some stranger who had called him about giving some extra lectures in Massachusetts, where everybody was afraid a terrible strike would soon start in the woolen mills.

Fee thought angrily, Strangers never dream how he is with his own family. At the paper, or the people at lecture halls, laughing at his way of putting things, growing serious when he got serious, looking up, adoring Stefan Ivarin . . .

Down the dark hall the sounds swelled and rolled, full-throated and deep and animal. Only in Russian prisons did they flog people with the knout. A knout was a huge rope with thick brutal knots in it.

She jumped up and ran to his room. "Papa, wake up, wake up." As always she had to reach out to touch his shoulder, had to feel his body leap with his last terrible cry.

"All right, all right," he said then. "I had a bad dream."

(1 1 3)

She wanted to turn and go at once, without having to look at him, but he said, "What time is it?" and she knew that next he would tell her to turn on the light so he could look at his watch on the chair at his side.

But he did not. Instead he said dully, "It's very bad," speaking to himself as if he did not know she was there. "It's very bad," he said again, and his voice was the saddest voice she had ever heard.

The words sounded vaguely familiar but she couldn't place them. She tried to ask what was very bad, but she did not. *He is your father and he is a good father . . . you don't think he feels happy either, do you?*

Suddenly her heart filled and she forgave him.

PART

II

T E N

Letty looked down and away. "I can't see what good it would do," she said, "and I'd be so embarrassed."

"Seeing Dr. Haslitt about it?" Garry said unbelievingly.

"Not just 'seeing' him—but talking it all out with him."

"He's talked it all out lots of times, you can be sure of that."

"I suppose he has. But *I* never have."

Despite himself Garry laughed. He had remained mystified at her repeated delays in going to see the doctor about not getting pregnant; she had never told him the real reason before.

"You don't ever have to go if you don't want to, Letty." She looked very young with her averted eyes, and when she thanked him for saying she needn't ever go, he was stirred. She was lovely and appealing, and he should have found fullness in their marriage and everything a man could wish.

And yet so little was of equal importance to each of them. Tonight, coming home from work through the ringing cold of the worst February in years, he had been sure that at the right moment he would talk out his special problem of Aldrich Chemical Co. and what was happening there, but, again he had delayed, and now at the end of dinner he half-hoped the right moment would not come at all.

(1 1 7)

The fire leaping in the old marble fireplace, the warm reds of the draperies Letty had made, swinging slightly with the swoop of the gale through Eleventh Street, even the tree scratching frozenly at their bedroom window in the back of the house, all surrounded him with peace, and he was reluctant to risk it.

When she began to talk about Dr. Haslitt, it was like an unexpected release, and he looked ready to discuss Dr. Haslitt all night. She rarely talked about having a baby any more, and she had stopped reporting to him each month. But tonight when she talked of the doctor, what she said was, "see him about not having a baby."

She was unaware of her phrase, but Garry heard it and his heart contracted that she should use it, instead of saying as she always had, "see him about having a baby."

"Or if you decide to see Haslitt," he said, "I'll go with you. I want to."

She looked forlorn at his ready offer. "Have you been thinking about Dr. Haslitt all along?" she asked, and before he could answer she said, "Oh, Garry, you *are* disappointed about it, only you don't want to make me feel worse, so you never let on or say a word."

"Disappointed in the way you are, nothing else." He waited until she nodded, accepting what he said. "Haslitt might know a specialist to send us to."

"He *is* a specialist."

"Once you're pregnant, yes. But there's a whole new field, a new kind of medical research about why some people don't have children. I mean one of those specialists."

She gazed at him in dismay. "You've been looking into the whole subject," she said. "You've been miserable about it for a long time, and you've been looking into it without telling me."

"I've not been 'looking into' it," he said matter-of-factly. "Just talking it over a bit with Otto; I talk about everything else with Otto, don't I?"

"Otto and Luise have four children," she said, disqualifying Otto by her tone.

Again Garry laughed. She knew what he thought of Otto Ohrmann, and of his envy of Otto's learning in a dozen areas besides chemistry. "I'd have to visit the specialist too, you know, not just you."

"Have to?"

"After Dr. Haslitt saw you, he'd send for me, and then he might know what specialist you should see, and what one I might see."

A look of distaste and panic came to her face. Her unwillingness to have Garry go to any doctor at all became insupportably worse—the notion of what his examination might entail repelled her.

"Let's not think about it any more," she said in sudden entreaty. "It's all mixed up with—with—oh, Garry, I'm starting to feel sort of sick."

She looked away again. Here was the Puritan in Letty, he thought, the New England world of her childhood, dwelling within the modern New York girl she had become.

"I hadn't even dreamed," she said, "of specialists and examinations and all that scientific rigmarole. I'm not old-fashioned, but it's too soon to go to such extremes, isn't it?"

"I didn't mean tomorrow morning. But if we just drift along—"

"Some people get married and have a baby the first year and others wait a while—perhaps they're the luckiest in the long run, not to be raising a family from the first minute."

"They might be," he said easily, though he was vexed. "Any marriage has plenty of problems to iron out first, at that." He thought, This is the right moment after all to tell her about the lab. But the syllables, "the lab," thudded in wooden doubt, and his vexation grew. There were problems you couldn't iron out, it seemed; in any marriage, you also had to keep a lot to yourself, and it could be wearing and abrasive.

"You clam up whenever it suits you," Letty sometimes said; it was an accusation he had heard all his life, from his roommate at college, from his parents, and now from her. He did fall silent, not because it "suited" him, but because he could not help it. When he was annoyed or angry, something snapped shut within him and he had no key that would open the closed place. It was like a time-lock arrangement, with nothing to do but wait. Then whatever had snapped shut finally came open once more.

The telephone rang just then, and Letty reached it first. At her "Hello, Dad," Garry put his hand out for it. He knew it was not her father in Maine; she always called Mr. Brooks "Father," though there was nothing forbidding or formal about him or the way the Brooks children felt toward him.

But Letty ignored his outstretched hand. Instead of her usual, "He's right here," she kept on talking as if the call were meant for her, and as if it were delightful.

"She didn't!" she exclaimed after a moment, her eyes alight. "I can't believe it, Dad . . . did she *really?*"

"What's up, Letts?" Garry said, but she waved him off, clutching the telephone to her breast. "She could have got it from Information, but I'm glad she called you—I'd rather hear this from you first so I can get used to it . . . *How much?* oh, no, I don't believe you."

"Hey!" He made a lunge for the telephone and at last she said, "Here he is, Dad, but please don't give him even a hint. *I* want to tell him."

Garry took the telephone and demanded, "What are you two up to, anyhow?" but he knew he would get no answer. His father's first words to him were interesting enough.

"I may be sent out to California for a couple of weeks, Garry."

"What for, Dad? When?"

"Pretty soon, I think. We had a meeting today and Schroeder suggested it. They've organized a League out there, and he and Abbott thought one of us ought to go out and get to know them, our first affiliate."

"And you're the one they picked!"

"I'm the one IF." Evan sounded cautious, knowing that his very caution would reveal to Garry how much he wanted to go. "The big IF is finances. It would cost a lot, and our year-end report isn't ready yet."

"It's not due until April, is it? They're not going to wait around until April before they decide, are they?"

"Not that long, no." Evan hesitated. "How did you remember April?"

"I don't know. I just did. Suppose I sent in my dues for this year ahead of time—would that tip the scales right away?"

"Not enough, but thanks." He hung up, pleased that Garry remembered just when the Free Speech League had begun. It was like Garry to be imaginative about his parents' interests—many children were not—and Garry always seemed eager to hear about his father's new work as counsel on the special cases handled by the League he had helped organize.

"Hurry," Letty whispered as Garry said good night to his father.

"*You* hurry. What did he tell you?"

"You'll never never guess," Letty said. "It started with a call this afternoon to ask for our number."

"From whom?"

"Mrs. Aldrich."

"Mrs. Aldrich?" He knew of one Mrs. Aldrich only, the wife of his employer.

"Cynthia Aldrich," Letty said, her voice rising. "She wanted to talk to *me.*"

"What *for?*"

"She wants to buy my lowboy."

"Buy it?"

"She saw it just that once," Letty said, stressing each word, "at our lab party. She told Dad she couldn't take her eyes off it all the time they were here. And she's been out hunting the best shops for one ever since. She'll pay me eighty dollars for it—oh, Garry, isn't it crazy?"

He produced a long impressed whistle and she whirled away, crossing to the small chest of gleaming pale walnut in the far corner of the big room. The party had been for Otto Ohrmann and several other lab people and their wives, and Mr. Aldrich had asked if he might drop in for a while. Though his entrance, with Mrs. Aldrich in furs and plumes, had made everybody stiffen up, they had given an extra fillip to the afternoon, a sense of high occasion. And especially for Letty.

Several times Mrs. Aldrich had told her how delightful "the drawing room" was, and several times Letty had caught her gazing at the breakfront, at the lamp tables and particularly at the walnut lowboy, her most recent triumph, a piece she had bought for three dollars from a junk dealer, and then restored with what by now had become almost professional skill.

"Eighty dollars," Letty repeated to Garry slowly. "Mrs. Aldrich said she has a lowboy that's Queen Anne also, and near enough to make a good pair with mine. Ours."

"You say 'mine,' darling. God knows *I* never would have carted the old wreck home, and spent weeks over it the way you did."

"It was so *beautiful.*" She laid one hand on its surface, as if its beauty and sheen were alive.

"And God knows *I* didn't believe you when you first said it was." He went over to the lowboy also, and saluted it.

"Eighty dollars," he said to it wonderingly. Then, turning to her, he saluted again. "Vive Queen Anne. Vive la France. Vive Letty Paige."

"Oh, Gare darling," she cried, "I'm so happy."

The next morning, Evander Paige reached his office half an hour earlier than his usual nine o'clock. He liked the first hour of the day, and he took pleasure in his large office, though he understood that some of their younger clients found a certain old-fashioned look in the suite of rooms occupied by Turner, Paige, Levy and Payson on the third floor of their old building near Trinity Church, and even thought it quaint to have to walk up two flights of stairs.

"But there's nothing quaint about our law," he had said once, for even in their regular flow of work, on the usual fee basis, the four partners were apt to be involved with "modern" cases, akin in spirit to the voluntary work they did on the outside. Most law firms still would not accept a labor union as a client, nor one of the Woman Suffrage groups, but he could never have remained interested in one such, nor done well enough to have become a partner within five years.

All four had their own "hobby" work that they did for motives of their own—Payson with his domestic court cases, Levy with his censorship ones, and Turner with juvenile offenders—but there had been noticeable curves and shifts in his own deep interests. He still devoted a great deal of time to prison and parole cases, but the ones he found most compelling now were these far subtler, far more complex cases usually lumped under the one label, "Free Speech."

It was a natural development, predictable enough perhaps for a man who had gone to Brown before Harvard Law, and who therefore had felt personally involved when the attacks had begun on old Professor Andrews.

"Elisha Ben Andrews, may his tribe increase."

The long-forgotten collegiate jest sounded in Evan's mind, as it had so often in the eighteen-nineties when Andrews, one of the greatest teachers he had ever had, had been so viciously attacked the country over as a scoundrel, a corruptor of student minds and of potential patriots, virtually a traitor. All because he believed in international bimetalism.

Today, in 1912, it was comic to remember the furor over this crime of old Andrews, but in the nineties it had been anything but funny on half the campuses of the United States, in most of the newspapers, and among the agitated members of Brown University's faculty and Board of Trustees.

International bimetalism, Evan thought now. He himself had been a young lawyer then, still conventional enough to be going back to good old Brown each June for Reunion, delighted to see classmates and a few favorite professors. But the increasing conservatism that was supposed to be inevitable as one's youth vanished, had apparently by-passed him, and he remained attached to "radical" ideas like academic freedom and free speech and the waste and futility of war. Not to speak of socialism in general.

All his grandfathers had been rebels, hadn't they, soldiers and officers in the Continental Army in 1776? And much later, all over Roxbury and Newburyport and Boston, his ancestors were noted for their "independence of mind" about nearly everything, including his own mother who flouted the Presbyterianism of her family, became a Unitarian, but still forbade the reading of any secular book on the Lord's Day.

"Good morning, Mr. Paige."

Evan greeted his secretary and entertained the vagrant thought that it was rather quaint to have a young man for a secretary in this day and age. A moment later, his telephone rang, and he picked it up himself. It was one of the League members, but the call was not about his trip to the Coast.

"You're right, Evan," he began. "We are topheavy with lawyers and it's high time we balance out a bit. Did you talk to your friend?"

"I haven't seen him yet—he's only there Friday nights as a rule, or in the afternoons when *I'm* not."

"A morning paper—you did say that."

"Maybe this weekend. He's not a man to rush, anyway; he'll want to consider it."

"It's just that I'd like to know before I start on this new membership drive. In New York at least, his name would help."

"Give me until Monday."

"The Paiges may drop in later," Alexandra said. "I think Evan has some news."

"What kind of news?" Fran asked. News about Garry?

"How should I know till I hear it? But it's nearly noon already, and this place is like a pigsty."

"I hate Saturdays," Fee said, not looking up from the book she was finishing. "Nothing but housework."

"Every family does the heavy cleaning on Saturdays," Alexandra said sternly. "Come, let's do it with a will, and we'll be finished before you know it."

Neither girl stirred. "Do it with a will" was another one of their mother's special phrases like "oh, my goodness" or "it's delicious," and they had learned long ago not to hear it. Fran was trying to repair her ivory-handled nail-buffer, one of the first purchases she had made for herself, now showing its hard use in the greyness of the once-yellow chamois, held taut to the long oval frame by a thin steel hoop.

Alexandra waited patiently for some response from the girls, busying herself with the everyday cleaning up of the breakfast table. As an afterthought, she added, "But Evan's news might have something to do with a nice trip to California for his League."

"To California?" Fran said.

"Alida said last week, they might send him, though he won't know for a while. Maybe by now he does know."

"I'd give a million dollars to go to California," Fran said dreamily, "or to Palm Beach or Paris or Monte Carlo."

Fee turned her book face down on the kitchen table. "Would he go all the way to California in a train?" she asked.

"How else?" Alexandra said.

"Steerage?"

Alexandra laughed. "Steerage isn't a—a *thing* to travel in."

"I know what steerage is," Fee said explosively. "I just said it instead of boat." She was mortified at being caught in an error of language by her mother, an unheard-of turnabout.

"Don't be so sensitive, Fira," Alexandra said. "It's what you've heard so often, 'coming by steerage,' or 'they came by steerage.' Why shouldn't you say 'steerage'?"

"Maybe he'll go by Pony Express," Fran said.

Fee ignored her. "How long does it take to go all the way there in a train, Mama?"

"Five days and five nights," Alexandra said, relieved that Fee's flash of temper had succumbed to the cure-all of new interest, "It must be delicious to spend five days and nights in a big warm train," she said, glancing out at their snow-laden back porch and back yard, the clotheslines bright streaks of ice between the frosted trees. "You sit in a lovely plush seat, or at a real table if you can afford the dining-room car, with a white tablecloth and silver knives and forks, and you look out of a real plate-glass window and watch the scenery going by."

The girls' silence begged her to go on. "All day long the towns go by, and the villages, and the cities, and then the farms get bigger and bigger, as big as whole states, almost. And at night, your seat turns into a berth, curtained off like a queen's bed, and you undress and get in, and read and sleep while the train keeps going, on and on in the darkness."

"How do you know?" Fee said. "Did you ever go to California?"

"I've never been further than Philadelphia and once to Scranton," Alexandra said. "But Papa told me how it is on long Pullman trips, and the rest I know from reading it." She looked fearful that this admission had reduced her status as an authority on transcontinental travel.

"Do lots of people go all the way to California?" Fee persisted.

"If they have money for fare. At last you come to the Rocky Mountains. They're as beautiful as the Alps in Switzerland—and the train crawls around and around, higher and higher until you're in the clouds."

"Does it just go and go, and never stop once, the whole way from here to California?" Fee asked.

"You bonehead," Fran said pleasantly. "It has to stop at stations, doesn't it? Like the el going to New York?"

"It *isn't* like the el. It has a locomotive and sparks flying and black smoke streaming out and winding up to the sky. Hasn't it, Mama?"

"Some day we all must travel," Alexandra said.

"How much would it cost?" Fran asked.

"Heavens, a fortune. But maybe when the mortgage is paid off, and you're both older—" She paused and then went on, the lift of hope in her voice. "We must manage it somehow, and see the Mississippi and the mountains and the deserts and then at last the Pacific Ocean. Just imagine, looking out at big breakers, and knowing it's not Rockaway or Coney, but the Pacific Ocean."

Her eyes gleamed and both girls looked faintly embarrassed. "I'd like to go just for the train ride," Fran said hastily. "It must be fun every second."

"It would be fun to go by motorcycle too," Fee said. "If Eli ever wanted to go, I'd beg him to take me."

"Darling, you'd die of exhaustion before you got halfway there," Alexandra said.

"I would not! Eli says I'm the only one who never gets tired when he gives me a ride."

"You'd sit on those hard stabbing handlebars all the way, with your little legs dangling, I suppose?"

Now Fee sounded superior. "Some motorcycles have a sort of swing on the side, like a short bathtub. Maybe Eli would get one before we started."

Fran snorted in derision. "Eli might take you to California! Eli won't even take us for a ride around *here* any more, he's getting so stuck-up."

Alexandra said, "He's busy. He's trying to get some extra teaching too."

Fran ignored this. "Ever since he became Eli Eaves," she said, "he snoots us about everything."

"Nonsense," Alexandra said briskly. "Now we all have to hurry or we'll never get through before the Paiges ring the bell. Come, both of you."

As she worked, Alexandra thought of a dozen things she herself would ask Evan about, if he were to take the trip she had dreamed aloud for the girls. Silly things, some of them, even embarrassing, like what the Pullman bathroom looked like on the California train, but she could ask the Paiges anything. They had become much closer friends since that night she had maneuvered Stiva into translating his famous editorial for them.

Months ago, that had been, a few weeks after the terrible night of Eli telling about his name. One afternoon the Paiges had stopped by during a walk, as they sometimes did, without telephoning first, and Stefan had been right there when they came in.

He greeted them almost formally and turned away with some flimsy excuse about a rush of work. He was still in his bad mood—that was it; she had forgotten—it was this very visit of Evan and Alida that had finally brought him out of it. Their visit, not to be too modest about it, plus her own sudden inspiration as she saw he meant to leave them to her.

She had given him no time. At once, almost as a greeting, she said, "You know, my dears, Stefan has started something like one of Evan's cases."

"Like a parole case?" Alida asked him, "or a free speech case?"

Stefan stopped; he had no choice. "It's not precisely—"

"Unprecisely then," Evan prompted. "It sounds interesting."

Alexandra avoided Stefan's eyes. "It's like freedom of the press," she said, "for a book he simply detests, that's one reason it's such a vital case, so similar to—"

"Alexandra," Stefan said.

"Yes, yes," she said. "I'll go start some tea; you'll tell it yourself—after all it's *your* editorial, and *your* printing fund."

With alacrity, she left them together, and from the kitchen she could hear him talking about "Assassinate a Book?"—at first reluctantly, then warming up as he gave them the background for it and answered their questions about the public's response to it, and the plan to print the book privately.

Dawdling over the glasses and spoons and biscuits and quince jam, Alexandra smiled. It lifted her heart just to hear Stiva speaking warmly to somebody, talking again in sentences, in lively inflections, not in the dead wood he had been using for speech ever since his mood had begun.

When she judged his improvement irreversible, she went back to the dining room with the loaded tray. As she saw the concentration in their faces and the satisfaction in Stiva's she felt amost a physical jar as the second half of her inspiration nudged her. Without a word of explanation, she departed again, this time to her sewing room.

In a moment she was back, holding out a copy of the *Jewish News,* folded back on itself to an inside page. "Stiva, translate it for them," she said. To Evan and Alida she added, "This is the very editorial. I sometimes save a special article for years."

"Do translate it, Stefan," Alida said.

"Is impromptu translation fair to your work?" Evan asked.

"Fair enough," Stefan said. He took the paper from his wife's hand and read a few lines over to himself. Then he began swiftly, as if he were reading a piece printed in English, "This paper has fought anarchism for twenty years. It still does. Yet it is a shock that in this free country—"

He paused only once or twice to search for a word, to re-phrase a sentence. Evan sat motionless and Alida spoke once. It was after the part about readers who still remembered the tyrannies they had escaped by coming to America. "They say again and again, 'It's a free country,' and their hearts hammer with gratitude and love. But that great banner 'A free country—' "

"It's wonderful, Stefan," Alida murmured. "Truly wonderful."

When the translation ended, Evan sat on without speaking. He looked at the folded newspaper, then at Stefan, then at the newspaper once more as if its physical size and conformation interested him.

"Stiva," he said at last, "would you write it out for me, when you can find time?"

Alexandra thought, He's never called him Stiva before.

"Write out the translation?" Ivarin said. "Yes, of course, yes, if you want it. I confess I'm pleased that you do."

"I'd like to show it to the League people. And to some of my law partners."

Evan had twenty copies made at his office, and had circulated them among everybody he knew; he even sent a few out to California, to the new group of Free Speech people who were organizing their own League there.

With a start, Alexandra returned to the present, to the mop in her hand. She had forgotten the cleaning, remembering that other visit of the Paiges and forgetting the one they were paying today.

She began to slash around her with the oiled mop, sliding it over the parquet squares of the floor as if she were in a race. Last-minute cleaning was so undignified—she disliked it on principle. Rushing against time, so as not to be caught at it by the expected guest or pupil. Or was there a hidden snobbery behind it—hating to be caught red-handed with this proof that she didn't have a nice Polish servant girl to do it for her?

Outrageous idea! She slashed the mop around twice as fast.

Fee raced for the front door at the ring of the bell. "Do you know yet, Mr. Paige?" she cried, while Evan and Alida were still on the porch, stamping the snow from their rubbers. "Are you going in a train all the way to California?"

"Fira," Alexandra said. "Can't you wait until they're in the house before firing your questions?"

"Yes, I am, Fee," Evan answered. "It was settled at last."

"When? Tomorrow?"

Her mother was welcoming the Paiges now, but Fee kept talking to Evan as if nobody else existed.

"I have to wait a while," he said. "A case of mine finally reached court, and I can't drop it flat and go."

"You can't?" Fee asked unbelievingly. Her father came down and it became clear soon that whatever Mr. Paige did want to talk about wasn't his trip at all. Fee knew with the familiar falling weight inside her, that it would be the kind of talk where children didn't count.

"Come on," she whispered to Fran.

Fran shook her head. She thought of her birthday party at the beach, and the churning rolling excitement in listening to Garry talk about the railroad strikes in England and Ireland. Perhaps listening to Garry's father would start up the same wonderful feeling.

"Stefan, I said on the phone I had something I wanted to tell you about."

"Alexandra was sure it was your trip."

"It would have been about that too," Evan said.

Hastily, Alida said, "If I hadn't told Alexandra about it first."

Both men smiled at this flutter of apology and Stefan said to Alexandra, "So you're not the only chatterbox! Forgive me, Alida."

They separated for a moment into two men united in common cause against two women, then at once joined again as two couples, four neighbors.

"Come on, Franny," Fee whispered again.

"Don't pester me. You go, if you want."

Alexandra said, "Franny, we might ask the Paiges if they'd want you to go out for a while, don't you think so?"

"Not at all," Evan said before Fran had time to resent being chided, "but I don't imagine the girls will be interested." He had grown serious and addressed himself directly to Stefan, and Fran settled back in triumph over her mother.

"What I want to discuss, Stefan," Evan Paige said, "is something important to me, and to the League. We have too many lawyers and we need editors, writers, lecturers. We need to find the right man, and nominate him and elect him as a member of our Board."

"And you want Stefan," Alexandra said, her pleasure uncomplicated and unconcealed.

"Not just I," he answered. "When I told Theodore Schroeder and Brand Whitlock and Abbott about knowing Stefan—they wanted him as much as I do."

Stefan, too, was pleased—Paige would not imply that Whitlock and Abbott and the rest knew of him unless it were so, but a frown pulled together the lines above his nose.

"I'm not the man for it," he said.

"Oh, Stefan, my dear," Alida said, her color rising a little, "you are just the man for it, just the man they want." As she ended, she saw the intent faces turned to her, and she looked flustered.

"Now, girls," Alexandra said, "I think we'd like to discuss this by ourselves."

"Please," Fran said, "just a little while longer. Mr. Paige said—"

"No, dear," Alexandra said calmly. "Now, we want to be down here ourselves."

"But, Mama," Fee protested. She still wished Fran weren't pig-headed about staying, but being put out was another matter.

"Now, now," Alexandra said, standing up and signaling to Stefan to leave this familiar business to her. "We've had this before. I don't hang around when Trudy is here to make fudge, do I, Fee? Not every single minute until you scrape the pot? Or you, Franny, when you come home after school with Jack Purney—"

"Oh, all right," Fran interrupted, to head off any Mama-ish comments about Jack. "Come on, Fee."

She walked off in ladylike poise, Fee at her side, but when it was safe, she made a face of deadly disapproval in the direction of her parents and their friends. Fee giggled. Fran glided toward the door and then ran up the stairs two at a time. Fee raced after her, stopping only to unlock the back door, whistle for Shag, and let him dash up at her side as if he too were glad to escape the dopey world of parents.

Downstairs, Stefan repeated more firmly, "No, I'm really not the man for it. By nature, I'm sorry to say, I don't work well any more in a committee. When I was young, at the University of Odessa, with Drubhinov and the others—there, to work together was priceless; we all found it so."

"It *is* harder to be flexible as we grow older," Paige conceded. "But I am sure you would be flexible enough, Stefan; this is a rather remarkable group."

"That's the trouble," he said. " 'A remarkable group.' I'm too used to being on a lecture platform, perhaps, the kingpin for a lot of poor devils, too hortatory perhaps, too much the eternal teacher, you follow me?"

At his last three words, Ivarin suddenly laughed, holding up a cautionary finger. "See there? I didn't mean it, it slipped out, it's the betrayer, the trademark of the lecturer and the teacher. 'You follow me' indeed."

Paige laughed also, his eyes lighting with a private pleasure in the way Ivarin's mind operated. "It is the phrase of a teacher," he said comfortably. "But they know about you and what you do. And they want you very much. By now they are counting on it."

"I thank you," Stefan said. "I thank them." He shoved his tea from him, stood up, and began pacing back and forth on a small track, remaining part of the group, yet finding the comfort of motion he so often needed. By now, both Paiges had become accustomed to this habit, and neither one remarked it as they had done in the first stages of their friendship, when it had invariably made them wonder if he had grown so restless that they ought to take their leave at once. Now they merely watched him idly, as if he were polishing his glasses or rolling a cigarette.

Alexandra said, to nobody in particular, "It is only a phrase, after all. They want him as he is."

"Yes, yes, I don't doubt it," Stefan answered vigorously. To Evan, he said, "You will be able to explain to them, I'm sure. They will understand, because—if I am wrong, please correct me—because *you* understand."

Evan nodded. He looked up at Ivarin affectionately, not challenging or pursuing the discussion. Then he said simply, "We need your help, Stefan."

Ivarin stopped pacing. "I'm not refusing to help." He sat down at the table, addressing himself to Evan with heightened seriousness. "There is another point, if I may raise it."

"Please do."

"Aside from my own fitness or unfitness, I must tell you—I disagree that your League needs writers and editors to mix in with its lawyers."

"But we're topheavy with lawyers, and we could be more effective in our work if—"

"Permit me, less effective by far!"

"Why less?" Paige asked, nettled. "You seem so positive."

"Your Free Speech League can be effective only *if* it stays topheavy with lawyers. Your work is with courts and judges, with witnesses and juries—the devil with adding members who cannot work inside courts and who are not qualified to deal with judges and juries."

"I see what Stefan means, I think," Alida said dubiously. Alexandra agreed, but a wary expectancy stood in her heart.

"I see too, and I disagree with every word of it," Evan said flatly. "You're dismissing writers pretty lightly, and editors and lecturers. You also overlook the weight of what people think after they read and hear them."

"Of course not." Ivarin stressed each word. "Of course I am not."

"But you do dismiss them from our Board," Evan said, also with extra vigor. "Rather high-handed, I would say."

"They would add nothing but talk and more talk." Stefan leaned forward across the table. "They'd be nice willing believers in free speech who would hamstring your specialists in endless ropes of words and clever suggestions. Throw them out in advance, I tell you."

Suddenly Evan Paige laughed. It was the laugh of a man amused and pleased, free of irony, free of resentment.

Alexandra glanced quickly at him and then at Alida. Both of the Paiges were worked up, in much the same way as they got worked up over pacifism, about which she and Stefan could never agree with them. It was a level-temperature "worked up" that was as foreign to Stefan or to herself as cool water to boiling oil. A moment ago, when Evan had been irritated, and showed it, he still was anchored to some solid reserve underneath. With the Paiges, the fear of a scene never occurred to you. It was remarkable.

Was this one more result of being born in America instead of in excitable Russia? For a moment there stirred in her the old forgotten sense of apology about being "a foreigner among real Americans."

"You fooled me, Stefan, by your sudden attack," Evan said. "But I just remembered the basic point: you did say you would help."

"I was never refusing that, you understand," Ivarin said. His words were quietly spoken again, as if in a victory he did not want to press. "If there is a free-speech case someday, that you are angry

(131)

about, you might perhaps like me to write about it." He glanced at Evan with a new gleam in his eyes, and added, "Even though I'm not also on your Board, talking. You follow me?"

Again Evan Paige laughed, but this time he stretched in his chair, his left hand kneading the back of his neck as if it had felt cramped for a long time.

Aloud he said only, "Yes, I might like it, Stiva." He thought, We are so different, but at bottom we're allies.

Upstairs Fee said to Fran, "Why does Mrs. Paige stay so thin, while Mama stays so fat?"

"Keep quiet," Fran answered from the doorway. "I think Mr. Paige and Papa are having a fight. It would be fun, wouldn't it?"

"You're spooky," Fee said, trying to see how Shag would look in her navy-blue middy. When the flannel touched his ears, he flung himself free of middy and Fee both. She righted herself on the floor, and he lay full length beside her, his tail thumping, his dark eyes fixed on hers.

At the door, Fran said, "Shag, stop that noise," but it was no use. That one promising flare-up downstairs had led nowhere; now they were all back to company-is-here voices; Papa never shouted at the Paiges or anybody Christian the way he shouted at the family or people from the paper or the unions.

"Can't Mama stop being fat *ever?*" Fee asked when Fran finally deserted the doorway.

"She's not fat. She's just stretched out."

"What stretches her?"

"I've told you a million times, and you can't remember a thing."

"You haven't told me a million times! You don't ever finish."

Fran sighed in exaggerated woe. "All those baby questions."

"They're not baby! You just want to get my goat."

Fran waved four fingers languidly, and then took up her nail-buffer, still unmended. She pried its steel hoop off and tried shifting the chamois so that the grey nubbled part would move off dead center and be replaced by a smoother part. But then she could not slip the hoop back. "Pull on this side, will you?" she said. "Then maybe it'll stay put while I get this metal thing back on."

"If you tell me, I'll pull it for you," Fee said, looking at the buffer with professional competence. The steel hoop fell to the floor and in despair Fran said, "Oh God, I just hate the old thing." Fee took the denuded buffer from Fran's discouraged grasp, saying conversationally, "What *did* stretch Mama out?" Her conciliatory tone implied, This is a fair offer; accept it and it'll be good for both of us.

"When you're having a baby," Fran started tentatively.

"The baby is inside you," Fee said energetically. Don't start with that stupid old stuff. But Mrs. Paige had a baby inside her twice, and she didn't get stretched."

Fran was nonplused at this crisp exposition and hesitated over her next words. At once Fee set down the buffer.

"Go on," she ordered. *"Why* didn't she?"

"Mrs. Paige was allowed to wear a special thing," Fran said, "and Mama wasn't. That's why Mrs. Paige didn't and Mama did."

"What sort of special thing?"

"A maternity corset."

"Why don't you stretch in it?"

"It holds up your stomach when you get bigger and bigger, the way Joan got. Remember?"

"Sure I do. Did Joan wear it? I never saw it."

"Joan wouldn't leave it around where anybody could *see* it. They're horrible big pink things with a million laces up the back and a sort of pouchy balloon up front."

Fran made a face and Fee said, "Icky." She was pressing the hoop in place, along one side of the frame, and now she gripped an edge of the dirty chamois with her teeth, pulling back on it hard. The hoop clicked; the chamois held; though the tapered ends of the buffer were uncovered, the buffing center was smoothly yellow.

"Goody," Fran said admiringly. "Oh, Fee, you're grand."

"Right up in front of you like this?" Fee said, touching her finger tips and extending her curved arms forward as far as they would go.

"Not up at your shoulders. It has to hold you *up* so the baby won't stretch and sag you way way way down to your knees."

Fee again said, "Icky," and looked down at her knees apprehensively as if she were fearful that her own small stomach would be billowing about her kneecaps.

Fran said, "Not exactly knees, either. It straps you up *under,* and holds you up so your stomach won't go floppy forever. Like this."

Fran placed her arms hard against her sides, elbows close in over her hipbones, making a basket-like circle of her arms, a sling to support a mighty weight.

Fee watched in total interest. "You're a good explainer," she said warmly. "I wish I could just ask you one tiny other thing."

"Well, you can't," Fran said.

"Why not?"

"Because."

Fee lunged at the buffer but Fran said, "You know something?"

"I don't want to hear it."

"I think Papa has a crush on Mrs. Paige."

"You *what?*" Fee cried out.

"I think he's got a real crush on her," Fran repeated, relishing the sensation she had made. "And I think she has a crush on him. Did you hear her down there? 'Oh, Stefan, my dear, you are just the man for it, just the man they want.' " Fran let her voice climb, in mimicry of Alida.

Fee looked stricken. "Don't do that, Franny," she said.

"And did you see her blush while she said it to him? She always blushes now when she so much as looks at him."

Fee clapped her palms to her ears and shouted, "I said *don't.*"

"Old people can fall in love too," Fran went on authoritatively, "and I think Papa has a crush on her for fair, and—"

"He couldn't have," Fee whispered. "He just couldn't." Suddenly she burst into tears. She heard Fran's exasperated, "For Pete's sake," but she couldn't help it.

The idea was so horrible, so overwhelming that her heart exploded with pain. Papa *couldn't* have a crush on Mrs. Paige, he couldn't, he couldn't. He loved Mama, and if he had a crush on anybody else in the whole world, then he couldn't love Mama any more.

A desolation struck at her, over and around her like a frozen lake closing over her head. In this bottomless icy sinking, she knew Fran was talking to her, but the separate words could not get through the numb and icy skin encasing her.

Fran suddenly put an arm around her. "I'm sorry I said it, Fee—I didn't think you'd take it so awfully."

Fee leaned against her. It was new to have Fran so sorry about something she had done to her, but she couldn't stop crying. She saw her middy blouse on the floor and at last she put it on again, as if it were morning and she were dressing for school. Then she started for the door, not knowing why she wanted to get out of the room or where she wanted to go.

"Fee," Fran said in an urgent whisper, "are you going down and do anything crazy?"

"No."

"It'll be terrible if you do."

"I won't." She started slowly down the stairs, holding the banister and going down one at a time, still now knowing why she was going. She would not go into the dining room where they were, but she could not turn around and go back either. Every third or fourth breath she took came out in a long pulling flutter, but she opened her lips, so it made no sound. On the bottom step, she could hear them: they were talking about the frightful strikes in the woolen mills in New England, and the lecture Papa had given up there, and the extra lectures he was going to go back and give every minute he could until the strike was won.

"It's been nearly a month already, hasn't it? How long can those poor people hold out?"

That was Mrs. Paige, in her familiar soft voice, and the sound of it pulled Fee down from the step to the little hall and past the edge of the open dining-room door.

Mrs. Paige was facing her, but she wasn't looking toward the doorway. Her eyes were unhappy, and she sighed, and made little sounds of worry and sympathy. But the one she was talking to was Mama, not Papa. The one she was looking at was Mama, not Papa. It was Mama's answer she was waiting for, about how long the poor people could hold out. She wasn't even bothering with Papa.

And Papa wasn't bothering with her. He was standing over by the window, making a cigarette, and talking to Mr. Paige.

Suddenly Fee's heart jumped and danced and glistened. They were all just the way they always were, so it wasn't true. She raced upstairs to tell Fran.

ELEVEN

During the night it snowed, so heavily that neither the morning milk nor the newspaper had yet arrived when they waked up. For the first time since they had moved into the apartment, the heat coming up was slow and inadequate, knocking against the pipes in thumps of protest that the task assigned on this bitter morning was too great.

Garry said, "Don't get up yet. Let's have a fire in here and feel pampered."

"Ooh," Letty said.

He built a husky fire. In the small fireplace in their bedroom, the logs they always used seemed massive, but this was the first fire they had ever had while they were in bed, and they found it intimate and charming.

"I could bring our breakfast in here," Letty said, not moving. She gazed past him to their stretch of garden. "Maybe you can't get to the lab at all today," she said. "Just look at it out there."

The garden lay foamy and glistening under their windows. Where drifts had sloped up against the dark-green wood fence separating the Tenth Street gardens from their own and from their neighbors, he could have stood in snow up to his shoulders. For a moment, as he put on his bathrobe near the frost-traced windows, he wished he could keep away from Aldrich today, and wander about the city's muted, fluffy streets instead.

A brisk ring at the bell told him the newsboy had come at last, and he ran down for the paper, hoping as always that he wouldn't be caught in his bathrobe by the owner of the house or by another tenant. Every morning since they had moved in last summer, he had run the same risk.

The *Morning World* welcomed the snow too, it appeared; its front page had been blown nearly clear of its usual grey freight of warnings and reports and threats from Germany and Italy and Turkey and the rest of Europe. There was the fresh sweep of the blizzard instead, pictures of impassable streets, of stranded carriages, hatted and cloaked in billowing white, of trolleys and store windows grotesque or beautiful in arabesques and swirls of snow and splinters of ice.

He raced up the steps in the draughty hall of the old mansion. The headlines said the blizzard would probably last until night and the cold wave most of the week. He was glad. It was a sort of recess provided by God. He had still not discussed the continuing rumors at the lab with Letty.

She was no longer in bed, but in the window-missing kitchenette, wearing her blue robe of a thin flowered wool, ruffled at the hem; it couldn't possibly be warm but it was pretty and becoming. She looked as she had looked since the sale of her lowboy a few days ago, happy and self-important and full of achievement.

He returned to the bedroom, pulled the one armchair close to the fireplace, the newspaper on his knees, still folded as if it had no interest beyond the pictures of the storm. It wouldn't be the right moment to have a serious discussion, he thought. He stared into the fire and wondered how one knew rightness or wrongness of moments.

"Queen Anne, ma'am" he called out, "where's that coffee?" She said, "You're so silly," in a voice he hadn't heard in a long time, the voice of just-meeting, of flirtation, the voice of that first summer in Maine.

For an instant the white brilliance of the snow gave way to the green and blue of a lake under a summer sky, and a shaft of longing bit into him, to have that Maine summer again, warm and beneficent, free of problems, filled only with a wild desire and the leap of love.

He unfolded the paper, and turned to the news which the blizzard had displaced.

LORD HALDANE REJECTS BERLIN DEMAND

The smaller headlines and subheads tumbled after the main one: Haldane, of the British War Office, had gone to Berlin for unofficial talks with German ministers, hoping to reach an understanding to ease the tension between the nations.

Germany demanded a guarantee that Britain would stay neutral in any war "into which Germany might be drawn."

Lord Haldane had summarily refused.

The War Office would issue Britain's formal refusal before the day was over.

Instantly Garry froze in the grip of unwillingness to accept the news, the real news, the endless news that had piled shoulder-high in every paper for the past weeks, months, years . . . demands, rejections, treaties, armies, navies, the Triple Entente, the Entente Cordiale, the Kaiser, the Czar, the King, the Generals . . .

Letty came in, carrying a tray with her prettiest china, fragile and translucent. He watched her pour their coffee, and said, "I wonder if the rink in Central Park is going to be cleared off by afternoon."

"They sweep it the minute the snow lets up," Letty said. She was an expert skater and loved skating "spang in the middle of the city." "You're not going to go to work today," she added, positively. "I can tell."

"I have to try."

"Not too hard though."

"I may not be going to Aldrich much longer, anyway."

"What does that mean?"

"That I'm pretty sure I'll quit soon and find a job somewhere else."

"Quit?" She refilled his cup. "But why?"

There were no easy words. This was what stayed unsaid when he felt that so little seemed of equal importance to each of them. For months now, whenever he had tried to share with her his uneasiness about Aldrich's emerging plans, Letty willfully, or in an amazing lack of perception, would brush it aside as "just worrying" or else listen with a patient indulgence that reduced his words to mere petulance.

"It's hard to explain, but it's wrong for somebody like me, and I don't think any more that it might get right. It's about their converting the business to synthetics."

"You said that was marvelous."

"I still would. But now it looks as if that's being by-passed completely."

"You said the new plant was purposely for that."

"But things are changing so fast that Aldrich is changing pretty fast too. They're going to make explosives instead."

She started to deny it, as if she knew their plans. He told her of new shipments of cellulose and of the absence of comparable quantities of sodium hydroxide and carbon disulphide for turning cellulose into the artificial silk that had become his specialty for the past fourteen months.

"We're getting sulphuric acid and nitric acid instead," he said. "Do you know what you get from cellulose when you go at it with those two?"

She shook her head. She hated this talk; she hated having to have it now when they had been so happy.

"You get something they used to call 'guncotton,' " Garry went on. "The technical name is cellulose trinitrate, also trinitrotoluol."

"Are they explosives?"

"They can make bombs that could blow up a field full of soldiers."

She glanced down at the newspaper, and hated it too. In it was the timing mechanism that had set off this talk at a moment when she couldn't force herself to think of such things. How could he?

Garry began once more. He went through everything he had told her, this time making it as non-technical as he could, though he knew that Letty had acquired far more knowledge of chemistry than she suspected, and of the chemical research into new processes and new products that had been so absorbing to him ever since he had been promoted past his first work of making collodion and other drug products that bore the Aldrich label.

"Otto and I," he added, "have facts to go on, not just suspicions. There's nothing secret about any of this, if you put it all together. The Acids fellow showed Otto the jump in our in-shipments, and Barclay bragged to me about the huge new orders on his books."

"Who's Barclay?"

"That fat salesman. He's head of sales now, and pleased as Punch."

She understood why Barclay was, and why everybody but Garry would be pleased as Punch too. Each month Aldrich grew, its profits and sales grew; the new plant was to be twice as large as this one. People were always getting raises, new people were being hired, Garry was making more than they had dared hope even a year ago.

"So now you know," Garry ended. "If they *are* converting to explosives a hundred per cent, that's the end of it for me. For Otto too."

There was silence. Letty thought, But maybe they won't. Even big companies change plans when their calculations take new turns and new directions.

She wondered whether to say that; she stole a glance at him; he shook his head and drew his breath deeply, as if he were tired.

"There," she said.

The single word pulled him up short. She had said it soothingly, sweetly, as if to say, "You'll feel better now for having talked it all out with me."

"Damn it," he said, and stood up abruptly, not looking at her, and went to the windows.

It had begun to snow again, but the wind had dropped; the flakes were aimless, uncertain. The garden looked melancholy now.

Letty could resist his deepest needs, as he could resist hers, by being willing but unable to feel them. She wanted to understand and share each single emotion, belief, conviction that he held, but she could not because they were too alien to her own interior conformation.

Just as he wanted to achieve a sharing passion for shining silver and crystal, for furniture that was old and honored by use and time, and just as he failed to know what she reveled in or despaired over.

Behind him, he heard the pages rustle. She did try to share his interest in the news; if he began now to discuss Haldane with her, she would listen like a dutiful child, eager to please him. A dozen times he had decided not to discuss what she called "politics" at home, and at last it was becoming second nature to wait until he could talk to Otto or to his parents or to some of his other friends who also were gripped by the rise and fall of drama in the dispatches and headlines.

The small clock on the bureau struck eight. "I'd better try to make it to the lab," he said. Her face was sad and he thought, I've ruined her morning. An impulse drove him to close the distance between them, and without planning to, he said, "Listen to this," took up the paper and read aloud the headlines on Lord Haldane. Then he began to read the story itself to her. In a moment he forgot why he was doing it, he forgot himself, forgot Letty; the lines of type were straight magnets drawing him one by one to the end.

Only then did he glance at her. She sat erect, her face squeezed and tight, her eyelids pressed shut as if to avoid any glimpse of him, lost in news she could not follow and danger she could not believe in.

"I didn't mean to read all of it," he said. "I get carried away with it because if there should be war in Europe—"

"War, war, war," she said dully. "It's all you ever think about."

"That's not fair. You know it isn't."

She didn't acknowledge or disavow it, but her rigid body and un-yielding voice held neither truce nor forgiveness.

"It's you and me I think of," he went on. "Our life would change if there was a war and America got into it."

"So would everybody else's life."

"But ours in a different way."

"Because you wouldn't enlist?" she said. "That's what you say now. You might change."

Anger whipped him. "I will not change," he said. It sounded too noble. "I don't *think* I'll change, let's put it that way. That's why—when I think ahead—that's why I want—"

"You want," she burst out. "It's always what *you* want, and what you believe, and *your* ideas about the factory and explosives and Germany and England and being a pacifist and Heaven knows what else."

He was astonished. She never accused and blamed; yet this tirade came smoothly, as if she had long rehearsed her bill of grievances, and could recite it fluently, with no pause to search for an item or a word.

It was bitter, this discovery, bitter in a deeper place than any other where pain had yet reached him. In the living room, the sharp bell of the telephone rang out like a cry, and he sped toward it as if toward someone in catastrophe.

A moment later, he called out, his voice false-gay for the benefit of the receiver in his hand, "It's an admirer of yours, darling, Mrs. Aldrich."

The office was in an uproar. To Stefan Ivarin, it was contemptible to be discussing sales problems when a great strike was involved, but thus far there was no sign that Joseph Fehler would yield, and he himself saw not the remotest chance of giving in on an issue of this kind.

To this meeting of the policy staff, Isaac Landau had also invited the two writers who were the paper's special reporters on the city's unions and on labor matters in general, as well as his lawyer, Joseph Steinberger, who had been in his office most of the day. The writers as well as Ivarin, Fehler and Abe Kesselbaum were all arguing at once.

Landau thwacked his desk with the flat of his hand for quiet, but nobody heeded him. He raised his voice, but his words carried no solidity. This was his first week back at the paper after a debilitating stay at Polyclinic Hospital for tests and treatment of his recurrent stomach trouble, and so turbulent a meeting tired him. Like all people, the others had forgotten that he was still weak; each of them was intent only on his own words, his own beliefs.

"It does make a difference to our readers," Fehler was saying to Ivarin for the third time. "They live right here in New York and they're sick of the Lawrence strike by now. Look at the newsstands if you won't take my word for it."

"The newsstands!" Ivarin said irritably. "The returns. The sales sheet for this week, for last week."

"This is the fifth week!" Fehler instantly answered.

Isaac Landau thumped his desk twice with his fist, using it as a gavel. Pain stung his flesh but this time they heard him and came to some semblance of order. Ivarin said, "Itzak, don't get worn out, it's too soon for you," and his concern in the midst of turmoil shook Landau unexpectedly. He was always uneasy when the business side of newspaper life was forced on Ivarin; occasionally in the past he had asked Fehler if he could manage not to discuss figures, sales, costs, profits with Stefan. But such matters did need to be brought up at the monthly meeting of the policy staff, and this time, unhappily enough, he himself agreed with Fehler rather than with Ivarin, a state of affairs that added to his private wretchedness.

He looked about him, reassessing the chance of a clear-cut decision, if he were to cut short the meeting and call for a vote. Abe Kesselbaum, a member of the group only since last November, had made it clear enough that he stood with Ivarin; the two reporters had no vote. But if they had, the split would continue, for one of them seconded Fehler's complaint that the paper had played up the Lawrence strike too insistently.

"The fifth week," Fehler repeated. "Did I raise any sales questions the first week, the second, even the third?"

"A noble silence," Ivarin said. "Thank you."

Fehler flushed. "This is a New York newspaper," he went on, "not a Lawrence newspaper or a Boston newspaper or a special organ for labor. It is a daily *news*paper, for all the news every day."

"We carry nothing on Page One except Lawrence, Mass. I see."

Ivarin said "Lawrence Mass" as if it were a hyphenated term; since the middle of January when the strike had started in the first of the mills, the three syllables had taken on a new identity, a trio in a tragic key. Often the chords of protest and refusal had blended with those of hunger, despair, sometimes violence. But though two hundred thousand strikers and their families were now penniless, the bleat of surrender had not yet been heard.

To Stefan Ivarin, it was unthinkable that his readers, so many of them workers and their families who had lived through strikes themselves, would or could stay deaf to a private clamor of recognition as they read about those on strike in another city.

"Fehler wasn't being literal when he said the readers are sick of the strike," Landau said pacifically. "He's raising a question of the future. If the strike went on for another five weeks, let's say, or ten weeks, then what?"

Fervently Fehler said, "This question of the 'future' is here already. Not one edition has sold out on the stands for six days. They see headlines about Lawrence and they think it's yesterday's paper."

Ivarin pushed back his chair.

"Are we to worry about selling out editions—or selling out labor?" He stood up, replacing his fountain pen in his vest pocket, and turned to Landau with finality. "You know how my vote will go. I'll miss my train if I don't get to my desk. By the way, I think your young man Borg will develop very well. He's still fumbling a bit, but an assistant is a godsend just now." He gave the room a general nod of farewell and left.

"Your suitcase, Mr. Ivarin," Abe Kesselbaum called out as he reached the door. "Let me."

"I have it." He had come straight from the street to Landau's office for the meeting, and his bulky suitcase stood just beyond the arc made by the opening or closing door. He had tossed his overcoat and hat atop the bag, and now the mound of evidence at his feet testified to the arduous trip ahead, the two days and nights of lectures, meetings, discussions with local authorities, harangues with the men leading the strike. Extremists too, the I.W.W., but in a different sense from Fehler's extremists.

. . .

At supper on his first night at home again, Stefan Ivarin saw without surprise that the girls were forcing themselves to appear interested in his report of his trip. It did not offend him; it was to be expected in youngsters. But this was one time it disappointed him.

Alexandra hung on each detail, asking, prompting, urging him to go on whenever he paused for a forkful of food. But Francesca and Fee, saying "Oh" or "Gee" at what they deemed the appropriate places, soon took on the glassy look of dutiful listeners. As he talked, he wondered how to break through the glaze and reach them.

"There was a little boy caught cheating on the bread line," he said ostensibly to Alexandra. "There was a hullaballoo, I can tell you."

"Cheating how?" Fran asked.

"What did he do, Papa?" Fee added.

"He had a plaid coat," Stefan said, "a lumberman's jacket, I think they call it. He wolfed down his bowl of soup before he was off the line for more than one minute. Then he stood right near the big steaming pots, watching every ladleful."

"Couldn't he get any more?" Fee asked.

He shook his head. "So at last, he turned his plaid coat inside out to disguise himself, and went back to the end of the line."

"Poor child," Alexandra said.

"But the plaid squares showed through the cloth, his coat was so threadbare. Just behind him there was a woman. She saw the squares—"

He looked at Fran and then at Fee. Why did it matter so immensely tonight that he had found the way to their involvement? He was no Alexandra, proselytizing in all directions at all times.

"This woman had four children of her own—and when she saw the inside-out squares she knew what the boy was doing. She screamed at him and cursed him, and hit him. She threw him off the line, acting like a wild animal, as if she didn't know a child could be so hungry he would try anything for a little more food."

"Oh, the poor starving child," Alexandra said. "How old was he, Stiva?"

"Six or seven."

"How much food is he supposed to get, Papa? Couldn't they give him a little more?"

That was Francesca, looking more sympathetic than she usually did about the hardships of strikers and their families. He had never been moralistic about blaming any of the children if they stayed remote from the hardships of workers in sweatshops or workers out of jobs or workers on strike; from babyhood they had heard about all of it so often that perhaps a new tale of poverty and struggle was like crying "Wolf." But Fran's face now struck him as sweeter, even prettier, than it had ever been; it had a warm and loving softness that was new.

"They have no more to give him," he said. "Thousands and thousands are on the bread lines and at the soup kitchens. Men, women, boys, girls, babies, grandfathers, grandmothers—almost nobody has a scrap of food in their house any longer."

"Do they die, Papa?" Fee asked.

"Some have already, babies mostly, of malnutrition and cold. It was five above zero both nights."

Alexandra shuddered, and glanced at the silver radiator near the kitchen window. "What happened to the little boy in the plaid coat?"

"One of the women at the relief station took him home. There's a new committee being formed now, to search out any families who could take in a striker's child, perhaps two, as long as it goes on."

"Anybody with a shred of humanity—" Alexandra said.

"It's not just humanity; it also is sound strike-strategy." Almost as if the girls weren't in the room, he added, "I don't know if *I* could stand firm and not surrender to the owners by now, if I knew my little girls were so hungry."

He spoke gruffly and Fee stared at him in surprise. Would he really choke up about her and Franny and lose a strike because of them? Even if all his own ideas were mixed up in it? It was a new idea, a new possibility, exciting in a new way. She almost wished she could get right on a bread line or into a soup kitchen, and turn her coat inside out, just to put Papa to the test.

When it came right down to it, she decided, her spirit sinking, he probably would stand firm day after day. Even if she turned into a skeleton right in front of him, he would never let the owners win and let the workers lose.

Principles came first. No matter what, if you had a principle, it came ahead of everything and everybody.

"If this new plan to board out the children does go through," he said to Alexandra, "we'll take a child in with us, won't we?"

"Here? So far from home for them? Oh my goodness, of course!" She sat up straight, her entire bearing expectant and active. "Why, I thought you meant only in Lawrence, in the neighbors' houses there."

"It started that way, but it's no longer enough. Nearly everybody is hit by now, and some families who did take in a child are forced to send him back."

(144)

"Why are they all hit, Papa?" Fee asked. "Is everybody a striker?"

He shook his head, not in negative reply to her question but at his own difficulty. How to explain enough and not too much? How discourse to children on wages and hours and exploitation?

"At the start only the workers in three mills went on strike," he said. "Eleven thousand spinners and weavers. But on the very first day there were riots and violence—"

"What kind of violence?" Fran wanted to know. "Who did it?"

"At first, the workers, I'm afraid. They were so furious—they had hoped for so long to escape a strike, and when it came they hurled their bobbins and shuttles around, they cut pulleys and opened sprinklers, they smashed windows and gates—"

"And the company police," Alexandra put in bitterly, "instantly began smashing heads with nightsticks and pistols. A fair exchange."

"Did they?" Fee and Fran asked together.

Ivarin nodded. "That was at American Woolen, a big company. Then strikes or lockouts started at smaller places, the Pacific Cotton Mills and the Everett and Arlington Cotton Mills. Not only spinners and weavers, but carders and teasers and twisters and blenders and rovers and felters and strippers and winders—every kind of worker everywhere, in a dozen different towns."

"What they are striking for is a living wage!" Alexandra said. "When you're older, you'll realize what it is to work yourself to death and yet not earn the barest living wage."

The girls hardly heard her; they both concentrated on Stefan, as if they had never known him to speak before.

"So you see why the neighbors are hit too," he said, also ignoring Alexandra's interpolation. "Every grocer used to sell to the workers; now he can't sell anything. Nor can the butcher, or coal dealer, or kerosene dealer, the milkman, the bakery store—it's hard times for all of them."

"Do they get on the bread lines too?" Fee asked.

"Will it stop soon?" Fran wanted to know.

Stefan shook his head, this time meaning "no" for each question. He looked angry, and he sounded angry when he spoke. "Whenever the papers say a blizzard is coming, or a new cold snap, the bosses of the mills stiffen up on the smallest demand we're making."

"Brutes," Mama said. "Every one of them must have a heart of steel and iron."

"Is every boss a brute, Mama?" Fee asked.

"Not every one, no," her mother said, going to the window and looking anxiously out at the starless February sky, begging it not to send more blizzards, more gales, more zero nights.

"Isn't there one *good* one anywhere?" Fee persisted.

"Yes, darling, I suppose there must be."

"Are all workers good? And all strikers?"

"Of course not. There are bad people and good people everywhere."

"Is any capitalist good?" Fee asked. "A real capitalist?"

"Stiva," her mother said. "Why shouldn't we take in more than one child?"

"Don't run away with it, Alexandra. I beg of you."

The plan might fall through, Stefan cautioned; out-of-state transfer of children might not prove feasible; the Board of Education in Massachusetts would surely object, unless temporary schooling could be arranged during a child's absence.

"Schooling?" Fran suddenly asked. "Go to school even if you're living in somebody else's house?"

"Of course, school," Stefan said. "A child can't be a truant from school in *any* state."

All at once Fran looked cautious. "If we did have one of them live here, what school would he go to, I wonder?"

"It depends on how old he is."

"How old are they, mostly?"

"Such a thing to worry about, Franny," Alexandra said.

Stefan Ivarin looked at his older daughter carefully. The sweetness had fled from her face; now she was thinking only of herself again and her precious friendships. She would be so relieved, he thought, if he told her that no children of high-school age could be involved in this plan, that it was the young ones only, none that she would have to take along with her to that academic paradise of hers.

"They'll be too young for high school," Stefan assured Fran. "Those your age work in the mills too, most of them, so now they're on strike themselves. You have nothing to fear."

Fran flashed a look of inquiry at him, bracing herself, but he had snapped open his watch and was selecting a small key from the bunch he always carried on the same chain. It was for his big portmanteau, still in the hall.

Alexandra jumped up from the table to unpack it for him.

"I hope the committee does arrange it," she said. "We have so much room in this big house. We are so fortunate."

Fran looked at the unpainted plaster walls about them, but Fee with sudden authority said "S-s-s-sh," and the word "fortunate" hung like a lamp in the air as their parents left them alone and went upstairs.

"If it goes through," Alexandra said on Friday afternoon, "the Paiges want to take two children, too. Isn't it marvelous?"

Fee had come home from school first, and her mother was waiting for her to tell her this great news.

"Does Mr. Paige know about his trip yet, Mama?" Fee asked. The one thing the name Paige made her think of was California, and how much longer that law case was going to drag on and keep him off the train. She didn't know how he could stand it this long, though his case must be pretty important, because even the *World* had a piece about it and said it was setting a precedent for freedom of assembly, whatever that was.

"His trip, his trip," Alexandra said. "You didn't even hear what I told you. Does Miss Roberts let you ignore everything she says in class?"

"I just asked."

"I told you that when Papa gets to Lawrence tonight, if the plan did go through, he'll say he has found homes for four children, not just two."

"The Paiges and us?"

"You did hear, then. Isn't it marvelous, Firuschka? When I phoned Alida about it, she instantly said, 'It's a lovely, lovely thing to do'— you know the sweet way she sounds—and then asked if they might do the very same thing."

Fee wondered if taking in two children at the Paiges' house could turn into one more reason for putting off the California trip. On Monday afternoon, she worried about the trip again. Somebody in a union telephoned Mama to say the children were all arranged and on trains that very minute, two with Papa on one train, and two others, the ones for the Paiges, on a different train, coming from some other town, not Lawrence. Those two were traveling with a representative of the Danbury Hatters' Union who had been up there, and he was taking them downtown to Mr. Paige's law office, so they wouldn't get lost.

It would be queer to have two strange new children right in the house, and the last hour of waiting for them to get there became prickly too. Fee kept looking out of the window for the first glimpse, but it was too dark to see down the hill.

At last the front door opened and there they were. Fee didn't look right at them at first. She saw the icicles hanging down from the porch roof behind her father as he came in with them, leading them in, and she knew they were both girls. But she kept looking past them and around them, until with a kind of yank she made her eyes look straight over at them. They were homely and skinny, and they weren't looking at her either. They weren't looking at anybody; they both stared down at the floor.

Papa said, "Well, this is Damosina and this is Josephine Jablonowski. Here's Francesca, my older daughter, and here is Fira."

He didn't have to explain Mama. She went up to them and said "Hello, children," and took the big paper bag Damosina held strangled in both of her hands, and then she helped them both to take off their funny coats and stocking hats and thick blue sweaters. They had no rubbers and their black shoes were icy-wet all the way up their ankles as far as the laces went.

"You both must be frozen," Mama said to them. "Come warm up in the kitchen. And I'll get everybody something to eat, too."

They didn't move. Damosina was an inch taller than her sister. They both looked as if they were going to cry. They let Mama take their coats and the paper bag, but they still wouldn't look at her or anybody else, not even around at the room.

"Damsie is eight," Papa said after a moment, "and Josie will be seven next month. They like my suitcase."

The girls nodded at that. They still stood just where they were, but now they stared at his bag instead of the floor.

Fee hated the portmanteau her father always took on his trips. It was of thick brown leather with knobby warts sticking up all over it, and it looked high-shouldered and queer and foreign.

"Should I open it, Josie?" he said.

Josie shook her head but Damsie took a step forward and said, "Open it, mister. Sure, open it."

"Let me do it, Pa," Fee said, and was proud at the immediate way he handed over all his keys and put her in charge.

"Why, Stiva," Alexandra said with approval. "You're like Madame Montessori today—the one familiar thing to them."

Fee was fitting the tiny key into the brass lock. Alexandra took several surreptitious looks at Damsie and Josie, fleeting ones, so they would not feel they were being inspected.

They were so thin, it was impossible to know if they were pretty or ugly. Their stringy hair was an unnatural yellow, as if it were dyed hair on vain old women who refused to be grey.

(148)

The lock stuck and Fran spoke for the first time. "Push down while you turn it, Fee," she said, and then turning to Damsie and Josie, she added, "Here's a wonderful new record." She wound up the Victrola for "Alexander's Ragtime Band," and hummed along with its jumpy little tune. Damsie leaned down closer to the suitcase.

Josie stood exactly where she was when she had come in. The heat of the house had made her nose sting, and now it began to drip, but she did nothing about it. Alexandra again went to her, offering her own handkerchief, but Josie reached instead for the hem of her dress and wiped her nose with it.

"That's fine," Alexandra said, putting her handkerchief away and smiling at Josie as if in praise of her superior method.

On the floor the lock of the bag clicked open. Damsie said, "Do it?" and Fee said, "She wants to lock it, Pa."

"Let her lock it then." To Alexandra he said, "Some hot tea would be nice," and he left them and went upstairs. Josie said, "I want to go home," and began to cry.

"You'll go home after a while," Alexandra said. "Come eat something, and tell me about your train ride to New York."

"No," Josie said. Her crying grew more intense.

The Victrola boomed on and Josie ran across the room and kicked it. The music kept coming out of it, and she leaned close and spat full at it.

"Franny," Alexandra said, raising her voice, "I'll get something good to eat. You stay here with little Josie, dear. Tell her about school. I'll hurry."

In the kitchen, she cut two slices of bread, buttered them and spread brown sugar thickly on top. She took them back to the parlor. Damsie and Fee still hung over the suitcase, Josie was crying less frantically, and Fran was turning off the Victrola, careful not to touch the place where it was wet.

"Here, Josie," Alexandra said. "This one is for you." She lifted Josie's hand, opened it flat, palm upward like a tiny tray, and set one piece of bread on it. The brown sugar had begun to run molasses-dark into the butter.

"Can I make one too?" Fran asked. "It looks peachy."

"Make one for me," Fee said, the sixth sense of special occasion telling her that Fran would do any favor she asked just now.

Josie bit into the sugary slice, and her crying petered out. Damsie abandoned the suitcase and with a swift snatch took her slice from Alexandra's offering hand.

"I have to give the key back," Fee announced. "My father will be

(149)

sore if I forget." Jangling the keys, she ran upstairs, calling out, "Here they are, Papa. We're all through now."

She felt busy and older, as if she had just had a birthday. It was lucky Josie and Damsie were only seven and eight, and though she'd die rather than admit it, she was glad their father was on strike.

"The truancy laws will just have to wait," Alexandra announced next morning. "Alida and I just decided we couldn't send either their two children or our two off to school without a hurry-up shopping trip first."

Fran said, "To buy what?"

"Some rubbers and mittens, and perhaps a few other things they really must have."

Damsie and Josie showed no interest in the promise of shopping, but Fee said, "Gee, things to wear." The news made her cheerful; no lugging them to school today anyway.

Not that she was nervous about taking them. She had asked herself straight out during the night whether it made her nervous and the answer was no. But putting it off a day was dandy, because she hadn't had a minute to think what to say to Trudy or any of the others, or even to Miss Roberts. Being crazy about Miss Roberts made it important to say the right thing, and now she'd have until tomorrow to decide just what the right thing would be.

"Can we run over to the Paiges' for a minute?" she asked. "I'm dy·ing to see what their kids are like."

"You and Franny go," Alexandra said. "We're not ready yet, are we, girls?" Neither Damsie nor Josie answered, but she gave them an encouraging smile and a second helping of Scotch pinhead oats, irrationally vexed at the cereal for not instantly yielding a year's worth of minerals and proteins to these poor bony mites.

Fee and Fran ran all the way to Channing Street, and both decided the Paiges' children were much better-looking than theirs. They were Federico and Maria Callavini, with bright dark eyes and curly black hair. They were ten and eleven, but like Damsie and Josie they were much smaller than anybody in Barnett of the same age. Their clothes were full of mended places and different from kids' clothes at school, but there wasn't anything woebegone or scared about them and they chattered and laughed, acting as if this was a great adventure they wouldn't have missed for anything.

"The lady says you have a big dog," Rico said. "Why'nt you bring

(150)

him?" He sounded bossy and fresh, the way most boys did, and Fee promised to produce Shag at the first possible minute.

She liked Federico. It was he who was eleven, only six months younger than she, yet nearly a head shorter. She envied him for that. Nowadays she was jealous of any boy or girl who stayed small because she was growing so fast that Fran predicted more often than ever she'd be a hefty old Amazon by sixteen.

She thought about Rico in class during the day, wondering if her shoulders were wider than his. For the past few months, she had taken to measuring her shoulders once a week, and so far they were all right, the same as Trudy Loheim's, but sixteen was so far off.

By coincidence that afternoon when she got home, Mama was thinking and talking about people's sizes too. The shopping trip with Mrs. Paige had revealed that all four children took one or two sizes smaller than they were supposed to for their ages. To Mama and Mrs. Paige, smallness was a calamity, especially for a boy, and they both agreed it was the capitalist system that was to blame.

"It's because Rico's father never could make a living wage," Alexandra explained. "Not in Italy, and not even in America. Rico never got enough milk. Under socialism, every baby would get enough milk."

"At least he's good-looking," Fran grumbled. "And so's Maria. The Paiges have all the luck."

"S-s-sh," Fee said fiercely, "they've got *ears.*" . .

Damsie and Josie were playing in the cellar, where Alexandra had just shown them the ironing board and the two white tubs for the laundry. It was warm down there, and they had never seen anything like the big furnace with pipes branching out of its top in all directions, nor the slippery, sliding mountain of coal, nor laundry tubs that were shiny white enamel instead of slimy old wood.

"Even now in America," Alexandra went on, "I'm sure Rico and Maria eat nothing but macaroni and spaghetti made of denatured flour. Damsie and Josie may get brown kasha once in a while, or whatever they call kasha in Polish. I must ask Papa; he would know."

Fran would not be deflected from her pronouncements on comparative beauty. "Just the same, Damsie and Josie are the homeliest kids in the world. And the dopiest. Whew."

"They're *not* dopey," Fee said. "They're a million years younger than Rico and Maria, that's all."

"They'll open up like flowers," Alexandra promised, "after I can feed them up a bit. Their cheeks will be pink instead of like lard, and their hair won't be like yellow strings—you'll see. Why, last night when I bathed them their ribs stuck out like washboards."

(1 5 1)

The shopping trip had been successful indeed, and after adding flannel middies to the necessities, Alexandra had become enamored of a bolt of bright red plaid that she was sure she could make into pleated skirts "in less than an hour each."

She had been at it ever since, leaving the sewing room only for trips to the pantry to fetch milk and cookies and fruit to tempt Damsie and Josie into the usually frowned-upon delight of nibbling between meals.

"I also washed their heads, and doused them with larkspur," Alexandra added. "Just in case."

Both girls looked knowing and said, "Well?"

"They didn't have any," their mother said. "A blessing, I must say."

From the cellar Damsie's voice rose in a shrill laugh. Fee said, "Could I show them Shag *now?*"

Alexandra hesitated, looking out to the back yard where Shag had been banished all day, so as not to risk his frightening the girls.

"But, Mama," Fee said urgently. "He'll just freeze if we never let him in until they go home to Massachusetts."

"I suppose we have to, sooner or later."

"I'll go too," Fran offered. "I wish we had his new collar, to hold him by."

Fee indicated her opinion of anybody who could distrust Shag and without bothering to get her coat, darted out to him. Fran followed, and they made for the cellar door in the yard, imperfectly cleared of its slope of new snow.

"Now you behave," Fee admonished Shag, clutching a fistful of his fur as she led him sedately down the stone steps and into the cellar. "We're coming with our dog now," she shouted by way of preparation. "Don't be scared—he's nice to everybody."

"Wait, Fee," Fran ordered. "I'll go first, in case he gets stupid and jumps all over them." Inside the dim cellar she couldn't see the girls anywhere at first, but when she did make them out, she laughed and said, "That's *cute*—stay inside them."

Damsie and Josie were kneeling in the white porcelain washtubs, one in each tub, and at Fran's approval they squealed and shouted and looked happy for the first time since their arrival.

"Shag, that's Damsie," Fee said, pulling his big head to the left, "and this one is Josie. Remember what I said, now, and behave yourself."

Shag barked resoundingly several times and then collapsed on his haunches. His tail thwacked the concrete cellar floor and Fee hugged him because she could tell he liked the little girls in the tubs.

"Lean down and pat him, Damsie," she said, pulling Shag closer to the tub and guiding Damsie's hand under hers to help her stroke his great head. Damsie said, "I'm not afraid," and kept on patting Shag after Fee dropped her own hand.

"Let me too," Josie shouted, "Dog, come here."

Fran performed the patting honors with Josie, until Josie also ventured it alone. "He's the most conceited dog in the whole world," Fran said a moment later, "look at him."

Shag was clearly wallowing in self-importance, and when Fran and Fee lifted the children out of the tubs, he sat immobilized, his eyes expectant and the top of his head slightly twitching, as if at the homage about to be showered upon him.

From above, Alexandra called, "Is everything all right, dears?" and Fee shouted excitedly, "He just *loves* them, Mama."

The whir of the sewing machine began again, and for no reason Fee skipped around in a big circle. "We can all come down here every single day, if we want," she announced, addressing herself equally to Damsie, Josie, Fran and Shag.

By suppertime, Damsie and Josie seemed done with any sense of strangeness. As Alexandra served them juicy meatballs and gravy, a baked potato, string beans, a tall glass of milk, two slices of thick dark bread and big pats of pale-yellow butter, they both fell to and ate with head-lowered intensity, free of constraint. Fee and Fran watched them for a moment, but Alexandra felt that neither was being critical or unkind. Above the lowered heads of the strangers, she smiled at her own girls, begging them wordlessly not to be lofty and unmoved at the sight of these who had been too long deprived.

Then Alexandra started to eat, and in a moment Fran and Fee began too. For most of the meal there was hardly a word spoken. Then suddenly Josie let her clumsily-held fork drop to her plate, and nodded in a swoop of drowsiness.

"She's sleepy," Damsie explained, herself overcome a second later by fullness and warmth and the need to sleep.

Alexandra said, "That's nice," and signaled to Fee and Franny, who half-carried, half-pushed the children up the stairs to help them undress and have their bath.

At the table, Alexandra sat on, ignoring the spread of dishes to be done. She could hear Josie's protests about another bath, and Fran explaining it was like brushing your teeth every single day, then

(153)

switching to a big propaganda about the fun of being so little you could get into the tub with your sister and splash water at her when she wasn't watching.

Fran was being unexpectedly sweet with them, Alexandra thought. For all her disparaging comparisons with Rico and Maria, she was kind and patient with them. And Fee actually enjoyed them!

If only school would not be another ordeal, when Fee took them with her tomorrow morning.

Never had Fee mentioned the black bunting of a year ago, not once. But it was not something a child would go through and then forget, surely not. Did she think of it in secret, in silence? Did she think of it now, when she looked at Damsie and Josie and knew she would be taking them with her when she left for school in the morning?

Alexandra left the table in sudden determination to finish the two plaid skirts. She hoped Stiva wouldn't ask about costs when he got home. Two pairs of rubbers, heavy mittens, long drawers, black stockings—then the middies and the nice red plaid. She had gone at it with a rich woman's recklessness, but Alida was getting as much for Maria, and even more for Rico, since he had to have a jacket.

She glanced at the clock on the sideboard in the dining room; between the grooved gold columns ranged along its polished green marble body, its bland face said it was nearly eight o'clock. An hour had passed since supper.

"Franny," she called, tilting her head back and addressing the plaster ceiling of the little room. "Fira . . . what's taking so long up there?"

"We're coming," Fran answered. But as usual the words meant nothing. Alexandra whipped her foot up and down on the treadle in a burst of impatience to end her task. It sounded so simple, "I'll make little plaid skirts for them to wear on their first day at school," but as always, the crackle and rustle of the paper pattern was the signal for a dozen pesky delays. Every time she made a dress for Fran or Fee, it started out as "something simple and quick" and ended at two in the morning, with her eyes stabbing and her back breaking, while the girls slept in the untroubled ignorance of the young—and in their serene sureness that all her labor would end up in something Dutchy and awful. When they did love what she made, they were so surprised it infuriated her almost as much as when they hated it.

They came down at last, both looking at her with serious eyes.

"Josie cried herself to sleep the way she did last night," Fran reported. "I sat on her bed until she stopped."

"Damsie didn't," Fee said. "She played jacks on the floor. I gave her my old ones and told her she could keep them."

Alexandra smiled. "You've both been very sweet with those poor little creatures," she said, "and I'm proud of you." She seemed to be searching for something better to say. "You're turning into real Ivarins, both of you—it's simply wonderful."

"Oh, Mama," Fran said. But this wasn't her usual "Oh, Mama"; now the two words were surprised and shy, as if a boy had just called her beautiful.

Fee liked it too. Compliments from parents were silly, mostly, but this was different. Everything about Damsie and Josie being there was different. Different from what, she didn't know; it just started being different when they arrived and it still was different.

"I'll tell Papa all about the way you've been," Alexandra went on. "He'll be proud of his two girls too, I can tell you."

"He won't forget to write the note I have to give to Miss Mainley tomorrow, will he?" Fee asked.

"He won't forget it, dear. Don't worry."

"I'm not worried a bit."

She meant it, and she reminded herself that she did while she was getting ready for bed, and again in the morning when she woke up. Here it was, the morning when she was going to have to cart Damsie and Josie along to school with her, and she wasn't nervous or worried at all.

She *was* sore at Fran for not having to take one of them to Barnett High with her, instead of sliding out of the whole thing, but that wasn't the same as a hard knob in your stomach about what was going to happen.

At the corner where Fran had to turn off and leave her alone with them, her heart did thump a bit, and when she finally pushed Damsie and Josie through the big front door of P.S. 6, into the hall with the usual mob of kids, it thumped and banged a lot.

She had them by their hands now, and she was glad they had new clothes to wear. Their hair still was that funny yellow and their skin all pasty, but she made them take off their coats and hats right inside the door, and they did look nice in their new middies and skirts.

At the principal's office, Fee tapped twice and at Miss Mainley's "Yes?" she led the girls in and straight up to her, handing over Papa's letter, and explaining who was Damsie and who Josie and that you had to say Jablonowski as if it ended uffski not owski.

"JablonUFFski," Miss Mainley said without ado. She read Papa's letter in a flash and shook their hands and asked what grades they were in back home in Lawrence, though she acted as if she knew herself that it was 2-B and 1-B.

Then she said, "Come along, everybody, and we'll see where you belong." She marched ahead out of her office, and then down the hall with Fee right at her side, and Josie and Damsie running in spurts to get caught up when they fell behind. And as they went, boys and girls in the hall had to fall back and make way for the principal and everybody with the principal, as the school rules made them do. It was delicious.

"Mrs. Paige got here ten minutes ahead of you," Miss Mainley told Fee in a sort of side-voice without turning to look at her. "I went along with her and the Callavini children also, to establish them in their proper classes. No visitors are going to skip a grade in this school the very day they get here!"

Fee thought it one of the funniest remarks she had ever heard, especially for a principal, and especially in that side-voice and with the sideways smile Miss Mainley gave her as she said it. It was enough to make you brag, dashing along while everybody in the halls could see Miss Mainley smiling and talking at you a mile a minute.

"Here's Two-B," Miss Mainley said. "I'll take you in, Damsie."

Through the open door, Fee could see Miss Mainley explain to the teacher and introduce Damsie. Damsie took to 2-B right away, and there wasn't any fuss about leaving her there.

But when they reached 1-B, Josie wouldn't go in. She hung on to Fee's hand, and reached for her bookstrap and hung on to that too.

"Come in with us, Fira," Miss Mainley said, "Josie is younger, you know—"

But when Josie was introduced all round and led to her desk, she collapsed into it, looked up at Fee without speaking and began to cry. It wasn't loud and embarrassing, just soft and miserable.

"School is fun, Josie," Fee whispered, but she glanced up at Miss Mainley in appeal. Josie looked so tiny, sitting there, huddled inside her middy as if she wanted to squinch her bones together and disappear.

"It will be fun later, Josie," Miss Mainley said. "Here's a present for you, and I'll be back soon to see if it *was* fun. Now come along, Fira."

Miss Mainley departed briskly, and Fee followed. The present was a bright-yellow pencil, new and sharp as a needle. In the corridor,

Miss Mainley said, "She'll quiet down," and then waved Fee off, saying, "Skedaddle, or you'll miss the last bell."

It was so unexpected that Fee waved right back, as if she were a principal too. Then she ran off, in a panic that she had been fresh, and she reached her own class just as the bell clanged.

Miss Roberts said good morning in her special way and seemed interested in watching Fee arrange her books and pencil-box. Then she said, "Are they your cousins or friends of your family, Fee, the little girls you brought to school today?"

The old stupid whisper shot out of Tommy Gording to Jack Dryer across the aisle, and his cackle of a laugh too, but when Fee stood up to answer, it came out in her everyday reciting voice.

"No, ma'am, they're not cousins or anything," she said. "They're from the Lawrence strike, and Mr. and Mrs. Paige took two strike kids to live with them too."

"Why, how nice, Fee," Miss Roberts said.

There was a whole hiss of whispering then, but Miss Roberts put up her "Attention" hand and it stopped. She looked at Fee as if she were waiting for the rest of her answer, and her "Attention" hand made the whole class wait with her.

"Lawrence is in Massachusetts," Fee added politely. "And everybody up there is cold and starving."

"I remember now," Miss Roberts said. "The newspapers haven't had much about the textile strikes for quite a time." Once again the whispers boiled up but Miss Roberts said, "Silence, please," in her strict tone and they stopped at once. She gave Fee her "Be seated" nod, and kept looking past her over the whole room, taking her time, as if she wanted to look at everybody there, first one row and then the next row. Nobody moved.

Then Miss Roberts said softly, "Perhaps you have forgotten your manners, Class. But Fira Ivarin's family have not. Helping people in trouble is the highest kind of manners."

Fira felt wonderful.

By lunchtime the whole school knew about the Paiges' Rico and Maria and about her Damsie and Josie. It was comfortable, having it all happen together. And it was different.

Tommy Gording and Jack Dryer and the rest of them could whisper and cackle as much as they pleased, and the minute Miss Roberts' back was turned they'd start right in again, as sure as sure could be.

But the Paiges weren't crazy foreigners and they were doing exactly the same thing her family was doing.

(157)

Let Tommy Gording and Jack Dryer put *that* in their pipes and smoke it.

And if it came to that, Miss King could put it in *her* pipe and smoke it too.

TWELVE

When you suddenly stopped being the youngest it was wonderful, Fee thought, and the way people started behaving as if you'd become lots older overnight was marvelous.

By the end of the first week, Fran stopped paying much attention to Damsie and Josie, maybe because it wasn't her school that they went to. Then Mrs. Paige telephoned and asked to talk to Fee. She wondered if Fee could take Rico and Maria along with her and Damsie and Josie. "Just for a few days," Mrs. Paige said, as if she were coaxing. "They're older, and pretty soon they'll go and come themselves."

And when the bell rang that afternoon, there they were, waiting out front in the schoolyard by the big stone statue where her own kids were already waiting. They *are* mine, she thought. Fran hasn't one thing to do with the school part of them, and Mama and Papa haven't either, except the one letter to Miss Mainley. At home, everybody had to ask *her* what had happened during the day, because when they asked Josie or Damsie, the answers were mostly little shrugs.

"Is your teacher nice, Damsie?"

"All right."

"And yours, Josie? Is she nice too?"

"Kinda."

Fee liked it when Fran or Mama took her aside and asked about Damsie and Josie and school. She liked to hurry out to the statue; it was important not to be late. One day she *was* five minutes late, and it was awful.

By then, Rico and Maria were going home by themselves, so Fee knew Damsie and Josie would be waiting all alone. There was nothing she could do; when the bell rang, Miss Roberts was at the blackboard, explaining something, and nobody was ever allowed to leave a class if a teacher was still talking.

It took Miss Roberts forever and when Fee dashed out, they were waiting in the empty yard, standing tight together as if they had been pasted to each other along their sides. They shrieked, "Here's Fee, here's Fee," and ran to her as if she were the Queen of Sheba or Ethel Barrymore.

One afternoon, without saying a word to anybody first, she took Damsie and Josie off with her to Gray's. They had never had a soda or a frappe, either one, and she even had to order for them, because they didn't know what to say. "Three chocolate frappes with vanilla ice cream, and grated nuts and whipped cream," she said and laid three nickels down on the counter. She had never spent so much of her allowance on a treat before. They both lapped up the last dribble, and it made her feel wonderful in a brand-new way.

Not everything was wonderful, but even the bad things didn't last long. Once, leaving class, Trudy Loheim said, "Some people certainly are fickle, aren't they?" and informed Fee it was the saddest thing in the world if your best friend turned into a traitor. Fee said, "I've asked you over about a million times since they came," but Trudy dismissed it. "It's no fun if we can't be alone," she said, turning it into a second accusation.

It ended in tears of rage for Fee, but that afternoon was Damsie's and Josie's turn to go play with Rico and Maria in the Paiges' big high attic, and she had to hurry them over. She loved the Paiges' house; it was all grey stucco on the outside, with ribs of dark-brown wood a few feet apart, and a roof of curved red tiles, one overlapping another all the way up to the top, like starched red ruffles on a dress.

It was time to say good-bye when Mrs. Paige asked them to stay for supper. Mr. Paige had something important to finish at his office, she said; he wouldn't get home until ten.

"That's not considered working late, over at your house, is it, Fee?" she asked, with her nice light laugh. Fee shook her head, and into it popped the memory of Mr. Paige's trip to California. She hadn't remembered it since goodness knew when. How was that possible, when it mattered so desperately?

"I'd love to have you three stay," Mrs. Paige said.

"Stay here," Damsie begged Fee, and Rico said, "There's chicken."

"I'd have to phone my mother," Fee said, as if that hurdle might defeat the whole idea.

"Go ahead, dear."

It was while she was saying "one-seven-one-eight-W" to the operator that she wondered if there were some offhand way she could phone Trudy too, and tell her she'd just been invited to have supper with Mrs. Paige at the Paiges' house, without her parents being there. If Trudy was going to be mean and jealous, she ought to have plenty to be jealous about.

Fee sighed. It was impossible to phone Trudy and tell her. Why it was, she didn't know, but it was impossible, and it made her sore to know it was.

The voices turned into shouts and Fee thought, They'll scare them to death. She ran into the children's room, and leaned down over Damsie and then over Josie. They were drowned in sleep; if the roof blew off with the racket below, they wouldn't know it.

She closed their door in relief and stood in the hall listening, wishing Fran wasn't off at Jack Purney's sixteenth birthday party. The shouts were booming up through the funnel of the stairs from the kitchen, mixed of her father's voice and her brother Eli's, mixed with weeping that was not her mother's and terrifying because it was not. She wondered what Mrs. Paige sounded like when she cried, but Mrs. Paige had gone home with Rico and Maria before supper, after all the rides on Eli's motorcycle. Eli and Joan had left Webby with the people in the upstairs half of their house and had come over to meet the children, because Mama had nagged at Eli on the phone a lot, saying it was heartless not even to come once in three whole weeks and show a little concern for the poor things.

Eli must have wanted to prove he wasn't heartless because one by one he took all four kids out for a ride. Not one had even touched a motorcycle before, and each one came back buzzing with excitement. The fun spread to everybody and there was a jolly mood right through supper, with Papa joking about his empty agnostic office on Fridays, and sitting around like anybody else's father.

Now this! It was getting worse by the minute, with bursts of words like bullets. The familiar plunge of worry drove downwards inside her, and Fee stood, holding the knob of the children's door as if the door might fly open. She was half undressed and her underwear felt sticky with sudden perspiring. She pulled at it, away from her moist skin, deciding to go back to her homework but not moving. The voices grew louder.

"I did say that," her father roared. "Mama was quite correct."

"But you didn't mean it." It was a terrible accusation as Eli said it, flung like a rock.

"I meant every word. I did smash my parents between the eyes, just as you did, Mr.—Mr. Eaves." Mr. Eaves was a rock too, hurled right back.

"But you can forgive your own actions," Eli said. "There's some God-given difference between your actions and everybody else's."

"And that difference, if you please—"

There was a pause and Fee realized it was Joan crying, not Mama. She had never seen Joan cry except once a long time ago, before Webby was born. It was more terrible to know it was Joan down there with tears running down her face, not Mama.

"That difference eluded me," her father said, "when I first heard this news about Eaves. Until now, until this evening it eluded me."

"For God's sake, can't we drop it?" Eli said. "It's done, and it isn't going to be undone."

"That difference is that when *I* thrust those so-called daggers into my parents' hearts, I was running some sort of risk or danger myself."

"I must admit," Alexandra said, "I think Papa is right, Eli. He *was* arrested and he did go to prison—"

"And you, sir," Papa said, "were running *away* from risk and danger."

"Running away—what are you talking about?" There was the sound of a chair being shoved back hard. Eli must have sprung to his feet.

"Running away from the risk of being a foreigner, of having a foreign name, of being a Jew, different from so-called real Americans."

"Exaggerate," Eli said. "As usual, blow it all up."

"Pardon me, I do not wish to exaggerate." Papa was suddenly as cool and formal as if he were addressing a stranger. "You do not regard a foreign name as a risk or danger, merely as a nuisance, an inconvenience. Hooray. What remains, nevertheless, is that *you* thrust your daggers to spare *yourself.*"

On the last words, coolness vanished. He shot out each one in fury, with a thump on the table to mark it off. Outside, Shag began to bark in sudden warning, trotting back and forth on the porch, growling and watchful. Another chair was shoved back. They must be facing each other like wild animals.

Fee shivered. She sat down on the top step, her forehead on her knees, her eyes squeezed tight as if to banish the scene she could not

(1 6 1)

see. A moment later there was the click of a switch below her and the whole staircase was lighted. Her head flew up, but she sat rigid as her father started up the steps. He saw her and stopped short.

"What are you doing here?" he demanded.

"Nothing." She jumped up and ran into her room. She sat on the edge of her bed, expectant and afraid in a terrible familiar afraidness.

It never was being afraid he would spank her, even way long ago when she was little. He never spanked them, except that one wild funny time when she was four that she and Franny still could go into stitches about.

She could still see the doll that started it, the beautiful blond thing, with eyes that opened and shut. An English lesson of Papa's in New York, who worked in a toy factory, gave it to him one night "for your little girl," thinking he had only one.

Apparently she and Fran used to fight like tigers, about whose turn it was to have the doll, though neither of them remembered that part. But one day, Papa was at his desk and they were at it about the doll and kept at it even though he kept ordering them to be quiet, and then without warning he marched in on them and spanked them, first one and then the other, with the doll tumbling like an acrobat between them because neither one would let go of it.

All of a sudden it seemed so funny to be spanked by a *father,* that they got the giggles. The harder he spanked them, the louder they giggled, and if they looked at each other, it started them all over again.

He gave up at last, talking Russian to himself, and he took the doll away by force, carrying it with him to his own room, slamming his door. The idea of the doll in there with him set them off worse than before, and they laughed until their stomachs hurt.

The next day Papa said, "From now on, it is *my* doll. You can play with it any time you like, every day, if you like. But if you start fighting over it, I will take it away in one minute flat. Do you follow me?"

After that, Fran and she always called it "Papa's doll," and it became a family joke that Mama told everybody. What Fee liked best of all was one part she didn't remember herself, but had heard so many times, she almost *did* remember it.

"It's my father's doll," she had once explained to a visitor. "I think he plays with it at night when we're asleep."

Even now, rigid on the edge of her bed waiting to see what would happen when he got upstairs, that part made her smile. He came up heavily and stopped, and her heart stopped too. But then he went straight to his room. She waited another moment to be sure he wasn't coming back, and then ran down to the kitchen.

Joan had stopped crying but Eli was saying the wildest things about "never coming to this damn house again," and about Papa's sarcasm and inhuman logic and being a big fake about children having the right to live their own lives.

Mama said "Stop it, Eli," but she didn't seem to be thinking about Eli.

"We scared you, poor child," she said when she saw Fee, but she didn't seem to be thinking about Fee either.

"We'd better start home," Joan said.

"Don't stay upset," Alexandra said. "You know how he is."

"She sure does," Eli said. "And *I* know too. God!"

They left, and Alexandra came back from the door looking vaguely around as if she were searching for something. Fee was putting away the rest of the dishes, but instead of praising her for being a good girl, Alexandra hardly saw what she was doing.

Fee glanced at her once or twice, but Alexandra did not notice that either. Then she said, "Oh my goodness! I knew something was making me furious at him."

"At Eli?"

"At Papa. I knew it all the time. But I couldn't separate it from everything else. I listened, I agreed with every word he said to Eli, and yet, under agreeing with him, there was something burning in me about him."

She pulled her lower lip in with her teeth and then let it go and then pulled it back in. Fee said, "Don't do that, Mama," and Alexandra said sharply, "Stop ordering me about!"

Fee didn't take it as a scolding. Her mother probably didn't know she had said it. She was still puzzling out whatever it was Papa had done to her.

"When Eli said 'inhuman logic,' something sounded familiar," Alexandra continued. "But I couldn't *think* then, not until a minute ago. 'Inhuman logic'—why, those were the very words I used to Papa, that night Eli told me he'd changed his name."

Fee wished her mother wouldn't talk about that horrible time. It was so long ago and so frightening—

"That night," Alexandra said, "I waited and waited for Papa to come home, with my heart breaking for the way he would feel at the news that his only boy—"

Her voice thickened, and Fee begged, "Don't, Mama."

"But Papa didn't feel that way," Alexandra went on. "With his inhuman logic, he made me look like an idiot. And *now,* half a year later, after I finally got over Eli's action by myself, now he shows he was just as heartbroken as I was." Her eyes filled and she added, "It was unspeakable of him that night to be so noble. Posing as a philosopher and sage, married to a simpleton and booby."

Fee shook her head in total disapproval of her father, still not sure what had been so unspeakable in his long-ago behavior. Her mother looked at her with new misery.

" 'Euphonious,' he called their new name. 'Well, it's euphonious enough'—oh, Firuschka, he can be so hurtful, he can really torment the soul."

Her tears now spilled over and she wiped them harshly away with the checked kitchen towel. Her shoulders shook, and her round stomach shook, and Fee couldn't think of anything except how awful it was to be fat and old and floppy instead of young.

She hated thinking it now, but she couldn't help it. She looked away from her weeping mother, wishing she could go up to her room where she needn't see her. Did Papa sometimes think she was disgusting too? Did they love each other any more, Papa and Mama? Was *that* what really was the hurtful thing, tormenting the soul?

Maybe Papa did have a crush on Mrs. Paige and Mama knew it, and knew that Mrs. Paige had one right back.

Fee suddenly remembered how it felt when Fran told her about it, how her heart exploded in a terrible new kind of pain, and later went all shiny with joy when she saw for herself that they didn't look the way people with crushes always did look.

But now, standing off watching while her mother cried so—"he can really torment the soul"—now the explosion happened again and then the icy skin encasing her and she wondered if old people were different when they fell in love, different and hiding and secret so you couldn't tell just by looking at them. If she and Fran had been able to keep Eli's secret from that night on the beach, maybe Papa and Mrs. Paige had a secret *they* had to keep.

"Oh, Mama," she cried out, rushing to her mother, "I love you so."

Joan transferred Webby from their neighbor's bed to his own, adoring his sleepy gibberish, and then made two cups of steaming malted milk for herself and Eli. In a winter like this the motorcycle ride home from Barnett was all anybody could bear.

"This will warm us up," she said. "I hope it won't give you a heartburn."

"Only the powder does that," he said. "And if I didn't have to make a pig of myself when I open the jar—"

He sounded like a child confessing an orgy of cookies and jam, but it was more serious than that. He did make a pig of himself; whenever he felt like a snack, he went straight to the huge jar of the powdered malted milk, as big as the ones you saw in soda fountains, and ate spoonful after spoonful of it, just as it was. She had tried it a couple of times, but she didn't like the grainy dry feel of the powder, nor the way it stuck to her teeth and caked on her palate. Eli did; he couldn't remember how far back he had formed his taste for it, but it never left him. If he overdid it, he knew he'd pay the price with an upset stomach, a heartburn, often the first steps toward an attack of asthma. And he overdid it at least once a month.

But now Joan smiled in absolution at his confession. She was glad he was getting over his fury at his father. What an evening! What a family! Whenever she thought she had learned not to let them shake her to her smallest nerves, they could fly into some new crisis that jangled a hundred tinier nerves she never knew she had. Tonight she had felt like one huge scream from the moment it began until Eli kicked over the motor on the Harley for the trip home. In the rush of freezing wind, talk was impossible and she wished it could stay impossible forever.

Everything at supper had been so smooth until the very end. They'd all laughed over her new stories of Webby's doings, and both the Ivarins were happy and dear that she was to have another baby in August.

"If it's a girl," she started to tell them, but Eli interrupted.

"Since Web was named for Joan's father," he said happily, "we're going to call this one Stefan if it's a boy, and Alexandra if it's a girl."

"Stefan?" Father Ivarin asked instantly. "Why not change it to Steve?"

In one swoop the nightmare was on them.

Joan stole a look at Eli now, but he was finishing his drink, stretching and yawning. "If it is a girl," he said, "we won't be up against it in August."

All she answered was, "It's five months off. Let's not think about it."

"The damn old crank, nothing will satisfy him. Remember when you said my being the only son is why he picks me up no matter what I do? You wait till the girls get bigger."

"Boys often clash with their fathers more than girls do," she said. "That's all I meant."

"But you just wait," he said. "Let's say if Fran decides next year, she isn't going to Training School and be a teacher, if she sees how great it is to earn what I earn. Or, wait till Fee is sixteen. Fee's a spunky kid with ideas of her own. She can get mad, too—and she won't always knuckle down to him."

"She's awfully stubborn sometimes."

"You stick around, Joanie," he said. "There'll be fireworks just like the ones I had to stand for."

He coughed slightly. Illogically Joan said, "I wish I hadn't cried so tonight. I was a disgrace."

"I could kill him when he's that way, the God-damn tyrant. The Great Ivarin, the Champion of the Suffering, the Noble Fighter for a Better World. Sure Mike—in public. But at home, why, he's the biggest czar of them all. If you agree with him, good. If you don't, by God, if you argue against him or act the way *you* think is right instead of the way he does, by God, down comes the knout on *your* back."

"Oh, Eli, don't get worked up again."

"*His* knout is words. And rages. And then the hell of living with his bad moods."

Fee woke up with the decision made. It would be only fair to prepare Damsie and Josie. They had lived there for two whole weeks, but they hadn't ever seen Papa in a mood, and they might be frightened. She didn't know how to explain, but she *had* to. Perhaps, she said, as they dressed, her mother might seem nervous or sad, and might even stay that way for a day or two, but it would pass, and it wasn't anything they need be upset about. Her father might be grumpy and slam doors and things, but that needn't be scary either.

"Why?" Josie asked.

"Well, last night they had a big argument—"

"Did he hit her?" Damsie interrupted eagerly.

"Hit my *mother?*" Fee cried.

"My Pa hits my Ma like that, that, that, that, when they get in a fight." Each "that" was Damsie's clenched fist hitting herself vigorously on the jaw, on her ear, on her mouth, under her chin so her teeth clacked together.

"He hits me," Josie said calmly.

"Ma hits us most," Damsie said. She pulled down her black stocking halfway to her shoe. "Look." She pointed to a scar circling the lower curve of her kneecap, which Fee had once asked about without getting any reply. "My Ma hit me so hard that time, I fell against the big black pail of coal, and the shovel slit me open and all the blood and everything—"

"You poor little thing," Fee cried. An unusual stir went through her, a strange sense of safety and sureness about her own life compared to Damsie's, no matter whether Papa was in a horrible mood or not.

When they came in that afternoon, he was not in a mood at all. At the front door, they could hear Mama laughing in the kitchen, and he was talking about something in the papers, and laughing too.

Fee stopped in the doorway, listening. Brief resentment rose in her, as her father's voice went on so merrily, and her mother's short little laughs, like commas, broke in at spaced-out moments. They really were the craziest parents anybody could imagine. You never could count on them, even when you explained them first.

THIRTEEN

A few days later, Fee tapped on her father's door. For the first time in her life, she was seeking him out in the privacy of his study to ask him a question about capital and labor.

She offered him a newspaper she had brought with her, pointing to an article about Lawrence on an inside page, and standing close to him while he glanced at it.

"Is it true they demand a twenty-five-per-cent raise, Papa?" she asked, her eyes somber, her tone worried. "And would it really wreck all New England?"

Stefan was taken aback. He looked at her above the paper, not knowing what made the small familiar face newly appealing. For a moment he was conscious of how his desk must appear to anyone but himself, with its usual storm of clippings, letters, papers, pages laden with the beautiful hieroglyphics of mathematics, and the hateful flock of household bills, that swooped in upon him like vultures in the first days of each new month.

"Are you too busy now?" she asked at last.

"No, no, I was thinking." He was careful not to show that what he thought amused him: Her two children have turned her into a student of economics.

He put out his cigarette as he read the article, remembering it at once; it was in one of the papers he had brought home last night. Reading its black warning in the subway at two A.M., he had found a sour amusement in its devotion to the percentage mark.

RAISES UP TO 25% DEMANDED

THREE MILLS OFFER 5%
LEADERS DEMAND 15% AND UP
DICKERINGS PROCEED ON 7½%

TO COST OWNERS $5,000,000 YEARLY

"—THREAT TO ALL NEW ENGLAND INDUSTRY"

"Is it true," Fee repeated, "about the twenty-five per cent?"

"It sounds like a bonanza," he said, nodding judiciously to her. "A big fat jump, all right."

He was being sarcastic, she knew, but she had been so sure he would denounce all of it as another big lie directed against the strikers that she was vaguely disappointed.

"This bonanza," he went on, starting to make another cigarette though his last one still sent up a curling thread of smoke, "this would be twenty-five per cent, at the highest. BUT—" At his loud BUT, he picked up his chunky inkwell of black coal. It was empty; he never filled it, but it was as much a part of his workroom as his chess pieces and books; he used it as a paperweight or else as something blocky to throw from hand to hand while he was thinking out a problem.

"But twenty-five per cent of *what?*" he asked. "The paper didn't tell you that, did it?"

"No."

"Twenty-five per cent of nine cents an hour!" He glared at the offending headlines. "Nine cents an hour—do you hear?"

She glared also and said nothing. He wanted to tell her in his own way, and with a faint indulgence, she wanted him to.

"So this sky-high jump would be from nine cents an hour to about eleven."

"Gee, that's awful."

"Mind you, fifty-four hours in the mills and your pay now leaps from four dollars and eighty-six cents to five dollars and eighty-four cents. Every single Saturday! I tell you, labor is downright piggish."

He banged the desk with his gleaming chunk of coal. Behind his glasses his eyes shone, and he was shouting, but he was in a good mood, so Fee found the noise exciting.

"And, mind you, this twenty-five per cent isn't for everybody—let's not be extremists, I pray you. Skilled workers with their twelve cents an hour and a handful of specialists getting twenty—no bonanza jump for them!"

"How much are the special ones striking for?"

"A one-cent raise—fifty-four cents more every week." He raised a finger in admonition. "Do not ask me to put it in per cent marks—I'm not mathematician enough."

She returned his look of private jesting, and then said, "It sounds so different in the paper."

"It always does. In the big newspapers, it nearly always does. Even in those that intend to be honest."

"But would it wreck New England, Papa, if we win?"

My child, he thought, my little daughter. We. If we win. A storm of love rocked him, and he turned abruptly toward the window, saying, "It's stuffy in here. Too many cigarettes." He rose and went over to it, opening it from the top. The air that blew in over his head had no frost in it. Winter was going.

"It won't wreck anything," he said, as he returned to his desk. "Here, there was something you didn't see. Let me show you—it's important to see these, every time they appear in print anywhere."

With his fountain pen, he began to ink in the quotation marks around the last headline, making them very prominent. Fee leaned down over his right arm, watching his pen.

"They're like signals," he said. "Whenever you read something in quotation marks, remember you've had a high-sign that somebody said it or wrote it or warned it. If you want to believe this fearful threat that some giant intellect is making about New England, go ahead and believe it. But, Firuschka, *I* believe it's a godforsaken pygmy lie."

Fee laughed, and the last of her confusion and worry evaporated like steam from a windowpane. "I believe it too, Pa," she cried, wishing you could kiss fathers the way you could kiss mothers, without seeming babyish. "Just an old godforsaken pygmy lie," she chanted, and ran out of his room.

. . . .

In the street a grocery wagon went by, and the horse's hoofs made fat squashy sounds in the slush. It was the second week in March, and all of a sudden you could believe that the sun and the air knew all about the calendar and the end of stiff crusty old February.

They were all out on the porch, Fran and Fee and the girls and Shag. Nobody would allow Shag near enough to touch; his thick fur was muddied and soaked from his lunatic dashes all over the meadows and fields around the house; he was silly with spring. Damsie and Josie were spinning a metal top that made a whizzing sound.

"There's Rico," Fee said, seeing him race by with another boy a block away, where Channing crossed their street. Rico had been a trouble to the Paiges of late; half the time he wouldn't mind Mrs. Paige, staying out long past supper without even telling her where he was.

"Mrs. Paige comes over here an awful lot of afternoons before Papa starts for New York," Fran said. "Haven't you noticed, Fee?" The instant the words were out, she wanted to snatch them back from the air. How *could* she forget the way Fee had carried on that time she spoke about Mrs. Paige's crush on Papa? "Mostly," Fran hastily added, "she's just looking for Rico."

Fee stared at her sister, glad she had never told Fran about her seesaw of doubt and sureness and doubt and sureness. Illogically, she remembered the Hippodrome and the hot chocolate at Letty and Garry's afterward. Mrs. Paige had taken all of them on Saturday, and at Garry's apartment, Fran sat staring at him like a lovesick cow while he did a smoky chemistry trick for Damsie and Josie and the Callavini kids.

"You're getting hipped on people having crushes," Fee stated clearly, in a faraway sort of teacher voice. "And it's kind of disgusting, hinting at things all the time."

Fran was astounded, and Fee was astounded herself. Never had she dreamed she could talk to Fran like this.

Fran said, "I wasn't hinting at anything."

"Just because *you* have a big crush you think nobody knows about," Fee said in the same level tone, "you run around suspecting everybody else has crushes too."

"What big crush?" Fran demanded.

"Never mind."

"What crush I think nobody knows about?"

"I said never mind." An echo of some old clamor reminded Fee that big sisters could be terrible if they got furious, but it vanished in the din of joy over standing up to Fran.

(170)

"What's got into you?" Fran crossed the porch to Fee and yanked her shoulder.

"Nothing. And don't nag at me."

Damsie looked up uneasily, and Josie held the metal top to her eyes like a screen. Fee ducked out of Fran's reach, and sat down on the step next to Josie. Behind her she heard Fran mutter something and then slam herself into the house.

"It's all right," Fee said to the children. "She gets me sick."

"Can we play lotto?" Damsie asked.

"I'll see," Fee said. "I have a lot of homework."

Inside the vestibule behind them, the telephone rang, and they could hear Fran answer it, saying Hello angrily and then shouting, "It's for you, Papa."

"Can't we play lotto?" Damsie begged, and Fee eventually gave in. "We better go in the side door," she said. "My father's still talking on the telephone."

He sounded worked up, but he was talking in Russian and Yiddish, so there was no way to know what it was about, except that he was happy. In a minute Mama went and stood right next to him at the phone too; she kept saying things and asking things, and she sounded happy too.

"Come on." Damsie begged again.

The first lotto game was half over when Fee heard her mother start upstairs, calling out, "Girls, girls, it's won, it's all over, the strike is won."

Fee flung open the bedroom door, and saw her mother's joy, but a bleak apprehension rose in her, grey and ghostly. "Will the mills open right away?" she said slowly. She had known that the strike would be over someday, but she hadn't thought of that for a long time.

Damsie and Josie watched Fee and her mother, as if this were just another family scene that had nothing to do with them.

"Don't you understand, Damsie?" Alexandra said. "And you, Josie? Your Papa won, and everybody's papa won, isn't it wonderful?"

Damsie nodded her head up and down, up and down, as if somebody were pumping it. Then suddenly she jumped to her feet and screamed, "Can I go home to my Pa right now?"

"Of course, you'll be going home, dears, the moment we can arrange it," Alexandra said, taking each of them into her arms and kissing them in ecstatic triumph.

Damsie shook free by jumping up and down, now as joyous as Alexandra. She ran to the chiffonier, yanked open her special drawer, and started to pull out her jacks and red ball, her extra stockings and hair ribbons and the other belongings she would have to pack for the trip home.

Then Josie shouted, "Going home, going home," and started hauling and tugging at the things in her own drawer, dumping them into a scramble on the floor.

Fran could not withstand the noise and shouting and at last she came in, too. Fee looked away, and her mother told the news to Fran and everybody went wild all over again about how wonderful it was that the strike was over, and that the strikers had won enough of their demands to make the terrible nine weeks worthwhile.

Suddenly Fee ran out of the room and down the hall to the bathroom. She slammed the door and pushed the hook into the round steel eye as hard as she could, grinding it in, to lock it the tightest it could be locked.

She flung cold water at her face until she had to gasp, and then she pressed the end of her pinky until it began to burn.

It wasn't fair. One telephone call and they were going to go away and never come back. Without a minute's warning, without even caring what anybody felt.

Alexandra was worried. She had been worried for two or three days without admitting it, but now she thought, Something is wrong with Fee. Maybe it isn't just a cold. Maybe she's really getting sick.

All her staunch theories about bringing up children commanded her to stop *that* line of speculation, and she obeyed.

She wound up the Victrola again, and continued with her dancing. One unexpected result of Damsie and Josie's departure was the renewed freedom she found, dancing without once wondering whether two extra pairs of astonished young eyes were watching from another room.

She smiled at the idea. She had opened all the windows as far as they would go to the sweet warmth of the delayed spring, and it cheered her just to look out at the sparkling young grass and the nubbins of buds on all her bushes. Even though March had thumbed its nose at the maxims and gone out like a lion, these soft days of April were all the more delicious now that they at last were here.

Soon, Fran would start work at making her tennis court, and the field to the south of the house would be overrun with her friends who were all filled with zeal to help with the leveling and grading and rolling, since that was their guarantee of using it as their own when it was ready. Or nearly their own. The agreement was that Fran or Fee could play in the first set each day, but then they had to wait turns like everyone else.

Jack Purney had suggested the arrangement, and Alexandra fretted a little about his basic assumption that Fran and Fee had superior status as owners. But undoubtedly she was being utopian; after all it was Fran and Fee's father who had sought out the absentee owner of the property, who was paying the rent the man demanded, an exorbitant three dollars a month for land lying useless! And it was their father who had donated money for two spades, a cast-iron roller, a tennis net from Spalding and the proper oak stakes to hold it up.

Luxuries like wire screening for backstops would of course have to wait. Perhaps next year, next April, no longer.

Optimism and confidence, as always, swept her hopes high. She felt well, and her strength seemed unflagging. Hop, hop, hop on the right foot, change; hop, hop, hop on the left. Slide and jump to the right, slide and jump to the left. The hops once more, then a deep bend to the right, another to the left.

How old, she wondered, was too old to learn tennis?

A vision of herself racing around on the court made her frown, running after a ball with her grey hair flying, wearing some sort of gym suit, with those baggy bloomers beneath her bulging stomach and a white middy over her pendulous breasts.

They would never forgive me, she thought.

Tennis was for the young, and even though she felt so strong and vital and aware of her endless energy, she was fifty-one and time seemed speedier and more evanescent with every year.

Well, she would enjoy watching the girls play. They would make new friends when the court was finished—that had been their strongest argument: anybody's tennis court always swarms with all the boys and girls for miles around.

It was a great moment when Stiva finally abandoned his nonsense about "aping the rich" and gave in to Franny's entreaties. Fee's too, for even though Fira had never held a tennis racket in her hand, she had backed up Fran in every attempt to persuade him, from the first try more than a year ago, hurling herself into the fight with all her young might and boundless energy.

Alexandra paused and let the music run on. These last days Fee had no energy at all.

Something *is* wrong with her, she thought, theories or no theories. An ordinary cold wouldn't account for it.

She silenced the Victrola with a determined click and clapped the lid down hard. Wallowing in ignorant fear over every cough or sneeze or stomach ache was one thing; facing the truth in Fee's wan little face was another. Something was wrong.

She tried to recall when this sixth sense of all mothers had first told her so. Last week? That was when Fee's cold began. The week before that? Fee had been rather quiet then, it was true, reading every night until her eyeballs must have jigged. It was natural enough, all that reading; at that time, Damsie and Josie had been gone only about a week, and like the whole family, Fee still missed them.

Like the whole family.

Alexandra Ivarin drew in her breath, held it like a precious commodity, and let it out only with the whisper, "Oh, my goodness."

Fee *wasn't* like the whole family about Damsie and Josie, hadn't been during their four weeks in the house, nor after their return to Lawrence, Mass.

Why, the child had suffered heartbreak over their going, and nobody had been humane enough to guess.

Alexandra's throat knobbed with sudden pain. She had been blind and stupid, abysmally, criminally stupid. How often during the month Damsie and Josie had lived with them, had she spoken to Stiva of Fee's warmth toward them, her growing maturity as she took care of them, the fun she had with them because they were like the one thing she had never had—little sisters to play with and lord it over and love.

Fee *had* loved them; her whole nature had gone out to them from the first hour, and though Fran had been sweet also, it was Fee who had become their center of gravity.

And they had become hers.

Then how could Fee's own mother, how could she, Alexandra Ivarin of supposed intelligence and knowledge about the ways of children—how could she have failed to prepare her own child for eventual parting and change and a natural period of missing them? And how could she have failed once again after they went off?

Fee was eating her heart out for them, that was the truth of it. Fee was knowing her first loss and sorrow. No wonder she was listless and pale and wan. And not one soul had tried to help her.

With a fury of purpose, Alexandra flung herself into her clothes. She *had* to do something to help. What, she had no idea, but something. An idea would come.

During the entire morning she concentrated, but her mind remained empty of plan. She thought back to the day Damsie and Josie had left for home, but no clue appeared to guide her. It was a Wednesday afternoon when the victory news came, but as it turned out, they didn't leave until Saturday, and neither did Rico and Maria. She and Alida Paige had consulted with Miss Mainley, and her ruling was firm: the school week had to be finished out.

They were interminable days for all the children, and for everybody else. Stiva nearly exploded the roof off at the *Times* for calling the strike tactics "the greatest menace since the French Revolution," and denounced "this blockhead idiocy, not in the yellow press, mind you, but in the *Times*."

Fran and Fee quarreled, Damsie and Josie were like jumping jacks, and by Saturday when they at last said good-bye and went off, it was actually a relief all around.

Alida took them with Rico and Maria, and later reported every detail of the trip and the children's homecoming. But, Alexandra thought now, hadn't there been a dryness in her way of phrasing things? A subdued note, a bit lifeless?

Lifeless. Listless. Did Alida miss the hustle and bustle of Rico and Maria, as she went back to her lovely house, again to be empty all day? Perhaps Alida, too, was still mourning the loss of the children.

It was days and days since they had seen each other. They had grown closer while they were sharing the experience of having strangers' children live with them, and it had been pleasant, but since their departure—

I'll take a walk, Alexandra thought. I'm beginning to feel as unhappy as poor Fee.

"Come in, Alexandra," Alida said eagerly. "What a nice surprise!"

She was warmed by Alida's delighted welcome, and her doubts about dropping in unexpectedly, which had accompanied her as the route of her walk kept drifting closer and closer to Channing Street, vanished before she had taken the hatpins out of her old spring hat.

"You're busy," she said a moment later, startled at what she saw.

"But I need a rest; I can't take in another word." Alida led the way into the dining room and said, "Sit down, while I make tea. Read some of them, and you'll see what I've been doing for the last few days."

The table had been extended by two leaves inserted at its center, and its surface was covered from edge to edge with neat piles of letters, clippings, notes written by Evan on pad paper, and a few telegrams.

Each pile had an oblong label on it, like a shipping tag, with a crayoned name or date or phrase. The label nearest Alexandra said, "Jails," and the second "Single Taxers." A third was "Traffic Ordinance," the next "Socialists," and another, "Anarchists." Beyond that was "Beatings" and by its side, "Deaths."

A shiver moved Alexandra's arms and shoulders. She picked up the first assortment, "Jails." Alida had said, "Read some of them," and she began with a small page in Evan's writing, disconnected notes, like words and figures jotted down as reminders for a lecturer.

"First test of const; 41 jailed. Incl. League att'y, Smithers. March 4 Total-200; Overflow to Santa A., Riv., etc. S.D. *Tribune* public stand: Taking men out of jails, hanging and shooting them."

Attached was a clipped editorial from the *San Diego Tribune,* of which she had never heard. Underlined in red crayon were phrases like "hanging and shooting them." In actual print, she thought, in an American newspaper.

Alexandra put it down in a strange sudden fear, and set the rest of the pile down too. She looked at the stack marked "Beatings," without touching it. Under the label she saw more penciled jottings: "Hoey, 68 Third Degree; kicked stomach, groin. Rupture—may die."

"Isn't it frightful?" Alida said as she came in with a tray.

"What *is* this?"

"I'm trying to help Evan, organizing it by subject, and doing a summary for him to use in California."

"His trip, oh yes." She sensed that Alida expected her to understand perfectly by now, but she was still bewildered.

"It's a good thing he had to put it off this long. By now the Free Speech League in San Diego is battling a new case every week, and a second California chapter is forming. He may have to stay on for quite a time."

Alexandra was silent. Somewhere she had heard or read of free-speech riots in California, but it had slipped away as if it had nothing of importance for her. Suddenly it was near and intimate; Alida's grave manner, Evan's involvement, all made the transformation.

"Stefan must have told me what's going on there, but I'm ashamed to admit—"

"Hardly anybody in the East does know about it," Alida said, "but it's spreading like wildfire out there."

"Do they know how it started?"

"It's so strange," Alida said thoughtfully. "Ever since San Diego was settled, it had a tradition about open-air meetings and then overnight the tradition vanished."

"Meetings for labor?" Alexandra asked.

"And for everything else. Civic reform, the I.W.W., church revival meetings, socialism, anarchism, Single Taxers, Votes for Women—"

"I never knew that either," Alexandra said, suddenly approving the inner spirit of the Far West. "I usually think of Bret Harte or the Gold Rush when I—" She broke off hastily.

Alida was absorbed in her own train of thought. "There always had been heckling and shoving, but since January the heckling has been transformed into brawls and riots, with mobs of roughnecks and vigilantes, and finally the police, ordered to keep the peace, keep traffic moving, and no questions asked about how."

"And since then," Alexandra said positively, "it's been like Russia, more and more every day."

"It's sickening, it truly is."

"I wish Stefan were here," Alexandra said impulsively. "We've never heard *you* speak out on such things, and you make it fascinating. And so clear too. Please go on."

Alida blushed a little, but she was touched. How lovely, to speak so freely and sweetly to a friend. In praise and kindness, words became blessings; how infrequently were such words used.

It was not until they were parting an hour later, that Alexandra remembered her desire to discuss her worry over Fee. It was just as well, perhaps, that she hadn't been able to. Was it possible, after all, for any mother to report on the lonely sadness of a child?

At the door, Alida said, "We'll see you before Evan leaves next week."

"So soon?"

"Next Thursday—didn't I say that, with all the gabbing I did? His Pullman tickets are in his wallet."

"Only four days from now. May I tell Stiva?"

"Tell anybody—and I'm so glad you dropped by, Alexandra. Thank you, I had a lovely time."

Alexandra suddenly laughed. "I could live in America for three hundred years," she said, "and I'd never learn to send off a guest the way you do."

Alida's responsive little chuckle drifted after her, and she walked away in elation. She had had a lovely time too, though so caressing an adjective would never occur to her, for a visit that included revelations of beatings, jails, prisoners, death. But it had stimulated her and sent her away refreshed. Soon now her instincts might yield up a hint of how Fee—

She stopped on the sidewalk. The April wind had grown playful and its fingers snatched at her hat and her skirt. It was nearly dark; the wide sky curled at its edges with pink and golden plumes. She stood still, not daring to move lest the idea drift away.

Then she hurried the rest of the way to the house. Stefan would be demanding supper any minute.

Fran said, "Hello, Mama, I decided you were lost," and Alexandra said, "I'll be down in a minute, Franny. Light the oven, like a good girl."

Upstairs Fee's door was closed; she knocked twice before Fee said, "Who is it?"

"I have some news, Fee," she answered. "You'll be interested."

Alexandra could hear her throw down a book, grumble as it slid to the floor, and then get up from bed where she doubtless had lain motionless, reading, hour after hour since she had come home from school.

"What kind of news, Mama?"

"You look worse, Fee, what's wrong, dear?"

"I'm not worse, honestly. I haven't even coughed."

"It's just an impression probably," Alexandra conceded. But her heart ached at Fee's appearance—eyes strained, skin without color, hair disheveled. "My news," she said importantly, "is about Evan Paige and a trip."

"What trip?"

"To California, *that* trip. He's leaving in four days."

"Really and truly? Are you sure?"

"Positive. His Pullman tickets are in his wallet this very minute."

"Oh, Mama!" Fee's voice rose in excitement. "Will he tell me every single thing about the train when he gets back?"

"I know he will," Alexandra said unhesitatingly. "He will notice each detail, so he won't forget anything and when he comes home he will describe every single one."

Fee's face was transformed, and Alexandra thought, I can explain that she needed something to look forward to, and Evan will do it for her. Aloud she said, "And you ought to start a secret list right away. Put down all the things you're going to ask him about. Don't show it to me or Franny or anybody—it's only for you and Evan."

"It'll be a mile long," Fee said. "I would start it tonight if I had a special notebook—the kind you can lock."

"Tonight's a good idea, Firuschka. I'll give you some money and you go downtown after supper and buy the right kind."

"Right after supper—oh, I'm so happy."

Fee hugged her mother with such vigor that Alexandra's bones winced.

FOURTEEN

For a moment, Evan Paige stood at the edge of the pitted dirt road, too shocked to move or speak. In the hot darkness of the California night, the only light came from the crescent of moon above them, and from the dimmed headlamps of one of the four cars making a semicircle around the cleared place where the vigilantes had dragged their prisoner.

"Sing it, you anarchist bastard," one of them shouted, "or you'll get kilt with this here gun."

There were fourteen or fifteen of them, armed with rifles, whips, metal piping, and they had ordered Ben Reitman to sing "The Star-Spangled Banner."

As they dragged him from the first car, he had gone limp, but now he was pulled half-upright on his knees, his bald head gluey with sweat, his glasses hanging from one ear, his shirt torn from his body.

"Damn you, sing."

With each note that squawked up from his tight throat, they kicked him, beat him, shrieking and shouting in their indomitable glory, while the single victim, alone, attempting bravery, attempting dignity, tried to produce the syllables and even the melody.

" 'By—the—dawn's—' "

He gulped for air, and one of the vigilantes struck Reitman with his gun; the butt hit his eyebrow and blood jumped forward from bone and flesh, leaping down over his eye.

"Go on, sing it," one of them shouted. "You quit singin' again, I'll kill you, you goddam red bastard."

Paige rushed forward, all at once released from the prison of his horror. "Let that man alone, you animals," he shouted, and heard his

(179)

voice carried off in the din of their savagery, heard it reduced, made puny, impotent, foolish.

" 'Early—light—' "

Paige charged at the line of circling backs; two of them turned toward him, and in a perfect harmony of timing, without apparent effort, lifted him off the ground by his arms, forcing them to bend at the elbows, lifting him, half swinging him between them as if he were a happy child in a happy game being swung through the air by loving grownups, indulgent, ready to play.

"You stay the hell out of this, Pop," one of the men said in his ear, "or you get the same as this here red bastard anarchist."

They pitched him like an awkwardly baled package to the edge of the road. A shout of laughter tore the hot dark air, as Evan got back to his feet, and Reitman's voice stopped, sheared off on a syllable. A man in overalls was stuffing a small American flag down Reitman's throat. Sounds of retching, hideous, unending, took the place of the strangled singing.

Evan started forward, his convulsive muscles going into spasms of retching too. He controlled the spasms, thinking, Not now. Bitterness invaded him. He had been so sure that some of the reports were far-fetched. Now, after three weeks with people he trusted, he knew that the truth had outdistanced the reports.

"Don't let him choke hisself," somebody said with a voice of authority. "Yank it out quick now."

The sounds stopped except for a moaning from the road. Evan inched forward, and for the first time saw that beyond the immediate ground was a wispy hedge and then a farmhouse. From the privy at the back of the house, there now came one of the youngest of the vigilantes, a boy, straw-colored, and downy still. He carried a newspaper made into a giant scoop, and he roared with joy as he called out, "Who's got a spreader? Anybody got a lathe or stick or somethin' to spread with?"

"Hold it a minute, Ernie," somebody answered, matching Ernie's roar with exploding laughter of his own, appreciative, admiring of Ernie's ingenuity and cleverness. "I'm just heatin' up the tar bucket a bit, won't be a minute. That'll hold it real good."

Evan dived into the wall of bodies blocking him off from Reitman. Instantly he was trapped, thrown to the ground, kicked in the ribs, stomach, head. He could not rise beyond a kneeling position; a thick-bodied giant with hands of stone pushed down on him with tons of power, grinding, sending him flat once more.

The tarring began. Evan saw that it was not heavily or evenly put on, but it was viscous, brutal, sinful as nothing he had ever seen in his entire half-century of living. Ernie had found no lathe, no stick or spreader, but with a newspaper folded over and over, he was covering over the strokes of tar, spreading the stench and foulness of human excrement over it on Reitman's flesh, shrieking in savage whoops all the while, bellowing and gasping at his own joke.

Ernie's wildness ignited the others. One tore up fistfuls of grass and threw them, like confetti at a Mardi gras, making patches of young green on top of the filth.

"Herbie, wait a minute," somebody else shouted at the grass-flinger, "lemme get near the stinking anarchist son-of-a-bitch—I got a real great thing here."

Herbie obligingly moved aside. "What real great thing, Bobbo?"

Bobbo did not answer. He was already kneeling on the dark earth, reaching for Reitman's head, stabbing at his ears and neck with something he held in cautious fingers.

"Cactus?" Herbie said. "Them little acorny needly ones? By God, you're the one, Bobbo!" And as Bobbo tried to jam the cactus more accurately into Reitman's ear, Herbie begged and wheedled, "Save me a few for his anarchist asshole; don't forget now, Bobbo."

Paige rose uncertainly. He was sure he had not lost consciousness, even for a moment, but the semicircle of cars was gone, and with the cars, the armed lords of creation and their prisoner.

He had not moved from the spot where they had ground his face and shoulders into the pits and pebbles of the road. From somewhere to his right, beyond a planted field, came shouted obscenities, ending ". . . promised the Chief of Police not to kill you . . . that's the hell of it." He heard it clearly though his head rang and buzzed within its protecting layer of bone. He put his hand up to his face, feeling it wet, but the light was too dim to let him see whether the wet was his blood or some of their tar. He did not care just then. He started for the car he had borrowed from Jonathan Smithers of the League, by luck a Reo like his own, but a new one. He had been foresighted enough to leave it under a tree a hundred yards away.

He walked with a blurry unsureness and wondered how much time had passed since their assault. His right foot kicked into a piece of white cloth; as he stooped to pick it up, pain tore through the base of his skull. He wondered if they had injured his neck or given him a concussion, but his attention was not fully engaged by the possibility, as if he did not care about that either.

The white cloth was Reitman's torn and bloodied shirt, and he rolled it into a packet, clenching his fist about it as if it was suddenly dear to him. He moved on again, thinking, I mustn't lose it, I'll need it.

"I'll need it," was what he had said to Smithers at the lecture hall. "I'll probably need it."

The beginnings of this vile night suddenly were clear again. He and Smithers were at the hall because Emma Goldman was to speak on—of all things—Henrik Ibsen's *An Enemy of the People,* and they had reason to expect furor or worse. Vigilantes had crowded the San Diego railroad station hours before, when she arrived from Los Angeles with her manager, Dr. Ben Reitman, and by the time the two were in an autobus for the Ulysses S. Grant Hotel, a typical storm of jeers and threats had blown up to roaring proportions.

From the hotel, word was sent to Smithers by a member of the League. Other vigilantes, some openly armed, were there, jesting with the Chief of Police. The Mayor was on his way, and in the street, crowds were already gathering.

"You stay here," Paige had said to Smithers. "I'll come back as soon as I can."

Smithers insisted that Evan borrow his car. "I suppose I'd better, Jonathan. If there's trouble, I'll probably need it."

Their four cars were pulling away from the hotel as he drove up. He didn't know they had Reitman tied and covered over, on the floor of the first one. He saw their flags, heard their curses and shouts, and inside the hotel, he saw the police clearing the way for the last of the vigilantes. His decision to follow the fourth car was automatic, as if the steering wheel in his hands had turned by itself.

That's how it had been—each detail stood out as the buzz and noise in his ears and head died down. He ran the last yards to the tree and the car.

Smithers' car was still there. But its four doors were hanging crazily from their hinges and its tires were slashed deep and wide in gashes that showed the metal of the rims beneath.

How had they been so sure the car was his? They had stopped their procession to take this vengeance but he had heard nothing, no twisting of steel as they wrenched the doors in their vandal hands, no hissing of air from slaughtered tires. He *had* gone unconscious after all.

He turned from the dangling doors and flapping strips of rubber and sat down on the running board, as exhausted as a drowning swimmer. This dirt road must be twenty miles from the city; he remembered passing a painted sign, "County Line," while he was trailing their cars, and they had not begun to slow down until they had left the sign well behind.

He tried to empty his mind of image and memory, to stop speculating about how he could get back to his hotel. First, he needed to rest, to regain himself.

Hardly a moment passed before he was up again, searching for further damage to the car. He could find none. Four new tires, four new doors—their vengeance had come in specific terms and tidy quantities. Had they been inspired further, they might also have bent and pierced and scratched each fender, all the shining glass and metal, gouged out the faceted lenses from the brass headlamps, smashed the engine itself.

The cloth packet was hurting his hand. He loosened his grip; he had been jamming two buttons against the bones of his fingers. As if the buttons tapped out a coded order, Evan instantly retraced his steps to the open space where they had ringed Reitman, and began to search the ground, inch by inch.

The last of the blur was gone from his vision and in the light of the high stars and the bright crescent of the moon, he found a long scrap of dark wool that might have come from a man's trousers, and he pocketed it. He saw a gleaming section of curved glass, and knew it would fit the face of a dollar watch. He found, innocently clustered in a clump on the road, some small-scaled cactus, "them little needly acorny ones."

He saw what might have been the newspaper spreader, but he was wrenched by the spasm of vomit again and decided that Exhibits A, B, and C would be evidence enough for any court of law that *was* a court of law.

He stood still, breathing deeply and quietly, resting once more. The farmhouse was little more than a shack, he saw now, but he moved toward it until he was sure that there was no barn, no stable that could contain a horse and wagon.

Then he began to walk toward San Diego.

The doctor sent by Jonathan Smithers said, "Nothing broken, and I think no concussion." But he refused to let him get up, no matter how urgently Evan said he had to go to the League office, finish his report and turn over his exhibits.

"Apart from the manhandling, Mr. Paige," he said diffidently, "there's your walking most of the night before the milk wagon showed up. Twelve miles for anybody out of training—well, you see. I'll give you something for pain."

Dr. Grimes handed Evan a domed pill, poured water from the white crockery pitcher on the bedside table, and said, "You take this pill, and I'll look in on you after supper."

Evan nodded, thinking, I'll be back in an hour. He swallowed the pill with the complacent knowledge that he was going to disobey, the moment the doctor's back was turned. As long as the hurricanes of pain blowing through his neck and legs meant no internal damage to brain or body, he had to see Jonathan and the others at once, to fill out the rough account he had telephoned the moment he had reached the hotel. They were already tracking down Ernie and Herbie and Bobbo, but he could give them descriptions, details, clues that might make it easier, faster and surer.

"In case you have any lawyer's plan worked out about getting up anyway," Dr. Grimes added conversationally from the doorway, "you'll be giving it up in about two minutes. The pill I gave you was a real persuader."

He nodded pleasantly and left. Evan wondered if he could have prevented Grimes from out-maneuvering him so handily, and decided he could not. The few seconds that had slipped by had taken some of his urgency along with them. His eyelids seemed thicker already and he leaned back into the pillows' support with gratitude.

At his side he could see Alida's letter, a flash of white on the table, and he reached out, to read it again. But his hand fell an inch short of it, and he let it rest there, soothed at its proximity. She had written ten days ago but the letter had reached him only yesterday. Parts of it were funny, especially about her secret fear of joining the great parade up Fifth Avenue from the Arch up to Madison Square.

"Alexandra was nervous too, but she kept my courage up," she wrote, "telling me ten times over that once I marched in public for something like Woman Suffrage, I'd like it so much, I'd do it every chance I got."

Evan smiled. Sleep was all about him now, slowing his breathing and adding weight to his head, but he made another effort to pick up Alida's letter, and this time he succeeded. The last page had saddened him, about Garry and Letty and their weekend in Barnett. He turned to it again.

"They worry me so," Alida had written at the top of the sheet. She had crossed the words out, and crossed them out a second and third time, but the paper had taken her pen's first pressure to its heart, and

(1 8 4)

still revealed the curves and lines of every word she had tried so insistently to unsay.

"Last night we were talking about the *Titanic* again, and I said how unbearable if a warship or submarine had done it *on purpose,* instead of a submerged iceberg in a horrifying accident. Garry didn't do anything except agree—in an instant, an iceberg of our own was right there in the room! I have the heaviest feeling that Letty freezes up about all sorts of things now, and if I say a word about the news or politics, I get that faint embarrassed sense that they've just had a quarrel but want me not to guess that they did. If this happened only once, I'd decide they *did* have a whopper, and think nothing of it. But it's a persistent impression, and I pray I'm just imagining things."

Evan bowed his head, as if to second her prayer. Immediate pain ringed his throat, sending waving tendrils up into his brain, and he wondered if Grimes could have overlooked some hidden injury that his own doctor at home would have detected. He put Alida's letter down on the bed beside him and fell asleep.

Voices and lights struck at him from everywhere, and he opened his eyes unwillingly. Jonathan was coming in, closing the door behind him quickly. Beyond him in the hall were several policemen.

Jonathan came close, asking how he felt, was the pain less? Beyond him, Evan saw bright light at the two windows, despite their lowered blinds; his disappointment was like a child's anger. It was still daylight; Dr. Grimes and a second pill were a long way off.

"What time is it?"

"Ten, Evan. It's morning."

"Grimes said he'd come back after supper."

"He did come back. You were still under and had fever. Grimes gave you a stronger sedative. I was here with him, so I know."

Evan tried to see his watch. It had been moved from the table, together with the thick white pitcher and Alida's letter. Two small bottles stood there now, nothing else.

With a start he said, "Who took my things away? Is my coat here?"

"I took your exhibits with me last night; they're in the office safe, locked up." He pointed to a sheet of paper tacked to the closet door. "I left you a signed receipt in case you woke up and thought you'd been robbed."

"Good man." He glanced toward the hall door, alert in a flash.

"I thought of the police, too," Jonathan said. "Especially since the

Citizens' Committee will affirm on oath that they know no Bobbo, no Herbie, no Ernie, and that all their members were in their trundle beds right through the entire night."

Evan didn't answer. The Citizens' Committee. How innocent, how upright.

"I'll get up," he said slowly. "I suppose the police out there are armed with a fine warrant, to arrest *me* for disturbing the peace?"

"Not by all the warrants in this sovereign state. You've got a lawyer, sir, who's qualified to practice before the California Bar, as you are NOT. You also have a physician who has attested in writing that you are to remain in this room until he says different."

"That's good too." He got to his feet, and moved his head in a tentative circle, and then slowly backward. "I'm all right," he said.

"Coffee is coming up in a minute," Smithers said. "And some eggs."

"I'm all right now," Evan repeated. "I'd better be, with what's ahead."

He didn't mean for that one day, he thought as he shaved. He didn't mean only in San Diego, or even Los Angeles where the new League chapter had just formed. He meant in the Governor's mansion at San Francisco, he meant in Washington, D. C., he meant in New York, he meant in courtrooms and in judge's chambers and wherever he would be spending all the hours he meant to spend on this fight until he could again come to some possible pause.

June was half over before Evan Paige was at home again. His homecoming dinner was at Garry and Letty's apartment, but afterwards, on that same evening, he and Alida went down to the Lower East Side to meet the Ivarins at the all-night café they had so often heard about.

Evan himself had arranged the midnight meeting. As he and Alida were leaving for the city in the late afternoon, he had telephoned Stefan, and almost his first words were, "Do you remember what you said that time—'if there is a free-speech case you are angry about'?"

"Yes, certainly, yes." Ivarin was obscurely pleased that Paige had remembered and meant to hold him to it. "What is a convenient time to talk about it?"

"We're starting for Garry's house now," Evan said. "You'll be at the paper tonight, won't you?"

"Did you say 'the paper'?"

"I wondered if you might manage half an hour later on in the evening, *this* evening. Then Alida and I could go downtown when we leave Garry's, and perhaps see you at your office."

"Excellent! But wait—"

Stefan was charmed at the unexpected suggestion. He had guessed Evan would be returning in a fury from California; there had been some Sunday pieces in *The Call* about the free-speech riots there. But it had not occurred to him that Evan would be driven to act the first night he was at home. That was more like his own character than like the equable and controlled New Englander Paige invariably seemed to be.

"Tonight is excellent," he said, "but my office is no good for talk, quite bad in fact. How would it strike you if we meet instead in the café next door? Nobody would interrupt us there."

"That would be even better. Alida will be coming too—you did understand that?"

"Do I understand about wives? Has Alida ever been in an East Side restaurant?"

At his side, Alexandra said, "Stiva, what's going on?"

Stefan looked around, and thought, Now I'll find out about wives all right, I never even considered it. Into the telephone, he said, "If Alida would enjoy it, perhaps Alexandra might also like an East Side rendezvous, for the sake of change."

He brushed away Evan's thanks and smiled at Alexandra as he hung up. "It's been several months," he said, "since you've stopped in at the café. I thought you'd enjoy meeting them there tonight."

Alexandra said, "I would not." She turned abruptly and left him.

He thought, I knew it. But he went after her and said, "Now see here," in his most cajoling voice.

"You never *thought* of including me," she said, facing him suddenly. "If I hadn't wanted to say welcome home to Evan, and come over to tell you not to hang up, why then, you would have thought nothing of meeting them there by yourself, without one word to me until afterward."

"Damnable nonsense," he said in Russian.

Since she was so correct, he was outraged. His pleasant emotions about Evan's desire to hold him to his word, his sense of comradeliness, even his small proprietary pleasure at being the Paiges' host in *his* domain—all this was riddled with holes by her spattering outburst.

"It is not nonsense," she said. "I won't go, like a—an afterthought."

"Then don't. If you're going to dish up a bowlful of anguish, it's better that you don't."

(187)

He started up the stairs. He could hear her hurl herself on the narrow bed in the sewing room, and he thought, Like a child, like a debutante. Each notion deepened his resentment. No matter how intelligent she was, no matter how fine and good, she was also a damnable nuisance with her hurt and her tears, and he wished he could call off the entire evening. It was ruined in any case.

He wondered about Evan's specific plan for his help. An article, of course. Would Evan renew the other suggestion, about signing him up as a member of the committee? Surely not. But would a man of Evan's temperament come downtown on the very evening he arrived back East, to ask him to write one article? Improbable also.

He rolled a cigarette and thought, How interesting human behavior is. Paige knows enough of press time to know it could not be in tomorrow's paper if he doesn't see me until midnight, yet he wants to come down tonight, not wait until tomorrow.

Human behavior. He wondered where Alexandra was, and why no sound of tears. He had been sure she would follow her sudden passion for etiquette and pursue him upstairs to belabor it until misery enveloped her like thick dark velvet.

He bent his cigarette double and jammed it into his crowded ashtray. His hand slipped and the red end of the cigarette nipped his thumb. He cursed at it, at the ashtray, at himself for smoking too much and at Alexandra for being so unreasonable that she drove a man to excesses that would kill off his health.

Then he went to find her.

She was out in the garden, hoeing the earth around her tomato plants, apparently contented and untroubled. In the late sun, Shag was the color of a red fox, and his dripping elongated tongue told of June and summer. Beyond the peaceful scene were the strenuous shouts of five boys and girls helping Fran and Fira to make the tennis court—if tennis court it was to be. The grass was certainly gone from the plot, but there was no more tennis court as yet than there would have been at the ruins of Pompeii five minutes after the eruption. Hills of loose earth straggled over half the area, where the rise had been which Franny had so complacently predicted would be leveled off in "a day or two." Who could have suspected the rocky stratum under the grass and dandelions?

Alexandra said, "Well, what is it?"

He smiled and his irritation vanished. She had won a victory, and she had been aware of it when he came out to find her in such splendid calm and serenity, instead of in the tears he had expected. Now she had thrown it away by being Alexandra to the nth degree—unable to wait it out and force him to speak first, apologetic, contrite. He loved her for her failure. She was a marvel.

"You were right," he said. "I was so interested in Evan's inviting himself downtown, I hadn't yet thought about anything else. But in another minute, I would have. You must know I would have."

She looked at him, hoe in her hand, suspicion in her eyes, but also trust and willingness to believe him. Shag trotted over to Stefan and he scratched the dog's head absent-mindedly. "You must know I would have," he repeated.

"I suppose so," she said. "Perhaps I'm too sensitive." She dropped the hoe and shook earth from the hem of her skirt. With a bound, Shag leaped toward her, crashing through the even rows of her tomato plants. "Bad, bad dog," she scolded, "you're always sorry afterward, but you always manage to mangle things first. Go away, go, I say."

Shag miserably obeyed. Stiva watched him go and thought, At times, she can be quite witty.

It was like meeting a new man, Stefan Ivarin decided as he finished his coffee and signaled to the waiter to clear and tidy the littered table. Evander Paige had never shown himself this way in the three years and more that they had known each other, never so angry, so fierce, so close to hatred.

As Evan told his story Alida seemed nearly as stunned as Alexandra, though Alida was not hearing it for the first time, while Alexandra was raw under its first impact. She was always so unguarded about showing what she felt that now as she flinched or squeezed her eyelids tight in shock, Stefan found it hard to look in her direction.

Nobody interrupted Evan with question or comment. When the waiter approached, Stefan whispered, "Now, some tea," but only by gesture did he ask the others if they would join him or order something else.

His flesh did not retract as Alexandra's did, but violence tore him. He was a student again, a youth bending over a secret printing press in a Russian cellar; at the sudden stomp and thud of the Cossacks he was riven again with fear; he was in a stone cell again under the whistling descent of the knout.

Evan must have guessed it, for now he spoke directly to him, as one speaks to a co-survivor. And soon Stefan Ivarin felt that he was also Evander Paige, also standing in the ringed circle under the high crescent of the western moon, hearing the brutish laughter, feeling the iron hands grinding him down into the pocked and pitted road.

Suddenly he seemed to be manifold, ribboned and interlaced, the terrified boy in Russia, the grown man and editor listening, the native-born American lawyer telling. This extraordinary interlocking of memory and fact, of youth and man, of himself and his friend shook Stefan Ivarin in some new depth. It was as if they now shared the same corpuscles and muscles, briefly but forever, as if the lobes of their brains could be interchanged, as if they were a new creature, single, various, but one.

And as Evan went on to the aftermath of that May night, Stefan Ivarin hardly needed to wait for his words to sound and his sentences to form. His contempt for "San Diego Law" chilled Ivarin's bowels but the contempt was familiar, his own, seen and known long before.

Yet he hungered for the specific, for date, place, name, and urged Evan on through the shabby farce of affidavits and depositions and sworn testimony, the deadening delays, the languid police. He could hear the raucous patriots in meetings swearing to protect the beloved city, see the local press blazing at the anarchists, foreign agitators, vagrants, bums, radicals, free-speechers.

Fleetingly, Ivarin's heart lifted that the *San Francisco Bulletin* had at last made the issue state-wide, with a full-page attack on "Gag Law in San Diego," and that the A.F. of L. and the young unions of the West finally joined forces, the copper miners and silver miners, the dockhands and lumbermen and seamen and shipbuilders.

"And then came the great news," Evan said. "Up at the State Capitol, Governor Johnson ordered a full investigation of the riots and the vigilantes by a Federal grand jury."

Ivarin nodded, but quickly looked away again.

"You know how it ended?" Evan said.

"I am sure," Ivarin answered.

"The grand jury indicted thirty people," Evan said quietly. "Thirty I.W.W.s and socialists and union leaders. And not one vigilante, not one." He looked at Alida and at Alexandra. Then he addressed himself again to Stefan. "Not even one."

Stefan said nothing.

All around him in the restaurant beat the loud voices of the East Side, of Europe, untrained in American composure, unaware of American manners, voices rising and falling in talk and argument, in bursting laughter or noisy discussion. Dishes clattered, waiters rushed back and forth, metal trays clashed against each other. The smells of Europe's food were there—spiced meats, herring, dill pickles, cabbage soup, the rind of lemon, the sweet freshness of cherries, the baked sugar and honey of small cakes.

It all spoke to him as a call from his own beginnings, a memory, a recognition of a promise made long ago, to whom he did not remember, for what he could not say. He looked at the somber face of the man before him, born in New England, grown in the unflurried sureness of an American youth, educated to a profession of justice. And he loved him as he had never yet known he could love another man.

Various, but one. He himself the American born in another land and become an American by choice, by law, by document; Evander Paige the American by birth, his first papers issued to him with his first breath—yet each knowing that a lifetime might go toward validating those papers and being worthy of them.

"One article," he said at last. "Yes, one fine article about your acorns and your 'tar' and the flag. You are asking for more than that, I think."

Evan nodded and said nothing. Alexandra put her napkin up to her mouth and then to her eyes; they were dry but they were on fire. She dipped the napkin into the ice water in her glass and then pressed it to each eyelid again. This wasn't anything she would like her pupils to see her doing in a restaurant, but it didn't matter.

"Tell Stefan, dear," Alida said to her husband.

"Let's take your 'one fine article,' " Evan said. "It will appear in your paper first, but as fast as possible in twenty more. It would be translated the next day—I'll arrange that—into English and other languages besides. German, Italian, Polish, Swedish."

"Twenty papers?" Ivarin was genuinely startled.

"Here's the twenty we'd like to use—I started drawing up a list out West where some League people could advise me—San Francisco, Duluth, Milwaukee, Chicago, St. Louis—probably you know most of the papers already."

"An article of yours appearing all over the whole country!" Alexandra exclaimed. "Imagine!"

Stefan reached for Evan's list. He knew the Wisconsin *Vorwaerts* and the San Francisco *Tageblatt,* both printed in German, and of course the *Appeal to Reason,* that stout native voice from Kansas. Some other names had the ring of the familiar, some he had never heard of. The Swedish paper was a weekly, published in Duluth, and the Italian was *La Prensa,* a neighbor of the *Jewish News* right in New York.

Evan Paige was a good campaigner, Ivarin thought; there was a large design here. The English translation he would do himself; Evan wanted to spare him the extra effort, but that was not to be considered.

He was aware that Evan was waiting for an answer, but Ivarin remained meditative and absorbed. Touching at the edge of his mind, like a tentative finger, asking for silence, for attention, for another moment of time, was an idea, and he held still, inviting it, wanting it, valuing it.

There are pogroms in California.

The phrase leaped at him. As if he saw it in print, he knew it for the opening line of his opening article. There are Cossacks in San Diego, czars of the streets. They call themselves by pretty names like "The Citizens' Committee," but they are the Armed Tyrants of Europe sprouting again in the sweet soil of this free land—

Aloud he said, "You have a good plan, Evan. It strikes me very strongly."

"I think it is strong. San Diego isn't the only city with vigilantes."

"So you are suggesting a series of articles," Ivarin said matter-of-factly. "The first right away, then a few days later, a second one, and so on. San Diego leading to episodes you fellows know about in other cities. That must be it."

"That *is* it, Stiva."

Stefan Ivarin took off his glasses, nodding to them as if in greeting, as if to signal them of duty and work and late hours ahead.

Evan said, "At first, I thought one piece only. But that led me to a second and a third, as I hoped it would lead you. I don't know how much work it will be—a good deal, I am certain."

"Yes, yes, of course." Ivarin said it without stress, as Evan Paige had spoken without apology. Stefan squinted through the lenses he had been polishing and was satisfied with their brilliance. The ostensible target of these vigilantes, he would write, is always an anarchist, but along with anarchists, or instead of anarchists, the victims turn out to be strikers, workers holding grievance meetings, union organizers, vagrants, and of course socialists. Socialists who by definition oppose all anarchists as extremists, just as they oppose all vigilantes as extremists.

Yes, it could make a powerful series. Perhaps two of Evan's articles, then one of his continuing pieces to get Berkman's book printed, then back to Evan's. He put his glasses on and with total illogic reached across to Alexandra and pinched her cheek. To Evan he said, "Can your people at the League send me material for subsequent articles?"

"I'll select it myself," Evan said. "If the League sent it, they would swamp you. But I will sift out what you'd be interested in. I think I'll know."

Ivarin said, "It would be fine if you could do it yourself, Evan." He thought, He will choose what I would choose.

A singular contentment invaded him.

F I F T E E N

Long after his parents had left to meet the Ivarins, Garry's surprise persisted. This was a new Letty. He had never seen her this way, his parents had never seen her this way.

"It's cooler in here," he said as he came back from the front door. "Let's sit around a while."

How good it was, this swift bridge between them tonight, this reaching across, one to the other over an idea. It was the first time it had happened. Letty could have been strait-jacketed and drugged while his father told them about the vigilantes, but she would have managed to express her wrath. He was proud of her anger and glad his parents were seeing it too. For the first time they had reached common ground for all four of them to stand on.

"Anyway," he added as Letty settled back in the big chair near the open window, "I love you too much to want to go to bed. How's that for a paradox?"

He turned off every bulb in the room for added coolness; the street lamp sent a yellow paleness toward them, like a whisper of light. Outside nothing stirred; the long windows, denuded of their red draperies weeks before in the fast-quickening city summer, stood wide open, but they were like elongated maws, sucking and gaping at air that was diverted elsewhere.

"Who do they think they are?" Letty had cried out at the vigilantes. "Who made them anybody's keeper?" This wasn't "politics" but a family matter; it had happened to them, to the Paiges, to her, Letty Paige, who was one of them.

Wasn't there a lesson for him in that? There was a hitch or delay at Aldrich about converting to explosives, but if the company did go ahead later on and he did pull out, wasn't it possible that she would be this family-Letty of tonight, and not the distant Letty of the morning papers? After their bad quarrel on the blizzardy morning, he had told her he was "through talking about the news," and had stuck to it. Over this "clamming up" she had never protested.

Who do they think they are? Who made them anybody's keeper? How easy and good marriage must be, Garry thought, if always there were this sharing with your wife of feelings and ideas that were basic to you.

"I talk too much, Letts," he said suddenly.

"What makes you say that?"

"I pave the way too much."

She could see only his outline and position; she could not see his expression. But he sounded relaxed and contented. Recently they had been happier, as if God had willed new patience and a new start for them. She still had not gone to Dr. Haslitt, but she had promised to go once the heat was over. She still hadn't told Garry of her daydream for next fall, not out of secrecy, but only to find out more about it before she did.

"I've been mulling over a thrilling idea," she said, "wondering whether to tell you now or wait a bit more."

"Tell me now."

"Oh, Gare, since we're not having a baby for a while, I want something to do all day. Not just a hobby, but something real."

"Like what?"

"A shop, an antique shop with beautiful pieces in it, like all of ours here. For sale to people. *My* shop."

"Why, Letty." He suddenly reached to the lamp nearest him and relighted it. She looked intense and eager. "When did you think that up?"

"I don't know. It seems forever. But I didn't know how you'd feel about it."

"I'd be proud of you, for having the gumption."

"You wouldn't!"

"Did you think I'd start spouting 'Woman's place is in the home,' and denounce Mrs. **Pank**hurst and Carrie Chapman Catt?"

"Of course not. But I thought you'd think I ought to take a job in a store first, instead of starting my own business."

He gazed at her. Women were no longer a novelty in the world of business, but their "place" was still pretty well limited. Clerks, salesladies, telephone operators, bookkeepers—certainly they could succeed at more enterprising projects than these, but he didn't know a single one who had ever tried. The Woman Suffrage movement was worldwide and irreversible, and far more than votes was involved, but to have Letty actually practicing what it preached had never occurred to him.

"You'd be a pioneer, Letts," he said.

She could tell from his voice how pleased he was. "I've sort of done some hunting around for the kind of store I'd want."

"Where? How much would you need to start you?"

She looked off into a space far beyond him. "I wouldn't want a pokey little place like a little neighborhood hat shop. I'd want to start right out uptown, a fashionable place, a fashionable address, as if it were the best antique shop in New York."

"Do it," he said. "I want you to; how much money do you think?"

"Fifty dollars a month for rent, and maybe three hundred dollars for special finds, to restore and put in as stock, and I might even rob *us* for extra pieces—I wouldn't sell them."

He laughed as she eyed the sofa, the chairs, tables, crystal ornaments, even the old andirons in the black fireplace.

"Back to crates painted red and your five heirlooms," he said. It would be like starting their marriage anew.

"Maybe I'd swipe an heirloom now and then," Letty said, matching his tone. "My show window is going to have nothing but one perfect piece in it. Nothing. No knickknacks, and no price tag showing."

"Is *that* the Four Hundred style?"

"Mrs. Aldrich told me of *the* antique shop all her friends go to, and I've been there. Ten Eyck and Hoque, off Fifth Avenue. Mrs. Aldrich said lots of her friends would switch to me. They love her lowboy!"

"You little close-mouth, you've been scheming for a long time."

She laughed. "I can see my shop whenever I close my eyes. A shining big window and one wonderful chest or breakfront in it and small gold lettering at the side: 'Mrs. Garrett Paige, Antiques.' "

"I can see it too. I'll probably drop a curtsy at your front door the first time I go through. Go ahead and *do* it."

"He has something for me from the train," Fee shouted as she hung up. "Can I go right over? He said Franny should come too. It was Mr. Paige."

She did not pause for permission or for Fran. She washed her hands and face at the kitchen sink, sifting grey Dutch Cleanser on her skin as liberally as if she were scouring pots and pans. Then she ran the tines of a kitchen fork backwards through her hair, a private system of combing which satisfied her private standards.

"Come on, Fran," she said. "I said we'd start this minute."

"Fee," Alexandra said, "whatever Evan has for you, don't forget to thank him, *really* thank him. If you knew what he endured out there —and still he remembered his promise to a little girl."

"She'll thank him, Mama," Fran said with a meaningful glance, one disciplinarian to another. To Fee she said, "If you think *I'm* going to swab dirt around on my face and go!"

Fee moaned, but Fran went upstairs, wishing it were evening instead of noon. When she returned she was in the dress her mother had taken her to New York to buy for Jack Purney's party. It was crepe de chine, so full and sheer it swirled like chiffon when she danced, and so faint a yellow it looked almost white. She had put her hair up, and used a touch of Ashes of Roses, hoping her mother would not notice.

"Francesca! You can't go that way."

Fran's hands flew to her cheeks, rubbing them unmercifully but Alexandra said, "Not in that dress."

"Why can't I?" Fran demanded, abandoning her cheeks.

"You look overdressed and foolish, that's why. It's *morning.*"

"Oh, Mama."

"Never mind that 'oh, Mama' either. A silk dress like that isn't for early morning, go put on something else."

"She'll take another hour," Fee protested.

Look who's turned into a fashion expert, Fran thought, staring at her mother. Aloud she said, "If I can't wear a decent dress to the Paiges', I won't go at all."

Fee looked from one to the other in an anguish of entreaty. Neither returned her glance. Neither moved nor spoke.

"Mr. Paige might think we're not coming," Fee said desperately, "and he might go out, and I'll just die."

"You can go alone," Fran said.

"Wear your polka-dot," Alexandra said. "It's new and you look lovely in it."

"That thing." Fran sat down heavily.

Alexandra thought, That thing. The million polka dots blinding me when I made it for her, racing the machine like a sweatshop, she was so crazy to wear it. Now it's "that thing" and only a ball gown will do for Mrs. Astorbilt. Obscurely she wished she had never raised the issue, let Fran wear a hundred yellow crepe de chine dresses. How opinionated, how unyielding daughters became as they grew up. A son never raised such a ruckus over what to wear.

"Can I Mama?" Fee nearly screamed it, at the edge of tantrum. "Can I go by myself?"

"No. That would be an insult to the Paiges. They asked both of you. Call them up and say Mrs. Astorbilt has a sudden headache from her diadem." She marched out of the room.

"Please, Franny, It's been a million years since Mr. Paige's trip on the train, and I can't bear it if we can't go over now."

"All right," Fran said suddenly. "Stop acting like a sick cat. I'll be right down."

In pure hypocrisy, Fee smiled at her; privately she vowed to get even the first chance she got. Mr. Paige had something for Fran too, and she hoped it would be terrible.

Shag sidled in and collapsed at her feet. "You poor thing," Fee said to him, "you haven't one decent thing to wear, even your horrible new muzzle for the beach." Shag was going with them this summer, but at the price of wearing a muzzle whenever he was allowed off his leash.

"I'm ready," Fran called. Fee flung Shag away from her, and skipped out of the house lest new delays develop.

At the Paiges', even while they were saying hello, Fee could look only at the two packages on the dining-room table. One was big, wrapped in Manila paper and tied with stout cord, the other little and frilly-silly with a pale-blue bow.

"Do you like Eau de Cologne, Fran?" Mr. Paige offered the little one.

"I love it," Fran said. "It's my very very first—ooh, thank you— ooh, it's from Paris."

"By way of California," he said, while Mrs. Paige added, "I had my first when I was sixteen, and you're almost, aren't you, dear?"

Fee was oblivious to all of this; if they had been talking in Attic Greek, she would not have absorbed less of what they said. She was staring at the big package, inching toward it, still impatient but no longer desperate, now that she was In Its Presence.

At last Mr. Paige put his hand out and pushed it toward her. "Fee," he said, "you had me committing crimes for this." He sounded mysterious and a little ominous, and her curiosity blazed once more. "Petty theft, bribery, premeditated larceny," he added dolefully.

"Oh, Mr. Paige," Fee said, clapping her hands just once, holding them stiff upright as if they were welded together by her fiery excitement. "What's *in* it?"

"Open it yourself," he ordered. "Enough of my fingerprints are on it already." At her squeal of delight, he cut the cords with his pen-knife.

Fee tore away the wrappings. It was a Weber & Heilbroner box, marked "Navy All-Wool Overcoat, $22.50," but under the lid lay a tightly packed jumble of paper, metal, cloth, a green something and invisibles carefully wrapped in white tissue. She reached for the folded cloth on top, plucking it out as if somebody might snatch it from her. It was a small oblong huck towel, with PULLMAN woven right through it in a center stripe.

"A special one," Fee cried, "just for trains."

"No crime involved so far," Mr. Paige said. "I paid the porter for it."

"It's beautiful," Fee cried. "I'll never never use anything else as long as I live. Oh, I just love you, Mr. Paige."

Fran laughed, but it wasn't nasty and Fee didn't mind. She pulled out a bronzy-looking matchbox stamped PULLMAN too, and then a nest of a dozen waxy drinking cups, all bearing the magic name. Next came an unknown of shiny brown paper, folded and folded again in sharp-creased oblongs; it opened into a yard-wide expanse of crackling paper bag, with sawtooth edges across the top.

"That's for women only," Mr. Paige explained, "to hide their hats from the cinders and smoke flying in from the engine."

"You blow *that* bag up and explode it," Franny warned Fee, "and the hook-and-ladder engine will come dashing."

Fee was already opening something wrapped in the white tissue, and she gasped when a crystal goblet emerged, tall, airy, like an oval bubble on a stem. Then came a smaller one, matching it in shape and in the seal or crest blown into its side.

"Those entailed bribery," Evan said cheerfully. "They're on your table in the dining car, Fee, the big one for water, the little for wine."

By now, Fran was as entranced as Fee, and watched avidly as Fee drew out the next unknown in tissue, something solid and heavy.

"Bribery again," Mr. Paige said. "My only out-and-out thievery was the drinking cups and hat-bag and matchbox. Bribery is more soothing."

Fee was solemn as she discovered that this was silverware, piece after piece of it, polished and gleaming. There were a silver knife, two forks of different shapes and sizes, a funny round soup spoon, a teaspoon, and a blunt-tipped flat little knife of a kind she had never seen. Each piece bore the same crest, and gazing down at them, Fee saw herself seated on a throne-like chair at some unknown table, its priceless lace cloth set with these bubbles of glass and pieces of silver, and she a queen dining in a glory unknown.

Evan Paige drew a small card from his pocket and consulting it, he said, "Each place at the table is set for dinner as follows: two knives and three spoons at the right of your plate; two forks and two spoons at the left. Nine pieces of silverware per diner per dinner." He looked unsmilingly at Fee. "I promised details, didn't I? Each table also has a thin vase for three flowers, a glass carafe for water, the engraved menu—there it is, under that green netting—and mahogany chairs with leather seats and backs and brass studs outlining the leather. There are no spittoons in the diner; those are in all the other cars."

Alida was laughing in soft short spurts, like trills of music to accompany his phrases. She took the silver from Fee and set it out on the table, at either side of an imaginary plate.

Mr. Paige said, "One last haul, Fee. Half legal, half criminal." He drew out the green netting, taking one end of it and giving Fee the other. Then he moved back, to stretch it taut between them.

"It's a hammock," Fee said, bewildered. "A tiny hammock."

"The porter hangs it up every night on two hooks in your berth, and you put your clothes in it, and nothing falls out no matter how hard the train sways or swings." Whereupon Mr. Paige surrendered his end to Franny, proceeded to take off his jacket, fold it lengthwise and lay it inside the tight webbing. "I don't know what you can do with this contraption in Barnett, Fee," he said, "but to me it says sleeping car and berth and train and overnight travel more than all the rest put together."

"It's marvelous," Fee said, awed. "I've never seen—I never—I— oh, you're the most wonderful—"

She wheeled around, ran into the parlor through the open double-doors and swiftly turned two somersaults on the carpet, the half-kind where you start with your shoulders touching the floor, so you're not too wild and uncontrolled.

She heard the Paiges laugh, and Fran calling her a tomboy and laughing too, and she was so happy, she lay on the floor for a minute and laughed right along with them.

It was the end of June, with the household in the usual demented joy that meant school was closing and Alexandra and the girls going off for the summer, and though Stefan would acknowledge the heresy to no man, he could hardly wait for them to be gone.

Evan had been correct about the extra work, but work didn't matter. Late hours, extra reading, research, inquiry, nothing mattered in his preoccupation with the new series. Each day was more demanding than the one preceding it, but nothing was beyond his powers. From the moment they had all parted at the café, energy kept boiling up as if from a hidden geyser newly erupted to bless and freshen him as he wrote.

That same night he had gone straight to his office, straight to his desk, needing no pause, no inner discussion. Across the top of his writing tablet, he had blocked out a title for Evan's first piece, a title he was never to change.

POGROM—California Style?

He had omitted nothing, softened nothing. He could hear himself arguing later on with Alexandra that a newspaper's readers were not children, to be spared shock or revulsion, arguing it more irritably with Fehler, who was raising the issue of disapproving readers on any handy pretext these days.

But issues and arguments didn't matter either. For nearly two hours Ivarin wrote on, aware he was running long but not checking himself, stopping once for some twenty minutes when his assistant brought in changes and new leads for the morning's Final, and then finishing the sentence under his pen without needing to reread it when Borg took himself off again.

It was nearly three in the morning when Ivarin started for Delancey Street and the subway. The streets of the East Side were dim and sleepy and as nearly quiet as they ever became, but he was too elated to be tired. The pain in his back was sharp, as always now when he stayed writing too long, and he paused occasionally, leaning slightly forward from the waist, rounding his shoulders, lowering his head, gently, purposefully, as if this rite could outwit his one enemy.

As he walked, he read in memory from the folded pages in his pocket, wishing that Alexandra were not asleep so he could show them to her as soon as he got to the house.

The Triangle Fire, he thought, it's something like that night. Then too he had had to write on and on, unable to delay until the sensible hours of the morning, sorry too that she was asleep when he had ended. He had wandered around the house, he remembered, forcing himself to let her rest, sure she would like what he had written, yet absurdly eager to hear her say so.

Tonight—he suddenly realized it—he wished Evan were not asleep either. He was even more eager to show his pages to him.

(200)

That's something new for you, Stefan Ivarin thought, amused. Now Evander Paige also. Life grows thinner as one grows older, or else it multiplies. My damnable back is not in total command yet.

Two days went by before he did show it to Evan. Though he could be as ruthless about cutting his own work as he was with the work of others, this San Diego material gave him no obvious superfluities that made cutting a wholesale assault. This was precision work, challenging all the way. Then came the English version; there could be no hurrying over his translating either.

Borg was only too happy to be trusted with new duties, and Stefan turned over an assortment of them, generous in praise at the young man's quickness and growing ability.

"Good work, Saul," he said as Borg showed him a list he had made of the next day's assignments for the staff, something Borg had never done before and had undertaken on his own. "Post it on the board."

"Without any changes, Mr. Ivarin?" He had gone a damp pink like a schoolboy though he was twenty-six, with four years of experience on a magazine printed in Yiddish.

"You have learned at breakneck speed since Landau hired you, Saul. How long ago was that?"

"Six months. You're a wonderful teacher."

"A good pupil makes a good teacher."

Again Borg flushed. "There's only one thing you have not taught me," he said, turning away quickly. "How to write like Ivarin."

Ivarin thanked him but was vaguely annoyed. A moment later he forgot Borg and telephoned Evan. When they met, the two men were alone. Stefan had suggested this himself, naming Paige's house as the place he would prefer for their meeting, and Alexandra startled him by not being hurt. She had read the piece twice and the translation twice, saying that even in translation it was unmistakably Ivarin, and Ivarin at his greatest. Stefan did not find her language "too volatile."

Evan read the article slowly. Then he said only, "I knew it." He sat thoughtful and still, with the pages sprawled face down under his hand, as he had set them one by one.

"I knew this could happen, Stiva," he said, "but I suppose you can never be sure until it's written."

"With material as dramatic as that, anybody—" Ivarin broke off and added, "Listen to this holy modesty," but the truth was that Evan's praise pleased him remarkably.

By the time his second article was ready, unfamiliar newspapers began to arrive at the house from all over the country with "Pogrom —California Style?" The sight of his own words translated by the pens of other men sent his hidden geyser into a greater leap and thrust and he felt that he would stay strong and productive for another fifty years.

"Well, Stefan," Alida greeted him as she came over with Evan a few days later, to read the second piece, "I do believe Evan brings up your name with everybody he meets, just so he can get your clipping out of his wallet."

"You'll make him conceited, Alida," Alexandra said. She saw the two men exchange glances, and a brief envy invaded her; they were becoming deeply attached, in the way men could when they embarked on work together that each held important and that each felt was partly the other's to do best. Women so rarely could find that specialized warmth of colleagues or comrades-in-arms. Though of course, when Suffrage was won, that too would change.

Envy fled before the fair breeze of hope. Evan was reporting on the mail forwarded to the Free Speech League from the out-of-state papers.

"Some of them are vile. Not all; some are splendid."

"The vile," Ivarin said, "will outnumber the others five to one."

"Well, the League has had plenty of vile letters since the day it was formed."

"Hurrah and hooray rarely take pen in hand," Ivarin said amiably.

"What a clever way of putting it, Stiva," Alexandra said.

He frowned, turning to discourage further praise. To Evan he said, "It will be interesting to see whether your series acts like a catalyst on my series for printing Berkman's book. Another appeal for funds is scheduled for Wednesday."

"Could it hurt your Berkman campaign?" Paige asked quickly. "I never even considered that possibility."

"Quite the contrary," Ivarin said. "I've been irritated at the way the initial response has been dribbling off. Your series may wake it up again. There's not much time left if the book is to come out this fall."

"Stefan, it's sweet," Alida put in, "the way you always say 'Evan's series' as if *you* hadn't a thing to do with it."

Ivarin laughed, but Alexandra looked pensive. Yet apart from Stefan's annoying courtliness, she was happy he would be so involved with the Paiges for the next month or two. No steady diet of hard-boiled eggs like rocks this summer; Alida had already invited him over for supper whenever he and Evan were to see each other.

It would be the first summer she could go off with the girls without worrying about leaving him all alone. Tomorrow afternoon when the girls dashed home from the last day at school, they could all set off for the beach without one twinge of conscience. This summer, Stiva might even enjoy himself.

But the afternoon came and they did not set off.

Instead Fee sobbed as if her heart would break, Fran was pale and shaken, Alexandra was beside herself with guilt, and Stefan Ivarin was transformed into the executive, the managing genius, the pillar of strength and the one hope of the family.

Shag was missing.

He had been absent at breakfast, but everybody took it for granted that he was off on an ordinary tour of the neighborhood and Fran and Fee had gone off to school without a glimmer of tragedy ahead. His new license had been bought and paid for at last, and though there had never yet been time to buy him the large collar he had long needed, to which the narrow metal plate would be attached, Alexandra was to get it today, as well as the muzzle demanded at the tent city.

And when the girls reached home shortly after three, there indeed was Shag's new paraphernalia—the new collar and leash, the license plate neatly riveted into place, and the muzzle as well, a humane one, made of leather strips, not metal.

But Shag was nowhere in sight. He had not been seen since morning. He had not been seen, when their anguished reckoning was completed, since the night before. They called, whistled, shouted, raced through the entire neighborhood, but there was no sign of Shag, no report of him, no trace of him.

"He's killed," Fee cried in terror.

"Don't say that," Fran said, terrified too.

"Poor Shag, where *is* he?" Alexandra asked, tears starting as she put her hand out to comfort Fee and Fran.

"Wait, wait," Stefan Ivarin shouted. "You are calamity-howlers, every one of you. Keep quiet and let me think."

Fee was sobbing too wildly to stop, but Fran managed to stifle her grief in a frantic attempt to be adult. Alexandra dabbed at her eyes, but her obedient larynx and vocal cords followed her husband's command.

"Where is that confounded dog pound?" Stefan asked.

Nobody could tell him. For months they had referred darkly to the dog-catcher's wagon and its periodic excursions through the innocent streets of Barnett, but nobody knew whence it came nor where it returned with its living catch of uncollared, unlicensed pets.

(203)

"Are you all blockheads?" Ivarin shouted. "Not to know the simplest matter? He's your dog, and you've put off his new collar for six months, couldn't you at least *ask* where it is?"

If there were any *non sequitur* in this, nobody questioned it. All three kept shaking their heads from side to side until Stefan rushed from the room to consult the telephone book. His search through the endless listings of city departments was like an assault on the mild columns of type; his eardrums rang with Fee's agonized fears about Shag lying crushed and bloodied in some gutter and his fury at all procrastinators pounded in his temples. Moreover, a black fear for that big clumsy fool of a Shag attacked his whole nervous system.

At last he summoned Information and learned that there was no dog pound in Barnett, nor in Jamaica, and that the one serving Barnett would be, most likely, the main one in Brooklyn, at the far reaches of the borough.

He called the number given him and was promptly told what he already knew, that his quest for any dog could not be made by telephone since nobody could be sure which animal he was interested in, no matter how he described it. He restrained his vocabulary and emotions long enough to discover that this dog pound did indeed "serve" the town of Barnett, would remain open for two more hours, that if the dog in question had been there for less than one day, as claimed, it would still be alive and could be freed at proof that a current and proper license had been procured and upon payment of a fine of one dollar.

By this time Fee was clutching at his sleeve so that he had to fight her off to hold the telephone at speaking position, and Fran was breathing praise and adulation of his talents and goodness such as she had never yet produced in her nearly sixteen years. Alexandra merely murmured, "Thank goodness you were at home, Stiva, I would have no idea where to start."

His own hopes had taken one small leap upward at the "less than one day." He summoned Information once more, for the telephone number of the public school in Brooklyn where Eli was so unwilling a teacher of the young.

It was now four o'clock, but if there was any truth in Eli's summaries of the slaveries endured by the teaching profession, why then, his release on this the final day of the teaching year was still many hours off. Ivarin hoped devoutly that this was so, told the principal crisply that there was an emergency, and could Mr. Elijah Eaves be called to the telephone, please, irregular as that was.

"Eli," he said an instant later. "Don't worry, it's Pa—it's great luck they caught you at the front door."

"Pa—is somebody sick?"

Eli was so immediate in his concern, Stefan nearly thanked him for seeming like a son again. Instead he told him about Shag, asked him to go straight to the dog pound to see if Shag was there, and then to call back one way or another without losing a moment.

"Good boy, Eli," he ended. "I won't stir from the phone. I'll be thinking out the next move, in case he *is* there."

The waiting was insufferable. Eli's school was no more than twenty minutes away from the dog pound, but each of the twenty might have been an hour to the Ivarins. The first wild hope that all would be well faded for both girls before half the twenty were gone, and when the full period was over with no sound from the telephone, Fee said, "Eli can't bear telling us Shag isn't there," and burst into hopeless sobs once more. Fran tried to comfort her, but her own fear was too evident, and Alexandra's voice shook even as she spoke her most Montessorian words of calm wisdom to both her daughters.

"How can a man keep two and two together in this infernal racket?" Stefan demanded. "I still have to think, don't I?"

Upon dispatching Eli, he had telephoned the Barnett License Bureau, explaining the difficulty of sending the actual license plate to the end of Brooklyn before closing time, should their dog Shag prove to be there, and asking if the Barnett dog licensers might check their records of this very morning, see that license 421 was indeed sold to a Mrs. S. Ivarin, and then telephone this fact to the dog pound, thus permitting Elijah Eaves, emissary of Shag's owners, to pay the one-dollar fine and leave with Shag at his side.

The answer was no. That was not what the statute said. That way anybody could walk into the dog pound and claim the best dog there as the dog for 421, see?

Stefan Ivarin did not see and began to elucidate with vigor and clarity. At a warning from Alexandra, he desisted. Her look said that if he got the Bureau furious and something then happened to Shag because of that fury, he would be Shag's executioner.

By now thirty minutes had elapsed and the telephone in the vestibule remained inert and insufferable.

Stefan Ivarin glanced at his children from time to time and was twisted by their grief, but he did not know what to say that might comfort either one. Whenever he did speak, it came out as rage at statute-quoting idiots, blame at Eli for being so all-fired slow in calling back and putting an end to this killing suspense, and even sharpness at Fee's crying because it prevented him from deciding what to do next.

Five more minutes went by. Another five. By now, Fee was no longer sobbing; she sat as if paralyzed, upright, staring, her cheeks wet under the unpausing flow of her tears, looking only toward the vestibule where the implacable telephone faced her.

Then it rang.

Stefan raced for it. "He is?—Oh, good boy, good boy—"

He never finished that sentence. Fira, Fran, Alexandra, all of them incoherent, tumbled into the vestibule so that his footing was precarious. Each one had to grab the telephone in turn to hear Eli say that as the guard opened the locked door to the expanse of iron cages, he had whistled his special signal and at the first note "Shag just about pulled the place down."

"Let me talk to Pa again," Eli ended. "I can't get him out because of the license, but I said somebody would be there first thing in the morning."

"First thing in the morning," Alexandra promised. "I'll leave here by eight."

"The morning?" Fee cried in new alarm. "Something might happen overnight."

Alexandra said, "Now, dear, it's so wonderful he's found, be reasonable."

"But he'll be so scared when Eli leaves him. And all night long he'll think—"

"But we can't help it, Fee. It's nearly five o'clock right now."

Stefan interrupted by taking the phone from Alexandra, muttering about mothers who do not see the absurdity of talking reason to a grief-stricken child.

"Listen to me, Eli," he said. "If you will simply stay there in the building, so they cannot take it into their heads to close a few minutes early, I will come there myself with the godforsaken license."

"Tonight, Pa? I told them—"

"Yes, yes, but I never trust officials—if an error can be made, they'll make it and chloroform the wrong dog tonight. So it's better to get him right now. Can you wait there? I should make it by six."

Eli promised, and Fee flung herself at her father in gratitude so intense that he finally yelled at her not to delay him for these precious minutes or he would certainly be too late. She jumped back and away, and off he went, trying without success to stuff Shag's collar, leash and muzzle into his pockets as he hurried out of sight.

Two full hours had to elapse before Stefan Ivarin could possibly be expected back, but long before it was sensible, Fee and Franny went out to the porch to keep watch. It was a clear day, and the late-afternoon light was brilliant and open; the streets stretching away from the house to the brow of the hill were like pale ribbons, every inch visible except where the deep shadow of some tree scooped away a strip and left a long dark gap.

Once or twice there was a false alarm as a figure appeared in the distance, and Fee or Fran cried "There they come," but being wrong was delicious when the outcome was so exciting to wait for. Alexandra unpacked a nightgown for each of them and herself, and then came out to the porch also, rocking back and forth, back and forth, overjoyed that tragedy had only brushed instead of striking her children.

Occasionally she smiled at the reason Eli had been so slow about calling them back: 1718-W was a party line and it was busy. He had tried it every other minute, he said during her short turn on the phone with him, and the buzz-buzz drove him mad. Not one of them, waiting as the minutes dragged by, had thought of this simplest of all reasons, neither Fee nor Fran, nor herself, not even Stiva, splendid though he was through the family's torment, even Stiva's brain had failed on that everyday point. He had been splendid and she loved him for going off to Brooklyn then and there. If she told him so, of course, he might twist it around into a hidden accusation that he was a good father so rarely, it was like a national holiday when he actually did something for his children.

Fee cried, "This time it's *them*."

Just at the crest of the hill, Stefan appeared with Shag. Even that far away it was clear that Shag was virtually hauling him off his feet by his pull on the leash. Fee and Fran flew toward them, screaming "Shag, Shag," whereupon Shag leaped into the air in a pure perpendicular ascent. When he hit the ground again, Stefan shouted, "You half-wit, you," and dropped the leash entirely.

Shag became a reddish blur racing toward the girls. He bounded at Fee with such abandon that they went down together, Fee squealing and laughing while he dashed around her and at her and over her. Franny called him, and he repeated his performance, though Fran managed to keep upright. He raced back to Fee, beyond her to Stefan, then hearing from the distance Alexandra's voice, he abandoned all three and turned reddish streak once more until he hurled himself at Alexandra, who had had the foresight to sit down firmly on the porch floor to await the onslaught.

Later, as Shag lay under the kitchen table at their feet, a place usually forbidden him when they were at supper, Stefan supplied the details they begged for. He had been lucky with connections from trolley to train and had reached dog pound and Eli with ten minutes to spare. Eli stood leaning on the outer door as though he would put his foot in the way if they tried to lock up early. They had presented Shag's license plate to the man in charge, with its 421 and 1912 shining up like all the stars of heaven, and handed over one dollar.

"Then he took us inside," Stefan said. "It's an unhappy place, with the dogs all whimpering and howling and running back and forth. Before I could spot Shag, I called out, 'Here, boy, here, Shag,' and Eli whistled for him. Down at the far end, that crazy fool nearly beat his brains out with excitement, and when the guard unlocked his gate, Shag must have scraped half his fur off his sides, pushing through the first inch of space—"

"He was so relieved," Fee cried, "and so happy."

"He flew straight for me—my life was at stake, I tell you, and then Eli's. You saw for yourselves how he can be. I never knew such a maniac of a dog."

"He was so happy to see you, Papa," Fee repeated, her eyes suddenly wet again. "He must have loved you so for going after him yourself."

"He must have," Alexandra said ardently, not looking at Stefan. "Who could help it?"

SIXTEEN

The catalyst theory was correct, Ivarin thought, but Fehler astonished him by his gloom over the final spurt of donations for the Berkman Printing Fund.

Apart from the paper's activity, Berkman's own group had been holding fund-raising "readings" of the manuscript, and at last a specific day could be announced for the book's appearance next month, in September. But still Fehler gave no sign of triumph, and Ivarin was puzzled.

He had little time for speculating. Mail from readers had been mounting week by week in volume and intensity, and by August, he was reaching a wider readership than ever before in his whole life as writer and editor. The praise, the disapproval, even the abuse was elixir indeed, whether it was evoked by one of "Evan's articles" or by one of his last-call pieces on *Prison Memoirs of an Anarchist*. Deeply, in the unknown place where generals know a battle is being won, Stefan Ivarin knew he was crossing new lines in his fight to make the Jewish East Side see what America meant by freedom of speech and freedom of the press.

"Not afraid to print a book of its enemies—what a country!" one letter ended, with fifteen two-cent stamps enclosed for the book fund. The letter was shaky in its writing, misspelled, a little soiled, and somehow more valuable on all three counts. Ivarin underlined the final sentence, and tacked the letter on his bulletin board where people could glance at it as they passed.

Here, too, Fehler surprised him. "And what a relief," he said sourly, "not to be a post office any longer, for thirty cents' worth of stamps."

Ivarin exchanged glances with Abe Kesselbaum and Saul Borg. They were all in his office to see some new formats Abe had developed for Page One, and at Fehler's words, Ivarin found a sardonic gleam in Abe's eyes. Behind his thick lenses, he winked at him. To Fehler he only said, "I can't write my review until they send me Jack London's preface—they haven't forgotten, have they?"

"They'll send it when they're ready," Fehler said shortly.

Ivarin went wrathful on the instant. "If you please, you will not take that tone. Next you'll be telling me I've damaged our newsstand sales to help get your damnable book printed."

Again Fehler surprised him. Conciliatory at once, he said, "I will admit—sometimes I wish you had let it alone, sink or swim. The police may investigate us over the Berkman fund; that could damage us everywhere, not just at newsstands."

"The police? Is it so?"

"I hear rumors."

"Let them. It would be a routine nuisance at the worst, a good story at the best." He sounded gruff, but Fehler's emotions struck him as delectable. Fehler the Business Manager versus Fehler the Faithful—that was a jousting bout worthy of Ivanhoe.

"Well, the book didn't sink," he said, thinking, My review should help do that. He had read the final manuscript a few weeks ago; it was just about what he had foreseen. But Fehler had read it also without perceptible misery. Was the unseen preface the new element contributing to his gloom? Suddenly Ivarin wanted to get hold of it at once, tonight if possible.

"Do you agree, Mr. Ivarin?"

That was Borg, and he came back to the business at hand with all his attention, for Abe Kesselbaum had labored like a miner to dig out these new ideas on format. Passing by the open door, Isaac Landau said, "May I see too?" and joined them. He looked tanned and well, his stomach troubles forgotten under the new regimen set up for him, and for the next half-hour, Ivarin's office was filled with the impersonal give-and-take of preference and discussion.

But the moment he was alone again, Ivarin returned to the absentee preface. Everybody knew that Berkman and his cohorts had induced the world-famous author of *Call of the Wild* to write a special foreword for the book; they treated it as a *grand coup,* the final guarantee of success. Even if it had been late in getting to them, it must be in proof by now. Were they withholding it from all reviewers, or just from him, whom they had lauded to the skies for his campaign on behalf of free speech and free writing? Fehler would never tell him.

His nerves tightened; soon irritability gave him a headache. When the first press run began, he went down reluctantly to the café for his usual bite and for the ending of a game of chess begun the night before.

His opponent, a neighborhood expert, was a violinist at the Metropolitan Opera, a night owl by necessity for most of the year and by predilection for the rest. He sat at a side table, the board before him, the pieces in tidy rows along its side, and as Stefan appeared he began to set up certain pieces and pawns, consulting the notations he had made when they had finally called a halt after two hours of play.

Lucky man, Stefan had thought then, needing to write them down, instead of seeing them on the chessboard of his brain all night.

Now, approaching the table, he said, "Your move, Feifel. I had moved Queen to Queen's Bishop Four."

"Yes, a big attack," the other said.

The game went slowly. It is abominable, Ivarin thought, that Fehler and his comrades keep me from my final connection with Berkman's opus. They've known all along I would blast it the day it became a duly published book, blast its idiotic "defense" of assassination as a political principle, blast the stupor of its reportage on life in prison.

A child in kindergarten could write the review. But London's preface might yield something worth a man's time. London is a socialist, not an anarchist, a man of reason, moderation and talent; whatever he writes is worth a reviewer's attention.

I've become obsessed with this preface, he thought, and the recognition soothed him. He was; he was correct to be. This decision made, Ivarin gave himself completely to the game at last.

From a nearby table an old man rose and came over to watch. He wore a black skullcap, and his shoulders were huddled up, his head lowered between them and his eyes peering, as if he were running a seam in dark cloth by dim light. He was soon engrossed in their game, and when he was joined by another watcher from another table, he whispered proudly, "It's Ivarin, when he sometimes plays with Capablanca, all Capablanca gives him is pawn and move."

"You don't mean it? Capablanca?"

The old man said to a passing waiter, "He doesn't believe that a world champion like Capablanca gives Ivarin only pawn and move."

The waiter snorted. "Lasker, too," he said, casting an appraising glance down at the nearly emptied board, holding his tray aloft above the violinist's head.

Suddenly Ivarin sat back in his chair. He lifted his glass and tossed off the cold final inch of tea from it. Lemon pits slipped into his mouth and unceremoniously he popped them back into the glass.

Absentee preface indeed. He would not wait around one more day for them to send it; he would travel *to* the preface. He would go uptown himself in the morning, directly to Berkman or Emma Goldman or Johann Most in their Mother Earth Publishing offices, and read the preface there. Prolixity was not a characteristic of Jack London, and his much heralded preface surely could be read through in a measurable time.

Measurable time, Stefan Ivarin thought, is precisely what is at my command to finish off this business. He felt better than he had all evening. What had been needed all along, to borrow their lingo, was a little Direct Action.

"Check," his opponent said.

He looked back at the chessboard. Feifel had said "check" in a mild voice. Too mild. A disagreeable sensation rose inside Ivarin; he was not what was called "a good loser," and doubted that anybody else was. He examined the new positions, waiting only long enough to be sure. "Check?" he said. "I beg to differ. It's checkmate."

"No, no," the spectator in the black skullcap protested. "You have many moves, Mr. Ivarin, to get out of check."

"Useless moves, all of them," Ivarin said, and laid his king on its side to signal "I resign." Again he felt better. Reality was good, always. Waiting tactics, futile moves to stave off the inevitable—pah. That was for children.

The thick letter alarmed Alexandra. She had grown increasingly worried about Joan's condition in these final days of waiting for the new baby, and calling Eli and Joan for news only convinced her that they were hiding something, "not to upset her." Yesterday she had called Stefan to ask the truth. He had been busy and brusque. He had heard nothing. She should know that all confinements need not go as quickly and smoothly as Joan's first one.

She had hung up resentfully. Premature labor pains had sent Joan to the hospital twice already; twice she had been sent home the following day and told not to worry; but compared with the simple time she had had with Webby, it was inevitable that such a difference should worry them all.

Now Alexandra took the heavy letter from the postman and said, "I hope everything is all right."

"Don't you worry," the postman said. "It's a nice big love-letter from your husband."

She ignored his witticism. It was of course from Stefan; his angular handwriting on the envelope was unmistakable even upside down. But his letters were never more than single pages, usually to ask some question about a bill that he was sure was an error since it was too large.

This heavy a letter was not about bills. In a flash she visualized it filled with words of pain and grief, descriptions of disaster and ambulances—

She ripped the envelope open and at Stiva's opening salutation, her worries departed.

Assassinate a Preface

He had printed it like a headline but right underneath it, he reverted to ordinary letter style.

Dear Alexandra,
    It is too good to be true! I have chortled—

She closed her eyes in relief and thought, Thank goodness it's not about Eli. Immediately she corrected this to "not about Joan," thoroughly ashamed of herself, and returned to the letter. She was still standing beside the mailbox at the rear of their tent, and the wind whipping at the sheaf of pages in her hand made a pleasing chitter-chatter. She decided to stay outside in the sun and enjoy Stiva's chortling together with the heart-lifting August day.

Dear Alexandra,

It is too good to be true! I have chortled for three days now, and if that barbarian tent where you immure yourself had a telephone as per solemn promise each year, I would have called you when I finally untangled the brave shenanigans of our friends, Berkman, Goldman, Johann—that special group of screamers about the Free Speech they are denied in America.

They have denied a bit of Free Speech themselves. To Jack London no less! Because he dared to say—but I don't want to get ahead of myself. You'll discover his crime in the enclosed.

The comedy is too great for me to write in a letter—if you were at home, we could enjoy it properly over a good glass of tea. But I want you to know of it and relish it even off there in Thoreau's palace, so I am sending you my editorial, which will run the same day as my review of Berkman's book. I may put the editorial on Page One.

So here it is; *do not lose it;* I did not wait to have a copy made at the office, because then Sunday would interfere and you could not see it until next week.

Please return it as soon as you have read it. Don't forget to put your return address on it. Even though I know most of it by heart, it would be a nuisance to lose it. And do not read it aloud even to one of those hordes you describe as my admirers out there by the sea, by the sea, by the beautiful sea.

Alexandra smiled. He would never realize how much he had revealed to her in this impatience to have her read his editorial, in this willingness to send it without having a copy made, he who would raise the roof looking for a misplaced page of anything he had written.

Difficult, unreasonable, hurtful, moody—but he was the most glorious husband and friend and comrade and sharer of her life.

She read his letter once more, but deliberately put off the editorial itself, the longer to savor its promise of pleasure. She went around to the front of the tent and settled comfortably into one of the brightly striped canvas camp chairs that were a new luxury for their summer life this year.

It was a gleaming day, cooler than it had been, with the air promising September and then October. Her spirits sparkled like the points of mica that seemed to be strewn all over the white sand, and her heart rose and leaped like the blue box kite some boys were flying at the edge of the surf.

For a moment she watched the kite, smiling at it, and then she could wait no longer before turning to Stefan's piece.

Assassinate a Preface?

Alexander Berkman, author of *Prison Memoirs of an Anarchist,* denouncer of all American publishers as crass suppressors of freedom for writers whose ideas run counter to theirs, has just indulged in a little crass suppression of his own.

He has suppressed the work of a great writer, work done at Berkman's invitation, at his urgent and repeated request, a preface for his book.

The great man is Jack London, whose work is known and welcomed on the printing presses of the world.

Nearly a year ago, this editorial page contained a piece that raised a large question. It was called, "Assassinate a Book?"

"To assassinate a book," that piece said, if it is pardonable to quote from it, "we need only refuse it print . . . In a free country, all writing and speaking and thinking must remain free, even that which we detest, despise or fear."

It was for that principle, and standing on that platform, that this newspaper then campaigned for contributions from its readers to get Berkman's book privately printed.

The campaign succeeded, as did other efforts of people elsewhere, many of whom had other motives. The book escaped the death of suppression; it appears today; it is today reviewed by a member of the staff of this paper who, it appears, does detest and despise it, though "fear" is as yet not evident to the human eye.

Not evident either is Jack London's preface.

For the author of this rescued book, living by the nasty code of extremists everywhere, is quite willing to assassinate the writings of others. The preface in his book is *not* the long and thoughtful piece written by Jack London. It is by one Hutchins Hapgood, whose wisdom surely rests on something other than his willingness to substitute his talents for Jack London's.

Bombed, destroyed, assassinated: one preface.

Killed because in it, the illustrious Jack London used his inalienable American right of free speech for his own beliefs as well as Berkman's. He upheld Berkman's right to speak, to write and to publish, but he did not uphold Berkman's anarchism. And he explained why not, inevitably expounding his own moderate principles as a socialist while doing so.

Which obviously, by official ukase, put him beyond the pale.

Free Speech yes.

Free Speech always.

Free Speech, however, says Alexander Berkman by this singular piece of hypocrisy and hilarity, "only for me."

To assassinate a preface, we have only to refuse it print.

Alexandra said aloud, "It's simply wonderful," and looked around for the girls. She could translate bits of it for them, tell them enough about it to make them see how splendid it was, how forthright and uncompromising, yet how ironic. Lethal but funny.

Berkman would be the laughingstock of every real believer in freedom. It would be a delicious jest that would be talked of far beyond the readership of the *Jewish News*. Sooner or later all of Stefan's best things became the talk of the socialist and labor movement, wherever Yiddish or Russian was read and spoken, and since Evan's list of papers for the vigilante series, the name of Stefan Ivarin was known far beyond those linguistic limits. This editorial on killing Jack London's words would be a sensation anywhere it appeared and surely Evan's Free Speech League would want it in every paper on their special list.

It was lovely to feel so much a part of a future success, and Alexandra read his pages again, more slowly this time, pausing over each phrase Stiva had scratched out, comparing it with the one he had written in its place, testing each in her mind to see if his choice was always right. Invariably it was.

Again she looked up and down the beach. The girls were nowhere in sight. It was annoying to be so full of pride in their father's latest work and be unable to tell them about it. He had made a big point about not reading it to a soul, but surely that prohibition didn't extend to his own children.

She put the folded pages into the envelope, counting them first to be certain they were all there, as he always counted his chess pieces before putting them away in their box. Then she started toward the curling edge of the sea. She would enjoy a walk anyway, and when she spotted the girls she would say not a word about the editorial if they were with friends. She curved the bulky letter into the circle of her hand and it felt like a chunky white club. Just like the what-you-call-it, she thought, in those relay races in ancient Greece. Cheerfully she swung the cylinder of the letter against her thigh as she walked. Baton, she remembered. Like a conductor's at a concert. Like music to move one's soul.

Except for these last days of worry about Joan, it was being a lovely summer once more, with Fran at sixteen an absolute belle, imperiously snubbing nearly all the boys who were ready to worship and dance attendance on her day and night. And little Fee, suddenly twelve, was losing some of her tomboy wildness and maturing in subtle ways, though the poor child still went purple with jealousy whenever one of her contemporaries confided to her about the start of menstruation. Despite her sympathy for Fee's despair, Alexandra had to laugh at the boastful girls, every one pretending it was so awful, such pain, and every one ruthlessly lording it over Fee or any other girl who had not yet arrived at the moment of womanhood.

Apart from the children and her own extraordinary peacefulness at the sea, happy with her swimming, her dancing, with the feeling of wet hair on her neck and salt drying on her body, happy each day as a child is happy, for no good reason—

Aside from all this, there was again this summer, as if it had been lying dormant under the winter waiting for her, the same unparalleled discovery that the beach women came to her for guidance, about how to become American women instead of remaining immigrant women from the steerage of a hundred ships coming from a hundred cities and villages in Europe.

Again their turning to her was an experience like wine, like the moment of love, like the discovery of music. Anna Godleberg was still her star pupil, her devoted propagandist, indeed her circus barker advertising to one and all the thrills and delights awaiting them inside Mrs. Ivarin's tent.

It was easy to smile at Anna Godleberg but just as easy to cry over her. Longfellow's poem, whose opening line was all anybody seemed to know, always came to her mind, somewhat embarrassingly, whenever she had a pupil like Anna Godleberg, so eager to learn, to change, to grow.

> And what is so rare as a day in June?
>   Then, if ever, come perfect days;
> Then Heaven tries earth if it be in tune,
>   And over it softly her warm ear lays;
> Whether we look, or whether we listen,
> We hear life murmur, or see it glisten;
> Every clod feels a stir of might,

An instinct within it that reaches and towers,
And, groping blindly above it for light,
Climbs to a soul in grass and flowers; . . .

Anna Godleberg with her Morris and Louis and baby Reba would
never stop groping now, and to be the one who had helped that groping, fostered it, made it less blind—there was a sweetness in that
which must be kin to the sweetness of prayer.

This year twelve women came on "Mrs. Ivarin's evenings," and
only two were repeaters from the summer before. Since rentals were
usually short-term affairs "until the money was gone," the group constantly shifted and changed and remained fluid, yet there was an astonishing consistency about the women in each new group.

"You must write a book, Mrs. Ivarin," one of them would always
say.

"You should give lectures in a big hall, Mrs. Ivarin—every mother
would come to hear you."

"You simply have to write it down—I could make my sister read
it. She has one child, oh God, a brat you want to kill."

"Please—a book."

So last summer had not been a fluke after all, Alexandra Ivarin
thought. There did seem to be some unchanging response to her from
these poor souls of Delancey Street and Rivington, of Gouverneur
Street and Orchard, of Avenue A and East Broadway. Street by street,
tenement by tenement, they were asearch for the ultimate difference
between life in America and life in the ancient ghettos from which
they had fled. And many also searched to keep up with their children,
"American born," at home from birth in the great and beloved land.

Alexandra looked off at the shining sea and loved it. Foaming,
leaping, curling, it was nevertheless a bridge for the hopeful. It would
always be a bridge and she would always love it.

She had walked the entire length of the beach and the girls were
still nowhere in sight; they must be inside somebody's tent, and Shag,
who often gave her a clue to their whereabouts, must be inside with
them. Sharing things was best while the impulse was warm, but now
she would have to wait until evening to tell them about Stiva's letter
and his not waiting to copy out his editorial before mailing it to her.
Disappointed, she walked home.

"Mrs. Ivarin, I decided you flew away in an aeroplane!"

It was Anna Godleberg, waiting for her return. Alexandra was delighted, as if Mrs. Godleberg had magically changed into the most
desired friend on earth. As she invited her in "for a few minutes," she

heard an extra cordiality in her own tone, and a gong of warning sounded in her mind. But Anna Godleberg said she had come for the special rice-pudding recipe with natural brown rice and brown sugar, and the gong had a faraway tone, with no urgency.

Alexandra laid her husband's letter on the table and as she wrote out the recipe her hand was only inches away from it. "And this cup of raisins," she said at the end, "they mustn't be white raisins. Those are bleached with sulphur and lose all their minerals. Be sure you get dark ones like these."

She reached for a box on the open shelf which was the tent's pantry, tasted a few raisins and said, "Simply delicious," as she offered the box to her pupil. "Everything seems delicious right now," she added in the same breath, "I'm so excited about something I just read."

"In today's paper? Can I borrow it if you're through reading it?"

"No, it's not in today's paper."

"Something by your husband?"

"An editorial."

Mrs. Godleberg was electrified. "In yesterday's paper then. I didn't see that either. Could I please borrow that one? I'll send my Morris back with it right after supper."

"It hasn't been in the paper at all yet." Alexandra heard the gong more clearly, but Mrs. Godleberg looked confused, and she added, "It *will* be in the paper of course, perhaps in two weeks. I wasn't supposed to speak of it. It slipped out."

Her visitor's face was transformed. Like a child with its first glimpse of an unheard-of toy, Mrs. Godleberg was radiant with discovery. "You said you just read it—you mean just *now,* in that letter?"

Her hand moved forward toward the letter so prominently in view, but Alexandra said, "I'm afraid I can't. I promised."

Mrs. Godleberg halted her hand and stood still, nodding in obedience, not speaking, as if she had been caught in some indecency.

"Sometimes, he sends me an editorial ahead of time," Alexandra said, uneasy as she saw Mrs. Godleberg's radiance give way to a somber look, as she watched her move back a step, away from the table.

Alexandra understood. It was the look of respect, a return to deference that was part of the uneducated European's automatic posture to those in high places.

Oh, my goodness, Alexandra Ivarin thought in dismay. I made her feel she's a nobody.

Suddenly she was miserable. *Why* had they started on Stiva's editorial? Had she brought it up herself? She hadn't, she was sure; she was on her honor to confide in nobody about it.

Yet somehow they *were* talking about it. Had Anna Godleberg asked her what Mr. Ivarin was writing? She often did ask questions about "the great Mr. Ivarin"; perhaps it was all Mrs. Godleberg's doing.

"I didn't mean to butt in," Mrs. Godleberg said, wretchedly nodding at the letter as if she were indicating a third person with whom she had found Mrs. Ivarin involved. "I wouldn't have asked—if I had even dreamed— Excuse me, Mrs. Ivarin, please."

"No, no," Alexandra said contritely. *"You* must excuse me. I feel ridiculous, embarrassing you over something which, after all, is public property."

Hope shone forth again in Anna Godleberg's face, and eagerness, but she said nothing. She was waiting for the rest of the reprieve Mrs. Ivarin was going to give her. Alexandra added, "I mean will *be* public property when it is printed."

The niceties of this retreat were lost on Mrs. Godleberg, who still looked expectant. Alexandra suddenly thought, There's no way out now. I can't hurt her again and send her off empty—how I ever got so tangled up, I'll never know.

Aloud she said, "Let me read you a bit here and a bit there, but you must promise first—"

"Not one word. Wild horses couldn't drag it out." She leaned toward Alexandra, whispering. "I'd be so, I'd feel, I'm so excited *already,* even to see you open the envelope, see you take it out, and know it hasn't even been in the paper yet. Oh, thank you."

Alexandra read the headline, and the first paragraph. She would skip everything after that, go straight to the end and read another line or two from the last page. That would give Mrs. Godleberg enough to restore her, and still permit her own conscience to stay calm.

But at the end of the first paragraph, she somehow could not skip. It would mutilate Stiva's beautiful piling up of effect, his way of moving inexorably from point to point, his perfect interplay of cold fact, icy sarcasm, hot wrath.

She read the second page to Mrs. Godleberg, and the third. With each one her heart felt an anchor of guilt unwind and sink through fathoms to hold it firm to a dark regret, yet she was helpless until the last syllable Stiva had entrusted to her.

"God in heaven, he is the most brilliant writer in the whole world," Anna Godleberg said then. "What a privilege!"

(2 1 9)

Her rapture almost repaid Alexandra. But as Anna Godleberg took her departure, Alexandra detained her for one final word of caution.

"Remember, I read it only as a real secret," she said. "I think my husband wanted me not to speak of it to anybody."

"Don't worry, Mrs. Ivarin. I'm like the grave."

SEVENTEEN

Webster Martin Eaves, aged a year and a quarter, proceeded on plump legs toward his Aunt Fee.

His right hand clutched four orange-yellow asters which he had just pulled from a round flower bed in his front yard, and he held his hand stiffly toward her during his journey, as if he were pushing the flowers through the air against stubborn resistance.

"Annie Fee-fee ha!" he said.

Fee laughed. "Ha" meant "have" and she kneeled on the dry grass, her arms out, ready for his final lurch. "Come on, Webby, all the way to Auntie Fee."

His last steps were a stagger and she caught him, took his flowers, and rolled him on the ground like a smaller Shag. "Say 'Auntie Fee,' " she said, stressing the T.

"Annie Fee-fee," he said amiably.

"Not Fifi," Fee said. "That's like a French novel."

"Webby wants." He got up and lunged for his orange-yellow asters and Fee moved them just beyond his reach. "Webby wants," he said again, and stamped his foot so that a flurry of white powder flew up from his square-toed shoe. "Indian giver," she said, returning the flowers as she watched the white flurry. It reminded her of the soft puff from a dandelion, after it stopped being a yellow disc and became a ball on a greeny-grey stem, and she said, "Stamp your foot again," and laughed.

Everything made her feel good today. She had come all the way to Brooklyn by herself, to stay with Webby while Eli was at the hospital with Joan and the new baby, Alexandra, that they had been so scared about, and when Eli got home it would be too late for her to start back to Barnett, so she was going to stay overnight, even though it was a school night when she was supposed to go to bed early.

She never did go to bed early when she stayed overnight at anybody else's house, and certainly not to sleep early. Even when she was allowed to spend the night at Trudy's, it was such fun she never felt sleepy at the right time, and for Trudy's she didn't have to take a trolley and then a train.

But sleeping in any house that wasn't yours was exciting. There was an adventure-feeling from the moment you packed your toothbrush and nightgown to the final moment of getting home the next morning.

Nobody could explain why it was so special, but they admitted it was. People loved change, Mama said, new surroundings, getting away from the humdrum. But Mama warned her not to get "Wanderlust" too soon, and not to be in too much of a hurry for life. If she was too *much* in a hurry, trouble was sure to strike.

"What kind of trouble?" she asked, but her mother went vague and pretty stupid and so did Eli and Joan. As for Fran, she was now so crazy about herself and being sixteen and a senior at High, and she had such a crush on a new boy, Tom Ladendock, that she wouldn't say a thing you could make any sense out of.

Actually it was perfectly clear what her mother meant; she had uttered a thousand solemn warnings all their lives about the White Slave Traffic, and they both knew perfectly well that if *that* happened to you, trouble certainly had struck.

But of late, other people said she shouldn't be impatient to grow up and be independent, and they weren't all thinking of the White Slave Traffic. Trudy said her mother thought Fee was restless, and predicted she would want to leave home for good when she was sixteen or eighteen, and then that would give Trudy ideas, and Trudy would leave home too.

That was stupid too, Fee thought. She wasn't restless or in a rush or anything—she always had loved staying at Eli's house, and sleeping on the sofa and eating from their thin blue and white dishes. Pot roast or chicken or meatloaf that Joan made always tasted so much better than the same things at home; having white bread and white sugar, just being away from Mama and Papa and their accents and their principles and protests and wild ideas about everything—all together it added up to a feeling that was wonderful. Like riding a bike downhill without the handlebars, with the wind whistling through your hair and your skirt pressing back against your legs and past them. Or like being on roller skates and going faster and faster and then suddenly standing up straight, coasting along on the spinning wheels with no effort of your own.

"Auntie Fee loves you," she suddenly said to Webby, who had been busy pulling the four flowers apart.

"Webby did it," he said, pointing to the wrecked asters.

"Webby's a bad bad good good boy." She scooped him up, staggered a step under his surprising weight, set him back on his feet and started for the house.

"No," he shouted. "Webby stay here!"

"Look at that," she said, "the way the sun is going down right behind Webby's back."

He wheeled. "Where?"

Just above the roof of a neighboring house, the orange-yellow sun seemed motionless, but in a tick of an instant, its bottom edge was clipped straight across, then another slice of it, and another after that.

Fee watched her nephew. His total attention was on the sinking sun, his total life given over to it. When at last its uppermost edge disappeared Fee took his hand and said, "Now it's gone, so we can go inside," and Webby trotted along happily beside her.

Miss Montessori, Fee thought. She felt happy too. Feeding Web and bathing him and putting him to bed was an adventure also. Joan had written out step-by-step instructions, but everything seemed so natural and easy. When she was married she was going to have a lot of children and never do one thing to make them feel awful like the black bunting or being socialists. Damsie and Josie she would do, but absolutely nothing else.

She wasn't too sure about Damsie and Josie either. Once a letter came from Lawrence, with a friend putting down words Damsie and Josie's mother had spoken aloud in Polish to say thank you for what you did, and it didn't have one interesting thing in it. Papa translated it, and Mama said Fran and she ought to keep in touch with them, and answer soon, or else, with their resiliency and youth, they would forget all about each other.

Resiliency and youth, Fee thought, as she listened to Webby making spit noises in his crib, nice sleepy spitty noises that she liked when he made them but hated if somebody old sitting next to her in a trolley made them. Resiliency and youth—the two words had a sound she loved, a springy bounce hidden inside that made her tingle and stretch as if she were reaching up toward something on top of something high.

Down the street, Eli whistled and she ran to the door to meet him. He would praise her and say she was dependable and grown-up and she would love that.

"How did it go, Fee?" Eli said. "Everything jake?"

"He's fast asleep. He's an angel."

"So are you," he said. "Joan never worried and neither did I."

"Is she still red? I mean Sandra."

He shook his head. "She'll be a real beauty, Joanie says." He slumped into a chair. "Whew, Sis, I'm worn out, and starving."

"It's in the icebox. Just a jiffy."

He hardly ever called her Sis. As she went for the platter of cold ham and potato salad Mrs. Martin had prepared that afternoon, the word "Sis" said itself over and over. It also had a sound she loved, secret like a word in a private code, different from just a regular name.

"They might let them come home this Saturday," Eli said as they began to eat. "Three weeks in that place already—can you imagine how good home will seem?"

"What *is* a breech birth, Eli?" She kept her voice careless. Joan's mother had left tiny rolls too, and a raisin gravy that was better than candy, and when Eli didn't answer, she hoped it was because he was helping himself to everything, too.

Nobody ever answered her about Joan, except her mother, but that was a principle, and she did it in her Latin-words kind of explaining-to-your-children, which was no real good. Something about Caesarean and breech presentation and twenty-six hours of labor and Joan's father demanding a consultant specialist.

"It's when a baby starts feet first," Eli said, rather suddenly.

"Starts what, Eli?"

"To get born."

"Oh," she said. "Is it awful, starting that way?"

"The head is supposed to come first."

"Come where?"

He pushed back his chair and said, "Now look here, Fee, do you know about babies getting born, or don't you?"

"Certainly I do," she said. "They're inside the mothers and they get born and then they're out."

He looked mollified and said, "Well, all right." She waited for him to go on, but he said, "Is there any more milk?" and went to the icebox to see. He was gone for a long time, and when he came back, he said, "All these hospital bills and doctor's bills and specialist's bills —how are they ever going to get paid?"

He looked angry. There was a notice in the Teachers' Bulletin, he said, about a man who got you extra teaching jobs for summer vacations, and even before Joan had left for the hospital, he had gone to New York to see him about next year.

"He wanted to know if I was sure I'd be willing to give up my summer vacation. Willing! Trapped is more like it."

Fee couldn't think of what to say; he was scrunching one hand into the other, and she watched his fingers twist and grab at each other.

"Don't ever be a teacher, Fee," he burst out. "Do anything, work at anything, be a stenog, but don't you ever be a teacher. All those lies —'free every summer,' 'travel to Europe,' 'take courses at a college,' 'your job is safe even in hard times'—it's pure guff. Fifty-one a month! You're always so poor, you have to teach your heart out, year in, year out. Free time? God!"

Fee was almost frightened. She didn't want to be a teacher, everybody knew she didn't. She had no idea what she did want to be, but long ago she had confided to Trudy that she was never never going to teach no matter what her family did when they found out she wouldn't be the one thing she was supposed to be.

But just the same, it was terrible to hear Eli talk this way about it. As if he was spitting out acid.

"Hello, Franny," Garry said. "Well, for the love of Pete."

Fran stood back to let them come in, but his greeting put speech beyond her. Tonight nobody could have forbidden her the pale-yellow crepe de chine dress and it still was as floaty and shimmering and beautiful as if it were brand-new. Garry hadn't seen her since his mother took them to his apartment after the Hippodrome, and that was last April, and half a year had passed since then.

Well, for the love of Pete. It meant, I don't recognize you; you really are grown up now, and you're beautiful. She swallowed, and to her horror, her swallow was audible, like a marble in a box.

But Garry turned to Fee and said, "Are you going to dance with me *this* time?"

Fee said, "It's a cinch," and was so delighted with her worldliness that everybody laughed, and Fran felt safe and hidden. All the Tom Ladendocks in the world disappeared at the sound of Garrett Paige's voice, and all the Jack Purneys and every other boy she knew. Tom Ladendock had just moved to Barnett, and he was handsome and lived in a house with seventeen rooms, and he had picked her out to fall for. She fell right back, even though Tom always wanted to do things she would have died over afterward, if she ever gave in.

(2 2 4)

And then this morning Mama said the Paiges expected Garry and Letty for the weekend. "They want to celebrate the big success Letty had this first week in her furniture store."

"Antique shop," Fran automatically corrected, but it was lost. They had all heard a hundred reports from Mrs. Paige about Letty's new venture; Mrs. Paige simply loved to talk about Letty's courage and Letty's plans. They had heard of her ceaseless search for the perfect little shop, even more exciting to Letty than her search the year before for the perfect little apartment. They knew all about her scouring the city for old wrecks of antiques and about her back-breaking labors in restoring them. Never once had Mrs. Paige called Letty's new place anything but an "antique shop." But never once had Mama called it anything but a "furniture store." Mrs. Paige, of course, was too polite to say anything, but Fran squirmed every single time.

"The Paiges," her mother went on obliviously, "are all coming over before Papa has to start for New York, the first visit from the whole family since last year. Garry himself suggested it. He wants to tell Papa and me what he thinks about the articles."

She said it in a conceited way, Franny thought, as if she had written them too. Garry might have another reason for suggesting a visit, one that her mother could never guess in ten million years.

And now here he was, telling her father how it felt to be able to read him at last, and how much he admired his free-speech series.

Letty said, "I read them too, all six pieces. They really grip you." There was something new and attractive about Letty, Fran decided. Her clothes were expensive-looking and fashionable, like the Society pictures in the Sunday rotogravure. Even though it was still October and not very cold, she had a muff of creamy fur when she came in, and the collar of her coat matched it and stood up around her neck like a puffy little necklace.

Fran thought, Imagine how clothes like that would look on somebody young. *Well, for the love of Pete.* It was his way of saying, You're somebody I could be in love with, you're somebody I could kiss, my lovely girl who grew up when I wasn't looking. I would be quiet with you and not full of Tom's sudden pushes and grabs and high-school words like "What about a kiss?" But I *would* kiss you, and you would kiss me—

Again she swallowed, and again the marble rattled. But they were all talking now, their usual talk, not about Papa any more, but about Wilson and Taft and Teddy Roosevelt in the election next month, and working day and night so Debs would pile up the biggest Socialist vote in history—the whole endless rolling talk they seemed to find more fascinating than anything else on earth.

Even Garry. That was the one thing, the only thing ever, the single possible thing she ever wished was different in him. By now they were off on the war news, and that fascinated Garry even more. It was dazzling, the way he could remember about the Turks declaring war on Bulgaria and Serbia one day, and Greece declaring it on Turkey the next day, and Italy's demands and the joint note from Austria and Russia and Russia mobilizing in Poland—

Dazzling, but the one thing about him she didn't want to think about. Somehow he changed from the Garrett Paige who was so romantic and thrilling. And as he changed, he became more like, like, well, it was crazy but he became something like Papa and Mama when *they* were all excited and blazing about an idea.

He does not, an insulted voice protested inside her. What a horrible thing to say about him. He absolutely does not.

"He's a good boy," Stefan Ivarin said many hours later, and though he had gone to New York to work and come home again, Alexandra knew he was talking about the Paiges' visit in general and about Garry in particular.

"A wonderful boy," she said. "Such a clear mind, they must be so proud of him."

"Not always clear," he said. "But he thinks for himself and knows how to stand up to you if you disagree."

"Not clear? Why not? What about?"

"Let's say, in his pacifism."

"Stiva! Are you suddenly becoming militaristic?"

He looked at her indulgently. "Do you think I am?"

"Then what's unclear about Garry?"

At this elliptical progression, he shrugged. "In blueprint, his principles are perfect," he said, "but life sometimes alters blueprints, and this Garry will not concede." He saw that Alexandra was about to launch a large defense of Garry, blueprints and all, and he added quickly, "But he's a fine young man. The more I see of him, the more he impresses me."

"I thought the very same thing tonight," she said, and sighed. "If only Eli found politics so interesting, and could talk about it the way Garry does."

Stefan frowned. He disliked any comparison of their children with other children and at the first sign of it from Alexandra, he always did his best to head it off. He particularly wanted to avoid any dissection of Eli now, in relation to Garry or alone. Often he felt that despite his usually painful run-ins with his only son, he understood more closely than Alexandra the essentials that made Eli's character, and thus could forgo any continued disappointment in him or any persistent hope for basic change.

Eli was not notable and that was the sum of it. He was not bad or silly or especially weak; he had been a clever student, with easy good grades always, and apparently he was now a good teacher. But he was a deadly average in concepts, principles, ideas; he was, moreover, just weak enough to be eternally unready for concepts or principles that might call upon him for even minimal strength or independence.

"In a word," he said, "he is not a notable man."

"Who isn't?" Alexandra demanded.

He looked at her in consternation. Had he spoken aloud?

"You said 'he is not a notable man,' " she continued, slightly truculent, "and I didn't know whether you meant Garry or Eli."

"Did I say 'notable man'?" he said mildly. "I must have been thinking aloud." Before she could speak, he changed the subject with a skill and celerity he wished might always be his in a pinch. "Tonight at the office, Fehler expounded a new plan, far from notable, mind you, but probably harmless."

"Don't trust any plan of his," she counseled, "harmless or not."

"Do you find me falling into many of his traps?"

"Of course not, Stiva," she said, her truculence of a moment ago swept away by apology.

He forgave her, and told her that Fehler thought the *Jewish News* should assign somebody to "prepare a survey" of every innovation adopted in the last twelve months by any English-language newspaper in New York, "new cartoons, new funnies, new departments, new exposés, new anythings."

"It's not a bad notion," Stefan said. "We all do it, of course, every day of our lives, Landau and Kesselbaum and Borg and I and even Fehler himself."

She heard the edge in his tone and wished she could get him back to Garry and the Paiges. It was so pleasant to talk over a happy evening—that was why she had stayed awake waiting for him to get home tonight while she was so full of it. Fee had danced with Garry when they turned on the Victrola after Stiva's departure for the paper, and the child had behaved delightfully, not silly or giggly any more, but almost self-possessed. And Francesca, waltzing with him, was a vision to delight the heart, her delicate body swaying to the music, a faraway look in her eyes, the embodiment of youth's joy and promise.

"We don't call it 'a survey,'" Stefan continued drily. "That's the businessman's vocabulary, no doubt. But if Hearst or Pulitzer or Adolph S. Ochs has ever slipped an innovation past the gang of us, what with the stack of papers we each devour every day—"

"Survey!" Alexandra was scornful. "Fehler catches hold of a fancy word and he's proud of himself for weeks. I'm sure he's still trying to make up to himself for the fiasco of Berkman's book. Just to look at you must turn him green with anger at how you polished it off."

Briefly Ivarin considered returning to Eli and the notable man, but he vetoed it and let her talk on. He had already seconded Fehler's plan by saying it deserved a quick start if Landau approved, finding it restful not to need to dispute him. Fehler then asked that Borg be assigned to do the survey, waiting of course until the election was over, with its extra rush and extra work. Again he seconded the idea; Borg was the obvious choice.

"How does it strike you, Saul?" Ivarin asked later. "Mr. Fehler knows you're my candidate, too."

"What an opportunity!" Borg exclaimed, amost shouting. "How can I ever thank Mr. Fehler enough? And you, too, Mr. Ivarin?"

His eagerness was youth, Stefan thought now, eagerness to advance himself, to earn another raise. But something else had flamed in Borg's eyes along with his eagerness. Saul had been born in the slums of the East Side, educated in the city schools and in night classes at City College, the despair of his parents because he refused to become either rabbi or cloakmaker, the two vocations they held seemly. Yet he was their greatest pride, their darling, their joy, because he had done so well for four years on a magazine they could read and for nearly another year on their favorite daily newspaper.

Of course Borg was eager to try this special task. At twenty-six he probably felt there was no time left to make a name for himself while he was young. But had the other flame been the hot one of ambition? The consuming one that could so swiftly reduce standards to ashes and clinkers?

No matter, Ivarin thought. Where there's fire, it's never sure who will get burned. Next day, he commended Fehler's survey to Landau as "a useful idea that might consolidate our separate impressions," and then said, "I only hope that this survey won't end by convincing all of us of the vast superiority of yellow journalism."

Landau said, "Now, Stiva."

"Always the pessimist. True enough."

Their talk veered to the campaign and the rising venom of its final stage. Though his paper was supporting the Socialist ticket, Isaac Landau kept worrying about wasting his vote, casting it, not for Wilson who might win over Roosevelt and Taft, but for Debs who could not conceivably win over any one of them. He knew the folly of expressing this worry to Ivarin, who was forever glorifying "the protest vote," but now he heard himself talking about it just the same. And Ivarin, who knew the futility of arguing with Landau on this issue, as on the other issue of religion which forever separated them, was irresistibly drawn into battle. Only Landau's clock striking the hour proclaimed a truce and rushed Ivarin off to the two campaign speeches he was to give that evening.

In both he hammered at that one point of the protest vote. He had done so in every lecture he had given thus far in the campaign, and he knew he would redouble his efforts as his speaking schedule was doubling and redoubling itself. From now until Election Day, he was putting himself on a sweatshop routine of speaking engagements; rather, he was permitting Debs Headquarters to pile up an incessant list of appearances for him, in the drive to poll the largest Socialist vote ever known in New York City.

Everywhere he spoke, he pounded home that theme, the beautiful power, in a free country, of a protesting minority. On a platform, on a soapbox at a street corner, speaking to vast audiences or to groups of fifty, he harangued and pleaded and yelled that a vote for Debs would be not a wasted vote but a real vote, a good vote, a strong vote.

"I tell you," he shouted, "that every senator and every congressman, from every one of the forty-eight states, will pay more attention to the demands of labor, if there is a big, a tremendous jump in the Socialist vote this year."

Sometimes he said "forty-six states" and instantly corrected himself, saying he kept forgetting that Arizona and New Mexico had been admitted to the Union this year, saying he was a bad student to forget, a numskull to forget. Each time there would come delighted denials from the crowd, signals to his lecturer's sixth sense that he had won his audience. Then he would thunder at them to realize that in a great free country like America, a man's protest vote was a big instrument, that it could sledgehammer a big dent in the steel walls of politics as usual, profits as usual, poverty as usual.

Day after day, night after night, Stefan Ivarin kept on; during the final week before November fifth, he never went home to Barnett at all, sleeping wherever and whenever he could, campaigning around the clock. At the paper, he turned over all routine editing to Borg, blessing him again for his willingness to assume twice the normal burden, forgetting his brief clutch of doubt over his ambition.

By Election Day, Ivarin felt his vocal cords ready to split over one more syllable, and he was unable to utter an ordinary word to a waiter, a streetcar conductor, to Alexandra on the telephone. But three more times during that final evening, as crowds gathered before the lighted glass doors of the *Jewish News,* he climbed up on an improvised platform made from a shored-up pushcart in the gutter, and there, by sheer need, by will, by magic, he again found the huge hortatory voice of the campaigner.

Never had an election meant so much to him before. This would be the eighth time he would vote for a President of the United States. It was in 1884, when he was twenty-three, that he had first known the tremendous emotion of walking into a curtained booth and there, unbeknownst to any ruler alive, to any employer, policeman, magistrate, civil official, to any enemy or friend, there cast his secret, protected, inviolate vote. He never could forget that emotion; he knew now that it would clamor within his veins and cells every four years for the rest of his life.

"It's glorious, Stiva! What a day! Did you dare to dream—nearly a million?"

He shook his head. Debs had indeed polled the greatest Socialist vote of all time, and the whole world of labor was joyous. Out of every sixteen men who had gone to the polls across the vast stretch of America, one man had voted the Socialist ticket, and Debs' total was more than twice his vote of just four years before. Woodrow Wilson with his six million votes, Teddy with his four and Taft with less than that—suddenly it shone forth that workingmen held an edge of history in their hands. The country would grow and factories would grow and capitalism would grow, but labor would grow as well, and the voice of labor, the right to be heard as equals are heard.

"It's a turning point, all right," Stefan said, his voice again torn and thick. "The whole year, if you think back."

He turned to his columns of printed figures. As each new edition of each paper arrived, he had checked the endless lines of numbers himself, his fountain pen skimming down their plunging slopes not because he doubted their accuracy but for the delight of adding such unheard-of sums, such muscular, such life-filled sums in the column for Debs and the Socialist Party.

Alexandra's eyes gleamed as she watched him. It was a turning point; he was right. A sweep for everything they both believed in and worked for, right through the year from January onward. The terrible strike in Lawrence—that had started in January and gone on for bitter bitter weeks, but it was won. The steel strike, the anthracite strike, the railroad strike—won. The hatmakers, the bricklayers, the cloakmakers, the cutters, the furriers, out in the West the lumber strikes and the copper strike—won. Everywhere, in a hundred kinds of labor, all over the great growing land it was the same: the strike vote taken, the picket line started, the soup kitchens and bread lines set up, the jeers and taunts and curses, the clubbings and arrests, at times the blood flowing—but at last, the strike won. Nine cents an hour gave way to eleven, ten bowed to twelve, twenty to twenty-one. Ninety-hour weeks had already gone down the slide of history, eighty-hour weeks following them, now even sixty-hour weeks were beginning to go—

Won, won, a step here, an inch there, a right acknowledged, a dignity no longer denied—all over America change was afoot, hope renewing, the tiny patient tallies entered in the unseen books.

And now this soaring shouting vote for Debs. Alexandra wanted to say something to Stefan and his columns of figures but she was afraid to go too far, afraid she would not find the right word, so she said nothing.

Early in the afternoon, Stefan left for the office. He was still unrested except for a snatched couple of hours of sleep just before he voted yesterday morning and again at about dawn this morning. But he was drawn toward the office and she understood that. In the evening she was to meet him there, for a round of celebrations with old friends they had known in New York when they were young, when a socialist victory such as this was so far off in the unborn years that they had not dared to imagine it as something they might all live to see.

The round of celebrating was called off an hour before it was supposed to begin. When Stefan arrived at the office, it was still alive with excitement and discovery as it had been through the night before while the results kept streaming in from the AP ticker. Because it was still afternoon, Isaac Landau was there, and he sought out Ivarin in his office. "Shall I confess something," he asked.

"Confess away."

(231)

"It will make you conceited."

Ivarin studied Landau's expression. "At the last moment you decided it would *not* be wasting your vote."

"But it was God who helped me decide, not you, so why need I worry about making you conceited?"

"Perhaps that you find me on God's side, politically at least? From you, Itzak, that's big praise."

Landau smiled, but he looked meditative, and Ivarin waited. Itzak was no intellectual, and below the level of practical affairs they had never found a deep kinship with each other, but he liked Landau and Landau liked him.

"Politically on God's side?" Landau repeated disapprovingly. "That's too blasphemous for me."

"Forgive me," Ivarin said quickly.

"Forgive, of course I forgive. But sometimes I think it's a big hoax, your being such an unbeliever."

"I'm afraid not."

"A hoax, at least, that you feel nothing."

"Feel nothing? When did you get that idea?"

"Feel no pride in being a Jew," Landau said. "I wonder if it isn't a bluff when you deny that you're proud to be a Jew, as every Jew must feel proud."

"Neither proud nor unproud," Ivarin said unemphatically.

"You must admit there *is* something, Stiva, a secret pride that you were born a Jew, that you share a glorious heritage," he said with emotion. "I think of my heritage as a Jew and my heart burns with joy; I feel uplifted and grateful. For my children, too, and their children."

"I know you do, Itzak."

"An endless riches in their blood. Just think, Abraham, Isaac, Jacob. The Ancient Prophets, and Moses, David, Solomon. Think of Jesus. Then down the ages—Spinoza, Heine, Disraeli, and this Dr. Freud who some people say will revolutionize all medicine."

"An impressive list," Stefan said.

"You don't have to admit it openly, you old argufier," Isaac Landau insisted. "But in secret you must feel proud that your own children share this great heritage."

Stefan shook his head, half-wishing he could let Landau think himself unanswerable, but aware that nothing could make him hold back any longer.

"I'm afraid, Itzak," he said, "that if I did feel all this pride on behalf of my children, that then I would have to balance things by feeling a little quiver of shame as well."

"Shame?"

"That I give them no heritage of Galileo or Descartes or Thomas Jefferson or Shakespeare or Abraham Lincoln."

Isaac Landau said, "I should have known there was no use."

"Why, I couldn't look my children in the eye," Stefan went on, now enjoying himself thoroughly. "If we are starting to measure off glorious heritages, then I tremble to have them accuse me about Michelangelo, Dostoevsky, Tolstoy—"

"You're a madman, Stiva," Landau broke in, clutching his forehead in mock despair. "You are no Jew at all. Agnostics are all madmen."

"You bet your bottom dollar I'm a Jew. As long as there's one pogrom in Russia, I remain a Jew, agnostic but a Jew. As for you, my dear Itzak—"

"Don't tell me again. I'm a synagogue chauvinist. I know it by heart. A Jewish jingo—"

There was a tap at the door and Fehler joined them. They discussed the starting date for the survey and then the basic meaning of the election of Woodrow Wilson, the first Democrat to become President in twenty years. Suddenly Landau put both his hands to his stomach, his gasp almost a cry.

"Boy, boy," Stefan Ivarin shouted, "get a doctor."

A week later, in the hospital where he had undergone so many tests for his digestive ailment, Isaac Landau died of heart failure. Stefan's shock was deep, and the tenacity of his sorrow surprising. For weeks he felt the loss of him, sometimes too sharply to credit, sometimes in a muted way. It was a melancholy deprivation, knowing they would never sit together in a meeting, never greet each other in the hall, never resume their insoluble problem about blood-pride in one's religion. Through the whole life of the *Jewish News* they had worked together; they had shared those years and grown older sharing them. Now it was over for Landau, and he felt something over for him too.

The inevitable reorganization of the paper would begin as soon as a decent time of mourning and legalities went by, and Stefan dreaded the discussions with Landau's family and heirs, with their lawyers and advisers. His children were all daughters; none of their husbands had shown any desire for a job with the paper or any inclination toward the field of the foreign-language press. Eventually, since the largest fraction of the ownership was Landau's, they would select some person to safeguard their interests and they would install him in Landau's place. Perhaps it would be a figurehead. One could hope for a strong and able man, a man one would not need to persuade or proselytize.

It was depressing to speculate about, and Stefan Ivarin preferred to avoid it. After the first days, he knew he could not. Uncertainty was everywhere. The Landau lawyer, Jacob Steinberger, had posted a large bulletin inside the front door, countersigned by Fehler and himself, stating that nobody's job was at stake during the reorganization period, but after a day or two, the words of reassurance might have been written in invisible ink.

Throughout the paper the sense of change hung like a thin sour gas in the air. Groups gathered in the corridors and around desks, broke up, formed anew. A quickening anxiety was noticeable in every office, on every floor, in the pressrooms below. It was understandable but demoralizing. During the peak rush each evening, work and the clock cured it, but as the first edition went to press, it seeped back through the crevices of each partition and each personality.

One night for no particular reason, Ivarin found himself recalling the quarrel he had had long ago when he had overruled Fehler for interfering in some purely editorial matter. They had bickered like young girls until at the end he had reminded Fehler that for years the owner had approved of his business management and the growth of the paper's sales and income, just as he had also approved of the paper's writing and editing.

"So has it been for five years," he had told Fehler, "so let it be for another five years."

"Perhaps," Fehler had answered.

The "perhaps" had congealed in his mind before Fehler was out of the door, taking shape there, a lumpish possession to be cast out without ado.

Yet here it was, Ivarin reflected now, his possession still. *Perhaps.*

EIGHTEEN

By the start of the Christmas season, Letty's success was proved, and before the end of the winter it was clear to Garry that it was self-generating and as irreversible as the suffrage movement itself.

"You don't look like a New Woman," he said when she brought him her year-end figures. "But I'm proud of you."

"Gare, the *profit!*"

"From wrecks to riches," he said and ducked. They were happy; the opening of the shop on East Thirty-seventh Street, "around the corner from Tiffany's," had opened a new period of their marriage, with their other problems forgotten or tabled. For Letty, the shop was far more than something to work at all day, and for him, it was a surprising source of new satisfaction that he spoke about often.

Unexpectedly too, it swiftly became an influence on the basic shape of their social life, a life filled now with new activity in new circumstances neither had ever known before and that both found fascinating to explore.

It was the world of fashion, the world of wealth, and it was Cynthia Aldrich who led them into it. Regarding herself not only as "Letty's first customer," but as her natural mentor and adviser, Mrs. Aldrich had started by offering herself as a partner, ready to "put in any percentage of capital you'll let me have, child," but Letty had gracefully rejected this offer even before hearing Garry's explosive "no."

"The shop's yours, and only yours," he insisted.

The shop remained Letty's and only Letty's. Apart from a token share bought for a hundred dollars by her parents and another bought by Garry's, it was hers even in a legal sense, the lease signed in her own name, the books and credits and special checking account in her own name, without the usual countersignature or endorsement by her husband. Garry's "no" had also been explosive each time she suggested that since she was using their money to launch herself, the new project really belonged to both of them, "for richer or poorer, profit or loss," which made him laugh but did not change his no to yes.

And as the weeks and months passed, Letty found new pride for herself by feeling the mantle of his around her, and new reasons for a sense of well-being and achievement. When she came each month to the day that told her again they were not yet to have a baby, she no longer wept in desolation and sense of failure, accepting the fact and not dwelling upon it. All she knew was that she was happy again as she had been in the first year of their marriage and that Garry seemed happy with her.

One night early in February she thought, In a way he's happier. It was a mild Sunday evening and they were both in the closed and locked store, finishing the largest task that had ever faced them, each weary but each stubbornly unwilling to quit before it was done. Garry had just heaved an empty crate atop half a dozen others at the rear exit of the shop and was mopping his grimy arms and face with a filthy rag that had been tucked into his belt. Out front in the gutter, where the street-cleaner would get them in the morning, were a dozen more, and he decided to add these newly emptied ones to their outdoor brothers.

"Do you remember," he asked as he banged the door behind him at last, "when I promised to drop you a curtsy the first time I came in?"

"And then never once did!"

His hands were stained with varnish and oil, his shirt dark with dust and sweat, but at her reproving tone, he promptly sank in an elaborate maneuver that he took to be a curtsy and said, "Queen Anne, ma'am."

"And me looking like the washerwoman. Oh, Gare." She gave his shoulder a push while he was jackknifed at her feet, and he collapsed willingly on the littered floor, stretching out on the packing straw and shredded newspapers from the barrels and boxes they had been opening for hours.

"It feels good," he said. "I'll stay down here a while."

"You must be half dead," she said, "and starved too. But I'm so glad." She looked around at what they had accomplished. "It would have taken me forever without you."

She was as disheveled and grimy as he and as unconscious of her appearance, unworried about the hair coming loose from her high pompadour, about her skirts turned back and pinned up at her waist with a safety-pin like a slavey's. The backbreaking part was done, and now she could manage quite easily and get the entire shipment on display in a couple of days, a week at most. The barrels and crates and cartons had been filled with an unrelated assortment of decorative objects that even Garry's untutored eye recognized as beautiful or unusual or old or costly, or all of these at once. There were clocks and barometers and lamps, silver trays and bowls and candlesticks, crystal candelabra and wall sconces, andirons and firedogs and fireplace screens and fenders, several small tables and tiered stands and footstools, and then dozens upon dozens of those unknowns he always thought of as bric-a-brac, these ranging from fragile porcelains and china to indestructible bronze and marble.

Now, for all their dissimilarity, they were taking on a certain unity because, though they were a shipment on consignment, they were in a sense hers, in her control, set out in groups and clusters in her place, behind the two handsome screens she had installed across the width of the store to conceal from customers the mundane necessities she had begun with and still used in all her spare time: her scrapers and brushes and rubbers, her varnish removers and waxes and stains and polishes, the cracked old washbasin on the back wall, next to a gas plate where she made tea for the sandwich she brought from home each morning.

At her feet on the floor, Garry propped himself up on one elbow and looked about him. "Even I can tell it's quite a collection," he said.

"I could sell every single thing right off the floor, they're so marvelous." She leaned forward to pick a wisp of straw from a fluted vase and to blow dust from the face of a gilded wall clock, with an American eagle spreading brass wings across its top. "What luck that Cynthia thought of it."

Mrs. Aldrich had arranged the shipment on consignment, the first Letty had ever had. It came from the estate of a millionaire banker named Will Harrett, of Fifth Avenue and Oyster Bay, whose widow was a lifelong friend of Cynthia Aldrich. "It wouldn't take a cent of added capital," she explained to Letty, "and your commission would be thirty-three per cent, and on some things fifty. You would be doing Olive Harrett a kindness, too, my dear; she simply has to give up that enormous place out there, and she does have the loveliest things."

Her timing was perfection itself, for Letty had been taking inventory, her first attempt at that "store-wide inventory" that she had so often read about, and Mrs. Aldrich's talk of "the loveliest things" made her glance around her Christmas-depleted shop.

"It does look awfully empty, doesn't it?" she said. "I never will get used to that."

Last fall when success had still seemed a mirage, Letty had been constantly astonished that so small a store could swallow up all the pieces she had collected and restored throughout the summer and early fall. Each departure of a chair or table or chest left a gaping space that hurt her newborn proprietary pride, and now, even with new things due to arrive daily, she longed for those small odds and ends to "fill up the holes" and restore the fullness and variety she wanted.

"I'd love to go out to Oyster Bay," she said tentatively to Cynthia Aldrich. "Could I?"

"Of course, Letty. To make your own selection?"

"It's just that—"

"No explanation's necessary, child. When shall we go?"

"It's just that I've noticed that if I am really crazy about something, it always seems to sell. But if I can't quite make up my mind about it, customers can't make up their minds either."

Cynthia Aldrich patted her shoulder, nodding approval, and later that week enjoyed the long day at Oyster Bay as much as Letty did. She relished the role she had adopted for herself, and enjoyed Letty's gratitude immensely. Last October, on Opening Day, she had appeared at the shop with another of her close friends, who soon turned into Letty's "second best customer," and each day or two thereafter Mrs. Aldrich would show up with yet another. These friends in turn brought in their friends, or sent them in, and in some ways they were all alike. None of them fussed over cost. None showed surprise even at a price that Letty once would have called "scandalous."

Very soon Letty saw "social importance" turn visibly into commercial importance, and she never knew when she herself began unknowingly to put a private label upon each woman who came through the door. As with the price tags hidden away inside a drawer, or glued to the underside of a table-leaf, these private labels were unobtrusive and concealed, so artfully concealed that she remained half unaware of their existence on the retentive undersurface of her mind. She would have denied that she was impressed by one customer more than another, but she regarded this ticketing of the women she dealt with as "just business" and never questioned it.

Nor did it seem strange when Mrs. Aldrich invited her and Garry to dinner. The Aldriches lived in a wide stone house facing Gramercy Park, and Letty had been there once by herself for tea, afterward giving Garry a lyrical description of the beauty within it, its paintings and rare books as well as its fine furniture and carpets, its dignity as well as its elegance.

The dinner was planned for the young; the Aldriches' married daughters, Constance and Lucinda, both in their twenties, asked their friends too, so that seven young couples were at the table. Later, a five-piece orchestra played for them to dance to; the evening was a delight.

Neither Letty nor Garry had ever dined in such surroundings before, nor did they often go to parties where evening dress was taken for granted, where four wines were served at the table, where a butler and a footman in livery served champagne or liqueurs or whiskey afterward into the night. It all was new and exciting and carefree; Lucinda Aldrich was married to a man named Hank Stiles, who sold stocks on Wall Street and who kept coming back to Letty after dancing with any other girl, to ask for the next. Constance's husband was an assistant professor of history at Yale, Ronald Yates, whom everybody called "Proff," and both Proff and Connie were diverting and companionable from the start.

It was three in the morning when the Aldrich door closed on Letty and Garry and two other couples, and it was clear that this evening would lead to other evenings. At the curb several hansom cabs were waiting patiently, drawn there by the light streaming from the windows, their owners knowing that if a ball was in progress, customers would be sure and payment generous.

"It was wonderful, wasn't it?" Letty asked Garry happily, as the cabman spread a thick lap robe over their knees. She leaned against him, feeling herself newly valuable because she had been his introduction to the Aldrich house, even though it was he and the lab and his job that had brought the Aldriches into her life to start with. Garry agreed that it was a fine party; all evening he had worn that look which announced that he liked every moment of the evening, at dinner, over liqueurs, while he was dancing. Because he so openly showed what he felt, people responded and liked him in return.

All their new friends did that, Letty had frequently reflected since that night, at all the places they had been asked to since, and she was always aware of it, soothed and reassured by it. Garry was changing into a more social being; he didn't get started on the gloomy news from Europe while he was at a party, just as he no longer carried on about it at home the way he used to do. He was changing, and maturing, and that was wonderful too.

"Hey, what are you thinking about?" Garry said, and for a moment she thought they were still in the hansom cab, still in their new evening clothes, he handsome above his white tie and she still too conscious of how deeply décolleté her cerise gown actually was. Then he stretched and groaned and got to his feet from the littered floor of the shop and she came back to the present, to her pinned-up skirts and straggling hair.

"Oh," she answered, "about Mrs. Aldrich and this shipment and the first time she had us for dinner, and Lucinda and Hank's party and the Grintzers' theater-supper."

"Let's hurry and finish up now," he said. "It's nearly nine, and we're both giving out."

Outside on the street they stopped for a last look at the outer face of the shop, and Letty said, "It's prettiest at night." Even to a casual passer-by the shop proclaimed itself different, an individual among shops, unwilling to be like a thousand other small shops in the city. Letty had never changed her decision to keep the big window uncluttered, and there was in it now only one oblong dinner table of flame mahogany, its rounded tapering legs ending in the claw-and-ball feet characteristic of Chippendale. The window itself was framed by a pair of draperies of the same red damask Letty had used at home, and these gave an unexpected and personal warmth to the shining window. Instead of the usual store lighting, she had installed a crystal chandelier, hanging over the table on a long linked metal chain, lighted, not by candles, but by tiny frosted bulbs shaped like candles and imported from Belgium. It remained alight every evening of the week until midnight, when a watchman for the neighborhood turned an outside switch on the back door. Separated from them by the smooth expanse of glass, it blazed with a hundred twinkling brilliances, casting reflections into the depth of the old mahogany below it, sending radiance out to the guide lines of red damask at its left and right.

"I love it most of all at night," Letty said.

Garry pulled her hand through his arm and led her toward Fifth Avenue, past the grand shuttered solemnity of the Tiffany store on the corner. Had *that* begun as a small shop, he wondered, with the sparkle and dazzle of quick success? Or had it been a tedious halting growth, as most successes were? Even yet, it was hard to credit the reality of "Mrs. Garrett Paige, Antiques," but any doubt was evanescent. Long before Christmas it was clear that Letty would have to employ people to help her, but thus far she had hired only a handyman, Josh Flick, who could not get a regular job because he limped rockily and "looked peculiar." For a dollar a day, Josh kept the shop clean, the furniture dusted or waxed; he polished the great brass plate on the front door with its six-inch doorknob, washed the plate-glass window after every rain or snow, and packed and crated each item

(240)

so skillfully that nothing was ever scratched or injured by the trucking wagon hired for deliveries.

Letty agreed long ago that she needed a salesman or saleswoman to take over when she was away from the store on her endless searching through her ever-widening "sources," which now included regular antique dealers as well as her old dealers in junk. But she had hired nobody, and apart from some temporary help for the holiday season, she had rarely even interviewed anyone who seemed "right."

"It has to be somebody who's really lived with lovely things," she explained to Garry once, when he urged her to widen her idea of "right." "So she would feel in her bones *why* my things are lovely, and not just memorize what I said about them." The process of interviewing was an ordeal that made her feel as if she were the suppliant, she the one being measured or on trial, and she was invariably glad when the moment came to say, "Thank you for coming in, and I'll decide in a day or two."

The day or two was another of Cynthia's contributions. "So you can check up on references. You're not to risk being cooped up with *anything* that answers your Help Wanted ad."

"When are you going to advertise again, Letts?" Garry asked now, as they sank into chairs at the nearest Childs Restaurant. "Too many days like today would kill you off."

"I know. Do you remember Hank Stiles' brother Peter?"

"Sure I do."

"His private hobby is collecting antiques, mostly eighteenth-century." She looked pensive. "He said Wall Street bored him."

Garry laughed. "He's forty or so, isn't he? Could a young chit like you be *his* boss?"

"Why couldn't I? I could have salespeople of fifty or even sixty. Most antique dealers do."

"Would any Stiles ever become a salesman in any shop?"

"I suppose not." Again she looked pensive, but in a moment her face brightened. "If I ever did find somebody like Peter," she said, "he wouldn't have to be a salesman. I could call him Assistant Manager."

"You clever girl," he said. "I guess you could."

The decent time of mourning and legalities went by, and still there was no announcement about the reorganization of the paper.

"Any news?" Alexandra asked every time Stefan Ivarin came back from New York.

(241)

"None."

A dozen times in the past weeks she had promised not to ask the question any more; a dozen times he had promised that the moment there was news of Landau's successor, he would let her know, even if it came in the middle of the night when she was bound to be asleep.

The inclusiveness of this promise always set her mind at rest for a day or two, but then again she would greet him with that instinctive question. "Any news?"

Landau's death had made Alexandra weep, and these tears had touched Stefan to the point of pain. She was grieving, not only for an old companion of his last twenty years, but for the years themselves, gone now as Isaac was gone, irrecoverable as youth itself, as its limitless energies and hopes.

She had gone to New York to the funeral, though neither of them believed in religious ceremonials for the dead, regarding them as leftovers from primitive rites, just as they felt about religious ceremonies at weddings. One was a sanctified orgy over sex and procreation, the other a sanctified orgy of self-laceration and agony in public.

She herself had emerged so wrecked by the experience of Landau's funeral, to which he had not gone, that she kept returning to it as a topic of discussion for days, and at last he had drawn back in some reflex of distaste. Was she weeping for Landau's death, or in a self-pity of worry about her husband's future at the paper?

The moment the thought was born, it proved itself a giant, a Gargantua, not to be vanquished in a few casual bouts of reason. "The more you fret and worry about what will happen at the paper," he finally burst out at Alexandra, "the harder it is for me not to."

By that time a month had gone by since Landau's death. At the paper, the word "reorganization" had become virtually an oath. By the New Year, it could no longer be doubted that Miriam Landau and her four daughters and their four husbands and their several advisers, lawyers and relatives were in some inexplicable paralysis at reaching a solution of the problem death had presented to them. By then the acuteness of first anxiety throughout the staff had diluted down to a milder form, but there was an almost daily display of temperament or quarrelsomeness among the reporters or press crew or stenographers.

Late one afternoon Jacob Steinberger, now Miriam Landau's lawyer, came to the office to explain matters to the three remaining members of the policy group. Steinberger had been Isaac's friend as well as his attorney for some twenty years, and he was chagrined at his inability to get Isaac's family to agree. It was partly his doing, he told Ivarin and Fehler and Kesselbaum. He was not satisfied with the man finally selected by the four Landau daughters and their husbands, and he had persuaded Mrs. Landau to hold out for somebody else. With the mother's veto of their candidate, all semblance of family solidarity had disappeared, and thus far had not been recaptured. In the circumstances, he could not predict when and where they could find the person they would all agree on. The makeshift techniques they had been following since November would have to continue.

They did. The paper kept appearing day after day with no official owner at its head, with everything in abeyance, with a standing alibi for every grievance unanswered or denied. Once a week Mrs. Landau signed a check, countersigned by Steinberger, so that wages were paid on Friday mornings as they always had been. But promptness ended there. The old bookkeeper, Dov Moskowitz, held back all the weekly and monthly bills that used to go to Isaac Landau for approval and payment. With fine impartiality, old Dov kept them out of sight as long as possible, whether they were for a box of pencils or tons of newsprint, typewriter ribbons or inks for the presses, the Associated Press wire service, telephone and electricity or erasers and rubber bands.

Only when the first bill was superseded by a Statement of Arrears, and then with incredible speed by an ominous *"Final Warning"* did he appear in Joseph Fehler's office, slap the threatening notices and bills on his desk and demand, "So?"

"I'll see to it, at the policy meeting, Dov."

As always, Ivarin showed himself so bored by "these trivia" of invoices, bills, arrears, first, second and final warnings, that Fehler soon offered to take them straight to Mrs. Landau and her lawyer without bothering Ivarin at all.

"A capital idea," Stefan said, grateful that Fehler for once understood his basic emotions. Kesselbaum shook his head in disapproval, but Stefan said, "Don't you agree, Abe? It's a capital idea."

Later that night, Abe came up from the press room to Ivarin's office, frowning and uncertain. "Can I speak up about your decision?" he asked.

"Speak up," Ivarin said, but Abe hesitated. Stefan waited without impatience. Abe was a good boy, a good man, rather, with his birthday this month proclaiming him thirty-six and his dark hair so thin now that although he had no bald spot, the sheen of his scalp could be seen pinkly through the black sparseness, everywhere except around the base of his skull. His wife had had another baby re-

(243)

cently, their fourth child, and their oldest boy was now fourteen, the age at which Abe had first begun to work in a press room. It was inevitable, Abe's ferocity of determination that Freddy should stay in school and go on to the education he himself had never had. For Kesselbaum, Landau's death had been a particular misfortune; he had been promised a long-awaited raise on December first, which had been automatically halted when Itzak died.

"Your decision to not bother with the bills," Abe said at last. "It makes me nervous. Fehler and Mrs. Landau going over them together each week—"

Ivarin saw the effort it cost Abe to put his fear into words. "But would you have me tag along with Fehler each time, with his bills and invoices?"

"Of course not," the younger man said. "You are an editor. What have you to do with running to widows to get bills paid?"

"Precisely nothing."

"But that is why I worry. He will get to know her so well."

"He knew Landau well for years."

"Much good it did him." Abe suddenly grinned.

Ivarin developed a philosophical detachment toward Borg's elation over his survey. Borg had lost no time starting it, and during the darkest gloom and uncertainty for everybody else, he basked in the new sun of his private opportunity. He was collecting a mass of material in five large proof-books: one for funnies and cartoons, another for exposés and running series, another for scientific articles, another for women's specials and one marked, "Human Interest."

"What other kind of interest would a newspaper be likely to attempt?" Ivarin asked mildly one night when Borg ran on over this latter category. "Animal interest? Fish interest, tree interest, bird interest?"

"You *hear* words, Mr. Ivarin, that nobody else hears. I've said 'human interest' a thousand times but not one person—"

"Editors are lunatics about words," Ivarin said. "But, if you'll permit a suggestion, Saul, these are not days to talk a thousand times of your beloved survey in any way at all."

Borg said, "You're right, I won't," but Ivarin knew he would. The next day he passed Borg's cubbyhole and saw him showing his newspaper-size portfolios to one of the stenographers, who was listening with interest and resentment mixed.

Poor Borg, Ivarin thought, as deluded as an illicit lover who swears prudence but reveals his ardent secret with every breath and every glance. What makes it worse is that a hundred people wish they were as well-off as he just now.

Whereupon Ivarin went down the hall to Fehler's office. "I think it would be a wise health precaution," he began, "if you called a temporary halt on Borg's survey."

Fehler did not look surprised. "Temporary for how long? Until the new management is announced and the staff settles down?"

"Long enough," Ivarin agreed. "Borg can't restrain his enthusiasm, and fevers are developing all around him."

"It's true," Fehler said unexpectedly. "Bunzig said the same thing yesterday." Bunzig was one of the older reporters, who had been on the staff a long time. "I'll tell Borg we're calling it off for a few weeks."

"Until this damnable announcement is made."

When the announcement did come, Stefan Ivarin learned of it a day before it was made official. His informant was Mrs. Landau herself.

"I want to explain something to you," she said in an agitated voice on the telephone. "May I come to the office tonight to see you? Itzak would have wanted me to explain it myself."

"Any time, yes, surely." A wave of heat pumped through him and he knew. But he asked what time would suit her and then waited for eight o'clock and her arrival. She was still agitated, and constantly glanced about the room and over her shoulder. She had been a handsome woman, but time and grief had harrowed her face and it was destroyed. Ivarin had seen her twice since Isaac's death, but her appearance now shocked him.

"You know how I admire every line you write," she began in a tumble of words, looking at his thick lenses gropingly as if she was searching for his eyes, "and my daughters, too, and their husbands."

"Thank you."

"But the only man we can agree on," she sped on, "at last we admit it, the only one. He has to like business, almost like a banker, a real strict businessman."

"Yes, he has to."

"You don't like such things, you wouldn't even be interested in that part of the paper."

"And I would be no good at it." He was sorry for her, even as he hated what she was going to tell him. Futile, awkward, her preparatory lotions of honeyed apology. He almost blurted out her news at her himself, to cut it short.

"So we agreed finally," she pressed on. "He has been the Business Manager—now let him be the General Manager. Mr. Fehler."

"Yes," he said. "Fehler, of course."

"My lawyer suggested it," she said. "He said he'll keep an eye on things for me, and we can change again later if it's no good. But to go on this way any longer—"

"Impossible."

There was a pause. They sat looking at each other, silent, and the pause lengthened. Then she leaned toward him, her hand out, but not touching him.

"Nothing will be different for you," she said, beseeching him to believe her. "What could be different on this paper, for Ivarin?"

NINETEEN

I must go and congratulate him, Stefan Ivarin thought, but he did nothing. And I must call Alexandra at once, as I promised. But he turned his back on the telephone.

In the half-hour since Miriam Landau had left, he had done nothing except pace the familiar length of his office. Fehler knew already, she said at the end of her palpitating visit; Steinberger had told him that afternoon, and made it clear that nothing was to be different for him, Ivarin.

"Ivarin is a big name," Steinberger had said, "part and parcel of the paper. Nothing must disturb him or his work." It was language Fehler understood, business language. Talk of a paper's big assets, and the need to protect them. Fehler was part and parcel, too, in a different area, Steinberger had said, and they would all keep remembering both sides of this long-established truth, as they had done while Isaac was alive. Fehler had been in total and instant and unreserved agreement with every word Steinberger said.

Why not? Ivarin thought now. It is so easy, agreeing with a plea for eternal peace, when you have just won a victory.

His own cynicism irritated him. Fehler would avoid any immediate war between them in any case. To find another editor was not the work of a moment, and whatever Fehler might do later for larger sales and profits, he would not lightly tackle so thorny a proposition.

I am like some young reporter, Ivarin thought angrily, canvassing the situation, checking it, deciding, My job is safe. The devil with "safe."

He left his office and walked along the corridor to Fehler's. Ordinarily nine o'clock would be too late to find Fehler still at the paper, but tonight would be different. The door was wide open and for a moment Ivarin stood looking in at him, seated in profile at the broad flat table he used, preferring it to a desk. This was the man who would now be boss of the entire staff. His boss. At least, to the extent that Landau had been his boss.

"Congratulations," Ivarin said, offering his hand as he went in. "I've just heard the news."

"Thanks, Stiva," Fehler said, jumping up. "So she did come? She was worn out and thought she might wait a day."

"She was uneasy about how I would take it," he said. There was a pause. As always, he wished he could forbid Fehler the use of "Stiva" and as always he did nothing. "I'm not sure," he went on, "how I do take it."

Fehler smiled faintly. He was being careful to show no triumph or undue joy, and Ivarin gave him unheard applause for that show of taste.

"You will take it as it was intended," Fehler said. "They did not come rushing to me; I'm not forgetting that. Only as a compromise, three months after Itzak died."

Ivarin waved that aside. The pumping of heat that had begun with Miriam Landau's telephone call had died away but now it began again; he knew that Fehler was reading his reddened color as accurately as a doctor. But a rise in blood pressure was stimulating, as well as uncomfortable, and he was alive to his nerve ends. This modesty of Fehler's was a wise move, a useful lubricant for the days ahead.

Fehler offered a typed sheet of paper, the notice to the staff, to be posted in the morning. This time it was over the joint signatures of Miriam B. Landau and Jacob Steinberger, announcing "the long-awaited decision" and stating that Joseph Fehler would be known, not as General Manager, but as Publisher, a term more widely in use in the changing practices of modern journalism. Below this was an added message.

NOBODY'S JOB
IS IN JEOPARDY AT
THE JEWISH NEWS.
NO CHANGES
ARE IN VIEW
ON THE STAFF.

The notice was dated February 15, 1913, and Ivarin was sure that on the bulletin board next day it would be greeted with nearly universal relief. Though only the most unsophisticated would take its promise to heart, there would be a stir of reassurance throughout the paper. Better Joseph Fehler whom everybody knew by sight than a total stranger from the outside world.

Ivarin handed back the notice and drew his watch from his pocket, his automatic signal that unfinished work was on his desk, waiting for him. He said, "Well, we'll all have a go at it," not quite knowing what he meant by that.

"One small point, Stiva," Fehler said, again rising, and strolling to the door with him. "Mrs. Landau doesn't seem at all interested in political questions. Had you noticed?"

"I never thought of it, one way or another."

"I did only recently. And Steinberger, too. He does not seem even inquisitive about where I stand."

They had reached the door of his office and Ivarin stopped. A sensation he did not like invaded him and for a moment he could not put a name to it. Then he knew it for embarrassment. Fehler was going to ask, as a favor—

"It's the paper's politics that can matter to them," Ivarin said hurriedly. "Not yours."

He raised a finger in final salute and departed. But inside his mind he suddenly gave way to mirth. It was abrupt and lavish, not feigned, but a burst of delight.

It was the first relief, the first balance wheel of the evening. The new Publisher of the *Jewish News* was shivering in his pants that his benefactors might discover he was an anarchist. Or that Stefan Ivarin might go and tell them.

He did not call Alexandra. If it had been anybody else they had chosen, a relative, a businessman, somebody from any other news-

(248)

paper, he would have abided by his promise and called her. But Fehler would be a shock to her as it had been to him, despite its having occurred to him more than once during the deadlock, and he could not deal it to her by telephone. He would have to endure the scene she would put him through.

He was angry at her in advance but he resolutely picked up his pen and went to work. March 4 was to be a historic day, apart from the inauguration of Woodrow Wilson, and he meant to write a ringing editorial about it. For on that same day, for the first time in the history of America, labor would be officially elevated in the scheme of government; a Department of Labor was to be established, with its own seat in the Cabinet.

It was rich material, but he could not write two sentences easily. His pen stuck as if it were filled with mucilage; he struck out phrases as soon as he set them down. At last he tore up what he had written and leaned back in his chair.

He was tempted to tell Abe Kesselbaum the news, suggesting a visit to the café for a thorough talk about what it might mean. But he decided not to.

Borg came in at his usual intervals, but Ivarin had no thought of saying anything to him. Each time he glanced over the copy Borg brought in, asking "Do I need to read it?" and when Borg said "Nothing to bother about," he scrawled his initial in the lower corner and gave it no further thought. Whatever Borg's faults, his editing of routine stories constantly grew faster and more expert. In that respect he was still a godsend.

Once or twice one of the rewrite men or reporters came in, Bunzig, who had been on the paper as long as he had, and the labor specialist, Kinchevsky. Each time Ivarin was tempted, and then thought, Let them find out tomorrow, with the rest of the staff. What a parade there would be then to Fehler's office, to offer congratulations and best wishes, express delight, wish him well, and incidentally to consolidate positions already held in his esteem or attempt to wipe out past mishaps and make a fresh start.

You'd think I was jealous of him, Ivarin thought. Back there I was like a cub reporter fretting whether my job was on thin ice; now I begrudge him the plaudits and bravos and excitement tomorrow. The new Publisher, the big man on the paper.

And the editor? When was the editor demoted?

Again he was invaded by mirth, but this time there was less conviction in it. It was far-fetched, that "jealous"; it was unlikely that what he felt in the pit of his stomach was the shabby squirm of jealousy. But if this persistent unwillingness was something nobler than that, he did not know it, so let it be dubbed jealousy and the devil with it.

Alexandra surprised him. She took the news without dramatics, without tears. She listened in nearly unbroken silence to his whole story and fastened onto Miriam Landau's passionate question, "What could be different on this paper, for Ivarin?" She relished the lawyer's amplification of the point and virtually memorized it.

"It's a guarantee," she said.

"They meant it for that."

"And a warning to him."

"We'll see," Ivarin said.

"See? Is Fehler rash enough to flout such clear orders? What is there to 'see'?"

He shrugged, relieved that she was being so matter-of-fact about his news, yet puzzled too. She who could read untold menace into Fehler's plan for something called a "survey" now accepted with serene confidence the absence of all menace in his appointment to the executive post the owner himself had held for twenty years.

Yet there was something soothing in her sunny decision that Joseph Fehler in any post whatever was Joseph Fehler still. The tight chain of his own thinking soon loosened and he told her of Fehler's parting remark.

"The coward," she cried, transformed on the instant. "The sniveling coward. Is he going to run around to the whole staff, one by one, hinting to them to say he always voted for Taft?"

He said, "Now, now," as if he were soothing an excited child. Only Alexandra would have produced "Taft" that way, like a cat spitting. But her notion of Fehler in delicate conclave with all the staff, one by one, amused him and he said, "You cheered me up."

"The sniveling coward," she repeated, compressing her lips, a perfect mime of Scorn. "A guarantee is what it was, Stiva. He wouldn't dare, but with cowards you need guarantees."

This time he laughed, though the convolutions of thought that had led to this pronouncement were beyond him. "Was Fehler one of the possibilities you had already thought of?" he asked, and the question so clearly mystified her that he added, "While the deadlock held on, I did wonder if it would end up Fehler."

"But he's not good enough and they knew it all along."

"They decided he was."

"They grew desperate, so they took him for the time being, *knowing* he isn't good enough. If he actually *were,* Landau would have named him in his will, or in some codicil, or told the lawyer."

How clever she was, to put her finger on that point so promptly, so effortlessly. His own phrase, "convolutions of thought," sounded in his mind, with its patronizing affection, and he disowned it.

"The will or the codicil or telling Steinberger," he said. "I think you must be right. It never occurred to me."

She beamed. Her pleasure in his praise glistened on her skin like the sheen of summer's first burn. She longed to touch him, to kiss him as if they were still young. How happy people could be even in times of change and trouble if they were close in what life meant to them. The word "socialism" began to sound in her mind, but for once she rebuked it as inappropriate and halted it at the end of its first syllable in a soft protracted "Shhh."

They sat on for a long time, talking.

The weeks of early spring were easy ones for Stefan Ivarin and for the rest of the staff of the *Jewish News*. No changes were announced in procedure, none in personnel. Once the initial furor engendered by the bulletin board had petered out, the most noticeable change was the sight of Joseph Fehler in the office that had been Jacob Landau's.

"There is no rush," Fehler replied to people asking his plans. "I am considering certain matters, but there is no rush."

With Ivarin he took pains to be more specific. "What would you think of getting the first edition out an hour earlier? They are all doing it." "I'm thinking of how the policy staff should be enlarged— what do you think?" Day by day, or nearly so, Fehler would seek out Ivarin in the early evening, the end of his own working day and the beginning of the editor's, and tell him what he was considering and ask for opinion and discussion and advice. Sometimes he would ask Abe Kesselbaum, too, and they would all three talk for a while, thoughtful, agreeable.

"A new Fehler," Ivarin said one night to Alexandra. "A diplomat, a pourer of oil. If it's an act, he does it well. If he means it, so much the better."

"Don't trust him," she said, her old air of being menaced again upon her like a soubrette's agony in a low play. "It's some sort of trap."

"And I the fool to walk into it?" He turned away. Her serenity

(251)

had been too good to last—the real trap was his thinking it might.

"There *is* no new Fehler, a man like that never changes for good."

"Alexandra, I beg you."

"Then don't tell me another word about him! If I'm not permitted to say what I think, without 'Alexandra, I beg you.' "

She walked out of the room, and straight into Fee and Franny. They must have heard, for they were standing stock still, their schoolbooks in their arms. They knew enough about what had happened to understand; she had told them about Fehler's selection, adding that it was probably a better choice than some total stranger, who might turn out to be a capitalist at heart, against labor, against unions, against Papa's whole life.

The girls *had* heard, and Fee whispered, "Did Fehler do anything to Papa?"

"No, darling, of course not." She was too vexed to be amused at Fee's use of the name, Fehler, but at other times it made her laugh. Neither of the girls ever said "Mr. Fehler"; naturally not, since they had never heard him called anything but the unadorned Fehler. But coming from Fee, it was as if she had spoken of King or Roberts or Mainley.

Stefan came out, saw them clustered at the foot of the stairs, and silently went off to the city. He usually went in earlier now, and so did many of the others; he would have to stop this soon or get fraternal protests from the photoengravers and typesetters who already did have unions and saw no reason why writers, reporters and editors could not get a union too.

When he reached the office he found Borg in a state of distress, and half-guessed what it was. To a degree he rather sympathized with him: Saul had confidently gone to Fehler with the question that had been in his throat since the notice went up on the bulletin board a month before.

"Now that the staff *is* settled down, can I resume work on it?"

"There's no rush, Saul. I couldn't examine it right away, a big survey like that, and all your exhibits would go out of date before I could. I'll give you the signal later on."

Borg looked at Ivarin as he finished telling him about it. " 'Later on,' " he said. "The vaguest date in journalism."

"True," Ivarin said. "And well put, too."

The first meeting of the enlarged policy staff was put off by Fehler also, and April was half-spent before it actually took place. Two of the seven members were not yet selected, but Steinberger was there and Miriam Landau with him.

"Steinberger wants her to come always," Fehler had explained beforehand. "She should know something of the working problems of her paper."

" 'Her paper' sounds funny," Abe said.

"Hers it is," Ivarin put in. "By the inexorable law of ownership and possession, the *Jewish News* is 'her paper.' What it would be without *us,* God only knows, but our paper it is not, except by courtesy of the language we use—" He broke off, and said, "I sound like my wife."

"Could Papa ever get out of work?" Fee asked.

"Of course not," Fran answered. "Stop worrying, will you?"

"I don't."

"Ever since Mama told us about Fehler, you've been as scared as a rabbit."

"I haven't even thought about it more than once or twice."

"Once or twice a minute." Fran hooted. She was getting dressed for a high-school dance, the last one of the senior class except the Graduation Dance in June, and Fee, with Shag at her heels, had come in to watch her put on her rouge and lipstick. Fran didn't have to do it in secret, now that she was almost out of High; she was allowed to, if it wasn't too red. And no round circles, like red quarters, on her cheeks. It had to blend in, like Nature.

Suddenly Fee said, "Put some on me, Franny." She cocked her head and held her right cheek up at a sharp angle toward Fran's hand; her tongue stiffened to ramrod usefulness and pushed the center of her cheek outward.

"It's like a crab apple," Fran said. "Stop that." She rubbed rouge lightly over Fee's cheeks. Fee was already moving toward the mirror but her sister yanked her back and said, "Wait till you're finished and gorgeous."

Fran applied lipstick, and then said, "Now let's see how you look with a pompadour instead of that drippy old hair."

Fee giggled. Fran was already working at a section of Fee's dark straight hair, combing downward in quick, choppy strokes.

"You're teasing it," Fee cried. "I'll hate it."

"No, you won't," Fran said. "High will look good on you," she pronounced, and brushed it smooth and high up on Fee's head. "You're going to be pretty, Fee."

Fee whirled toward the mirror and a high grunted "Oh" came out of her reddened lips, astonishment first and then delight. There in the mirror was somebody who looked like her but also didn't look like her at all. It was Fira Ivarin, but a different, grown-up, *lady* Fira Ivarin. "Oh, Franny," she said.

Fran was watching her, smiling as if Fee were a new toy, a doll after all the grown-up years when she was too old for dolls. "You're pretty already," she said, in a burst of generosity she had never had before for her little sister.

Fee was peering at herself so closely now, her breath clouded the mirror. It's me, she thought, it's the way I'll be all the time when I grow up. She put both her hands up, cupping them, to feel of the raised-up curve of the pompadour. Her hair was suddenly wonderful, not her usual horrible hair, like brown rain falling, but a curving dark crown upon her head, weighing nothing, rounded and rising, like a diadem without diamonds.

"And once you *begin,* and everything," Fran said behind her, "you'll be prettier fast."

"But suppose I never *do* begin!" Fee's voice went rough with terror.

Fran turned brusquely away. "Don't start 'suppose I never.' I'll scream if I hear that one more time."

"But Trudy's mother knows somebody who's *twenty-eight* and hasn't begun."

Fran ignored Fee's fear that some hellish design had singled her out for the same extraordinary fate; by now she had to finish dressing. She opened her precious cologne from Paris, but in the mirror she caught sight of Fee's face. Distress lay on it, together with the delicate pinks and reds, and Fran for the first time felt remote and yet enmeshed with that distress. She herself was so lucky, almost seventeen and almost a high-school graduate. It was unfair, being a kid of Fee's age.

"Listen," she said, "why don't you run down and show Mama?"

Fee's misery vanished. "I'll surprise her," she squealed, rushing for the door. "She'll take one look at me and just die."

One drifts along, Stefan Ivarin thought. To pretend that all is well is work for a fool, but to assume that it may be a long time before all is *not* well is an adjunct of wisdom. Here it is, May, and no monumental explosions. One cannot keep girded up forever.

The second meeting of the enlarged policy staff had gone very well, as had the first. Bunzig and Kinchevsky were to be the other permanent members, and Miriam Landau was getting over her initial diffidence, though she still expressed an opinion only after preliminary whispering with her lawyer.

Thus far, Joseph Steinberger had added a considerable definition and dimension to their discussions. Across the years, Isaac had talked often of his abilities, and now Ivarin was seeing them for himself. With all his clients, Isaac had told him, it was Steinberger's nature to investigate the structure of their businesses or companies; it gave him the wider base he needed to serve their interests, and if in certain cases he thus was able to offer a client some opinions or advice that led to increased profits, he was usually well rewarded, by gratitude, and then perhaps by increased fees or even a few shares in the company's stock. He was a rich man, and his wealth was a direct harvest from his deep-sowed devotion to those he served.

After two meetings, Ivarin could well believe it. He was quick and perceptive; he brought with him an amount of background information the others did not expect. Once, Steinberger asked about the apportionment of space for Russian news, German news, Polish news, and had at his own fingertips rather exact figures about how many of their readers came originally from Russia, from Germany, from Poland.

Ivarin was impressed. Both meetings were devoted to "the money side," and he found nothing to interest him deeply. Nor to antagonize him deeply. The paper always had taken advertising; Fehler was hiring two extra men to try to get more. They were called "salesmen" and the usage amused Ivarin. He had always thought a salesman sold shoes, a hat, a quarter-pound of tobacco and the papers for it, but these salesmen were to sell empty space in an unborn copy of the *Jewish News*. A rather metaphysical sale, he thought, yet devoutly to be wished.

At home, Alexandra had adjusted to things as they were, and the girls had returned to their normal belief that nothing connected with parents could be interesting for long. Fee had decided he was not yet due to appear on the nearest corner with a tin cup and a case of pencils, and Fran had retrogressed to her assumption that fathers were created in heaven to provide private tennis courts, nets, iron rollers and the rest of the paraphernalia now cluttering up the back porch while Fran and all her friends, mostly boys, labored to finish the court once and for all.

One splendid small labor of his own had unexpectedly offered itself through Evander Paige's outfit at the Free Speech League.

"We'd like to publish the vigilante series in a pamphlet," Evan announced on the telephone one afternoon, calling him from his law office in New York. "The English translation."

"What a fine piece of news. When did you decide on that?"

"I'm just back from the League luncheon. They voted unanimously Aye. Do you remember the San Diego lawyer whose car I borrowed to follow the vigilantes in?"

"Smithers," Ivarin said promptly. "He took your exhibits overnight for safekeeping from the police."

Paige said, "That's right." Ivarin's memory for details of a story always surprised him. "It was Jonathan who suggested the pamphlet. He's come East for a few weeks, and I took him to the meeting. In California, they used your series with membership appeals and got better results, so he thought we might try it in all our chapters, with a national drive for new membership."

"I'll give the pieces one final editing," Stefan said. "When's your date with the printer?"

"You needn't," Evan said. "I reread them all, and they hold up just as they are."

"I won't do much. Just look for rough spots."

"The editor's privilege," Evan conceded. "If you damage these, though, we'll make trouble for you."

"Thanks, Evan, and that gang of yours." Then, as an antidote to the warmth in his voice, he ceremoniously added, "Tell them I am deeply honored."

One drifts along, he thought, and the days go and the weeks, and the only panacea is work at something your heart rushes to.

TWENTY

"But the minute it's ready to play on," Fran said in despair, "I'll have to go away for the summer! Can't I *please*? Just for two weeks?"

Alexandra said nothing. Day after day since the start of June, this argument had run along until the sight of the tan expanse beyond the windows made her angry. To stay behind when they started for the beach was what Fran was nagging her to death about, to stay behind by herself, so she could preside like a queen over the tennis court.

"If it was my fault," Fran went on. "But you know how much rain there's been."

"You can *not* stay all alone, no matter whose fault."

Fran looked away, hating her mother for being so pig-headed. She glanced at her father, who was insensible to what was going on around him, in that way he had, and then at Fee, who was almost as miserable as she was. Fee understood. They had worked all spring a year ago and all spring this year, and now at last the court was nearly ready, would positively be ready by Graduation—and bang, the next day she had to turn her back on it until September.

"It's like being a prisoner," she cried out. "Dragged off to the beach no matter what."

"By apron strings," Stefan agreed suddenly. "Fran is nearly seventeen. Is she to be tied hand and foot regardless of her own desires?"

"Apron strings," Alexandra retorted. "Could any mother believe more in free will for her children?"

"Free Will and White Slavery!"

Alexandra was infuriated. She wheeled toward the girls and said, "Must you both sit there enjoying this spectacle? Go upstairs or go outside."

Neither moved.

Fee sat as if tacked to the chair and Fran stared at her father, mute, afraid to break the spell and see him return to indifference. To have him as her ally and defender was an unimaginable glory. Maybe *he* could see the tremendous necessity of being right here for the court's first two weeks of life, so Tom and Jack Purney and the whole neighborhood would get it fixed in their minds forever that it was her court, not just any old tennis court but her private court, inextricably a part of Fran Ivarin, no matter how many of them played on it with no matter what equal rights. Maybe he could make Mama see it, too.

"Aping the rich," Alexandra flung at him, forced to accept the girls' immobility. "You said it a hundred times—they'd want tiaras next, you said. And now you're the big defender and I'm suddenly the Czar's jailer who wants to tie Fran up in apron strings and lock her away on the beach."

A faint smile moved across his mouth and Alexandra was infuriated anew. If he said a word about her being volatile, she would leave the room, leave the house, and they could all three get along forever without her. Her eyes stung with a hundred points of hotness and she started for the back door and the sight of her garden just beyond.

"There's nothing so frightful," Stefan said more amicably behind her, "when a girl chooses to stay at home with her father for a couple of weeks, is there?"

"That's right," Fran said urgently to her mother. "I can cook breakfast and supper for Papa and take care of the house. I won't be here all alone."

"You'll be alone half the night while Papa is at the paper," Alexandra retorted. "With Tom or Jack and ten other boys right here in the house with you!"

"Oh, Mama," Fran said. Her tone said that mothers could be revolting.

Fee suddenly spoke for the first time. "All spring long, Franny hurried with all her might, Mama, but the weeds and rocks and raining-all-the-time!"

Alexandra sat down heavily. "All three united against me," she said. The kitchen towel lifted to her eyes was the signal for Ivarin's abrupt departure, but Fran exulted in her heart. The struggle was all but won. She signaled Fee to follow her and they both left their weeping mother with alacrity.

The miracle that spelled total victory came the next morning. "How would you like to be a visitor every evening at the Paiges'?" Alexandra asked, ignoring Fee and addressing herself to Fran. "Every night till the middle of July?"

"What kind of visitor?"

"An overnight visitor—just to sleep there. You could be back here every morning to play tennis, stay here all day, then go to the Paiges' again for the night."

"Mama!" Fran cried, winds of delight blowing through her. "Did you ask her, or what?"

"Of course I didn't ask!" Alexandra said. "But we talk over things, you know how we do, and Alida agreed, a girl staying alone every night till three in the morning—"

"You didn't say those terrible things about ten boys, did you?"

"Don't be ridiculous." Alexandra sighed enjoyably. She had regained the upper hand in this matter of a daughter's behavior, although Fran would not see it that way. Nor would Fee, nor perhaps even Stiva. "We were discussing modern ideas about letting young people do anything and everything, without any adult nearby, and Alida knew exactly how I felt. So she invited you."

Fran kissed her mother and then raced over to Channing Street to thank Mrs. Paige for her marvelous kindness and goodness. In her excitement she almost blurted out the question churning in her heart. "Will Garry come out while I'm here?"

Even thinking it and holding it choked off was exciting. Victory? It was unheard of. Not only had Mama been beaten about carting her away from her court, but she had unwittingly arranged a sort of *assignation* for her daughter and Garrett Paige!

"Sweet girl graduates—two of them the same day," Alexandra cried, kissing first Francesca and then Fira as they came down for a quick breakfast before dressing. Fee's graduation exercises at P.S. 6 were scheduled for nine o'clock and Fran's from Barnett High at noon, a schedule that avoided the unthinkable for Alexandra.

A twin graduation day. What a happy quirk of fate, her two lovely daughters approaching two of life's milestones on the same glorious June morning. Even Stefan's refusal to go with her to their separate commencement ceremonies could not becloud the entrancing hours just ahead. Play no favorites indeed. Nobody could expect a man who worked all night, he had said, to be up for commencement exercises at the unholy hour of nine A.M., and since he could not attend Fee's, he would play no favorites and stay away at noon from Fran's as well.

But she had accepted it without discussion. Up and down, up and down, his internal barometer about the climate at the paper had recently begun to change from one day to another, and it was wiser to let him alone on as many other things as possible. He was still reasonably free from agitation about Fehler's doings, but in the last two or three weeks he had lost that seeming trust that "it could have been worse." He was not moody or agitated; if anything, he seemed to have lost interest in what was going on. Not that anything big *was* going on; the only news he had to tell her recently was that Borg was happy at last, ordered by Fehler to get his survey going again, and at all possible speed.

"Fehler changed the plan of it somewhat," he said. "Borg has to go beyond innovations and collect samples of big popular appeal."

Big popular appeal. Stefan mistrusted words like that, and she did too. Hearst! The name went hissing through her mind.

But this morning she was not going to let anything spoil one moment. Fran's court lay out there in the sun, like a silken tan carpet. They had finished it only yesterday afternoon, when Fran had mixed the plaster of Paris for the white lines, and then watched inch by inch while Tom Ladendock ran the little marking machine over the nailed-down lengths of string stretched along the base line, service lines and alleys. The white fluid came out of a square spout, to even it off at its edges, but the lines wavered a bit anyway, looking homemade. Just the same they had dried hard overnight and this afternoon was to be the official start of the tennis season at the Ivarins'.

"Fran," she said, "if you can take your adoring eyes off your court, eat a little breakfast."

Gazing at her beautiful court, Fran thought, It's all too much for one day. The moment the two graduations were out of the way, everybody was coming over for the "tennis christening," as Tom called it. She was to be the first one on the court with her brand-new Spalding racket that was her graduation present, and three fuzzy white new balls. Excited as she was about the last day of Barnett High, the first day of her own tennis court made her even more excited. She had waked up all aquiver and the feeling was so sharp it was like a thrill, the kind of thrill that always made her feel ashamed because she liked it so terribly.

Well, for the love of Pete. Another half year, even more, had gone by since the heavenly night in her yellow dress when he had taken one look at her and said it. And not one single thing had happened since then. Once or twice, he and Letty had been in Barnett on a holiday or over Easter, and he might have seen her just by saying he was going out for a walk. For all she knew, he had tried to, had said right out, "I'll be back soon, I feel like some fresh air," and then had seen the look on Letty's face and stayed in rather than quarrel.

But now, with two whole weeks just ahead, with her invited to sleep at the Paiges' every single night, it simply had to be that she'd see him at least once. And she'd be wearing her new graduation dress, white eyelet batiste with ruffles, rows and rows from the hem way up nearly to the waist and then around the neck and tiny puffy sleeves. Fee had a new white dress too, and it was all right for graduating from public school. Fee was just thirteen, but the poor kid didn't have the shape to wear anything but a straight dress anyway—she was still flat as a board and nutty on the subject.

"Girls," Alexandra said. "Drink your milk, at least."

Fee jumped up and raced up to her room. Let Fran go on acting insane about her ruffles; yesterday Fee had tried on her own graduation dress for Trudy, and Trudy said it absolutely made her look sixteen. It was a stiff white silk and had accordion pleats, like a million knife edges until you walked, and then they spread apart and jumped together again with wonderful little crackling noises.

Everything was wonderful anyhow. No more P.S. 6. She was already registered as a freshman at Barnett High, starting next fall. Class of Nineteen Seventeen—they reckoned four years ahead from the first minute. Maybe she could get a big red turtle-neck sweater with white felt letters stitched to it saying '17. That is, if you were allowed to just "get" the letters. Maybe you had to win them in athletics; then she'd have to go out for girls' basketball or field hockey. She would go out if you had to win them, and she would win them. She always did a thing if she really *had* to do it.

Fran never won anything. Fran never even got A's. Getting A was fun, like playing jacks better than Trudy or riding your bike faster. It was really interesting to know things and have that crazy feeling at the end of a test that you mostly hadn't made one mistake. At Barnett High it would be more fun. Imagine taking algebra and German and French instead of arithmetic and grammar and all that baby stuff at public school; no matter whether Fran loved High or not, *she* was going to. Nobody ever was more different than she and Fran, and what Fran was so conceited about, nobody could figure out.

Figure! Figure out. Your figure will soon fill out too. In the whole class of 8-B graduating today, only three of the girls hadn't filled out one bit yet, Anna Kogel and Clementine Sarto and herself. *Why* couldn't she have been one of the lucky ones? Trudy was. Trudy was going to be a big fat slob in a few years. You could tell, just looking at her in a middy.

Fee turned sideways to the mirror and thought of the night she had the rouge and lipstick on and her hair way up, and tried to remember the way she looked then. But now there was nothing in the glass except *her* and the way her nightgown plastered itself to her chest, straight up and down like wallpaper. It was enough to make you puke.

"Who's going to be late?" Fran said, and Fee jumped. She was pulling her nightgown out in points a few inches below her collarbones, and Graduation was a million miles out of her mind. "Gee, I'll hurry, Franny," she said, and ripped off her nightgown and dived into her underwear. Suppose she was late—could a principal refuse to give you your diploma if you were late for Graduation?

Three minutes later, she was dressed and ready.

"You look nice," Fran said.

"You too."

She started for the door and heard the silky whisper of the pleats in her new dress. Suddenly she felt as slinky and seductive as the actress in the novel Trudy had loaned her last week.

The two diplomas stood on the sideboard like tall white candles, but Alexandra no longer thought of them. Eli's last day of teaching coincided with the girls' last day of school, of course, so he and Joan had missed the morning, but now they were due any minute, with Webby and little Sandra too, and she kept listening for the first sound of the motorcycle roaring up the hill.

It was nearly five before she caught it. Fran's party on the tennis court was going full blast, with boys and girls calling and shouting silly flirting remarks back and forth, but despite them the motorcycle announced itself at last and she went out to the curb to watch Eli drive his family the last couple of blocks.

Once her heart would have stopped at the sight. But one lived and learned, and this time she only thought, How beautiful they all are. The tandem seat behind Eli was empty, except for a basket strapped to it, full of Sandra's bottles and diapers, for at two Webby was still too young to be buckled on by himself back there. In the sidecar Joan was holding Sandra in her lap, and down on the floor sat Webby, propped by his mother's knees and folded in three like a chubby little zigzag. His blond hair was flying and his handsome face was already so tan that his eyes looked like bluing that was too light. The baby was fair, too, and as plump as a piglet, sitting up in her mother's arms looking strong and sweet and good-natured. Joan was a sunburned schoolgirl compared to summer a year ago when she was pregnant, and Eli looked as if he had never had an attack in his life.

The "Eaves" family, she thought. Maybe they were right in some terrible hidden way. Maybe it's part of evolution, that the father and mother cannot bear to accept, but that Nature easily accepts, like Darwin.

Alexandra paused, not certain about her meaning. But she did not question herself arduously—a brief comfort had brushed her heart, and it sufficed. It was another touch of goodness in one of the happiest days of her life. At Fee's school, Miss Mainley had come up to congratulate "the mother of one of our brightest students," and said that Fee would sail right through high school and college. At Barnett High, Fran looked like a princess, and Alexandra saw with delight that Tom Ladendock hung around her like her special owner. Might it be that Fran would never finish out her two years at Jamaica Training School for Teachers?

But it was better not to permit such questions to tap at one's mind. In the Ivarin household, much better not. Why, when she told Stefan what Miss Mainley said about Fee sailing right through high school and college, she had actually left out the part about college. Four years of college? That was for the rich, too, and Stefan had often said so. To be a teacher one did not need four whole years after the four years of high school; that was like going on the Grand Tour in Europe; it had nothing to do with getting a good education and preparing for an honorable profession.

A good education, Alexandra thought. From the moment of birth, all their children were guaranteed a good education. Eli had had his, in two years Fran's would be complete, and in six the whole glorious process would be finished for Fee, and all the Ivarin children.

Life with nobody rushing off to school? For sixteen or seventeen years, since Eli was five, one child or the other was always racing off to school, with the house full of homework and talk of teachers and tests and marks, with school supplies to buy every fall and all the good things and bad that seemed to happen to every child in every school everywhere. It was hard to imagine a life with all that done forever.

There would, of course, be Webby and Sandra. But they would be little Eaves going to school, not little Ivarins.

"Hello, Ma," Eli called. He kicked down the big iron triangle that held the Harley upright at the curb, and she helped Joan with the children. Webby shouted, "Grammy," and Sandra beamed and bubbled saliva and came into her arms with the supreme willingness of a good-tempered and healthy baby. Alexandra's heart bubbled with gratitude; no woman ever had led such a blessed life, nor been so blessed as she.

Stefan was happy to see all of them, too; he was clumsy with the baby, making silly noises too close to her face, which made her draw back, but with Webby, he was charming, better than he had ever been with his own children, as if he had improved in the thirteen years since Fee was born.

"You can lecture too, Webby," he was assuring the child at one point, when Alexandra came back to them from the kitchen. "Here, stand up on this chair."

Webby chortled and laughed and climbed onto the dining-room chair Stefan had pulled away from the table.

(263)

"Comrades, workers," Stefan orated, standing a few feet away. "You say it now, Webby."

"Com-mads," Webby shouted, imitating the lift of the first syllable, his face gleeful.

Stefan nodded approval and raised a forefinger. "The right to organize—"

Webby raised his forefinger. "The wight—to—"

"Organize."

"—gan-ize."

"—is a basic right in a free—"

"—basic wight in a—"

"That's fine, Webby. You're a born lecturer," Stefan said. "In a great free country like America."

Webby looked confused for only a moment. "—great free country—"

"Like America."

"Like Uh-Merica," spacing the words and half chanting them as he had heard his grandfather do.

Eli and Joan laughed, and Alexandra said, "It's simply remarkable, a child of two, simply wonderful."

Webby jumped up and down on the chair in delight and Stefan said, "That's all for now, Web. Maybe sometime when I give a big lecture, I'll take you along to help me."

He put his hands under the child's arms and swept him off the chair. A twinge nipped his back and Stefan said, "This pain," reaching behind him to massage his muscles. But in the next moment he forgot them and was answering Eli's question about how things were going at the paper.

"It still seems pleasant enough," he said. "I tell myself *en garde* once in a while as if it was chess, but that's all." As if to change the subject before it was well started, he asked about the private school at Lake Winnepesaukee in New Hampshire where Eli had signed up for his first summer of teaching.

"If only you could rest for a week or two first, Eli," Alexandra said.

"I can't," Eli said. "I have to report up there in two days."

A crash of metal and smashing glass in the kitchen brought them all to their feet. Webby had wandered off and Eli reached him first, the others right behind him. The tea glasses that Alexandra had left on the kitchen table were in a heap on the floor, and the large tin tray that had held them had skittered off toward the sink. Webby's leg was bleeding, right through his white stocking, and he was shrieking in terror.

(264)

Eli saw at once that the cut was superficial. "It's nothing," he said. "What happened?" Webby cried louder. "You tell me what happened," Eli said, seizing his son's shoulder.

"Webby doesn't know!" It was a scream, growing louder as Eli shook him. Behind them, Alexandra said, "The glasses don't matter, is he all right?" With the scream was Eli's sudden hard breathing, and the two intermingled sounds pierced her heart.

"I said, tell me what happened," Eli repeated, suddenly twisting Webby around and spanking him hard.

"Eli, don't," Joan cried.

He suddenly stopped, as he had begun, and Joan put Sandra into Alexandra's arms and led away the sobbing Webby, murmuring comfort to him as they left.

Eli avoided his parents' eyes; there was absolute silence. On the floor, the tray slipped from the support of the sink's leg and stretched out flat, surrounded by slivers and curves of the broken tumblers. Sandra was crying too, and Alexandra rubbed the baby's back and whispered, "Don't cry, darling, there, there."

"You will make a liar of him," Stefan said to Eli, and his voice was controlled and harsh. "Next time he will say they fell by themselves, and when he's older, he'll say 'the other fellow did it, not me.' "

Eli turned away.

"You spank him too often," Stefan said. "I know about it."

"You *what?*"

"Joan didn't tell us, don't accuse her."

"What right have you to interfere, anyway?"

"He's my grandson, *that* right. And he's a clever child who will learn soon enough to be a liar to escape a beating."

"For God's sake, spanking isn't beating him."

"Then you will spank him for telling lies." Stefan turned and left the room.

Eli's breathing toughened. It took on its ropy sound and came in short hard breaks. Alexandra wished to all the heavens she had never told Stefan of the time she was visiting Joan and Eli when Joan's mother was there, and Eli lost his temper and spanked Webby. That time it was Mrs. Martin who had cried out in protest. "But, Eli, you spank him every time he does the slightest thing. Every time I've been here, you've hit that poor baby."

Shame had engulfed Alexandra that her son should deserve such a rebuke. And now again, shame went hotly through her at Stefan's protest. What had happened to Eli to turn him into a father who could strike a child so often?

(2 6 5)

Was it the asthma alone? Or was there something wrong and unhappy in his life with Joan? This teaching job for the summer in New Hampshire—was there a clue in that? He was going up alone for the first week or two, because the small school had no accommodations for a teacher's family, but he planned to rent a cottage somewhere nearby for Joan and the children, so they need not be separated until Labor Day.

Was he looking forward to a week or two of solitude? Did something in him cry out for a rest from parenthood? A father at twenty, again at twenty-one—perhaps he secretly grieved for the larky young manhood he had never had, free as the air, the gay young blade chasing after this pretty girl for a while and then another, with no thought as yet of wife or children.

My poor Eli, Alexandra thought, rushing headlong into marriage and babies and worries over doctors' bills. Eli was still seated at the table, staring down at it. Perhaps it was the down-turning of his face that made him look not like a boy of twenty-two but far older, thin, harried, with faint lines straining to show in his face.

So soon? She glanced down at the baby in her arms, sleeping now, her head heavy against Alexandra's shoulder, and the tides of memory swept in to engulf her, carrying with them the very feel and smell of another nine-month-old baby she had held against her breast, the first of her own to reach that age, the first to fill her with joy and love.

If only she could reach out to him now, as she had done when he was a child. But children grown were not easy to reach.

"Eli . . ." she began.

"I have to check up on my bike," he said, starting for the door. "An oil drip was starting."

She made no move. In a moment, from the street in front of the house, came the metallic clink of tools, and she sat down, listening. She was alone, with her namesake in her arms. Stefan's footsteps sounded above her, evenly spaced; Joan and Webby were silent; probably he had sobbed himself to sleep, with his mother sitting near him, alone too. Outside on the tennis court, a tightly fought game was in progress, with players and spectators for the moment silent, intense in their concentration on the white ball going back and forth, back and forth. Beyond them, coming toward the house, Fee and Trudy came into view, with Shag trotting sedately beside them.

They at least look at peace, Alexandra thought, and her harried nerves quieted. Gently she began to rock the sleeping baby in her arms, back and forth, back and forth. She glanced once or twice at the splintered glass on the floor and knew she should sweep it up. But there was, despite everything, a placid goodness about staying just as she was, and so she stayed just as she was.

TWENTY-ONE

En garde, Stefan Ivarin had said, as if it were chess. He thought it a fortunate phrase, vague enough to cover anything, including his obligation not to worry Alexandra needlessly, as well as his own inalienable right to keep things to himself when he saw fit.

If it were a chess game, there had been an imperceptible change in the overall position. It could not be explained to a beginner, but Ivarin saw it. The middle game is on, he thought. The opening lasted long enough, and it was too smooth, too sedate, to be arresting. Now it is another matter.

The change began with nothing more tangible than a feeling of hurry. Fehler no longer said there was no rush; he sounded rushed when you spoke to him, and he hastened from one appointment to the next. Nor did he take time to seek Ivarin out for his opinion or to pass along some information. When he suddenly resuscitated Borg's survey, and widened the scope of it, he dealt only in vague talk about current trends in the press.

Big popular appeal, Ivarin thought. He means big popular trash. He means yellow journalism. This could be the end game, not the middle game.

Ivarin asked Borg for further elucidation, but Saul also took recourse in generalities.

"Anything that made a real hit, or that's making a real hit." With a young glint of mischief in his eye, Borg added, "This time, I'm remembering my promise not to talk too much."

"Good for you."

"You'll admit I've stuck to it so far, Mr. Ivarin?"

"Keep it up."

After which small exchange, Borg kept his mouth shut. He was adroit, Ivarin conceded, at pulling himself over to a new line of behavior when his superior officers indicated distaste with the old. A valuable trait for any young man. And confoundedly impudent, if too assiduously practiced.

A few days later Fehler asked Ivarin whether he could manage without Borg entirely for two weeks or fifteen days.

Ivarin said, "I could," in an unwilling tone. "I did without him for years until Landau hired him. What's up?"

Fehler would like the July meeting to steer entirely away from the money-minded topics of their first three meetings, and talk about the paper as a whole. The survey, if it were completed in time, might prove a point of departure.

"Even as a whipping boy, it would be useful," Fehler said. "Parts of it we certainly will all attack."

Ivarin looked at him skeptically. "Why include them?"

"To steer us toward things we can agree on."

He expects me to lash out at it, Ivarin thought. He is counting on me to. As to releasing Borg for two weeks, he agreed with a show of good will he did not feel. In the old days, true enough, he had had no assistant at all. But the flow of news had doubled since the old days, trebled, quadrupled. The two weeks would be frantic.

The prospect rather appealed to him. He shoved his eyeshade back from his forehead and reflected, a little sheepishly, on his willingness to slave for untold hours over the paper. Some men drew strength and substance from music, from painting, from the competition of moneymaking, from prayer and faith. But he renewed himself from this fountain pen in his stained fingers and the endless pulsing rush of the news.

The pulse and beat and rhythm of life on this newspaper had so long ago become the timepiece of his universe, that he no longer wanted the more leisurely world outside, where more time could usually be had for the asking of it. Here, time was the driver, the commander; the first edition's presses were the lords of the afternoon and evening hours; their sworn subjects were all the people in the building, from the foundry men and machinists and typesetters in the basement all the way up to the reporters, the rewrite men, himself.

He drew his silver watch from his vest pocket, opened it and propped it up on his desk, the triangle of space made by it and its hinged cover suddenly a wedge of time, five minutes of time.

So the next meeting was to concern itself with the "paper as a whole." It should be illuminating. And more basic than the money topics that had thus far engaged them. Basic to the paper, basic to him.

(268)

Stefan Ivarin picked up his pen. It had gone dry and he gave it a sharp flick. Its tip went moist; the gold nib glistened through the blue-black fluid, winking up at him.

Alida Paige said to her husband, "She's the most studious girl. Vacation just starting, and taking an armload of newspapers to her room every night, making notes on them!"

"Maybe she fell behind on current events and has to make it up," Evan said. "Or maybe she's going to be an editor like her father."

"Not Franny," Alida said. "She hasn't the faintest idea of doing anything but fall in love and get married."

"I like watching the boys walk her over here. Remember Garry at that age?"

"I wrote Alexandra about Tom," Alida said. "Any mother of girls likes to hear about things like that. Standing out there in the street looking up at her lighted window."

"Hoping the shade was up."

It was the fifth night since Francesca Ivarin had been their "bed-time guest" and Alida had found the arrangement no trouble and unexpectedly interesting. She would have thought it rude to inquire into Fran's strange pursuits with the newspapers she brought with her each twilight when she arrived at Channing Street, but she rather wished Fran would volunteer an explanation. All she had offered so far was a slight wave of her hand at her folded papers, and a vague, "It's so thrilling."

That had been on her first evening, and Alida had thought nothing of the papers at all. But soon it became obvious that they were an inseparable part of Fran's evening existence, and she began to wish Fran would explain them. But after a polite half-hour of chatting, mostly about the glory of tennis when you didn't have to go to the public courts in the park and wait and wait and wait, Fran would say good night and go upstairs to bed. Alida had put her in the guest room, originally Van's room, next door to Garry's, and despite Alexandra's warnings of Fran's untidy habits, Fran was keeping it as neat as a room in a convent, the bed tightly made each morning before she left, her nightgown hung up, everything dusted. Only the papers crammed into the wastebasket were a mess.

It was rather intriguing, and at last Alida sat down on Fran's perfectly made bed one morning and fished the papers out to have a look.

How odd, she thought, Fran is making a study of war news from Europe. Fran had underlined certain headlines and subheads on the front pages, certain names and dates, and they all dealt with Germany or England or France. The Reichstag's frightening new bill for big increases in the German Army, the newest defeat of Bulgaria by Rumania and Turkey, even the heated predictions that the House of Lords would vote down Irish Home Rule next week—all these Fran had marked with her pencil, circling key phrases and quotes as she went, as if she meant to copy them out or learn them by heart.

The misleading little creature, Alida thought. With that face and figure, a secret passion for this kind of thing! How perfectly extraordinary.

But never a solitary word about it. Was she shy about her own ideas, as so many children of forceful parents so often were?

It was a startling discovery. But it *was* odd that Fran left the papers behind, like Hansel and Gretel leaving their clues in the wood. Did she long to be found out? Might it perhaps be a kindness to draw her out?

"This awful hypocrisy," Alida said gently the next morning, pointing to a headline in the *World*. "Holding an international peace conference right here in Washington, and now here's General Pershing fighting the Moro in the Philippines. Again!"

"Really?" Fran sat down at the table looking distressed. She wanted to ask what the Moro was, or were, in the Philippines, but she did not, in case she ought to know. "It's terrible," she said. "Is it a big war?"

Mr. Paige arrived for breakfast and the talk shifted to his newest free-speech case. For a while Fran listened because it was a murder case, too. Two migrant farm workers who were witnesses to the murder were being held illegally in prison, and had been for 158 days in a row, without any lawyer and with bail set at something wild like $10,000, when neither one had a cent. This was in Rhode Island and Fran heard familiar phrases like "due process" and "illegal search and seizure," and her attention wandered.

Being in the Paiges' house, though, made even this kind of talk seem different. They ate in the kitchen, too, but there was a real tablecloth instead of tacked-down oilcloth, and fresh napkins for everybody each morning, without a napkin ring in sight. All the cups and saucers and dishes matched each other, and there was always a little silver bowl of nasturtiums or cosmos or whatever was in bloom in the garden. Never had she been in a house where they had a centerpiece of flowers always on the table, and it filled her with the shyness she hated most, the kind she always felt when anybody new saw her own house for the first time.

"—address up in Canada?" Evan Paige asked his wife, and Fran's heart dropped.

"Letty's mother would forward it, dear," Mrs. Paige said. "She'll know if they decided on the new Laurentian place or the one they went to last year."

Fran nearly gasped out her sudden terror. Canada? Letty's mother? Were they off for Garry's summer vacation, and would they be gone during the entire fifteen nights she was sleeping at the Paiges' house?

Yes they will, something told her heavily. They went to Canada last year over the Fourth of July. She had forgotten that. Probably Garry's vacation always came over the Fourth of July. He was a million miles away and would be for the whole time she was there.

"Are you all right, Franny?" Alida asked.

"Me?"

"You haven't touched your food, dear."

"I'm fine, honestly. I just can't eat, I don't know why not, but if you won't be mad at me?"

"Of course I won't." She looked closely at Fran, hoping she wasn't catching cold. "Perhaps you're playing too much tennis in this suffocating heat, Franny."

"I'm all right, honestly I am." She sipped from her glass of milk and then stood up. "I'll only play doubles today, no singles."

Alida watched her run down Channing Street a few minutes later. If something had upset Fran, it doubtless would never be understood by any adult alive. Girls almost seventeen, though she had never had daughters, were very much like boys almost seventeen: indecipherable most of the time.

It was two or three days before Alida again admitted her lack of skill at deciphering. Then as she glanced into Fran's tidy room one morning, it struck her that the marked-up mess of newspapers was not there. She paused and stared at the empty wastebasket. It had been empty yesterday and the day before, she realized. Perhaps ever since she had told the child about General Pershing and the Moro in the Philippines.

Alexandra Ivarin felt like a traitor to her own flesh and blood. For the past ten days, only one member of her family had been with her on her beloved beach and she didn't miss a soul.

Fira and she—plus, of course, Shag—were in sole possession of the tent, and it was remarkable how much she was enjoying it. How calm the place was, without the girls' talk or bickering, how easy and quick to cook only for two, and most astonishing of all, how rarely she missed her darling Franny. Not to speak of Stiva and Eli and Joan. It was almost shameful.

She did think of Webby from time to time, because an idea kept nibbling away at her mind that could apply only to him—that is, if they had not all left already to join Eli in New Hampshire. Baby Sandra was too young to be able to live in a tent, with its limited facilities, but Webby? With him there would be no bottles to boil, no diapers to wash, no warm bath to give every day; he would eat like a little horse and paddle in the sea and play in the sand from morning to night.

The picture of him, ruddy and tanned on the beach, a shiny red pail beside him while he squatted on his strong little haunches, sent her into a reverie and then to the telephone booth, still the single booth serving the whole of the tent city, larger by twenty new tents than it had been last year.

It was still early morning, not yet eight. It had rained heavily during the night, but the wet grey of the sand was already changing to a dry shimmering silver in the hot sun. She ambled along, seeing from afar that there was no one ahead of her waiting for the telephone. There hardly ever was. How many of the poor souls who scraped together dollars enough for a week or so out here, knew anybody at home with a telephone at their beck and call? In the stinking summer tenements of the poor, a telephone was unheard of, and in their sweatshops and pushcarts too.

Telephones are still for the rich, she thought, it's a crime. Hastily she added, And of course for editors and lecturers and people like that, who have no choice. Again she felt like a traitor, and she hurried her pace for the rest of the way. In the booth, at the operator's lilting "Number please?" her qualms dissolved. It always made her feel good, that "voice with a smile," even though it was nothing but a calculated artifice to get more business. Joan's number rang again and again, and when the operator chirped, "Your par-ty does not ans-wer," she chirped back, "I'll call a-gain, thank you," and felt herself rather clever.

Outside the booth to wait, she realized that if Eli had found a cottage up there, Webby was in no need of his grandmother at all. She returned to the telephone, hurt in some unexpected way. This time the ringing had a sad useless sound, a confirmation of the message her heart had already given her.

She started home, the returned nickel moist in her hand. Married sons did not need rescue by loving mothers, and neither did their children. She should never have obeyed this simple impulse to phone about Webby, as if she alone could provide for his welfare during a blistering heat wave. As if *she* were aping the rich! Lady Bountiful to my suffering grandchild . . .

"Mrs. Ivarin, please, a moment."

A woman was calling out to her from a nearby tent, speaking in Russian. It was unexpected, out here where Yiddish was the common language, and she answered happily in Russian though she could not clearly see the figure within the flaps of the tent. "I'll wait, don't hurry."

In a moment a young woman came out, about thirty, Alexandra guessed, with a little girl of perhaps four at her side. The child's face was tear-stained and pale, with no sunburn, and the center of her forehead was swollen and purplish blue. The woman, agitated by shyness, introduced herself as Sonya Mikhailovna Vladinski; her child was Natasha Stepanovna, and there was a baby asleep in the tent.

"Sophie Jabrowsky," she said, "told me about you."

"Oh, yes, Sophie," Alexandra said with pleasure. "Is she here again? I hope so."

"Later. But I can't wait for her. She told me I should ask you about a private time for myself, but in Russian." She raced ahead, afraid to be overcome with her stiffening shyness if she spoke slowly. Her Russian was a country Russian, Alexandra decided, not an illiterate's speech, but not that of a much-schooled person either, and some of her words were hard to catch.

"Why, I would enjoy it," Alexandra said. "I give so many lessons in English to foreigners, but not often English to Russians."

"Not English lessons," the young woman said. "Lessons about everything. Like the lectures, in your tent at night, for Sophie and all the women. Only, I will come alone, and pay."

"You needn't pay! Just come with the others; you would be welcome, as they are."

"But I can't understand except Russian."

"You don't know Yiddish at all?"

Sonya Mikhailovna did not. "In my town, Jews were not allowed. My husband is learning it now for his business."

They had come to America only a few months before, and had met Sophie and her husband, who were Polish and could speak a Polish-Russian mixture they understood. One evening Sophie saw little Natasha banging her head on the floor in a fit, and Sophie told her that it was no fit, nothing but anger, and that there were modern ways to bring up children, different from the ways of Poland and Russia.

(273)

Then Sophie told her all about Mrs. Ivarin and it made her half-sick with jealousy, until Sophie suggested that Mrs. Ivarin might take her as a pupil, for pay, for bringing-up-a-child lessons. Her husband said yes, he was making good money, what was twenty-five cents an hour, or even fifty cents, as some of his friends were now paying for their own lessons.

"He is a master jeweler," Sonya ended. "He told me I should stop you right in the ocean, or anywhere, and ask you, beg you."

By now Alexandra was dumfounded. From shyness, her new acquaintance had shifted to loquacity, unhalting, free of self-consciousness. It was a novel idea; never had she given "a lesson" in so formless an area as she covered with her immigrant women in the evenings.

"It would not be a strict lesson," she said. "It would be more like a chat."

Sonya gave a small jump. "When can I start? Tonight?"

"If you like. My tent is in the first—"

But her new pupil knew where the tent was. She had found that out from the postman, who had been helpful enough to point out Mrs. Ivarin, so she would know whom to stop in the ocean.

Alexandra laughed, and as she moved off, she remembered the nickel, now moist in her palm, and went back to the booth once more. When Joan did not answer, she called home.

"Hello," Fran answered at the third ring. "Papa's not up yet."

"Of course not. How are you, Fran?"

"All right, I guess. It's so hot."

"You've been running. Could you hear the phone out on the court?"

"I wasn't out. I just ran down from my room."

"Why, dear, is it still raining there?"

"No, I just wasn't playing."

"Waiting your turn, like a good girl?"

Something was wrong, Alexandra thought. Fran sounded solemn, not the overjoyed young mistress of the glory and grandeur that was Rome. Or was it Greece?

"Mama? Are we cut off?"

"I was thinking. Do you know if Joan and the kids are up with Eli yet?"

"No, they're still waiting around. Every house up there costs too much, he says."

"Well, I had an idea, about Webby, and whenever I see our empty cot in the tent, it comes again. Maybe when you come out on the fifteenth, you could bring Webby out too."

(274)

"Gee, that is an idea."

The way she said it was strange; by now Alexandra was sure of it. But to ask one question was to be instructed on the importance of any daughter's privacy. "Yes, it is," she said, and waited.

"I just wondered," Fran said finally. "Is there any reason you want Webby to wait until the fifteenth? That's five days off."

"It's the day you're coming."

"But suppose I came right away, and brought him, I mean tomorrow."

"But the tennis?"

"Well, I suddenly thought."

Alexandra thought, Is the child crying? "Is everything all right, dear?"

"Yes."

"Is Papa in a mood?"

"No. I hardly ever see him."

"And the Paiges in the evening—is that nice?"

"Oh yes, they're just wonderful. But I—" There was a pause, and then Fran said, "I'm sort of blue, that's all, and I kind of miss everybody."

This was tribute. This was accolade. From Fran it was the sweetest praise Alexandra had won for a long time. Doubtless some romantic upset had soured Fran's plan to stay and queen it at her precious tennis court, but the sweetness remained.

"Come out the minute you can," Alexandra said firmly. "I'll try Joan until I get her, and I'll phone you around five tonight, to arrange things. Tell Papa."

"Is it silly, changing my mind about the tennis and all?"

"Not one bit. Only fools stick a thing out just because they said they would."

"You won't tell anybody about me being blue?"

"Don't worry, dear. I'm like the grave."

The phrase set off distant echoes in Alexandra's mind, vague and accusatory. But she was too contented to worry about what they could mean.

When she called back at five, two disappointments awaited her: Webby had a cold and could not come, and Fran had changed her mind about leaving at once. But Alexandra's spirits remained high; tonight she would give her very first "private lecture" for pay. It was going to be another wonderful summer.

· · ·

Garry and Letty did decide on the same place in the Laurentians they had chosen the year before, but a variation sprang up after they started.

While they were with Letty's family, a note arrived from Lucinda and Hank Stiles, forwarded from New York, asking them "to come up to this heavenly place for a weekend, preferably this one."

The heavenly place, they both knew, was the Stileses' cottage on Mt. Desert, but the weekend was the one just beginning. Letty promptly called Lucinda, and explained.

"I knew you'd be in Rockland or Augusta or some place near," Cindy said, "but I couldn't remember when. Can't you start a day later for Canada, and stop over with us for Monday?" Their weekend guests would be gone, but Hank's brother was staying on, and so was her sister Connie. "You let me talk to Garry," Cindy ended.

It took little persuasion. They loved the iced waters of Maine and the islands and bays and coves washed by them, and their one-day stay with the Stileses stretched to three. The cottage was really a cottage, and not one of the vast estates along the shores of Bar Harbor that often went by the same name in the stylish snobbery of understatement. It had been built twenty-five years before by their parents, when Peter was fifteen and Hank a toddler. Now they owned it jointly, and they took turns at it summer by summer. This summer was Hank and Cindy's turn, though with Peter still a bachelor, and a Wall Streeter as well, all summers now tended to be their turn.

Cindy and Connie welcomed Garry and Letty as if they were the first attractive people to appear for years. It was a trait of all the Aldriches, Garry realized, absent only during business hours at the Aldrich Chemical Plant, where the relationship of employee and owner was always clear, except on those rare occasions when Mr. Aldrich appeared in the laboratory. There, where Garry had again been promoted and was now second-in-command of research in synthetics, they met more casually, as men of unrelated but essential abilities who were both doing rather well.

Garry and Letty had celebrated his promotion by buying a new $500 Ford runabout for their trip, and she had chipped in from her own profits, so they both had a sense of high occasion over it. This vacation was also the first time she could leave the shop in charge of somebody else, a Mrs. Everrett ("two r's and two t's") a saleswoman with "social and antique references both." That was a milestone too.

Now, looking out at the choppy Maine sea, Letty thought, I'm so lucky. Everything she had longed for was hers, really, Garry, and her own success, and through it getting to know people like these, born to a life that was amusing and endlessly charming. It had been lucky, having Mrs. Aldrich take her under her wing, but luck was only the start of anything you wanted. Then it was a decision you could make, about caring enough for people to remain close for a good long time. She did care enough.

"Want a swim before lunch?" Hank asked. They were down at the edge of the water, all of them except Hank and Cindy's baby, and they were in bathing suits, sitting around, talking and joking. Whatever anybody said seemed funny, and they laughed easily and often, like children.

"Let's go out in the boat first," Peter Stiles said, "that wind's going to turn into a blow." The boat had belonged to their parents too; it was a thirty-foot sloop, old and slim and beautiful; its mainsail was patched in three triangles that seemed blind-white against the weatherbeaten grey-white of the rest of the canvas. Peter sailed it as if he were showing off its skills to restore its own awareness of eternal youth, and Letty thought, He doesn't have to memorize what somebody else tells him about it being a good little ship.

"Why the funny smile, Letty?"

"Was I smiling?" She looked up and flushed. It was Peter, and she realized she had been gazing at him as if he were an actor on a stage, staring straight up at him as if she had paid for a seat, and with it the right to watch his every gesture. "I didn't know I was."

"It's not a crime. Smile some more."

Letty did, but looked past him out at the sea. Her face and throat were reddening, and it bothered her to know it. As she watched the edges of the waves blow white, she thought he said something more to her, faintly mocking or teasing, but she did not look up again. Garry's back was to her. She was glad, and immediately flustered that she should be glad.

The three-day visit sped by; the long lazy hours of vacation one read about were lies, for these were short busy ones, flying by like balloons in bright colors. And then, on the last evening of their visit, at the table in the airy dining room facing away from the sea, the balloons burst. It started casually, with Peter saying something about a Congressman Underwood and what his tariff act could do to Wall Street.

"President Wilson running around making personal pleas for it," he said with the first annoyance he had shown about anything, "wanting tariffs knocked down all over the place."

"I gather you're not a Wilson man," Garry said.

"Good Lord!" Peter said. "I voted for Taft."

"Don't sound so righteous," Hank said sharply.

"Hank, please," Cindy said, elongating the "please" so it was a moan. "No speeches for Teddy Roosevelt. That's over and done with."

"No speeches," Hank agreed, still looking at his brother. *"But* if Garry did vote for Wilson, I fail to see why he should be given the 'Good Lord, no' treatment."

Peter said, "I didn't give him anything of the sort, and Garry knows it."

An instant of pause followed and then Garry said, "I didn't vote for Wilson. I voted for Debs."

"You what?" Hank said.

"Didn't vote for Wilson," Garry answered. "I voted for Eugene V. Debs."

As Garry repeated it, Letty blushed and glanced quickly from one to the other. Cindy was asking for the salt, Hank was suggesting second helpings, and Peter was refilling his wine glass from the old English carafe at his right hand. She looked down at her plate, praying they would all get talking about something else, searching for a way to start them, all words stoppered up inside. How could Garry, up here? How could he possibly, with this crowd?

"I wish Proff Yates were here," Constance said brightly. "Ron did vote for Wilson, and another instructor he knows in the history department at Yale did vote for Debs. So there!"

Garry laughed. "Thanks, Connie. I knew Gene Debs polled more than my one vote."

They all laughed at the way he stressed *my one vote* and the subject shifted. And when the time came next day for their final good-byes, Letty decided it hadn't made a whit of difference. Or was it simply their flawless good manners?

"The latchstring's out for next summer," Hank said.

"Lovely," Letty said.

"Next summer, the latchstring is *mine,*" Peter said to his brother. Then to Garry and Letty, he said, "And you two couldn't be more welcome, so is it a date?"

"It sure is, Peter," Garry said, "and thanks."

But when they were alone in their car again, Garry suddenly said, "You wouldn't have me stay discreetly mum, would you, Letty?"

"About what?" she asked.

"About the way I vote, or what I think, or anything."

"Why, Gare, of course I wouldn't."

.   .   .

(278)

The unseen social yardstick, Garry thought. I'll be damned if we're going to measure our lives by it.

It was the end of their first week in the cabin they had rented in the Laurentians, and he had been off hunting most of the day, with a paid guide and one of the other vacationers. He had enjoyed male companionship, liked the rough muscular fatigue, and come back at sunset ready for food and sleep.

"Let's not stay any longer," Letty greeted him. "It's so pokey."

He had been expecting it; they had got as far as mentioning it. The truth was that Canada was not being much of a success; they blamed themselves for coming back to the same place as last year, instead of trying a new one. The sense of discovery added spice to a vacation, they agreed; they would remember that for future summers. Here, it soon grew plain, they were finding it quiet and uneventful and stodgy, as if they were placid and middle-aged already. At first they joked about it being a letdown from Mt. Desert, with the large cottage and the sloop and private beach, with the constant companionship of Hank and Peter, Cindy and Connie. But they soon found it better not to pursue the joke.

"It *is* a letdown," Garry said now. "Let's not run away from the fact, if that's what's eating us."

"I just feel sort of stuffy here, that's all." This wasn't the time to get serious, she thought, he still was annoyed about that last dinner at the cottage, about her looking embarrassed. Not that he had said so, but the way he had clammed up on it told her enough.

"Then let's leave," he said briskly. "Any ideas?"

"Oh, Gare," she said. "You sound angry."

"I'm hungry and worn out—I've been on my legs since dawn. That's all."

"You've been angry since that night at the Stileses'."

"I didn't enjoy the way you acted, no."

"I just couldn't see—" she began. He was busy unlacing his high hunting boots and looking down at them; she could never make him understand when he wouldn't look at her. "They're the best friends we've found," she started again, "and I couldn't see the point—"

"Of my shocking them with Debs." He yanked off his boots and faced her. "*My* best friends are never going to be people I've got to be careful with on what I think."

"Mine aren't either."

"We're agreed then. Fine."

It wasn't fine, he thought, and again saw the glaze of her awkward-

(279)

ness at the table. It had caught him short, and it kept coming back to disturb him. He had enjoyed the dances and parties of this past year as much as she had, but a sudden doubt had been growing since Mt. Desert. With the Aldrich girls and their world of Society, did you have to be a little cagey about keeping in good standing? If you did, then the hell with it.

They went to the main lodge for supper and he picked up yesterday's papers, just in from New York, glancing at the headlines as they went into the dining room. At the table he found himself talking about the endless stream of visits and consultations between the Chiefs of the General Staffs of the British and French and Russian armies; she looked at him in astonishment.

"I don't know how long it's been since you even mentioned the war scare," she said.

"I said I wasn't going to harp on the news any more, so I quit. It's worked pretty well, hasn't it?"

"But I thought you were changing about it."

"Well, I wasn't."

The waitress came and they fell silent. Then Letty said, "About the shop, Garry. Wasn't that real either?"

"Of course it was. But it's your *doing* it that I'm proud of, not who your customers are." She sounded so desolate that he suddenly softened. "Let's eat and then look at some maps. We'll pick us a new place and be out of here at daybreak."

TWENTY-TWO

The heat took on its weight of wetness, took it unto itself as fiber absorbs moisture, grew heavy and sullen with it, and the city sweltered.

In the city's parks, sleepers appeared each night, stray figures walking about tentatively, then lying down on the grass, to remain until dawn. Or whole families would come, like picnickers, a mother and father with two or three children, the parents sometimes carrying a basket with a baby's bottles and something to eat themselves, should the fiery wakefulness of the tenement pursue them to the night secrecy of the park.

Along the city's piers and wharves, too, the sleepers lay each night, sometimes propped against fences and poles, sometimes lying prone along the safe edges of warehouse or dock or factory, away from the clomping hooves of truck horses and the tires of a new delivery auto.

The heat wave had lasted for days and the city's stone never cooled completely, even during the interludes of darkness. On the Lower East Side, as Stefan Ivarin walked slowly day after day to his office from the Delancey Street station, not one window was closed above the level of the fixed glass panes in the stores, not one bedroom window but was raised as far as the sash would go. Each fire escape and stoop was crowded, and later at night, when factory and machine were stilled, the tenement roofs sprang to life with voices and shouts and sometimes the songs and laughter of the young, managing gayety and flirtation and hope in the paltry ugliness about them.

It was during the twelfth day of such heat, late on a stupefying afternoon, that the July meeting took place in the office that was still often called "Landau's office." Fehler's large square table, the one change he had made on taking possession, seated them all easily, though Borg was present along with his exhibits. The five newspaper-size portfolios were ranged against one wall, but at the start nobody seemed aware of them. For the preceding days, they had been circulated among the seven members of the policy group, to allow time for examination; Ivarin had made his own estimate clear to Borg in private, surprised at how insulated Borg seemed against any criticism.

"Just so you are warned in advance, Saul."

"You have been fairer than fair, Mr. Ivarin."

Now Fehler was explaining that today's discussion of popular successes in other newspapers was not necessarily a prelude to change for the *Jewish News*.

"Let us say," he ended, "that these exhibits of current practices in the English-language press have one main goal: further edification for some of us in the modern and changing newspaper world of today."

Stefan Ivarin said, "Further edification is always welcome."

Fehler asked Borg for a résumé of the methods he had followed, and with surprising authority and lack of nervousness, Saul rapidly outlined his work. He started with his attempts to trace the shift in funnies from their original once-a-week version to today's six-a-week pattern, and went on to his study of humor columns, from the earliest right up to the new one in the *Sun* by a young man who signed himself Don Marquis. He talked of the special material for women readers and went on to his "Pinkerton" tactics, sleuthing for jumps in newsstand sales after some new exposé or feature appeared. It wasn't too hard, getting actual figures; the papers involved were only too ready to brag about success.

Of Borg's seven listeners, only Miriam Landau and Jacob Steinberger were untroubled by the comfortable air of the meeting thus far. Bunzig and Kinchevsky spoke occasionally in undertones; Fehler wondered about Ivarin's apparent disengagement; Abe Kesselbaum concentrated on a pad before him, drawing circles and interlocking triangles, not looking up from the tip of his pencil, waiting for the editor to speak out, and Stefan kept checking his emotions and behavior, like a hypochondriac taking his pulse. Still all right. Still regular.

"Borg has done a big job," Ivarin said easily when Borg ended, "the very job Mr. Fehler assigned him to do. If we may start with the humor columns, I agree *in toto,* but whenever I thought I had found a humorist for us, he turned in mere babble."

Fehler thought, Is he going to tell us he thought of it first? He said, "Do you know anybody we might approach now?"

Still easily, Ivarin said, " 'Anybody' won't do. It should be a man with a flair. I'll of course keep on the lookout."

"You never told me," Fehler said too heartily, "that you have been considering something for pure entertainment."

Ivarin turned his calm, pale face toward him. "An oversight," he said. "Or perhaps my old habit of thinking we both do best when we don't cross over the line between editorial and business. As for the funnies, you will have to do the searching without me. With funnies I would not trust myself for flair."

Fehler said to Mrs. Landau and Steinberger, "There are syndicates that sell them. Some funnies can be bought on a contract, and translated. We could look into it."

They both looked surprised. "Mutt and Jeff talking Yiddish," Ivarin said solemnly, not knowing whether this applied to well-known funnies or not. "I dare say it's feasible. But Jiggs? The Hall-room Boys? Happy Hooligan? Krazy Kat?"

Abe Kesselbaum burst into raucous laughter, and the others turned toward him. So far Abe had said almost nothing. Now his shouted laughter was an assault on the quiet room. Stefan Ivarin thought, It's pure relief, like the grave diggers in Shakespeare, but Joseph Fehler, staring past Abe, kept his astonished eyes on Ivarin. Jiggs? he thought. Krazy Kat and Happy Hooligan? A man who never reads the funnies?

The meeting went forward. A few more exchanges maintained a fairly amiable air, and then Ivarin said, "Matters like these will give us no trouble, but—"

He had not raised his voice, but the others paused as if he had asked for complete attention. Mrs. Landau leaned forward, and at her side her lawyer instinctively knew they had come to a key point, as if the preliminaries in a trial had been dispensed with and the case was about to begin.

Joseph Fehler heard Ivarin's "but" and thought, Here it starts, now it comes. Ivarin will show himself to Miriam as he did to Isaac all those years, the idealistic editor with purity of motive. More success, more profit? Only the base and vulgar could want that.

"But there is more involved," Ivarin said, "than funnies and a Don Marquis. I do not edit funnies; their galleys never need reach my desk. The Don Marquis? I'd edit that, but it would be a gifted writer, presumably, and one does little editing with gifted writers."

He went to the side of the room and brought two of Borg's portfolios back to the table with him. Stacked together, their weight was considerable, and he grimaced as his back felt the pull of them. The others watched him; no one spoke.

The constraint, Ivarin thought, is because Miriam and Steinberger are here. Company manners, instead of our rough meetings with Landau. We think, Miriam is new at this, why upset her? And we are impressed, perhaps intimidated, by Steinberger. The one rich man among us. His voice never rises and so we are muted; he does not commit himself and so we are unwilling to fight anything out.

"But beyond funnies and humor columns," he said, "there, the trouble starts." He opened one of the portfolios, standing, pointing down at it as he turned pages. "This stuff for the lovelorn, the heartsick? Never. Not if Dorothy Dix and Winifred Black and Beatrice Fairfax melted into one and gave their outpourings to us free. Never in any paper I am the editor of."

"Of course not," Fehler hastily said. "Borg included things we would never use, as a record of competitive methods. I told him to."

"Competitive!" For the first time Ivarin's voice rose and he did not care that it rose. He yanked open the other portfolio and said, "Science Features, if you please." He gestured to a vast picture of a lush brunette lightly draped in veils.

(283)

ACTRESS SPARED HIDEOUS DEATH. The headline swept from left to right of the page. Under it a more reticent subhead added, BY GENIUS OF PASTEUR.

"One tenth 'Science,' " Ivarin said. "Nine-tenths Sensation."

"Look at my note above it," Saul said, pleading.

"One tenth of the page," Ivarin went on, ignoring him, "for an interview with this unknown actress and her unfortunate bite by a mad dog. All the rest—this picture of a half-naked whore, to excite every ignoramus who flings a nickel on a Sunday newsstand."

At the end of the table, Joseph Fehler stood up also. With emphasis he read aloud Borg's note, " 'This would be equally readable if toned down as we would demand,' " and said, "We would handle it in our own way, but what's wrong with popularizing a science story?"

"Story?" Ivarin demanded. "Twenty, nearly thirty, years out of date, and still a *story?* Wasn't it 1885, 1890, something like that, when Pasteur got his serum?"

Ivarin's derision was too marked. Fehler clapped both portfolios shut and sat down. Miriam Landau put two fingers tightly across her lips as if to keep them from trembling, and Jacob Steinberger gazed at him uncomfortably.

Ivarin knew he had gone too far and it faintly pleased him. What's wrong with popularizing a science story? Fehler should ask Hearst and Brisbane and Pulitzer his hypocrite question, and get the answer he wanted. Since the nineties, their little wars for circulation gave all of them the proper answers to their eternal what's wrong with doing this, doing that, doing the other, to boost their precious totals of copies sold.

"Nothing is 'wrong with popularizing,' " Ivarin said to Fehler. He was still on his feet, and his voice took on the iron ring of the lecturer. "Popularize anything on earth—science, art, politics, even an idea! But trash like this, by reporters who carry out the boss's orders, who interview dope fiends, lunatics, White Slavers, get pictures of executions, lynchings, rapes, murders? That's what your naked whore with the mad dog always leads to, and always in the holy name of circulation."

"Bravo," Abe Kesselbaum whispered.

It was like a blast of sound. The room tingled with it, and nobody spoke. But Jacob Steinberger had lost his uncomfortable look; he watched Ivarin minutely, attending to every syllable, seeing every play of expression on his reddened face.

"Mr. Ivarin," Borg said urgently, "science stories like these were all I found in the papers I was clipping."

"He knew we would tone them down, change them," Fehler said.

"That's a farce," Ivarin said angrily. "You can't compete against trash with modified trash. Either you print it or you spit on it."

He sat down. Again he was faintly pleased. Miriam and Steinberger, he thought, know that this quarrel is not over these portfolios but over the meaning of the *Jewish News* today, yesterday, tomorrow. There is no puzzle about what's fit to print and what not fit to print, to quote the one paper Borg ignored. True, the *Times* sells two hundred thousand copies while the *World* sells seven hundred thousand and Hearst's damnable sheets are well over the million mark. But there's next year and the year after and then another, and who's to know which paper is on the way down and which on the way up?

Fehler had turned to the others, discussing what was in the other portfolios, but Ivarin scarcely listened. His high energy of a few minutes before seeped away and he was suddenly tired. He let them talk on.

"Mr. Ivarin, would you?"

It was Miriam Landau, and Stefan came to with a start. Sunk in his own feeling, thinking in his own terms, he had seen a moment he had never before seen, even in his darkest times. It was a moment that might never come to pass, but in the flashing of time from one thought to its following thought, he had seen himself walking out of the room, walking out of the building, walking out of the paper for good.

"Would I? I beg your pardon, I missed it," he said to her almost formally.

"Would you give in a little, as a favor?" she asked. "A *little,* for the test period?"

"The test period?" Had anybody mentioned a test period?

"A most informal one," Steinberger answered, his manner instructing Miriam Landau to let her attorney take over. "I have suggested to Mr. Fehler that he merely test out some physical changes, changes in format, type, a wider use of pictures. These are areas that would not disturb you, Mr. Ivarin. True?"

"They are outside my domain," Ivarin answered. He turned to Kesselbaum. "Abe, you're boss of format and layout, how do you feel about this proposition?" But Abe only shook his head and said, "We'll have to see." Was he thinking of his four children, of the raise he had been promised for last December that had not yet come through?

"That's right, Abe," Fehler said. "We'll have to see. We may never change by one iota, but we'll make a start and see." He could not suppress the exultant note, and his smile was broader than the day

(285)

the notice went up five months before. There was no need for a vote since an experiment was not binding.

Ivarin took his leave while the meeting was breaking up. A big name, he thought as he walked slowly to his office. Ivarin is a big name. Nothing must disturb him or his work.

That night Stefan Ivarin left the city the moment he could, without his customary stop at the café. During the evening it had rained, and the heat had become fetid. He thought ahead to the first breath of country air awaiting at home in Barnett, hot, too, but clean and quiet. How long it had been since the decision to move away from New York had struck him as a personal sacrifice of everything he valued. On a night like this, the thought of the house on the hill, his house, set back from the street behind its three young maples which had shed their supporting wires long since—it was surcease and haven. Even the train ride was worth enduring.

For the first time this summer he missed Alexandra. Shag, too; it would be nice to have the great oaf leap to life at the sound of his approach and come hurtling along the street toward him. Fran and Fira were not to be compared to Shag as companions; at this stage of their lives, they took everything, absorbed everything, and offered nothing. He remembered the Lawrence strike and Fee's "if we win," and thought, Most of the time, nothing. Maybe later, when they are grown, they will be companions to whom I can talk about things like this.

They are going to change the paper.

Not just the way it looks. The *paper*.

First, big type, bursting headlines, huge pictures. Then later, the explosion into trash.

That is what he was bursting to say. That was why he missed Alexandra. They will make it over, he would tell her, you will see. Not tomorrow, not next week, but soon.

This is his arena; here's where he will try to tear me apart.

We'll make a start and see, Fehler had said; we may never change by one iota. A test period. For a little while. But corruption had no time limit. And it never went back. Imperceptibly, the experiment became the mold of the future, beyond fluidity or shifting, became the hardened mold into which the hot metal of tomorrow would be poured.

Ivarin rose in the lurching train and took off his jacket. He loosened his necktie and opened his cuff links so that his shirt sleeves hung free

(286)

of his wrists. It was hotter than ever. The forward rush of the train under the river and into the humid earth caused a blowing of air, but it was like the blast of some chemical gas, noxious and sickening.

He did feel a little sick. After the meeting, he had had three private talks, all brief, all but the last unwelcome. First had come Borg, to explain again that he was merely carrying out orders, and Ivarin had cut him off without ado. "Your boss praised you. What more do you hope for?" Then Miriam Landau had fluttered in, to beg him to believe that it was not she, but her four daughters who were so insistent that the paper try a few ways to make more money. "I am not so young," she had said, "and when I go, the paper will be theirs, so it's only natural they should look ahead."

He had agreed that it was natural and escorted her to the door. Only with Abe Kesselbaum had he let his feelings show. "There have been storms before," he had ended, and Abe had replied, "But then we had Isaac, not her." They had each gladly escaped to their work.

Now there was no escape. The emptying train was taking other night workers home to rest and sleep, but he would not sleep too soon.

Steinberger might restrain Fehler in the fight ahead. He was a man of the world, a man of taste. And he had been faithful to Isaac and Isaac's paper for twenty years.

He had restrained Fehler already, in the meeting, in public, and he had done it with ease. *Merely some physical changes, areas that would not disturb you, Mr. Ivarin.* But he was counsel to Miriam Landau; he was in her service and on her side. Whatever his private tastes, that whispered "Bravo" had come from Abe, not from him.

For perhaps the eighth day in a row, Alexandra came back from the postman with nothing but the rolled-up copy of the *Jewish News* in its tight skin of wrapping paper. Disconsolately she went to the low shelves under the angle of hot canvas, and set it down unopened with several similar rolls. She usually saved the paper to read at night, but she had fallen behind and wanted to catch up in the proper sequence.

"Not even a postcard," she said. "I tell you something's the matter with Papa."

"He's all right, Mama," Fee assured her. "He's just busy."

"He'll write soon," Francesca added.

Alexandra thought, Much they care, but she kept this dark decision to herself. They knew nothing of life, for all their maturity and wisdom in things at their own level. For the first time in their four summers at the beach, Fee had become friends with a boy, and though the experience had not brought forth any feminine wiles, it did give her a new poise when she was treated to Franny's superiorities about crushes and romance.

The boy was a whole year younger, however, and this Fee took to be an insuperable chasm between them. His name was David Herzog and his father was a baker. David was starting high school right after Labor Day just as Fee was, despite being only twelve, and was going to go to college and study engineering.

"He knows all about electricity," Fee said the day she brought him to the tent for the first time. "Engines and dynamos and everything."

"Do you, David? That's lovely," Alexandra said. "Would you like some lemonade?"

"O-o-oh, he'd love it," Fee cried and flung herself onto the nearest cot, scooping both her legs up in her arms so her knees touched her chin.

"Get up, Fee, your bathing suit's still wet," Alexandra said, glad she had a legitimate reason for correcting this tomboy performance.

Fee jumped up, in a fit of shrill laughter that set David off into paroxysms with her. In the galley-like section at the rear of the tent, Alexandra busied herself with hacking slivers of ice off the block in the zinc-lined oak box that never held enough to last through the night. Behind her, their laughter raced on like a river, widened and narrowed between banks of words, first from Fee, then from David, though more frequently from Fee.

The realization troubled Alexandra. Fira must be told, somehow, not to out-talk a boy, not quite so obviously at any rate. David seemed a willing victim, even egging Fee on with his frequent sounds of approval, which came out sounding like "yare, yare," with the r's left out. Idly, Alexandra wondered how she could go about suggesting to David's mother that elocution lessons could be as important to a bright young boy as engineering lessons, and that parents owed children an education in the native speech of their native land, as surely as they owed them an education in general. David was a native-born American, but he spoke in the accent of the Jewish East Side, where he lived fifty weeks of the year, and where all his friends and classmates spoke in the same intonations and inflections. His teachers, from kindergarten onward, had doubtless decided it was hopeless to try to change the way these ghetto children talked English, and whatever attempt they did make probably was limited to "the elocution period" instead of extending through the entire school day, school week, school year.

(288)

Poor David. His voice had not yet deepened, and to an eaves-dropper who did not see him, he might have been another girl in the tent with Fee. Now, the two of them sounded like a pair of birds twittering and cajoling each other, rilling and trilling away as merrily as on the first day of spring.

"Here's your lemonade," Alexandra said as she went back to them, "and here's some jelly sandwiches. The cookies are all gone."

"What's that funny bread?" David asked, after one great gulp at his lemonade. "It isn't pumpernickel, isn't rye—" He picked up a sandwich but seemed unwilling to try it.

"It's delicious whole wheat," Alexandra began. "Refined white flour, David, even though your own Papa bakes with it—"

"I'll tell him, Mama," Fee said hurriedly. "Ow, my nose hurts, I drank the lemonade so fast, it froze."

She set her glass down and clapped both hands over the bridge of her nose, going off into squeals of sound, mixed of simulated pain and silliness.

David imitated her, and then with his hands still cupped over his face, he alternately raised and lowered the fingers of his right hand while he began a whooping sound, rising and falling.

"You're an Indian chief," Fee cried, joining her war cries to his. On the floor, Shag began a howl of protest, abandoned it, and lay in-ert, one ear twitching, eyes aggrieved.

It's enough to pierce an eardrum, Alexandra thought, backing out of the tent. David's shrieks fell away into high hysterics, but Fee kept on whooping and pounding her feet on the wood flooring of the tent. Bedlam, Alexandra thought. They're still babies, without an idea of what's ahead.

Fee would discover soon enough that she ought not out-talk a boy, but how would David discover English diphthongs and vowels and consonants in their native shapes and sounds?

She wondered if Evan and Alida happened to know any expert speech teacher in New York who might be persuaded to start a small class next fall for David and a few of his classmates, charging no more than a nickel or dime a child, since higher fees would kill off the idea before it could be tried.

The idea appealed to her and in the next few days, as Fee and David became inseparable, she began to feel it incumbent on her to do something to help him. The perfect speech teacher, that was the first step. On impulse she wrote Alida, to enlist her help in finding one. Not all parents could move to a small town for the sake of their children's speech and mannerisms, but not all who stayed put could be happy about it. David's mother, still young, would surely be only too pleased if some such community teaching could be arranged. David's little brother also talked the way David did, and in due time their baby sister, still in diapers, would start singsonging too.

Alida's quick reply lifted her heart. It was so kind, so willing. She was inquiring among all their friends, and had already asked Garry and Letty to canvass all theirs as well. The moment there was news, she would send it, special delivery; it was a lovely idea and she wanted to be of use for it in any way she could.

With the letter in the pocket of her alpaca bathing suit, Alexandra set out for the Herzog tent. At the store or in the public bathhouse, Mrs. Herzog was rather shy and withdrawn when they met, but shyness was so usual among the women in the tent city. And showing them you were interested in their children was unfailingly the magic sesame that dissolved it.

"May I come in?" she asked David's mother, pausing at the wide-open flaps of canvas. "It's about your David. He's the brightest boy!"

Mrs. Herzog was sweeping and her broom halted in mid-stroke. "The highest marks in the whole class," she said. Pride warmed her face fleetingly, but she made no gesture to invite her visitor inside.

"He's as impatient for high school this fall as my child," Alexandra said, stepping in as a matter of course. "And he'll get good marks there, too."

Mrs. Herzog muttered a fragment of prayer, but said not a word in direct reply. She remained standing, almost in Alexandra's path, as if waiting for the real purpose of this visit to reveal itself. The tent was arranged like their own, with the addition of a crib for the baby sister, but Mrs. Herzog ignored the wooden chairs and made no move to offer one of them.

Suddenly, Alexandra was abashed. David's mother had not asked her to come in, though she was actually in, had offered her no tea, not even ice water. She realized she was smiling at a young woman who had not smiled even once. "If this is a bad time to drop in," she said, "I'll come back later."

"Bad time, good time, it's the same. If you have a complaint about David, I'm ready."

"It's not a complaint, anything *but,*" Alexandra said warmly, and then faltered for words. It had seemed so natural, so simple, but now standing this way, face to face, unsmiling, it suddenly was hard to lead into the subject of singsong nasalities. "You know, a group of women from the tents come to my place twice a week, sometimes three times—"

(290)

"I heard," the other said. She shrugged slightly. "I'm too busy."

"Oh my goodness," Alexandra said. "I didn't come here like—like a salesman, to get another pupil." She was embarrassed and a little resentful at being so misunderstood. "I mentioned the women to explain that I'm not exactly an amateur about bringing up children in an American way."

"David isn't brought up right? Did he break something? I'll pay for it. Did he do something dirty with your little girl?"

"Heavens, nothing like that. I simply had an idea I want to talk over, about children losing their foreign accents."

"Who said David has a foreign accent? I know him like a book and *I* never heard it."

Alexandra was nonplussed. She wished she could turn on her heel and walk out. This young mother was either stupid or rude, and as unresponsive as a mule. "People *can't* hear it themselves," she said in one further attempt. "There's a brand-new play, on that very point. About a professor who teaches a little English girl to speak English without an accent. An Englishman wrote it, a brilliant man, a socialist, and it's a wonderful play, so human and so funny. The little girl didn't know she had an accent, of course, nor did her father or mother. They couldn't *hear* it, because they heard it all the time."

She had been carried away in her pleasure at finding so apt a way to make her point, so impressive a colleague in the world of phonetics. It apparently had got through to David's mother, for she seemed at last to be thinking and receptive, mulling this over.

"You listen to me," Mrs. Herzog said suddenly. "Just two words, *you* listen."

"Why, you're in a fury," Alexandra said. "I'll go. Forgive me."

"Mrs. Buttinsky!" She spat it out, and then repeated it in a shrewish scream. "Mrs. Buttinsky, that's who you are. Get out of my tent, and leave my David alone."

Alexandra shook with anger at the onslaught. "Good day," she said with dignity. "I wanted to—I hoped to—to interest you in an idea. But good day."

She did turn on her heel and behind her she heard a storm of language, ending in another "Mrs. Buttinsky." The words lashed at her and her own anger whipped back at them, but, she thought, It's impossible. Never, not once in all the hours of her life, as a teacher, as an adviser, an informal lecturer out here on the beach—never had she met anything but eagerness, never had she heard anything but words of thanks and desire for more. Now without warning, on this lovely hot clear summer morning, a woman she had approached with an open heart had turned fishwife and called her names and ordered her out. It was unbelievable. It was dreadful.

Back in her own tent, Alexandra sat down heavily at the kitchen table. A sadness suffused her, an emptiness she usually escaped, except when Stiva was in a mood that hurt her and would not let her go.

Her worry about his not writing swooped down upon her like a dark grey gull, wings outspread, blotting out the sweet normal sun. For a few days she had almost banished it, but now this raw abusive encounter brought it back, raw and abusive too. Was he merely too busy? Or was something seriously wrong? By now it must be more than two weeks since he had sent a line. And both times she had telephoned him he had given her a curt "Nothing's wrong," and shut her off as only he could shut her off.

She went over to the unread copies of the *Jewish News,* now stacked in a neat little pyramid by Fee. There must be ten or twelve of them, still rolled up; somehow she never could find time to start at the oldest one and read them until she did catch up. It might be a way of getting back at Stiva for not finding time to write to her.

She opened the top copy, to keep Fee's pyramid from collapsing, though starting with the latest issue was the exact opposite of reading them in sequence.

The moment she slit open the skin-tight wrapper and spread the paper wide, she forgot Mrs. Buttinsky and everything that had happened to her that day.

No wonder he hadn't written. No wonder he had to say nothing was wrong when she phoned. His only alternative was to say everything was wrong.

The paper was wrong. It was different. It glared up at her like an excited stranger. It was another paper.

It was splashed and splotched with headlines and pictures and captions and boxes. A big thick streamer of type, seven columns wide, topped the entire page, as if war had just started or a terrible strike, or the Triangle fire. But it was only a follow-up story about Becker in the death house at Sing Sing, where he had already been for months for killing a gambler named Rosenthal, by now the stalest story in New York City, even though the yellow press kept pumping air into its lungs with the artificial respiration of their tricks.

Under the screamer of a headline, there was something explosive and strange about the entire page. There were four photographs, three of them big, with heavy captions underneath. The columns of type were chopped up into short chunky paragraphs, wedged apart by black subheads, everything combining into the "crisis look" of it, the fire-alarm urgency.

Alexandra did not read the page; she stared at it as if reading were not part of the expected thing to do with a newspaper. Was it possible, she wondered, that her own low spirits because of Mrs. Buttinsky were dragging down her judgment in general? In her surprise at finding any change at all in the paper, was she exaggerating, being "volatile" in her response? She looked away for a moment, out at the sand glistening before the tent, and then looked at the paper once more.

It was not so terribly different after all, was it? More emphatic, certainly, as if it were thumping a fist on the table to make a point. In a way, there was something about it that looked easier to read, more coaxing to the eye, like a novel with lots of conversation as opposed to a book on economics.

I'm trying to like it, she thought. I'm trying to pretend there's nothing to be angry about. As if I was already face to face with Stiva and had to hide my feelings about it for his sake.

She stood up uncertainly and went back for the pyramided cylinders atop the bookcase, carefully bringing them all to the table with her and setting them down as if it were vital not to disturb the symmetry of their arrangement. Using a paring knife to slit and rip off the tight wrappers, she opened them as they came off the top, going backward in date and sequence, so that Thursday's paper gave way to Wednesday's, and Wednesday's to Tuesday's, this week to last week. One by one, their front pages flared out their strangeness at her, and still she did not read. But as she looked down at it, she began to realize that this strangeness diminished in degree as she went backwards in time.

The change had been planned to be gradual. She had missed its earliest stages; perhaps if she had been reading the paper regularly every day, she would not have found this morning's paper so startling. If you got used to it, you might not even see it.

"They couldn't *hear* it," she had told Mrs. Herzog about the little English girl's parents, "because they heard it all the time."

Alexandra at last stood up. She had been sitting over the papers for a long time and her legs were cramped and tired. When she had finally begun to read, she could find nothing to pause over; the news stories sounded much the same as always. The editorial page reassured her; it was Stiva in each leading piece.

So far they were changing only the quiet strong face the paper had always worn, not its heart. Would that come in time?

She walked out to the front of the tent. The sun had disappeared under mackerel clouds and the air was cool. Suddenly, she wished the summer was over. Normally she was content to stay at the beach until the last moment, enjoying the sudden briskness of August nights, the need for sweaters and an extra blanket for each cot, hearing the ocean pound more meaningfully, promising gales ahead, storms, winter. It was lovely, this quiet falling away of summer, and she valued it as she valued its beginning and ripening in June and July.

But suddenly she was homesick. If Stiva were enraged about the paper, home would be miserable, but all at once she was tired of the lazy life at the beach, and her heart filled with longing for home, for the late nights when she sat up waiting against all reason for the moment when she heard the front door open and Stiva come in.

TWENTY-THREE

Before September was out, Fira Ivarin decided she was the happiest girl in the world. Nothing in her entire life had ever been as wonderful as being a freshman at Barnett High.

From the first morning, she loved it. She loved having an armchair with a side rest instead of a babyish desk with a lid, loved leaving a classroom when a bell rang at the end of a period, and going to a different one for the next course, instead of staying at the same place in the same room all day long.

She was thrilled to have one teacher for algebra and a different one for English, another one for American history and a different one for German. The one for German was the most thrilling of all. He was a man, the first man teacher she had ever seen, except for Eli who didn't count, and the first man teacher she had ever had as her very own. His name was Ludwig Wohl, and you said it with a V and a very big O, and you called him Doctor, not Mister, Wohl.

He was rather tubby, but good-looking, with a reddish mustache and a beard that was as pointy as an ice pick. He called every girl in the class *Fräulein* and every boy *Herr,* rolling the r's until it must have tickled the tip of his tongue. When he called on her to recite and said "Fräulein Ivarin" as he did the first day or two, rolling both the r's as if he loved doing it, she felt grown-up and all set to giggle at the same time. Later, he switched to first names, and she became "Fräulein Fira," and though there were no extra r's, he seemed to get more roll with "Fira," and that was even better.

From the start, she knew she was going to get an A with Dr. Wohl, because classes with him were such fun that it was impossible not to do your homework and be able to reel off the new vocabulary you had to learn by heart overnight, or write out German words on the blackboard, or even read something aloud, which was hardest because of the crazy sound of words ending in *ich* or *och* or *ach.*

She said, "Gee, I don't know," when anybody asked why she chose German instead of French for her modern language, but the reason probably was that Trudy never had any doubt about what to take, and Fee took it too.

But being best friends wasn't the same, now that they were at Barnett High, though neither one of them admitted it. They kept on saying they were best friends; if anybody mentioned Trudy to Fee, it was automatic to say, "She's my best friend," and Trudy did the same thing. But it began to sound funny and young. Nobody else said it.

That was before Fee met Juanita Endoza and Anne Miller, so liking them had nothing to do with it. You could have a best friend in high school without calling her your best friend; it was another change from grammar school. Every day was a change, even going past the chemistry lab and smelling the awful sulphuric acid and knowing you'd be taking chem next year, even that was exciting.

Anne Miller was different from Trudy or anybody else she had ever known before; she was from Iowa, and she was fourteen. And Anne talked about boys, and could answer anything you asked about *anything,* and even if you didn't ask, she seemed to know what you didn't understand about, and she would tell you. Anne always dropped her voice, or even whispered, when she talked about boys, and her whisper made what she said twice as interesting. She had an older brother and maybe that was why she knew so much about boys, but compared to Anne, Trudy Loheim never said one thing worth listening to any more.

But talking about boys wasn't the only thing that made Anne Miller so fascinating. The other thing was being religious. She went to the

Grace Episcopal Church down on Main Street and she really truly believed so hard in God and angels and life after death that she talked a lot about that, too, almost from the first day they had started to know each other. She couldn't believe Fee had never been baptized or christened or anything and when Fee said she was agnostic and Jewish, Anne wouldn't believe her. You could always *tell,* she insisted, and she knew Fee wasn't. After a while she did believe it and then she asked if Fee would be allowed to go to church with her some Sunday, to see what it was like, and Fee said she'd love it.

"Will your mother and father let you?"

"Sure."

"My mother said they wouldn't."

"For heaven's sake!"

"Heaven's sake" made them laugh, but that same afternoon, Fee telephoned Anne and said, "I told you they would."

"What will your father say when he gets home and hears it?"

"He was right there." She had forgotten to tell Anne what her father worked at, so Anne didn't know about his being at home all day when regular fathers were off at work. Anne's father was a salesman of faucets. "He said sure I could, and when my mother said she'd make me a new dress, he said he should hope so, she made a new dress for unimportant things, of course she should for me going to church the first time."

"They didn't even have to think about it awhile?" Anne asked.

"They always said we could decide for ourselves when we got bigger, about being religious or socialists or anything."

"But right off the bat, the *both* of them. Gosh."

Fee was surprised that Anne was so surprised, but not the way she used to be when Trudy talked about religion and what her mother thought Fee's mother must think about Eli marrying Joan "outside your religion." She still felt a tight little excitement stir around inside her if anybody talked about Jews or Christians, but by now she knew she would, so it didn't surprise her the way it used to. It wasn't especially pleasant or unpleasant; it was like some familiar dopey friend you were going to run into every once in a while.

"What Sunday should we pick?" Fee asked. "Not this next one, because of getting my new dress."

Two days before the Sunday, the new dress was finished and Fee was so happy she said that if Grace Church was as wonderful as Anne Miller said, she probably would get converted.

"Converted?" It was her father, and he put his paper down on the table and looked at her, as if nothing was more interesting.

"Anne said I could be. Her minister said so. She asked her mother and her mother asked their minister, and he said yes, by all means."

"Quite right," he said. "You could be." He thought for a while and then murmured, "By all means." Under the table, his heel began to tap against the floor, but it wasn't angry, just concentrating, and he pushed his paper away from him. Fee was proud of herself; usually he acted as if all talk at the table was a thing he had to put up with. And she was glad in another way. For the longest time, he had been sort of pulled-away to himself, not in a mood, just far off, and not happy. It had something to do with the paper, Mama said, and anybody would be upset about it.

But now he seemed really absorbed and interested in what Fee said about conversion and Anne's minister. "Can I?" she prompted him.

"It's a long process, conversion," he said. "You don't go to church one morning and then, hickory dickory dock, you're converted."

She laughed at the sound of it, the sort of thing Mama would say, but she also was surprised. The things her father just knew about! "Do you know how long it would take me?"

"Not precisely," he said. "But in most religions, you do need time, a good deal of studying and thought. And to have real meaning, it should take a long time, don't you agree?"

"Studying and thought?"

"Well, Jews would want a convert to study Hebrew and the Talmud, Catholics would give instruction in their catechism and the Bible, and Protestants would have their own methods of teaching their prayers and beliefs, especially to somebody who wasn't born right into them. You follow me?"

"Anne Miller didn't say anything like that."

"Don't look disheartened, Fee. You gobble up studies, and get famous grades whenever you want to."

She cheered up. "Anyway, if I do whatever I'm supposed to, then I can be converted, is that right?"

Fran and Mama were at the table listening, but Papa ignored them and so did she. What they thought didn't make a bit of difference, not to him and certainly not to her. She knew that if she were going to be converted, Papa was the one that mattered. Mama would decide the way he did. "Can I, Papa?" she repeated.

"You're thirteen, aren't you? It might take a year or two. Then there would be a special ceremony, as in all religions. And since conversion is not anything to be taken lightly, or to make mistakes about, let's allow an extra year."

"Two or three years from now," Alexandra said sagely, speaking for the first time.

"So when you're sixteen, Firuschka, if you still want to be taken officially into the Grace Episcopal Church, why then, 'by all means,' to quote the minister, and Mama and I will not object in the slightest."

"I told Anne you wouldn't," Fee said triumphantly.

On Sunday morning she was up an hour early and when Anne and her mother came to get her, she was so excited, it almost hurt. Her dress looked like thin chocolate wool with sand scattered over it, and she was wearing last winter's white beaver hat, even though it was still Septembery outside. Just yesterday Anne mentioned hats and said you couldn't go to church with just hair, but the dirty old beaver was the only hat she had. Mama was too busy finishing the dress; she told Papa he simply had to lend a hand and clean up the hat. He was so surprised he started right in.

It was funny to see him dousing a rag in benzene and rubbing and rubbing and rubbing, not even smoking a cigarette because of the benzene. But it was sort of nice too because he simply never did *anything,* and she didn't know how to thank him.

"Whew, what a smell," was all she said when he handed the hat back. "Like a kerosene stove or the Paiges' car or something."

"It will evaporate by tomorrow," he said. "Anyway, there's no smell of sulphur and brimstone."

She looked up quickly, but he wasn't being nasty and sarcastic. He just said it, watching her try the hat on to see if it still fitted. It did, and he said something about heads changing size at a different rate of speed from arms and legs and bodies.

"That's why babies' heads look so top-heavy," he explained. "They're almost adult-size long before the baby is an adult."

"What a lot of things you'd never even think of if nobody told you."

"You look at Webby's head next time," he said. "Or Sandy's."

Having him so offhand and nice about the size of people's heads made her even happier about Grace Episcopal Church, though she couldn't see any connection, and when she did start off with Anne and her mother the next morning, she felt sweet and happy all over.

It was a beautiful shiny day, with the clouds way up and wispy against the blue. Downtown at Grace Church, she and Anne followed Mrs. Miller up the shallow stone steps, so old and used they were wavy at their front edges. Ahead, through the wide oak doors, Fee could see a big wide space. The nave? she thought. The apse? I don't even know what they call anything.

For the first time she felt nervous about doing something wrong and making a fool of herself. Mrs. Miller led them to a pew about halfway between the rear and the front of the church, and Fee watched to see if they crossed themselves the way Juanita Endoza sometimes did, or did anything else with their hands. But they just sat down, and she did too, and Anne gave her a little book from a rack in front of them, and Fee opened it for a minute and saw it was a hymnal. Then she could look around and upward, without anybody noticing.

The church was larger and higher and dimmer inside than she ever had dreamed it would be, just looking at it from outside. And it was beautiful. Sitting there in the pew, you were half-hidden from everybody behind you or in front of you; you could look up and up in the dimness, broken by the streaming colors from the long stained-glass windows. You could see the stone ribs of the arches creeping up the walls and coming together above, like fingertips touching in prayer.

Music flowed under the reaching praying stone fingers, and Fee wondered how she knew about hands reaching up like that to pray. She had never seen her mother's hands do that, nor her father's, nor any teacher's, but she knew. There must have been something in a book she read long ago, and she remembered it as if it was something that had happened right in front of her eyes. There was something beautiful about it, and suddenly something sad too.

Fee's eyes filled with tears, though she was happy, and she was surprised to feel them hot in her eyelids. She looked upward again; now the arches seemed to waver a little, as if the praying hands shivered, and in the stained-glass windows, the blues and yellows and reds of the saints and the angels seemed to blur and quiver, too.

Great bells began to peal and Fee recognized them. How often she had heard them from outside. But now she was inside and she loved them.

Wondrous, Stefan thought later that day when he heard Fee's rapturous account of her foray into organized religion. When I had to rebel and overthrow my parents, I turned atheist and later agnostic. She, poor child, was cheated of that chance through the misfortune of being born to parents who were already lost souls. So she rebels by turning back toward religion.

There was a mathematical purity about it that pleased him. He had spoken of it to Alexandra several times during the collective preparations for Fee's churchgoing, for he suspected that underneath

Alexandra's staunch principles about freedom of thought, she retained a certain classic tremulousness about her youngest child's desire to exercise it.

Alexandra detected his suspicions and argued against them, largely in her own mind, for this was no time to be at outs with him. Privately she found herself wondering again and again about what this first step might lead to for little Fira. Maybe parents should not agree to certain things after all. Maybe they should not permit a child to dabble in the opiate of the people, or was it the opium, she never could remember.

But listening to Fee's racing joy about her experience at church, she forgot any doubts she had had. Nothing mattered but a child's awakening, and this was an awakening, a blossoming for Fee. What happened later on, how long her glory and intensity would last, remained to be seen. But for now, she had burst forth into an incredible world of wonder and trust and longing. It was beautiful to watch, because it was watching your child try her wings in one more new direction.

If only they were strong enough to carry her. When it came to religion, a fledgling could be so easily swooped upon and wounded. It went without saying, in a family like theirs, that broad-mindedness was guaranteed the children from their mother and father. But once they left that warm safety, there was no guarantee the world would continue it. Like Eli.

How shocked poor Eli had been to discover that the Martins were filled with grief over their daughter's hurry-up marriage, not only because of Joan's condition but also because she was "forced to marry a Jew." Eli "a Jew" was always so unexpected an idea, or Fran or Fee, brought up as they were, small-town Americans and nothing else, all acting and looking and talking like all the other small-town Americans they had ever seen.

Assimilation was so natural an idea when you had no superior feelings toward other people, and it was such an American idea, the melting pot and all men are created equal. Some Jews looked on it as a dirty word, and some Americans didn't want it to touch their own family. If Joan hadn't been pregnant, goodness knew what opposition her parents might have put up. Now, of course, with two such grandchildren as Webby and Sandy, the Martins were happy over Joan's marriage, but there was no real friendship between the families. Nothing like the closeness between the Paiges and the Ivarins.

Why, they had become such friends that she could sense something wrong with Alida's mood, as she could with Stiva's. When Alida heard that Fee was going to church, she said it was sweet and good to find people like her and Stiva, who had principles like religious freedom and stuck to them. Then she said something about Garry's sticking to his guns about changing jobs, but she sounded troubled and perplexed. Garry's company, Alexandra knew, had abandoned the idea of explosives; were they returning to it now, after the slaughters in the Balkans and the bloodthirsty talk from Germany and Russia and France?

"Stiva," she suddenly said.

He looked up. The Sunday papers were growing too big for a man to manage. The *Times* gave you ninety-some pages per nickel, about twenty pages for one cent. Twenty was normal in the daily *Times,* and perhaps Ochs felt it behooved him to stay with the usual ratio on Sunday. Was there dissension and struggle and an eternal play for power at the *Times* too?

"Stiva," she said again. "You don't actually believe there will be a big war, do you?"

He blinked at her, taking off his glasses and peering at her, myope intentness in his gaze.

"Yes, I do believe it," he said. "What's all this about? I thought you were still lost in Fee's clouds of glory."

"But somehow I began to think of explosives and bombs," she said, "and then of Garry and Eli and all the young men beginning life." She shuddered and added lamely, "I suppose a million mothers in Europe think of it even more than I do."

"France has raised its conscription from two years to three," he said.

"When? What made her do it?"

"Germany raised the standing army to nearly a million. And Belgium insists that the Germans are calling up an unusual number of reserves."

"And Russia?"

"The biggest peacetime army in history."

He returned to the paper, and absent-mindedly she drew the first section of the *Times* toward her, folding it and rolling it into a tight cylinder, curling her fingers around it closely. She wished he would tell her more of what was going on at the office but it was dangerous to dig at him about it.

"It's about two months now," she said, "since Fehler began going crazy with the front page."

(301)

"The terrible thing is, it sells the paper."

It was unexpected. Usually he avoided being that specific. In the weeks since she had come back from the beach, the one thing they thought of was the office and the developments there. For brief stretches, for unexpected reasons like Fee and church, they could be absorbed by other aspects of living, but inevitably they returned to the paper. Talking openly about it was another thing. That depended on him.

" 'Sells the paper,' " she prompted. "How much more?"

"Fehler says a thousand copies more a day."

"I don't believe it."

"It was his big news at the September meeting. Mrs. Landau almost jumped up and down on her chair, like Webby."

"I can't stand her."

"Fehler also announced something else," he said. "He hired a man to be the first Picture Editor and General Art Director, one of Hearst's young geniuses, who's Jewish so there's no language problem. He'll be Abe's boss."

She stared at him, shocked. "Poor Abe, it's a public slap in the face."

"After being top man so long, yes."

"Can he do anything?" she said. "Will he quit?"

"He has four children."

"It's a crime," she said. "What things can happen under capitalism."

"This is a socialist paper," he said drily.

"But Fehler is an anarchist, no matter how he cringes and lies about it now to save his skin."

Here it was again, the unending wonder of her logical progressions. This time it didn't amuse him. He wished he had kept quiet about that thousand a day.

"I asked Otto and Louise for dinner Saturday," Garry said. "Is that all right?"

"Saturday?" Letty asked. "This coming Saturday?"

"Have we something for Saturday?" he asked. "It's Otto's birthday."

"The Harretts are coming, and the Grintzers, and Peter. I asked them two weeks ago, don't you remember?"

He looked disgusted with himself. "Of course I remember." He glanced at their dining table; more than six was crowded, and they were already seven. "Well, I'll tell Otto they can come afterwards."

"Afterwards?" She hesitated. "You mean some other night, after Saturday?"

"No, I meant after dinner."

"Oh," Letty said.

Garry almost said, "I can un-invite them," but an unwillingness kept him back. "What's wrong with asking them to drop in after dinner for coffee and some drinks? I thought you liked Otto and Louise."

"I do, only—" She was opening a large box delivered by an expensive dress shop that afternoon, and as she peeled away layers of white tissue paper from the top to reveal a glistening green satin, she said, "Isn't that heavenly, that color! I loved it the minute I saw it."

He admired the new dress and predicted she would look beautiful in it. Then he said, "About the Ohrmanns. We haven't had them here since spring."

"I know," she said. "But I was just wondering how they'd get along with everybody." She waited for an answer and then said, "Otto and Louise are so different, that's all."

"Does that mean," he asked carefully, "not well-off and fashionable?"

"Why in the world would I care about anything like that?"

"I can't imagine. Just the way you said it."

"You *are* imagining," she said.

Again he thought of the unseen social yardstick. Since the summer it kept poking at his thoughts at unexpected times. The table and its limits—was that now being measured by it, too? He was willing to make the usual concessions to the social graces, but beyond a point they didn't count enough. "I could stall Otto off until after dinner, nine-thirty or ten," he finally said.

"Wouldn't it be better asking them for Sunday, *for* dinner? It's awful inviting people, but saying 'you eat by yourself first.' "

"What's all this fiddling around?" he demanded. "You don't want them here with the others. Why not come right out and say so?"

"Otto is a—a radical," she said, flinging it into the room between them. "Most nice people just can't stand—" She turned away, saying something he couldn't catch about "free speech and all the rest," and left the room.

A radical. A single word to damn all dissenters, from the lunatics hurling bombs to the most moderate of socialists like his father. She would exempt the family from such a labeling; it would be too embarrassing: My father-in-law a radical! My husband a radical!

He stared down at the dress box and with a wrench of the string of memory remembered their trip to Canada. Were they going to keep on hitting rough spots whenever their path crossed the path of the Stileses and the Aldriches, the Harretts and the Grintzers?

From the other room, Letty called to him, and a moment later she appeared in the bedroom door. "I'm sorry, darling," she said.

He nodded and she withdrew once more. Soon he grew calmer and went into their room. She was lying down, facing the tall windows. The last afternoon light was yellowing the October-dry garden, and a shaft of light struck warmly across his eyes.

"Come on, Letty," he said. "I didn't ask Otto on purpose, but since I did." He made a complete statement of it, and she sat up, ready for compromise.

"I shouldn't have called him that," she conceded. "But take people like Jerry and Kay—apart from being friends, they're awfully important in business. Jerry is Olive Harrett's pride and joy, and he tells her absolutely everything, and I may get a second shipment on consignment from her any minute."

"They're not such boobs, though, that they'll fall apart at Otto's ideas. Or at mine. We'll have a fine time, dance and be merry. You'll see."

On Saturday, they were done with coffee before the Ohrmanns came, and Otto accepted everybody's congratulations and a special bottle of Rhine wine from Garry. Louise told a story about their youngest child, who had bought him a penny's-worth of licorice shoe-strings as a gift, and burst into tears when he ate one. Then both Ohrmanns withdrew into a shell of shyness that Garry had never seen, built, he thought, on Otto's self-consciousness, among these strangers, about his still-heavy accent, and Louise's uneasy lack of small talk. He waited for it to pass, but after another round of chatter by the others on books and plays, he saw that their shyness was worse. It was impossible to let them sit and flounder.

"What's new from home?" he said, and was rewarded by Otto's look.

"It's been a three-day orgy there," he said, and explained to the others, "I have a brother still in Germany. With I. G. Farben, you know them?"

"They're in steel, aren't they?" Jerry Harrett asked.

"That's Krupp," Peter Stiles answered for Otto. "They make machinery for heavy industry, heavy arms. The Farben people are mainly drugs and dyes and chemicals, isn't that right?"

Otto said it was, and Letty looked impressed at Peter's ready

(304)

knowledge. "Otto's brother is a top salesman at Farben," Garry said, and then asked Otto, "What kind of three-day orgy?" though they had already talked it all out over their sandwich lunches at the lab. A fever of military self-love had seized the country, a public frenzy of boasting about German might and German power, all in the guise of a national celebration of the victory over Napoleon at Leipzig a hundred years ago, and the invasion of France that followed.

" 'We did it once, we can do it again,' " Otto said. "That's what they're all shouting. Bismarck foams up at them in every stein of beer."

"Good old Bismarck," Garry said, raising his glass as if in a toast. "Likewise, good old France." It was heavy-handed and the knowledge irked him.

"There won't be war between them," Bob Grintzer said positively. "Another Balkan mess, maybe, and let them stew in it."

"It might be a bigger stew next time," Otto said. "As big as all Europe."

"They're busy fixing up for it," said Garry.

Peter looked at Otto and then at Garry. "Socialists," he said too casually, "are always against war, aren't they? Automatically against it? Justifiable war or not?"

"Not all socialists," Garry said quickly, "but I sure am."

Peter shrugged and the others said nothing, but their heightened attention excited Garry. This was the way it should be in a man's house.

"Is that glass empty, Jerry?" Letty asked brightly. "Gare, would you fix people's drinks, darling?"

He refilled glasses, but he thought, This is what counts, what really counts. He was oddly elated, and he urged Otto on. There was already a "war prosperity" in many pockets of industry, Otto said; shortages of raw materials were now so acute that every factory from Krupp and Farben down was aswim with overdue and undeliverable orders. The hunt for raw materials went far beyond the borders of Germany, and everyone in the field knew that England was buying up the waste products of spinning mills in Egypt and Indian cotton waste called "linters" for making cellulose and the new explosives and expellants.

"And over here," Garry added, "everyone in the field knows how many of our own Krupps and Farbens are getting ready right now." Ironically he went on, "Business is business, and it doesn't say 'Thou Shalt Not Do Business.' "

(305)

"That gets my goat," Jerry Harrett suddenly said, but his wife Kay said, "I'm sick of all this business talk. Let's put on that new record and dance."

" 'The International Rag,' " Letty said, jumping up. "It's too cute for words."

Peter Stiles jumped up also, with a quick glance at Letty, a look of understanding, even of sympathy. Garry saw it and it enraged him, a tacit assurance to his wife that he, Peter, knew what she had to put up with. The music started, people moved about, laughter and snatches of talk filled the room, and Garry found himself repeating, Just the same, this is what really counts. He had no time to decide what "This" was, which counted, but he knew he would recognize it when he could think the evening through.

He sat on with Otto and Louise, apart from the others now, as if they three had floated off on an unseen current, and before too long the Ohrmanns said good-bye and left. Then he asked Betty Grintzer to dance, and later Kay, and when he said "May I dance with my own wife?" she looked happy.

But the moment they were alone in their bedroom, she glanced at the clock on the dresser and said, "Not even twelve."

"They had a lovely time, Letty. And we did have two hours of dancing too, didn't we?"

"It was awful. They mixed like oil and water and I hated every minute of it.

"You hated me," he said, and remembered the way Peter Stiles had looked at her.

She flung herself into the process of undressing, not answering, not giving any sign she had heard his three words, not denying them. As the silence extended, he gave up and undressed also.

She went to the bathroom and the small familiar sounds of tooth-powder and toothbrush, of the heavy cold cream jar, the rapid brushing of hair, all came to him but brought him no warmth of intimacy or love. He got into bed and his eyes kept closing. He was not acting; his lids were weary and his heart worn. When she came in and said "Good night," his own "Good night" was muffled and far away. A loneliness and sadness had come to him when he had first insisted on inviting Otto, and though he had had his way, it had been no happy victory. And yet, he had come to where he had to be. Tonight talking with Otto, talking of things that might make for life or death of God knew how many people in God knew how short a time, he had known a terrible rightness that was almost like being happy.

(306)

This is what counts, he had thought repeatedly. This, the truth of life, the fear and reality of it, the blind spinning folly of the powerful, and the meekness of the rest. To see it and to think about what a man has to do, that is what matters.

The rest is vanity. One fools with it and accepts it on a summer day or a snowy evening when the orchestra plays, and nobody is the worse for it. But ultimately one has to set it aside again, a lovely tune, a scarlet ribbon, a glass of wine.

TWENTY-FOUR

Stefan Ivarin was late. The trolley from Barnett had trembled to a stop about three miles short of Cypress Hills, where one changed for the train.

After some minutes of waiting for repairs, passengers began to leave, despite the raw weather outside, but Stefan stifled his disgust and concentrated on the work he had brought with him.

Conjectural work, rather, since he was undecided whether to accept the offer of a small publisher, to translate into Yiddish a little-known Russian novel, *What Is To Be Done?*, from which he often quoted in lectures. He had never translated an entire book and the idea appealed to him as a new hobby. Nobody had translated Tchernyshevsky's work for Jewish readers, and though his fee would be nominal and future royalties problematical, he was tempted by the idea of a prolonged piece of work. It would take over a year, since he would do it in spare time, and there would be a continuity about it that, in these days of surprise and change, might well be soothing.

"All out," the motorman cried, and Stefan called, "No hope?"

The power failure had now affected the entire line, the motorman explained. Everybody could get his nickel back. Stefan frowned and asked how far he'd have to walk.

"Around sixty blocks, mister. Maybe you'll hitch a ride."

The blustery November twilight gave little promise of good samaritans in wagons or automobiles. It was only half past four but it was already nearly dark, and as Ivarin stepped down to the gutter, his mood darkened too. For no reason, he stood beside the trolley, watching the other passengers come out; then he abandoned the car's oblong helplessness and set forth, squinting as the roughening wind nipped at his ears and eyes, turning up the velvet collar of his black overcoat and wishing he had listened to Alexandra about rubbers and gloves. After ten blocks, he paused briefly to rest and thought, Fifty more, best not to count them. The wind began to come at him in uneven sweeps and gusts, and he bent into it, aware of his back grudging the extra effort and strain.

Strain nearly always gave him a backache now, both kinds of strain, physical or mental. He could feel his muscles tighten up if his temper tightened, feel them grow shorter as they pulled together and closed in on themselves, not precisely in knots, but in their entirety, like wool socks shrunk with too-frequent washing, not yet worn through in holes at toe or heel, but tight in their fibers.

He stopped once, to telephone the office, and then trudged on. By now the wind had gained further force, and he wondered what the precise point was at which the weather bureau began to use the term "gale." It was the first bitter weather of the fall. By the time he reached Cypress Hills and sat down in the train, he was shaken with cold and physical weariness and when at last he reached the warmth of his own office, he actually thought of stretching out on the floor for ten minutes to rest.

Just then Joseph Fehler came in, saying he had waited for him, and could he spare a minute now before settling down. "It's something I've been giving a lot of thought to," Fehler said. "It *should* please you."

Ivarin's private semaphor signaled DANGER. "If you have planned something to please me," he said, "let's hear about it. And thanks in advance."

They had both spoken with raised voices. The gales hurling themselves at the windows rattled and shook them in their frames, and Ivarin's "Thanks in advance" was almost a shout. Fehler now looked up at the ceiling as if he hoped for a sign about how to proceed. Then he went to the door and closed it.

"It's not an original idea with me," he said, "and I'm not claiming originality. It's another step in modernization, copying from the *World* and the *Times* and the *Sun* and all of them." Again he gazed at the ceiling.

Stefan Ivarin waited. The sense of danger intensified. He drew out

is cigarette papers and tobacco pouch and sifted tobacco carefully
nto the transparent trough of rice paper. The paper held steady; the
ain of fine brown shreds was even and steady too.

"I want to create," Fehler went on, "a special City Desk, the kind
hey have for the daily flow of the news, the routine stories. It would
be under its own City Editor."

"Not under me, if you please."

"Of course not. You're too valuable." He took a typed sheet from
his pocket, unfolded it and offered it. As Ivarin took it, he remembered the night in February when he had gone in to congratulate
Fehler, and Fehler had handed him the public announcement the staff
would see the next day.

> As with all New York's English-language newspapers, there is
> to be created a City Desk on this paper, responsible for the daily
> flow of the news, under its own City Editor.
>
> The famous editor of the paper, Stefan Ivarin, thus released
> from the routine editing of routine stories, will be sole editor of
> the editorial page, and continue as the paper's illustrious Editor-
> in-Chief.
>
> The new City Editor is Saul Borg.
>
> > Joseph Fehler
> > Publisher
> > 11/10/13

Stefan Ivarin read it twice. Automatically, as always when any
form of manuscript was handed to him, he had picked up his fountain
pen, but he made no move to use it. Unpredictably he suddenly recalled an old man in a skullcap, sidling up to the table in the café
where he was losing a chess game to the violinist from the Metropolitan Opera House. "You have many moves, Mr. Ivarin," the old man
had said, when Feiffel had said "Check" in a quiet voice. Ivarin had
swiftly run over the positions of the pieces, considering the possible
plays still open to him. Useless moves, he had decided, futile, staving
off the inevitable. Pah, that's for children, he had thought, and turned
his king over on its side.

Now he handed the typed sheet back to Fehler and laid his fountain pen down on his desk. He hadn't realized how tightly he had been
holding it, but an emptiness proclaimed itself in his fingers as if he
had let a welcome support slip from his grasp.

"Does Borg know?" he said.

"Only that I am considering it. I wanted to ask your opinion before reaching a decision."

Ivarin looked at him. "And Mrs. Landau? Steinberger?"

"Also on a preliminary level. I saw them, it so happens, the other night for supper."

Ivarin said briskly, "So you came in to tell me of a *fait accompli*." Unceremoniously he stood up and began to pace the floor. He did not look at Fehler as he passed him and there was silence except for the thud of his feet on the linoleum floor. Within his skull, a pulse thudded more importantly; he knew that the fork of veins over the bridge of his nose was rising bluely and he could feel his face inflame.

Pah, that was for children, he had decided that night. Futile moves, childishly delaying the inevitable. A man resigns.

A prima donna leaves the cast, he thought in rebuttal now. A baby throws a tantrum. The matinée idol makes a splendid speech and a noble exit.

Perhaps a man stays.

He stopped in front of Fehler. "So be it," he said. "We'll have a go at it and see." The phrase sounded familiar, but he could not place it.

"That's fine," Fehler said quickly. "Look at this shorter version. I can't decide which one is better."

As with all New York's English-language newspapers, there is to be created a City Desk on this paper, responsible for the daily flow of the news, under its own City Editor. To this post I have appointed Saul Borg.

> Stefan Ivarin
> Editor-in-Chief
> 11/10/13

Ivarin read the signature aloud, on a rising inflection and with a hint of drollery. "A little face-saving?" he asked, but before Fehler could speak he said unequivocally, "Use either version, suit yourself. But my signature cannot be used in either case."

Fehler said, "Since you're his boss, I thought perhaps, coming from you it might—"

Ivarin said nothing, and in a moment Fehler left. At once Ivarin telephoned to Borg and asked him to come in when he could. In a matter of seconds Saul was there, his eyes alight. "Congratulations, Mr. City Editor," Ivarin said, rising to shake hands.

"Thanks, Mr. Ivarin. I can hardly believe it."

"I remember," Ivarin said, "nearly two years ago, I told Landau you were a godsend. You had a lot to learn, I said, but you were a godsend. Oh, yes, it was during the Lawrence strike." Unexpectedly he patted Borg on the shoulder, as if he were a clever and dear child. "You've learned a 'lot' by now, more than a lot. Let's hope you remain a godsend."

"Let's hope."

Almost undiscernible, a change came over Borg as he said the words, the faintest insolence. Ivarin thought, From now on he's his own godsend—that will be quite enough for him. Unknowingly he moved toward the door, as if to usher Borg out, and in a moment the new City Editor departed. Ivarin returned to his desk, permitted himself a few minutes of nothingness, not really thinking, but sitting quiet in a kind of empty stupor.

It's a bad business, he thought then, and returned to his work, driving through it all evening. At about midnight, the gales began to abate, and the infernal racketing of the windows died down. That helped. He had forgotten the three-mile walk which had begun this evening, but he knew he was more tired than usual. On his way out at last, he stopped a few paces from the front door. On the bulletin board, the typed announcement was already thumbtacked in place. His peripheral vision told him it was different from both versions he had seen, and he stopped.

After consultation and discussion with Stefan Ivarin, it is decided to create on this paper a City Desk, to handle the routine flow of the news. This is the universal practice among English-language newspapers, and becomes mandatory with the sharp increase in today's volume of news. The City Editor is to be Saul Borg. He will be responsible to Mr. Ivarin, the paper's illustrious Editor-in-Chief.

It was signed with Fehler's name. That's smoother, Ivarin thought. More unprincipled, since Borg will not be responsible to me in truth, but to you. Nevertheless a more polished bit of craftsmanship.

Editor-in-Chief indeed.

He flung open the front door to the street, thinking, Why, it turns out I've been promoted.

As he approached the house and saw the lighted windows, he thought, The lights are always on now. No matter what time I get home, she's waiting up.

"Is that you?" she called as he unlocked the front door.

(3 1 1)

"I wasn't sleepy," she said.

It's become a ritual, he thought, I hadn't realized it. Always the same words, like a vaudeville turn that's too rehearsed to vary. "Is that you?" "I wasn't sleepy."

"Anything to eat?" he asked.

"In a minute."

"It's good you're still awake," he said. "I feel wide-awake too." He waited only until she had set out two glasses of tea and then he told her.

This time Alexandra took the news badly. She stormed and railed, her voice breaking and her eyes filled. But when he said his first impulse had been to resign, she cried out, "Run with your tail between your legs? Leave it all to Fehler, give him a free hand? Of course not!"

He did not answer. Only on the long way home did he remember that the first mortgage payment of 1914 would fall due in a few weeks; he was glad this doleful fact had not intruded itself during his first shock about Fehler's news.

With each hour, the shock grew stronger. A shock was what it was, the second shock he had had to absorb this year, just as he had had to extend congratulations a second time with some show of grace he did not feel. Not that Borg mattered much one way or the other. He was to be Fehler's tool, that was the surly part of it, but Borg himself did not count. Fehler did, and now Fehler was more than ever the victor. The arena at last had a name.

"Modernization, Fehler calls it," he said. "Everything goes by the innocent name of 'modernization.' Whatever he does in the future—that too will be called 'modernizing.' Or Americanizing. I call it Fehlerizing. Maybe I should have walked out after all."

Again she cried out in protest. "And let him lord it over those poor devils who can't fight back, like Abe? Please, don't consider it, please, never."

"It's quite a lot of dancing on the point of a needle," he said, speaking more to himself than to her. "To stay or not to stay," he said mockingly. "That is the question. To quit and call it honor, or quit and call it pique. To stay and call it maturity, or stay and call it expediency. How's a man to know?"

As he was speaking, a blackness seized him, weighted and blind, and he went upstairs. In his room he slammed the door with a ferocity he had been able to stave off for months. Leaning against the door, he put both his fists hard to his throat, his knuckles ridging into his jawbone, his shoulders rising and hunching forward as if to fuse with his stiffened thumbs.

The damnable conflict. He would live with it, sleep with it, work with it, write with it, try to ignore it, try to face it, try to solve it. But there was only one way to solve it.

If he had no children, no wife, no installment on the mortgage, there would be only one way to solve it and one time to solve it. Now. A letter written now, mailed now, sent on its way this night.

Then what? He was fifty-two and editor of a great paper, of what still was a great paper underneath its whore's paint and powder. The only other paper with a large following was the *Forward,* and to him it already was so far from the kind of paper he could be proud to work for that he could not walk through its front door in a hope of finding the next chapter of his life there. There the barter of almost anything he believed in had already been made for the painted beads of success.

There was no place he wanted except his own place, editor of the paper he had given twenty-two years to and had always counted on giving the rest of his life to, the core of himself for whatever years there still were to be.

Fee didn't care whether her father was in a mood or not. She kept out of his way and tried to keep out of her mother's way too, because no matter what was wrong with them, she couldn't help it. Not now, not when she was so happy she could scarcely breathe.

She was in love. Anne Miller's brother had come to church with them at Thanksgiving, and he took the hymnal out of the rack and handed it to her, and her heart rang out the way the bells did when they began to peal. He was fifteen and his name was John and he wouldn't let anybody call him Jack.

"Does anybody call John D. Rockefeller 'Jack D.'?" he demanded when she asked him why, and she had to laugh at the sort of fresh way he said it. But that wasn't what made her fall in love with him; she was already in love before she had the nerve to ask personal things like that.

It wasn't anything all by itself anyway; it happened when he handed her the hymnal that first time, and then it kept on, and then one day when they were walking home from Grace Episcopal, with his mother and Anne separated from them to cross the street, he suddenly said, "If you meet me at Gray's, I'll treat you to a frappe."

"When?"

"Right after I get home and get out of this Sunday suit. Can you?"

(3 1 3)

"I don't even have to go home first," she said. "I could go right now."

"If we went right now, guess who we'd be stuck with," he said grimly, and she felt idiotic to have to be reminded of his mother and Anne.

Feeling idiotic was so wonderful. She always felt smarter than anybody she was with, and to feel the opposite was strange and new and glorious. John made her feel absolutely tiny, too; he was a long stringbeany boy and next to him nobody could be scared about turning into an Amazon. Ever since she fell in love, she had stopped measuring how wide her shoulders were, and the only thing left to worry her was not seeming too smart for a girl. Lots of times, instead of doing her homework, she'd just read a book from the libe, to make sure she'd stop getting the best marks in her whole class.

John was a sophomore and wouldn't be able to keep track of her grades, but things got around in the most mysterious way. Trudy was one way. Ever since they had stopped being best friends, Trudy began to say things about her, and somebody would always tell either Juanita or Anne, and then Juanita or Anne would feel it a sacred honor not to keep her in the dark. That was how she knew Trudy had gone around telling everybody in Barnett High about the black bunting all over the front porch and how Miss King asked if Shag had died and were they socialists. That time she was so furious at Trudy, she told Juanita and Anne about Trudy's father getting slobbery drunk on beer every single night and falling half off his chair and how her mother and brother Carl had to heave him and lug him and pull at him to make him get up and be carted off to bed, with the two of them pulling his clothes off for him.

But she only did it that one time. It made her go icky afterwards, and she hated Trudy for making it happen. She never mentioned drunk Mr. Loheim any more, but if anybody made fun of Trudy's thick ankles, she felt glad.

She took a vow not to risk having John Miller hear gossip about her being smarter than any girl in the freshman class, and the surest way was to stop being it. She didn't do her homework half the time; she didn't study her German vocab the way she used to, and she couldn't write some of the new words out on the blackboard when Dr. Wohl called on her. A couple of times he struck his forehead with his palm and said, *"Fräulein Fira, was ist los?"*

She still got B and B-plus in everything, but no A's, and John stopped calling her too smart for a girl, and it was lovely. Once he called her "Skinny," though, and she almost came right out and begged him not to tease her about being too thin and flat.

"That's what *you* think," she said instead, and some sort of miracle must have been wrapped up in the words.

"What does that mean?" John asked, blushing down to his collar.

He looked straight at her chest and automatically she caved herself in, as if she *had* started to have a shape and wanted to hide it from him. He took both her shoulders, trying to force her to un-cave, but she wriggled free and hunched herself up again, thanking her lucky stars for her heavy winter coat and laughing at him. The beet-juicy color of his face and neck, and the way he kept glancing sideways at her as they walked up the hill, and the way his books kept touching her books as if books could have a crush on each other—it was the most thrilling heavenly moment of her life.

When she got home and had to go in, she hid just inside the window of her mother's sewing room, so she could watch him walk up to Channing before he had to turn. She wanted to tell Anne about it, and Fran, but telling it to anybody would be like tearing a wonderful book in two and giving half of it away.

"Then resign," Alexandra cried. "If life is one long misery because of it, what good is it to stay there?"

" 'Resign and leave it all to him?' " he said, mimicking her voice of a week ago. " 'Let Fehler lord it over those poor devils who can't fight back'—you seem to have changed remarkably since you begged me to stick it out."

"But nobody dreamed how it would be. Now I'd rather starve—"

"For God's sake stop bawling." He banged his fist on the table, once, twice, a third time. Alexandra ran out of the room, and still he banged the table. He knew Fira and Francesca were near enough to hear, but he could not stop. He had been in this hellish depression since the night Fehler had carved out half his territory and handed it over to Borg, since the night he had forced himself *not* to resign.

Now she was nagging at him as if she alone had principles. Day after day he felt hammered at, enraged that he should have no shelter from the incessant attack upon his nerves. At the office his blood was whipped to a froth; at home his nerves were twanged and plucked until he felt himself at the edge of breakdown.

"I'd rather starve." It was a recurrent refrain, like a line in a rag-time song. Whenever he forced himself to smash through his black prison and talk to her, she said it—but wept buckets of her damnable tears if he talked not at all. "You'd rather starve," he answered once, "but what about the children?"

"Let them starve too," she cried.

"Do you know how long our savings would last?"

"I'd rather scrub floors in City Hall than have you stay at a paper you despise."

He could not tolerate her moralizing. He left the house earlier each day; that act lengthened the hours he spent at the office. No knout had ever had this backlash.

By the end of Borg's first week, at least six front-page stories offended Ivarin. The worst was one he would have given no more than a stick or two on an inside page; it appeared as a four-column screamer with two large pictures.

CIRCUS FAT MAN
ASSAULTS
GIRL OF 12

The man weighed over three hundred pounds; the very notion of this creature in the act of sex—

I will vomit, Ivarin thought. Up until now it's been only the look of the paper that they have raped. Now it's the essence.

No, the essence is still the editorial page.

"Borg," he said abruptly, flinging open the door to Borg's new office, and flinging the wet proof on his desk, "this lechery doesn't go in."

"But Mr. Ivarin—"

"You are responsible to me. It is part of my responsibility not to permit this trash." His finger flicked across the headline with such vigor, the flimsy paper tore.

Borg again started to speak. Instead he picked up a black crayon, held it poised in the air and then printed at the side of the proof.

CIRCUS FAT MAN
CHARGED
WITH ASSAULT

"Would this be better?" Borg asked. His tone was not as conciliatory as his action.

"At least the nastiness is delayed," Ivarin said, and left as abruptly as he had entered.

By the end of the week, the circulation jump was two thousand a day.

(3 1 6)

The second week of Borg's new glory brought new clashes, and the third week imitated it. At the end of his first month as City Editor, Ivarin sent a note to him, with a copy to Fehler.

"Borg—you may think yourself responsible to me as per the bulletin board, but from now on I am not responsible for you. Henceforth, you are to check all news stories with Mr. Fehler."

He's been doing it all along, Ivarin thought in a sweep of clarity. Had Fehler come right out and told him to? "Never mind Ivarin's objections, this is what we want. He'll get over it sooner or later."

They've left me my one page, but they pour their filth on every other. They keep their paws off what I say, but I am standing on a platform of dung to speak from. In the end, what kind of audience will gather around a platform of dung?

By mid-December the daily jump was at four thousand, and by the close of the year, it was close to five thousand. In the nineties, Ivarin thought as the whistles and horns of New Year's Eve died down below his office window, when Hearst hired Brisbane away from the *World,* the *Journal* shot from forty thousand a day to quarter of a million in a few months—is Fehler dreaming of grandiose achievements like that?

He reached into his inside pocket and drew out the little oblong wafer that was his savings book at the Barnett Bank and Trust. He had taken to carrying it around with him; he was never sure when the mood would strike him to recalculate their general financial situation. Once it had been in the subway coming home, and he fumed because he hadn't the book at hand. Not that he didn't know precisely the fourteen hundred and sixty dollars recorded there, but it had long been ritualistic to open up the little bankbook whenever he had to plan for future expenses or change the family budget. Not too bad a sum, over and above the amount they had saved for buying their piece of ground and building their own house. The first entry in the bankbook was 1902, when they had moved away from New York to make Barnett their home for life.

For life? If he could no longer earn his living as an editor? He could get lectures, he could give private lessons again, he could write articles for other papers and magazines, in Yiddish, in Russian, in English. Through Evan Paige and the Free Speech League his work was now known to twenty socialist papers in the nation, and if he told Evan that it had become a question of writing articles for those out-of-town dailies and weeklies to augment what he could earn in New York, then Evan would turn himself inside out to arrange it.

Exactly $1460. Allowing for coal and gas and light, for the three interest payments after this one in January, they could still draw out fifteen to twenty dollars a week for food for over a year. They need not starve, not for a year, not through all of 1914, even if disaster struck him down so he could not earn a penny for those twelve months. In fact, one of these days, merely as a precautionary measure, he might line up a private lesson or two in English to foreigners, just as an experiment in regaining his touch.

It had been twenty-five years since he had given lessons. But he had earned extra money as a teacher when he was a young man, and he could earn extra money as a teacher again, now that he was getting old.

The moment came sullenly, as everything at the paper did now. Some days later, Fehler asked him into his office; they were alone there, and Fehler said, "I do not expect you to be too happy with this."

Ivarin thought, I knew it would come. It's almost a relief.

"But the facts," Fehler went on, "force us to experiment with the one page we thought should be left as is."

"The editorial page," Ivarin stated, as if in warning. Fehler did not acknowledge the three words; he aligned several pencils at the edge of his desk blotter, and placed his telephone carefully back on a round felt pad tailored to fit its base.

"The editorial page," Ivarin repeated, "may be experimented with only in type face, arrangement, appearance. Not in any other way. You follow me?"

Fehler looked up. "There is such a trend to short lively editorials, in short lively jabs of phrases. Like Arthur Brisbane."

"I am unlike Mr. Brisbane."

"No sane man," Fehler said, "would ask you to change your style. We only wanted to ask—" He lowered his gaze to his table. "—That is, Mrs. Landau and her lawyer and I, we would like to ask you, as a matter of providing the space, to write only two editorials a week for the time being. At the same salary, it goes without saying."

"It goes without saying that I refuse."

He spoke without heat. For a moment the two men gazed at each other and then Ivarin started for the door. Behind him Fehler said urgently, "Don't decide yet. This needs discussion. It is too serious."

"It is a farce. I am through."

He walked out slowly. In his own office was the smudged proof of an editorial he had just written denouncing the rising call for compulsory military service in the United States. Automatically, he began to read it through, uncapping his pen at the same time. After one sentence he stopped, dropped the galley on his desk, rolled up his eyeshade and eased it into his pocket. He opened the drawers of his desk rapidly, but took nothing from them. Then he walked over to the coat rack in the corner and lifted down his things, stomping into his overshoes but carrying his coat and hat. He clicked off the light switch at the doorjamb and his office went dark. He felt the darkness as if something had hit him. It was not yet seven o'clock.

He did not wait for the elevator to achieve its deliberate climb from the press rooms in the basement, but started slowly down the stairs. On the main floor, he paused briefly at the bulletin board, staring at it absently while he put on his hat and buttoned up his coat. There was nothing new there.

Then he walked swiftly out of the building.

TWENTY-FIVE

"I have something to tell you," Alexandra said the next morning when Fran and Fee were done with breakfast. "It isn't very happy."

Fran said, "What isn't?" but Fee asked quickly, "Is it about Papa?"

"It's about all of us," Alexandra said. "We must all stick together now, no matter how hard it may be."

"Whatever happened to him, I don't wonder," Fran said resentfully. "He's been in a bad mood for a hundred years."

"You're heartless," Alexandra cried out. "You never did try to understand him or think that he suffers too when he's in a mood. And now that this terrible thing happened—"

She bowed her head and closed her eyes. Fee looked at her grey curly hair parted in the middle, pulled down tight into the two braids Mama always went to bed with; this time the part was jagged and uneven, as if her hand shook when she drew the comb down the middle of her scalp.

(319)

"Did you have a fight with Papa?" she whispered.

"Oh no, darling, no." Alexandra raised her head and said, "In fact last night was the first night in I don't know how long when we agreed about everything, because at last he did something we both think is right."

"Did he have a fight with Fehler?" Fran asked.

"This time there was no fight," Alexandra said proudly. "Fehler suggested one final indignity and Papa said no and resigned."

"Is he out of work?" Fee asked.

"When did it happen?" Fran added.

"Yesterday. There was one more change Fehler suggested, but by now Papa knows that each time he gives in, something new develops a few weeks later. Last night was the end. He left for good."

"Can he be an editor of anything else?" Fran asked.

Alexandra did not seem to hear it. "If you both knew," she said, "what torment Papa has been through, for months now, trying to decide. But at last he knew he could not face himself another day, so he did it."

"Are we going to be poor?" Fee asked.

"Oh, my poor child, of course not. Papa will get lectures, and he'll teach again, and write for all kinds of magazines and papers. You'll see. And of course, I'll get a few more lessons too."

"Gee," Fran said. "No wonder he's been in a mood."

"At last," Alexandra said sternly. "At last you are able to think that maybe he has a reason, and isn't simply a bad father. He *always* has a reason. I've told you a thousand times, it's like a killing disease that swoops into him—can a man's children hate him, because he has a terrible sickness?"

"Do editors ever go on a bread line?" Fee asked in a small voice.

"Never, darling," Alexandra said, getting up from her chair and going over to Fee. "A brilliant man like Papa, a famous man, why he'll have more lectures than he can fit into a schedule. The A. F. of L. keeps begging him to give some lectures, ever since the Lawrence strike, they've said a hundred times he's the most effective lecturer they ever found. And they will pay him ten dollars for an hour's talk, even for a shorter one. And the Socialist Party will too."

"If he gave only one a night," Fran said hopefully.

"Lectures aren't like that, one a night on a regular calendar, like clockwork. But when a strike is looming, or when they want to organize a new union, like all the times Papa went to Scranton and Wilkes-Barre or out to Milwaukee, why then, he'll have more lectures than you can imagine."

"That's good," Fee said, expelling a large breath. "Gosh, having your father out of work."

At first Stefan went to New York every night. To stay at home would quickly demoralize him, he said; it was better to follow his ingrained routine of walking down the hill, taking the trolley and then the train, reaching the city and spending the first half of the night there.

By the end of the first week, he had lined up two pupils, at the now generally accepted higher rate of fifty cents an hour, and two paid lectures, one to be given before the month was out, the second in February. He had discussed an article in English with the *Call* on the growing viciousness of the fuel and iron workers' long strike in Colorado; there had already been shootings and deaths and he would write his reasons for saying it was headed for historic proportions and historic bloodletting. The *Call* could not pay more than a few dollars, but they were "eager to see a piece by Stefan Ivarin."

It was hopeful, he told Alexandra. He even had "headquarters" in New York for giving his lessons or for any appointment that might come up. Abe Kesselbaum had instantly offered the parlor of his tenement flat on Essex Street for as many evenings as Ivarin would honor him by using it.

"The news about you flew from one man to the next," Abe said the first time they met after Ivarin had left. "Like when Landau died. Everybody is uneasy, scared of his job again, asking what's next. They think Borg is too stuck on himself, and Fehler, you know what they think of Fehler."

"Who's writing the editorials? Bunzig's style is easy to spot, so I know he's done some of them, and I think Kinchevsky has filled in on several. Has there been any decision yet about a new editor?"

"Not that anybody knows of." Fehler was interviewing men almost daily, without apparent success thus far. Abe sounded despondent; he was getting along well enough with his new boss; he had schooled himself in masking his real feelings, but with Ivarin off the paper, he knew that his own chance for regaining a higher status had gone forever.

"Life changes," Ivarin comforted him, more out of desire to comfort than out of conviction. "Even on newspapers, it sometimes changes for the better. You are still young, Abe."

Still young, Ivarin thought, lucky the man who wears the description. He himself was no longer able to. And yet? A burst of young energy had erupted in him; there was an excitement he had not expected in telephoning people in the newspaper world or the labor movement, and saying, more or less abruptly according to impulse, "This is Ivarin, I've just quit the *Jewish News,* and I would like to talk to you."

Not yet old, he thought. That's the phrase for me. "Still young" would be whistling in the dark, but not yet old is quite the thing. Apart from the flare-up of his lumbago, which had remained high and fairly constant since his enforced three-mile walk against stiff winds a month ago—only a month?—he actually felt in better shape than he had since the sweltering day last summer when the first "little test period" began.

In better shape emotionally, too. To be active was always a cure for him, to start a new project, begin a new series, even line up appointments and lectures and lessons. The despair that was born in that July meeting half a year back, had vanished like a puff of oily smoke. Occasionally an ache for the office seized his heart, irrational and inconsolable, like the longing for the dead, but time would ease that, he knew. He wrote his article on the Colorado strike with ease and authority, and sent it off, thinking, They'll surely take it. The thought unexpectedly jarred him. To hang on another editor's decision about a piece he had written? To write "on speculation"?

I'm boggling over phrases, he thought, feeling disgraced at being a free-lance writer, as if all writers were not exactly that.

You never were a free-lance writer, came the instant rebuttal. You never had to calculate some editor's probable acceptance of what you wrote. You wrote because you *were* the editor.

He thundered at himself not to be a debating society. Then he turned his full attention to the translation he had already begun of Tchernyshevsky's novel. He had not liked the fee of only a hundred dollars, in ten monthly payments, but he regarded the undertaking as a lucky piece of timing. He had to keep busy. If he was idle for only a few hours, anxiety and foreboding seized him. Already there had been minor disappointments with several of his evenings in New York; when his lessons were over and he had nobody to see, he would go back to the café, hoping for a hard game of chess or some good talk with an old crony. But that too had a tendency to demoralize him; in the café he could almost feel the throb and thump of the presses next door.

At the end of his first month off the paper he had earned $38, ten from the lecture, ten from the *Call,* ten from his translation advance, and the rest from his two pupils. But further encouragement came just then. He had had some cards printed cheaply, announcing that he was available for English lessons to those speaking Russian, Yiddish, French, German, or Polish, and the owner of the stationery and newspaper store in Barnett, who had seen years of service in the men's coat trades, and knew all about Ivarin, perched it right beside the cash register. With barely suppressed triumph, the old dealer sent him two pupils within the next five days, and boasted that he would undoubtedly send along two more. The only snag was that these two would have to take their lessons right in Barnett, after coming home from work at night.

"It can't be helped," Stefan said to Alexandra. "If they lived in New York it would have been better, but they don't." And he added slowly, "Anyway, to go to New York religiously every night, and perhaps just sit around there—it's none too cheerful when it happens. I may as well stay home and give some lessons."

She knew it was none too cheerful. How could it be? A phantom New York.

Fee stood still, watching. Even though she knew about it in advance and hadn't thought it was going to be anything, it was awful. Seeing him there at the kitchen table with a pupil, not Mama but *him,* was the most unexpected sight. Her own father giving a lesson—it was so sad, she felt like crying. She knew he used to teach when he was young, but that was in a real school. Not *this,* doing what Mama always did.

Side by side, at the kitchen table, so pupil and teacher could see the exercise book at the same time, her father and a man who was already pretty old were leaning forward while her father corrected what was written on the page. She could not understand a word because they were talking in Yiddish, but her whole life had gone by to the accompaniment of lessons. The mistake in the exercise book, the pause for explanation, the correction put down by the teacher above the writing of the pupil, the pupil's nod or further-question-and-then-nod, the united moving ahead to the next word or line or page.

But to have her father doing it was just terrible.

She didn't want him to look around and catch her watching him; on tiptoe she went up the stairs one at a time. Fran was out and Fee hoped she would stay out until the lessons were over, so Franny wouldn't see him and get going about it. Fee didn't want to say a word about Papa giving a lesson. It was not only sad, it was sort of a disgrace.

(323)

Did people his age ever get blue or unhappy the way you did when you were young? Last week John Miller didn't even look at her in the cafeteria at lunchtime, and she stayed blue and unhappy all afternoon. He had been there with the whole sophomore basketball team, and she kept telling herself it was natural for him not to look over even once, but it did no good. Nothing stopped the dragging blueness, and it was the first time in her whole life she had ever experienced anything so thick and sad.

Could her father and mother feel that way, at their age? The idea had never occurred to her, but now she couldn't stop it. She could still see him sitting there, stiff and ramroddy, talking in that special teacher-explaining voice to a pupil who was almost as old as he was.

She threw herself face down on her bed. Her throat felt as if a cord was knotted around her Adam's apple.

Eli wouldn't come out to talk to him about it. "He'll just get into a shouting match over something if I do," he said to his mother on the telephone. "He can't accept sympathy from anybody any more than he can accept an idea from anybody."

"You're heartless," Alexandra said. "You seem not to care what happens to him."

"He'll get another job. 'The great Stefan Ivarin.' "

"Sarcasm comes easy now," she said. "Are you trying to get even with him?" Her wretchedness at his refusal to come to Barnett for an evening was growing worse. Every few days she suggested it to him or to Joan, to take the trip and "cheer Pa up," but he was adamant. In some dark unknown way, Eli seemed glad that his father had come upon evil days. But Eli could never be so nasty, so spiteful, she thought. He was still a boy, unable to feel what his father was going through, how brave Stefan was being, how determined to make a new life without self-pity.

"Try to come soon," she said now.

"It's no use, Ma. I'd get riled as hell and then start another attack of this damn asthma."

"Have you had another attack?" she asked in alarm.

"I'm over it."

"Was it one of the terrible ones?"

"It's over," he said. "You know how I hate to talk about it when it's over."

"Did they inject adrenalin?"

"They do that more often now. But that's nothing to worry about, no kidding." His voice and his manner softened, as if he were not bereft of consideration for how parents could feel. Don't depend too much, she thought, on any child for acts of kindness. They probably meant them; she must not be too easily hurt. It was one of her greatest faults.

She hung up, absolving Eli. Hours later, she suddenly thought, He didn't even offer to help with a few dollars. Not that they would have accepted. They had both sworn never to be dependent upon their children for support, and even this calamity could not make them crumple up and forget that vow. They were at the start of making a new life; Stefan was like a young man starting out to make a career.

But Eli should have offered. It would be a sweet thing to hear your son offer to stand by you when you were in need.

"That was Mrs. Vladinski," Alexandra said to Fran and Fee exultantly one morning as she came back from the telephone. "You know, the pretty young Russian woman at the beach last summer."

"Sonya Nikholovna," Fran said knowingly. "She only talks Russian."

"Sonya Mikhailovna," her mother corrected. "That's right, and you'll never believe why she called me." She sounded so cheerful and bouncy that both girls were as interested as if she were one of their friends instead of their mother.

"I've been feeling in my bones that something good would happen soon," Alexandra said. "This may be the start of it."

"What may?" Fee exploded.

"She wants me to go to New York twice a week to give her the private lecture at *her* house, a dollar each time."

"Gee." Fran looked at her mother with new respect.

"Her husband is doing very well," Alexandra went on, "and she has nobody to leave with her children, so she can't come out here, and she realizes she has stopped learning about bringing them up, and all the other things she was getting from me and can't get from anybody else."

Fran saw "the conceited look" settle over her mother's face, but she forgave her. "Will you like going to New York twice a week?" she asked.

"A big change is what it will be. I'll go right after breakfast, Mondays and Thursdays. It's all arranged, even the days."

(325)

"Will Papa like it?" Fee asked.

Alexandra looked upward toward his room. "I wish he'd come down, so I can tell him. He'll be as delighted as I am."

But some of the elation left her face as she said it, and Fee wondered if this was sad too. Mama sounded so jolly, but was there a hiding place inside the jolly for being sad?

"One new thing like this with Sonya," Alexandra said, "and I feel sure about everything again."

When the girls left, the sureness grew. She waited impatiently for Stiva to appear. He was sleeping lightly these days, and getting up at unheard-of hours; sometimes he could be heard moving about while the girls were still at home, though he never came down until they were off for school.

"Stiva, I have a nice little surprise," she greeted him, and even before he had his coffee, she tumbled out her news.

"It is a surprise," he said. "Twice a week, a dollar each time!"

His voice warmed her. "Something could grow from this," she said. "I don't know why I never thought of it before except at the beach."

"You may be right," he said. "It is a new kind of instruction, and there is a need for it."

"Maybe I could gather a little group in New York, for the same kind of evenings. But now there would be a charge, a few pennies from each one."

"I don't see why not," he said. "They flock to you in that tent city."

"Why should it only be the beach in summer?"

He looked cautiously at her. "The beach in summer?"

"Not this summer," she said quickly. "I haven't given this summer a thought."

"We better face it ahead of time," he said. "Fran and Fee better face it also." He had been looking for an opportunity to get in an early warning that there could be no luxuries this year. Nevertheless when he finished his warning, he wished he had not chosen this moment of Alexandra's triumph to raise the subject.

"It's a nice little surprise, all right," he repeated with enthusiasm, to make up for his lapse. "Monday and Thursday, one dollar each time." He asked for more coffee and then suddenly added, "It's good news for us right now. You're a good girl."

Anna Godleberg closed her copybook and English Grammar. Then, with the swift embarrassed gesture she had never been able to overcome, she darted her hand into the pocket of her skirt, slipped out a twenty-five-cent piece and laid it on the table, pushing it close to the saltcellar and sugar bowl. She never yet had managed to hand it directly to Mrs. Ivarin.

Alexandra watched the familiar motions. She had long since given up any hope of changing her pupil in this respect. At the beginning, she had spoken to her about it matter-of-factly, as if Mrs. Godleberg were stumbling over a diphthong, or forgetting to purse her lips to produce a W that would vary from a V. But now after nearly three years of weekly lessons, lessons which had wrought heart-warming changes in Mrs. Godleberg's reading, writing, and speaking of English—by now Alexandra Ivarin herself was vaguely uneasy at the appearance of the quarter and glad when the ritual of payment was over.

"The teacher vanquished by the pupil," she had remarked philosophically to Stefan one night. It was not her fault if Mrs. Godleberg who could learn so much, could not manage this, too.

But in the weeks since Stefan had left the paper, Mrs. Godleberg's embarrassment had grown more acute, and tonight it was tinged with an agitation so noticeable that Alexandra was upset. It's because she knows I really need it now, she thought, and for a moment she was suffused with longing *not* to need it, for Anna Godleberg's sake as well as for her own.

"Don't worry about us," Alexandra said, removing the coin from its hiding place by the sugar bowl. "We are so fortunate anyway."

"Oh, I know, yes, my husband told me about Mr. Ivarin's lecture last month, and about giving his own lessons; I know he has a thousand different ways to earn a living without that accursed paper."

Her face was moist with effort, and Alexandra said, "There's even one more way for me—perhaps you could help me with it."

"Me? I'd die of being proud."

Alexandra told her of Sonya's phone call. "Maybe you could start up a little group in New York," she said. "Perhaps Sophie would help you."

"I'll see Sophie, I'll see everybody." Anna Godleberg sprang to her feet in excitement. "Even people who have never been at the beach know about your little lectures. It will be such a success, you'll see, Mrs. Ivarin."

"It would make me happy," Alexandra said. "Will you really try to round up a few of the women? It would be the biggest favor."

"A minute is all it will take me. You can't believe how we've worried already, some of us, about losing our evenings in the tent this summer—" She looked ill at ease again over this revelation that they had jumped straight to the financial meanings of Ivarin's disappearance from the *Jewish News*.

"I shouldn't have said it. Excuse me. It's none of my business, what is to happen with your summer. If you took me for a common gossip—"

She strapped her books together with the schoolgirl bookstrap she always used, shellacked canvas with a brass tip to keep it from raveling.

"It can't be common gossip," Alexandra said, "with so much kindness in it. Gossip is always cruel."

It was one of the days when Stefan Ivarin would not be going into the city; he would be at home teaching instead. He had begun to dislike these evenings, though he resolved not to question them. He was at work on another article in English, this one on the outcry from all organized labor at the news that Henry Ford would pay every one of his workers a five-dollar wage per day. Ford said he wanted to share some ten millions of his 1914 profits with his thirty thousand workingmen, as a matter of good will. "Good will" indeed. It was an outrageous sop to labor, a bribe, a handout, yet half the world took it as an unheard-of magnanimity.

The article was giving Ivarin trouble. Was there another side to this, other plateaus of economic truth, that needed further exploring and further thinking through?

Even the classic problems of capital and labor could suddenly shoot off into new complexities. A five-dollar minimum, not won by the workers themselves, but handed out like a slice of birthday cake. To hail it as manna from heaven was craven, but to expose the interior treachery of so disarming a move would need an extended analysis he had not yet been able to achieve. Nor had anybody else in the field of labor. He could not write his piece yet; it would be premature.

It was a bad feeling always, to be balked when he sat down to write. It seemed to happen more often now. That other editor, waiting somewhere to pass on his work, to accept or reject, loomed larger; the habit of half a lifetime was not so easily filed away in the cabinet of necessity.

He rolled a cigarette, lighted it and drew sharp smoke deep and hard into his lungs. A paroxysm of coughing seized him and he was helpless, waiting for it to subside. It did not, and suddenly it was as

(328)

though a hot sword stabbed through his back, low and to the right of his spine, forcing a cry of pain from him. From another room Alexandra called, "What is it?" and came running down the hall. Both his hands flew to the small of his back, his pen splashing ink on his old grey smoking jacket, making two ragged blotches low in the center, like knobby vertebrae suddenly exposed.

"Stiva, what happened to you?"

He clutched his body as if hands and back had hardened into a single unit. His head was thrust forward, his mouth distorted with effort. He saw Alexandra's stricken face, and he grunted "Soon," but he made no move to return to a normal position. The muscles of his neck stood out like cables curving outward on a suspension bridge, visible from his earlobes to his shoulder blades, and when she said, "Is it more than your lumbago?" he could not answer.

Lumbago. It could mean a hundred different things, from a nagging ache to something like this. He tried to lean forward and again the hot iron shot through to his spine. "This is worse than any other," he said. He moved his hands an inch away from his stiffened body, to see if he could manage without their encircling support, without his thumbs pressed inward like grappling hooks on his hipbones, as if to hold them together. He could not manage; with another cry of pain he locked his hands into position again.

"I'll call a doctor," Alexandra said.

"No, wait."

"We must get somebody," she said. "It's frightening."

"Wait."

She moved toward him as if to help him, but he shook his head and said, "Not yet." He still sat rigid as a rock, a man carved from granite, but he said, "My pen," and loosened his fingers so that she could take it away from him.

He began to move his right foot backward, flexing his knee and trying to rise. Inch by inch he moved forward to the edge of his chair and his face went white with the effort of it.

She thought of Landau's heart attack and her own heart contracted. "Joan's father, Dr. Martin. He can come quickly."

He nodded but she was afraid to leave him until he was lying down. He was clear of the chair now, still bent and angled forward, unable to straighten up. Had he broken his spine? Was it possible to deal oneself the blow of death itself? Please, she thought, please.

Stefan was nearing his narrow bed. She stripped the blankets and top sheet down with one sweep of her hand. Then she moved out of the way because he said, "It's safer if I do it alone."

He lowered himself to the edge of the bed and then with one final spurt of decision fell over sidewise, still doubled over as if his knees were lashed by wires to the upper part of his body.

She covered him as he was, with his clothes on, with his shoes on. His face and throat had gone wet, and she ran to the bathroom, moistened a towel, and came back to bathe away this visible look of pain. His eyeglasses were still on and she lifted them away.

"I'll call him, Stiva," she whispered. "Later, we can call Alexis, if it looks necessary." She ran downstairs. Dr. Martin was out on calls, but would telephone her the moment he returned. She was too terrified to wait, and called Alexis, in New York. He was the Alexis Michelovsky who had refused her a maternity girdle but he was far more than a "woman's doctor," and though he was now over seventy, he was as active as an interne in his beloved medicine.

"It sounds like a jarred vertebra or a squeezed nerve," he said when she finished. "It can be agony. He needs sedation, maybe morphia, as soon as your Dr. Martin gets there. I can start out in an hour—the office is full of patients—but that would be two hours before I could see Stiva."

"Is there any danger?" she asked. "Tell me the truth."

"I'm only guessing, but with his history of back trouble, I can hope not."

"But what caused it? It's as if he's paralyzed."

"It can start when you pick up a match. But diagnosis on a telephone is impossible."

"Then I better hang up. Dr. Martin may be getting a busy while I talk."

"Alexandra," he said authoritatively. "Explain how it happens that another doctor presumed to suggest morphia, or Dr. Martin will be offended. There is a protocol in these matters. Tell him I'll be there at four."

As she held down the pronged hook, the telephone bell rang and she jumped. "Oh, Dr. Martin, please, could you come right away?" Again she told what had happened, and why she had called their old doctor in New York.

"I'll be there in ten minutes," Webster Martin said. "Try not to worry, Mrs. Ivarin."

"He's never sick, never. I've never seen him this way."

She sat down for a moment after the call ended. Fear ran through her, that this might be real disease announcing itself in another guise.

Please, she thought again. He's had enough to bear already.

. . .

"Tell me the truth," Alexandra said once more as soon as she and Webster Martin were alone. And she repeated it again to Alexis in the late afternoon.

"He has high blood pressure," each doctor said. "Not an immediate danger, but serious."

He would have to live a different life, Dr. Martin said. There was a certain hardening of the arteries, not unexpected in a man nearly fifty-three, and not dangerous if he would follow orders to the letter. The acute attack in his lower back was almost inevitable, what with his long-neglected "back condition," too chronic to be dubbed a simple lumbago any longer, and badly aggravated by his three-mile walk against heavy winds. Morphine and then lesser drugs, plus total immobility, would heal the inflamed areas to a marked degree in perhaps a week, when he could be measured for a made-to-order supporting belt or harness, but it would be out of the question for him to travel by trolley and train for a much longer period. As to the regimen of special diet and the like, to bring down the blood pressure, he would like to discuss it first with Dr. Michelovsky because Mr. Ivarin might feel more inclined to obey unwelcome orders from a lifelong friend.

Mr. Ivarin, Alexandra thought fleetingly. Even in this awful time of sickness, it stays Mr. Ivarin and Mrs. Ivarin. And I call him Dr. Martin. How can we remain so distant, so formal, when our children are married, when we are all grandparents of Webby and Sandra?

Resentment at Dr. Martin mingled with her gratitude for his speed in coming and for the thoroughness of his examination, but it was not until Alexis came and saw Stiva that she felt safe again. He reinforced everything Dr. Martin had said, and since Stiva was deeply under the injected drug, wrote out a series of instructions for her to give him, when he could understand them. For five days, he was not to be propped up in bed, even to read or eat; he was not to get up, not even to walk to the bathroom. If he disobeyed, it could end in his being moved in an ambulance to a hospital, perhaps to be "clinically immobilized" in spinal traction. This was not stated as a threat, merely as information.

Unequivocal pain made Stefan obedient. Even to shift his position in bed was out of the question when the drugs thinned down. He read Alexis' orders without interest; Alexandra held the prescription blank straight above him, and he read upward. He ate so little of what she tried to feed him that he never suspected the absence of salt or red meat nor the weakness of his morning sips of coffee. His lessons had to be postponed, his February lecture canceled, and he seemed not to care. He lay in a torpor hour upon hour; Alexandra was glad both doctors had ordered her to say nothing about his high blood pressure, for she could not have dealt him further pain.

After five days, they were both there in consultation. When they told him and talked of "mild arteriosclerosis," he said listlessly, "A synonym for getting old, isn't it?" To Michelovsky he added, "You found my blood pressure high that time, when was it? Since then, over and over, I've been warned, 'Your face is getting red.' It's an old story."

But hardening of the arteries, they told him, was a progressive condition, and by now radical measures were indicated. Apart from the prescribed diet and medication, he was to forswear activity that excited him, to remain calm, almost lethargic. And it was essential that he reduce his sixty cigarettes a day until he could give up nicotine entirely.

That was Webster Martin's pronouncement. Dr. Michelovsky said, "I agree, Doctor, and there will be no difficulty with keeping to the diet and medication. Perhaps he will also cut down on his smoking. As for giving up activity, remaining lethargic and tranquil in his activities, it would be Ivarin's death knell. I know this man."

They talked as if he could not hear them. He drew shallowly on the cigarette he had lit when their discussion began; he did not inhale deeply for fear of another paroxysm of coughing. During the revolution, he suddenly remembered, was the first time Alexis had discovered that he had some elevation of blood pressure. Nineteen five that had been, the last time he had been sick enough to see a doctor, and Alexis had joked sadly that half the Russian colony in New York, revolutionaries all, had fallen sick at the collapse of their hopes. An inflamed larynx and windpipe he had had, that was it, of no real consequence. Nineteen hundred and five, nine years ago, and he had been at the top of his powers, as a man, as an editor.

Hate for the passing of time took him, a spasm of longing to be young again, strong, tireless in his work. In this, his second month off the paper, he would earn exactly ten dollars. With his lecture canceled, his lessons not given, he would "earn" only the fee on his translation. Thirty-eight dollars last month, and ten this. This single reality outweighed everything the doctors were still saying, in a melancholy reiteration, about the vital necessity of avoiding flare-ups or overexcitement, the necessity to limit himself gradually on tobacco.

He reached for the ashtray on the chair near his bed, brought it toward him, and set it on the blanket drawn tight across his chest. He pressed his cigarette into the stale ashes already there, grinding it down, twisting it down. Alexis Michelovsky saw him and put his old hand out to steady the saucer crammed with butts.

" 'Gradually' won't work," Stefan said. "Better to get it over with."

"You mean *now?*" Michelovsky asked.

"Why not?"

"But you've smoked all your life," Alexandra cried.

"I'd rather get it over with," he repeated.

By nightfall, nothing mattered to him but not smoking; by next morning he could think of nothing but a cigarette; by the next night he was reliving the hunger strike and tobacco strike in prison in Russia when he was a boy of seventeen.

Now, as then, he bit into his knuckles in a wildness of need, but now, after one day, the network of nerves, tendons, ligaments, muscles that bound his flesh to his bones tightened up with whistling pain again, and he shouted for Alexandra to get the drugs still available from the original prescriptions Dr. Martin had given him.

He did not smoke. By the end of the first week, he had almost forgotten how to eat more than a mouthful of food, how to think, how to speak. He lay, concentrated on the vow not to smoke, on the knowing that he would not smoke, on the dream of comfort there had always been for him in the making of a cigarette, the lighting of it, the deep drawing down into himself of its mysterious nerve-feeding yield.

It was unwise, perhaps, his instant deathblow to his dependence on smoking, not conducive to the calm and placid existence prescribed for him. But he could not tolerate gradual change any longer. From the first moment the tearful Miriam Landau had peered into his eyes over a year ago to explain away her choice of Fehler, he had acceded to the hell of gradual change, in an unending sophistry of so-called patience and self-control and even dignity. It was enough.

It had been the darkest period he had yet known. It must be bad for Alexandra, for the children, but he could barely think of that now. All his first hope of remaking the structure of life, his first quick encouragement drawn from signing up for a lecture, a lesson, an article —all that first hope had fallen sick with him, and during this siege of pain and illness had thinned and weakened and drained away.

It was very bad. To be sick, to be old, to be squeezed out of the job you loved—it was bad. Perhaps too bad.

TWENTY-SIX

At Aldrich Chemical, on March first, an official memorandum informed all personnel: "Your company's Number Two plant, now approaching completion, will manufacture commercial explosives, such as dynamite for blasting, powder for drilling, charges for tunnel and harbor work. Number One plant will continue on established lines."

Garry read it and looked at Otto Ohrmann. He saw skepticism take command of Otto's face and said, "Have you no faith in the mimeographed word?" Otto muttered something he did not catch, and Garry added, "Too obvious a dodge, hey?" He went to his locker, drew his unfinished morning paper from the pocket of his topcoat and turned to *Help Wanted Male*. At his side, Otto read along with him.

"We toss a coin," Otto said, "if we both like the same one."

Six days later, a Saturday, Garry said, "Thanks, Mr. Molloy," and took his hat from the elongated window sill. Across the twenty-foot width of plate glass ran the legend, Synthex, Inc., presenting the back of its flowery cursive script to the office.

"Think of it as a starting point only, why don't you?" James Molloy said. "I have this one other fellow to see on Monday and after that we'll get in touch with you."

"I'm doing that already," Garry said pleasantly, though he was disappointed. "But it would be more of a cut than I expected, even as a starter. Anyway, thanks again."

He left and went down into the warm drizzle and looked about him. Long Island City was a flat plain that might have been a hundred miles from New York, instead of just across the new bridge to Queens, and the only buildings that stood out above the ugly three- or four-story plateau of brick and concrete were the two ten-story factories making Sunshine Biscuits and Aeolian Pianos. The Synthex plant, modern as it was, was only four stories high, but it occupied an entire square block, and a billboard proclaimed its ownership of the adjacent property, used now as a parking area for two trucks and a few cars.

Before meeting Molloy, he had been interviewed by the head of their New Products Development department, who had shown him around the laboratories and the factory at large; it was a satisfying experience. Synthex was not as up-to-date as Aldrich, but it was equipped for extensive projects in the field of synthetic fibers and substances. One of their major goals, in the experimental division, was to achieve a composition as tough as the black Bakelite of telephones but in a wide range of pale colors, a predictable achievement but still in the future.

Garry had offered a minimum of explanation about his reasons for considering a change of jobs. Aldrich would soon concentrate on manufacturing in a field that did not interest him, he said; he wanted to stay in research. Artificial silks and allied products had become rather a specialty with him, so the Synthex ad had appealed to him.

Garry liked Mr. Molloy. He could be described as "a scrappy little Irishman," except that he was six feet one or two. He was pugnacious and vigorous in the way he spoke, and he dismissed Aldrich by saying, "In the trade they say he's got a good head." It did not interest Molloy why an Aldrich chemist was looking for another job, and Garry was relieved; he had been uncertain whether Aldrich activities were still a business secret on the outside.

He glanced up again at the grey sky when he reached his car. The drizzle was little more than a pervasive mist, and in the west, across the river, there was a brightness that meant the March sunlight might soon break through. He obeyed an impulse, lowered the canvas top for the first time this year, and headed for the city.

Rushing the season, he thought. It won't be official spring for two weeks. Thank the Lord this winter is over and done with at last; it's been the longest one ever. The fifth year of marriage—is that it? Maybe this happens to most couples in the fifth year, especially if they don't have children.

Recently he and Letty had been drifting along, like two becalmed sailboats separated by a small stretch of water, hailing each other easily enough when necessary, but most of the time intent, in a separate watchfulness, for the missing force to send them skimming along again.

The day after Christmas, she had decided to take a few days off from the shop and visit her family up in Maine, and he had spent New Year's Eve alone for the first time since their marriage. Undressing alone, going to bed alone, he had had the strangest sense of recognition, as if he and the quality of aloneness were not strangers in truth,

(335)

but good friends who had been separated for a while and now were rejoined.

The car was approaching Thirty-seventh Street, where he turned right if he were going to pick Letty up at the shop. He thought of taking her off for a drive in the early spring chill. It was only three o'clock, and Saturday afternoon was always too busy for her, but he drew in at the curb, fished a nickel from his pocket and went to a telephone.

"Oh, Gare, I wish I could," she said. "But you just caught me in the middle of an appointment."

"Can you let Mrs. R's-and-T's do it for you?"

"Would that I could," she said airily, signaling that she couldn't talk freely. "I'll tell you about it at dinner, darling."

"I have something to tell you too."

He waited until they were alone before he told her about Molloy and Synthex. This waiting to speak was another new phase in their life, brought about by their having their first maid, a Frenchwoman named Blanche, who had once worked for the Harretts at Oyster Bay. Letty had hired her during the winter and the thirty dollars a month for her wages were well spent, now that Letty scarcely ever got home before seven, but Garry rather disliked having Blanche in the odd little extra room next to theirs. *Don't worry about this little one, darling, I'll make it into a cunning room for a baby.*

Twice during the winter, Letty had made an appointment with Dr. Haslitt; she had broken each one. She was busier than ever. Recently she had ventured into a new side line, again abetted and endorsed by Cynthia Aldrich. "People are too timid to do a house, Letty, without an expert's say-so, and the fees for interior decorators are tremendous." Already it was clear Letty would succeed in this too. For the first time, Garry's attitude toward the shop began to change; its increasing success and dazzle were becoming a rival to her longing or need for a baby.

"I did see the Synthex people today," he said when Blanche had given them a final *"Bon soir."*

"Oh, Garry, you should have warned me."

"I did. I showed you the ad and said I was going to see them."

"I suppose you did."

"Well, this afternoon I went."

"Did you get a job?"

"They only pay thirty-five dollars to start. I said I'd think about it." She looked distressed, and he didn't think it was about the smaller amount of money.

(336)

"Actually being interviewed for another job," she said. "If they hear about it at Aldrich, you could be fired. We've all been such *friends*."

It caught him unawares: if he quit he would overturn the applecart of their friendship. She was accusing him of ignoring what was important to her. *All you think of is what you want. All you think of is war, war, war.*

"You really would take a job with this Molloy?" Letty asked. "If they come up a little bit?"

"Yes."

"When?"

"I'd have to give Aldrich enough notice, and stay until they got a new man."

"Oh, Garry," she said, tears coming suddenly to her eyes. "We've been so happy this way."

"We'll be happy again, wherever I work," he said roughly. He pushed away from the table and went to the fireplace where an unneeded small fire was dying out. It will get better, he thought, once it actually happens, like the time Dad came back from San Diego. She'll line up with me, just the way she did then, a kind of family feeling. She knows as well as I do what's shaping up at Aldrich and she knows I'd never have a hand in it.

Unconsciously he stretched out his hands before him. On the left was a two-inch scar, still livid, running from the base of his thumb in a jagged line to his middle knuckle, the result of an acid burn he had got in the laboratory, which had unaccountably festered until finally it had required minor surgery. Eventually, the surgeon assured him, the scar would turn white and scarcely show.

He stared at it now; he rather liked it as it was, red and angry-looking. It was like a possession to be valued, the credentials of a research chemist.

There was no further word from Molloy, and day by day Letty prayed that there would be none. After ten days or so, Garry said, "I guess he hired the guy he saw Monday," and never spoke of Synthex again. She was not base enough to be glad he had lost out, but it was fortunate he would have more time to think, before he played ducks and drakes with his whole future.

Cynthia Aldrich herself talked of Garry's future, not long after. Mark had told her that Garry was "being difficult" around the lab, had given notice that he was looking for another job, and said openly that he had already had one interview which led nowhere, but that he was keeping an eye out elsewhere.

"You simply must dissuade him from making such a mistake," Cynthia said gravely.

"I've tried to dissuade him."

"A wife never knows when she gets her licks in, Letty, and you mustn't give up. If you could have heard what Mark said about Garry's future with the firm! To have him chuck all that away because of some idea about the wickedness of war! Everybody hates the wickedness of war, child, it's inhuman to do anything else."

Letty tried to think how best to tell Garry about Cynthia's "warning," but soon she gave up. Nothing would change him. Even those Ivarins weren't the out-and-out pacifists he and his parents were. One night recently on a visit, Mr. Ivarin was shouting away at Garry and his father. In the blueprint, he yelled, pacifism was as wonderful an ideal as Christianity in *its* blueprint, but life was soon going to tear up the blueprints, no matter how wicked and foul war was. For the first time in her life Letty had liked the old man.

The wickedness of war. Now the news was all full of Mexico and our Navy bombing Veracruz, and about Ireland's fight for Home Rule, and the Irish landing forty thousand rifles and half a million rounds of ammunition. She wasn't sure whom they were to shoot or when, but it was all over the papers, and Hank and Cindy and Peter talked about it almost as much as Garry and Otto.

She even tried to read the papers every morning again, the way she did when she and Garry were still in love.

The words thwacked against the floor of her mind, and she thought, We still are, we still are.

It's too big a risk, Alexandra thought. The third week in a row is too much to put off Stefan's two pupils in New York. With the two in Barnett there had been no dilemma; from the start, she had given the lessons for him, and though they were disappointed at having a substitute, they showed understanding and even some awe at the idea of his lying ill right above their heads. Soon he would be permitted downstairs again, she had promised them, hoping she was not telling a flagrant lie.

If these two had accepted her in Stefan's place, why shouldn't the two in New York?

She went upstairs to his bedroom. By now, the pain had decreased enough so that he was taking no analgesics but he was not permitted out of bed for more than ten minutes at a time. His blood pressure had come down somewhat, and both doctors were encouraged. He never questioned his diet, and so far had not made one exception about smoking. He had lost weight and appeared exhausted, but both doctors assured her that he would regain strength when he became more mobile.

"It's Nature's automatic mechanism for safeguarding him," Alexis said. "Using a minor collapse, to force a thoroughgoing recuperation. Don't let him rush."

Stefan showed no sign of rushing. He still lay inert for hours at a time, asking only for the papers, nearly always silent. Now when Alexandra came in, he showed neither interest nor concern about his postponed New York lessons.

"It's too risky to skip a third week," she said. "They might lose their determination."

"I suppose so."

"Let me try going in your place."

"As you like."

Despite his indifference, she went to New York, and was waiting in the Kesselbaum parlor when the pupil arrived. "My husband asked me to come," she said, "and give the lesson for him tonight. I'm a teacher too."

It was like a trick, but there was nothing shameful in it; in giving English lessons to any foreigner she was Stefan's equal. She exerted herself to find amusing ways to explain a word or a point of grammar, even to praise the pupil enough to keep his spirits high. Only after the lesson was over did she say, "If my husband is still not well enough next week—the doctor says the jouncing of the trolley and the train could send him straight back to bed—if so, should I come once again in his place to give you your lesson?"

"Of course, Mrs. Ivarin, of course."

Poor thing, Alexandra thought, he couldn't very well say anything else, but I can't help that right now.

It worked as smoothly with Stefan's other pupil. She set about shifting Anna Godleberg's lesson to New York, and those of other pupils, fitting them in before or after these of Stefan's. Switching them around like marbles, she thought, it's a crime. Then she started to rearrange her Monday and Thursday morning trips to Sonya, and felt her first trepidation, for her little lectures to Sonya had taken on a special importance, forcing her to read up on all sorts of authorities besides Madame Montessori. She bought a child's copybook and began to keep notes. It was as if she, too, were taking lessons, a postgraduate course of her own, and to jeopardize her agreement with Sonya would be a loss of more than money.

But Sonya proved as flexible as the others; perhaps a time of sickness and trouble brought out the kindness in people. One evening Sonya asked if her husband might listen, and Vladinsky sat, mute and absorbed. Alexandra regarded him as a special feather in her cap.

Why? she scolded herself. If I get a bigger satisfaction because a man responds to my little talks, am I not betraying the principle of suffrage and equal rights?

She was. But it was delicious.

"It's your turn," Fran said.

"It is not," Fee answered. "Mama said you'd do it, to make up for yesterday when I did it so you could go out with Nick Fanelli."

"But she didn't say today or any other day that happens to suit *you*. So leave me alone. I have an exam."

"So have I," Fee said, though she had none. In half an hour, Papa's supper had to be ready, and this was a perfect example of how Fran managed to sneak out of things. "If I do it, it would be two nights in a row, Monday and Tuesday."

"If *I* do it," Fran said scathingly, "it would be two nights in a row, Tuesday and Wednesday. Or is that too much for you to figure out?"

Fee stood still, helpless. She was beaten because she was afraid of her father and what would happen if he didn't get his food; Fran won out because she wasn't afraid. Fee ran down to the kitchen, wishing she could slap Fran's face, or push her over. It was always Fran who won out; Fran always knew how to twist things around so she could get out of doing things she didn't want to do. Like hanging their things up in the closet. Fran never hung up anything, never. And Fee hated skirts and dresses draped over the chairs and the bedpost, or underwear and petticoats and nightgowns in round little pools on the floor.

"Fran, you're supposed to hang your own things up," she would say. "It looks horrible."

"I don't think it looks horrible at all."

"But it *does*. I always hang my clothes up."

"I like mine this way."

"But it's my room too. It isn't fair to make me live in a pig pen."

"If you feel so awful about it, then hang things up yourself. Just stop yapping about it."

(340)

Tears of rage came to Fee's eyes. She reached for the kitchen towel, but the touch of it was like a burn. She was getting to be as bad as Mama, crying over everything, a million times a day.

Only Mama didn't. Not any more.

Come to think of it, Mama was different, now that she was going to New York four nights a week. Mama was being just wonderful, Mrs. Paige said once, and Joan and Eli said it too. "You have to hand it to her," Eli said on the phone. "But secretly she's enjoying herself too, don't forget."

How could Mama enjoy *anything* with all the things that had happened? Fee went to the door and let Shag in. Even he knew something had changed everybody's life in the Ivarin family. He wasn't allowed in the house at all any more unless he was on a leash, in case he raced upstairs and flung himself against Papa's bed and wrenched his back all over again. Poor Shag drooped around, acting as if he had done something wrong. Actually, Papa liked it when somebody took Shag upstairs on the leash to visit him; he didn't want to see anybody else in the family except Shag, and when you took his meals in on a tray, he just looked at the dishes, as if he didn't know for sure what they were there for.

Fee flipped open the petcocks on the stove and lit the gas. Then she read the list of directions her mother had written out and left on the grooved enamel dish rack that hooked over the edge of the sink.

"Heat ch. in g," it read, in her mother's most hurried writing. "St. b. about 15; carrots same; sweets in ov. to warm them. Slice Orange, ap & ban."

Fee proceeded to follow orders, heating the chicken in the gravy, after the string beans, carrots and baked sweets had had ten of their fifteen minutes. She also peeled and sliced two oranges and two bananas and two apples; it looked like lots more than three portions of dessert, so she spooned some off into a fourth plate and put it in the icebox. Mama might come home hungry.

The bell rang, and she flew to the door, not forgetting to shut Shag into the kitchen first. It was John Miller, and her heart skipped. He came in nearly every day, on his way home after basketball or baseball practice. With Papa out of the way upstairs for sure, and Mama in New York, it was lots more fun to have John in the house than it used to be. Fee didn't know why it was nicer; they never did *anything*.

"I'm busy," she said at the door. "I'm fixing supper."

"I'll go on home, if you're so all-fired busy."

"Don't be so mean."

(3 4 1)

"Who's the mean one? You didn't even say hello."

"Hello," she said and giggled.

They always said the cutest things to each other, Fee thought happily. She always *felt* clever when he was around, the way she didn't feel with ordinary people. John piled his coat on the top of the coat rack, and the way he stacked it up there was cute too. She led the way into the kitchen, and Shag jumped all over him; the big lunk treated John now as if he were a member of the family and Fee wanted to hug him for doing it.

"I'll just take my father's stuff up," she said. "Here's something, if you're hungry, I made it myself." She fetched back the plate of sliced fruit she had put aside for her mother, and John said, "Gee."

"That was great," John said, when she came back. "You're some cook."

"Poo-ey," Fee said, and it made him laugh. It was a wonderful visit, and after John went home, she was suddenly scared that she was as selfish as Eli, who still hadn't come out to visit Papa. She couldn't stop being happy, no matter what had happened to Papa, and what an awful time it was for Mama too. One day her mother had heard her singing, and sort of sighed and said, "Youth is a time for enjoying life, Firuschka, go ahead and enjoy it, no matter."

It made guilt rush through her, but Fee kept on forgetting to feel awful, even when her mother talked about Papa's not being a famous editor any more, or when she said he looked ten years older. Fee looked at him hard when she took his next tray in, but he always looked so old, she couldn't see any difference. She thought her mother would feel encouraged when she said so.

"Children never look at their parents," Mama said. "You never know whether I look well or not, you never know whether Papa does."

"I do so."

"If you came downstairs and found another woman right in the kitchen giving you breakfast, you wouldn't notice it for ten minutes. Children never *see* their parents, I tell you."

It was one of those typical Mama remarks, but you didn't know how to prove it was wrong. And maybe there was nothing wrong in singing if you felt wonderful. It was glorious to be in love, and to adore high school, and church every Sunday, and even to be able to look in the mirror and see that you weren't *absolutely* as flat as a board any more, even if you still weren't anything to brag about.

Another wave of joy boiled up in Fee, a bubbling up of hope and expectation. At once, a new rush of guilt shook her, and almost as an act of revenge, she pushed Shag out the door for the night. Then, because the wind suddenly felt so fresh and inviting, she ran out too, and raced him all the way up to Channing Street and back. Shag won, but it was grand.

It happened about a week later. It happened during the night. Fee did not know it until she awoke in the morning and started to take off her thin nightgown. Then she saw the faint sign, like a delicate brush stroke on the white batiste. She knew at once and her heart jumped with relief and joy.

Her mother had always said there was nothing to fear, that Nature had planned everything wisely, without anything horrid or nasty. Only superstition and ignorance misled girls into imagining ugly and unlovely things, she said, but actually it was sweet and normal, with nothing to dread.

It was true. It had happened while she slept, so quietly, so easily, and she had at last, at last, at last, begun.

She didn't get dressed and she said nothing to Fran, who was stirring in the first moment of waking up. Instead, she ran down to the kitchen where her mother was already finishing her own breakfast.

"Mama," she said, "look." She fanned out her nightgown on each side of her body, like a little girl about to curtsy. She watched the expression change in her mother's eyes.

"My darling," Alexandra said, and came around the table toward her and kissed her.

All day Alexandra felt warmed and happy because of Fee, and then that same evening dear loyal Anna Godleberg sprang her great surprise.

For the very first time, she was not at home when Alexandra arrived. Her son Morris could only explain "She's out," a fact which was all too obvious, and Alexandra said, "I'll wait." But so unprecedented was it to be kept waiting by this of all pupils, that the minutes stretched out inordinately. Then the door opened, and a breathless Mrs. Godleberg rushed in, her hands already on the hatpins in her big pathetic hat, with its imitation plumes and shabby velvet.

"Well, Mrs. Ivarin," she announced with a hitherto unheard cadence of triumph, "you will have twelve in your audience the first time."

"Oh my goodness."

"Monday night, *next* Monday."

(343)

A month had passed since Alexandra had asked her favor, and not once had Anna Godleberg mentioned it. Now "an evening in the tent" was arranged. Eight of the twelve women were from the beach, including three Alexandra barely remembered. The others were unknowns, recruited either by Anna Godleberg or her eager co-organizer, Sophie Jabrowsky, galvanized into action at the chance of "going to hear Mrs. Ivarin again."

The lecture was to last an hour and each woman was to pay fifteen cents, but from the first Monday, Alexandra found herself talking and answering their questions for nearly two hours. And each time, the old surge of joy rose in her again, especially when they burst into self-conscious applause at the end of a lecture, when she heard again, "Oh, if you would only write it down in a book."

Long ago she had sat at the edge of the tent at dawn with the sand cold beneath her bare feet, thinking that life emptied so much earlier for women than it did for men. Now, in the midst of hardship and sadness, her own life was becoming full again, with a lovely fullness as if she were young enough to be pregnant, looking ahead with hope and eagerness.

You're a good girl. The words often sounded again when she pocketed her dollar or two dollars after an evening of lessons or the little lectures and started for the Delancey Street station of the subway. These midnight streets of the East Side—how often Stiva had walked them on his way home. This was the same subway station he had entered and left a thousand times since they had moved out to the little country town, as it was then, of Barnett. Undoubtedly he had sat in the very seat she now had, in this same lighted car swaying on the curves, rushing through the city earth and then emerging into the air of Long Island. Now it was she who made the trip in the middle of the night, who walked up the hill, carrying the first edition of all the papers, including that one.

She thought of it as "that" or "it" now, never as the *Jewish News*. She had come to hate it, for what it had done to him more than for what it had become. But he wanted to read it every day, sick as he was; his interest in what they were doing to it was as fierce and strong as a ruffian boy on a street corner.

And he was more eager for the Russian papers now, as if, in his decrease in strength, he looked homeward and backward to his first years. He always had kept up an unflagging watchfulness about what the socialists in Russia were doing, their victories, their defeats; he never wavered in his faith that the czars would go, and only grew agitated at the fear that the extremists might win out in the supreme moment of victory, reducing it and robbing it. "Betraying it," was what he said.

Alexandra shifted the papers to her other arm; they grew heavy as she walked uphill. Suddenly, from afar, came Shag's double bark of excitement, and she smiled at the familiar sound. "Here, boy, here," she called, though she knew he was already racing toward her. He really did know how to make you feel welcomed home.

"Down, you silly fool," she cried at his first impact, but he paid no attention until she patted his head and talked to him and started toward the house again.

He probably wonders why it's me and not Stiva, she thought, who comes home late at night now.

But you'll see, she thought, as if she were addressing Shag. He'll be doing it again the day he is well enough. He will be active again and happy again, you'll see.

Like me, she added. It was amazing, unimaginable beforehand. Four nights a week, and it was marvelous.

You're a good girl. He had said it before he fell sick, during his determined new start at earning a living, without the fifty dollars from the paper every payday.

And now she was the only breadwinner the family had. Eight dollars a week was no great sum, but in her thankful heart, she knew the glory of accomplishment.

Forty-two days, Stefan Ivarin thought, and I still have not. He glanced at the bag of tobacco with its thin cord drawn tight, like a miser's purse-string, and touched the half-empty packet of papers beside it. His trophies; he had refused to let Alexandra remove them. In his fingers was a tactile memory of how fine and crisp a sheet of the rice paper felt, curved into a three-inch trough waiting for the pebbly fall of the tobacco. And in his nostrils was the strong appealing aroma.

Forty-two days and nights. Not once had he come close to rolling one and lighting it and smoking it, but not once had he experienced the moment of release when it no longer mattered. The moment would come, he knew it as one knows the theorems and propositions of mathematics, but he had not the faintest idea when it would arrive and let him move on to some more important issue.

How interlaced were the importances of a man's being, when once their normal shapes and balances were distorted by disaster or disease or despair.

(345)

The longing for tobacco was more acute than the longing for a paper to edit, yet it was not as involved with his true necessities. The compulsive gambler like Dostoevsky, the compulsive drinker, the compulsive smoker, they all had in common the singular disgrace of being captive to their own folly, whatever elegant excuses they might adduce for their consciences. If he had any virtue in this whole shabby agony of forty-two days, it was only his refusal to make any excuse whatever for it. He was like a dope addict, of a milder persuasion than the poor devils who took heroin or opium, but an addict.

It was a shock, among many shocks, to face the fact.

But he was surviving it, and he had survived the others. Little by little, more slowly than one could imagine, he had begun to recover himself from the series of events which at times took on the aspect of assaults upon his total being. At seven one evening, during the third week of his collapse, he had begun to "earn" again. He had obeyed Michelovsky and waited for the contraption to be made for his back, but the day it arrived, he had taken back the first of his two Barnett pupils from Alexandra, and given the lesson himself. The next night he had taken back the other, and at his urging, each of them had suggested several other stores where the proprietor would display his special printed card. Three more pupils and a dozen inquiries had already resulted; but one had to allow time for these things to build up.

Stefan put on the "contraption." It was a steel-and-leather belt or holster, a handspan in width, that circled him at his hipbones. It laced with thong-like cords, and was padded with a spongy wool inside, over a crosshatching of steel ribs. Made to his measure by a surgical outfitter, it had cost an outrageous thirteen dollars.

But with it he could begin to manage again. It did protect him in part, from the tearing, ripping feeling he had had for the first days of moving about. It would save him from a new wrench or twist, and it permitted him to walk for as much as a quarter of each hour, or to sit at his desk for that amount of time, and write. And then at last it let him go slowly down the stairs, to teach and earn and be his own man again.

His own man again. There was a farcical quality to so large a phrase for so minor a beginning, but he was not willing to edit it. "His own man" would not sound farcical forever. Step by step he was on his way once more.

But there were decisions to make that could not wait for the unknown length of that journey. The time was coming when they could not be put off any longer.

(346)

Alexandra saw the light in the kitchen windows, and she guessed. When Shag hurled himself at her, more excited than usual, she said, "He's downstairs, boy, isn't he? So late at night."

She hurried the rest of the way. "Is that you?" she called out as she unlocked the front door, and from the kitchen his voice came, "I wasn't sleepy."

"I'm not sleepy either."

With deliberation, he came toward her through the dining room. He was straight again, with the artificial straightness the steel-and-leather belt gave him. Though he had been coming down once each evening to give a lesson, he had always been upstairs again and in bed long before she arrived from the city.

She touched the switch in the parlor and saw his pale face, his thin neck, his careful slowness. Old, she thought. It's the first time he looks old—we are getting old at last. The one sickness they have no drugs for, the one attack they can never fend off. She didn't want him to grow old, never, never, she didn't want to herself, she could not bear it for either of them. They loved life, they loved the struggle and challenge of their kind of life, throbbing with hope for a better world, furious with fire and resolve, not like the thin empty lives of people who accepted poverty and injustice as if God himself were a capitalist.

"You look surprised to see me down here," Stefan said.

"Oh, Stiva, the worst is over, I feel it."

"Today I even did two sessions of the translating. A second one this evening, and none the worse for it. And the blood pressure stays down."

"For once they were right."

"Maybe they know something about certain sickness," he said grudgingly. "Give me." He reached for the papers and preceded her into the kitchen. On the range, steam curled out of the spout of the aluminum kettle, and she raised it to see how full it was.

"You're not to lift anything that heavy," she scolded, and he chuckled in pleasure at his own prowess.

"Yes, yes, but now we can have tea without waiting."

He sat down carefully and she fetched what they would need. He glanced at the headlines but did not give himself over to reading, as if he were waiting to finish something else first.

"What did you mean, 'the blood pressure stays down'?" she asked. "How do you know?"

"Joan's father came by after supper," he said. "I rang him up to ask

(347)

if I could go to New York. I told him it was getting more imperative, about money. So he came and checked up and said 'next week.' I can give two lessons on the same evening, but he orders a half-hour rest between them, and again before starting for home."

"It's wonderful. What you've been through, and now it's beginning to be done with."

"By June," Stefan went on, "he thinks I could even lecture. It would be welcome, I can tell you. Getting up on a platform again . . ."

"I know." His longing set off an answering sharpness of desire in her, that he should be himself again, at least Stefan Ivarin the lecturer, if not Stefan Ivarin the editor.

"But even though I'll be earning some money again," he added, "I have reached a decision at last. It can't be put off any longer." He waited, but she would not ask him what it was. "It's the house," he said slowly.

"The house?"

"There is no way for us to keep it any longer." He turned his face so she would not see his expression. "We will have to sell it." She said nothing; she had been thinking of it too. "Offer it for sale," he added.

"Must we? Are you sure?"

"I calculated it a hundred different ways. Even with your help, there is no way out."

She wanted to protest, to cry out, argue. But they had warned her: he could not stand dissension, scenes, storms of emotion. "I've been trying to prepare myself," she said. "I knew it was coming. But I hoped we could put it off—"

"You can't sell a house in one day," he answered. "We can't put it off any longer, the first step, listing it with the real estate people."

The first step. The blueprints were the first step; she could see them again, the strong blue of their sturdy paper, their lines and labels and dimensions in white. The quarrels and crises over them were long ago forgotten, the stairs, the icebox, the bedrooms like cubicles. What folly to have been miserable over such details. What mattered was the house they had built, the house they loved, the house they now had to sell to strangers.

Alexandra's eyes filled with tears, but this time she made no move to hide them, and was not surprised at his hand upon her shoulder.

TWENTY-SEVEN

The white sign, HOUSE FOR SALE, stood at the crest of the rise of earth that sloped sharply back from the sidewalk. It was made of wood on a painted metal spoke, and under its unwavering arms the lawn was tender and green in the early June warmth. At the curb, the three maples, still supple and slender, bent toward it under a brisk west wind, as if to acknowledge its sudden presence.

It's like a cross over a grave, Alexandra thought. It will be death itself to the girls, the end of everything they have always taken as immutable.

She had come down early, unable to sleep. Another few weeks had gone by since Stefan and she had agreed that it was inescapable, and at last they had gone together yesterday to buy it. They had felt the need to go together, though they had found almost nothing to say to each other, either on the way to Beck's Hardware or on the way home. Stefan insisted on carrying it, and as he trudged silently on with it, unwrapped because it did not lend itself to neat packaging, she wondered if he and all other human beings also found an infinite sadness linked to the shape of any cross.

"I'll tell the girls in the morning," she said.

And now the moment had come. "Fran, Fira," she said, and they looked up. If only she need not give them one more thing to accept as best they could. How many there had been already; how good and brave they both had been most of the time. Even about staying home all summer long, the first summer of their lives without the mountains or the beach. "It's nearly half a year," she began, "since Papa got sick. Longer since he left the paper."

"What's wrong, Mama?" Fran asked. Fee sat up straighter.

"He's getting well, he's earning again, signing up a few lectures, writing a few articles, but even so."

"Are we poor now?" asked Fee.

"Not as the poor are poor. But we do have to take a certain step;

we finally decided we must. We argued it from every angle; there's no way out."

"What step?" Fee asked.

"To sell the house."

"*Sell* it?" Fran cried.

"Where would we live?" Fee asked.

"In a smaller place," Alexandra answered. "For what we get from the house, we could pay rent for a long time, low rent."

Her heart chilled at the look on their faces. Fee had been a tiny thing of three or four the first time they had begun to talk and plan about building their own house; even Fran had been too little to remember the rented houses they had had before this, the only home they could regard as permanent.

"How do you sell a house?" Fee almost whispered it.

"You advertise it, and you tell real estate people. And usually you put out a little sign saying it's for sale." She wet her lips and unclasped her hands. "Papa and I went down to Main Street together yesterday, while you were still at school, and we bought one."

"Where is it?" Franny and Fee said together.

"Outside on the lawn," Alexandra said. "Late last night we went out and put it up."

Franny and Fee left the table as if at a signal. Alexandra followed only as far as the parlor, and then waited at the window. Unwilling, unbelieving, the girls stood face to face with its stiff unyielding whiteness. HOUSE FOR SALE.

Alexandra turned away from the window. Then she heard Fee begin to cry and Fran try to comfort her.

Alida Paige saw the sign and told Evan that evening. "Is there nothing we can do?" she said.

"They'd refuse, if we offered."

"Why should they? They know us so well."

"When it comes to money, and being out of a job, a man—" he broke off, thinking about it. "Stefan's an easier man to ask help of, than to offer it to."

"But it's a poor friend who makes no offer at all. I'll talk to Alexandra, and feel her out a bit."

"I'd go pretty lightly," he said.

Suddenly Alida knew that Alexandra, like Stefan, would refuse a loan. As she herself would refuse. Going into debt was the unthinkable, in the tenets of behavior which had guided her own parents and grandparents. Undoubtedly it was just as unthinkable to the Ivarins. "The Puritan background," her family would have named it, "the New England tradition." Yet here were Stefan and Alexandra, as far from the Puritanism of New England as the North Pole from the South, but a loan would seem unthinkable to an identical degree. Alida pointed out this paradox to Evan. "How alike the four of us really are."

"Maybe they're Russian Puritans," he said.

"You're laughing at me."

More seriously he said, "There's something of the ascetic in any idealist, don't you think?"

"I suppose that's it," and almost without pause she added, "Garry hasn't been sounding right, have you noticed?"

"Not particularly, no."

"He really has not. When he telephones, he never has those little teasing things to say, the way he used to, and the last time they were here, he seemed quite edgy."

"I did notice that," Evan said. "I thought Letty did too."

"Oh, dear," Alida said, and they fell silent. Then she called 1718-W, but when she went over, she had no better idea than to offer to lend the Ivarins some money.

"I came over," she said, waving vaguely toward the front lawn, "to see if there's anything we can do to help."

"You're upset about the sign," Alexandra said.

"Evan and I were talking about it."

"You're lovely to worry about us, simply lovely. It makes me feel better, just hearing it."

"He said a man doesn't like to borrow from a friend, but I do think illness makes it different." She looked earnestly at Alexandra. "If men can't understand that, it's a lack in *them,* don't you think?"

A comfortable look passed between them, but Alexandra said, "Still, it's true. Stefan wouldn't like it."

"I'll be darned if I wouldn't," Alida said defiantly. "As a practical stopgap for a while—" she stopped short and said, "That does give me an idea."

Alexandra waited. Through the open windows came the sweet smell of summer meadows and trees; for all the speed with which downtown Barnett was being built up, the hill was still blessed with great patches of openness. The last week of school was beginning for the girls; in other summers they would already be more than half packed for their move to the beach.

"Suppose you rented the house," Alida said, "instead of selling it.

(351)

Then it would still belong to you, and the rent from it would be just enough to pay for a small stopgap place that you could rent for yourselves." Alexandra was staring at her, her face brightening. "Only until Stefan is all settled again, and when he is, then you would still have your own house to move back to again."

"Why, Alida." It sounded so simple, so rational—why had they never thought of it themselves? Alexandra, faintly troubled, thought, There must be a reason why it's wrong, and went to the window and looked at the sign. Its back was blank, but she could imagine it saying HOUSE FOR RENT. How much softer the words were.

Stefan refused to consider it. To be a landlord was to be a capitalist. "Alida is fine to think about us, to worry about us, but to rent the house and become a landlord like John Jacob Astor—impossible. Paige will see that, if she didn't."

"Nobody meant becoming a capitalist," Alexandra said. "If you charged only enough rent to pay for a stopgap place, it would be like a temporary swap."

"A swap, indeed. Plus enough on the side to pay for the interest on the mortgage here, to pay for repairs here, to pay the water taxes here. Enough to pay for a moving van out, and then another moving van back in. The chicanery, if I used our house as capital and denied I was playing capitalist."

"It wouldn't be like unearned increment—"

"No textbook jargon," he said, too patiently. "I beg you, let it alone."

" 'I beg you,' " she retorted. "Whenever you beg me, that means you command me." She had been at the point of being hurt by his tone, but this observation struck her as so apt, so spirited, that she suddenly felt invincible.

"Let me read about this assassination," he said, turning back to his paper. "There must be an article for me in it."

Still triumphant, she went outdoors to the garden. How neglected it was compared to other summers, how scraggly and scratchy. With her four days a week in the city, she could not spare the time it needed, the calm, loving work early in the morning and last thing in the afternoon. Her neglect showed, and her skimpy little tomato plants were chiding her, her thin little lettuces and radishes reproaching her. She glanced up at the hot blue sky and then went around to the side of the house for the hose. The grooved black rubber was sweating, and Shag was lying stretched across the metal nozzle so that it was out of sight. The spigot must have been incompletely turned off; he always discovered it on a hot day and treated himself to the contraband coolness.

She had known that Stefan would say no to offering the house for rent instead of sale. She had been uneasy about the fundamental principle herself, but she had not his faculty for putting things into precise words. That was one thing that made him so strong a writer—

She wrenched the hose unceremoniously out from under Shag, and he sprang erect with a yelp of protest. It upset her these days to think of Stefan's writing; something was going wrong with it.

Not with his translating; he was forging ahead like a fanatic on that, now that he was permitted at his desk again. Not only had he made up all the time he had lost on it, he was far ahead of any normal schedule.

It was different when he wrote an article. The piece he had finally completed on Henry Ford and his $5 a day—"Turning-point or Bribe?"—had come back from the *Wahrheit;* excellent though it was, most unfortunately it was no longer timely, since the news had broken three months before, in January, and the *Wahrheit* had commented on it on several occasions since then.

"They're right, quite right," Stefan said, but he was infuriated. He wrote the piece all over again, in English, and sent it to the *Call,* and then to the *Leader* out in Milwaukee, but both times it came back, with much the same explanation. At last he tore the piece to ribbons, and dumped them into the garbage pail.

He began an article the very day twenty strikers were killed in Ludlow, in a pitched battle between the miners and the Colorado State Militia; he had foreseen violence months back, and now Federal troops were being sent in, not to protect the starving miners, but to protect that most sacred of all gods, property. He was going to finish this piece in one day and mail it that night, as if the mailbox were the press room in the basement. Then no one could say "untimely" about it.

But it didn't work out that way. He himself was dissatisfied with it, and he set it aside to do over. It was forced, he said, stilted. "In your own paper," he told her, "you know what the reader knows; it's been right on your own front page. But with somebody else's readers, you have to stop, explain, fill in background. You are writing an essay, not an editorial."

She asked to see what he had written; he refused. The next day he said it still needed more work; once again he did not mail it. On the third day she saw that the color had begun to rise in his forehead and it upset her. He was discouraged, he was angry, he was bored. It was not the kind of writing at which he was best. She almost wished he would not write a word on the assassination of the young Austrian Archduke, in that place in Serbia.

If he pressed too hard with these free-lance pieces, and if too many of them were rejected?

Fee wished she could put on blinders whenever she passed the white sign on the lawn. Nobody seemed to feel the way she felt about it.

The first time some people came to look at the house, she wanted to slam the front door in their faces. It was a man and a woman, and they looked things over as if it were their house already, staring, amazed at the plaster walls, talking to each other about them, ignoring Mama, who was explaining about letting a house settle before you put up wallpaper. Then they saw the stairs starting up from the back hall, and they laughed. For the first time in her life, Fee loved the stairs.

They finally said they would have to think it over, and it was like a last-minute escape. They hadn't even asked the price, her mother said, and it meant they were *not* going to think it over at all. They were not interested at all.

"That's good," Fee said.

"Good?" Alexandra repeated. "You call that good?"

"What *is* the price?"

"Exactly what it cost us, not a penny more," Alexandra said.

"How much did it?"

"The lots were four hundred dollars each," Alexandra said proudly, "because this is 'select property,' up here on the hill, and no stores allowed, just houses. So that's eight hundred, and building the house came to five thousand, two hundred."

"Six thousand dollars," Fee said. "Whew."

"Minus the mortgage, of course. But even so, it's wonderful, isn't it, that we could save and put aside so much? And now when we are in such need of it, there it is."

The next people did ask the price, but the house wasn't exactly what they wanted. Some real estate people came, and they went about things like machines, zip zip and out. It was "a slow market," they said; business hadn't picked up from the dip last year, but any house with copper pipes and the best materials would find a buyer soon.

Each day that passed was like a present, Fee thought. Maybe it would take a long time before it actually happened. Fran said it would. After the first few days of getting used to the white sign, the tennis court worried Fran more than the house. Papa had written the owner of the land practically the minute he got off the paper, sending a final $3 check and saying he no longer wished to rent the property from him. Fran had been positive the unseen man would wreck the tennis court so they couldn't play on it free of charge, but it was still there, and still "her court."

"Selling the house isn't even necessary," she burst out to Fee one day. "He has enough money saved to last a year, but he's too stingy to spend it."

"How do you know?"

"From things," Fran said with authority. "I can figure out our budget too, you know."

"He never never would sell this house if he could help it," Fee said, with equal authority.

"I don't give a hoot any more. I'll be earning my own living in one more year, don't forget, and then I'm moving straight to New York. If I'm appointed to a school there, they can't even kick up a fuss."

"You're getting to be more like Eli every minute."

Fee walked away, wishing she could make Fran shut up about having only one more year at Jamaica Training School for Teachers. She herself had three more years at High, and then two at Training. *If* she went to Training.

But I won't, she thought, I never will.

If she did go, she would have to teach, and the one surest thing in her life was that she would not be a teacher. Let Fran teach, let Eli teach, but for her, never. All her life she had said that, and it was truer than ever. What she wanted to do, what she wanted to be, she didn't know. But it was something you started to be by going to college first.

Anne Miller was going to college in three years, and John, in two. Tom Ladendock was just back from his first year at Cornell, and he wasn't even jealous of Fran and Nick Fanelli, because Nick went to Jamaica Training too, and if you were a college man, you didn't mind about boys in places like that. Tom called Nick terrible names like Dago and Wop and he upset Franny horribly too by saying nobody like Nick could belong to his fraternity at Cornell. "He might as well be a little Jew-boy." He remembered right away, and blushed deep red, and tried to take it back. He said Fran was different, and so was her little sister, but Fran said Cornell had certainly made *him* different, and she left him flat. That night she cried like anything.

Fee felt pretty horrible herself about it. And about being stuck right there in Barnett for the summer. Next month it would be worse because Anne and John were going back to Iowa for August, to stay at their grandfather's, and she would have to get through a whole month without seeing John once. Fran might go flitting from Jack Purney to Tom Ladendock to Nick Fanelli—and then forget all of them the moment she saw Garry Paige again—but Fee wasn't fickle and flirty, and how she could stand it after John left was impossible to figure out.

"Are you going to go to church every Sunday when we're not here?" he asked one day, looking at her sideways.

"What a thing to ask," Fee said with dignity. "Of course I am."

"I'd never, if nobody was watching."

"You wouldn't?"

"But there's one place I would go," he said. "If somebody cute went with me."

"Where?"

"To the new theater downtown."

"When?"

"Tonight. Unless you have a previous engagement."

Fee flew off to ask if she could. The few times she had ever been allowed to see vaudeville and a moving picture, her mother had taken her and Fran to Jamaica, but the new Barnett Theater had just been finished right on Main Street, and now she had been asked to go alone with a boy, which made it even newer.

"You're fourteen, aren't you?" her mother said, looking pleased herself. "Of course you can go. But, your word of honor: straight home afterwards."

"But if he wants a chocolate frappe at Gray's—"

"Naturally, a frappe at Gray's too."

Going out with a boy was glorious, Fee discovered. During the vaudeville acts, they sat and laughed and joked, but when it got dark for the picture, John took her hand and held it and put his fingers between her fingers, moving them around and squeezing them together, and she didn't pull her hand away. She could hardly stand it after a while; this was what everybody meant about being thrilled; it was like the time he had taken her by the shoulders and tried to un-cave her chest.

Thrills weren't always lovely. If the wrong people had a thrill, it was disgusting. A few nights ago, Fran and Nick Fanelli went out, and without knowing they had come back, Fee went to the kitchen for a drink of water, without bothering to put the light on.

There they were, out on the back porch, and she could see them. Nick was in the big wicker rocker out there, holding Fran on his lap, and they were kissing and doing things and it was sickening. She tiptoed out of the kitchen and up the stairs, but she couldn't forget them down there, and couldn't get over the feeling that she was going to vomit. Fran was nearly eighteen, but even so. Her own sister. It was awful.

The hall was jammed to the last row, and Stefan Ivarin stood there waiting for the applause to die away so he could finish his sentence. The lecture was half over, and they had stopped him ten or fifteen times.

It was in an old loft building on Hester Street, on the night a strike vote was to be taken in the men's cloak industry, and the A. F. of L. had done a big job of publicizing his appearance, "the first lecture this year by the East Side's most famous speaker."

With his first sentences, his old "feel for the audience" came back, unchanged, undiminished; their response was unchanged, undiminished. Here at least he was none the worse for wear, none the older, none the weaker.

He talked not only about their strike but also about the bloody strike in Ludlow; he contrasted the methods of a moderate union like their own with those of an extremist union, their leadership with I.W.W. leadership out West. The labor movement, the socialist movement itself, he warned them, was in danger of a split, a division, a mortal cleavage between the old-line socialists who believed in progress wedded to responsibility, and the newfangled "action boys" who thought that terror tactics were excusable if they themselves used them.

"Terror gives birth to terror," he shouted. "Violence by strikers, wrecking property, smashing machinery—I say to you, these only breed a smashing of workers' heads by company cops and state militia and even Federal troops."

The heat climbed in his face as he spoke, in his body, along his whole flesh, but he felt it glowing and beneficent, not threatening. The pressure in his veins now was a kinetic energy, not anger and revolt and scorn at himself or at Fehler or at his own situation. On this platform, facing these poor devils who looked up to him for guidance, for the spirit they would need for what they had to do, here he felt strong and free of concern about sickness or age. Since medicine was still half quackery, he would take his chances now with his own diagnosis: when your heart begins to be high again, a high blood pressure can do you no damage.

Alexandra was in the audience. She had temporarily lost three of her pupils and four of her lecture group, off with their children for their annual snatches of sea and clean air, and she had a free evening. She had asked whether he would mind having her there in the hall for his "first lecture," and he had said he would like it. He meant it. She's been a wonder, he thought, as he so often had in their long and tumultuous years. A little pain was in it when he had thought it while he was still a prisoner to helplessness, but that pain was gone now. She was a rock. During those months just past, she had dropped her maddening faults, her tears, her hurt feelings, and become a rock for them all to cling to.

Now, during a particularly wild burst of applause and stamping from the audience, he glanced at her, sitting in the first row. She was gazing up at him, responsive, enraptured for all the world to see, her eyes the shining eyes of the girl, Alexandra Bartschoi, who used to come to every lecture he ever gave when they were both young.

Letty looked at the postmark and tore open the letter. It was from Mt. Desert and it was signed, "Please do, Peter." A lightness entered her heart.

Dear Letty and Garry,

This is to remind you about the latchstring being out. I can't recall when you take your vacation but I hope this isn't too late. Hank and Cindy are still off in England, as I think you know, and it's been mostly their kid and the governess up here so far. But now I'm hoping to have a few amusing weekends, and this is to ask you for either the first or second in August. They'll be back by then, and it will be like old times if you say yes.

Please do, Peter.

They had already taken their vacation, starting as usual over the Fourth of July, and they had got back only two days ago. Neither of them had suggested Canada this year; neither had remarked on the absence of an invitation from Hank and Cindy, Connie and Proff, or Peter himself, but Letty knew the lack of it in her heart and wondered if it had some special meaning.

(358)

She never spoke of it to Garry, and all he thought of was where to go for their holiday; she was glad to leave it all to him.

"White Sulphur Springs," he finally said. "There's a new hotel down there, very fashionable, very expensive."

"It sounds lovely.

"We drive through Washington, and we could take a day for sight-seeing."

"I've always wanted to see Washington."

"But what about our visit to the family?"

"I'd write Father and Mother and say we're heading for the Sunny Southland instead. Maybe we could manage a weekend later."

"If we took a Pullman up instead of driving, we could."

Maybe during the first or second weekend in August, she thought now, and combine the two. That would mean Garry asking for a couple of days off at Aldrich, and so soon after his vacation, he wouldn't want to.

She leaned back and let Peter's letter drop on the table. She was still at breakfast; during the hot weather, with her best clients off at their summer places, she did not hurry to the shop the way she did at the height of the season. Mrs. Everett could manage the ordinary customers, and it was lovely to dawdle around a little after Garry left for work each day.

"Is there any more coffee, Blanche?" she asked. "I'll take it in my room, please."

She took Peter's letter with her. The tall windows were bright with summer, the tree leafy and full in the sun. The sea around Mt. Desert would be aquamarine on such a day, Peter and Hank's lovely old boat would slip across the water, with the slap-slap of the sea on her hull, and of the wind on her canvas. She could feel herself, lazy and sunburned in a bathing suit, sitting on the deck again, gazing up at Peter until she realized she was staring as if he were an actor on a stage and she a member of the audience who had paid for the right to watch his every gesture.

Perhaps the only way would be for them to visit her parents in Rockland as they planned, and then have her take another day or two by herself to go on to Mt. Desert, while Garry went back to town for Monday morning. He was always sweet about that, no matter what else went wrong between them. Women were more than appendages of their husbands, he said; had he ever acted as if it was just talk?

Blanche appeared with fresh coffee, on a Sheffield tray laid with her best Georgian silver, by Emes and Barnard, 1792. A sense of luxury suffused Letty, and slowly she read the letter once more.

"Please do, Peter."

It had a a special sound in her mind, not insistent and yet rather commanding. Maybe I will, she thought.

Sixteen days of the summer vacation had gone by, when Stefan Ivarin suddenly thought, Nothing is worth this. Poverty averted is excellent in theory, but if insanity is the price, then let poverty come.

For sixteen days there had been no school for his daughters and all their energetic friends. He glanced out at the tennis court, which seemed to lie just under his window, as if it had developed the faculty of creeping closer during this first summer of having the whole family at home. There were six or eight of Fran's friends there, going off in their particular style of laughter, insufferably full of sex awareness as well as noise.

Fee and her religious duenna, Anne Miller, were close at hand, too, on the back porch. At the moment they had forgotten their twin devotions to God and Boys, and were playing some thumping game that shook the house. It involved Shag, causing frenzied rushes and whanging against the copper screening, so that Stefan kept awaiting the whining tear of metallic mesh.

And in the parlor, mysteriously delayed long past her usual schedule, Alexandra was doing her morning dancing to the accompaniment of that eternal Strauss lollipop she called a waltz.

Suddenly he consulted a narrow strip of celluloid propped against his inkwell. The 1914 calendar was there in entirety, and showed him there were nearly two months to go before education would again claim the daytimes of the young. An intolerable stretch of time for a man at last making some headway as a functioning human being.

He stood still, listening. Fran, Fee, the Strauss waltz.

He had to get rid of them.

They had taken it very well, all three, the dictum that there could be no extravagances this year like going off to the seashore. But, to his surprise, he had not.

Was there any way, now that he felt a little less pessimistic about what lay ahead, to get them out of the house for the rest of the summer? Perhaps for three or four weeks, if not for the rest of the summer?

The vision of them gone was entrancing. The familiar lost sensation of being alone in the house suddenly returned, floating into him

(360)

like a silken fog. Alone, silent, untended, asked no questions, offered no solace. He could feel himself going downstairs in the morning to start the coffee, going out for the two papers, folded into thirds and interlocked, waiting for him on the porch in their pristine lumpishness. Since the Sarajevo affair, he had stopped telling himself he ought to cut the morning newspaper bill in half by giving up either the *World* or the *Times;* it was impossible to give up either one now. Never had an extra penny been better spent, nor the extra nickel on Sundays.

In any case, the saving of pennies and nickels no longer seemed so imperative. Where did optimism lie buried when it was gone, and why did it seem so natural when it returned?

In hard reality, there was not yet much to be optimistic about, and yet here he was, daring to think of using up fifty dollars of their savings to send them off to their tent for at least a month.

His one lecture, after all, was not the only one he had on the schedule. The A. F. of L. had signed him for no less than six during their annual convention in the early fall. More than that, he had their assurances, backed up by word from Gompers, that they would count on him for two appearances each month throughout the year, usually in New York, but occasionally a night's trip away. That was the minimum, at ten dollars each, and since when did a year go by in American labor where a minimum of lectures could suffice?

The Democratic Party had approached him just last week for their campaign in the city elections in November. Thirty dollars each was their rate, but to talk to labor not as a socialist but as a Tammany boy was not to talk to labor at all.

The devil take their thirty; even at an honest man's ten, he would build up a schedule of three or four lectures a week, and with the growth in his list of pupils that he was already seeing, he would be supporting his family again before he was through.

If he did not lose his mind first from the hullaballoo.

He took out his savings book; the steady earnings of Alexandra had put a big stretch into his earlier calculations; there was no doubt about it. He opened his checkbook and flipped the pages backwards, going through his check stubs until he came to a year ago May and the name of the landlord of the tent city. Were all the tents rented by now? He thought of the slow season and depressed business of the last months and then went down to the telephone, closing the vestibule door behind him.

When he emerged, he called all three of them together, in the parlor. They came warily, each face studying his for a clue to what might be coming.

(361)

"How soon could you all get packed for a vacation at your heavenly beach?" he said.

"The beach?" Alexandra cried.

"When?" Fee said, jumping to her feet.

"You said we couldn't afford it," Fran put in.

"I think Mama needs a little rest," he said hypocritically. "Maybe a month out there, to the middle of August, would break up the summer in a good way."

"I'd love it, I'd just love it," Fee squealed, whirling around and then rushing toward him, as Shag did, but stopping an inch away. Her face was flushed and pink; she had been less of a child recently, he realized, in this instant of seeing her revert to a total childishness.

"What are you saying this for?" Alexandra said. "As a theory, or as a real thing?"

"Do I dare theorize, when it comes to beaches?" he demanded. "There is an empty tent. I just telephoned the tent landlord, to find out. Your old one in the front row is rented, but the end one in the second row is vacant, and so is the middle one in the last row."

"I can't believe this," Alexandra said. "But my lessons, and my little lectures—"

"Oh, Mama," Fran said.

"Please," Fee begged. If she were going away before John left, if it weren't she who had to stay behind—"Please say yes, please."

"But my lessons," Alexandra repeated wretchedly.

"Some of them you can give right there," Stefan said. "The ones you thought were temporarily lost for a while. Your Sophie Jabrowsky, for example, who always goes to that beach for two weeks, and Mrs. Godleberg for four this year, and Sonya Mikhailovna, with her husband, the jeweler, doing so well."

She looked at him, flabbergasted. "How did you know, how could you figure out all these schedules?"

"You forever talk about which pupils you will lose for which times, don't you? I remember what you tell me."

She gazed at him. Was there ever another man like this one, to be in command of every detail of her pupils and their plans, in case he needed to make an unexpected new calculation?

"Thus," he went on, "you need not interrupt *all* your lessons, merely a different group. You follow me?"

"And in fact," Alexandra said with a sudden lift to her voice, "I always seem to meet a few brand-new women out there who—" At this naked commercialism, sudden embarrassment appeared in her face, but it gave way to a seraphic look of acquiescence. A yearning

(3 6 2)

awoke within her, for the white sand stretching as far as she could see, for the twinkling spray over the crest of the waves, the flaky crackle of hot canvas at the touch of a mid-morning wind. "Oh my goodness, what wonderful news," she said, and for the first time in all that troubled and frightening year, an unqualified serenity possessed her.

"There is one condition," said Stefan, suddenly stern.

"What condition?" she demanded, while both girls went motionless.

"You must not shilly-shally over ten thousand getting-readies. You are to start tomorrow afternoon."

"But, Stiva—"

"But, Papa—"

"I just can't, my clothes are all dirty."

"Tomorrow," he said.

A vast enlightenment entered Alexandra's soul. She looked at him for an instant. He suddenly had had enough of them, he suddenly wanted to go back to his hard-boiled eggs like rocks, his unmade bed, his ability to get along without them. That was what was behind this whole change of mind, this entire remarkable performance. He was getting well at last, within himself where it counted most.

"We'll go tomorrow," she cried happily. "We'll take our dirty clothes with us."

One morning nearly three weeks later, Fee was lolling in one of the striped canvas chairs in front of their tent. It was barely past eight, but the sun was already ablaze.

Suddenly she looked up and could scarcely believe her eyes. Way off, at the end of the trolley line, where the wooden sidewalk started for the tent city, was her father, dressed in his dark wool suit and stiff white collar, and holding his felt hat against the wind that blew toward him from the sea. He was walking slowly toward her.

He's sick again, she thought, something terrible must have happened. And at this hour of the morning! He must have been up all night.

She began to run toward him. With the first steps, she wished she had a towel or a sweater over her bathing suit; sometimes she was suddenly embarrassed at the way she was filling out day by day. She jackknifed her arms up in front of her, with loosely clenched fists under her chin, and then ran on. She called out to him, but he had his head down against the stiff breeze, and her voice carried past him.

She could see him now, really see his face, and it was dull and grey. He had an armload of newspapers, about ten different ones; his whole right side sagged with the weight of them. Maybe that was why he looked sick again, infirm, and so old. He never came out to the beach, simply never, even if Mama begged him to come for a day, not even once in all their summers in the tent had he ever been there. Yet here he was now, with everything still hushed and quiet around him, like a scarecrow in hot black wool. She was frightened, and called out again.

This time he heard her. "Firuschka," he said eagerly, actually sounding glad to see her.

"Are you all right, Papa? Are you sick again?"

He shook his head. Then to her astonishment, he bent down and kissed her. "The war has started," he said slowly. "All over Europe." He spread out the papers a little and she saw that they were black with big headlines, but he held on to them, as if he couldn't let go.

"It started at last," he went on, half-closing his eyes, the way he did when light hurt them. "I came out to tell Mama, and be here for today with the family."

PART
III

TWENTY-EIGHT

The world had changed. Month after month since that summer day when Fira Ivarin had run toward her father on the wooden sidewalk of the tent city, the world around her had kept filling with new words, new places, new phrases.

The rape of Belgium, the Huns, the Allies, the Battle of the Marne —at first the war in Europe was a barrage of sounds, strange sounds spoken by her parents, by the Paiges, by teachers and newsboys, and passers-by on the street.

Then the sounds gave way to feelings, feelings of her own, although she could not remember why they started, or when. Perhaps it was the day she gave ten cents of her allowance for Belgium Relief, and knew for the first time in her whole life that she was part of something bigger than herself, something right and good. It must be what her mother had always meant about the way to be happy. This was different, of course, not like socialism and strikes and labor unions; this was joining with *everybody,* instead of just a few "idealists" everybody laughed at. And this was joining in on something of real use, helping to win the war this year or next, not something that might be of use a hundred years from now.

Belgium Relief. Soon that seemed far away too, familiar as if it had always been there. The awful news kept sweeping on, the awful battles and the awful numbers of the dead and wounded piled up higher each spring, each summer, each fall and winter. She could never keep the figures straight because they were always erased from the blackboard of memory by new totals of the dead and wounded. But the names stayed, like great bells ringing in a dark and terrible hymn . . . Flanders and the Somme, Jutland and the Dardanelles, the Western Front, the Eastern Front, Ypres and Verdun.

Even the *Lusitania* seemed years back already, but when she stopped to reckon it out, it was less than two years ago. She wasn't even fifteen that spring, and she kept getting it mixed up with the *Titanic,* and was ashamed because once she made a mistake and said "When the German sub sank the *Titanic.*" Now she was sixteen and a half, and registering for the last half of her last year at Barnett High.

Stopping to reckon out dates about the war was a sort of a lie, anyway. What she really felt was that it had been there always. When people said "before the war," it was like their saying "before you were born," and she couldn't imagine it for herself any more than she could imagine the Diet of Worms or the Crusades. As the second year passed and now half of the third, she couldn't even remember newspapers without the big maps of this battle line or that, without dispatches from "Somewhere in France, " or believe that people had ever dismissed bad news from Europe as "just another war scare."

And there was one good thing about the war.

It was lovely not having to be brave about her own parents. To have them feel the way Anne and John's felt, or Juanita's, was so new and so comfortable, it was wonderful. *This* war, they said, was inescapable; they despised war, but this one had to be, and had to be won, to rid the world of Prussian militarism and mailed fists, and balance-of-power deals, always on the necks of the poor.

This time it was the Paiges who were different from everybody, and somehow half of Barnett knew it and said snide things about them. The milkman tried it one morning and Fee was glad her mother slapped him down for being "a tattletale," and glad she gave him a little lecture on the Paiges' right to stick to their principles, yes, stick to their lifelong pacifism even now, and then said he ought to remember that America was a free country.

But it was exciting to have it somebody else that needed to be defended for what they believed. Whenever the Paiges came over to the house, the argument would start, and Fee always went pins-and-needles while she listened. Wonderful Mr. Paige could disagree so hard with her father—and yet they could remain friends. And Garry Paige had the same knack. The few times he and Letty came over, too, he would argue even harder than his father did. Even though he was about as young as Eli, he never budged an inch under all of Papa's pounding words or loud voice, and he never got sarcastic or sore either, which was such a dead giveaway about Eli. The war was morally wrong, Garry said, killing was wrong. And the war would not end any of the terrible things Mr. Ivarin thought it would end. It would just lead to another war, bigger and more horrible than this one, with bigger bombs and faster airplanes and faster, more terrible deaths.

Listening to him, Fran would look miserable, or bored, the way Letty looked, but Fee didn't feel that way at all. She noticed something about Garry when he talked up to her father that she had never noticed when she was little; he was handsome. His eyes looked bluer and his mouth went stubborn, and it made him twice as attractive as the old Garry she had seen around since she was a child.

"It's terrible," Fran said one night, after he had lambasted the "preparedness craze" sweeping the country. "Pacifists are even more terrible than socialists. It's just my luck."

"What's just your luck?" Fee asked.

"Nothing."

Fee looked at her with disgust; she was often disgusted with her. Fran might be grown-up, now that she was twenty and a teacher for nearly two years, but she was a sap about saying "just my luck," when nothing about Garry could possibly matter to her any more—she who could have crushes faster than you could count!

Fee was still in love with John Miller, even though he was off at Iowa State. Or anyway, she liked him better than anybody else. She wasn't the fickle kind, that was all, and never would be. Even if she forgot to write for a while when she was snowed under with work at school, or practice during the basketball season, she didn't go and fall in love with any new boy who gave her that special look or said she was a marvelous dancer.

And to have to listen to Fran say "just my luck" about Garry, with that moony tone in her voice—whew.

She knocked on the door marked *Principal* and Mr. Fitch called, "Come in, Fira." She had written a note to ask if she might see him, and she had rehearsed what she was going to say, but now she suddenly was stage-struck. If he said she couldn't, she would never get over it. "What's on your mind?" he asked as she sat down.

(369)

"Miss Mercer said I'd be allowed to," she began, "that anybody would be allowed to take over a Regents exam, if you didn't get a good grade the first time."

"That's true," Mr. Fitch said. "You are allowed to."

"How many?" She leaned toward him. "Could you take *a lot* over?"

"How many are you thinking of?"

She lowered her head, as if she were about to say something embarrassing. "All of them, except drawing."

"Drawing—that was back in your freshman year." Mr. Fitch looked at her sharply.

"I got sixty-two in it," she said, "and I'd get even worse now, so there'd be no use. But could I take all the other ones over?" A slip of paper showed at the top of one of the books she was holding tightly, and she drew it out and offered it to him. "I made a list of them."

He began to read it aloud, at first with rapidity and then with longer and longer pauses as the list lengthened. " 'English I, English II, English III. Intermediate Algebra. American History. French I, French II. German I, German II, German III. Geometry. Elementary Physics.' "

He gave a small whistle, and went through the list once more, this time with his pencil nicking off each subject as he counted them. "Why, Fira, that's twelve. And how many senior Regents?"

"Only three. English IV and German IV and French III. And they're not too hard." She added urgently, "I have real reasons for asking."

"Fifteen. Three hours each, and they'd overlap—you might have to take four in one day."

"Oh, please, Mr. Fitch, it's the only way I could bring up my grades and try for a State scholarship." With an effort, she added, "I used to have a crazy idea that if a girl got A's, she'd never be—popular."

"Are your grades very low? You've always been a good student, Fira."

"They're all right. Sort of average. But not good enough for winning a scholarship. That's why I got this idea—please say yes."

"You'd have to study up on all of the old ones," he said dubiously. "It would be like cramming an entire four years into five months. That's—a little excessive."

"But honestly I *like* having a crazy amount to do, if it's something I'm crazy about. And if I could win a State scholarship, then I'd have a chance of going to college instead of just Jamaica Training."

He read the list once more, this time in silence. Then he reached above him to a bookshelf hung on brackets and brought down a loose-leaf notebook. "I must say it's one question I've never been asked before," he said as he opened it, "and I've been principal of B.H.S. for sixteen years."

The notebook contained various official documents, Fee saw, and as she watched him leaf through it, a little hammer began to beat inside her, near her heart it felt, except that it also went tack, tack, tack inside her throat.

"—and it is expressly stated," Mr. Fitch read in a mutter as he came to the page he wanted, "—not to be construed—" He looked up at her encouragingly. "Let me just check this once more," he said.

By this time, the little hammer had grown heavier, and Fee's lungs felt crowded. Please have it say I can, she thought, please let me take them all. It's the only possible way to even try to persuade him. She saw her father's face, red with refusal, and she hated it.

"It seems clear enough," Mr. Fitch said at last. "Until such student has received his or her diploma—at any time prior—may take one or more Regents examinations again for the purpose of improving his or her grade for the final record—"

"I can," Fee cried. "I can, it says so." She jumped up from her chair. "Oh, thank you, it's marvelous news."

"Have you talked this out with your parents, Fira?"

"My mother knows," she said, sitting down again.

"And your father?"

She shook her head. "If I do win a scholarship," she said, "of course I'd have to tell him. But there's no use upsetting him—I mean, if I don't win one, then I'd have to go to Training next fall anyway."

Mr. Fitch looked disapproving for the first time. "If I'm not interfering, Fira, I'd suggest you get his permission now, before you start this—this big project."

"You don't understand how he can be," she said pleadingly. "Even my mother said I could wait until after Regents Week to tell him."

"I wish she hadn't." He closed the loose-leaf notebook and Fee thanked him again and left. She was filled with joy and gratitude. He had been wondrful, and let her see he was impressed with her— and yet she had told him a lie. Mama had said she could wait, only at the end of an awful quarrel, giving in because there was nothing else she could do to make Fee tell him right away. Fran thought she ought to tell him right away, too, and get it over with. The only one who agreed with her was Eli, the only one who advised her to say nothing, not one word, not until she actually had the official letter from Albany toward the end of August. "Why go through all hell with him, if you do *not* get it?" Eli said. He gave her a huge smile, as if something wonderful had just happened to him. "I used to say there'd be plenty of fireworks when you girls grew up and could give the old crank a real argument. 'Especially Fee,' I used to say, 'that kid's spunky and she's got a mind of her own.' I was right. Go to it, Sis."

For Garrett Paige, the phrase, "before the war," had a tenacious and evocative power, as if it were a phrase of music that would forever call up a memory, a time, a state of mind and heart that had once been his and was his no more.

Before the war he was an innocent. Before the war were all the years when he thought man could barter reason for unreason, with millions in every nation eager for the exchange.

But from the first weeks of the war, he was an innocent no longer. He knew. He would always date his first encounter with crime and sin from that August of 1914, with the first wounded screaming out their pain on foreign battlefields, the first dead going rigid and cold.

For that was when he discovered that men loved war.

He had always believed they hated it and that nations hated it. But within weeks—perhaps within days, even hours—he discovered that there was an excitement, a heightened life and importance among people who were at war, people who watched them at war, people who wanted to be at war with them.

The British newspapers revealed it, the French, the American. An exhilaration took hold of those who read the dispatches; it fired their talk. The phlegmatic disappeared, burned away by a hotness of opinion—we should be in it, we should steer clear of it, we can't stay out of it—

Life constantly notched up in tempo, in pressure and intensity. Around him, people were less bored, and therefore happier; they were making more money, and therefore happier; they snatched at papers, bought up Extras, swapped reports and communiqués like generals at military headquarters.

Like them, Garry snatched at papers, bought the Extras, talked of every advance, each defeat, the mounting statistics of the dead. But unlike them, he was solid with resistance; he could never grant that there was an ultimate good to come from this paroxysm of killing.

So many others had changed overnight. Within twenty-four hours of the first guns, H. G. Wells was declaiming that there never had been "so righteous a war," and that he was setting his pacifism aside. "Now is the sword drawn for peace," he wrote, going off into an ecstasy to explain how his "declared horror of war" had found the span of a single day long enough to overturn a lifetime's vow against it.

How did he manage with such rapidity? Garry wondered. Five weeks after that Wellsian flip-flop, his own life somersaulted, albeit differently. A mimeographed notice was sent around to all heads of departments at the plant, signed by Mark Aldrich himself. As of that day, the 11th of September, 1914, the Number Two plant, built to manufacture industrial explosives, would instead make only explosives and propellants for the Allies. Two ten-hour shifts were being set up; soon this schedule would be changed to three eight-hour shifts. Number Two would remain on a round-the-clock basis for the duration of the war.

Expected, expected, expected, and yet the actual moment had come as a shock to him and to Otto. War orders, they knew, were already vast; some rumors had them streaming in from J. P. Morgan, whose offices were the largest single agent for the sale of American war products to England and France, and other rumors insisted that Mark Aldrich had made a deal with the Du Ponts, and was putting both plants under their command. Either way, the orders were there.

At Garry's plant that same morning, a second announcement came from Sid Barclay, who had gone far since the days when he was "that fat salesman" boasting about sales. Just appointed vice-president in charge of foreign markets, he was now the operating executive of the older Aldrich plant. All work would stop at the end of that week in Number One, Barclay said, even where unfilled orders were still outstanding. Angry customers could lump it; there was priority on all orders from the Allies, and the plant was shutting down to rush conversion, so it could join Number Two in record time, as the European war crisis demanded.

"Nobody loses a day's pay around here," Barclay said, coming into the synthetics laboratory, beaming with the joys of generosity and mounting profits. "With double and triple shifts at Number Two, just move over there, and add ten per cent to your pay envelope. We're putting it in across the board."

Garry could still remember that moment. While Barclay was talking, he and Otto exchanged glances.

"I won't be moving over," he told Barclay. "I'll call Mr. Aldrich, and go see him."

"See him for what?" Barclay sounded suddenly chill.

"For good-bye," Garry said, chill too.

"You needn't bother," Barclay said. "He told me that if you were going to speak up again, you might as well save your time and his."

Garry picked up the telephone and asked for Aldrich, his face revealing his fury at Barclay's insulting delivery of Aldrich's insulting message. Barclay walked out as a hum of talk began among all the others—Otto alone remained silent. Garry asked Aldrich's secretary for an appointment. "I won't need but a minute."

"He's all tied up today, I'm afraid," she said. "Let me see, why, that's too bad, he's all tied up tomorrow too, and Wednesday. How would Thursday be, Mr. Paige?"

"It would be posthumous," Garry said, suddenly able to laugh. "Tell him I said 'so long,' will you? I'm quitting now."

He called across to Otto, "I'll call you," waved to the others and left the lab. Otto was not going to leave today, it appeared, but Garry had to be off, at once, alone, as fast as possible. He had no plan except to leave the building.

When he reached the street, a blaze of late-summer heat struck him, but he did not slacken his speed. A plan had formed and grown to maturity in the minutes it had taken to get downstairs. He walked at top speed to the subway, and then half ran from the station near Wanamaker's across to Fifth Avenue and Tenth Street, where he had left the Ford, over a year old and no longer babied by being kept in a garage. It caught with one flip of the crank, and a moment later, he was driving up the Avenue. To be off in his car, with the canvas top down, bareheaded under a hot September sun, at ten o'clock of a Monday morning gave him a high sense of adventure. He did think of stopping to telephone, but decided against it and drove across the bridge to Long Island City. Nothing had changed there. The vacant block beside the Synthex plant was still vacant; there were a few more cars there, and an oversized new truck backed up to the loading platform on the ground floor.

Garry parked near it and went in search of a telephone.

"You probably won't remember me," he told Molloy, "I answered an ad of yours last spring before the war started. My name's Paige."

"I do remember. You're with Aldrich Chemical."

"Until half an hour ago," Garry said briskly. "Could I see you again about a job with Synthex?"

"Sure," Molloy said pleasantly. "When would you like to come out?"

"Well," Garry said, "I'm calling you from downstairs, the phone booth in your lobby."

"The hell you say." Molloy's laugh was sudden and loud. "Come on up. I'm on the third."

It was over in five minutes, and Garry still warmed at the ease with which they had arranged it. Molloy told him he had taken the other applicant, the one he was to "see on Monday," and had never been too pleased with the results. "Good enough fellow," he told Garry, "and maybe I was right, to pinch some pennies then. But now with this war boom, we're full blast, so what's your pay been at Aldrich?"

Before he left, Garry found the opportunity to ask whether Synthex "might be converting to making war supplies too," and the primary sympathies of Molloy boomed a "Never" at him.

"I sure want to see those Heinies beaten, Mr. Paige, but if I raised one finger to help the Allies, sure as hell those damn English would grab off most of it." Molloy then talked hotly of the Rebellion, as if Irish Home Rule outranked all other struggles in the world.

Garry left with a flashing pleasure. It was done. The move he had so long ago begun to think of, to speak of, to discuss with Otto, to try to persuade Letty into endorsing—at last it was done. He had enjoyed his five years at Aldrich, had learned much, had earned his pay and promotions, and it had been a good beginning of whatever career in chemistry research he was to have. Now those years were behind him, for cause. That was the only good way to leave a job. For your own reasons.

He paused at the telephone booth in the Synthex hallway, and gave Letty's number to the operator. But as she repeated it, he said, "Hold it. I think I better make another call first," and gave the Aldrich number instead. In a moment he was talking to Otto.

"You'll never believe it," he said. "I've got another job!"

"Where?"

"Synthex. I drove straight out here and saw Molloy."

"*Verdammt*—" Otto's delight matched his own. They talked technicalities, about the equipment at Synthex, and Garry's probable first project for Molloy.

"When do you start there?"

"Tomorrow."

"Luck," Otto said. "I wish you the best good luck. You will despise me?"

"Probably," Garry answered. "What for?"

"I'm going to stay here." Otto was suddenly agitated. "I face myself and I know I live for nothing except to kill it off forever, there in Germany."

H. G. Wells, Garry thought, but for a different reason. The telephone booth became insufferably hot.

"Are you still there?" Otto asked.

"I was thinking," Garry said. "We'll make a date later this week. I'll talk you back to our side."

"Yes, well," Otto said, and then in a sudden spurt, unlike his familiar deliberate speech, he added, "Armament-makers don't make wars, Garry! They only make profits from them."

The rationalizations, Garry thought as he hung up. For the moment he felt bereft, stripped of something he had valued and counted on. And when he and Otto had their evening two nights later, he ended by feeling bereft again.

With Letty—

Their quarrel over Otto and Louise had become a pattern for others, especially after the war started; each left an acid residue for both of them; always they got over the specific quarrel, as man and wife always did. But each time the residue hardened, calcified into a stony memory that became another milestone on the road they were traveling.

He decided against calling Letty, and went to her shop in the afternoon instead. Customers were there, and he had to wait with his big news until she was free. They went to a Huyler's, ordering sodas and pastry, like children. Then he told her.

"Oh, Garry." She looked desolate and he understood, but as her silence continued, resentment climbed in him.

"What did Mark Aldrich say?" she asked at last.

"He wouldn't see me. He was 'tied up' until Thursday."

"Did he know you were leaving?"

"I told his secretary to say 'so long' for me."

"But you always said you would give them plenty of notice," she said. "Is it right to walk out before they can get somebody else?"

"I gave them my notice in March. This is September."

"You needn't shout."

"I'm not shouting."

He put his fork through the éclair on his plate and half of it shot away from him and skittered across the table and to the floor.

Looking back across the distance of two and a half years, he could still see that skittering éclair, feel again the lurch of his anger. He no longer hoped to find a magic that would make Letty share his beliefs. As he had done when she had first gone without him to spend a week with her parents, he felt familiar with aloneness.

But one February afternoon in 1917, on his way home from Synthex, he felt its grip with a fresh insistence. A newsboy at the foot of the subway stairs yelled his gibberish and a glance at his papers made it clear. In the train going to the city, voices were raised to a new level; whatever the words, the mood was the same: "Thank God, at last."

U.S. BREAKS WITH GERMANY

WILSON ADDRESSES BOTH HOUSES

—SEVERS DIPLOMATIC RELATIONS

BERNSTORFF HANDED PASSPORTS;

GERARD ASKS FOR HIS IN BERLIN

It is all but, Garry thought. All but war, and that will come soon enough. He stared down at the great black lines marching across the page like armies. Within him an excitement beat, too, different in kind, but a rhythmic beat just the same. My damn clock, he thought. The sense of time closing in was frequent now, and each headline of American crisis sharpened it and hurried it, for when the time came to act, his own crisis would arrive. Would he also exult and say, "Thank God, at last" or would he too find out how quickly the marble of resolve could melt into the pulp of acquiescence?

He stared at the subway flooring, and stamped his right foot, to get warmth back into it. He was seated too near the sliding door, and a stream of frozen air slipped under its lower edge; idiotically, his left foot remained warm. He picked up his newspaper, still unread on his knees, and folded it lengthwise. The armies of type instantly were chopped in two—a sudden killing, as in a trench in France.

He began, at last, to read the story under the headlines. It was, of course, inevitable, and had been all week, since the Germans tore up their year-old pledge to leave American ships untouched on the high seas, announcing unrestricted submarine warfare. Germany had invited this break; they knew it must follow; why did they want it, and to what military end?

He wished he could buy all the late editions and stay in and read them, but they were going out to dinner at Hank and Cindy's and there wouldn't be time. Connie and her Wilsonian husband, Proff Yates, had never forgiven him for his departure from Aldrich; they took it as a slur on the family ethics. But Hank, the lesser thinker of the two brothers-in-law, had thumpingly told Cindy that she wasn't responsible for one damn thing her father did, nor for one damn thing his chemists or ex-chemists thought about what he did, so why break off old friendships?

When he got home, Blanche told him Madame would be delayed, and set out a silver bowl of slivered ice near the carafe of whiskey. He made himself a Scotch and soda, mildly surprised to find himself eager for it, aware that the glow of the first swallow loosened the tightness of his nerves the way a hot sun on the beach eased aching muscles.

Letty was often delayed these days, often telephoning Blanche to delay dinner for half an hour or more. The war had made a big change for her, doubling her business, nearly trebling it. "You'll be a wealthy woman any minute," he had exclaimed when she showed him her final figures for 1916. Somewhere along the unbroken line of her success, he had put a halt to their earlier sharing of all earnings. "You make too much by now," he had said once. "I'd feel like a kept chemist." Thereafter, her profits were her own; she paid for Blanche and her own clothes, and he paid for everything else.

He was still proud of her "as a new woman," though he couldn't forget his newer feelings about the shop. Still, his work was his own substitute for other kinds of happiness, and he could not begrudge her hers. At New Year's she had moved to a larger place, farther uptown, with twice the space of the old one. Her Mrs. Everrett now had a younger colleague. "Very Four-Hundredy," Letty said about Miss McNaught. "She *knows* why a piece is good, without having to memorize what I tell her about it."

Garry sipped at his drink and thought idly that she had said the same thing once about Peter Stiles. Impossible—she couldn't have. Yet the notion stuck; she had said something to the same effect about Peter, a long while back. Funny, that he should remember it after all this time. "He has a hobby of collecting antiques," she had said. "If only he weren't a stockbroker."

Garry suddenly remembered the long-ago Sunday they had spent contentedly unpacking her first shipment on consignment. They had had problems before then, even quarrels, but they had not yet really mounted the tightly held animal of pain they had been riding so steadily through the years of the war.

He made himself a second drink and leaned his head against the high back of the great wing armchair that now stood by the fireplace, a comparative newcomer to their apartment; "Eighteenth-century and important," Letty had called it. It was still the same apartment, but in many ways it too had changed in the five years they had lived there. Every month or two, Letty altered it in some particular: a lamp she had not been completely pleased by would disappear and be replaced by another of crystal, with a dazzling circle of pear-shaped pendants just below its shade. Their familiar dinner plates would vanish and the table would blossom in a banded and encrusted china which Letty told him was Royal Worcester. A vase, a small table, the andirons in the fireplace, would suddenly not be there, and something finer and costlier would appear in their stead, always a something from one of the great names, and dated "circa" one of the great years.

How far a distance was this perfection of a room from their early talk of Letty's "five heirlooms" and of barrels and boxes she would paint red and gold. How young they had been then, and how unwarned.

"Read all about it," the old man with the papers shouted, as Letty came out on Madison Avenue. "Break with Germany, lady?"

She waved him off, not hearing his words. There was always an Extra. She wished he would keep quiet and give her the chance for one last peaceful look before she started for the Waldorf. They had changed the windows during the morning, as they always did on alternate Saturdays, and she loved this "outsider's impression" after a few hours had gone by. The niggling uncertainty about this piece or that was forgotten, so this look could be pure response, like a passer-by's, knowing nothing of the conflicts there had been, all so imperative in the morning. In this double-width window, she could do entire groupings, instead of "one major piece," and the problems had multiplied.

But so had the rewards. How wonderful to have taken this second huge step and have it start off so well. War prosperity was zooming the sale of antiques as if they were something needed in the trenches. She could not feel wrong about being so delighted; as long as her clients were more than ever prosperous and in the mood to improve their houses, she could hardly help doing everything to accommodate them. And if she did not, somebody else would.

She stepped back to the curb to get a larger view. It was so stylish to be way up here on Madison at Seventieth, and to have a second floor that was hers as well, half for an extra showroom and half for her own workshop. Last fall she had followed a hunch and sent Josh Flick to a trade school to learn upholstering, and faithful Josh, for all his limp and "looking peculiar," had turned into an expert at rebuilding old sofas and chairs, from the frames and springs and webbing up through the final covering with the costliest of fabrics. Now he left the packing and cleaning to another man she had hired, though he still insisted on polishing the brass doorknob outside—"for luck." He made three times the dollar a day with which he had started, and was worth every dime of it.

The window was superb. The lemony sweep of the satin draperies at each side was so much more elegant than the red damask of old; it was more formal, rather cold, but much more fashionable. The red damask would seem obvious to her now; it did at home, in the living room, but Garry still liked it and there was no point in rushing things. Next fall, if they renewed the lease, she could broach the idea of the same lemony-yellow satin there too. Duplication again. As Josh might say, "for luck."

But who knew what would happen by next fall?

Letty turned away from her windows. She hailed several cabs before she got one, and realized she would be late. She kept forgetting that she wasn't around the corner from Tiffany's, where it had taken only a flash to walk to Thirty-fourth and into the great lobby, either to find him already there, or to seat herself and wait for him to come.

She liked it when she got there first, despite the advice in the ladies' magazines about not seeming overeager about a man. She could watch for him to come in, and when Peter did catch his first sight of her, she could see the change sweep over his face, and it made her happy. He was forty-five now, distinguished and wonderful-looking, and as the sudden gleam took charge, vital and command-ing. For nearly a year they had been seeing each other for these secret meetings, usually at the Waldorf or the Vanderbilt, usually for tea, occasionally for lunch, and in absolute innocence, except for the central fact that they were in love.

Did anyone suspect? Did Garry never doubt the message from Blanche, nor wonder at the frequency with which Mrs. Everrett or Miss McNaught told him she was "out shopping with a client," if he telephoned while she was meeting Peter for lunch?

Luncheon. Tea. Once in a while, an hour in his entrancing house, conscious of the servants. But even without them there, they would have limited themselves just as they did. Peter wanted nothing clandes-tine and guilty, any more than she did. He would rather wait. He was so sure.

Letty sighed. Sudden sighs, deep and slow, were a new part of her life; she couldn't stop them or head them off. She knew it was pure nerves, but it worried her. Did she sigh the same way at home, in front of Garry?

"At last," Peter's voice said. She looked up. The cab had stopped and he was there, on the curb, paying off the cabbie.

"Darling," she whispered.

She was late getting home, too, and Garry seemed strange when she did get there. He was just sitting in the Benjamin Randolph wing chair, finishing a drink, not reading, not dressed to go, not even shaved and showered. He looked at her in an especially thoughtful way as she came in, and a squirm of fear went through her. She would collapse at the first word of where were you? whom with? Not that Garry ever would. Even if he did suspect that she was in love with Peter, it wouldn't be his style to "prosecute" her. He probably would call it quits instead and break up for good.

"You haven't forgotten Cindy and Hank?" she said.

He shook his head and glanced at the new watch on his wrist but still made no move.

"If you'd rather stay home," she blurted out unexpectedly.

"But you want to go."

"I could go anyway. I could tell Cindy you were running a cold and a fever, or something."

Relief was mixed with his surprise, and as she went off to dress she felt relief herself. How often she had wanted to go by herself without saying so, and here she had blurted it out and it was so easy! It was no longer that she wanted to escape war talk at parties. There was no way of shutting it off any more, no matter where you went. Now it wasn't just the Garrys and Ottos who talked about the war—it was everybody, everywhere. Half had voted for Wilson because he kept us out of it, and half had voted against him because he was being mushy-headed, with all his peace offers and his talk about all the nations forming a league. Garry, of course, still didn't fit in with either group.

She no longer really listened to any of it. It bored her, they bored her, all of them, every one. Garry, yes, Garry. She probably was becoming a "little peculiar" herself. The first time she had ever given herself away had surprised her more than it did Garry. It was terrible.

Letty shuddered, remembering. It had been New Year's Eve, the first one after the war began, and there was a big dance at the Grintzers'. People said it was the gayest, wildest New Year's Eve anybody could remember, especially people who had been to Times Square and Broadway, with mobs gathering early for that new trick the *Times* had, lowering a big lighted ball from its top at the last sixty seconds of the old year. By then, they all knew it wasn't going to be "out of the trenches by Christmas"—but they were gloriously happy anyway. And at the Grintzers', that same excitement kept building up, and a few minutes before twelve, the dancing stopped and all the husbands and wives moved close to each other, watching the big ormolu clock. When it started to strike, she said, "Happy New Year, darling," and Garry said, "Happy New Year, Letts," in his old way, and they kissed.

Then Garry said, just under his breath, "Dear God, end it for them," and though she knew that his religion was a deep part of him, a ball of anger exploded in her that even at this happy moment he had to lug in the war and the wounded. Without meaning to, without knowing she was going to say a word, she heard herself say, "And for us too."

Garry thought that she was echoing his prayer, and he said something sweet, but she was staggered at what she did mean.

Since that night it had grown within her, like an enemy-tumor, until by now it was unbearable to go around carrying it. She didn't have courage yet to tell him she wanted to end it between them; she couldn't get herself to the point. Never had there been a divorce in the Brooks family; her father would be indignant and her mother heartbroken and mortified.

And then came Peter, and a hundred new emotions, and time passed like flashes of lightning.

Letty raced through her dressing and Garry took her down and found a cab for her. The moment she drove off her spirits lifted; she was wearing her new pink crepe and could hardly breathe, but she knew how she looked in it. Peter was not to be there; he insisted that they should not "manage" to be asked to the same places, and this was a group of Hank's classmates and their wives.

But Hank talked about his brother at dinner, and it was a delight to sit there and listen. Peter had put all his own holdings into things like Hercules Powder and Bethlehem Steel, and Du Pont, at the very start of the war, and persuaded his clients to let him shift their portfolios the same way. The results were uniformly unbelievable, often as high as two or three hundred per cent up in a year. Somebody implied that Peter and Hank were millionaires, and Hank did not deny it. But his brother deserved the credit, he said. "There isn't a war baby Peter doesn't check in on. He's one of the men the Street watches."

A new joy took possession of Letty, oddly proprietary, but at the same time submissive, as if she were a little girl and Peter her superior in every way. A superior who was also her petitioner. The paradox added a private delight to her evening.

When she got home at two, Garry was asleep, and she undressed without turning the light on. Though it made him restless to sleep in a closed room, he had kept the window shut so that the freeze of the February night wouldn't fill the apartment, and she was suddenly irked that he should be so considerate. He must know something was wrong; he simply must. Why, the last time they *had,* must have been —when? How long back? Two months? Three?

No matter how modern she was, she could never think about these things or put words to them the way other wives did. It had been months, that was all, and Garry hadn't even tried or asked.

"Is that you?" Garry said, turning over in bed. She murmured yes and stood still, waiting for him to sink into sound sleep again. But in another second he turned on the light and asked whether she had had a good time, and who was there.

Again she was irked. To tell him about the evening was risky; she could not say it was full of business talk and war talk, but the ordinary kind, the all-right kind. She might blurt out that Proff and Connie were there and that Proff asked, "If we do get into it, will Garry be like those conchies in England?"

"It was wonderful," she said. "But I shouldn't have stayed so late. I'm so sleepy."

It didn't work. He was wide awake, and soon he got out of bed and put his bathrobe on. She said, "Can I fix you something to eat?" but before he could answer, she suddenly cried out, "Oh, Garry, I can't bear it any more. I don't know what's happened, but it's been happening so long and I just can't manage it any longer."

"Manage what?"

"We're both so unhappy, if we'd admit it," she said.

"Manage what any longer?" he repeated.

"I don't mean get a divorce," she said, "just not live here any more, not be together here any more." She was not looking at him. At the word "here," she waved her hand at their two beds, at the tall windows and the familiar garden beyond, then back to the fireplace.

He watched her hand carefully, as if he needed to remember which items she indicated. "You want us to break up our marriage," he said. Then he went into the living room and turned on all the lamps, one by one. Through the corridor of space past the kitchen, she could see him. He did not look surprised; he was calm, as if he were thinking about an experiment in the lab.

"Maybe for a while," she said, following after him. "Maybe until the war is over—"

"Some wars are never over," he said.

"What do you mean?"

"It doesn't matter."

She began to cry, softly. "I'm so unhappy," she said, "it's so terrible—"

He said, "I'll move out in the morning."

"I can go," she said. "I never even thought who would be the one to leave."

"Letty, cut that," he said, suddenly angry. "So far we haven't made a fool of the other's intelligence. Please don't start."

They looked at each other without moving. Then she said, "I suppose you wouldn't consent to staying here and let me be the one to leave." Her words seemed to make him angry in a new way, and she wished she had not said them. He went quickly back to the bedroom, dressed, and left the apartment. "I'm going for a walk," he said. It was nearly three.

She stared at the door as it closed behind him. A hundred times she had come close to telling him, usually after some awful evening they had been through at somebody's house. And now tonight, when he hadn't even been at the party, tonight it had come spilling out of her throat.

The telephone rang and she ran to it. "Oh, Garry, I'm so sorry—"

"Let's not go into feelings now," he said. "I changed my mind about the walk; I'm at the Brevoort. I'll send for my clothes tomorrow—get Blanche to put them together, will you?"

"Of course, but I—"

"I'll stay here until I can find a place to live in. I'll keep the car. You can have everything else."

"That wouldn't be fair to you," she protested. "All our lovely things."

"You keep them. Good night."

(384)

TWENTY-NINE

Stefan Ivarin stood still, considering the sign on the rising bank of ground in front of his house. Against the new snow, it was no longer a clear strong white, but a listless grey, its legend, HOUSE FOR SALE, rather faded and blurred. It tilted over at a slight angle, and a lazy indifference seemed to exude from it, as if it no longer took itself seriously, nor expected anyone else to take it seriously.

"We ought to take it down," Alexandra kept saying, but he always said, "Better leave it alone."

"But we're both doing so well, Stiva."

"Yes, but I'd leave it there."

"We wouldn't accept the best of offers by now," she said.

"Just the same, if you don't mind."

It was a talisman, he thought with some amusement, gazing at it, and then continuing on his way to Main Street for the first evening editions. In those first days of despair nearly three years ago, the sign had been for them both a reminder that they really had something set aside, more solid, more substantial than the $1460 in the bank. Their equity in the house had given them courage and a sense of safety when they needed it most. That equity, of course, had proved an unavailable blessing. But putting the sign out there had been action; it revealed their willingness to take steps, no matter how drastic, and that in itself had been a source of new vigor and confidence to each of them.

It also was a valuable object lesson to the girls; it told them as words never could tell them, that there were not limitless quantities of money available to fulfill their every wish, whether it were Fran's endless need for new clothes and new trimmings for her tennis court, or Fee's periodic spasms about going to college, which she doubtless soon would outgrow.

Now that Alexandra and he would reject any offer for the house, it was pointless to keep the sign there. Yet he clung to it, like an ignoramus who thought it had proved its power to ward off the evil eye.

(385)

Between them, he thought comfortably, they had indeed warded off the worst. Since they had put their house on the block, their fortunes had climbed upward—in every particular except his writing. Miraculous though it seemed, his heavy schedule of lecturing did not shoot up his blood pressure in any lethal way; both doctors had to agree that he was physically better when he was not in a black mood, and lecturing always lifted his spirits, elated him, made him feel at his best. These mysteries were beyond the medicos, that was certain; if, because of holidays, he had periods with no lectures, and did nothing but rest and stay quiet, his blood pressure soon was at an alarming high. When he was up on the platform, excited and concentrated day after day, it behaved remarkably well.

The second campaign for Wilson last year, and the wartime attacks on the slightest demands of labor as "unpatriotic," both had sent his speaking schedule to new heights. By the end of the year his lectures had brought in very nearly the same money as he would have made had he still been on the paper.

The Paper. No longer did a snake leap and writhe in his bowels at the thought of it, the sight of it, the mention of it. No longer was it a painful pleasure to see Abe Kesselbaum, and hear the latest news of it, a pleasure vitiated at first by an insensate envy and rage, yet a pleasure he could not deny himself because it satisfied his undiminishing interest in what was happening to Fehler, to Borg, to Mrs. Landau and Jacob Steinberger, a man he could have enjoyed getting to know had Steinberger not been bound to Miriam Landau, that female Uriah Heep.

The paper's circulation, Abe kept reporting, was "up again." It kept rising with cliff-like abruptness for over two years and then had leveled off, holding steady at 200,000, second by a few thousand only to the *Forward*. The profits, despite the greater costs and much larger staff, had gone up sharply too. Nothing was too cheap to get by, either in text or in pictures, though Steinberger had finally balked and persuaded Mrs. Landau to vote against one exposé of working girls seduced by factory owners, not on the ground of vulgarity but on the livelier one of possible libel suits. This had been rather recent; Abe had told him of it the last time they met, told it with relish, as Ivarin had heard it with relish. He found himself mortified that he should be pleased, but pleased he was.

"You know Borg and how he'd take it," Abe Kesselbaum said with a malicious grin.

"I suppose so."

"He had talked it over with every living soul on the paper beforehand. Remember the way he talked to everybody about his damned survey until you had to call him off?"

"I remember."

"He's ten times worse by now. Whatever idea he gets, he chews off every ear on the paper about it, from the press room up. So when he was voted down on his seduced girls in the January meeting, he took it as a public kick in the teeth, thank God."

Ivarin laughed with unfeigned pleasure. With Abe he had never dissembled; he never would. Of late they were meeting again in the café next door to the paper. Ivarin still had a special sensation each time he walked the familiar route from the Delancey Street station, but for a long time now the "specialness" had been free of that early bitterness of longing to be back on the paper as its editor. There was still a faint sadness, a deprivation, but no longer anything strong enough to be destroying.

This easing-off was not true of his feeling toward Fehler. It was Fehler who had killed him on the paper, and he had no ability to love his enemies. He was delighted that the *Times* had climbed even higher than the *Jewish News,* to a steady 325,000 circulation and five millions in advertising, and all this without any of the trashy tricks and gaudy splash of Fehler's paper.

Well, Ivarin thought now as he approached the newsstand, I've done well enough, despite Mr. Fehler. We've done well enough, rather.

Alexandra had been remarkable, and that was a fact. Not once had she tired or complained of working too hard, and by now she was ready to lord it over him when the word "lecture" was used. Three separate groups of immigrant women she had now, on three separate evenings, each group held about twenty, and in the war-born prosperity, the fee was twenty cents, so some twelve dollars a week came in this way, in addition to the ten or twelve more from her many lessons.

Prosperity, he thought wryly. In a way we are both war profiteers. He had reached the stationery store where he went twice each day for the latest papers, unless he was out of town. The owner had his three papers ready for him, the *Evening World,* the *Sun* and the miserable *Journal* with its thousand distortions, that he read as if he were still an editor and bound to keep track of the entire field. For him, in truth, there was no such thing as a glut of reading about the war. For him it was not only the war it was for everybody else: for a man born in Russia more than half a century ago, it was also the incredible possibility he had dreamed of and youthfully worked for and endlessly believed in. From the first days of the war, he had found a never-slaked thirst and hunger in him for news, but in addition there was a special passion for war news involving Russia. Ever since the loss of a million men on the Eastern Front, since the rumors of the demoralized army, the workers openly threatening strikes, his political sixth sense had been telling him that gigantic news was in the offing. History was on the march in Russia again.

Unconsciously, Ivarin speeded his pace as he walked up the hill. Drubhinov—was he still alive, that marvelous being who had drawn him into the movement, and then arranged his escape from prison? He had never written from America; it was their code. Foreign stamps and postmarks awoke the interest of the authorities too deeply, too fast.

Of course Drubinov is alive, Ivarin thought. Petya was my age, why shouldn't he be? He suddenly saw the fair-haired handsome young face, and longing stirred in him. They had quarreled about extremism as they became closer friends, quarreled over Stefan's conviction that even within a revolutionary movement, extremism was a proposal to exchange an old tyranny for a new.

"You and your tactic of moderateness, both of you belong in England," Petya once told him. "Or in France or America. Not here in Russia."

Had Drubhinov stuck fast to that rejection of moderation? In the 1905 Revolution, then, he would have sided with the Bolsheviki, opposed to Stefan and the Mensheviki. Enemies!

Stefan let his mind drift and speculate. Soon Shag was upon him, and in the house Alexandra greeted him as if she had been lying in wait for him. "Maybe you can help me remember," she said before he had shaken the snow out of his overcoat and overshoes. "I want to tell my other two groups that story about Joey and the pictures, but I can't remember how I started it. Can you?"

"Something about wanting to tell them of a little boy with the most wonderful manners—"

"That's it. Just a second—I'll write it down."

He watched her scribble it on the back of a bill from the grocery store, and he said, "I told you, you should always make notes so you *won't* forget."

She looked at him uncertainly. "I've tried, but it's no good. Later on, I don't know what the notes are supposed to lead me to."

"Then write it all out, like a letter. Make believe you are writing somebody all about it, perhaps in a letter to me. 'Dear Stiva, Today I told Sophie's group about a little boy named Joey who had the most wonderful manners.' Do you follow me?"

"And go on to the end?"

"The idea is to keep you from stiffening up and getting formal. Just you try writing down the two words, 'Dear Stiva,' and see if it doesn't help."

"I'll try it right now." Supper was late that night, and she looked weary when they had it. But at about midnight, she appeared upstairs at his desk, saying, "Could you glance at this?"

The pages she handed him were from his own writing tablet; he frowned at the larceny, and began to read.

Dear Stiva,

Let me tell you about a little boy with the most wonderful manners. His name is Joey. He is in kindergarten. In his school one day, the teacher was giving some of the modern tests, to tell whether a child was quick-minded and attentive to detail.

In order to do this, she handed Joey a picture, and said, "Tell me what you see, Joey."

The first picture was of a woman with two ears on each side of her head.

Joey stared at the picture, turned it upside down and then turned it right side up again.

"Thank you, it's wonderful," he said, handing it back.

"Is anything wrong with the picture, Joey?" his teacher said.

"No, ma'am, it's nice," he said, and with a polite little smile he accepted the next picture she gave him. This one was of a horse and wagon. The horse had the right number of ears, but he had only two legs, one in front and one in back. Joey stared at this picture, until his teacher said, "Is anything wrong, Joey?"

Then he said, "No, ma'am, it's nice," and smiled politely once more.

Then the teacher gave him a third picture of a dog with three legs, another of a tricycle with five wheels, and last of all, a top spinning on its thick bottom, with its metal point in the air. Each time, Joey gave the same answer. So the teacher decided he was backward about "perception" and she sent a report to the principal, who then asked Joey's mother to come to school to hear the sad news.

Poor mother! She was heartbroken about her little Joey, and when she got home, she asked him if he had not noticed that the woman had four ears, and the horse only two legs, and so on. Joey burst out laughing.

"Sure," he yelled. "But you always slap me if I say it's rotten, so I didn't."

From this little story of Joey, maybe you will see a moral: Tell your child to be honest and say just what he or she thinks. Don't, please, force the poor little one always to say "it's lovely, it's perfect, thank you."

Maybe you don't think you are forcing your own child to be such a hypocrite. But if you have ever scolded him for saying "it's no good," or "I don't want it," when you or anybody else gives him something, why, then you're in danger of having a little Joey on your hands, instead of a good lively little soul who says everything from the heart.

So stop nagging at your little boy or girl to say "Thank you, it's wonderful," and let them say what they think. In the long run, life will tell them when to be tactful. You needn't worry about it now.

Stefan began to smile almost at the first paragraph, and at the end he let her see he was delighted. "It's good," he said, "quite pleasant reading, human and natural all the way through."

"Oh, Stiva."

"You ought to do just this," he said, "every time you give your women some anecdote they seem to like. You know the other two groups will like it too, and you have it saved up as soon as you write it down."

"It does fix it in my own mind," she agreed. "I might even read it aloud to Anna's group tomorrow night."

"When you're through with Joey," he said jovially, "don't throw him away. Give him to me."

"What for?"

"A souvenir, should I say?" He looked at her mysteriously. "No, that's not it. I want to—" he broke off and said, with a touch of irritation, "Do I have to account for every impulse I may have?"

Several days went by before he said, "Are you through with Joey or not?"

"Yes, I forgot," she said and went to her sewing room for it. Forgot, he thought. She's probably beside herself wondering why I should want it.

"And here is another one I did," Alexandra said, giving him a set of new pages as well. "This one is about spanking, about what you said to Eli about making a liar out of Webby. But I didn't give any names."

This time Stefan did not seem amused as he read. But he read with attention, even absorption, and then said, "That's it too, a different genre, but it will catch at them."

He put the Joey pages into his pocket and as soon as he was alone at his desk, he inked out "Dear Stiva," and sent them off to the editor of *Abend,* a small evening newspaper that had been in existence since the first winter of the war. He signed the pages only "Alexandra Bartschoi," though on the back of the envelope, he wrote, "Ivarin, 800 Hill Avenue, Barnett, L. I."

Having written it in ink, he paused and stared at it. Force of habit, he thought, and wondered whether there were some motive mixed into this reflex action. He considered tearing up the envelope, and writing another. "A.B.I., 800 Hill Ave, Barnett" would be return address enough; "Ivarin" was not essential. But he had already put a stamp on it. Nonsense; he would mail it as it was.

Garry found a three-room furnished flat in the town of Flushing, not more than a twenty-minute drive from the Synthex plant. It was on the second floor of a two-family house, ugly as sin, with one saving grace: a view of Flushing Bay from the front windows.

Even in the denuded landscape of early March, with the low-lying ground still patched with smoky snow, there was a sparkle to the water that cheered him when he went about in the unfamiliar morning silence, shaving, dressing and getting his breakfast. He liked to cook, he discovered, but it was so new, so abnormal almost, to wake alone, to spend this first hour of the day in total solitude, that each day began with heaviness. He wondered if Letty was finding it the same experience; she had Blanche, of course, a human presence around. It must make some small difference.

He would get used to it. His parents had invited him—he had known they would, and he had known that he would refuse—to live at home again, but he was twenty-eight, a man who had been married for seven years, nearly eight, and he couldn't go back to being a child in his parents' house again, not even as a temporary thing.

He had stayed at the Brevoort for only a week, and had found his new place on the first day he had searched for it. Apart from wanting to be near his work, he had no specifications for the way he wanted to live; to his surprise, it was a relief to find himself in harsh and unlovely surroundings, plain and dull to the point of idiocy. He did enjoy fine furniture and the soft gleam of old wood and silver, but suddenly now, in their absence, he realized that there was a suction in them too, pulling at your independence of judgment about what you liked, what was good, what was attractive. Unless it were "important," you were obligated to disapprove of it.

He was exaggerating, of course; Letty would be the first to say, "Why, Gare, you never heard *me* preach any slavish following of period or that sort of thing."

"Why, Gare." He heard her voice saying the two syllables, and knew the sense of loss in a quick plunge inward and downward at the core of his body. The first days at the Brevoort he had been berserk with fury at her, and at Peter Stiles whom she had never mentioned, he realized at last, for a solid year or more, though she chatted often about everybody else they knew. By the end of a week he had cooled down, again surprised at the speed with which he could accept the end of their marriage. For longer than he liked to admit, he had known the end was approaching; again and again, after some miserable set-to, he had expected her to issue the ultimatum. How often had his mind gone waiting-empty then, like a beaker drained of its contents, waiting for refilling.

Even so, her words had come with stunning suddenness, and that suddenness could infuriate him still. There was a female cleverness to it, a particular kind of attack no man would ever think up or act upon. She must have known all winter that things were in their last moments between them; he had not made love to her for months, nor had she sought him, telling each other in the most blatant way that love had vanished. And yet that final night, she had made it seem, not a mutual parting, but as if she had dismissed him.

He looked about his ugly flat, as if assessing the distance there was between them. The sickly tan of the walls was matched by the unhealthy pink of the shower curtain in the bathroom, where he was shaving. Behind him, visible in the mirror, was the bedroom and a swathe of the parlor, with its "store-bought" furniture and pictures, its starched lace curtains, fancy lamps and endless knickknacks.

He thought of Letty seeing it, or their friends. "Or Cynthia Aldrich," he said to his image in the mirror and this time he smiled.

The telephone behind him rang, and his mother's cheerful voice asked him to dinner on Saturday. "Same time?" he asked, and thanked her, meaning it. It was already a habit, driving out to Barnett once a week, to have "one home meal" with his parents, and it was solidly pleasant, not a dutiful chore.

It wasn't that they agreed with him; it was that their terms were the same; wrong meant wrong, not unpatriotic. And when they went, as in the old days, to visit the Ivarins, who did not agree at all, who never yielded a point, there was a kind of good muscular strength in their arguing, unrelated to the vapid exchanges with most of his opponents.

The Ivarin girls were pleasant too. He did not think Francesca quite the beauty his mother called her; she was pretty but she was vain, and it flawed her. Fira was a surprise. She wasn't a child any more, and it was easy to see why his mother always pronounced her "striking." There was something intense in her and something original. He had never noticed until his mother spoke one night of "Fee's big secret," and even then he had been mainly amused at the idea of anybody taking fifteen finals over in a lump. But the amusement left its residue, and the residue made him notice Fee as an individual instead of as "the Ivarin kid," which she had always been. She did strike you, that was true.

Fee was ashamed about being so weak about her secret. She had told it to her mother, of course, and to Fran, because she had to, what with staying up studying night after night until at least two o'clock, and she also had to tell it in a letter to John at Iowa State, to explain why she hadn't written for so long. Then she decided he would probably say something about her plan in a letter back home to his family, so Anne would know, and it would be awful if Anne was hurt at finding it out in so roundabout a way, so she confided it to Anne too. And to be fair to Juanita Endoza, she simply had to tell her also. Then Ginny Smith, the captain of the girls' basketball team, bawled her out one day for not playing her top game at Center, and she was so upset at Ginny's tone, she found herself explaining just *why* she seemed lackadaisical on the court. Even Trudy Loheim, when Trudy smugly said that by fall she would be earning twenty dollars a week.

"Next fall," Fee said airily, "I might be in college."

"You're kidding."

"If I win my scholarship, I'm not."

"What scholarship?" Trudy asked suspiciously.

There was nothing to do but explain. But by now, so many people knew the secret of her extra study schedule that Fee began to worry about her father finding out. Mr. Fitch's advice about getting his permission kept coming back to her, and she was almost glad when her mother at last took a stand.

"You're putting a burden on me, Fee," Alexandra said sternly one evening. "I have never kept secrets from Papa, and I have never lied to him, and you are forcing me to do both."

"Oh, Mama."

"You sound just like Franny. I'm not a big boobie, and you needn't sound as if I am. Besides, you'll discover that this is the surest way of all to get him angry, when he discovers what's been going on behind his back for months and months. He thinks you're outgrowing this idea of college."

Her father was just back from one of his lecture trips, taking "a swing," as he called it, from Scranton and Wilkes-Barre to Milwaukee and St. Louis and Toledo and Buffalo, although she could never remember what order they came in. He loved his swings. He never came right out and admitted that they were fun, that he liked going to diners on trains and living at hotels and having all his fares and bills paid for him by the union or whoever was sending him. But everybody knew he loved the change and the travel, the crowds he drew everywhere, the applause.

Fee always thought of him as a lecturer now, and if anybody asked what her father did, she answered, "Lecture," and it sounded silly. She could remember him as an editor of the paper, but it was almost like remembering "before the war." It was that way, too, when she tried to imagine him rolling a cigarette and smoking it, though that bag of tobacco was still on top of his desk, and the half-empty packet of rice papers. Even the last box of matches he had used was there; when you were dusting his room, you had to be careful with these three-year-old relics.

The night before he had gone on this swing, she heard him complaining to her mother about the nightly waste of electric lights, and after her mother's explanation, he had said, "Am I supposed to take that literally—that she's studying each night until two in the morning?"

"It's true."

"Is this routine performance now at that high school of hers?" he said.

While he was gone her mother kept on at her: she had better tell him soon. "Oh, all right," Fee said, at last, none too pleasantly, "I'll tell him."

But when the moment came, she said, "Papa," and then stopped. He said, "Yes?" and she looked at her mother in a wild petition. "Go on, Fee," her mother said, "tell."

"What is this, a game of riddles?" he said good-naturedly. "Tell me what?"

"Why I'm up so late every night," she said. "I—well, you see if I could take over a lot of my old Regents exams—anyway, I am taking them over, all of them."

"Taking them over?" he said. "What for?"

"Trying to win a State scholarship."

"Good for you. How much is it worth?"

"A hundred dollars a year."

"Two hundred dollars." He looked at her in admiring re-appraisal, as if he had never realized that she could do anything that could be valued at so high a price.

"Not two hundred," she said. "Four."

"How four?"

"It's a four-year scholarship, for college," Fee said. "If you go to Training, you don't get any of it."

"But you are going to Training."

She shook her head. "No."

"What do you mean, 'no'?" he demanded. Gone instantly was his good-natured tone, gone his admiring appraisal, and in these five words there sounded instead the outrage and sarcasm that she had so often heard him direct at Eli or her mother, but never yet at her. Something went thick in her throat, and she couldn't answer him.

"What does that 'no' mean?" he insisted.

"I don't want to go to Jamaica Training," she said. "I want to go to college. If I win a schol—"

"You want what?"

"To go to college," Fee cried. "Because I—*please* listen to me about *why*."

"What can there be, for me to listen to? Are we so rich, that you can take two more years before you are self-supporting, two whole years more?"

"I can't bear Training School. I'd rather die—"

"You'd rather die!" he roared at her. "How many times have I asked you to do what *I* want in this world?" he went on. "And on this one point that I *do* ask, that your mother and I have always taken for granted—on this you flout us?"

"Stiva, if Fee does win a scholarship—"

"Keep out of this," he ordered Alexandra. "You are always ready to give in, supinely, spinelessly, whatever they want, no matter how shameless and selfish."

"It's not selfish," Fee said, her voice suddenly shrill. "There's nothing bad about wanting to go to college." She looked at him and thought, I hate him, he's horrible and unfair. She burst into tears, and at the sight of them, Alexandra's own eyes filled.

"For God's sake," Stefan shouted at Alexandra, "none of your tears."

"How can I help it?" Alexandra demanded, moving closer to Fee. "The poor child."

"If you can't help it, then leave me alone."

Alexandra clattered a chair out of the way and left the room. She banged the door so violently that her hand tingled around the knob. He was a czar, a Cossack, a tyrant. One by one, the children had come up against his will and gone through this hell of beating against its iron. First Eli, then Fran when she wanted to move out and live in New York, and now Fee. Fran had given in after a scene like this, but Fee would kill herself before—

The thought turned Alexandra motionless. In the kitchen Fee was crying convulsively.

"—Nineteen twenty-one before you are self-supporting," Stefan thundered, "not 1919, as we always calculated. That's too soon for milady who must do just what the rich girls do—"

"Don't you call me names," Fee shouted. "Don't make fun of me, I'm not going to Training, no matter what you say, I'm not, I'm not."

"Milady doesn't intend to obey her parents," he said, as if he were addressing somebody in the distance. "Did you hear that? She is no daughter of mine any longer, who spits on her father's wishes—"

The door flew open and Alexandra confronted him.

"Are you suddenly a patriarch in the Bible?" she demanded, tears wet on her cheeks, hair wild. "What's wrong with you?"

Stefan ignored her. His face was scarlet, the skin damp and burnished so that it shone. He moved toward Fee, facing her, standing inches away from her. "You are to give up this rich man's notion, do you follow me?" he demanded. "You need only two years to become a teacher and—"

"I won't become a teacher. I'll never be a teacher."

Hysteria flung the words at him, and Fee ran out of the room.

For a full week Alexandra spoke to Stefan only in monosyllables. He seemed not to notice, not to mind. But she knew that he did mind. She didn't know how she knew it, but she was convinced. Soon she began to find an exhilaration in this unprecedented experience. *She* was in a bad mood.

Day after day it continued. She left her food untouched on her plate, she muttered good morning and then fell silent. She could see him glance at her above his newspaper and then glance down, his foot pumping up and down on the linoleum in agitation. She would put his food before him and leave.

She would not forgive him. She would not, could not, dredge up the usual excuses for him and exonerate him. Never before had poor Fee faced her father in a battle, faced him head on. From babyhood onward, the worst times Fee could remember were when Stefan was fighting Eli or Fran, and of course, herself, Alexandra. Those times were bad enough, when his shouting, his unbridled rage and temper had terrified and scarified Fee as a bystander.

Now she was not a bystander, she was his enemy, facing him while his wrath and fury threw themselves at her like physical blows.

My poor child, Alexandra thought, my Firuschka. If this Dr. Freud is right, this war with her father can damage her for life; it will set off echoes she will always vaguely hear whenever she's in conflict with any man she loves—with a fiancé, with—with a lover perhaps, with her husband, and later on, her son. Dr. Freud might not be right in his more exaggerated views about what could go on in an infant's life, but surely he was correct and intuitive about the unseen damage done to children by the very parents who loved them.

Alexandra wished, fleetingly, that Dr. Freud had written more about the damage inflicted on parents *by* children. She thought of the night Eli had told her about changing his name to Eaves. Of his refusal to visit when his father was so sick. And of the family scandal when his infidelity was discovered that summer after the war began.

For a moment, Dr. Freud and Fee alike were forgotten, and Alexandra's heart squeezed in shame for Eli. During his second summer at the New Hampshire school, he had once again dawdled and delayed about finding a place for Joan and the children. But this time Joan suspected more than a lack of houses and when she finally joined him, she began sleuthing about. Sure enough, he had fallen in love the year before with a silly young thing, and was again carrying on with his pastoral paramour. Poor Joan—who could blame her for blurting out her pain to her mother? And then to Eli's mother?

But the pain children dealt out to their parents was dealt to full-grown people whose development could not be sent askew, in those hidden recesses of character, that loamy dark earth that held the roots of young plants and trees.

Alexandra returned guiltily to Fee. But Fee was not a baby plant, not a child of four or five. Perhaps her spirit would not be sent askew too far by this first primary struggle with her father. Fee had some inborn strength of her own to call on.

Alexandra cheered up. If the truth were known, she was rather enjoying this terrible period. It was as if Fee was seeing a lifetime's worth of what her mother had had to endure, how crushing Stefan could be, how cruel. It was a new bond between them, mother and daughter together, united in a basic experience.

"Don't worry too much," she said to Fee one day.

"I'm not worried," Fee answered briefly.

"You look tired."

"I'm just tired. I never think about it any more."

"Your light *is* on until two or three every night. You're doing too much."

"Even if I fell asleep, I'd leave it on, to spite him."

"Fira!"

"Well, I would. And don't tell me he didn't mean it, that he can't help being this way."

"Have I tried?"

"I know you're on his side. You always are."

Alexandra looked at her, dumfounded. When *she* was in a mood day after day, nobody in the house even noticed.

He does, she thought, and was comforted.

One morning a letter came, addressed to "Alexandra Bartschoi Ivarin," and Alexandra thought, There's a mistake, but how did they know my whole name? It was from *Abend*, the upper-left-hand corner said, and she finally opened the envelope and saw her name again.

Dear Mrs. Ivarin,

Thank you for sending us your sample column, about Joey. All of us agree that there is an undoubted audience waiting for such a column, amusing and instructive at the same time. We would like to discuss with you the possibility of running one like it on a regular basis, every Wednesday, on our weekly Women's Page.

It was signed by the paper's editor, Simon Tischmann. She read it twice, and then in a greed to prolong her joy, she raced through it a third time.

So this was why Stefan had asked for her notes about little Joey, to send them off on her behalf, without a word to her, in a professional submission of material. She had thought about them several times while he was away on his short lecture trip, but since his return and his terrible fight with poor Fee, he was beyond the pale so she couldn't ask if he was through with them.

And all this time, Joey was in a newspaper office, being read by editors. She started for the stairs, to show him the letter, to bless and praise him for what he had done for her. How kind of him, how generous, especially now in this period of his own life when he was so bitterly useless in journalism, and had been for more than three years.

Halfway up the stairs, Alexandra thought of Fee. She stopped. She was Fee's ally—could she forsake Fee and rush to praise him? Fee would feel forlorn indeed. Betrayed. A Judas mother and a patriarch father.

But she *had* to speak to Stefan now, tell him what a marvelous thing he had wrought, for it really was he who had done it. If he had not sent Joey in, she never would have dreamed of doing it. She was already slipping away from the task of writing notes down; it was hard, no matter how informal.

But to do it for publication. For pay? To see it come out in print? It would be the greatest adventure in her whole life.

"Are you going down or coming up?"

It was Stefan, and she looked up to see him at the top of the stairs, still in his underwear, looking straight at the letter in her hand. It was an act of God, surely, like a hurricane or an avalanche. Fee could not feel betrayed, when an act of God had intervened.

"Oh, Stiva, look—it's from *Abend,*" she said, rushing up with the letter extended. "How marvelous, sending it in."

He grunted and took the letter. As he read, his face lighted, and he said, in Russian, "I must still be an editor—I knew it would fill the bill."

"Did you do anything to it? Rewrite any of it?"

"Would I take liberties with an author, without specific permission?" he asked. Then he tapped the letter with authority and said, "You'll have an entire new career now as a writer. You'll see."

"I can't bear it."

"No question about it. Call them up and make an appointment. They'll offer you at least ten dollars a column."

The appointment was for that same afternoon, and they offered fifteen. Alexandra knew all about the war boom and how it was touching its wand of gold to all segments of life, even those not involved with guns, explosives, cotton, food, shipping and ten other matters. But it was with a sense of unreality that she sat before the

(399)

stranger named Simon Tischmann and heard him offer fifteen dollars every week for "anything" she wanted to write, in the general area of "guidance" to its women readers, help with their problems, "Americanization" in general.

"Fifteen?" she said. "My husband guessed you would offer ten, and *that* seemed like big pay to me." Her fingers flew to her mouth, as if she would cram back these unfortunate words. "I'm not much of a businesswoman," she said.

"Maybe that is why your first column is so human and warm," said Mr. Tischmann, and Alexandra loved him. The column was to appear as soon as they had three more, "in the bank," and the experiment was to last for half a year, probably from April first through October.

"We'll see how it's received," Mr. Tischmann said. "I'll mail you the contract tomorrow."

"A contract?" she said. "Why do we need a contract?"

"It's the usual thing."

She shook her head. "I have your word," she said, "and you have mine." She smiled, dismissing contracts. He had her pages on the desk before him, and as she rose to go, she said, "May I?" and reached for them, as if they no longer were hers. Page by page, she read what she had written, knowing that he was watching her, amused at her, as if she were not only an amateur but a child. He thought she was reading in a splurge of self-congratulation, and partly he was correct. Now that *Abend* was going to set it up in type and print it, it did sound a great deal better than when she had written it down at home.

But her real need was to see what Stefan had done to her pages before sending them in. Perhaps automatically he had improved her sentences here and there, substituting a word, editing out a repetition, without even recalling it later.

He had not. He had inked out "Dear Stiva" and added some punctuation. That was all. A relief rushed through her, and another burst of pride. It was really her work they were going to run. Stefan had respected it as hers and left it as hers, intact, an entity in its own right.

He was simply wonderful. Even when he was at his worst, he was still Stefan Ivarin.

THIRTY

With a start, Fee woke and saw them. It was barely dawn and yet her father and mother were both out on the sleeping porch, bending over a heavy rolled package on the floor. They were both fully dressed; they must have been up all night.

She recognized the package at once. That was what had awakened her, the sound of it being dragged over the floor and over the doorsill to the porch, the door banging open in the blustery wind, her parents' voices, low and yet excited, as they both worked at the heavy cord, undoing the knots. Inside was the flag, the awful bargain her mother had fallen for, so huge that when it hung out on the stubby gun of a flagpole up here on the second floor, it swooped halfway down the thin pillars of the downstairs porch. Every Fourth of July, or Lincoln's or Washington's Birthday, when the flag was out, she hated the hugeness of it; it belonged on a schoolhouse or a bank or City Hall, but on their long thin house, it was grotesque, like a giant in a baby carriage.

But hanging the flag out today? What was today, for Pete's sake? The sixteenth of March. What was *that?*

Fee started forward to ask them, but there was such an extraordinary look about their faces, what she could see in profile, that she hesitated. She hadn't forgiven her father, but by now her anger was like something set aside on a shelf, from time to time remembered, but at other times forgotten. The excitement about Mama's articles was a screen for everything else; you could be happy again, and celebrate with Mama, and even say a word or two to him, though nothing was changed about college or the Regents exams. He knew it, and she knew it, and they were in a kind of temporary truce.

"Franny," she whispered, crossing to her sister's bed, "look at them out there."

Fran didn't stir. The last knot was undone by now and they began to open up the stiff brown paper. As they stood up, shaking out the flag between them, Fee caught sight of their faces full on, for the first time. They both looked strange, and now their voices were louder as if they couldn't hold them down any more, no matter who was sleeping.

"Franny," she said again, tugging her awake. "Look at Papa and Mama." This time Fran awoke, took one look, and groaned. "Oh God, what damn-fool thing are they up to now?"

Stefan was threading the line through the wide white hem of the flag and again his back was turned to them. Then he worked the pulley arrangement and suddenly the flag snapped wide in the wind. He stood there watching it and then he turned to Alexandra and said something in Russian—

Both girls jumped forward. He was crying. Tears ran down his face, and his cheeks and mouth were pulled out and distorted. Never in their whole lives had they seen him cry.

"Papa," Fee cried, "what happened?"

"Is the war over?" Fran asked.

"Russia," Stefan started and then stood there gulping as if he had to fight for breath. "Russia is free. The Czar is gone."

"We were in New York all night," Alexandra said. "We just got home."

"The Czar gone?" Fee asked her father.

"It's revolution," he said. Then to both of them at once he said, "Do you know what it is, when a country becomes free?"

His voice broke over his last words and Fee forgot she hated him. To see him cry! Again and again she had seen her mother weep, heard her mother sob, but never, not once, never before this moment had she seen her father cry. She knew he was happy, but it was an unbearable thing to see. Her throat filled with the knotty ache it always got when a gigantic force pulled her, either happiness or sorrow, it made no difference which. They could be related, like that first day in church when she was little, and heard the pealing bells far above her.

"It's wonderful, Papa," she said. Then she made a half-turn toward her mother, and awkwardly added, "And you too, Mama," as if they had done something as a team and it wasn't fair to congratulate only one.

"Yes, darling," Alexandra said, and kissed her, and then kissed Fran, though Fran was still standing just inside the door, staring at her father.

He suddenly took out his big handkerchief and began to slap at his face with it, turning away to hide the fact that he was crying. He took off his glasses and dried his eyes, but the moment he put them back, he had to reach for his handkerchief once more.

(402)

Alexandra put a finger to her mouth as they looked at her. It seemed a long time before he turned back to them.

"And it's the moderates who did it, mind you," he said then. "That's what makes it so tremendous. *Not* Bolsheviki, but the moderates." He shook a finger at them, as if *they* were lined up with the Bolsheviki extremists he was forever haranguing about. "I knew something was up," he added triumphantly, "I kept telling Mama all week, 'No news from Petrograd? They're suppressing something—strikes, mutiny, maybe even bigger than that.' "

"It's true, he knew it all along," Alexandra said. "Come inside now, Stiva, it's quite cold out there."

"Yes," he said, but he turned away, resting a hand on the stubby flagpole, making no move to obey her.

"Let him be," Alexandra said. "Get bathrobes on, girls, and help with breakfast."

"Were you really in New York all night?" Fee asked, as they retreated into the bedroom.

"All night long. Abe Kesselbaum called Papa when the news came in on the ticker—you know it wasn't in the papers yesterday—and then Papa located me at Anna Godleberg's, and I dropped everything and rushed to meet him. All the Russians in New York were up all night, I can tell you."

There was nothing in the papers, that was true, Fee thought as she put on her bathrobe. She had Current Events class yesterday, so she knew. There was a lot of stuff about the Hindenburg retreat, and the railroads striking soon for an eight-hour day because it was the "eve of war" and their last chance, but the biggest news was about another American ship sunk by the U-boats, the fifth or sixth in a row.

Downstairs, one glance at the hurricane of newspapers all over the table told her that nobody cared about anything now except Russia. Even the *Times* looked as if it had exploded:

REVOLUTION IN RUSSIA; CZAR ABDICATES;

MICHAEL MADE REGENT, EMPRESS IN HIDING;

PRO-GERMAN MINISTERS REPORTED SLAIN

And the other papers went even wilder than that. Special boxes—pictures of all the Romanoffs—extra stories about the new cabinet forming—the papers were all shouting at the top of their lungs.

The start of the war must have had headlines as excited as these,

(403)

but she couldn't remember anything except her father walking toward her on the beach. Now she was grown up, though, and she knew she would never forget these. There was something private in them too, besides the public news, the something that was big enough to make her father cry.

He wasn't crying now. There he sat having breakfast with all of them—that was extraordinary too. At about eight, the telephone began to ring, and from that minute on it never stopped. At each ring it was he who leaped up to get the call, and even when he talked in Russian or in Yiddish, you knew it was all congratulations and joy.

"Evan?" he shouted once. "Yes, yes, of course—all night long— Please do, yes, I needn't even ask her, I assure you. She'll be as delighted." He suddenly burst out laughing. "You're right, quite right, like the call of the wild." Then he said, solemn for one moment, "No, if it had been the Bolsheviki, it would be a different matter altogether."

Fee watched her father as he talked. His face was younger-looking and his body as straight as a kid's, as if his writer's stoop was blown off his shoulders by the wind out there on the sleeping porch. When he hung up, he said, *"Their* flag is up, too," and for an instant his voice went shaky again. "Garry has been trying to call us, but our line was tied up. I wonder if Eli—" He cut the sentence off and substituted, "Evan and Alida want to come over tonight. That's what I meant about not needing to ask you first."

"Lovely," Alexandra said. "Simply the dearest friends—"

"And Garry's coming too. He also feels this is one of the great days." He paused for the time of a breath. "I wonder if Eli does."

"Stiva," Alexandra said. "You always say not to compare our children with any other children."

"All right."

"Not today."

"I forgot," he said. "I'm excited so I forgot."

Again the telephone rang, and she started for it, but once more Stefan was there ahead of her. A firecracker of annoyance popped off within her, that he should have *all* the pleasure this morning, but his first words restored her joy.

"Good boy, Eli," he said. "Beside ourselves is right." He beamed at the telephone, listening. "As you say, *not* the Bolsheviki—better not spoil the day with nightmares." He listened again and then said, "Good, fine. The Paiges will be here too, and Garry, the more the merrier . . . Here she is—"

Alexandra said, "See, I told you," and took the telephone in triumph, but nobody paid any attention. Somehow the whole day seemed to belong to him.

Fran could scarcely wait for the evening. The insane thing was that every time she thought she had grown out of her dreams about Garry Paige, something would happen to show she had not.

The day she heard that Garry had moved out and taken his own apartment, she felt that her whole life was involved, that the news was *her* news. She was no longer young enough to moon about him; nothing was going to happen overnight. A separation wasn't final; divorces took time; he might even be in love with somebody else already.

But she didn't believe it. Not Garry. He was the kind to stick to his guns—how often had she heard that—and that meant he wasn't fickle and fast either. She blushed. She had been called both, by angry boys, but that was all behind her.

Garry was twenty-eight and she was twenty. Perfect. It was only at school that boys were the same age as the girls they fell in love with. In real life the man was always six or eight years older, or even more. She'd wear her one black dress tonight; he had no idea of how sophisticated she had become. He would notice that she really had changed, in all the subtle ways that only the young ever recognized, one to the other, barred from parents as if they were not even there.

Fee had changed too, she suddenly thought. She tried to see her with Garry's eyes, and was relieved. Of course he would see that Fee was pretty now, and he might even know why girls always called her "a clothes horse." Everything Fee wore, from a gym suit to a sweater and skirt to a real dress, just looked wonderful. She acted as if she never gave a hoot about how she looked, but that was just an act. Fee knew what was right for her, and always got it or else wore her eternal middy. She was a whole inch taller than Franny now, and weighed the same, which irritated Fran, though she'd die rather than admit it. Fee had those long straight legs that didn't get wider up at the thighs, and they gave her the long skinny look that all the magazines now showed, especially when they ran pictures of coeds and college girls. The war had changed styles a lot, and the new ones were just made for people like Fee.

As if I care, Fran thought. Recently Fee got on her nerves. Everybody admired her energy all the time, everybody praised her "spirit" about the scholarship—except Papa, of course. Fran was on Fee's side a million per cent, but she did wish at times that Fee would ease

(405)

up a bit and be easier to get on with. Fee could be a damn crank too, just like Papa. She was always busy, or dead tired, or not at home when it was her turn to do things.

"Basketball," her mother said when Fran said it was Fee's turn to set the table. "How she can keep that up—and track and dramatics —that girl is killing herself."

With that insane schedule of study, Fran thought, Fee could at least have got off all the teams and dropped the senior play, but no, it had to be everything. "I'd lose my numerals!" she cried in anguish when Mama broached the subject of doing less. "And I have the *lead* in the play."

Fee always talked in that ferocious emphasis now. Nothing was so-so with her any more; everything was a crisis, climax, big headlines. Boy, if she ever falls in love, it'll be the end of the world, till death do us part and all the rest, ten times over. Ick.

Fran turned away from the mirror, suddenly disconsolate. She thought of lying down for a while before putting on her black dress, but then she'd have to do her hair all over again, and next time it might not come out as perfectly as this. What was wrong with her, she wondered, what was bothering her when an hour from now she'd be seeing Garry for the first time since he'd got rid of Letty?

It can't be, she thought, it simply is impossible. Fee would strike any man on earth as what she is, a schoolgirl, dying to stay just that for another whole four years of college. And in a way, she's a kind of nut. Men don't ever like girls that are the way Fee is.

A pleasant sureness returned. She just prayed they wouldn't spend the whole evening talking about Russia, that was all. Or how soon we'd be in the war. Good heavens above, there was more to life than that.

"I'd like my tea in a glass," Garry said, and everybody laughed.

"Good fellow," Stefan said, "a most fitting desire."

Alexandra had brought the tray, with the usual two glasses for Stefan and herself, and cups for everybody else, and Fran thought that this unexpected request was really darling of Garry. To see him try to nestle the glass of boiling hot tea on his curved fingers, imitating her father, was lovely, and her spirits soared. They had talked and talked about Russia, but with such a holiday kind of air, it really wasn't bad at all. Her father even managed to be funny when he got on his favorite theme. He cocked his teaspoon at his forehead as if it were a pistol, and went click-click with his tongue. "If it were the Bolsheviki, I'd be shot at dawn. Provided I was there." Now he was sipping his tea as if it were champagne.

"That's better," Alexandra said to Garry, "or you'll scorch yourself." She sounded as if he were her son as much as Eli, who was next to him. Garry's handkerchief was folded under the glass, and he was using his other hand to keep the glass from sliding right off it.

"You'd make a damn poor Russian, my dear sir," Stefan said to Garry, "unless you can dispense with that bandage over your knuckles." Then a moment later, in a different voice, he said, "I have to admit, since the news came, for the first time in forty years I've been longing to see Russia again."

"I too," Alexandra said. "Never did I dream of such a thing before, not once. Even when my poor mother died—it was too late anyway."

"To be there for the first free elections, see it with my own eyes?" Stefan said. "To speak up, with no secret police reporting you?"

He shook his head as if it were too much to envision. Garry stopped his clowning with the glass of tea. Eli said, "Maybe when the war is over, you could visit," and Fee asked, "How long does it take to get to Russia from here, anyway?"

"You want souvenirs of that trip too, Fee?" Evan Paige instantly demanded.

Fee said, "Will you *ever* forget what a baby I was about that Pullman hammock?"

Fran went to the phonograph and searched for a record. She didn't want to put on "Tipperary" or any of the war songs, because she didn't think Garry liked them, but a good dance tune might keep them from turning serious about this new business of going to visit Russia. So far, nothing had gone too far wrong. Eli and Joan arrived about a minute after the Paiges got there, so the first moments were all mixed up; with nine people around, she'd have to be clever to get any private word with him at all.

She wound up the Victrola, but before the first note, she knew it was too late. Behind her Eli said to Garry, "When we *are* in it, are you going to be one of those—those—?"

"One of those what?" Garry said.

Eli said, "Oh, nothing," but his voice was queer and hard. Everybody knew what he meant, and Fran held the needle at the edge of the spinning record without daring to put it down. The whole room had a hush over it; she forced herself to look around.

Eli was looking away from Garry, and straight at Papa. "I'm not going to wait around to be drafted," he said. "When we get in, I'll enlist the first day."

"Eli," Alexandra cried out. "Why do you say that? When did you decide? Joan, does he *mean* it?"

"I mean it," Eli told her, "and it's true. The day we're at war, I should think the one thing any man could do would be to enlist."

"Not quite the one thing," Garry said. His voice was quiet, but each word was clear.

"What else?"

"You could go right on saying war is useless and evil," Garry told him. "If you believe it is."

"Even if your own country's in it?"

But Stefan interrupted sharply. "Eli, what is this?" he demanded. "A military board of inquiry?"

"Of course not. Can't I ask a question?"

"I think not, unless Garry wishes you to."

"I was just—"

"Just having me on," Garry said, still quiet. "I'll be needing plenty of practice."

"Not in this house, you won't," Stefan said flatly. Without ado he turned his back on Eli and said to Evan Paige, "Is your new bureau coming along by now?"

Evan nodded. "We're up to our necks already."

Fran closed the lid of the Victrola, murmured an excuse and went upstairs. She needn't have bothered with excuses; nobody noticed her leaving. She could have killed Eli; he probably was still trying to make up for everybody's low opinion of him when they found out about him and that nitwit girl at Lake Winnepesaukee. And this was another selfish little trick to get attention as usual, not even thinking that he might be wrecking the evening for somebody else.

But wrecked it was. Garry stayed cool as a cucumber, but he must have been furious. Eli had as good as called him a draft-dodger and it didn't help to know that once the war did start, everybody else would be calling him the same thing.

Fran threw herself down on her bed, not even bothering to smooth out her black dress. Her eyes hurt and her stomach was squeezed and tight. I can't bear it, she thought, I can't stand it.

Suddenly she realized it was Garry she couldn't bear, not Eli. It was Garry she could never forgive. Why, *why,* couldn't he be like everybody else?

· · ·

(408)

Occasionally on Sunday morning, Garry would drive to New York to go to the church he had attended most regularly during the years he lived on West Eleventh. He knew he would not meet Letty there; she was a Presbyterian, and had gone to Unitarian services with him out of a wifely willingness, nothing more, but now she would see little reason for going uptown to Park Avenue and Thirty-fourth.

"He's a preacher who thinks my way," he told his parents once when they remarked on his "commuting" to church. "Don't most of us choose ministers who agree with *us?*"

"He's a good man, Holmes is," Evan said. "One of the ones you can count on."

As Garry entered the Church of the Messiah in the beneficent mildness of the first day of April, he was thinking, How characteristic, not only of Dad but of everybody, to weigh people in scales of their own making. "One of the ones you can count on," meant that the Reverend John Haynes Holmes, so much younger than his father's crowd—he was in his mid-thirties—was already a key figure in nearly every group his father had joined or helped organize since the first months of the war, anti-militarist all of them, against the preparedness craze, and of course against compulsory military service.

Garry sent dues and "belonged" to his father's particular groups, mostly to endorse his father, but he wondered often whether any group could ever budge history. An idea might, a man's work might, but a group, a committee?

The church doors softly closed behind him and the service began. Garry again felt the beneficence of the fresh April morning, and was glad he had come. Beneficence was not easy to come by these days, not in his private life, not in any other.

He gave himself to respite, seeking it, accepting it. But then the sermon began. Almost at once it was clear that this was to be no ordinary Sunday discourse, and Garry sat straighter, leaning a little forward. Around him men and women did the same; like beads on a string they all were suddenly looped on a current of excitement. Dr. Holmes was talking of the war, of the President working day and night in Washington, drafting his message to Congress, that message which would ask for a declaration of war. No man was in doubt any longer; no man still hoped it could be avoided. One day this week, America too would be at war.

The whole church waited; the minister's position was known. The pause was endless.

"If there is a war," said John Haynes Holmes, "I will not fight. No

(409)

order of a President can persuade me or force me to the business of killing." If the church found it an embarrassment for him to continue as its minister, his resignation was tendered then and there. But his position would not alter. "If there is a war, I will not fight."

When it was over, Garry made his way toward the man he had heard with such astounded awe. He was not used to making himself known to any public speaker, but there was nothing for it; he had to get close, he had to speak.

"I won't either, sir," he heard himself say, as Dr. Holmes at last turned toward him. "Thank you for the way you put it." He flushed, as awkward as a schoolboy, and added, "My name's Paige, I think you know my father, Evander Paige."

Later he drove his old car over to the Hudson River and then on up along the river. It was impossible to go home, settle down for the day, read. Vaguely, he longed for someone close, to whom he could talk. Not Letty, not anybody at all like Letty. He wasn't meeting new people; he went nowhere as yet, and was out of the mood for social life. When he was asked, anywhere and by anybody, whether he had a family, he always answered briefly, "I was married, but we're amicably separated."

"Amicably separated" was a lie. No matter how polite, how restrained, how calm their behavior, a man and a woman who had left each other were not amicable. They were filled with pain that they had failed; they were filled with questions as to whether it might have been avoided, if only one or the other had been less insistent, more flexible.

I'll be damned if I'd be anything, once I stopped being insistent, Garry thought. Without transition he began to compose an official letter in his mind. "Sirs, this is to tell you, I will not kill. No President, no public outcry, can persuade me or force me to this business of killing—"

He came to with a start. He'd have to figure out his own way of saying it. He wondered how much time there was left.

Three mornings later, in the anteroom to Molloy's office, Garry was waiting for the eleven o'clock appointment he had asked for. He was early, and though he had already read every word of the war message at home, he picked up the folded *Tribune* from Miss Alston's desk, saying, "May I?" Her nod was routine, but he was unaware that she watched him with interest as he read.

It would have surprised and rather pleased him. Victoria Alston had been Molloy's secretary for several years, proof enough of her intelligence and ability, but never yet had Garry managed a few words with her without finding the conversational burden too lop-sided to enjoy. Usually they said their good mornings or good evenings and let that stand for an exchange of the amenities.

THE PRESIDENT CALLS FOR WAR WITHOUT HATE

Garry stared at the banner headline on the *Tribune*. He read it once again, and there it was, unchanged. It was not a morning for levity, but the phrasing made him compress his lips in what looked like a smile. Kill but do not hate; eviscerate but do not hate; murder but do not hate.

"Now, come *on,*" he said half aloud.

"What was that, Mr. Paige?"

He pointed to the headline. "Did you read this?" he asked.

"Mostly I did. It's historic, isn't it?"

" 'War without hate,' " he said, in the tone of a bewildered man. "Loving little bullets, I suppose, sweet little bombs."

"Oh, Mr. Paige, you always say such things!"

"What things, Vicky?"

He glanced down at her; she was blushing. It was so unexpected a sight; he might have been loading her with endearing compliments. She fidgeted, staring at his hands holding the paper, and then beyond his fingers to the type itself. "It's just, well, it's a historic speech, and you're taking digs at it."

"At this soapy headline," he said.

"Soapy?"

"Mealy-mouthed," he said. "I didn't say a word about the speech itself."

"But you're not *for* it."

An authority suddenly charged her words, and Garry was interested. Was there a real person at this desk, not the automaton she had always seemed? "I don't think we can make the world safe for democracy through killing people," he said. "But I do think it's as fine a speech as anybody could make who does believe we can."

"That's what I thought you meant."

At that moment, Molloy came out with his caller. "Sorry," he said, "we took a bit longer," and then went on to the elevator with his guest. "You can go in now," Miss Alston said, and as he started toward the open door, she called in a fierce postscript, "You oughtn't talk that way, with people's relatives wounded or dying."

(4 1 1)

He wheeled around; her face was scarlet again. It wasn't a blush, he realized now, it was fury.

"I didn't know you had relatives in it," he said, as Molloy came back. "I really am sorry."

But inside, Molloy shut the door and said, "She hasn't one soul in it, Garry. She's just made it her own private war, and if it ended tomorrow, she'd cry her heart out, like being jilted at the church."

His venom surprised Garry. About everything but the Irish question, Molloy was generally in good humor. He was turning forty, and the first conscription would not reach him, so his edginess could not be the kind that was showing its ragged presence among the younger men at Synthex.

Molloy suddenly said, "Forget it. I'm fed up about something else, taking it out on Vicky. Now about those new tests you want to run, here are the figures of what they'll cost."

Garry ran through them, everything suddenly forgotten but the research he had been projecting for most of a year. A Swiss chemist had patented a process for making artificial viscose in transparent sheets instead of in filaments, and Garry believed he could go further and make such sheets so waterproof that they could be used for everything from a baby's milk bottle to a surgeon's hypodermic syringe.

"The figures," he said at last to Molloy, trying to subdue the entreaty in his voice, "aren't too far from my estimates, are they?"

"Mighty close. So get going, Garry my lad, and if it's a smashing flop, it'll be right on your own head."

Garry laughed. He was happy. Good Lord, he thought as he left the office, happy.

THIRTY-ONE

Before the week was spent, flags flew from every house in Barnett, from every house that had a flag to fly, throughout the state, throughout the nation.

Alexandra Ivarin wept for the young men who still had to die, and then she wept for Eli. She gazed at their own flag, remembering the joy with which they had hung it out at dawn just three weeks ago, and their somber pain when they hung it out at dawn this morning, the first day America was at war. Once again they had seen the sun come up, waiting through the night for the momentous news. It was half-past three when Congress finished voting and Abe Kesselbaum, sleepless too and at the paper, caught the news off the ticker and called them.

And this morning came the official proclamation of war on Germany, and the frenzy of rejoicing and recruiting and enlisting was engulfing the land. For the young and reckless, a blaze of glory and heroism lighted the skies. But for those with sons in their early manhood, there was the choke and gulp of fear.

"The day we're in it," Eli had said, "I'll enlist." Her only son, sometimes weak, sometimes hurtful, but her adored son. By now he might be in line at the recruiting booth nearest him; he might even be signed up, already the Army's.

She saw him as he would be in khaki uniform, the rakish overseas cap on his light hair, his blue eyes eager, his color high.

He married too young, she thought, he was trapped by life, and now it takes the risk of death to offer him the adventures he should have had.

Then she saw the khaki ripped apart by shrapnel, his blood pouring, his eyes glazing—she put her head down into the cradle of her arms and sobbed. The one pain not to be borne—how had those mothers borne it, the ones to whom it had already come?

Stop, stop, stop it, Alexandra thought. Do something, get up, go somewhere, and don't wallow in this danger you now have to live with. You're not the only one, you're not the only one.

Only then did she remember that she did not know for certain that Eli had already enlisted, nor that they had accepted him. If he were wheezing with his asthma, they would reject him, surely the Army would have to turn him away. The trouble was that between his attacks, he could breathe freely, easily; he might be just boyish enough, adventurous enough, not to say a word of his real medical history.

Alexandra moved to the telephone. It would be better not to ask Eli, but Joan might answer and she might know. Poor Joan, how different she had been since Eli's infatuation two years ago. Like all hurt women, Joan forgot that when she and Eli were the ones caught up in an infatuation too strong for them, she had seen nothing wicked in his desires, had found them as natural and good as life itself. But

(4 1 3)

when it was Eli and somebody else, of course it was agony and jealousy and outrage.

At least Joan had been clever enough to think twice before leaving him forever. Webby and Sandra were her "reasons," but she still loved Eli, so she did what women so often do, and took him back.

Alexandra's hand had come to rest on the telephone, but it still had not lifted the receiver. She never would try to hold Eli back from enlisting—never could she be so great a hypocrite, when she believed that there was no hope for humanity until this horrible war was won.

She rushed from the telephone and sought refuge in the garden. Her hobby of so many springs and summers was now, it appeared, an act for the good of mankind: the government called upon every citizen to grow as much produce as possible, to send more food to war, for our Allies, and soon for our own sons.

Remarkable, how her own enthusiasms all seemed to be coming home to roost now, bringing satisfactions the whole world could see. She had always loved her lettuces and tomatoes and radishes and corn, so now she had a head start on poor Alida who never had grown a thing except flowers for the table. And she had loved her little lectures on the beach years ago, so now her first piece had just come out in *Abend,* and she was actually an author, with four more pieces already accepted by them, "in the bank." And the first letters she had ever received from total strangers were already waiting for her replies! Five letters were received on Thursday, and then eight on Friday. Even on such a day as yesterday, somebody there had called her to tell her the number.

She suddenly hacked viciously at some weeds, chopping them down with her hoe. She ought to go in this instant to answer those letters; war news had let her put it off this long, but it was folly of the worst sort to fall behind. If she was going to be lax about answering such mail as the week's article brought, then soon she would be falling behind with the article itself. She had not been married to a Stefan Ivarin for nearly thirty years without learning what torture awaited any writer who had to race a deadline.

Inside the house the telephone rang, and it sent a nervous thrill along her skin as she rushed to answer it.

"I suppose you'll like this," Eli said heavily.

"Which?"

"They'd rather we didn't enlist until the term is out," he said. "Can you beat it?"

Her heart leaped. "Until the term is out?" she repeated stupidly. Respite, she thought, April, May, June.

"Registration Day will probably be before that," he said, "and naturally when that's decided on, they can't suggest any delay."

"But as for volunteering right away," she said, "the Board of Ed is asking teachers to finish out the school term?"

"That's about it," he said. "We heard yesterday afternoon."

She said not a word of her relief, and later she searched both the *Times* and the *World* for the school announcement. It was not there; it must have been crowded out of these early editions. But they would print it tomorrow.

There were two other students in the classroom when Fee arrived on Monday, and Dr. Wohl said, "Well, Fira, you are Number Three. For the grand total, we'll wait for the bell."

He didn't roll his r's any more, nor was he effervescent and amusing. Fee couldn't remember when he had changed into this somber man but it got worse as the war went on. There had been about thirty in the class at the beginning of it, and a year later there were only twelve. Four more had dropped out last fall at the start of senior year, and not a single freshman had registered then for German I. There had been pieces in the papers all along, angry letters to the editor, demanding that schools drop German forever, and Fee often squirmed at the idea of Dr. Wohl reading those wild-eyed attacks.

But all that was nothing to what he had read for the past two days and Fee watched him, without daring to meet his eyes, in a misery of worry about the way he must be feeling now. Sixty German spies, the papers said, were arrested the very day we declared war, sixty in New York alone, seized and jailed. All over the country, every police force was rounding up spies, too; in war, speed and no-escape was the first principle. The police didn't have to wait around for warrants or anything; they swooped down and hauled you off the way they used to do in Russia.

Fee hadn't had time to think of Dr. Wohl over the weekend. It was a crazy time for the whole family. Her mother shivered through half of it expecting Eli not only to enlist but die in battle any minute, and her father, grimly satisfied about our getting into the war at last to help win it, was absolutely livid about the fanatic spy hunt, and he was over with Mr. Paige half the weekend, yelling his head off even worse after he got back. All kinds of old laws of sedition and treason, from as far back as 1798 and the War of 1812, were being rushed back to life, he said, and every human being who cared a fig for decency and justice would have to enlist for this other war here at home, parallel to the visible one in Europe.

Out in the school corridor the bell rang, and Dr. Wohl closed the door. Nobody else had arrived; that meant the other five wouldn't stick it out until June. With a spark of his old style, Dr. Wohl counted them aloud, *"Eins, zwei, drei,"* and then bowed low. "A crowded classroom, under the circumstances," he said. "I thank you."

Fee felt awful. He rapped briskly on his desk with his knuckles and said "Page eighty-two, please, Class," and the word "Class" made her hate the five who had quit. One of them was Trudy Loheim, and she knew Trudy wasn't home sick because she had seen her in the hall. A couple of weeks ago, Anne Miller told Fee that the Loheims were going to change their name to Lowe because Loheim was so German, and then they hadn't, because they thought Lowe sounded Jewish. It had made Fee sore, but now all she thought was that Trudy was mean and cheap to walk out on Dr. Wohl. He was an American citizen and everybody knew it, and had been since before Trudy was born.

It isn't fair, she thought, it isn't. In a flash, like a dream, she suddenly saw Dr. Wohl as a little boy getting up in class to answer a question, with everybody giggling behind his back and making fun of him. Though the little boy was only about ten, he had a reddish goatee and a rounded stomach, but his voice went piping high as he tried to answer the teacher, and the giggling and laughing got louder. In another flash the little boy was gone.

"Another paragraph, if you please." This was the real Dr. Wohl, and Fee forced her attention back to the translation. But after class she hung around a minute; she wanted to say something nice to him. She couldn't think what, though, so she made up a question about the subjunctive mode, and they talked about that.

By the start of the next week, one of the others dropped out, and Dr. Wohl elaborately counted, *"Eins UND zwei.* Further casualties, and we may have to disband."

A different sort of distress flooded Fee, and she was furious at him for making jokes. If they disbanded as a class, maybe they wouldn't even give Regents exams in German—and her scholarship could go down the drain. Out of the fifteen she was taking, *four* were in German, and all the cramming she had been doing on the three easy Germans had done marvels for her work in Senior German, too. She was counting on a 90 to 95 in it, and even better in the others.

To lose these four! It wouldn't be fair, not the way she had been slaving. The other day, Mr. Fitch told Miss Mercer she had character, and Miss Mercer passed it along with a big smile. But now everything in her character focused on this one danger; she could not get it out of her head and she connected it with Dr. Wohl and couldn't bear him for being so offhand about it.

Nor could she wait patiently day after day for nearly three whole months, waiting to find out. It would drive her crazy; she might have a nervous breakdown or something long before then. Maybe it would upset Dr. Wohl to pin him down now. But she didn't care; she couldn't think about everybody in the world's feelings. She stopped at his desk again and said, "Would there be Regents anyway, do you know?"

He looked at her without asking what she meant. He always knew what she meant. Then he said, "Mr. Fitch says, this year without question."

"Oh, you checked up already."

"I knew Miss Fira would be thinking of her scholarship soon enough," he said.

He said it almost in his old twinkly way, but Fee blushed. "I was worried," she said lamely. "I mean, if *I* was the only one left—"

"A natural worry."

"Oh, Dr. Wohl, I was worried about other people too."

"That is nice," he said, as if he believed her. He let her get as far as the door and then called her back. "What would you say if I told you that I am also cramming night and day on something?"

"On what, *Herr Doktor?*"

"This coming Monday, I take over two of Mr. Burney's classes, in algebra." Her surprise delighted him. "Mr. Burney enlisted, and I wish him well."

"Enlisted?" Fee showed her astonishment.

"Why not? He's a young man, not an old tub like some of us."

"But the Board of Education ordered all teachers to finish out the term," she said.

"What's this?"

She only stared at him. Then she shook her head and said, "Just another rumor, I guess," but like an explosion in her mind was the realization that Eli had made it all up, about the Board of Ed not letting teachers enlist until June. That night she was glad her mother was off in New York. Mama could always guess if something had happened, and pry it out of you. She would make a big speech about how wrong parents were to dig and pry into their children's developing minds—she probably would make it a subject for her lecture groups, and then write it as an article later on. But in one way or another, she would pry it out of you just the same.

Fran was at home, but Fee never told her things like this any more. Fran probably hadn't even noticed Eli taking digs at Garry about rushing out to enlist. For a few seconds, she considered telephoning Eli and having it out with him about his lie, after his holier-than-thou dig at Garry about enlisting on the spot. But she made no move to the phone. Suddenly it came to her that the only person in the world that she really wanted to tell it to was Garry Paige.

She could see him balancing the glass of tea on his folded handkerchief, and then the way he changed when Eli started in on him. She could hear his voice too, not joking any more. *Just having me on . . . I'll be needing plenty of practice.*

Without warning, the painful knot rose in her throat, and the great force tore at her, half sorrow and half something else. This time it had no name.

She almost prayed that people wouldn't take digs at Garry about rushing out to enlist, but she was out of the habit of praying. She stopped saying prayers when she stopped going to Grace Episcopal, and that was a long time back. She couldn't remember when exactly, except that it was about two years after she'd started to go. John Miller was already off at Iowa State, so he never went with them any more, but she still hadn't ever skipped a single Sunday, except if she had a cold and wasn't allowed out of the house.

And then one time the minister bowed his head and begged God to keep the nation out of the bloody war that was raging across the sea, and it sort of sounded like a whine, moaning around to God, beseeching Him to keep our fine strong-limbed young men out of the carnage but not wasting a breath on the fine strong-limbed young men in Europe. It wasn't only a whine; it was so selfish, and somehow after that she didn't feel happy and good in church any more and began to stay away.

I don't have to pray about Garry, Fee thought now. I can just hope people won't take nasty digs at him, whatever he's going to do, that's all. Please don't let them, please.

From the platform that night, Stefan Ivarin was far too nearsighted to be sure whether the blurred uniforms in the rear of the hall were policemen or not. He halted so briefly at the idea, that his audience took it for one of his pauses.

"So for all my shudders," he went on, flinging his words out into the audience, "I was long ago positive that we must enter this inescapable war. At first, when it was just starting in Europe, many of us, most real socialists, condemned it out of hand. It is our tradition—it was always our tradition—to be against wars, all wars between ententes and alliances, wars which always ended by making new power blocs, new fortunes, and new exploitation of the working class.

"The only exception, the *only,* mind you, were wars of revolt against kings and emperors and czars—the French Revolution, our own Revolutionary War in America to throw off England, the Civil War to end slavery—these were the only wars a socialist could ever call—if not a good war, then a necessary war, an inescapable war."

He paused, and the crowd waited for the "But" that was to come. They knew what it would be; their papers and many of the papers in English, that they could read a little or which their children read to them, all had said it—since the news came from Russia a month ago: BUT now, defeat for the Allies would also be a deathblow for the young revolution, the return of the Romanoffs for another hundred years.

"But," Ivarin went on, "there is another inescapable war—and that also has to be won. This war too will have many battlefronts— The Espionage Act they call it, and it's before Congress now. Every word you or I say can be a target on *these* battlefronts, every opinion, each meeting, every newspaper or magazine. Already they are rounding up the work of the labor press, the socialist press, calling everything 'anarchist'—that damnable convenient label.

"While we're getting rid of Prussians in Germany and the secret police in Russia, are we to grow their brothers over here?"

From the side of the platform, a young man began to tiptoe out to the center of the stage. Ivarin stopped short at this unheard-of intrusion, but the young man whispered, "Important," as he came on. Behind him murmurs sprang up in the crowd and there was a sweep of new interest.

"The manager of the hall," the young man whispered, "made me come. There are four policemen in the audience, with a translator, to take down everything. Please don't be excited."

"I thought I saw them," Stefan said. "I wasn't sure."

"And outside, on the sidewalk, there are perhaps eight, ten, with high-powered rifles. But our permit is in order. Nothing overlooked."

"Are we sending somebody to the police?"

"They're on the way."

"So they want me to keep the audience calm. I'll try."

Throughout this colloquy, Ivarin's hand had been raised to the audience, in a signal to them to be patient, to wait just a moment. Now he nodded farewell pleasantly to the young man on the platform and then addressed his listeners in an easy voice, as if he had an amusing anecdote to share with them. "As if by a special favor to me," he said, "arranged by some helpful friend in the Mayor's or the Police Commissioner's office, we have been given a beautiful illustration of what I mean.

"Every good teacher—and I was a teacher long before I became a lecturer—wants the perfect illustration for his pupils, to make a point, to drum it into their heads. Now this is a point you need not be alarmed about—we have the legal papers to meet here, as we have met a hundred times before.

"But the fact is that the police seem interested in listening to every word I say. I did not know I was so fascinating as all that. There are also a few policemen outside in the street—but we have all learned from strikes and picket lines that never, never must we give these gentlemen what looks like any reason for getting rough, so not one of us will begin to shout or shove. Not here, nor later out there. Agreed? Your word?"

There was a roar of "Sure . . . Yes . . . You bet," but Ivarin's hand was up for silence through it all.

"These policemen were sent here tonight, just in case. In case what? Just in case. They know that socialists hired the hall; they know I am a socialist. And we are workingmen, after all. I do not think any policemen have been sent to any meeting that J. P. Morgan may be holding tonight, or John D. Rockefeller.

"But we are poor men, and we belong to unions. We will soon be making something like a million khaki uniforms for the new army, and a million or so overcoats, and another million hats, and a million khaki shirts. Up in Lawrence Mass, the workers will be weaving the cloth for these millions of pieces, and somewhere else, other workers will be making two million pairs of shoes, and digging a million tons of coal for the million ships to carry the fifty million shells and rifles and grenades, to win this war that must be won.

"Perhaps that is why the police are so fascinated with us. We are important. We are valuable. We must be protected and cherished.

"BUT—some of us are also cranks about a phrase we know by heart. We heard it in Europe before we bought our tickets in the steerage. We said it here a thousand times before we got our first papers. 'It's a free country' and we want to keep it free. Not only in peacetime. Even now, in war, with the necessary taboos on military information—even so, we want to go on saying 'It's a free country' and we will fight every inch to keep it free. Won't we?"

This time when the roar came, Ivarin held up no hand to stop it.

. . .

(420)

In some unlooked-for way, the actuality of being at war made Garry think more often of Letty. *All you think of is war, war, war.* Her furious phrases took to sounding again in his mind. *All you think of is what* you *want, what* you *believe, what* you'll *do."*

She was wrong. She was unjust and she was wrong. She had been wrong then, and she would be wrong now. At that time he had thought of their life, their needs and plans, the baby they both wanted, the children. And now, too, he thought of a thousand things apart from the war and his beliefs about it; he was absorbed in his sheet-synthetic experiments at the lab, mesmerized by their problems and quirks, on a deeper level than he had ever reached on any research of any sort. He still enjoyed people and easily made friends; at Synthex, there was nobody like Otto Ohrmann, but a chemist named Plevette was intelligent and likable, and they were soon sharing many free evenings. Plevette was devoted to the theater, and once a week or so they went to Broadway for dinner at a steak house and then a show. Plevette liked to dance, too, and several times lured Garry along for an evening, talking about a pretty girl he wanted him to meet. These evenings always held a special invitation in them, but the expectations were usually greater than the outcome. Plevette once told him he was growing monkish and virtuous, but Garry knew better, knew it with the wretched authority of his private misery.

It's a damn stupid way to live, he thought often. "A lonely way to live" was a phrase that offended him, and one night only was it formed by his treacherous mind before he could halt it. That was the night war was declared.

One evening a month later, he had a sudden impulse to take a walk past Letty's shop. He had no reason to find himself in that neighborhood and never had laid eyes on it since they had parted. The idea came to him at the theater and he told Plevette he had a late engagement. While Plevette gave him a knowing grin of farewell, he set off at a stroll for Madison and Seventieth.

It was nearly half past eleven as he approached the shop. From a distance he could see a mild square glow from one of the show windows; Letty still kept her display lighted until midnight, and the outside switch that would be turned off by the night watchman at twelve was still part of her life. The small unimportant fact took on a sudden poignancy.

He slowed down. He had chosen the opposite side of the avenue; if she were staying late at the shop, or were showing it to some friend, he did not want to come upon her, discomfiting them both. They had exchanged a brief letter or two on impersonal things like bills and charges, but they had not seen each other or talked by telephone. Neither had set forth these conditions; they seemed inevitable to each of them. It was more than three months since he had gone to the Brevoort. A quarter of a year.

Even from where he stood, Garry could see the gilt legend, "Mrs. Garrett Paige, Antiques," and again a small poignancy stabbed him. By now it was clear that the shop was deserted, and he crossed the street and stood, like any casual window shopper, gazing in past the gleam of its double plate-glass windows.

The display was beautiful. For a moment he tried to remember what he had learned from Letty, to be able to name the long slender settee or sofa facing out at him; the long flutings, the reed-like legs, but he gave up. It could be Chippendale or Sheraton or Hepplewhite; in some complex, convoluted way he was glad he did not know. The release he had felt in his ugly three-room flat was mysteriously heightened by his nearness now to this glassed-in perfection.

Letty's sense of release must be heightened too. Now, with the war, her long disapproval of him must have grown worse. Just about everybody else's had.

Extraordinary and unwelcome, a shaft of apprehension drove through him. "Now, with the war"—it was a ghoul calling the changes in a simple dance, a calm and simple dance that had been familiar and dear. Now, with the war. Long ago Letty had said he would change, if ever war did come, and he suddenly twisted with longing to do just that, to change, to be like others and run their risks with them, not a special set of risks of his own, risks that were not even codified, that were vague and unknown. The apprehension deepened and became so sharp it was fear. It held him as he stood there looking in at her beautiful scene made of polished woods and shining crystal and cool yellow draperies flowing untroubled down the outer edges.

Garry turned harshly away. He slept badly that night and next morning telephoned Cindy Stiles, to ask if she and Hank would let him take them out to dinner and the theater soon.

"We'd love it," she said promptly. "We miss you."

"It's nice to hear *that*," he said, with a laugh that undid some of his emphasis. "What haven't you seen? And what night?"

They agreed on Friday of the following week, and then Cindy impulsively added, "It's been so long, Garry, why don't you come on over and have supper tonight—we're stuck with the babies. It'll just be my cooking."

"The best kind," he said, a decided lift in his spirits.

Hank was equally glad to see him, though he said at once, "Bob Grintzer may drop in later. Are you and he all right?"

"I forgot Bob," Cindy said. "Did you know Betty's had another baby? She's still in the hospital and he passes here on his way home."

Garry hoped Bob would be sidetracked, but said he'd like to see him again. It was quite natural, neither forced nor obvious, to add, "Have you seen Letty? How is she?"

"Fine," Hank said. "She seems just fine."

"She had to hire a third woman," Cindy said, "to shop for fabrics and wallpapers, and write letters and bills and things. That's five people working for her!" She went on about the new complications Letty had to face, now that the supply problems that had plagued her for the last three years, about imports from England and France, were starting in all over again right at home. "She's already buying up bolts of absolutely everything in America, you know, of *anything* good to make curtains or drapes with, or upholster things in."

There was silence. Garry wished they would volunteer what he knew they were thinking about. Was she in love with Hank's brother Peter, or with anybody else? Was she happy? Did she go out constantly? Was she ever sad, or troubled?

"Who do you think's enlisted?" Hank said then. "My brother-in-law, Proff, that's who. In the Navy, like his father and grandfather."

"Connie gets me sick," his wife said, not explaining it.

"They'll have to come and get *me,*" Hank said. "If conscription passes, why fine, but—"

"You'll be exempted if it does pass, Hank," Cindy said sharply. "Married, and two children? Please!"

From that instant on, right through supper, which they had in the kitchen on the ground floor of the house, there was no break in their talk of the war, and when Bob Grintzer arrived, they were at it still.

But with Bob's first words, the evening changed. Maybe it's his name, Garry thought. Is he turning into another of these fool German-name apologists? "I can't see," Bob said truculently, "where anybody gets off, attacking conscription any longer. It sure is going to pass and be a key part of the war effort."

"Until it becomes law," Garry said flatly, "I can talk for it, against it, at it, under it, over it or any other way I choose."

"You sure can," Hank said. "They're still at it hot and heavy in Congress. Why shouldn't you?"

"When it comes to that," Garry added, straight at Grintzer, "after

(423)

it becomes law! What's wrong with saying it should be repealed, that it's unconstitutional? We've done that with plenty of other laws that passed."

"Not in wartime."

"Come on, Bob," Hank said. "The idea of it gets my goat, too—I don't even know why."

"Sure you know why," Garry said hotly. "Damn it, Hank, forced conscription goes against the grain in this country, that's all there is to it. It always has. Start it up now as an emergency measure, good Lord, after a while it gets to be taken for granted. Before long, you've got it in peacetime too, and nobody even gets up and argues any more."

"Sure, sure," Grintzer said, "go worry about fifty years from now, and lose the war today. The only *real* question is what you intend to do about conscription now."

"What I intend to do about it?" Garry now was truculent too.

"Yes, you," Grintzer said stiffly.

"That's my business, wouldn't you say? I'm not asking you what you'll do about it, or saying what I think you should or shouldn't do."

Bob Grintzer stood up. "That about finishes it," he said, looking only at Hank. "I'll run along."

"Take it easy," Hank said as he took him to the door. "That new baby must be winding up your nerves." He looked dubious when he came back. "He's sure hot under the collar," he said to Garry. "He'll get over it."

"I wouldn't bet on it."

The Selective Service Act passed, and as May inched gently into June, Garry called his father's office and said, "Is there any agreement by now?"

There was, Evan told him with obvious relief, and suggested that he come into town that afternoon or the next, "like a real client." He added, "It'll be nice to see you again anyway."

"Me too, Dad."

On his last two or three visits to Barnett, his mother had always greeted him with "More meetings," to explain his father's absence. It had been just as well. With his mother alone, he could talk in comfortable generalities; when his father was there, the specifics of law came up, and they could be uncomfortable. Since America had got into the war, he sometimes felt, his parents' classic and pure pacifism had shaded off in the faintest degree. No flip-flop, no flag-bestrewn speeches about patriotism, but an almost imperceptible retreat from the unequivocal position that had for so long been theirs.

If ideas were shifting and changing over at the Ivarins', he once thought, there'd be nightly boxing bouts, but we're not so noisy. Maybe that's too bad.

He didn't mean it. Day by day, as the details were announced for carrying out the sweeping new law, he felt less noisy, more muted. Apart from the Civil War Draft, with its riots and evasions and bribes, this was something the country had never condoned, had always denounced as peculiarly European, unacceptable to America, yet now one would think that forced conscription had been ordained by all the founding fathers and blessed by God as well.

Ten million men, the papers agreed, would register on the fifth of June. On that single day, from dawn to dusk across the land, one by one, yet thousand after thousand and million after million, those who had already had their twenty-first birthday but not yet their thirty-first, would register. One by one, alone for all the millions, each would go to a designated "local board" in his neighborhood grocery or bakery, schoolhouse or barber shop, fill out a printed draft form and come into possession of a little green card that might prove to be his official license to go forth and kill.

The fifth of June, Garry thought, as he started driving toward the city. Next Tuesday. Five days from now. Where did resistance start, and when? With a technicality, not unlike a census or the filling out of forms for a driver's license? Even in matters of conscience, of a man's immortal soul, there could be so practical a question to ponder, such a splitting of hairs. Preposterous. But there it was.

More than the splitting of hairs. The evaluation of the member-parts of the problem; put that way, it gained some dignity. In this hell of re-evaluation and re-defining, his own father had worn himself down over the past months; his relief was obvious, that they had reached agreement on the immediate issue of registration, and he would certainly assign all credit to the new member he was so impressed with, a man who had moved East from St. Louis the week war was declared, and who had almost overnight become a key figure among them all.

"He sees it," his father had said once, "not only as a theory of civil liberty, but as the war forces us to see it. Baldwin wants a separate bureau for objectors, because he knows we could never sandwich those cases in with the usual ones."

(425)

"I'd like to meet your 'sage,' Dad," he had said, only to have his father laugh and say, "Roger Baldwin is younger than *your* sage. Thirty-two or three."

Never sandwich them in, Garry thought now, as he looked for a space in which to park his car. It was getting harder every day to find one; people now talked about traffic problems and crowding of roads, even good ones like Queens Boulevard. A separate bureau for objec-- tors; did they expect much crowding there too?

In his new office, waiting for Garry to arrive, Evander Paige stopped any pretense of work and gazed out on the young green of Central Park. Turner, Paige, Levy and Payson had moved up to West Fifty-ninth Street only recently and the oily smell of paint and varnish was lively still in the warm air. A slight burn within his eyelids, for which Evan blamed the new paint, made him lean back in his leather chair with his eyes closed.

It had been an exhausting time, for him, for all of them, a time raw with dissension and readjustment, and new slow clarities. It was true not only for his own free-speech group, but for the larger groups, the anti-militarist, anti-armament groups all over the nation, wherever other men and women who had long been united to combat war were faced with the fact that war had come.

So much human effort, Evan thought now. So much idealism and hope about the power of citizen-opinion to alter or sway the decisions and acts of government. And now so much character needed to resist the paralysis of defeat. To go on instead, laboring toward new goals, beyond the immediacy of the war. Toward a just peace, without venge- ance, as Wilson put it, perhaps even toward some federation of coun- tries large and small, powerful and weak.

On his desk, the telephone rang, and he picked it up himself. It was Stefan Ivarin, and Paige said, "Did they issue it?"

"And every mail copy was confiscated at the post office."

Frequently now, Stefan called him for "the law" on this point or the other, usually about some socialist publication in the foreign-lan- guage press. Sometimes he called just to tell him of some new episode of censorship or suppression. The opinionated fellow still would never sit on the board of any league or union, and sometimes his convictions about the war's historic inevitability rode so roughly over any dissent, that it was hard not to resent him and go off in anger.

"But I called about something else," Ivarin said. "Have you heard about the girl and two boys they arrested today?"

"No, who? Where?"

"Students at Columbia. She's at Barnard. Secret Service agents pulled them in—I just heard it from my friend Abe at the paper."

"Is it in the papers? I know about the Madison Square affair, but I haven't seen a word about this."

"You will tomorrow. It's not a case for you fellows, I don't think—they'll have their own lawyers by the sound of it."

The three were members of the Collegiate Anti-Militarism League, he said, with chapters at most colleges and universities, and they had printed two thousand copies of a pamphlet urging men not to register, to defy conscription. Proofs of the pamphlet had been sent to the Attorney General in Washington by some informer, and the agents had found more on press.

"A sidelight," Stefan said, "is that only one boy is old enough to register; the other is nineteen, and then there's the girl. She's descended from a signer of the Declaration of Independence. I like that touch."

"Yes," Evan said, and he talked of other arrests in the past twenty-four hours, three in Kansas, two in New Jersey, two in Maine and several on the West Coast. As they hung up, Evan looked toward the door, as if Garry had already knocked. Zealotry spread fast in wartime. Again he closed his eyes and leaned back.

The Madison Square Garden affair last night was a magnified version of Ivarin's four policemen—with the Garden surrounded by no fewer than five hundred of them, all carrying rifles, training huge floodlights on every corner of the building, on each exit and entrance on Twenty-sixth or -seventh. Emergency police headquarters were set up in the S.P.C.A. nearby, with high-powered rifles, and temporary field telephones, as in the trenches. Inside the Garden, no fewer than seventy-five Federal government stenographers took down every word that was said, every question, every cheer.

It was a mass meeting of pacifists and socialists, where each speaker underlined the fact that he was not urging one man to break the conscription law. The meeting had only one goal: to call on the Supreme Court to pass on it, as to whether or not it violated the Constitution of the United States.

The fact that the meeting was held, said the Police Department to the press, was proof that pacifists and socialists were permitted free speech. The five hundred police, the rifles, the field telephones and floodlights were only to quell any unpatriotic demonstration that might arise. Five were arrested; no more.

"Hello, Dad," Garry said, suddenly opening the door.

Evan jumped up. "You look fine!"

"Shouldn't I? You sound surprised."

Evan laughed. "I expect everybody to look pale as a mushroom, the way I do. You haven't a care in the world, by the look of that tan."

"It's the car, with the top down." He looked at his father's tired eyes and pale color, suddenly aware of him as looking much older. "What do you say to taking a ride along the river right now? We can talk over dinner."

Evan smiled in appreciation, but he said, "Let me give you the gist of it, first. It's so precise now, it won't take but a minute."

"Sure, if you'd rather."

For a moment they just looked at each other. Then adopting an impersonal tone, as if he were addressing a client, Evan said, "Our bureau will advise any man to register, no matter whether he intends to claim conscientious objection or not. Especially if he does intend to. There can't be anything that looks like draft-dodging, not if we're to provide counsel."

"That's the official stand?"

"Roger Baldwin's very strong on this, and I think he's right. Not to register, we are saying, might look like trying to hide, or evade, and the government would have a much stronger case, contending that failing to register implies intent."

"Intent to lie doggo?"

"There's a watch on at all ports, for South America, Mexico, the Orient, so nobody can escape registration that way."

"You're kidding."

Evan shook his head. "The escapers and dodgers we won't defend. We'll take on only real cases. To claim conscientious objection is not a crime. And if the claim is rejected, there still is no crime. Not until the objector refuses to obey his draft board's order to serve."

"I get the distinction, I think."

"We'll provide counsel for any real objector—the religious objectors, political objectors, the partials, the absolutes. It's more complex than you ever dreamed, with more distinctions and variations."

"The absolutes?"

"They'll be the hardest cases of all."

Again they just looked at each other.

THIRTY-TWO

"I feel like a criminal," Alexandra said, her voice joyous. "To be so happy, on Registration Day."

The editor of *Abend* laughed into the telephone. "I could have held back the news until tomorrow."

"No, oh no. Oh, Mr. Tischmann, are you sure?"

Simon Tischmann laughed. "You're a delight," he said, "just like your columns. We're very sure."

"Then I'll go tell my husband. He'll be happy too."

She had no compunctions about waking Stefan. After only an eight-week trial, they wanted two columns instead of one. Thirty dollars every week, for something *she* wrote.

"Stiva," she cried in his darkened room, "it's good news, wake up."

"Yes, what—?" As she blurted it out, he sat up in bed, groping for his glasses on the chair at his side. Even then, while she was a large blurred something to him, he reached up and clutched her arm and then her shoulder with such ferocity that he hurt.

"What did he say?" he demanded. "How did he put it?"

His pleasure was so acute, one would have thought he had just had this triumph, about something *he* had written. She repeated every word Tischmann had said, and then Stefan exclaimed, "Of course they're sure, even after eight weeks. When you have a hit you know it the same day, the next day. Look at the mail you pull."

Alexandra drew back slightly. The mail was one thing she didn't like to remember. Do what she would, she could not keep the letters answered on time. It was the one blot, the one strain, the one miserable lining to the silvery moon of her new happiness.

"Can I keep up the columns?" she asked. "Two every week? Every Monday and every Thursday?"

"You'd better keep it up," he said. "There has to be one big writer in this family."

For an instant she paused, and then she said again, "I feel like a criminal though—when you think what day this is."

(429)

"The juxtaposition is bad," Stefan conceded. "But you can't be expected to feel glum."

"But at this very moment, Eli may be signing his life away, and Garry, and a million others. And I so happy."

"Life doesn't seek out its illogic," he said. "It merely accepts it and passes it along."

He was out of bed now and he kissed her. Then he said, "I'll be right down," and she left as if she had been summarily dismissed. Over and over as she prepared his breakfast, she heard Tischmann's "You're a delight, just like your columns. We're very sure," and the most extraordinary sensation came to her, as if she were a beautiful bird, preening its feathers. It was conceit, vanity, self-love, and it was simply delicious.

At the turn in the road, where the cars from New York had to slow down, Fee waved her arms wide, like a cheerleader, and shouted, "Liberty Bonds—come on, here's one for you."

Stationed near her were Anne Miller and Trudy Loheim and two other seniors, but Fee's sales were way ahead of theirs. At the side of the road, like a small recruiting station, was the Liberty Loan pavilion, plastered over with huge red, white and blue posters that said "Do your bit—invest," "If you can't enlist, invest," and things like that. Perhaps because it was Registration Day, this was turning into the most successful afternoon of the ten separate times she had been out on the Liberty Loan Drive, and she was sure she would win Barnett High's second prize for Biggest Total. Harvey Neill had first prize tied up tight as a tick, but his father had started him off with four thousand dollars' worth, and besides, Harvey didn't do anything much except the drive. He was only a junior and didn't care about Regents.

Fee put the thought of Regents promptly aside. She had recently collapsed about studying. Everything else was so exciting, and anyway if she hadn't crammed enough by now, it was just too bad. Last-minute, all-night cramming wouldn't work for the thing she was doing. But she was ready; she could feel it in her bones.

"Liberty Bonds," she shouted, coming perilously close to a car that was slowing down, so close that the driver yelled, "Look out, you," as he stamped on his brake.

"Don't be mad," she said airily, "shouldn't I give my life for my country? Would you sign for a bond?"

"Isn't that cute?" a man next the driver said. "Giving her life for her country." To Fee, he said, "Would you give a kiss for your country, if I sign?"

Fee knew how to handle the fresh ones. Before they were allowed out at all, the girls had been trained: laugh off anything you can, but if it's worse than that, just turn on your heel and go back to the pavilion until the car drives on. Mostly it didn't get worse.

It was fun, selling Liberty Bonds, a new and different kind of fun. It was wonderful to know you were helping your country; all the papers, and all the Four Minute Men giving speeches at the movies, were forever telling how vital every single bond was, what it stood for, what it could do, and how they had to go over the top on the two million dollars' worth before June fifteenth.

But there was another kind of wonderful in it, just as exciting, but private. Like being the lead in the play, hearing the applause, having people say you could become a real actress and go on the Broadway stage because of your vitality and personality. This was also a question of personality, Miss Mercer said, only in a business-y way, being a salesman.

It was terribly easy, Fee thought; maybe Mercey was right, saying she could become a crack salesman and earn a lot of money. That was another exciting thing about the war; all kinds of things that only men used to do were now being done by women, from being letter-carriers and traffic cops to belonging to the women's land army or working in munitions factories, putting the powder into shells and bullets.

"One more Liberty Bond," she sang out as another car approached her station. The girls were strung out about twenty yards apart, and the rule was that you couldn't barge in on a car that stopped nearer one of the others. But this one was definitely driving right past Anne and coming straight at her. Its top was down and a man—

"Garry," she cried out in delight.

"I'll be damned," he said, pulling off the road and stopping. "Since when have you turned financier?"

She gave a little laugh of pure pleasure and retorted, "And since when do you go touring on Tuesday afternoons?"

He laughed, too. "I'm on my way to the family. Everybody got the afternoon off to register."

"And did—?" She stopped herself. It wasn't anything you just tossed out, not at Garry. A hundred times she had wondered what he was going to do today, but she'd die rather than dig around asking. Her parents had talked of it a hundred times too, but they'd never dream of asking either, not Garry, not his mother or father.

(431)

By this time he was out of the car and standing next to her. He was as tan as midsummer, and he seemed taller. Anne's voice came singing out, "Get your Liberty Bond right here," but Fee knew Anne and the rest of the girls were keeping more of an eye on her than on the cars. Garry took out his wallet and said, "Have you seen one, Fee?" and offered her a green card.

"Oh, Garry," she cried, "you did register. Oh, that's so wonderful. I thought I'd die, *not knowing.*"

"Did you?" he asked, surprised.

"I worried so," she cried. It was too emotional, but it was out before she could stop it. He was looking at her, and she looked down at the card.

"Look," he said, "if you can call it a day, I'll give you a lift home."

"I'd love it," she said, but added uncertainly, "I have to report and turn back all this stuff. It takes about five minutes. Would you wait that long?"

"Of course I'll wait."

She started off for the pavilion, but he shouted, "Hey, my card," and she turned back to him with it. Her outstretched hand offered it, and then suddenly she said, "I was so *scared,* Garry."

He looked surprised again, and when she came back and got into the car and drove off with him, with all the girls watching, she was excited and proud. Not one of them ever had anybody like Garry Paige waiting around for her; it was so different from having one of the boys at school waiting for you. She had taken an extra minute to fix her hair, and put on fresh lipstick; since the war, nobody had to get permission any more, even during school hours. And she was wearing her new dress with the short skirt; she wore it every time she came out to sell Liberty Bonds; having your skirt halfway to your knees was the latest thing, and gave you the loveliest feeling if you had nice ankles.

"This is fine," Garry said after a minute. "Why don't we stop off somewhere for a soda?"

"To celebrate," she said. "The papers said today should be a festival and a patriotic occasion."

"That's right," he said. " 'A joyous pilgrimage,' too." He glanced at her quickly; she was serious, trusting him. To say the wrong thing now would be fat-headed. He asked how many Liberty Bonds she had sold, and when her fifteen Regents were to descend on her. Only after they reached the soda fountain, and ordered, did he find himself searching for something to say.

"You're not sorry you came, are you?" Fee said, after they had sat silently for a moment.

(4 3 2)

"I got thinking," he said. "I'm sorry, I often do that, and then I just sit and don't say a word."

"It's all right," she said. "I sort of like it. You look interesting. Some people just look dopey. My father looks angry."

He laughed once again, and glanced quickly at her in appraisal. This wasn't the first time she struck him as being oddly original; he had thought that of her before, when he did not know. Intense and original, he had thought. It was apparently true. She had meant it just now when she said she liked it, and before, when she said she had been scared about him. There was an openness about her that people usually thought childlike, but childishness had left her forever.

"How old are you, Fee?"

"Almost seventeen," she said. "Why?"

"No special reason."

"How old are you?"

"Twenty-nine last week."

"I've known you half my life," she said matter-of-factly. "But you haven't known me even a quarter of yours."

"Half your life? That goes back to—"

"Your father and mother stopped at one of our trees the year we moved in," she said, "and your father said the stresses on the wires were wrong. My father thought he was an engineer, and then he found out he was a socialist."

"Even better than being an engineer!" He grinned at her. "How do you remember things like that?"

"My mother always talks about how things got started. She's awfully sentimental."

Nineteen-nine, he thought, the year I married. "Was that about the tree in the spring or fall or when, do you know that too?"

She shook her head. "Anyway, that's how long I've known you, but I didn't start to worry about you until we got in the war."

He said, "Don't worry too much, Fee." Then he added, "But thanks, it's pretty nice of you." Again she looked unsure, as she had when she asked if he would wait five minutes, and he added, "You mustn't think everybody's kidding, if they say things like that to you."

She looked startled. "How'd you know I thought it?"

"I didn't know for sure, but I guessed."

She leaned toward him. "Oh, Garry, you are patriotic, aren't you?"

He waited for a moment and then said, quietly, "Yes."

"Then you're not going to do anything wild?" she said. "Please don't, *please*."

It was so unexpected, he made no answer for a time. Her dark

(4 3 3)

eyes looked larger, wide with their plea. Then he said slowly, "Have you noticed how hard it is, to talk about something very important to you?" She nodded, but he felt it was more to be obliging than because she knew what he was getting at, and as if he were suddenly a teacher at a key point in a course, it seemed essential to make himself clear. "For instance, have you ever said, right out loud in a conversation, 'I love my country'?"

"No," she said, thinking about it. "Why, no, never."

"Have you ever heard your father say, 'I love my country,' or 'I love America'?"

Again she thought about it before answering. "He's forever saying, 'It's a great country' or 'It's the hope of the world.' "

"But that's as close as he gets, isn't it? And your mother—sentimental as she is—?"

"Or he'll talk about how immigrants love it, and how native-born Americans sort of forget what it stands for, and they need immigrants coming here to remind them, to let them see it again with new eyes."

Garry leaned back a little, the unsuspected teacher within him satisfied. "Some words you can't say straight out, Fee," he said. "Some things may seem 'wild' to other people, but you can't talk out about what's back of them or inside them."

"I suppose not," she said.

"There are so many ways to show whether you love your country," he said slowly. "You can work for it, in some real way, or even suffer for it."

"Or die for it?"

He repeated, "Or die for it. But not kill for it."

"In a war—even then?"

"I wouldn't think it was the same, Fee. You could kill off one enemy, or ten, but that's not the same as doing something for your country itself, or its future."

He could almost see her mind working over what he had said. That somber, thoughtful look, he thought, you don't see that very often. People look interested or bored, happy or sad, annoyed or furious, but rarely thoughtful and somber. She's weighing and balancing, trying to decide.

Suddenly he said, "You funny girl," and smiled at her.

The call from Abe Kesselbaum early that evening puzzled Stefan Ivarin, but he willingly agreed to meet him late the same night. He was more puzzled when Abe rejected the café and suggested instead another restaurant several blocks away from the *Jewish News*. "Something happened today at the meeting," Abe said and that was clue enough. So often had Abe been the source of flash news—he was his last connection with the privileged speed of journalists the world over—that he had assumed this was another scoop from the ticker, but it was shoptalk which Abe didn't want to pass along too publicly. Ivarin told him about Alexandra's "promotion" and turned the telephone over to her so Abe could congratulate her himself, but he was already wondering what this news could be.

He arrived at the restaurant much too early, fortified with the early morning editions of everything. Each front page told of the ten-million registration across the country, still being counted but unprecedented, larger than any known before in any land on earth, told it, yelled it, shouted it. Two months of being in the war had made over the entire American press, English-language and foreign; roaring headlines were a daily affair now with all the papers, and there would be no return to a civilized mien for any of them until the war ended. Pure garishness was no longer the circus barker that brought people in; the human eye had deadened to the sight, the inner ear deafened to the shriek. Ivarin wondered if Abe would tell him circulation was off at the *Jewish News* and vaguely hoped so. Hearst's *American* and *Journal* were in a slump, their circulation down, their international wire service long barred from France and England, the rags themselves now barred from Canada, the Hearstian harvest of years of anti-British tirades and pro-German admiration, but proof too that sensationalism alone was no longer a guarantee for any paper.

"Am I late? Have you been here long?" Abe said, hurrying in.

"It's nothing, I was early."

"Have you heard anything, from anybody else?"

"Not a word." Ivarin saw Abe's pleased look and waited for him to order. Time and disappointment had done their work on Abe; he was forty now and looked it; the sheen of pink scalp that used to gleam through his thinning black hair now had no interference at all. But he looked better, stronger as a personality; his years of discipline as the Number Two man on layout and make-up had toughened him and taught him he could survive. A valuable tonic for any man.

"It starts with Miriam Landau," Abe said. "I told you she was sick? Well, it got worse. Last week she had a sort of paralysis in her legs, and she can't go anywhere, attend meetings, nothing."

Ivarin made a small sound of acknowledgment. He could feel no warmth toward her, but it was unpleasant to hear about the physical pain or destruction of anyone.

(4 3 5)

"She's nearly seventy, would you believe it?" Abe went on. "I never thought she was older than Isaac, five, six years older."

"I had no idea." He was startled; of recent years he had begun to be aware of people's ages, and to remember them, but when something reminded him of Itzak, he was the man he had been when he died. He had to calculate now: if he were alive, Itzak would be about sixty-five. "So she's seventy," he said, believing it at last.

"And Steinberger has to think ahead. Those four daughters, remember? And their four husbands?" Ivarin cast his eyes upward and Abe gave an unfeeling little laugh. "Steinberger is resolved not to live through another performance like last time, not to put the whole staff through it all over again."

An arrow of memory pierced Ivarin. That fearful waiting, that damnable wrack of not-knowing. Impatience seized him now. "Come, Abe, let's have it, has he a way out?"

"He arranged the succession *now,* you might say," Abe said in a sudden rush. "She's transferring her stock to the daughters now, and Steinberger is to represent all of them. He has a big contract, five years, renewable for another five. He's turning over most of his law office to his son, to do it."

"A contract as what?" Ivarin leaned forward.

"As the top Something, *over* Fehler," Abe said. "Oh, Fehler remains Publisher, nothing changes there. Borg stays City Editor, my boss stays my boss, everything stays the same, everybody the same. But the paper has a new top-story, that's all."

Ivarin thumped the table. "That *is* a piece of news, Abe." He ripped off his glasses. "A new top-story, by whatever name."

"President of the *Jewish News*—that may be Steinberger's title. Maybe Chairman. Does it matter?"

Ivarin said it did not matter. Involuntarily, dismayingly, his mind had already asked, Would this mean I could go back there? Could I be an editor again? After nearly four years, could it ever work? Never, not with Fehler and Borg and Miriam and Miriam's daughters. No matter who's the "top-story." Never. Let me not get into that torture chamber again.

"How did they take it, Abe?"

If Kesselbaum saw his agitation, he gave no sign of it. "They were full of joy, big congratulations. Fehler 'congratulated the paper' on its good luck. Since devoting himself to Miriam's interests, Fehler had said, Mr. Steinberger had become a true expert in journalism, as he always became expert in his clients' affairs. Et cetera."

"And Borg?"

"The same, and Bunzig and Kinchevsky. Even I. Just like a big bar mitzvah." He laughed, but Ivarin didn't notice.

"And Steinberger? Did he say anything special?"

"That there would be no changes. The usual. But then he said something else." Abe lighted a cigarette and went on more slowly. "He said he sometimes wondered if people didn't feel—now, in this time of war—feel the need for something in the paper that made it legitimate to suffer a little. Even if they didn't have a boy in uniform."

"A point," Ivarin said. "A good point."

A long time ago he had thought Steinberger might be an interesting man to know, had he not been tied to Miriam Landau. Now he thought it again. But that kind of thinking was trying the knob of the torture chamber, and he moved back from it sharply. After a time both men fell silent, Abe smoking, Ivarin intently watching the curl and twist of smoke from his cigarette. How long it had been, too, since he was tormented by a cigarette in somebody else's fingers. But he was free of it forever and would stay free. Life changed and curled and twisted, its problems and burdens took new shapes, and one grew accustomed to the new. Then there might be another twist, unexpected, unsought for, perhaps welcome, perhaps too late to be welcome.

Please buy one more," Fee begged her mother. "Harvey's Dad bought another thousand dollars' worth, it's so sneaky."

"One more twenty-five," she said. "That's the last."

"I'll take one more for twenty-five, too," Ivarin volunteered and Fee jumped.

"That's grand," she said. "There's only three days left; if it doesn't go over the top, I'll die."

"It will," her father said. "Closer to three million than two, the estimates say."

And when he was proved right, Fee felt it a triumph, apart from her private pleasure over winning the prize for Most Bonds Sold By A Girl. Now she could turn to study again; Regents Week was at hand.

From the first minute of the French I exam, she had the sure feeling; she raced on, hardly stopping to think. The only thing she was nervous about was proctoring. It would start the minute she turned in her French, because German I was given that morning too, in the auditorium, where all Regents were given. They had let her choose which to take first, but when she finished it, she saw the rub.

She wasn't allowed to leave the room. Or go to the basement cafeteria for lunch or anything. Somebody who had already done German I could tell her the questions.

"You're to go to Mr. Fitch's office for your German I," Miss Mercer said. "I'll go along. Do you want to stop off first?"

Fee felt her face go hot, but she had to say yes. In the girls' room, everybody looked at her when Miss Mercer came in at her side, because teachers had their own, and there was buzzing and giggling while Miss Mercer took up a post outside Fee's swinging door. But being proctored had to include every minute, like being in a spy story.

At one o'clock Mr. Fitch sent a freshman for soup and crackers and milk, and Fee told him she thought proctoring made exams fun. The whole week went on wheels, with either two or three Regents each day, but with eleven exams done by Thursday evening Dr. Wohl said, "You're the only one left who's still in the pink, *Fräulein Fira.*"

"Tomorrow, *Herr Doktor.* FOUR."

"Let's hope the faculty holds up."

She started in Assembly Hall with everybody else from nine to twelve and then one to four, taking French III and German IV. Then they made her go to Mr. Fitch's office again, to rest for half an hour, alone, with the door locked. Then from four-thirty to seven-thirty, Mercey proctored her on algebra, and at eight Dr. Wohl came back to school, just for her, and stayed through the geometry. By then it was eleven; even the janitor was gone.

For supper she had had sandwiches and milk Fran brought from home, but she was too wound up for more than a bite or two. She almost had hysterics when Mercey opened up each sandwich and looked inside before handing it over. "If anybody later on said you had a set of answers smuggled in, Fee, you could lose your entire scholarship, so don't giggle."

Again they had let her decide which ones she would do in the evening, and she had picked geometry and algebra, because with those, it was either right or wrong, no style of writing involved, not even any judgment about the best way to translate a sentence. She'd been smart to do it; tired or not, she just knew it was a 98 or 100 on each. The whole week had been grand; the only boner she knew about absolutely was that awful one about Longfellow.

And that was her mother's fault.

How many times had she heard her mother recite, "What is so rare as a day in June?" and call it Longfellow? All her life, every time the month of May ended! And then later on, when she herself

(438)

knew, how many times had she bitten her tongue to keep from blurting out, "Not Longfellow, Mama, Lowell."

Then, taking English IV, just before the bell, while she still had three questions to go, there was "What is so rare as a day in June?" and she wrote, Longfellow.

If she lost her scholarship by a fraction of a point, she would never forgive her mother.

The recruiting booth was a one-story white cottage, the size of a roomy vacation lodge up on Lake Winnepesaukee, and as Eli cut off his engine and propped his motorcycle at the curb, he glanced inside the open door and saw that it was nearly empty. Only three men were already in line, and the sergeant behind the desk still looked calm and unhurried.

What a box to be in, Eli thought; why did I ever get into it? School had been unendurable this entire month of June. Halfway through, the first Americans landed in France, at Boulogne, fewer than two hundred, and just four days ago, some fourteen thousand at St. Nazaire, mostly raw recruits who had volunteered the day war was declared. Half the teachers on the staff had stopped him in the halls, with some smart dig about those heroes "enlisting the very first day."

Eli loosened his necktie and went inside the booth. At each breath, the muscles at the sides of his neck widened and hit his collar; the attack was a pretty mild one so far, sounding like a rotten summer cold.

It was cooler inside than it had been on the bike, the air a little easier to get some purchase on. This was the last day of school, there was no putting it off any longer. He should never have said a word about enlisting, not to the family that night, not at school, not to his in-laws. There was always something about the Paiges and Garry that made him say the first thing handy. That's what had started this mess.

With the others it was easy to undo it, but he could hardly use the Board of Ed right at school, and if he didn't go through with it today they'd never stop the smart remarks for the rest of his life. It was all so needless; that's what riled him the most. By now nobody was enlisting, except the romantics and the bums; the rest were waiting for the official drawing of the draft numbers, still held up by politicians, still put off week after week. The whole business of exemptions was still way up in the air. There were four thousand exemption boards, as many as there were draft boards; nobody knew how fast exemptions would be acted on, or even exactly what for. Of course, with two kids, he'd never be drafted. Enlisting was something else again.

But he was in a hurry; he was due at the new summer school by the Fourth of July. Never would he catch up on expenses, and if he told Joan they had to cut down, she told him to sell the bike, the one escape he had from the eternal arguments and the kids' eternal banging around.

His breathing grew a little harder.

The sergeant at the desk said, "Next," and the man just ahead of Eli snapped out, "Yessir," and gave his name and address.

"Is that you," the sergeant asked jovially, "with the pneumonia?"

"Me, sir? No, sir."

Behind him, Eli opened his lips to make his breathing less stertorous. Within him, a first faint hint of pleasantness made itself known, like the first rise in a barometer after clamped-in weather. Visions of the night before plagued him, of Webby and the spanking and the rest of it, but he switched out the light in his mind and refused to see them. He concentrated on the official blanks on the desk, the bottles of ink, the flag standing in a pedestal off at the side.

The sergeant called out, "Next," and Eli took a slow hard breath. The next few minutes were the ones that mattered most. "Eaves," he said as he moved up. "E-a-v-es, Elijah Lovejoy Eaves." The sergeant's pen stopped dead on the blank form before him, and Eli felt the hint of pleasantness again. His voice was thick now, rope-hard yet clothy too, and glancing down at the sergeant, his own eyes could see the flare of his nostrils.

"Then it's you?" the sergeant asked, not making a joke of it this time.

"It's not pneumonia," Eli said. "It passes. My address is Two Twenty-nine—"

"You better get to a doctor till that's over, and then come back."

Eli shook his head. "It passes," he said again, leaning on the edge of the desk. "It's just an asthma attack. Sometimes I don't have a bad one for months. Forget it."

The sergeant looked at him, at the men in line behind him, and then back to him. "You can't enlist with a condition like that, mister. They'd call me for wasting their time."

"Fill it in," Eli said slowly, "and let *them* decide."

The sergeant finished printing his name. Now a paroxysm of coughing seized Eli, and behind him there was a scraping sound as a chair was pulled across the wooden floor. "Come on, better sit down," a man said, and the sergeant came around from the desk, addressing the others, "Anybody a doctor?" Eli sat down and they drew up another chair for his legs, relieved him of his jacket and goggles and offered him a paper cup of water, chilled, from a large metal canteen hung on khaki straps. "You take it easy, hear me?" the sergeant said. "I'll have to phone my captain."

Eli closed his eyes. His breathing slowed and evened in rhythm again, but the clutching for air went on, though he did not care. His rising spirits hit a peak. He had done it. He had said he would, and he had. There would be some delay, the phone call to the captain, perhaps more delay while the captain passed the buck to one of the doctors in the Medical Corps. But it was done, and nobody in God's green world could ever accuse him of just shooting his mouth off.

"Here, Mr. Eaves," the sergeant's voice came down at him, unnaturally clear and loud as if he were shouting. "A nice souvenir to show your grandchildren some day, how you wouldn't let nothing stop you, but you tried to enlist in the war. A brave man, you tell them."

It was the enlistment form of the United States Army. Nothing was written on it but July 2, 1917, EAVES, ELIJAH LOVEJOY. He folded it, got to his feet, and faced the sergeant. Then, with the snap and precision he had seen in the newsreels, he saluted and took his departure.

Fee took one fleeting glance at Eli's souvenir and looked away. She couldn't bear him when he got talking about himself and the war; she didn't feel that way about one other human being in the world, but with Eli, she couldn't stand it.

He didn't notice; he had enough of an audience anyway. Mama hung on each word, every syllable, of what the sergeant had said, what all the people in line said, what they did about the chair, about everything that happened. Fran was rushing off to another Soldiers Dance at the Masonic Temple, but she let the soldiers languish without her while she heard it all, and even Papa found it fascinating; you'd think he and Eli were like a father and son in a book.

She looked at her father and wondered if she had ever forgiven him. Even though they talked again, about Liberty Bonds and things, was he still furious at her? They never, either one of them, said the word "college" out loud, as if there were no such thing, anywhere. But after her four exams in one day, he said, "Well, how did it go?" and even seemed pleased. And by now he must certainly know she had *not* registered for Training in September, but he didn't mention that either, not even on Graduation Day when Barnett High was over and done with forever.

"He doesn't think of such things now," her mother said. Then unexpectedly she reeled off a list of names. "The *Call,* the *Appeal to Reason,* the *Milwaukee Leader,* the *Masses*—do you realize that eighteen, twenty, newspapers and magazines are just about finished, with these new rules that cover anything the mailman doesn't approve of?"

If it weren't for Mr. Paige, she'd know this was another of her mother's exaggerations, but the one time Mr. Paige had been over recently, he had talked about "omnibus bills that include everything in sight," and he simply never exaggerated.

"I'm going to bed," Fee said now, yawning largely, as Eli folded up his souvenir at last. "I'll never catch up on sleep, I guess."

"*C'est la guerre,* Sis," Eli said. "See you around Labor Day, if I don't get drafted."

Drafted, Fee thought as she undressed. Being married isn't, but having two kids *is* a ground, all the papers say that. But he still talks as if, any minute now, he'll be on his way to No Man's Land. She used to feel all melty and happy when he called her Sis, but that was ages and ages ago. Maybe she was a "simpering Puritan," as her mother called anybody who thought he'd been terrible about that girl in New Hampshire; it did disgust her to think about it. But even that was nothing to the way she felt when he opened up about the war or the draft or enlisting.

What is this, Eli, a military board of inquiry? She could hear her father saying it angrily that night; it was about the only thing he had done that made her like him, since her own horrible fight. But now when the words sounded again in her mind, they suddenly brought back her fear about Garry. He was going to do something wild, she knew it. Wild and dangerous and frightening. She loved to think about the day he had waited for her in his car and taken her to the soda fountain, and it kept coming back over and over. But each time, the fear came back too.

Garry gulped the last of his coffee, eyed his letter and thought, So it's today. He had foreseen this day a hundred times, yet he could not foretell the outcome of it. All he did know was that the letter was at last written, signed, ready to be delivered; he was going to deliver it by hand, not send it by mail. It had been twice as difficult as he had thought, ten times as difficult, and he had been writing at it for a long time.

"Writing at it" was exact; he kept making stabs at putting down what he felt ought to be put down, yet it never satisfied him. Weeks ago he had stopped imitating Dr. Holmes' sermon, but he could not get his tone right; sometimes it sounded portentous, sometimes apologetic. Last night it had come closer to what he wanted, and he had determined to let it stand. Even so he had stayed up half the night with it, and then had continued to write phrases during his five hours of sleep. He was excited in a strange subdued way, heavy, reluctant. After he saw his father, he would go and give it to the authorities and be done with it. Done with his part of it, the only part he knew about for sure.

It was being unsure that was so hard to manage; each case one read about or heard about was enough different from each other and from his own so that no "expectables" were being established, as to the range of discipline or punishment to be meted out. With the three Columbia students, the case had speedily gone to trial before a jury and been settled, at least for the one fellow old enough to register. He was found guilty of "conspiracy to interfere" with the Draft Act and his sentence, not published, could be two years in prison or a fine of ten thousand dollars, or both.

On the other hand, out in Ohio, where three men were arrested for anti-draft plotting on the same day, the charge was nothing less than Treason, and in the courtroom they were officially reminded that conviction might mean their death.

The pendulum could swing as widely when it came to lesser deeds, though to be an objector was not designated a crime at all. Garry picked up his letter and thoughtfully waved it to and fro, holding it only at one edge, so as not to smudge or soil it. Then he went to the telephone and called Barnett. "Dad, it's ready at last, with a carbon for you, as per instructions."

"When can I look it over?"

"I'd like to turn it in today, and get it over with."

"How about coming to the office around lunch time? Can you get some extra time?"

"I'll be there around twelve. Thanks."

The promise to show it to his father before turning it in had been made the night he had registered, over a month ago. "I'm your attorney, Garry. No documents delivered without approval by counsel." It had been a simple promise to give, a good deal simpler than the one to register. They had every right to establish their conditions for becoming involved, his father's group, but beyond that, he had finally

(443)

agreed that if they were right about what was coming, it would be foolish to fuzz over the main case with a preliminary one.

He hoped his father would have no changes to suggest. About delivering it before the official drawing of the draft numbers, he had never had any doubt at all. Only five or six men in a hundred, the papers agreed, would be summoned in the first draft—"twenty-to-one in the national lottery" one headline had said. But to deliver his letter before he knew whether his own number would be picked or passed over, this had never been open to question.

The drawing would take place in Washington at the end of next week; blindfolded, the Secretary of War would thrust his hand into a crystal globe containing ten thousand shiny black capsules, close his fingers around one, and draw it forth. In it would be a piece of paper with a number. That number would be flashed to the nation, and in each of some five thousand communities of the country, the man holding it would be the first man called up in his own small world. Then another capsule, another, another—

So simple. But they had put it off for all these tantalizing weeks since Registration because they could not devise equally simple machinery for processing the claims for exemption. Millions were expected, the papers said, for a dozen allowable reasons—including "Religious Objection for bona fide members of sects whose creeds forbid war."

"Get a signed affidavit from your clergyman," said the author of a feature article Garry had read somewhere, "and the chance is your claim will be duly allowed. You will then be assigned to noncombatant work, and remain a member of the U. S. Army in good standing."

The partials and the absolutes, Garry thought now. The partials and the absolutes. There was a swing to the phrase. He realized that he was again waving his letter to and fro. He drew it out and began to read it, trying to see its words as if he had never laid eyes on them before, trying to imagine himself a member of whatever Exemption Board would be the one to act upon it.

July 10, 1917.

Sirs:

I beg permission to make these statements, to complete my claim for exemption on my registration blank.

There I wrote down only "Conscientious Objector," I could not add "on religious grounds" for I am not a Quaker, nor a Mennonite, nor a member of the Dunkards, Molokani, Plymouth Brethren or other sects you listed. I am a Unitarian.

(444)

But as I understand my religion, I shall always hold it wrong to kill, in war as in peace, in this war or in any other. I shall not do it. I shall not fire a gun at any man with the purpose of taking his life.

Nor could I, in conscience, accept service in any of the non-combatant units of the Army, for these units are essential to the waging of war, and I could only interpret that service as becoming an accessory to war and killing.

I write this in full awareness of my position, and ask that I may have a hearing, with my father, Evander Paige, an attorney, as my counsel.

Yours most respectfully,

Dear God, Garry thought, it's still not right. He slid it, together with its carbon, back into its crisp envelope, suddenly dejected. Why can't a man say what's in his heart? The tearing, ripping struggle between the love of God's will, and that other love, My own, my native land?

He rose quickly, slipped the envelope into the outer pocket of his jacket, and started off in his car. Even though it was not yet nine o'clock, the heat hung low over the day, and the air blowing in limply across the water was steamy and sluggish. It had rained yesterday and the canvas top was still raised; if the ride were longer, he would have stopped and lowered it, to feel a breeze, such as it was. He did wriggle out of his jacket, while he drove, but to avoid crumpling his letter, he transferred it to the locked compartment near the speedometer. When he arrived at the plant, his shirt and collar were wilted, and as he reached for the compartment, his hands felt gritty as well as moist.

Let it stay there, he thought, until I get to Dad's. Though he usually never bothered, he did lock the car before starting for the rear entrance of the building, near the loading-platform. He was no longer required to punch the time clock in the employees' entrance by the freight elevators, but it was the shortest way in, and he always used it.

"It's going to be a broiler, I'll bet," he said to the loading foreman on the platform.

"Better go in at the front door," was the only answer.

"Me?" Garry asked, looking around to see if the foreman could have been talking to somebody else.

"That's right."

"What for?"

"There's somebody there, been asking for you," he said, gazing at the air above Garry's head. "From the District Attorney."

Garry's heart hammered at his rib cage. He turned away, crossed

(445)

the length of the lot to the street entrance, and then he saw a man in ordinary clothes, fanning himself with a straw hat. He was leaning against the building, standing on the single wide step that led to the front door. The man saw him coming but said nothing, simply waited and let him come on. Garry kept his pace even and unhurried, and he did not speak until he reached the wide stone step. Above, at almost every window, there were faces.

"I'm Garrett Paige," he said. "I was told you asked for me."

"That's right." He reached into his pocket and drew forth a card with a small snapshot of himself on it, impressed with an official seal. "Federal Marshal, from the U. S. Commissioner's Office," he said, restoring the card before Garry could more than glance at it. "I have here a warrant, sworn out by the United States District Attorney, under powers defined in the Wartime Espionage Act of June fifteen."

"For what?" Garry instinctively reached his hand forward, as if to receive a document. The man merely patted his breast pocket. "It's all in writing in here," he said, as if that were enough.

"What's in writing?" Garry asked. "I have the right to see what the charge is."

"Come along," the other said shortly. "They'll tell you when you get there."

"Get where?"

"The Federal Building, New York City." He put his straw hat on, and motioned to the curb.

"One minute," Garry said vigorously. "I want to see that warrant, and I want to phone my lawyer."

Somebody passed them on the way into the building, and Garry nearly shouted at the unknown back, "Get Molloy to phone my lawyer," not wanting to say, "my father." But the Federal Marshal cut that short by speaking even more briskly.

"This isn't any nice little civil action, bud. This is a Federal charge under the Wartime Espionage Act of June fifteen. I'd advise you to come along easy."

He put his hand on Garry's arm. Garry shook it off. "You won't need any of that," he said. "I'm not trying to escape. I do have the right to call my lawyer first." Ridiculously, he added, "And I've got a car in the lot there, I can't just go off and leave it."

"Better leave your keys," the Marshal said, "so somebody can drive it home for you, if you're held up a while." But he put his arm through Garry's and unceremoniously propelled him toward the curb. "You can phone when you get there." Garry did not try to break away; he knew too well what that would do. At the curb, a black sedan was waiting, with a small insignia on the windshield that said U. S. Department of Justice.

Fear came slowly. Anger held it at arm's length throughout the ride over the familiar bridge, and then as they started down the length of the city to the Federal Building. His anger was the immediate, specific kind, that was in itself holding at arm's length a larger anger which would come later. Now he was angry that he had been refused the telephone call to his father, that he had not been permitted to turn his car keys over to somebody, even that the man had called it the Espionodge Act. He was angry that he had been denied any proof that this stranger did have authority to force him to go with him, except for the flash of an official card and a pat on a breast pocket to indicate the presence of a proper document.

He clenched his fists. His hands were dry now, but he suddenly remembered the moist harsh grit of them when he was about to unlock the compartment and get out his letter. The letter and the carbon with it were still locked away, inviolate, with the keys still in his pocket. The Marshal had forced him to keep the keys; unwittingly the man had protected his letter.

An extraordinary confusion swept him. In an instant it was gone. So often had his father and he discussed what might happen when his letter was acted on, so fully had they discussed it without prettifying it, using words like arrest, arraignment, even jail—so often, that his sudden arrest had hooked itself into the letter itself, meshed gears with the letter, engaged with it in some marvel of efficiency. An efficiency that was all wrong, he saw, as his confusion departed. His letter was locked in his car. It had not been delivered; it had not been seen, not even by his father. No official had received it, none had judged it, none had acted on it.

Then why had they arrested him?

For something else. For something he did not know about, for something he had never discussed with his father. But what? What had he done? *This isn't any nice little civil action, bud. This is a Federal charge—*

Fear began at last, gritty too, and grinding. To be an objector was not a crime, yet he had been taken into custody for something. He glanced at the Federal agent beside him: he was absorbed in his driving, his eyelids lowered against the glare of the sun through the windshield. He would not tell him anyway.

By now they were speeding downtown, the light flickering through the ties of the elevated tracks above them, off—on, off—on, light—dark, light—dark, as maddening as the third degree.

THIRTY-THREE

As Evander Paige entered the outer office, the girl at the reception desk said, "Please call the switchboard, Mr. Paige."

"Is anything wrong?"

"She said, 'emergency.' I hope it's not too bad."

He did not wait for her last words. Standing at his desk, holding the telephone upright along his body, he heard that Mr. Molloy of Synthex had been trying to reach him for half an hour. "But it's not an accident, Mr. Paige, he said to be sure to tell you."

"Thanks, Elly, please get him." No accident, he thought, but an emergency. The vertical rod of the telephone clicked against his vest buttons.

"Mr. Paige, this is hard news," Molloy said a moment later. "It looks as if Garry was arrested. Somebody from the District Attorney was here and took him off in an official car."

"Arrested? Are you sure?"

"It looked that way. It was five minutes before I arrived, but there were people watching the whole thing. They saw the fellow flash open a wallet and they heard Garry demand a look at the warrant and say he wanted to call his lawyer."

"He was refused?"

"He never did come inside. The man took him off in the car. Garry's Ford is still here in the lot."

"Took him off where?"

"Nobody knows, but while I was waiting for you to call back, I checked with the local precinct here, and he's not there."

"Was it a police car? A Black Maria?"

"No, just a car. Somebody saw a seal that said 'U.S.A.' or 'U. S. Justice.'"

"Then it looks as if they've taken him downtown to the Federal Building on Park Row. That's a big help, Mr. Molloy. Thanks—I'll let you know."

He was hanging up but Molloy's voice rang in the receiver. "Mr. Paige, are you still there? Mr. Paige—"

"Yes, still here."

"I don't like to say this, now, but as head of this business, I do have to think of the reputation of Synthex, and if the newspapers—"

After part of a second, Evan said, "I'll do what I can to keep Synthex out of it." This time he hung up quickly.

At once he called an assistant district attorney he knew in the Federal Building, but was told he was in court. Was there a message? He tried another, but he was out too. He called the building's Information clerk, but the line was busy and stayed busy. He tried office after office, but nobody could get the first fact he needed: whether Garry was really there, and if so on which floor, in which room or office, and in whose custody. Through all his years as a lawyer, through his earlier years of parole work, his dealings had been with district attorneys and judges and commissioners of New York City or New York State; his answer now could come only from a United States District Attorney or Assistant, and he knew none of these well enough to say, "Drop everything and do me this favor because it's my son."

Two of his partners were also putting in calls to officials downtown. "Mel," Evan finally said to one of them, "I'm going down there myself. If Garry does get to a phone first, tell him I'll phone back here at eleven sharp for his message."

"I'll go with you," Melvin Levy said.

"Better not. But line up a bondsman, will you?"

Downstairs, the wide street was brilliant with light and heat, with flags, the navy-blue of sailors, the khaki of soldiers, the sudden brightness of foreign uniforms. Evan half-ran to the subway station on Lexington Avenue; seated in the train, he felt as if he were still racing. He was raw with the news and shock, already taut with delays and setbacks. *Is there any message? Information Desk is still busy. Mr. Jones just left for court.*

And the actual infringements. *Demand a look at the warrant. Wanted to phone his lawyer. He was refused? He never did come inside.*

He closed his eyes and was back in San Diego—the bland police, the refusals and evasions, the vigilantes in a ring under the high crescent moon. He wrenched away from the memory, but it held him; his muscles strained again against the country road, he was vowing again to fight them up and down the courts of California and in Washington and at home, he was hearing again the grand jury's indictment of thirty men, but not one Ernie, not one Herbie, not one Bobbo.

The subway jolted and then stopped. Once more Evan was half-racing through the crowded familiar streets, toward the corner of City Hall Park and the building which housed the offices of the Department of Justice. This was Park Row, not San Diego. This was New York; here in the several buildings clustered together in a vast complex of the machinery of justice, county and state and Federal, he had many times served as counsel in many kinds of crises. Faces and names here were part of his life, city and state district attorneys and assistant district attorneys, judges, commissioners and deputy commissioners and parole officers. His fellow lawyers of the old Free Speech League, and of the new Civil Liberties Bureau, knew them too. This time he wasn't a stranger on a visit; this time he was in his own proper sphere.

But this time it's Garry, he thought. And this time we're in a war.

He pushed open the front door and went to the Information desk. He showed his credentials; waited while a finger ran down a list of names; waited through interruptions and the resumption of the tracing finger down the list. At last he was in the elevator, rising toward the tenth floor; at last he opened a door, saw Garry jump up from a chair at the rear of the room, saw his lips part in the single syllable, "Dad." Relief seized Evan and an absurd sense of accomplishment. The first step was over.

It was a Detention Room, and it was crowded. About thirty men and a handful of women were there, seated on wooden chairs arranged in loose uneven rows. Garry was in the last row but one, and he must have been watching the door each time it opened. Now he started forward but a policeman standing guard moved and spoke, and Garry sat down again. Evan made for a uniformed guard just inside the entrance.

"I have a client here," he said, handing over a card. "He is Garrett Paige, and I am his attorney, as well as his father."

The officer studied the card. "You're his attorney," he said as if imparting information. "You got the right."

"Dad," Garry said a moment later, and put his arm hard around his father's shoulders. "How did you find out? Am I glad to see you!"

"And me you. Have you any idea what they're charging you with?"

"Not one."

"Is there anything you've kept back from me?"

(4 5 0)

"Nothing."

"Then start at the beginning." They told each other what had happened, Evan swiftly, and Garry with the detail his father insisted on. They stood together near the window at the rear of the room, inches away from the armed guard, who showed no interest in their words, though he managed an air of unfading vigilance every time either one took a step to shift from one foot to another.

"And when we got here," Garry ended, "I asked for a phone again. They said, 'Sure, but look at all who's ahead?' "

"And when you asked for the warrant?"

"Just the same. They sure make you into a zero the minute they arrest you." He had begun quietly enough, but as he went on with the story of the morning, his control gave way to agitation.

Evan spoke with a legal calm he was far from feeling. "Don't let yourself get too upset, Garry. We don't even know yet what this is for. We may need a lot of patience, both of us."

"I guess so."

"I'll see the warrant now," Evan said. "We've got to get to a U. S. Commissioner, or to a judge, to ask him to set bail. There will be some questioning first." He looked at Garry briefly and said, "I'll be back." Then he left. Apprehension had darkened Garry's eyes, along with the anger of that "zero." Evan forced it out of his mind for the moment; he had to be steady and clear-headed, and he had to hurry. He knew all too well how minutes could elapse in the preliminaries of any hearing, how half-hours could be lost, hours.

". . . the said Garrett Paige is hereby charged, under Section Three, Title One, of the Espionage Act, with willful and repeated attempts to cause insubordination, disloyalty and refusal to serve in the military or naval forces of the United States . . . with willful and repeated attempts to obstruct the recruiting or enlistment services . . . with willful and repeated attempts to interfere with the successful functioning of the Selective Service Act. . . ."

Evan's heart pitched and plunged as he read. No, he thought, no, there's a mistake, it cannot be. This is a criminal charge; this is ten times worse than anything we ever discussed. Compared to this, his letter is nothing. This could mean prison. It is not possible.

He had to think, but his mind balked. He had been kept waiting an hour before he had had his "turn" with the Assistant U. S. Attorney who was handling Garry's case, a man named Edmonds, who examined Evan's card, asked questions about his firm, dwelled on his relationship to "the accused," as if any man were suspect for being not only father to the accused but also attorney. Then at last Edmonds had handed over the warrant, and he turned aside to read it.

He was still holding it, in hands gone watery at the wrists. What charges had led them to this? What evidence had they gathered, from whom, where, when? He had to think clearly; he had to hurry; the morning was all but gone. Before his turn had come, he had called the office, had heard that a thousand dollars in bail was ready for his signal, and had cautioned everybody there to let no word slip if Alida should happen to call in. He had been logical, effective. He would have to get back to being that.

He turned back to Edmonds, who was busy with another man. The pitching and plunging had halted; the ship of feeling was grounded on a dark reef of necessity. Be his attorney, not his father, he told himself. His attorney, not his father. He stared down at Edmonds' desk, at the dossiers, documents, folders piled neatly there; they had been there before, but this time he noticed that nearly every one had a copy of a Registration form clipped to it. Garry's would be there too, with the unadorned phrase, CONSCIENTIOUS OBJECTION.

There was one other thing he had not noticed before. A sheaf of pages, stapled together at the upper left corner, came into view as Edmonds shifted one pile of dossiers. It was several pages in length. It was headed by a single word, ORGANIZATIONS.

The sight of it stiffened Evander Paige's spirit; it remobilized his forces. This was familiar, increasingly so in recent times. Whereas a man's attachment to or membership in any club or organization used to be a matter for his private interest alone, in the years since war had begun in Europe, some such handy little compendium had come more and more into favor with the enforcers of anything, in or out of context, in or out of testimony, in or out of a court of law. This was not entirely new in America; before the Civil War, lists of the Abolitionist damned began to crop up in the hands of pro-Slavery groups, but they had been secret guides for secret intelligence, used in stealth. Not right out in public. Not with official approval.

"If possible," Evan said to Edmonds, as the other glanced up, "I should like to see the charges which caused this action."

"You'll hear them when he's arraigned."

"Will that be soon? The question of bail—"

"You'll have to wait your turn." Edmonds returned to the man seated beside him.

In the smallest matter, Edmonds would be hostile, Evan decided, had been already, would go on being. He already had "testimony" against Garry: his lists doubtless told him that Garry sent in five dollars a year to the Free Speech League, another five to the American Union Against Militarism, perhaps that he went out of his way to travel to New York and attend the Church of the Messiah and listen to the Reverend John Haynes Holmes.

He went back to the Detention Room and told Garry about the warrant. He did not minimize it. "But that's impossible," Garry said, and he answered, "I know it is." He went off to the telephone again, calling his office once more and also the Civil Liberties Bureau, checking up on his right to be shown the actual charges, grateful in each case to hear that judicious attempts would be made to reach people who might ask Edmonds to speed up and loosen up.

At three he went back to Garry once more, and for the first time told him what might lie ahead if they were still waiting when the office closed for the night. He saw Garry blink, but neither went on with the subject. Half an hour later Garry was summoned by Edmonds and, with routine formality, put through a preliminary questioning. Whether any outside persuasion had come to bear was not clear. Edmonds still declined to inform "the accused" of the charges leading to the Federal complaint. "He isn't arraigned as yet," he said. "At that time, his attorney may see them privately." Garry went back to the Detention Room, but Edmonds was already dealing with another case. Again Evan waited.

It was ten minutes to five when the arraignment itself occurred, before a U. S. Commissioner, and Evan was at last given a folder, told that it could not be removed from the premises, that it must be read in the presence of a deputy who would see that nothing was mutilated or removed.

Evan began to read; within seconds the pitch and plunge began again. Apart from the usual documentation of Garry's life, from birth to his arrest that morning, there were four letters accusing him of disloyalty and treachery to the United States in its time of war, letters from four different people, sent at varying times during the three months since April 6th, sent either to the Attorney General in Washington, or to the Department of Justice in New York.

The first was from somebody Evan had never heard of, a Victoria Alston: ". . . and so I think it my duty to report that Mr. Garrett Paige ridicules our Commander-in-Chief, calls him soapy, and mealy-mouthed for declaring war on Germany, and constantly embarrasses people who are patriotic and proud of it . . . heard him say that the war is against the word of our Savior, and that the Conscription Act is against all our traditions . . ."

(453)

It ran on for three pages, and Evan hurried through the rest of it and turned to the next. This at least was not signed by an unknown, nor did it startle him as much. It was from Robert Grintzer, whom Garry talked about with irony. "The king and queen of England are self-conscious about Teck and Battenberg, why shouldn't Grintzer be about Grintzer?"

". . . my clear duty, since it goes against the grain of any American with red blood in his veins. Garrett Paige stated, before witnesses, that the Conscription Act 'got his goat' and that it was unconstitutional, and that he would not obey it. He ridiculed our hostess' brother-in-law for enlisting and . . ."

The letter also told of an evening when "a German-born chemist, Otto Ohrmann, with a constant stream of information from a brother with Krupp in Germany, drew from Paige the avowal that he was a pacifist, and that the war was for big profits, that 'the Bible permitted killing for profit.' "

The third letter was from Sidney Barclay. Evan paused over the name. Barclay? But Garry had left Aldrich in 1914!

". . . and because he was such a radical during the years when he was in our employ, I was interested in his attitude toward the manufacture of vital war matériel now. Under oath, in court, I will supply the names of those I checked with, co-workers in his current employment. He still talks the same way about manufacturing the wherewithal for our victory in the field or on the seas.

". . . further suggest examining a fellow chemist, Otto Friederich Ohrmann, still employed by us, a citizen, but with one brother in the German Army and one in the employ of Krupp Munitions. Ohrmann still sees Garrett Paige often, and does not refute statements that Paige is a pacifist to this day . . ."

Again Ohrmann, Evan thought, again Krupp, tacked on to all the rest. One expects it only of saloon patriots, corner clowns, and one is always wrong. He closed his eyes for an instant, and Woodrow Wilson's words came to him, offstage, from the wings of memory. "Once lead this people into war and they'll forget there ever was such a thing as tolerance . . . the spirit of ruthless brutality will enter the very fiber of our national life, infecting Congress, the Courts, the policeman, the man in the streets."

The very fiber, Evan thought. He began on the final letter. This was on the stationery of the Department of History of Yale University, and was signed Ronald Yates. Typed under the signature were the words, "Assistant Professor, now on leave for service with the U. S. Navy."

". . . do not imply that he would betray his country in the specific sense, but it is clear that he cannot distinguish between giving an opinion and conducting an insidious campaign of counterpropaganda to the entire war effort . . . therefore I feel it my duty to suggest that he be directly questioned as to his loyalty to the war effort, and if necessary be kept from further spreading his disloyal and disturbing negatives to dozens of men he works with, most of whom are young enough to be of military age."

Yates the historian. The Wilson-supporter, the man of liberal views. Yates also wrote of his duty. Each one of the four wrote of his duty to inform; not one spoke of a free man's right to think and speak.

It's going to be a dirty case, Evan thought. He wished he could take notes on the letters; he would be stopped if he tried. Quickly he went through them again, memorizing phrases, repeating names. Then he returned the folder and once more went down the hall.

Garry was astounded, then furious. "Who's Victoria Alston?" Evan asked.

"Vicky—she's Molloy's secretary. I hardly know her."

Evan told him of her letter. How many of her phrases he could repeat, how her whimper came through! "What's this about calling the President soapy, or mealy-mouthed?"

"I never did," Garry said flatly. "Oh, God, wait—there was one morning . . . Some saccharine headline somewhere about fighting the war with love in your heart. It was the paper I called soapy, the headline, I made it clearer than daylight, I—" He broke off and then asked, "Are they all like that? Who else?"

"I'm afraid so. The worst of it is that even under oath, people like this usually will be just as twisted as this."

Garry said dully, "Who else wrote?"

Swiftly Evan gave him the gist of each letter, and just as swiftly Garry produced at least one point to refute or confound the accuser. Evan pocketed each in his mind; each was a peg to hang later questioning on.

"It's nasty," he said, his voice strong. "But given elementary justice, there should be a solid case, and even with all of the delays, there should be complete acquittal."

Garry looked at him, and Evan said, "I'll try again, about bail. Remember what I said."

He hurried back to Edmonds. A man with a pad was asking questions and jotting down replies, another was sorting out the dossiers and folders, restacking them into smaller piles. Evan interrupted.

"There isn't much time," he said, "to attend to this matter of bail."

"It's way past time," Edmonds said briefly, looking at the wall clock and then at his own watch. "No judge is going to hang around waiting until after six. For tonight he'll be remanded to The Tombs."

Far off in the blackness, a bell clanged and Garry jumped and woke. There was no stir, no light around him; he had dreamed it. Except at first he had slept only in wisps and tatters; that first hour had been like anesthesia, unqualified, blessed. Then memory jolted back and he had lain on his bunk, staring, as if the air in the cell were a visible thing.

Again he saw his father's face when he came back from Edmonds for the last time; it told him before words did. For half the afternoon, he had known the day would end in defeat and jail; they had both known it, but neither had wanted to admit it to the other.

"It's bad news," his father had said, cursing himself for letting it happen. He turned aside for a moment, whether to hide his face or give Garry a chance to set his own in order, there was no way of knowing.

"Let me have your car keys," he said then. "I'll get it tonight and keep it in the garage at home."

"Read the letter, if you still want. Send it in." Already the letter seemed another world, another life. He had trouble detaching the two car keys from the others on his key ring. He wanted to ask what it would be like in The Tombs, what they would do, whether they would question him. But he said nothing. Down on the street, an ambulance siren wailed, and the sound engulfed him in melancholy, unlike anything he had ever felt.

"For one day they can put bail off," his father said, "but not for two. You'll be out tomorrow. If you can still believe me."

The words came back now, but at the time he had heard them with his eardrums only. By then he was intent on the door from the corridor. It was opening, revealing four armed men, letting them into the room. They went first to the slumped figures on the chairs up front, separating, one guard to one man. Then the fourth came back toward them.

"Which one of you is Paige?" he asked.

"I am."

"Then let's get moving."

Without a word to his father, without a word from him, he moved off alongside the guard. At the door, he glanced back. The way his father had looked came back to him and he gripped the iron railing at each side of his cot.

He tried to think of the warrant, the letters, but he kept seeing faces. Bob Grintzer's face came to him, and then Barclay's; he saw Vicky's flush of rage that he had misinterpreted, and then suddenly he was back in the cottage that first summer on Mt. Desert, with Proff Yates reproving Hank or Peter Stiles for taking on about how he had voted. "I voted for Wilson myself," Proff had told them, "and a man in the history department voted for Eugene V. Debs."

Could war change a man from that Proff Yates to this one? Sitting at a desk somewhere, finding it his duty to write this letter? That entire scene at the cottage, every word, every gesture, was still clear, but the man himself was no longer the same man—

Wait. Hold it. Something's wrong. It wasn't that way, it's not true, it's twisted around.

Garry lay rigid. What was twisted? What was eluding him, slipping off the edge of his mind just as he came near it? He had to know; he would never sleep until he did know. Start at the beginning, start with the minute you and Letty got there—

Letty, he thought, and for the first time thought of whether she would hear about this, and how soon. The newspapers were so full of wartime arrests, wartime suspects, of draft-plotting and draft-dodging cases; there had been such a haul in the Detention Room today. Poor Letty, he thought, the shop, all those people she cares about.

Start at the beginning. Again he saw the dinner table at Mt. Desert and again heard Proff—

That was it. He didn't hear Proff, he couldn't hear Proff. Proff Yates was not there. The weekend was over, and Connie Yates had stayed on for a few days, but her husband had gone back to New Haven. It was Connie who said it, Connie, quoting Proff, to restore the situation. "Ron did vote for Wilson, and an instructor in the department did vote for Debs—so there!"

And he heard his own laugh, and his "Thanks, Connie. I knew Gene Debs polled more than my one vote."

Yet just now he had been positive it was Proff; that he could still hear Proff himself saying it. He would have taken any oath on any witness stand and sworn it. If he had been in court just now, if the question had been tossed at him, an answer demanded, he would have given that answer and never had time for his uneasy feeling that something was wrong. The next question would have been tossed at him too soon.

Evidence, he thought. Evidence under oath, about what a man

(457)

said, the syllables he used, the tone of voice, the intent and meaning. Dear God, it's so easy to be wrong. But it still is evidence to pile up in a letter, to send off to authorities. Evidence to convict a man with.

It was late in the evening before Evan told Alida. Until then she knew only that he was detained "on a case," and might not be home until ten.

Then she saw him drive up in Garry's old Ford, and she ran out to the curb. "What's wrong, dear?" she asked and heard her voice tremble.

Standing out there in the street, Evan told her of the day, step after step, withholding nothing. As she listened she leaned on the car for support; she saw the way its headlamps lit up the lower branches of the trees and heard the buzzing of insects at the circles of lighted glass. When he told her of Garry's going off to The Tombs, she turned away from him and wept. He put his arm tightly around her, saying nothing.

The ringing of the telephone sent them indoors; she went ahead while Evan at last turned off the lights on the car. It was a reporter from one of the papers, and Evan answered his questions patiently and fully, even taking time to suggest that the name of Synthex be omitted, since it had no bearing on the story. As he hung up, he told her that newspapers had begun to call at the office in the late afternoon, and said, "We ought to warn the Ivarins, so they won't come on it out of the blue tomorrow."

"Later, Vanny," she said. "Don't, for a minute."

She had called him Vanny before they were married, far off back when they were young, when they had known no death of one son, no imprisonment of another. It moved him now, and he talked to her of his own pain and fear, seeing that it assuaged hers, and it was late into the night that they sat together.

Fee was the first one in the Ivarin family to know. She saw Garry's name shooting up at her from the newspaper. She was staring at the headline, CHEMIST ARRESTED UNDER WARTIME ACT, and the smaller letters under it, "Held in Tombs for questioning; Father acts as counsel," when his name, as sudden as two arrows, shot up at her.

"Acting under instructions from the Department of Justice in Washington, Deputy Federal Marshal Joseph P. Glover yesterday took into custody a research chemist, Garrett Paige—"

She cried aloud. At the stove, her mother did not hear her above the splatter and sizzle of the eggs she was frying, but underneath the table, at her feet, Shag growled. As usual Alexandra had brought in the papers from the front porch the moment their neighborly thud signaled their arrival; as usual, she had been unable to resist pulling out the two overlapping "ears" the newsboy still made, though papers were often up to twenty-eight or thirty pages now, and harder to fold into the familiar thirds. She saw the war headlines, and said to Fee, "Papa will be upset again," pointing to the news from Petrograd about the growing split in the new government. But then resolutely she had set both papers aside.

Behind her Fee suddenly rushed out of the room, and she called out, "Your egg is ready," but Fee was already halfway up the stairs. Alexandra grumbled that the egg could go frozen cold for all of her. She didn't notice that one of the papers was gone.

Upstairs Fee started all over again and almost cried out once more when she came to his name . . . "—Garrett Paige, 29, of 315 Turnpike Rd., Flushing, employed in Long Island City as a research chemist by Synthex, Inc., specialists in artificial silks and synthetic compounds.

"Arrested upon his arrival at the Synthex plant in the morning, the suspect was taken to the Federal Building, on the charge of alleged interference with and obstruction of the enlistment or conscription of male persons between 21 and 31 years of age.

"Preliminary questioning of the accused was conducted by Assistant U. S. Attorney C. A. Edmonds, but when Mr. Edmonds proved unable by six o'clock to arrange for a determination of bail, Paige was remanded to The Tombs Prison overnight—"

Fee dropped the newspaper on her bed. The Tombs—that's where they put murderers, and he's there in a cell, locked up, behind bars. If anything happens to him, I'll die.

Suddenly she cupped her face in both hands with such vehemence that the lobes of her ears were swept forward by her thumbs, and her eyebrows were pulled down by her fingertips until the top arc of her eyesockets burned.

If anything happens to him, she thought again, I just can't stand it. She dropped her hands and looked at the paper. Standing above it, rigid, not bending to touch it, she still could see the two words, "Garrett Paige."

(459)

Once again she forced herself to go on with the story. ". . . remanded to The Tombs Prison overnight.

"Counsel for the chemist is his father, Evander Paige, 22 Channing Street, Barnett, Long Island, a partner in the law form of Turner,
Paige, Levy and Payson. The attorney has been widely active with
the Free Speech League and the American Union Against Militarism,
which upon our entry into the war, allegedly abandoned its previous
pacifism and adopted the goal of 'a democratic peace' and 'world
federation at the end of the war.' This organization is now reported
merging with, or branching into, the Civil Liberties Bureau, recently
formed as a special wartime unit, with Roger N. Baldwin, 33, its
Director.

"The twenty-eight others taken into custody as wartime suspects
during the past twenty-four hours included—"

Downstairs her mother called out in exasperation. Soon she would
see his name too and say, "Oh my goodness," and carry on as if it
were *her* tragedy. It would be unbearable. Luckily Fran wasn't
around; she had been off at eight for New York every morning for a
week, secretly looking for a place to live in the fall.

Fee picked up the newspaper. Again the arrows flew at her, pierc-
ing her eyes, and this time they brought tears, burning all vision away.

Down in the kitchen Alexandra glanced at Fee's egg; the butter
was glazed, and it looked revolting. But she couldn't be bothered. Already she was at work, as she was from her first waking hour every
day, always searching for an idea for the column she had to start today, always clutching at something, examining it, growing fond of it,
then suddenly turning on it in discontent and tossing it aside. Maybe
she was already stale on her writing; perhaps she had been wrong to
say, "No beach this summer." Everybody was giving up vacation
trips because of the war; she had felt a hypocrite to have her decision
taken as self-denial by her pupils, by Alida, even by the milkman and
garbage collector.

"Where could I keep all my papers in a tent?" she had asked
Stefan when she had first told him they would stay at home. "Where
could I keep my books, the Montessori, Dr. Holt, the women's magazines, and all the rest?"

The glory of becoming well-known as a writer had never ceased; it
had grown, ripened, gained in meaning and inner joy, even in these
days of war. But the doubts grew too, and the confusion; she did not
have an orderly mind, nor a lifelong habit to substitute for it. She was
forever floundering, forever falling behind. Not only on the letters,
but on the articles themselves; two a week were four times as hard as

(460)

one a week, why she did not know. Even the house was neglected; half the time it was a shambles. The girls were only too happy to slide out of their share when she was unable to do her own.

"Fee," she called again, but there was still no reply. She sat down and surrendered to the newspaper; something did seem to be going wrong in Russia, and worry nipped at her. Day by day for nearly two weeks, Stefan had been saying there was difficulty, dissension, a play for realignment of forces. He denied that he feared for the revolution, but she knew he did fear it, and so deeply that he dared not say it aloud. The war on the Galician front was going badly, too; she prayed it would suddenly swerve toward a huge victory for the Russians, to unify them.

Otherwise Stefan would go on in this deepening gloom, and end in God knew what mood. It had been a long time since he had been in a bad one, but even longer since he had been satisfied and happy. He did not admit it; he was too busy with his lectures, too fascinated with the war news; he certainly was never bored. But when he did speak of himself, or of the future, he spoke of having less energy, of getting older.

"You're only fifty-six," she would protest.

"In four years, I'll be sixty."

It saddened her. She was the same age as he, and she never spent ten seconds on it. She felt strong, she was never ill, never needed a day in bed. She slept harder than she had in years, like one of the girls, all sleep, total sleep.

She heard a rush down the stairs, and then Fee was with her. "Mama, look, they arrested Garry. He's in prison."

"What are you saying?"

By now, Fee's tears were so ungovernable she could not see. She felt her mother rip the paper away from her, heard the thud of her body on the wooden chair. There was no "Oh my goodness," there was nothing. Fee finally saw her mother's stricken face, open lips, like Eli in an attack, saw her rush toward the stairs. In a moment she heard her fling open her father's bedroom door, heard his sharp "What? *What?*" and heard his feet thump on the floor as he sprang out of bed.

"Stiva, how can it be? What for? That wonderful boy."

"This damnable hue and cry. Here, let me dress, I must get to Evan."

Somehow their pain helped her own.

.   .   .

Stefan was nearer Alida when her composure finally broke, and Alexandra watched him try to comfort her, clumsy with his gestures. He patted Alida's bowed head as if she were his child, and put an arm about her shoulders, holding her awkwardly in an embrace.

It was a strange thing to see, a piece of sculpture cast not in marble or bronze but in the warm flesh of life, and Alexandra's heart ached with the seeing of it. A long time ago, she used to tease Stefan about Alida; it had amused him at first, even flattered him a little, and then it had begun to annoy him. "You sound like the girls, everything is a crush—it's barbaric."

She had stopped, not because of his strictures, but for the far sounder reason that not long after, she had overheard Franny discoursing learnedly to Fee, learnedly and lasciviously, on the theme that old people could get crushes and fall in love too. Franny's tone outraged her, and especially so, since among Stefan's multiple faults there had never been this meanest one of all.

Now, over Alida's head, he looked to her for help and Alexandra went closer. "If only you'd come back home with us," she said, "and not wait here alone all day."

"The phone," Alida said. She moved away from Stefan then, still keeping her face turned from them both.

The Ivarins looked at each other. From the moment they had arrived they had known what the night had been for her; her swollen lids and cheekbones had told them all too vividly. When Alexandra phoned to ask if they might come over, she said, "I'd be so thankful," and then added, "Evan left two hours ago," as if his absence might change their minds. "I mustn't talk about it too much," she had begun, and then had opened her heart to them as she had never yet done, unaware of herself, needing only to tell what had befallen her. She concealed nothing, not the warrant, not the four letters nor the things they said. It was only when she came to the final moment when Garry had to go off to the Tombs, that she broke down.

As she faltered, clinging to Stefan, he could see the final scene, the rows of vacant chairs, the morning crowd diminished to a handful of desolates, still waiting for something to happen, for somebody to appear. Then Garry hearing the news from Evan, his stone-silence as he heard it, Evan looking away to let the boy get control of himself. And then Garry's departure, out of the room, through the door, down the corridor off to The Tombs.

Off to a cell, Ivarin thought. No stomp of boots, no Cossack uniforms, but off to a cell, as once his own young self had gone off to prison in Russia. There was no knout waiting for Garry, but arrest in itself was an assault on a man.

For a young man, a man with a basic decency, it was an assault he would not forget through all his life. The moment of arrest, the words of the law, the start of the process, the start of fear—

Yes, the fear. Nobody need tell me, Ivarin thought, it's there still, that taste and tightness of fear as they marched me off to my first night in prison.

And now Garry has had it too. And for what? An arrest based on nothings, on the tyranny of orthodoxy, under the Czar Conformism, the Emperor Conformism. Garry was unorthodox—throw him in a dungeon.

"An American boy in Siberia!" He said it violently, and Alida shivered and moved away from him, closer to Alexandra as if to restore a balance. "I beg you," Ivarin cried, "forgive me. It was unpardonable. I was thinking of something—"

"I know," she said. "Don't be distressed."

"Would you like some coffee?" Alexandra asked, ashamed of Stefan's lack of tact. "Let me make some new, and perhaps a slice of toast." The women began to talk together and he stood apart, still flushed with his gaucherie.

Gaucherie because he had blurted it out to the boy's mother. That was all, that was the only trouble. Perhaps in some lecture soon, he might use it to express his point. There was a clang to it, a hard ring, like the hooves of a Cossack's horse on frozen cobblestones at night.

When could he see Evan and hear the whole story from him? Alida had left nothing out, but he had to hear it from him. And from Garry as well. Edmonds or no, bail couldn't be stalled off for a second day, and doubtless Garry would be here with his parents this evening; perhaps at some point later on tonight, he could talk directly to him, hear it directly, the best way to start anything.

"The carbon of his letter to the Exemption Board," Alida said behind him and he turned to see Alexandra already reading it. "Evan didn't mail it when he got it out of the car," she said. "There's no hurry now."

Ivarin moved over to Alexandra and they read the letter together. Then he took it and read it through once more before he gave it back to Alida. "He is a good man," he said simply.

Alexandra said, "He means each word. You feel it right through."

Alida stood, folding and refolding the letter.

Ivarin went on thoughtfully. "I disagree with him, mind you, but it's the letter of a good and upright young man. I am proud to know him."

"Oh, Stefan."

"There must be something I can do— There must be."

THIRTY-FOUR

It was from Cynthia Aldrich that Letty heard it. Since she had separated from Garry, she never did more than glance at the paper, but today with a new client coming early, she hadn't even done that. She was barely inside the door of the shop when Cynthia called.

"Have you seen it?"

"Seen what?"

"Don't tell me I'm to be the bearer of bad tidings. Oh, Letty."

She told her, and then read the story from the newspaper as if to lend authority to her words. She could hear Letty say, "Oh, no," and "It's too awful," but these phrases were not addressed to her, and she did not pause over them. When she came to the end of the newspaper account, there was silence.

"It's such a shock," Letty finally said.

"Mark saw it first, and made me call you. He told me to warn you, newspaper people may descend on you, right there."

"I suppose so. In the telephone book."

"If only it were 'The English Antiques Shop,' or some other name."

Letty said, "Yes," without taking it in. She knew she ought to think of the shop, but she could not, not yet. Through the window she gazed at the gold lettering, running backwards, "Mrs. Garrett Paige, Antiques." That was its name, not "The English Antiques Shop" or anything else. She stared at the lettering, but she also saw Garry's face. "I suppose I should have been prepared," she said, "but I always thought if war did come, he'd change."

Cynthia made a faint sound of dissent. "Should I come over for a while? In case there *are* newspaper reporters?"

(464)

The shop, Letty thought, I do have to protect it. "I'm so mixed up, I can't think," she said. "It's dangerous for the shop, isn't it?"

"Now, Letty, you're not to fret. We're simply not going to let the shop's name get dragged in the mud."

"I feel so dreadful, even thinking of business at a time like this."

"Of course you do, dear child. But we have to carry on, and I'll think about it for you. I've always been your special adviser, haven't I?" She went on rapidly, for she was not sure whether the soft sounds in the receiver were sobs, and she felt it best not to know.

As she hung up, Letty looked at Mrs. Everrett, and then at Miss McNaught. They averted their glances, and her heart sank. They both knew it. The whole world knew it. Peter knew it.

"Mrs. Everrett," she said, "Please see if you can cancel my appointment."

But just then, the door of the shop opened, and her new client came in. She was not only new, but one of the clients known as "important," with a town house to do over as well as an estate in Pinehurst for the winter months.

"I'm so sorry to be late," she greeted Letty with a charming smile. "All that traffic."

"It couldn't matter less," Letty answered, smiling too. Her client didn't read the morning papers either, and in a flash of decision she thought, Cynthia's right. You do have to carry on.

Fee was out on the porch, waiting for the newsboy and the Sunday papers. She had been up since six, as she had been every morning since it had happened, and except for Shag crouching uneasily at her feet, the house was motionless.

Only ten days had gone by but life had changed forever. Garry's had and so had hers. Even when he did get out on bail the next afternoon, the relief over "the good news" had lasted for only a little while, and then her black awful feeling came back.

Nothing mattered now except what was going to happen to him. Going to college, her scholarship, what she would do if she didn't win it—maybe she would care again at the end of the summer, when the time came near for the letter from Albany, but now none of it counted.

A whole month had to pass before the trial would begin, a whole month.

How could Garry stand it, not knowing for another thirty days and thirty nights? Even working with his father and the other lawyers

(465)

every day in New York, rounding up witnesses, getting the case ready—even so, how could he bear it? She saw him once in a while, for maybe a minute, never more than to say hello, and she was almost glad of that, because if she ever got talking, he would guess.

Just yesterday her mother said, "You're still upset, Fee, and why not? I always said, 'a real Ivarin, not deaf to the miseries of others.' Do you remember Damsie and Josie?"

"Who? Of course I do." She started out of the room, but there was something she had to ask. The draft numbers had at last been picked, and Garry's wasn't one of them. "Mama, since his number didn't come up this time, will his letter make any difference?"

"I asked the same question. Papa doesn't know."

"But it might be a year before the second draft," Fee said. "Maybe he could have kept it back until then."

"Papa thinks Garry was right to send it anyway. Mr. Molloy knew he wrote it; Garry told him in advance, because of working there. So it would come out at the trial anyway."

Fee couldn't stand the word "trial" spoken out loud. She didn't like to hear any of it spoken out loud. She was glad Fran didn't talk much about it. Fran had carried on a lot that first day, but then she had dolled up for the Soldiers Dance and rushed off to Masonic Hall. She stayed out way after it was over, and when she did get in, she yanked at Fee's shoulder until she awoke. Fran had met a boy named David Marks, a second lieutenant from Tennessee, the first officer she'd ever met. He wasn't supposed to be there in the first place, because the dances were for enlisted men only, no officers. He was an aviator, good-looking, and his father owned three big stores for electrical things and belonged to a country club.

"He's six feet tall," Fran ended in a sort of awe, "the only boy I've ever met who's a whole head taller than me. The only Jewish boy. Do you remember that dance at the Yipsels in Brooklyn?"

Fee had heard of it a thousand times, and she steered Fran right off it. As soon as possible, she turned over and pretended to fall asleep.

Sleep refused to come back, and every night since then it had played tricks, sometimes covering her with such weighted blackness, it was like being buried, other times, blowing at her like a spring breeze, hardly touching her. Last night had been one of the heavy nights, but she had awakened before six, as if God had touched a button to uncoil her.

Now she saw the newsboy at last, coming over the crest of the hill. She ducked inside until he had left his papers and gone on; she did

(466)

every morning. If he saw her out there waiting every day, he'd blab it all over town. Everybody knew they were real friends of the Paiges, and every human being in Barnett was talking his head off about Garry. They even went out of their way to pass the Paige house, gawking and snooping and gossiping.

When she went out again, she saw that at last there was no mention of Garry in either paper. Their front pages were still full of the lists of serial numbers in the draft-drawing, but not a mention of "The Paige Case."

Her relief lasted only a few minutes. Inside on one of the feature pages, she found it. It was a summary, step by step from the beginning, and this time with pictures of Garry and his father both. Under the pictures ran a single caption: DISLOYALTY SUSPECT WITH COUNSEL, HIS FATHER, ONCE ACTIVE IN CASE FOR EMMA GOLDMAN'S MANAGER.

It's a dirty trick, Fee thought furiously. Mr. Paige was active against the vigilantes, that was all. He was against Emma Goldman, against her manager, against all anarchists, and it was underhanded and nasty to drag in Emma Goldman or any anarchist alive.

Her fury stayed as she read the story. There was a pointing finger in it all the way, and part of it sounded as if Mr. Paige was arrested, too. Even when it told how Garry had telephoned Synthex to resign, the moment he was out on bail, and heard then and there that he had been fired instead—even then they dragged in Mr. Paige and his trip to California.

The reporter had asked Garry how he felt when he heard he was fired. "I'm not sure yet," was his only answer. Then they asked Mr. Paige.

"It came as a surprise," he said and hesitated to explain why it did. "If I said Mr. Molloy had been most courteous and helpful, it might lay him open to misunderstanding, in the climate today. Which is why we have opted for a hearing before a Federal judge, instead of a trial by jury. An impartial jury would be hard to come by just now."

The story "recalled that as far back as 1912, in California, Mr. Paige also questioned the impartiality of witnesses and jurymen. His allegations, upon investigation, were declared unsubstantiated."

But they were true, Fee thought. Mr. Paige would never lie, never. And neither would Garry.

She finished in a rush. She couldn't sit still. She couldn't go in and get breakfast. She refolded the papers carefully, so nobody could tell she had already read them, and started off from the house. Shag came too, looking around at her every little while, checking up to find out

(467)

if she were in the mood for a race or anything happy. Each time he would droop and walk on again.

She chose a route that led her directly away from Channing Street, and she walked until the sun began to burn on her hair, and people began to appear on the streets, going to church. On her way home, as she went by the corner of Hill and Channing, she glanced over at the Paiges' house.

Then she stopped.

A couple of boys were kneeling on the pavement right in front of it, kids of nine or ten, kneeling as if they were playing marbles. But she caught a flash of white chalk and thought, Not marbles. Tic-tac-toe or hopscotch. Suddenly they rose and dashed off, both whooping with glee.

She stood where she was. Shag came back to her and sat at her feet, somber and uncertain, too. She patted his head, but she was looking at the Paiges' house all the while. There was no sign of anybody awake as yet. The bedroom windows upstairs were all opened wide, as if they were still asleep. She tried to see if their newspaper was still out on their porch but she couldn't be sure.

She kept hearing the way the boys had whooped when they ran off, shouting in a smark-alecky way. And they really had had chalk. She began to move quietly toward the house. There still was no sign of anybody awake.

As she drew closer she saw that something was printed on the pavement, in tall, wobbly letters.

It was one word. SPY.

She spat straight down at it and rubbed at it with her shoe. If only she was wearing her sneakers; the rubber soles would be like erasers.

She spat again and rubbed harder. But in the hot sun, the spot went dry, and the chalked line still showed. A sense of hurry seized her, like in an exam. If they saw her, inside the house, they would come right out and discover it. Her mouth had gone dry; she picked up a pebble from the gravel driveway and sucked at it; they taught you to do that at field hockey, if you were dying of thirst. It worked like magic.

After a minute with the pebble, Fee knelt on the pavement. She lifted the hem of her dress and put it to her open lips. She felt it grow moist and she loved the pebble for helping her. Then with her dress, she began to mop the street.

"Shag, look," she whispered. "It works." He barked in joy; he always could tell the way she felt.

(468)

. . .

It's an illusion that I cling to, Stefan Ivarin thought in bitterness, this belief that somehow I can "help Evan."

Each time he came back to the house from a lecture, he was assailed by frustration, and he soon found it intolerable. Twice he had lectured about the arrest, not naming Garry, and each time he had aroused an anger in his listeners.

But how does it help Evan, or Garry, for my needle-workers to agree with me, or the men in the coal pits? Can I find no positive way to help now, at this crucial point? Can *I* round up witnesses, like this Hank who remembers that it was he and not Garry who said conscription got his goat, and thus may discredit Grintzer as a witness, and cast some reasonable doubt on his testimony?

Can I help prove that the secretary Vicky is a morbid romantic, in love with the war as a woman is in love with a young lover?

Evan has the case planned, controlled, ordered; everything now depends on this Judge Perkins and how stout a judge or how frail a judge he is; how infected with the prevailing disease, or how free of it.

I will testify, Alexandra will testify, yes, yes. We will say what we know of Garry, of his intelligence, his independence, his inner goodness. But will Judge Perkins remember what Thoreau wrote about a man and his conscience?

As the days passed, as August approached, Ivarin's sense of futility grew greyer. It's Russia, he thought at times; I cannot think straight while the Bolsheviki grow bolder. A *coup* to seize the government! They failed last week, but will they try again? Or, with Trotsky arrested and Lenin in hiding somewhere outside the borders, will their kinetic energy dwindle away to nothing?

Do not let your own energy dwindle away, he commanded himself. One positive thing you can do for Evan is the "patriot" data. Get back to that. Without plan, he had begun to collect printed data about cases like Garry's. Everywhere, "patriots" were doing to others what Garry's accusers had done to him. Evan had said the data was valuable; in the courtroom some bit or piece might come in strongly at the psychological moment.

Ivarin went on collecting samples from newspapers all over the country. A survey, he thought once, my own survey, a touch more vital than anything Saul Borg ever contemplated. At special newsstands that sold out-of-town papers, he got hold of papers from big cities across America, reading, studying, clipping.

Every day there was something. In Boston, just days before, Federal agents had pulled in six or seven people for "unpatriotic remarks." A parade of socialists, of workingmen from labor unions, their permit in order—and then, riot. A melange of the Naval Reserve, the National Guard, the Marines, and for a bizarre touch, Canadians in kilts— they had attacked. They seized flags and banners, they kicked people, pummeled them, beat them up—for two solid hours the riot went on, before law and order, those dilatory twins, came into play.

And there was in Vermont a minister handing out a pamphlet to five people, calling it unchristian to kill; he got fifteen years for it. Another man of the cloth, Bigelow, no pacifist at all, denounced the vast wartime profits of public utilities companies; he was publicly horsewhipped for it.

Ivarin grew interested in his collection. Did Evan know of those jailed for saying that war taxes would be wiser than Liberty Bonds? Of the benighted citizen in Minnesota jailed for telling ardent knitters that no soldier would ever get to see their socks?

Did Judge Perkins know any of it? There was a delirium abroad in the land, insidious as the mustard gas at Ypres.

And what was abroad in Russia? Ivarin always came to a halt at the question. The East Galician front was now shattered, and in the cities, the people were war-weary, sullen, hungry for food. Brusilove was out, Lvoff was gone, and suddenly the head of the government was Kerensky! A good man, a moderate, a fine socialist, but did Kerensky have the stature to head the country?

The need creates the stature, Ivarin thought. He will have to have the stature, or else—

That damnable "or else."

The suspense darkened his days. His encounters with Evan began to raise doubts of his own strength; Evan faced a suspense far closer than his own, yet Evan, and young Garry as well, managed an air of composure, admirable to behold.

A fierce longing seized him, for Garry to go free, for Russia to be safe. The days passed and the fierceness grew. He was on the periphery; once he would have been able to do something that would help.

The telephone rang, and he picked up the receiver. It was Garry, asking at once for Fee.

Ivarin called her, saw her mixture of eagerness and disbelief, and then ostentatiously left. If Alexandra were at home, she would have hovered. But he was not yet reduced to eavesdropping on a child.

"Fee," Garry said, "do you remember the time we went for the soda?"

"Of course I do."

"Could I come over and talk to you about it?"

"Oh, Garry, of course you could."

"I'll be right there. Try to remember what we talked about that day, will you?"

"I don't need to 'try.' I can hear every single word right now."

"Because, Fee, Dad's been asking me about talks I've had with all my friends, and I couldn't exactly remember what we said, except when I asked if you'd ever heard your father—"

"I remember."

"Dad said he might like to put you on the stand next week, if you would agree. I'll be right over."

Fee trembled at the idea of herself in a courtroom, herself in a witness chair, herself being badgered by the prosecution. She had read about it so often, in the newspapers, in mystery books and detective stories. She ran upstairs to fix her hair, and change her dress, and the trembling grew worse.

In less than five minutes, she saw him coming toward the house, heard Shag's welcoming bark, and she ran downstairs again, to reach the front door before he rang the bell. If only they could be by themselves while they talked.

"Let's stay here, on the porch," she said a minute later, as he came up the front steps toward her. The tremble was in her voice, too, but he didn't notice. He still looked tan, but he was so thin, with his cheeks caved inwards, and his eyes farther back in their sockets.

He understood about staying outside, and he talked in low tones, as she did. Then, bit by bit, she repeated what they had said that Tuesday afternoon when he had found her selling Liberty Bonds.

"Would you be too nervous, Fee," he asked at the end, "to say it in court?"

"Even if I am," she said.

"It might help. 'One part in the mosaic we're trying to build,' to quote my father."

"Would I say it this same way? Like just now?"

"Exactly. Dad might talk to you about it first; he couldn't today."

"Oh, Garry." She looked at him and then away. He stood up and she was about to stand up also, but suddenly she bowed her head, to hide her face. For a while nothing happened, and then he put his hand on her hair and said, "Fee?" as if it were a complete question. A thousand points of light ran from his fingers through her, and without looking up, she cried, "If anything happened to you."

This time he said, "Why, Fee," as if it were his answer.

. . .

(471)

Her father and mother, a man named Ohrmann, the people who wrote the letters—all day, people had been testifying, and now, in a moment, it would be her turn on the witness stand.

Waiting, dreading it, Fee felt her tongue stick to the roof of her mouth. She thought of the pebble that had helped her so much, that morning a month ago, and wished she could lean down in this frightening courtroom and find one now.

Everything about it was strange and the look on everybody's faces was, too. The prosecuting attorney, Edmonds, asked questions as if he expected lies for the answers, and, high up on his perch, Judge Perkins seemed distant and not very interested. At the special table for Garry and Mr. Paige and Mr. Paige's lawyer friends, Garry looked worn-out and even thinner.

The fifteen or twenty rows of benches for spectators were not full of strangers, and that too was terrible. Half of them were from Barnett; how had they got there early enough in the morning to get seats? "The joy in feeling superior propelled them," her father had said.

Mrs. Loheim was there, and Trudy, and Fee thought it cheap and mean of them to come. How long ago it was, when Trudy and her mother were part of her day-by-day world. Now here she was miles away from them, even though they were in the same courtroom. They were enjoying themselves, as if it were a moving picture, while she sat there hurting, listening to people attacking Garry, listening to his father try to pin them down, watching them slip around and attack from another direction.

There was something so old-maidish about that Victoria Alston, but even Mr. Paige could not make her admit that it was only a newspaper headline that Garry had called soapy and mealy-mouthed; Vicky stuck to it, under oath, that it was President Wilson, the Commander-in-Chief, and that she took him to task about it, but that he kept right on. It was her word against his. She swore that he said right out that nobody could make him wear a uniform or use a gun and that anybody who did was going against the word of God in the Bible. Many of the men employed at Synthex were of draft age, and he kept saying it to them, too.

None of it was a surprise; nothing all day was a surprise. Over and over for a month Fee had heard about the four letters, the people who wrote them, the preliminary examinations, and now here it all was for the last time. She could not believe a judge could really be taken in by them, but even her mother had told her optimism was foolish with the world gone mad.

"Miss Fira Ivarin."

She sprang up with a gasp, before she remembered all the things Mr. Paige had told her about not being afraid. She was sworn in, and put on the stand, facing the courtroom, but she did not dare look at anybody except Mr. Paige. He smiled at her.

"Now, Fee," he said in his ordinary voice. "I'm just going to ask you to tell us here about the day you had a soda with Garry. When was that?"

"The day he registered."

"June fifth. How do you remember so clearly?"

"He showed me his card; he said he had the afternoon off to register."

"You got talking about the war," Evan said. "Suppose you tell it in your own words."

She began with effort, but soon the words came faster. "And then we got talking about being patriotic, and he said it was hard to talk about things like that, and asked me if my father ever said straight out, 'I love my country,' and I said no, he always said things like 'It's a great country' or 'This wonderful country,' but never the other."

"Then what did Garry say?"

"Then he said there were so many ways a man could show that he did love it."

"Such as—did he say?"

"Not exactly. He said he thought a man could work for his country, or suffer for it."

"Anything else?"

"Or die for it." She stopped, trying to remember. The courtroom was very quiet. "He said a man also could die for it, but not kill for it."

"Did he say what he meant by that?"

She shook her head. "Not exactly. He did say you could kill off a man who was an enemy of your country, but killing him off wasn't the same as working for the country itself, or its future, not if you kept thinking of its future."

"Did he say what he was going to do?"

"I didn't ask him, Mr. Paige. He never said, and I thought that wasn't any of my business."

Even Mr. Edmonds was not as fast and snappy with her as he had been with the other witnesses when he was cross-examining them. Fee went over the answers once more, some of them two or three times. But no matter how Mr. Edmonds phrased his questions, she always said the same things; it wasn't hard, it didn't need any trick or wanting to outsmart him. All she had to do was to let herself think back. All she had to do was to remember, and it was as if they were still sit-

(473)

ting there together, with Garry saying the words right to her in that serious voice he had used then.

"—and this young lady," Mr. Edmonds said to the judge, "who is apparently in love with the defendant, and who, in her youth and innocence, was taken in by his words—"

"I wasn't taken in, not a—"

But Mr. Edmonds stopped her, and Fee saw Mr. Paige shake his head, as a signal. She was too angry to listen to what the prosecutor went on to say. Something that began, "despite this appealing faith in what she thinks is the defendant's independence and courage."

"It *is* courage," Fee said. And she looked at Garry for the first time. He was staring at her, and he didn't look away. He was staring at her in a new way; she had never seen him look at her that way before, and she looked down at the floor. Then she looked back, as if he had told her to. He was still looking at her. He was different. The whole world was different.

There was the waiting to be got through while the judge deliberated in his chambers. Unable to remain seated, Stefan Ivarin left the courtroom and went outside to the corridor, pacing up and down.

She helped more than anyone else, he thought again. More than I have helped, for all my wishes to be of use.

It's the inevitable sequence. The old cannot find the way; the young instinctively do find it. The old back down, the young take over.

Not yet, he thought, not yet. I'm not backing down quite so soon. Even if I was of no real help to Evan and to Garry.

How did I think I could be of help? How was I of help about San Diego?

Not for the trial, he suddenly thought. Never for a moment. I didn't know of the vigilantes until it was all over, the trial done with, the verdict known. Not until then, when Evan came back, after all his legal work was done.

Yet I did help. Not Evan, but the fight itself. His fight, mine.

Fights can be lost in a courtroom. But they can go on outside. That's what I knew then, that's what I have forgotten.

The recess lasted for a few minutes over an hour. Then Garry rose to hear the verdict. It was, "Guilty, as charged."

The sentence was a fine of five thousand dollars and imprisonment in a Federal prison for a term of three years.

(474)

He felt it, the ache changing to anguish. He walked out of the courtroom, thinking only, Go slow, don't look around. Slow, careful slow. Empty, no thinking, no feeling, you knew it all along.

Slow, careful, there it is again, the prison, the same until they ship you to the other.

Three years. Three, three, three, three. Dear God, help me.

THIRTY-FIVE

At two that night, Stefan Ivarin went to his desk and began to write. The house was silent, Alexandra long since sleeping the burning sleep of sorrow.

He had been unable to consider bed, he could not concentrate on chess, on his mathematics. Over and over he saw Garry's last quick look at his parents as he left for prison, heard Alida's sobs, Evan's voice stating the intention to appeal.

All at once he abandoned his attempts to settle down to some distraction. He drew one of his narrow white pads toward him, shook down his fountain pen to free the flow of ink, and without clear intention, without knowing to what end, he began to write.

Across the top of his page, taking great care with the formation of each letter, he blocked in a phrase.

An American Boy in Siberia?

It was when he put in the question mark that certainty erupted within him. That question mark was like a signal, a wave of a hand—it was his old style, it was his old self.

Assassinate a Book? Assassinate a Preface? Pogrom—California Style? A dozen headlines came back, his own headlines, that he had written atop his own editorials. He looked at this one and then wrote a subhead.

Arrest and Imprisonment
of a Youth
Who Talked

Once more he paused. Then he began; the sentences started to come; for a long time he wrote, with scarcely a correction or interlineation.

There is a boy I know who is dead wrong about this war. In my opinion, dead wrong.

I call him a boy, because he grew up near me, the same age as my son, his parents close friends of my family in the small town where we all live.

Today this boy, Garrett Paige, twenty-nine, was sentenced to a prison term that will last three years.

For what? For something he said. Not for something he did, but for something he said. For many things he said. Said to the people he worked with, said to the people he knew as friends, said for a long time before we got into the war, and continued to say after we were in it.

What he said was, "It is wrong to kill." He is a deeply religious boy, a Unitarian, which again is something I happen not to agree with, but to his religion he has committed himself with all his young heart.

And so, he often quoted the Bible and said, " 'Thou Shalt Not' means 'Thou Shalt Not,' and there are no exceptions."

(This is where I disagree. I hold this war to be inescapable if man is to rid himself of tyranny and oppression.)

Young Paige is a chemist, and when his boss first ordered shells and bombs and explosives for war, he quit his good job rather than make them.

That was three years ago. The world war was Europe's war then, not ours. Now it is ours. A big change.

It changed you and me; it changed Garrett Paige. What did not change for him was his faith in his Bible and what it said. What did not change was his belief in his right to say so.

He said so and lost friends; he said so and lost more than friends; he said so and on July tenth was arrested for the things he said. Things about war, about this war and all war. Things it is his right to say in a free country.

This free country.

His right, in war or peace, so long as he says only what *he* feels and does not say to one other man, "Break the law."

This he never did. Not once.

Busybody letters said that he did; busybody witnesses swore that he did. And they lied.

(476)

But this country is now partly enslaved to the Czar of Orthodoxy, the Emperor of Conformity. The Siberia I speak of awaits the man who says the unpopular thing—

For the first time Stefan Ivarin paused. A long time ago, years, he and Eli had been in a fearful row about conformity. The idiom of one's surroundings, Eli had said; one must protest within the idiom of one's surroundings.

Eli, my only son, Ivarin thought, and suddenly he felt closer to the imprisoned Garry than ever in his life he had felt to the son of his own blood.

You did not, he thought, addressing Garry in his mind, you did not make your protest in the idiom of your surroundings.

He was wrenched with regret for his son, wrenched with love for this young man in prison. Another night came back to him, that night in the café when Evan told of the country road and the needly little acorns and the ring of ruffians, told, and asked that he write not one piece, but several. That night, sitting there in the café together, the accents and odors and gestures of Europe around them, he had first felt that he and Evan were eternally kin, the foreign-born, the native-born, disparate and various, but one.

Now he felt the same toward Evan's son, a generation between them, but dividing them less than proving a continuity. A wheel had turned. In 1877 he had gone to prison in Russia for his ideas; in 1917 Garry was in prison in America for his.

Stefan Ivarin closed his eyes. For a while he rested, and then went back to his unfinished piece. He read it through quickly and was sure of it. It was too long, but that was nothing; so often it was too long to start with. Next day's light was a fierce critic, and his own blue pencil its most willing weapon.

More important was an omission. Should he work in Garry's letter which Evan himself had brought up in court, saying his son had no wish to hide it? If that went into this first piece, he could lead from it to a powerful paragraph:

And that is *not* why he was arrested. That is not why he was locked up in a cell. That is not why he faces his three years in prison. He was arrested before that letter was sent.

Ivarin considered the possibility as if the words were already written, with his pen hanging above them, ready to descend and scratch them out, or move on to their followers.

Not in this first piece, he decided. Time enough in a second one,

(477)

or a third. There will be others, about the appeal, perhaps a request for a government review—

A second piece, a third? A series of pieces? Ivarin shoved back from the desk, startled. He was not dazed, not daydreaming. He meant it.

Suddenly he thumped the table. Of course he meant it. He meant to try it, not in a magazine, not in Alexandra's paper, not anywhere but where he had always meant every word he cared about for most of his life.

And Steinberger said he sometimes wondered if people didn't feel the need for something that made it legitimate to suffer a little.

Steinberger, "the new top-story." Steinberger, who had said all the usual things when he took power—no changes, nobody in jeopardy—but had also spoken up of a newspaper's duty.

Especially, Ivarin thought with a faint interior amusement, when the paper has stayed on a dead circulation plateau for more than a year.

He went back to his work, and hurried on to the end. Before him stood his silver watch, its lid open, propping it up like a sliver of time. When he finished, it showed twenty after four.

How long it had been since he had stayed chained to his desk half the night, writing. How wild a joy there was in doing it again.

In the morning he would read it to Alexandra and translate it for Evan and Alida. And then—

Once more he stopped short.

Then he would go to New York and take it direct to Steinberger. The devil with Fehler. He would write this series not as a staff member; that was forever over. But a new phenomenon was appearing more and more in the American press: the outside columnist, with a space of his own, under his own by-line. Even Brisbane, after two long decades of refusal, first by Pulitzer, then by Hearst, was at last achieving his heart's desire, an editorial column that carried his name, not only in the Hearst sheets, but in other papers where he was not on the staff. It was another new phase in American journalism.

Why not in the *Jewish News?*

In the morning, to his astonishment, he overslept. It was nearly noon when he came downstairs, and Alexandra was already gone.

"For her letters," Fee reminded him.

"*Chortu,* I forgot her letters." It was he who had suggested this weekly trip to the offices of *Abend* for the secretarial help Simon Tischmann was willing to provide for her mail, and it had proved the solution to her growing problem. At first she had been tongue-tied and miserable, unable to dictate letters to a strange young woman, but so acute was her shame at being two to ten weeks behind, that she had persisted, and by now her weekly trip was her "life-saver."

Today Ivarin regretted the routine. He wanted her right there, right then. Her return at the end of the day would be too late. "I wanted her to read something," he said to Fee, "that I wrote late last night about Garry."

Fee was setting out his fruit and pouring his coffee. At his words, the stream of coffee missed the cup and splashed the oilcloth. "God damn it," she cried, so unexpectedly that he looked sharply at her. She's in torment, he thought, and a warmth of sympathy touched him, rare when it came to any of the children, because he scarcely ever could follow what mattered to them and why it should matter.

"It's nothing," he said, taking swipes with his napkin at the coffee spill. "I was going to let Mama read it"— he spread his sheaf of pages—"and then I was going to translate it for Evan and Alida. If they're up to hearing anything about it. It may be too soon."

Fee poured coffee into a fresh cup. At its side, the narrow white pages lay, written over in her father's heavy stub-pen strokes.

"Papa," she said. "Could you translate it now?" She saw his surprise. "I honestly would like to hear it." Quickly she added, "We're interested in things our parents do, after all."

He took a sip of his coffee. Then he remembered the sugar, and stirred in a heaping teaspoonful. She had seated herself across the table from him, and without looking at her, he sensed her eagerness and grief. He picked up his sheets, translating the headline and the secondary head. Then, easily, he continued.

"There is a boy I know who is dead wrong about this war. In my opinion, dead wrong. I call him a boy, because he grew up near me, the same age as my son—"

He heard Fee swallow, but he went on without looking up. Went on until he came to Garry's arrest. "—was arrested for the things he said. Things about war, about this war and all war. Things it is his right to say in a free country—"

"Oh, Papa," she cried, and she put her head down on her folded arms and sobbed until the table shook. He put his pages aside and came around the table, standing near her, uncertain, unsure of what he could do.

Suddenly he was again seeing her as a sobbing child of ten, hearing her mimic her own squeaky voice in the classroom, "I think we're socialists, Miss King." He had taken her into his lap then, held her, and he had made her know that he understood. "It is very bad," he had said, "for a little girl to be so unhappy is very bad."

He wanted to say it now, but he said nothing. He wanted to let her know again that he—terrible father that she thought him when he opposed her—that her father understood what grief was, and loved her for the capacity of it.

But he said nothing. He did nothing. Only when she grew quieter, did he make a gesture toward her. He laid his hand on her head, and was astounded that both her own flew up, holding it hard to her hair as if she would never let it go.

He left for the city without going over to Channing Street. Fee's response had keyed him to a higher pitch. After another few minutes, she had asked him to finish his translating, and as he came to the end, she said, "It's so wonderful! I never knew you wrote that way."

"It's good to hear that, from your own child," he said. "I'm going to take it to New York. I may meet Mama too, after her letters. Are you all right alone here? Where is Fran? She's never at home these days."

"At the canteen. Do you think I could go over to Mrs. Paige for a while?" Before he could answer, she said, "Oh, Papa, I'm so glad you wrote it."

She's forgotten how she hates me, he thought, as he went up to dress for New York. Now I'm a good father again. Well, and why not? There is an equilibrium in it; she is a good daughter again.

By some freak the weather was cool and dry, more like September than the middle of August, and Ivarin walked briskly from his house. The HOUSE FOR SALE sign was at last gone; a slashing rainstorm had finally toppled it to its side, and Alexandra had carted it off, moaning about the "trench" dug into her grassy lawn by its exit.

The briskness made him feel well. For everyone except poor Garry, life had to go on today. Garry and surely Alida. But Evan was already going forward, absorbed in the next move. In the same way, he himself was absorbed by the move he had just taken and what lay ahead. There was authority in his thinking now, not pensive wondering. Not once, in the train to the city, did he ask what he would do if Steinberger said no. Not once, as he started to walk through the streets from Delancey to the paper, so infrequently traveled in these four long years, yet so familiar still, not once did he weigh the possibility of trying it next at the *Forward,* or even at the small but flourishing *Abend.*

He did consider seeing Abe Kesselbaum before Steinberger, letting him read it first, even inviting him, if Abe liked it, to go to Steinberger with him. A dual effort, as it were, and were it to go decidedly well with Steinberger, perhaps Abe could feel himself its sponsor.

But if it should not? Saddle poor Abe with some invisible part of it? He scowled, fished out a nickel and went into a candy store to an open phone, hung on the wall. He announced himself to Steinberger with some formality, said that he was in the city and would like to see him if possible.

Steinberger was formal too, but cordial and even inquisitive. He was at Ivarin's service. In half an hour? Fine.

"We should be alone," Stefan said amiably. (It sounded too authoritative.)

"I was going to suggest it," Steinberger said.

For the half-hour Ivarin walked. Going into the building of the *Jewish News* brought his pulse up sharply. It was too early in the afternoon for the staff to be in the halls; he thought it just as well. When he knocked at Steinberger's door, no secretary let him in. It was Steinberger himself, his hand outstretched.

They looked at each other for a minute. Each thought, He looks older. Each said, "You look better than ever."

As Stefan Ivarin sat down, he took out his folded white sheets, and said, "Have you followed the Paige case?"

"Yes, and I often thought of you as I read it," Steinberger said. "I knew that you know the father."

"Here is an editorial I wrote last night," Ivarin said, and pushed it across the desk. "As a free-lance submission, you understand." Then he rose, went to the window and looked down at the busy street below.

It took Steinberger a long time. Too long. Then Ivarin realized that he must be reading it a second time, and he thought, Good man.

"Yes," Steinberger said at last, and Ivarin turned. They stood in silence, facing each other. "I want to run it tomorrow."

"As a free-lance submission," Ivarin repeated. "That's why I could permit myself to by-pass Fehler."

"An outside piece. Under your signature." He suddenly rose and shook hands.

"I am very pleased that you want it," Ivarin said, and found it unthinkable to suggest a possible follow-up piece, a series, a regular space of his own. It had seemed so rational during the night; now it was unsayable.

"It needs cutting," he said. "I haven't cast it up for length."

(481)

"Leave it. Let it run. Let them have enough to chew on." He looked at Ivarin. "I sometimes feel we don't give them enough to worry them. Many things wouldn't arouse them anyway, but I think that readers who remember Europe—I think they get nervous if it seems not so free over here."

Ivarin agreed. He wanted very much to question Steinberger about his way of proceeding—would he not make a gesture of consulting Fehler about the piece? the policy board? the Landaus?—but he forced himself not to. "You may run some risk, printing it."

"It's possible to get out, if we need to weasel. Maybe we will need to." He shook his head. "So far the press has been fairly strong, where it comes to their being badgered. Haven't you noticed?"

"For their own freedoms, yes."

"Let's try this and see." He put his hand out to press the buzzer on his desk, but then pulled it back. "Where do you think it should go?" he asked, smiling for the first time. "On the editorial page?"

It was *politesse* and Ivarin meant to take his cue from it. "Anywhere but," he said. "This is no try at a 'come-back.' You follow me?"

Steinberger laughed. "Then the front page," he said.

Less than a minute after Ivarin left, Joseph Fehler entered. He looked directly at the sheets on Steinberger's desk and said, "I hear Ivarin was here. How is he?"

"A little older, but fine." Steinberger was holding the telephone, but he set it back on his desk. With some effort, he kept back a smile. In Fehler's place he would have wanted to do the same thing, but he wouldn't have moved an inch from his desk. "I was just about to phone you," he went on, indicating Ivarin's pages, "about this free-lance submission of his."

"An editorial?"

"I want to run it tomorrow. I'm sure you won't object."

He handed it over, and made a point of not watching Fehler while he read it. From time to time he did glance at him; he was not surprised that Fehler's face revealed nothing.

"It's Ivarin, no question about it," Fehler said. "A 'free-lance submission,' you said. Just this one time?"

"I'm not thinking about anything except this one time."

"If it were to be more than that," Fehler said slowly, "if he were to get back on the staff."

Steinberger calmly repeated, "It is as an outsider that he wrote it. If you and I want one more piece, we might arrange one more."

"Also as a free-lance?"

"Of course. Perhaps other pieces, from time to time."

"On the same basis?"

"Ivarin will never be back on the staff. He stipulated himself that it was out of the question."

"Well, then—"

Fehler said something else that he did not quite catch and then withdrew. Steinberger drew the telephone toward him. "Borg," he said, "I want some space on tomorrow's front page. Would you come in, please?"

At about eleven that evening, Stefan and Alexandra went to the café next to the paper, to wait for the first edition. He had met her at *Abend,* waiting there dutifully for more than an hour, while she finished out the full eight-hour day. Like a henpecked husband, he thought with pleasure, married to one of the new women. A year ago I couldn't have made such a jest. Today changes it.

She still showed the strain and sleeplessness of the night before, but she was clearly stimulated at his unexpected appearance there, and at his cryptic explanation, "a piece of news about Steinberger."

On his way to meet her, he had stopped to call Abe Kesselbaum, still at home. Abe sputtered his excitement, but Ivarin said, "Don't blow this up in your mind. It's only one piece."

"Just the same. Ivarin again in the paper!"

"If that overseer of yours would let you lay it out, I'd like you to work on it."

"I'll tell him you said so, may I?"

"As you please. My wife and I will be in the café, late. Maybe you'll drop in at the break."

And now at any moment Abe would be coming through the door, with the wet paper in his hand. At supper, telling Alexandra what he had written, remembering some phrases exactly, losing others, Ivarin had felt for the third time that day the long-forgotten thankfulness. First Fee, then Joseph Steinberger, then Alexandra. It was still his; it had come to him again as if he had never lost it. The universal language. The language of protest.

Don't make too much of it, he thought. Two of them are your family, too close to you, too close to Garry.

What counts are strangers. What counts are readers.

And what about the trashiness of the *Jewish News?* That no longer

(483)

counts? The sensation-mongering, the vulgar screaming? Has it disappeared, replaced by a dignity and quiet?

No, Mr. Prosecutor, he thought angrily, it has not been replaced. It is detestable. It is a platform of dung for a man to speak from. No rationalizations, no pious excuses.

"What's wrong, Stiva?"

"Nothing."

"You're suddenly on Mars."

"I beg you, let me be."

Just then Abe appeared, with a copy for Alexandra and another for him. "Stiva, your picture," she cried, and he was equally startled at the small cut of his own face looking up at him, next the bold by-line, BY STEFAN IVARIN. The picture was his idea, Abe said, and his boss, thank God, had gone for it. They had set the piece in a two-column measure, with larger type than run-of-paper, and frequent subheads.

"Impressive," Ivarin said. Secretly, vanity burst about him like shrapnel. "I must say, Abe, most impressive."

"It's glorious," Alexandra corrected.

Later, on the way back to Barnett, Stefan Ivarin reminded himself not to triumph too soon. Tomorrow the readers would see it, the strangers, the only judges. But once again when the house grew still, he went to his desk and began a second piece, starting with Garry, but connecting Garry to the horsewhipped Bigelow, to the Vermont minister, to the benighted Minnesotan. In Bisbee, Arizona, a town heretofore unmapped in his geographical knowledge, twelve hundred Wobblies, strikers and their families, had just been hammered out of town by Bisbee vigilantes, again under some sweet-scented local name, had been kicked, shoved, pushed, hounded out. No trial was contemplated; the authorities conceded there was no chance of finding twelve people who could qualify for impartial jury duty.

Once again he sat at his desk far into the night, knowing he would not submit this piece for a while, but writing anyway. In the morning, he again slept late, as he used to sleep in the years of his old life.

"Abe says they already had six telephone calls and a telegram from the Cloakmakers' Union," Alexandra greeted him when he finally appeared. "He says to call him."

The telegram, Abe told him, was a rather florid greeting to "the return of labor's truest spokesman," and the phone calls were admiring. Ivarin thanked him. Was there anything to report from the staff? "The best," Abe said. "Everybody is full of it, except Fehler. Even Borg says he loves it. But so far, no word out of Fehler."

(484)

Ivarin chuckled. A nip of conscience asked how he could be so cheerful less than two days after Garry's sentencing. It's a different department, he answered, and asked Abe to report again, if anything developed.

If Steinberger would call instead, he thought, and began to listen for the telephone. Steinberger did not call.

But several days later, he did. "It caused a sizable to-do," he announced. "Almost fifty letters, postcards and calls."

"That is good to hear. Thank you."

"Actually, I would like to run a second piece. If deadline pressure is not unwelcome—"

"It never is unwelcome."

"Then could you do one?"

"My pleasure," Ivarin said. "I will write something today."

Steinberger thanked him and added, "Perhaps later, you might write another, on a different subject. Still on your terms, the outside columnist."

Ivarin said, almost stiffly, "Later is later." To reveal the exhilaration pouring along his veins would have been like begging.

"The situation in Russia," Steinberger said. "Some readers are getting frantic about it."

"As I am too," he said. "Five months, and the Bolsheviki show so much power. It freezes the blood."

He went straight upstairs to his desk. If there is a "later," he thought, the old alternating technique might still have the strongest impact. A piece in Garry's series, then one on the danger in Russia, then again Garry and what it means to stay free. This "eternal vigilance" they talk of. It is never sure when and where it will be called for.

Fifty-six, he thought unexpectedly. It is no longer young, true enough. But it is not necessarily old.

Letty said, "If one more person gives me that look, I'll close up the shop for a year."

"It must be dreadful," Peter Stiles said. "What you've been through!" He signaled the waiter, and without asking her, ordered a second drink. "I'm glad I could change our tickets. I don't want you sitting through any war play tonight."

"I'm glad too." He was waiting for her to say it first, but she kept drawing back from the words. Cynthia Aldrich had come right out with it, and her own parents, in the letter her mother wrote the day after the trial was over. "In all the history of the Brooks family, on both sides, nobody has ever served a prison term, never. When I remember I once said that we never had had a divorce!"

"I'm so tired of thinking," Letty said.

"It's time you let me do it for you."

"Oh, Peter."

Somebody has to, she thought, I can't any more. The day Garry was sentenced, she had thought about nothing but him, how he must feel going to prison, but then her own life claimed her again. Everybody's did; there was nothing wrong or heartless in that. This afternoon, before Peter came to call for her, she had gone out to Madison Avenue, as if she just wanted a breath of fresh air, and stood staring into the show window, like any admirer of some piece on display, wondering what the hidden price tag said. Actually she was staring at the gilt lettering, superimposing "Brooks" over "Garrett" to see if it would fit. There was one more letter in Garrett, but the two t's were thin and run-together. Two r's and two t's: she had never noticed that before.

"Mrs. Brooks Paige, Antiques" did sound smarter. Mrs. Brooks Paige. If she did go ahead, it would be her legal name. A widow went on forever with her husband's name, but a woman who had to get a divorce coupled her own last name with her married name. She had read that somewhere, or heard it, and after Garry was found guilty, when Cynthia talked flat out about his name damaging the shop's reputation, Cynthia had said it too. In a year, she said, nobody would remember that it hadn't always been "Mrs. Brooks Paige, Antiques."

But if I marry Peter, Letty thought now, would I have to change it again? Everything turned to problems. If only she had instituted proceedings way back, when Garry walked out that night and went to the Brevoort. Or at any time between then and his arrest. If she had started a divorce then, nobody could accuse her now of hitting him when he was down, nobody could call her cowardly or cruel.

But now if you do nothing, she thought, they'd only accuse you of trying to act like a martyr. A heroine. An angel with a halo.

"What, darling?" Peter asked. "You suddenly smiled."

Slowly Fee came to realize once more that time did pass. The first days of Garry's prison sentence had stood still, black rocks in a black desert. The first morning after the trial, hearing her father translate what he had written, somehow had managed to tear her hands loose from their clutch at the rocks, and for a while afterward, when she

(486)

was alone, she had been able to think of three years as something that would move away, grain by grain. Then the standing still began again.

She asked a few days later if anybody could visit Garry, and the answer was, "Only his family." The stillness grew thick once more, and everything was wrapped in it. She knew her parents were happy, or excited, about the paper, her father's paper. For so long "the paper" was her mother's; having her father on his own paper, was before the war, before everything.

Before Garry. Did everybody have a private calendar inside the world's calendar?

Once upon a time her calendar had taken in the wait from Regents Week until the end of August when the letter from Albany would come. And if she did win her scholarship, it stretched in a lovely hazy way over four years of Barnard College, where she had been entered, just in case, ever since Easter vacation.

Now the only real calendar was the one that said Three Years. Until August, 1920. The war might be over by then; she would be waiting to start her senior year, if she were at college, and she would be twenty herself. And Garry twelve years older. It didn't sound so much for anybody who was twenty.

When she went over to see Mrs. Paige, she felt about twelve, and even with Mrs. Paige being kind, the noose of shyness knotted tighter. After the first week or so, Mrs. Paige was something like herself again, talking in that same soft way, saying Garry's name as if he were still at Synthex and expected for one family meal over the weekend.

"Why don't you write to him, Fee?" she asked once. "Mail means a lot when you're a prisoner."

Fee looked away at the word. The two Paiges were allowed to visit him once a month, and he wasn't allowed to write more than once a week, but there was no limit about the letters he could receive.

"I started to write once or twice," Fee said, "but I always tore it up. I never know what to say."

"Don't tear the next one. Remember he thought you were the best witness of all; he said so again when his father saw him about the appeal."

"Did he really?" She had heard it from her parents already, but her heart flamed at hearing it from Garry's mother. Just sitting near her was important, a special event, like talking to Mr. Fitch instead of to a teacher.

Mr. Fitch. Teachers. The fifteen exams. Curiosity began to stir

(487)

again, and one morning she went out to the porch to wait for the mail-man. It was nearly Labor Day, it should have been here by now.

Maybe I didn't win one after all, she thought, and suddenly, longing for college took hold of her again. If there was any way to go on day after day for three full years, college would make it easier.

The mailman came and he had no long thin envelope for her, but he said, "Fine day," in his ordinary voice. Barnett was forgetting Garry and "The Paige Case." Words like "traitor" and "slacker" weren't thrown around so often any more. But she still kept to herself. She didn't see Anne, nor Juanita, she had no friends any more. Not just that they had said things about Garry. Mostly it was that she felt older than any one of them.

The next day there was no letter, nor the next. That afternoon she had promised to go to Brooklyn to stay with Webby and Sandra while Joan went off, and she was glad something forced her out of the house and away from the mailbox. Joan was only going to a beauty parlor, but it was to get an Irene Castle hair-bob, and it was a secret until she saw how she looked. Eli of course was in New Hampshire, again alone. Joan had decided to let him. "I'll take my chances," she told Fee once. "If he's going to fall in love again, let him. He thinks *he's* tired of marriage." She had talked on and then said, "You've grown up so, Fee. I think you're more mature than Fran will ever be."

Now she was ready to start out when Fee arrived. Webby had grown another inch, and Sandra too, and they were so tan that their eyebrows looked white; they all had spent a month at the Martins' new house in Long Beach, four blocks from the beach, where Joan's father could have a vacation and be a doctor at the same time.

"Auntie Fee," Webby cried, hugging her. "You can sleep in my room."

"In *my* room," Sandy shouted at him.

"No she can't," his mother said. "Not in anybody's room." Then, drawing Fee aside, she said, "I felt so awful about Garry Paige. We'll talk later."

"I sort of can't," Fee said and left it that way, turning to the tugging six-year-old at her side. "Webster Martin Eaves," she said sternly, "you are tearing my skirt plumb in two. How will I ever ride home again?"

The children began an assault on the threatened skirt, and Joan left. An hour sped by, and once Fee thought with astonishment that she was having a good time. A howl from Webby plus the thump and noise of a heavy fall put an end to her well-being. She rushed to the kitchen, and then almost laughed in relief. The heavy fall was

Eli's five-pound jar of malted milk, its cover unscrewed, its total contents in a pale yellow mound on the linoleum.

"It's not so bad, Webby," Fee said. "We'll scoop it up."

"He'll hit me," Webby screamed. "He'll spank me."

"He's not even at home."

But long after he stopped crying, angry questions about Eli still bubbled up in her mind. What was wrong with him anyway? Still spanking Web every minute, and Sandy too. Off there with his double exemptions, for the children and his asthma, feeling superior to everybody else!

There were three smart rings at the bell and Joan dashed in, her bobbed hair flying. "Look at me, I love it, do you?" The children were instantly excited, as Fee was too. How grand it would be not to have all her long hair to comb and wash and fix and pin up. "Maybe I'll do it too," Fee said, "when I get to college, if I ever do."

Long after the children were in bed, Joan and she sat talking. Almost as if we were the same age, Fee thought. Then she told her about the spilled malted milk.

"Webby's always so *afraid,*" she said. "Doesn't it mean something, Joan?"

"And especially about that damn malted milk," Joan answered. "He caught his father at it one night. The wrong night, and he really did get a beating."

"Caught him?"

"Caught him making a pig of himself over it, spoonful after spoonful." She saw Fee staring at her. "Maybe he only did it out of nervousness over the next day. Eli always overeats when he's bothered and upset. There's that possibility too."

"What was the next day?" Fee felt a feather skim down the back of her neck, and she shivered. Somebody's walking over your grave was what that meant; she had heard it all her life. "What was the next day?" she repeated when Joan remained silent.

"The next day," Joan said with care, "was the day he got the souvenir to show his grandchildren."

At last the letter came. Fee saw it in the postman's hand and ran out, crying, "Is that big one for me?" She tore it open, and then rushed back into the house.

"Mama, I *did,*" she called. "I got it, I won it, look at their letter. I can't believe it, I began to think—"

"I'm so proud of you," Alexandra said. "It's time you had something to be happy about." She read the brief letter. "The State of New York," she said. "One hundred dollars a year for the four academic years."

Fee wheeled and started upstairs. For once Fran was at home, still asleep but at home. Fee shook her awake and said, "I won my scholarship, Franny, I did, I really did. Here, look at this."

Fran sleepily reached for it, read it, and then surprised Fee beyond speech. She got out of bed, put her arms around her and kissed her. "It's just grand," she said, "simply grand and glorious. Oh, Fee, you crazy galoot, I'm glad."

Only later did they think of their father. "What about Papa?" Fee asked, and Fran said, "If you budge an inch, I'll never forgive you. He's had to take it about me renting a place in New York next month, hasn't he?"

"I can't stand another fight right now, I just can't." Fee ran downstairs again to her mother. "What about Papa? I forgot all about that."

"Don't borrow trouble," Alexandra said. "He's waiting for news of his own. I think he'll get it too. Four pieces so far and he's like a new man, a new writer, better than ever."

That night Fee wrote her first letter to Garry. This time it was easy to know what to say.

Dear Garry,

   I haven't written because I had no news, but this morning I found out I can go to college after all. Those fifteen Regents you laughed at were not so silly; they brought my average up to 91, and I won a State Scholarship. I keep thinking about you and every time I feel glad you're just the way you are.

She signed it "Love, Fee," and then had to write it all over again, to sign it simply with her name. Then she tore up the second one and addressed the one she had written first. She ran all the way down to the mailbox on the corner to send it on its way.

(490)

Thirty-six days had gone by, and Garry was no longer possessed by the voices of the trial, the questions, the answers. From his first hour as a prisoner, he wanted to forget them, but they came at him incessantly, day or night, awake, asleep.

In the second month they began to withdraw, particularly during working hours. He was assigned to the machine shop and while he was there, he could shape his thinking on the lathe—beveling, trimming, freeing it of its rawest edges.

But stupor, the vacuum of prison, that he had read about, once dreaded, still did not come. As if it were a companion, he sought it, but it eluded him. Memory, sentience, pain were his inseparables each night. His pain, the pain of others. His mother's he dared not think about, nor his father's; Letty's he thought of in many ways, entwined with his own, divorced from it.

Divorced. The word had taken on a hardness since his father's second visit to him in prison. "Garry, I have news about Letty," he said, a reluctance in his tone. "She telephoned me and asked me to tell you."

"She's going to start a divorce, is that it?"

"By now she has already. She started for Nevada that same day, to establish residence."

And a month has gone by since then, Garry thought now, and she's about ready to see the judge. *Intolerable cruelty and mental anguish.* For once, it's more than a legal slogan. Anguish, each to the other. Starting way back, each in our own fashion, never wanting to hurt the other, managing less and less each year to avoid doing it.

Who was to apologize for pain given or pain received? Pain was part of living, of feeling, of moving on from one stage to another. Some day he might be able to trace and examine the pain in their marriage, where it had risen, how it had gone along almost unnoticed, gathering power, cutting through their love, joining with little tributary troubles until it swept along in a force too strong to dam up or deny.

A river, he thought, and suddenly he saw his old geography book, with red lines wriggling down the great expanse of the nation. The schoolboy memory came strongly alive, why he did not know. In prison, one could not predict the mind's activity, nor the heart's. One day he was sure of what he had done, what he had said, what he believed; on another he would curse himself for it. Many men had found a way to make good their faith, to stand on what they believed, without getting themselves arrested, arraigned, indicted, convicted, sent to prison for it—but he had not. Had he blinded himself to any way but the way he had gone?

The schoolboy debater, unable to function, except when he blasted ahead with what he thought—was he still that?

He would slap the doubt down, trample on it. This had been no schoolboy debate; three years of prison and twice his total savings would testify to that.

Pain, defeat, hope again when his father visited and talked ahead to the appeal, perhaps by January. The hysterics were growing, but so was the awareness of it. Teddy Roosevelt had brought Madison Square Garden to its feet with warnings of "Huns Within," and at Carnegie Hall, La Follette was denounced for "disloyal and seditious utterances." Predictions were heard that Debs himself would land in prison; nothing was too outlandish, and no human safe who dared say it might *not* be the war to end war.

But in Baltimore, his father told him, Federal Judge Rose had directed a jury to return a verdict of "Not Guilty" for two men accused of "conspiring to persuade young men to evade or violate the Conscription Law," the judge stating for the record, on the record, for the press, that "Every man has a perfect right to any opinion he may see fit to form about any law that is proposed, or about any law that is on the statute books."

"If I had only lived in Baltimore, Dad."

"Or if we manage to get Judge Rose's kind of judge next time around. There still are some, even in all this."

Perhaps in January, that next time. A new year, and he would have finished five months of his thirty-six by then, a hundred and fifty days of his thousand and ninety-five.

Dear God, help me. He prayed often. He drew comfort as never before from his praying and from his faith. He drew comfort from his parents' support and approval, and from the things they wrote or told him about the widening support for his case. Clarence Darrow, Dr. Holmes, Norman Thomas, Senator La Follette, Roger Baldwin and his quickly growing Bureau—all saw in it an attack on a basic freedom.

His mother sent him translations of the two pieces Stefan Ivarin had written, soon to appear in the *Appeal to Reason* and the *Milwaukee Leader,* both excluded from the mails, but appearing in their own states. The two shook him particularly, not only because he could see and hear Ivarin in every phrase, but because he knew that if Ivarin and he were to go at it face to face once more, right here in this cell, Ivarin would still shout him down about how wrong he was on this inescapable war, you follow me?

And he also could hear Fee's phrases from the witness chair, and they too brought him comfort. *It is courage.*

When he least expected it, her words would sound again for him. Growing up in the Ivarin house, absorbing her parents' ideas all her life, she surely agreed with her father about the inescapable war, the justified war. But she had said, "It *is* courage," and for the first time she looked over to him.

He kept seeing her as he saw her then. She had changed. She was older, and he saw her as she would be some day, all warmth and all passion, for whatever she believed in, for whomever she loved.

The September meeting of the policy staff was going well. Circulation was on the rise again, Fehler announced, a thousand a day, nothing too dramatic, but a welcome lift off the recent plateau. The growing suspense about Russia doubtless accounted for it, he said. When Riga fell, over Labor Day, a thrill of fear went through their Russian-Jewish readers, and this week with General Kornilov and his counter-revolutionists marching on the government itself, the word "fear" was not enough.

"On such days the newsstands go clean, of course," Fehler said, "with no returns. And on certain other days, too. There have been six or seven such days in the past month." He paused for an instant. "These other days led us to a decision, Mr. Steinberger and myself."

The burr of self-consciousness caught at Fehler's voice, and there was sudden strain in his listeners. Joseph Steinberger looked uninvolved, but Saul Borg, the two reporters, and Abe Kesselbaum became self-conscious too. Abe concentrated on a pad before him, drawing circles and interlocking triangles, but he was smiling.

"Mr. Steinberger and I," Fehler said, "as you know, have been delighted with the reaction to the six or seven special pieces by Stefan

Ivarin—especially among older readers who remember his writings. Mr. Steinberger has already discussed this matter with Mrs. Landau and her family, who of course will defer to his—to our judgment. This week we discussed it fully with Ivarin himself."

At the last two words, Abe Kesselbaum exhaled, so forcibly that Fehler looked briefly at him.

"There has been no disposition to invite Ivarin back to the staff. However Mr. Steinberger did propose—Mr. Steinberger and I proposed—a daily column, to start at once. For some reason, though he never did before, Mr. Ivarin demanded a written contract for a period of years."

"How many?" Saul Borg asked quickly. He had not been called up in the first draft, but was training a substitute to be ready for the next. He constantly looked ahead now.

"Five," Fehler replied. "A five-year contract."

For the first time Steinberger spoke. "We agreed and signed yesterday," he said. "Ivarin starts next week."

"Bravo," Abe Kesselbaum shouted. The burst of talk began all about him and he had a dim memory of a Bravo at some other meeting. But that time he had whispered it.

For the first time in months, Alexandra stopped in front of the Victrola, considering it. In her hand was the record she had not played for those same months, and she shifted her gaze to its visible grooves, wondering whether it was possible now.

Since the terrible day they arrested Garry, she had been unable to do her morning dancing. The lilting music, the cheer and well-being that always came to her as her muscles responded to its rhythms, would have seemed an indelicacy. Instead she had reverted to her hated calisthenics with the deadly sound of her own voice counting off the one-and two-and three-ands.

But this morning, for the first time since early July, she was tempted. Perhaps the reckless step she had taken yesterday—so soon to be discovered—had left a residue of rashness urging her on.

She delayed a decision and opened a window. It was almost too much; the gust blowing in upon her naked body had a hint of December frost, though it was the first Sunday in October. A golden October it promised to be, but for the war, but for the cell in her heart which held Garry.

October. Harvest, fulfillment. A few nights ago with her "charter" lecture group, dear Anna Godleberg had raved about Stiva's return to print, but then had loyally switched back to two of her pieces, the first she had ever tried on older children, starting high school, starting with flirtation and dates. The old refrain again came to Anna Godleberg's lips. "You ought to put it all down, you ought to write a book."

This time Alexandra hadn't let it pass with silent thanks. This time she said, "I am, Anna, oh, I am. Each time I write a piece, it's a fraction of a book. Some day there will *be* a book."

Never before had she said it aloud; the sweet good words were like a promise of new youth waiting ahead. It was true. Only recently Stiva had made her see that when she had written enough pieces there could be a collection of the best ones in book form; he had promised to help her at that time, selecting and organizing her material into sections according to topics; he swore he would find her a publisher. Jewish women had never had such a book; it was her duty to give them one.

Duty—and desire. How fortunate when they were locked together like lovers, inseparable, one the same as the other.

Another frosty gust shot through the window and Alexandra remembered where she was. Naked and chilled through, she had been standing there gawking at the world, holding the Strauss waltz like a votive offering to it. With sudden resolve she opened the Victrola, and put it on.

Hop, hop, hop, slide and jump, bend to the left, bend to the right. She had done it wrong, the right came first, then the left. It had been so long a time, her starving muscles had forgotten. Hop, hop, hop, slide and jump, bend to the right, bend to the left.

The wonderful tuning up began, of all her nerves, like the little instruments in an orchestra, joining their companions, melting into them, flowing on together. It was right to dance again, not wicked or unkind. Garry would say so himself.

There was a clatter up above, and both the girls' voices, suddenly high, excited. This early, and on a Sunday morning? She remembered her nakedness and rushed to the sewing room, now her workshop and study, the sewing forgotten, since the girls no longer approved of any dress she made. She put her nightgown on again, and her bathrobe, and picked up her comb. They were dashing down the stairs, three at a time, by the sound of it.

"Franny has news for you," Fee shouted on the other side of her door.

"Good morning, Mama, hurry out." That was Fran.

(495)

"Just a minute," She couldn't compete with their news by forcing in ahead with news of her own. "I'll be right there, I washed my hair and it's dripping."

In a moment she faced them, a towel swathed around her head. Fee said, "Tell her, Fran, go on," and Fran said, "Mama, I'm going to get married on Thursday."

"Oh my goodness."

"There's a new aviation camp in Florida, and they're shipping Davey to teach flying, and he won't go without me."

"My little Franny, married. I'm so happy." And Alexandra burst into tears.

"You like him," Fran said, "you said you did."

"I did. He's lovely. I wish I knew him more."

"He's grand," Fee said. "I met him yesterday while you were in New York, and he's just wonderful. Lieutenant Marks, how do you like that? Mrs. Lieutenant David Marks, of Memphis, Tennessee."

Nothing could stop Fran after that. She talked too much, she told too much, she repeated things Davey had said, apologizing, granting that they were too personal, and going on anyway. She talked of his parents, of their big house and garden, the country club, and his father's three stores of electrical supplies. She broadly hinted that Davey not only was going to be terribly rich later on, but was far beyond a second lieutenant's pay right now, so renting a place off base was going to be no problem.

An hour passed like one of Davey's airplanes. Outside Shag somehow knew that extraordinary things were afoot and he barked himself hoarse until they let him in. He had instantly caught the general fever, and decided all rules were off.

"Down, I say," Alexandra shouted at him after an unexpected lunge. Her towel turban slipped over an eye and she remembered. "Wait a minute," she said, and left them. Once again she ran the comb through her hair. This time she looked at herself, smiled, and hurried back.

"Look at me," she said. "I did it last night in New York."

Her curly grey hair was short, bobbed in the Irene Castle style, cut straight around, on a line with the lobes of her ears. As they stood gawking at her, she tossed her head, as she had done a dozen times an hour since yesterday. "It's so light," she cried, "so free. You can't imagine."

"Oh, Mama," Fee cried. "I love it. You look just like Joan."

Fran loved it too, she said. But she thought of Davey, of his parents coming for the wedding. God, why did she have to do it now? It's for girls, not old women, not for people who weigh too much and have a foreign accent. I can't wait to get out of this awful place, where you forever have to die of shame.

Fee was the only one left at home now, and they treated her as if she were their equal. Hardly ever did they shift into Russian to discuss anything important, and if Mr. and Mrs. Paige did come over, they never suggested that she might want to go off and read.

Her father still never mentioned college as college; he did ask her what courses she was taking "at that school of yours," but that was it. As for putting up the rest of her tuition each semester, there wasn't even a mention of it.

"I'll do it, I tell you," her mother said. "You can't change him. I earn plenty, don't I?"

"If I only could figure him out."

"He can be wrong, can't he?" Alexandra flung it out as the ultimate challenge, and hurried on. "Tuition is two hundred and your scholarship takes care of one hundred—do you think I'm not good for the other half? If you need fancy clothes, get an afternoon job—fashion is not my worry."

"All I need is my cashmere sweater and saddle shoes."

College was unbelievable. From the first day, she wondered how she had ever liked High; this was not a harder High, with longer assignments, this was new, like the time she read *Wuthering Heights* for herself, by accident, when it wasn't on a Reading List.

Had Garry found a whole new world at college? She almost wrote to ask him, but his letters had to be mostly for his parents. She wrote every few days anyway, except when she heard about his divorce. She was afraid her fury at Letty would show. And also the bouncing ball of joy alongside the fury.

Garry had only written to her twice in the twelve weeks he had been there. She always carried both letters in her purse, wherever she went, but she did not need to take them out to read them.

Dear Fee,

Congratulations on the Big 91. And on becoming a Barnard frosh. And thanks for writing me, especially for your last line. There haven't been too many good things happening to me of

(497)

late, so your testimony in court and then that last sentence in your letter were pretty important. I don't know how to say thanks, but please do take it for said.

Always,
Garry

The second had just come this week, and it was even shorter. She had read it and read it and read it, wondering if it really could mean a fraction of what she wanted it to mean.

Dear Fee,
　　Your letters help more than you can guess. They remind me that there are happy things going on too, and that the time will come when I might share some of them again. Please write a lot —I find myself waiting to see if there's a letter from you.

He had signed this one the same way, but this time the words sounded like different words. *Always, Garry.*

Always and always and always. Tomorrow and tomorrow and tomorrow. It was so sad in the play, but Macbeth was talking of death and dusty yesterdays, not of love and time ahead.

Constantly Fee tried to think what "three years" was like. Three years from now, she would be twenty, but she could not think of herself as anything except seventeen. She could not remember herself at thirteen or ten or five; she had been all of them, but they were impossible Fees that no longer were true. The Fees waiting ahead were equally impossible.

The one thing she did know was that she was living in a new universe with Garry in each molecule of it, in each minute and half-minute of it. She would be in the middle of a class at Barnard, and suddenly she was back in the witness chair in the courtroom, seeing that different look come into Garry's face. She would get into the train at Penn Station in the afternoon, and then the conductor would bawl out "BAA-NET" and she would think, But we just started, I haven't even opened my book. And once a Columbia sophomore asked if she'd go out with him on a date, and she said, "Oh, I just couldn't," without stopping to think.

"Why not?"

"I can't explain. But I just couldn't."

Almost none of the people she met at college knew about "The Paige Case" and her part in it; in August, most of them were off on vacations, and not bothering with newspapers. But even if they did know, they could never guess what had happened to her because

(498)

of it. The trial was like a boundary line between two countries on a map; one country was the old way she had felt about Garry when she was a child, and the other was this vast new world she would never leave for the rest of her life.

On weekends, she went over to the Paiges as soon as her Saturday cleaning was done. Mrs. Paige never asked why she came; she would talk to Fee about Garry's last letter, and sometimes read bits of news aloud, like his making an improvement in the toolshop that the foreman liked and was adopting. And she would talk about the appeal that was almost sure to get on the calendar by the end of January or start of February.

Once Mrs. Paige let her see her cry, without sending her home or even turning away. Fee didn't know what to say; she put her hand on Mrs. Paige's shoulder, and under her hand, she felt the shoulder sort of thank her.

She still adored Mr. Paige, but there was something new in her feeling about Mrs. Paige. The sense of a special event, like talking to Mr. Fitch at High, was gone now; in its place was what she felt for her mother, but with an extra excitement to it.

One Sunday when Fee was there, Mrs. Paige happened to tear off a leaf of the calendar on her small desk in the parlor. "November first," Alida said. "I declare, time does move."

" 'The hypocritic days,' " Fee quoted, and added, "It's Ralph Waldo Emerson; I just learned it."

"Say it for me, Fee. I don't know it."

" 'Daughters of Time, the hypocritic days,' " Fee began, lowering her eyes in sudden constraint. " 'Muffled and dumb like barefoot dervishes, And marching single in an endless file—' "

She broke off, and above her head she heard a sound, but there were no words in it. Then Mrs. Paige left the room quickly, and water ran from the tap in the kitchen and a glass clinked against the brass faucet. I shouldn't have, Fee thought; just because I can't get it out of my head was no excuse.

She heard Mr. Paige come down and talk to Mrs. Paige, and she sat wretchedly still. Should she go in and apologize? Should she just go home? *An endless file,* an endless file of days.

"Fee, how's college going?"

It was Mr. Paige coming into the dining room, as friendly as ever. She jumped up and said, "Really marvelous."

"What's your favorite course?"

(499)

"Well, Baby Greek—it's so good-looking to write in." She answered his questions about teachers and new friends, and soon Mrs. Paige came back and they all three chatted a while as if they were three happy people.

Then Mrs. Paige put her hand out toward Fee. "I asked you to recite it, and then I made you feel as if you'd hurt me. I'm sorry, Fee."

"I wouldn't hurt you for anything," Fee said passionately. "I love you so, I just couldn't *ever*."

Evan Paige said, "Of course you couldn't, dear Fee." He kept looking at her, and she sat quiet under his scrutiny.

The instinct for love, Evan thought, the readiness to love—Fee has always had them. *Oh, I love you, Mr. Paige.* From five years back, a little girl's excited voice sounded again; he remembered the small green "hammock" and he saw once more the wild exuberance of Fee's joy over his assorted thefts and bribes and purchases from the Pullman car.

Who could have thought that the little tomboy turning somersaults in an abandon of thanks, would turn into this Fee, this girl Garry was clearly preoccupied with already, and the Lord be praised for it. When the young can still long for love—

"Fee, the appeal," he said suddenly, "may have a slightly better chance than we dared hope."

"Oh, Mr. Paige."

"Tell her, Evan," Alida said.

"Well," he said, his tone advising her not to overrate his news, "Molloy is going to testify this time. Basically, Molloy's a decent enough fellow, and he doesn't like the way he panicked about getting bad publicity in the papers. Now he sees that Synthex's good name wasn't damaged for all time, and he wants to speak up on Garry's behalf."

On the table, Fee's hands clasped as she listened, and she sat straighter, but she said nothing.

"Molloy wants to testify that he first heard Garry's beliefs about war back in 1914, when he came to work at Synthex, and heard them in '15 and '16 as well, long before we got into it, clearly a lifelong conviction of Garry's. He also wants to say that Garry never once urged any man to disobey the draft law or any other."

"Don't get your hopes up too much, Fee," Mrs. Paige said. "But a new character witness might impress a new judge."

Again there was silence from all three. Then Fee looked at Mr. Paige and asked, "If we lose the appeal anyway, is there anything else you could do?"

We, Evan thought, if we lose. For a moment he could not speak. Then he said, "At the worst, Fee, we might have to wait until the war ends. There would be amnesty on all these hysteria cases; it always happens. And Garry would come back to us then, at the very latest."

Several nights later, Fee looked at her watch, surprised. Midnight, and she still had half her paper to do for English Lit. Tonight should have been a good time to finish it. The house, for once, was quiet; it had been bedlam for the past week, with the Woman Suffrage victory on Election Day, and seven socialists elected to Albany, and the hue and cry against seating them, and the big victory over the Germans in the Aisne sector.

But the worst bedlam was over the ups and downs in Russia. Trotsky was free, no he wasn't, yes he was; Lenin was back, no, he's still in Finland, no, he's in Petrograd; Kerensky denies all rumors of Russia's weakness and swears there will be no separate peace—up and down, back and forth, and her father going mad with each new dispatch.

He was forever dropping in at the paper, just to watch the news ticker; he would hang over it hour after hour half the night. Mama was forever saying, "You'll kill yourself, just when your life is at its highest point, at a new apex."

"It's a killing time."

Tonight her mother was in New York, too. The house was empty as a barn. Fee had two rooms now, if she wanted them, with none of Fran's dresses and slips and skirts in rings all over the floor, like big quoits. Fran didn't write much either, but when she did, she drooled about her new life. She was learning to drive a car. It was her own car. Davey had bought it for her as a wedding present.

Good for Franny, Fee thought, and stretched. She would rest a bit and then finish her Lit paper, no matter how late it was. She stepped over Shag's supine body and went to the mirror over Fran's old bureau, slipping out her hairpins. She brushed out the teased-up pompadour of her hair, and then tried to fold it under at her earlobes. It kept escaping, and she couldn't tell; then she tried on one side only, using both hands at once, staring at the effect.

I'm going to, she thought. Maybe tomorrow. And I'll get Eli or Joan to take a snapshot. If the snap comes out, I could put it in my next letter. She tried to imagine Garry seeing it, opening a letter and seeing her face, and then looking at her.

(501)

She turned away from the mirror, and went downstairs. She wanted something, even though she wasn't hungry. *I'd like mine in a glass.*

"We'll have some tea," she said to Shag and put the water up to boil.

When she finally finished her Lit paper, it was past three and she went to bed. Still no sign of her mother and father. She slept hard, and when she sprang awake at the sound of their voices, she had a momentary feeling that it was the sleeping porch again, as on that dawning day in spring when they were out there with the flag. This time, too, it was just getting light, but they were nowhere to be seen.

For a moment she was still, listening, straining to hear. Their voices were agitated, just like that other time at daybreak, but they were downstairs in the kitchen, not out on the porch. They were not having a fight, and though her mother was in tears, it wasn't the usual hurt-feelings kind, or even the same as her weeping over Garry.

Fee got out of bed and reached for her bathrobe. She didn't have to sneak halfway down the stairs any longer; she could walk down and let them see her openly. Now only her father was talking, flinging words out, something about a *coup d'état,* about Kerensky fleeing for his life, the moderates being shot, the extremists triumphant—

The kitchen door was open, and they were both there. Something in the way they sat, in the way they looked at each other halted Fee on the threshold, where they did not see her.

"And now we'll see a terrorism," her father shouted, "now the whole world will see such a terrorism as the czars never dreamed of."

"Perhaps—"

He wouldn't listen. "Six months of hope, then the Bolsheviki take over."

"Perhaps it will fail too. Maybe Trotsky and Lenin—"

He cut her off once more. "This time it is real. We are finished."

"Stiva, perhaps—somehow—"

"There is no 'perhaps.' There is no 'somehow.'" He sounded like a giant shouting in anguish. Then suddenly there was silence.

Fee stood motionless, still in the doorway, still unwilling to go in. Her father suddenly put his head down, covering his face with his hands, right over his glasses. His shoulders were tight and high, and they were shaking. She remembered the time in spring when she saw him crying for the first time in all her life.

He spoke again, and this time his voice broke. "My poor Russia," he said. "My poor Russia."

About the Author

LAURA Z. HOBSON—the Z. is for Zametkin—was born in New York City and grew up on Long Island. After her B.A. at Cornell, she worked as advertising copywriter, newspaper reporter and, finally, in magazine promotion, which became her business specialty.

In 1935, as a spare-time hobby, she tried her hand at fiction; her stories appeared in many magazines. In 1941 she turned full-time author, and her first novel, *The Trespassers,* was published in 1943, here and in England. It was with *Gentleman's Agreement,* in 1947, that Mrs. Hobson took her place as a major American novelist. Some two million copies have been sold in various editions in the United States, and the novel appeared in about a dozen languages abroad. On the screen, it won the Academy Award for Best Picture of 1947.

The Other Father appeared in 1950, *The Celebrity* a year later. Then, in 1953, Mrs. Hobson began *First Papers,* a novel unlike any of the others. Under constant pressure of deadlines for a daily newspaper column and monthly book-page, writing short stories, novelettes and from 1956 on, again working at magazine promotion, she wrote on the manuscript only sporadically for some years. When *First Papers* reached its half-way mark, she again abandoned all other activity, and wrote the second half of the novel in the twelve months of 1963.

She lives in New York and has two grown sons. Their middle initial is Z. for Zametkin too.